THE PLEASURES OF
PEACOCK

The Pleasures

OF

Peacock

COMPRISING IN WHOLE OR IN PART THE SEVEN NOVELS OF

THOMAS LOVE PEACOCK

· HEADLONG HALL · MELINCOURT · NIGHTMARE ABBEY ·
· MAID MARIAN · MISFORTUNES OF ELPHIN ·
· CROTCHET CASTLE · GRYLL GRANGE ·

Edited with an introduction by

Ben Ray Redman

FARRAR STRAUS AND COMPANY

NEW YORK   1947

PRINTED IN THE UNITED STATES OF AMERICA
BY J. J. LITTLE & IVES COMPANY, NEW YORK

FOR FRIEDA

Uxor vivamus ut viximus

CONTENTS

INTRODUCTION

THE pleasures to be found in Thomas Love Peacock's short
novels are known to many readers, but not to enough. In a
way it is fitting that an author who disliked large social gatherings,
who preferred the company of a few convivial friends, should not
have become the object of wide popularity; yet this state of affairs
is a loss to all the fit readers who remain outside his circle, and,
to those who have long enjoyed themselves inside it, the loss seems
a pity. No more than the admirers of Jane Austen are Peacockians
a selfish breed. They are eager to share with a friend, or even a
passing acquaintance, what they consider one of the very good
things of life, and it is seldom, if ever, that they are not heartily
thanked for their sharing.

It is true, of course, that what Peacock has to offer is not everyone's dish, and he is not so great that anyone need feel under
obligation to pretend to enjoy him. Hence the phrase, fit readers.
If you demand the grand manner or the heroic tone, he is not for
you. If you must have an ingenious plot, or psychological subtlety
in the study of character, or a broad social panorama, do not look
to the author of Crotchet Castle. If you go to books for sober-sided
instruction, do not go to him. But if you like good talk, you will
hear in his pages some of the best that English literature affords.
If you have a relish for genial satire, you will find that he is one
of its masters; a marksman whose shafts speed straight to folly
on the wing. If you would meet a writer whose words are always
nimbly at the service of his wit, and whose wit is nearly unfailing,
you should not delay meeting him. If you would sit in the best
of jovial company, hour after hour, enjoying the lively play of language and ideas, with prejudice striking sparks from prejudice, and

crotchet meeting crotchet in eloquent collision, then Thomas Love
Peacock is your man. Richard Garnett, one of his devoted editors,
went so far as to call his style perfect. There is exaggeration in this
ultimate eulogy, but it should be noted that officials at India House
anticipated Dr. Garnett when they wrote on the papers which won
Peacock his post with the East India Company: "Nothing superfluous and nothing wanting." For is not this officialdom's way of saying perfect, in five words instead of one?

However, we may stop short of carrying praise so far, and still
praise abundantly. The rule of "nothing superfluous" was one that
Peacock seldom failed to honor in the observance. Writing in an
age of long-winded fiction, he made a practice of brevity. Only once
in his prose, in *Melincourt*, did he deviate from that practice; and
when he did, he erred. As for "nothing wanting," this is a description that may be attached justly to a piece of writing produced for
a specific purpose, but to the works of no author who ever lived
can it be applied with accuracy. Virgil wants Dostoievski's intensity; Rabelais wants Cicero's elegance; Jane Austen wants Tolstoy's
range, and Tolstoy wants Miss Austen's lightness. Even Shakespeare, who has come closest to writing in all ways for all men, has
left undone some things that other authors have done well.

Peacock's own lacks are obvious, as has been said. He cultivated
a small garden, while he let others attempt the heights, but within
that garden he worked enduringly. He did all that an author need
do in order to live, whether in the major or the minor ranks: he
gave, and gives, his particular, peculiar mixture of literary satisfaction. If we would enjoy that mixture, we must go to him. This is
not to say that he was born without ancestors or that he died without issue, but neither his vaguely identified progenitors nor his
possible descendants can supply us with the true, the unique
Peacockian essence. We find only adumbrations of it in the eight-
eenth century French tales from which sound critics would derive
his novels. We discover it somewhat adulterated in Mallock's *New
Republic*, come on traces of it in Norman Douglas, and taste it in
Aldous Huxley's *Crome Yellow*. We know that Peacock gave much
time and affection to Aristophanes and Petronius, to Rabelais and
Voltaire, that their humors chimed with his, yet we may look in

vain under those great names for the precise sort of thing that we find bearing his own less famous signature.

Like his masters, he was a satirist in all his fibers: in observation, thought, and utterance. There is a portrait of him at the age of eighteen which reveals the youth who was father to the man. In it we see a youngster of obvious and self-conscious intelligence, behind whose smile there lurks profound amusement at the world he is viewing, whose eyes are the keenest, the liveliest a picture ever showed. The whole expression is alert, sharp, shrewd, even impudent, and yet it is tremendously attractive. There is a saving warmth, a saving geniality. We can be sure that in this nature sharpness will never turn bitter, that shrewdness will never prove selfish, that impudence will not swell into arrogance. Geniality, indeed, is a prime ingredient, the very mark, of Peacockian satire. It has no place for the savage wrath of a Juvenal or the dark humors of a Swift. Even during the most violent verbal clashes between the fanatics who people Peacock's world, good-humor is always the presiding deity at the feast; there is always a handy bottle from which conciliatory bumpers may be poured.

The game of identifying Peacock's characters with their originals has long been an amusing one, and the present volume is furnished with a Key, which it is hoped will be used with discretion. For these identifications are partial at best. No one knew better than the author of Nightmare Abbey that he was not drawing a portrait of his friend Shelley when he depicted Scythrop. But he was giving fictional body to one aspect of Shelley's nature, just as, years later, he was to embody other characteristics of the same poet in Mr. Falconer of Gryll Grange. His originals seldom served any more thorough purpose than this, and their contribution was usually even more sketchy. There is something of Coleridge in the figures of Panscope, Mystic, Flosky, and Skionar; but really not very much of him in any one of these fuddled philosophers, or in all of them put together. Nor was there meant to be. The fact is that Peacock's favorite targets were not individuals but types, which came within the satirist's range as vulnerable personifications of humors, crotchets, theories, schemes, obsessions, and opinions of every hue and age. In the preface which he contributed to a collection of his tales in 1837, Peacock himself pointed to the general and perdurable nature of his butts.

"Headlong Hall," he wrote, "begins with the Holyhead Mail, and Crotchet Castle ends with a rotten borough. The Holyhead Mail no longer keeps the same hours, nor stops at the Capel Cerig Inn, which the progress of improvement has thrown out of the road; and the rotten boroughs of 1830 have ceased to exist, though there are some very pretty pocket properties, which are their worthy successors. But the classes of tastes, feelings, and opinions, which were successively brought into play in these little tales, remain substantially the same. Perfectabilians, deteriorationists, statu-quo-ites, phrenologists, transcendentalists, political economists, theorists in all sciences, projectors in all arts, morbid visionaries, romantic enthusiasts, lovers of music, lovers of the picturesque, and lovers of good dinners, march, and will march for ever, pari passu with the march of mechanics, which some facetiously call the march of intellect. The fastidious in old wine are a race that does not decay. Literary violaters of the confidences of private life still gain a disreputable livelihood and an unenviable notoriety. Match-makers from interest, and the disappointed in love and in friendship, are varieties of which specimens are extant. The great principle of the Right of Might is as flourishing now as in the days of Maid Marian: the array of false pretensions, moral, political, and literary, is as imposing as ever: the rulers of the world still feel things in their effects, and never foresee them in their causes; and political mounte-banks continue, and will continue, to puff nostrums and practise legerdemain under the eyes of the multitude; following like the 'learned friend' of Crotchet Castle, a course as tortuous as that of a river, but in a reverse process; beginning by being dark and deep, and ending by being transparent."

Here we may glimpse at least a few of Peacock's likes and dis-likes, and lightly sample his satirical temper in the reference to the "learned friend," whose original was Lord Brougham, a politician whose vanity, love of parade, and parliamentary methods were all nicely calculated to make our author's hackles rise. Brougham, indeed, was among the few individuals at whom Peacock aimed with anything like lethal intent. For the most part, he was out for sport, and he found it wherever he looked.

He was free to find it because his essential role in life was that of the detached observer. He had no vested interests to serve or to guard, no political commitments to respect, no ambitions that made it prudent for him to suppress occasionally his sense of the ludicrous. His inherited position in English society was nondescript, for his father was a London glass merchant while his maternal grandfather was a master in the Royal Navy; and nondescript it remained —save for the modest honors due to authorship and service at India House—from the day of his birth at Weymouth, in 1785, to the day of his death at Lower Halliford, in 1866. He formed no alliances that hampered, and he made no pledges that hobbled him. He was neither a climber nor a joiner; he was not even a fighter. In the midst of a self-seeking world, he sought after little, for he knew how to live by the rules that Horace could at least express. His was a great capacity for contentment, of both the sedentary and physically active kinds. His father, who died in 1788, left his widow and child well enough off for the latter to feel free to follow his own inclinations, after trying his hand at one or two uncongenial tasks, and, when the patrimony dwindled, he proceeded without fuss or bustle to get himself a good post with the East India Company, which enabled him to afford the luxury of a wife. Her name was Jane Gryffydh, she was pretty and she was Welsh, he proposed to her (after not seeing or writing to her for eight years) in a letter that is a model of rationality, and the happiness of their union was testimony to the eminent good sense of the entire business.

His formal schooling lasted some six years, ending when he was not yet thirteen. During this early period, spent on the edge of Windsor Forest, he exhibited the characteristics that were to mark his maturity: love of study and physical exercise, robust independence, and a taste for solitude. He left school early, but his education was a life-long activity, and no commonplace idiom amused him more than the one which referred to a young gentleman who was finishing his education at one of the universities. Whether Peacock's scorn for these institutions would have been less, if he had gone to Oxford or Cambridge, is a question. As it was, that scorn was considerable, for he had as little use for what he deemed fossilized methods of teaching as he had for the rising system of popular education, which he insisted was nothing but mis-education, certain to produce many unhappy results. And who can say that he would have to recall his words if he were alive today?

Books were university enough for him. After a brief bout of clerking, at the turn of the century, he headed for the reading room of the British Museum, where he spent the best hours of five or six years building upon the rudiments of Greek, Latin and French, which he had acquired at school, learning Italian, and absorbing the greatest literature to be found in the languages at his command. It was to books that he returned, in 1809, after a brief tour of duty as secretary to Admiral Popham, commander of HMS *Venerable;* they were always waiting for him when he came home from India House; and they remained the inexhaustible consolation of his last years, when death had taken the dearest members of his family from him. In his middle seventies he was still clinging to an old routine which called him from bed at five every morning, that he might read from then until breakfast at eight, and after that divide the rest of his day between library and open air, in proportions determined by the weather.

It is fitting that death should have laid its hand upon him just where it did, even if he was not struck down at once. For it was in his library, that inviolable sanctuary in his house at Lower Halliford which was his home for so many years, that he suffered the shock from which he could not rally. A fire having broken out in the roof of his bedroom, the octogenarian went straight to his books, probably as much with the thought of protecting them as with that of seeking refuge from the flames and water which were threatening the other end of the house; and there he settled himself firmly, until a nearer approach of danger made a perturbed curate beg him to desert his library for the shelter of another dwelling. Thereupon the old man eyed the curate with disdain and roared: "By the immortal gods, I will not move!" Nor did he; and the fire was mastered before it reached him. But shock was another matter. This put him to bed, shaken and sick, and there he stayed until he died a few weeks later, aged eighty years and three months.

Peacock was a bookman through and through, but he was no pallid worm. Handsome in youth and age, sturdy and above middle height, he was a tremendous walker, a good swimmer and a good oarsman. Landor, in his famous quatrain, put nature first and art second among his loves. It is hardly credible that Peacock would have placed nature above literature in a similar category, but throughout his life the two ran a close race for his favor. Perhaps it would be more accurate to say that they ran tandem. Good country in good weather was, for him, the one rival of good reading. Wales was made for walking, he thought, and so was Scotland; nor was there any doubt regarding the purpose upon this earth of Windsor Forest. Clear summer days saw him abroad from dawn to sunset, afoot or on the river, and then it was his books gave ground. But they were never abandoned. As he wrote to Shelley, during the summer of 1818: "I open to myself many vistas in the great forest of mind, and reconnoitre the tracts of territory which in the winters I propose to acquire."

Conducting his self-education early and late, decade after decade, he did a thoroughgoing job. His literary knowledge was wide and deep and well-assimilated, and when specialists say that his scholarship was not exact, they mean only that it was not textually or philologically precise when judged by the strictest professional standards. His reading of Homer and Horace, Aristophanes and Nonnus, Sophocles and Virgil, Tacitus and Ariosto, Cicero and Rabelais—to mention only some of his favorites—made these authors part of himself, of his own mind, of his literary equipment. If his admirations appear conventional, one must note that he valued these writers not for their fame, but for what he himself found in them. It was no truckler to convention who insisted that, next to the Iliad, the greatest poem in the world is Nonnus's Dionysica. He was learned enough to know that the oldest books are often the freshest and most vital, while the youth of those new from the press frequently goes no deeper than their covers, between which we find borrowings warmed over for the hundredth time. He was wise enough to know that the true contemporaries of a man of letters are to be found in all ages. If he was fastidious in his unwillingness to give his time to any but the best, he recognized the best when he met it, even if it belonged to his own day, as he proved when he picked up Dickens in his later years.

Men were less necessary to him than books, but this novelist of conviviality, this recorder of almost endless conversations and innumerable bumpers, this genial historian of mighty trenchermen and great drinkers, was in his own discriminating way a happy social animal. His friendship with Shelley is famous: it was intimate from 1812 until 1818, when Shelley left England for Italy, and after that it was maintained through correspondence until the younger man's death. That the inveterate idealist and the ingrained satirist should have enjoyed each other's company so much has puzzled some writers, but such puzzlement betrays a narrow view of the nature of friendship and an ignorance of the many bases on which it can securely rest. During these years, Peacock naturally saw a good deal of the numerous members of Shelley's circle, by several of whom he was held to be an unfortunately cynical influence; a judgment which he doubtless provoked, for he and Harriet Shelley had a way of laughing happily together at faddists and enthusiasts. Perhaps this shared fun played its part in making Peacock remain Harriet's stout champion until the end of his life.

For several years he dined once a week with Bentham, imbibing the utilitarian philosophy at its source, with interest and respect, but still with reservations of independent thought. He also saw a good deal of James and John Stuart Mill, both "Company" men, without any friendly warmth being generated. George Meredith became his son-in-law, but did not win his affection. However, with John Carr Hobhouse, later Lord Broughton, it was different. The office acquaintanceship, which began at India House about 1830, ripened into a lasting intimacy which gave deep satisfaction to both men as their years grew upon them. Indeed, it was only Broughton who could persuade the comparative recluse of Lower Halliford to leave his lares even for a night. But the full story of Peacock's few friendships must be left to his biographers, of whom Carl Van Doren is still the best.

For a man whose true interests were radically divorced from the world of affairs, Peacock proved remarkably capable in his business conduct during his many years of service with the East India Company. Entering the Examiner's office in 1819, he advanced steadily from a subordinate position, with regular increases in salary, until in 1836 he succeeded James Mill as Examiner, a post which he held efficiently for twenty years. His was no superior clerkship, but a position that involved him in the formulation and execution of the policies of an *imperium in imperio*. On several occasions he was chosen to represent John Company before parliamentary committees, and on these occasions he performed with distinction. His letters show that he could think in terms of imperial geography and imperial forces; his knowledge of Nonnus was matched by his knowledge of Far Eastern navigation problems, and those who have thought of him as being always a proponent of the old, as opposed to the new, should note the part his influence played in the substitution of steam for sail and iron for wood.

Yet he might have served his company with five times as much distinction as he did, and still be no more than a name followed by a curt entry in the *Dictionary of National Biography*. But for one fact, there would be nothing in the record of his life to attract and hold the inquiring eye. His existence was quiet, almost secluded; nothing remarkable happened to him. Oh, yes, he often saw Shelley plain; but so did a great many others. What is important about him, and important to us, is that he did one thing supremely well. He wrote seven little "novels" that are unlike any other novels under the moon.

He was slow in finding himself. In his youth he fancied his talents as a poet, and the fancy lingered, but he proved that he was one only after verse had become incidental to his fiction. There may be Peacockians who still read *The Genius of the Thames* and *Rhododaphne* with determined affection, but if there are, they are qualified candidates for their author's own band of crotcheteers. He also, when young, fancied himself as a playwright, and there too he was mistaken. His brief essays at drama are now read only by his biographers and editors; but they pointed the way to the novels, and vestiges of them may be discovered in a happier context than that in which they came to birth.

It was in 1815, in his thirtieth year, that Thomas Love Peacock set his feet to his destined path. He did it at the precise moment when he picked up his pen and wrote:—"The ambiguous light of a December morning, peeping through the windows of the Holyhead mail, dispelled the soft visions of the four insides, who had slept, or seemed to sleep, through the first seventy miles of the road, with as much comfort as may be supposed consistent with the jolting of the vehicle, and an occasional admonition to remem-

ber the coachman, thundered through the open door, accompanied by the gentle breath of Boreas, into the ears of the drowsy traveller."

No *exoridum* could have been more conventional. It might well have led into a novel of sentiment or adventure, or even a tale of the terror school. But it did nothing of the kind, for with it some-thing new was beginning in English fiction. This novelty started to show itself in the very next paragraph, with the facetious account of Squire Headlong's ancestry, and it came fully into view a mo-ment later, when the author named the four inside passengers of the Mail, all of whom had been invited to pass Christmas at Head-long Hall. "These gentlemen were, Mr. Foster, the perfectabilian; Mr. Escot, the deteriorationist; Mr. Jenkison, the statu-quo-ite; and the Reverend Doctor Gaster, who, though of course neither a philosopher nor a man of taste, had so won on the Squire's fancy, by a learned discussion on the art of stuffing a turkey, that he con-cluded no Christmas party would be complete without him."

Here are prime ingredients of the Peacockian mixture: three gentlemen of violently differing opinions, a parson whose name betrays his weakness, a genial host, and, at least potentially, the pleasures of the table. The three philosophers are the forerunners of a numerous company of faddists, hobby-riders, crotcheteers, and fanatics, with which Peacock will delight himself and his readers. The Reverend Doctor Gaster is a primitive version of a type that will flower to perfection in Doctor Folliott and Doctor Opimian; Squire Headlong is a model in his role of host; and the turkey is a symbol of all the good cheer that will be dispensed, in volume after volume, at various country seats. By the time the ladies have retired from the table at Headlong Hall, leaving the gentlemen with their wine, we are in the midst of a world that is unique in English literature. With the postprandial eloquence of Mr. Escot and Mr. Foster, we begin to hear the characteristic tones, and some of the themes, of the Peacockian dialogue. Doctor Gaster, tossing off a bumper, has just remarked that the antidiluvian patriarchs "knew not the use of the grape, happily for them." Whereupon Mr. Escot exclaims:—

"Happily, indeed! The first inhabitants of the world knew not the use either of wine or animal food; it is, therefore, by no means incredible that they lived to the age of several centuries, free from war, and commerce, and arbitrary government, and every other species of desolating wickedness. But man was then a very different animal to what he now is: he had not the faculty of speech; he was not encumbered with clothes; he lived in the open air; his first step out of which, as Hamlet truly observes, is *into his grave.* His first dwellings, of course, were the hollows of trees and rocks. In process of time he began to build: thence grew villages; thence grew cities. Luxury, oppression, poverty, misery, and disease kept pace with the progress of his pretended improvements, till, from a free, strong, healthy, peaceful animal, he has become a weak, distempered, cruel, carnivorous slave."

With *Headlong Hall,* Peacock shaped a form peculiarly suited to his own needs of expression: a short work of fiction, with a picturesque rural background, in which a little love and a little horseplay yield precedence to the marches and countermarches of opinion; the encompassing satirical climate being mollified by genial winds of humor. The author sought, without entire success, to expand this form in *Melincourt* (1817); used it most happily in *Nightmare Abbey* (1818) and brought it to perfection in *Crotchet Castle* (1831), the tale in which Folliott flourishes, which has been described justly as "an unconquerable fortress of wit and scholarship." Finally, after a long literary silence due to a complex of business and domestic causes, he returned to this same form in *Gryll Grange* (1860-61) and demonstrated that he had, in his mid-seventies, lost nothing of his quality, and only a trifle of his strength. Meanwhile, during the years of his greatest productivity, he had turned aside from his "house-party" novels to write two romances in which opinionated talk is less dominant. These are *Maid Marian* (1822); and *The Misfortunes of Elphin* (1829). They are both highly entertaining excursions into the past, the first into Robin Hood's Sherwood Forest, the second into medieval Wales: they are both entirely characteristic of their author, and either would have served to win him a respectable reputation, but because of their form they stand a little apart from the main body of his work. In form only, however, not in spirit. No one else could have written them. No one else could have drawn the people of Sherwood with the same nice mixture of sentiment and irony; no one else could have furnished that incomparable drunkard Seithenyn with his incomparable eloquence.

Since Peacock's characters are close at hand, waiting for the readers of this volume to join them, there seems little purpose in listing their names and traits here, or in setting forth their views on life in the large, and on all matters under heaven, great and small. Nor is there any more reason to enumerate the almost numberless objects of their creator's satire. It will be much better to turn the page, and use eyes and ears. It will be much better to walk straight into the liveliest series of symposia to be found in our literature, wherein everyone talks for victory and nobody wins any battles, where, at the end of every discussion, every character can join with unshaken conviction in Mr. Trillo's chorus:

> After careful meditation,
> And profound deliberation,
> On the various pretty projects which have just been shown,
> Not a scheme in agitation,
> For the world's amelioration,
> Has a grain of common sense in it, except my own.

And where, no matter how hot the jousting grows, there is always someone with sense enough to say: Pass the bottle.

There is, however, one subject that remains to be considered, and that is Peacock's own position amid all the opinions, ideas, theories, and persons which he assaulted with such impartial vigor. Because he directed his shafts as deftly at statu-quo-ites as at reformers, because he laughed as happily at the excesses of idealism as at the folly of reaction, he has been a sore trial to his critics. Where, they demand, did he stand?

His position, it seems, was arrived at by a sturdy common sense which was sharpened by an increasing scepticism. Only a part of his knowledge came from books: he was alive to all the movements and currents of his time, and his awareness of them confirmed the natural bent of his intelligence. The thoughtful reader of his novels will keep in mind the social background against which they came into being. When *Headlong Hall* was written, Liverpool was Prime Minister and Eldon was on the woolsack: a government, successful in war, faced profound social unrest with the smug assertion that reform of any kind was neither desirable nor desired. When

Gryll Grange was written, Gladstone was preparing to succeed Palmerston, the first Reform Bill was nearly thirty years old, and the second was only a few years ahead. Between these two books lay a period of change unmatched in English history. There had been great suffering among the people, and there had been threats of revolution. With the abolition of rotten and pocket boroughs, and the enfranchisement of towns and cities, the middle class had come to power by virtue of rights that were soon to be shared with artisans. Railways, new highways, new canals, steam navigation, and sanitation had changed the country's face, just as the triumph of the machine and the rise of the laboratory had transformed industry, while labor's position was being improved by factory reforms and the emergence of the trade unions. The electric telegraph, proliferating newspapers, and cheap postage were having their effects. The penal code had been humanized, the poor laws overhauled, Catholics emancipated and Dissenters recognized as respectable members of society. The Navy could no longer press men into its service, and householders could no longer send small boys up their chimneys. Free trade and laissez-faire had performed wonders so complicated that the necessity of increasing governmental controls over business was clearly foreseen. The dream of empire was paying undreamed of dividends. With the International Exhibition of 1851, the expanding period had reached the zenith of complacency and optimism. Then and there, as if in a mirror, it had stared with dazzled admiration and infinite respect at its own features. The six million visitors who crowded into Hyde Park's Crystal Palace knew that there was nothing, now, that man could not do; nothing that he would not do.

But Peacock was not one of the crowd, and never had been. He was sure that new goods often bring new evils in their train. He was aware that many solutions are themselves problems in disguise. His sentiments drew him affectionately towards the past, the imperfections of which he clearly saw, while his intelligence made him alert to present errors and evils, and sceptical of a future in the perfection of which he could not believe. His scepticism extended to his own prejudices, hates, and crotchets, but he still claimed the unalienable human right of hugging them to his heart. He did not share the mystical faith in science which possessed many of his contemporaries, yet he was willing to partake of the benefits which science bestowed, as when he became a commuter to and from town, thanks to the newly laid railway. If no one of his characters served him as a true mouthpiece, a good many of them enjoyed a distribution of his ideas; and we may be sure that the Reverend Doctor Opimian was far from distasteful to his creator when he delivered himself as follows, obviously envisaging a future that is our present.

"Science is one thing, and wisdom is another. Science is an edged tool, with which men play like children, and cut their own fingers. If you look at the results which science has brought in its train, you will find them to consist almost wholly in elements of mischief. See how much belongs to the word Explosion alone, of which the ancients knew nothing. Explosions of powder-mills and powder-magazines; of coal-gas in mines and in houses; of high-pressure engines in ships and boats and factories. See the complications and refinements of modes of destruction, in revolvers and rifles and shells and rockets and cannon. See collisions and wrecks and every mode of disaster by land and by sea, resulting chiefly from the insanity for speed, in those who for the most part have nothing to do at the end of the race, which they run as if they were so many Mercuries, speeding with messages from Jupiter. Look at our scientific drainage, which turns refuse into poison. Look at the subsoil of London, wherever it is turned up to the air, converted by gas leakage into one mass of pestilent blackness, in which no vegetation can flourish, and above which, with the rapid growth of the evergrowing nuisance, no living thing will breathe with impunity. Look at our scientific machinery, which has destroyed domestic manufacture, which has substituted rottenness for strength in the thing made, and physical degradation in crowded towns for healthy and comfortable country life in the makers. The day would fail, if I should attempt to enumerate the evils which science has inflicted on mankind. I almost think it is the ultimate destiny of science to exterminate the human race."

And, with that timely quotation, let us follow the good doctor back into the world from which he came.

BEN RAY REDMAN

New York City,
December, 1946.

A NOTE ON THE TEXT

The present text of the novels is based on the edition of Peacock's
WORKS, 1875, edited by Henry Cole. *Nightmare Abbey* and
Crotchet Castle are here complete, except for the quotations with
which the author headed his chapters, and some of his original footnotes. The cutting of *Headlong Hall, Melincourt, Maid Marian,
The Misfortunes of Elphin,* and *Gryll Grange,* has been so done as
to present large sections of these works in their entirety; the sections
being connected by narrative bridges, in square brackets which have
been designed to combine utility with brevity. Notes in square brackets
have been supplied by the present editor. The others are Peacock's
own.

Headlong Hall

THE MAIL

THE ambiguous light of a December morning, peeping through the windows of the Holyhead mail, dispelled the soft visions of the four insides, who had slept, or seemed to sleep, through the first seventy miles of the road, with as much comfort as may be supposed consistent with the jolting of the vehicle, and an occasional admonition to remember the coachman, thundered through the open door, accompanied by the gentle breath of Boreas, into the ears of the drowsy traveller.

A lively remark, that the day was none of the finest, having elicited a repartee of quite the contrary, the various knotty points of meteorology, which usually form the exordium of an English conversation, were successfully discussed and exhausted; and, the ice being thus broken, the colloquy rambled to other topics, in the course of which it appeared, to the surprise of every one, that all four, though perfect strangers to each other, were actually bound to the same point, namely, Headlong Hall, the seat of the ancient and honourable family of the Headlongs, of the vale of Llanberris, in Caernarvonshire. This name may appear at first sight not to be truly Cambrian, like those of the Rices, and Prices, and Morgans, and Owens, and Williamses, and Evanses, and Parrys, and Joneses; but, nevertheless, the Headlongs claim to be not less genuine derivatives from the antique branch of Cadwallader than any of the last-named multiramified families. They claim, indeed, by one account, superior antiquity to all of them, and even to Cadwallader himself; a tradition having been handed down in Headlong Hall for some few thousand years, that the founder of the family was

3

preserved in the deluge on the summit of Snowdon, and took the name of Rhaiader, which signifies a *waterfall*, in consequence of his having accompanied the water in its descent or diminution, till he found himself comfortably seated on the rocks of Llanberris. But, in later days, when commercial bagmen began to scour the country, the ambiguity of the sound induced his descendants to drop the suspicious denomination of *Riders*, and translate the word into English; when, not being well pleased with the sound of the *thing*, they substituted that of the *quality*, and accordingly adopted the name *Headlong*, the appropriate epithet of waterfall.

> I cannot say how the truth may be:
> I tell the tale as 'twas told to me.

The present representative of this ancient and dignified house, Harry Headlong, Esquire, was, like all other Welsh squires, fond of shooting, hunting, racing, drinking, and other such innocent amusements, μειζονος δ' αλλου τινος, as Menander expresses it. But unlike other Welsh squires, he had actually suffered certain phenomena, called books, to find their way into his house; and, by dint of lounging over them after dinner, on those occasions when he was compelled to take his bottle alone, he became seized with a violent passion to be thought a philosopher and a man of taste; and accordingly set off on an expedition to Oxford, to inquire for other varieties of the same genera, namely, men of taste and philosophers; but, being assured by a learned professor that there were no such things in the University, he proceeded to London, where, after beating up in several booksellers' shops, theatres, exhibition-rooms, and other resorts of literature and taste, he formed as extensive an acquaintance with philosophers and dilettanti as his utmost ambition could desire; and it now became his chief wish to have them altogether in Headlong Hall, arguing, over his old Port and Burgundy, the various knotty points which had puzzled his pericranium. He had, therefore, sent them invitations in due form to pass their Christmas at Headlong Hall; which invitations the extensive fame of his kitchen fire had induced the greater part of them to accept; and four of the chosen guests had, from different parts of the metropolis, ensconced themselves in the four corners of the Holy-head mail.

These four persons were, Mr. Foster, the perfectibilian; Mr. Escot, the deteriorationist; Mr. Jenkison, the statu-quo-ite; and the Reverend Doctor Gaster, who, though of course neither a philosopher nor a man of taste, had so won on the Squire's fancy, by a learned dissertation on the art of stuffing a turkey, that he concluded no Christmas party would be complete without him.

The conversation among these illuminati soon became animated; and Mr. Foster, who, we must observe, was a thin gentleman, about thirty years of age, with an aquiline nose, black eyes, white teeth, and black hair—took occasion to panegyrize the vehicle in which they were then travelling, and observed what remarkable improvements had been made in the means of facilitating intercourse between distant parts of the kingdom: he held forth with great energy on the subject of roads and railways, canals and tunnels, manufactures and machinery: "In short," said he, "everything we look on attests the progress of mankind in all the arts of life, and demonstrates their gradual advancement towards a state of unlimited perfection."

Mr. Escot, who was somewhat younger than Mr. Foster, but rather more pale and saturnine in his aspect, here took up the thread of the discourse, observing, that the proposition just advanced seemed to him perfectly contrary to the true state of the case: "for," said he, "these improvements, as you call them, appear to me only so many links in the great chain of corruption, which will soon fetter the whole human race in irreparable slavery and incurable wretchedness: your improvements proceed in a simple ratio, while the factitious wants and unnatural appetites they engender proceed in a compound one; and thus one generation acquires fifty wants, and fifty means of supplying them are invented, which each in its turn engenders, two new ones; so that the next generation has a hundred, the next two hundred, the next four hundred, till every human being becomes such a helpless compound of perverted inclinations, that he is altogether at the mercy of external circumstances, loses all independence and singleness of character, and degenerates so rapidly from the primitive dignity of his sylvan origin, that it is scarcely possible to indulge in any other expectation, than that the whole species must at length be exterminated by its own infinite imbecility and vileness."

"Your opinions," said Mr. Jenkison, a round-faced little gentleman of about forty-five, "seem to differ *toto cœlo*. I have often debated the matter in my own mind, *pro* and *con*, and have at length arrived at this conclusion,—that there is not in the human race a tendency either to moral perfectibility or deterioration; but that the quantities of each are so exactly balanced by their reciprocal results, that the species, with respect to the sum of good and evil, knowledge and ignorance, happiness and misery, remains exactly and perpetually *in statu quo*."

"Surely," said Mr. Foster, "you cannot maintain such a proposition in the face of evidence so luminous. Look at the progress of all the arts and sciences,—see chemistry, botany, astronomy——."

"Surely," said Mr. Escot, "experience deposes against you. Look at the rapid growth of corruption, luxury, selfishness——."

"Really, gentleman," said the Reverend Doctor Gaster, after clearing the husk in his throat with two or three hems, "this is a very sceptical, and, I must say, atheistical conversation, and I should have thought, out of respect to my cloth——."

Here the coach stopped, and the coachman, opening the door, vociferated, "Breakfast, gentlemen;" a sound which so gladdened the ears of the divine, that the alacrity with which he sprang from the vehicle superinduced a distortion of his ankle, and he was obliged to limp into the inn between Mr. Escot and Mr. Jenkison; the former observing that he ought to look for nothing but evil, and, therefore, should not be surprised at this little accident; the latter remarking that the comfort of a good breakfast, and the pain of a sprained ankle, pretty exactly balanced each other.

THE SQUIRE.—THE BREAKFAST

SQUIRE HEADLONG, in the meanwhile, was quadri-partite in his locality; that is to say, he was superintending the operations in four scenes of action—namely, the cellar, the library, the picture-gallery, and the dining-room—preparing for the reception of his philosophical and dilettante visitors. His myrmidon on this occasion was a little red-nosed butler, whom nature seemed to have cast in the genuine mould of an antique Silenus, and who waddled about the house after his master, wiping his forehead and panting for breath, while the latter bounced from room to room like a cracker, and was indefatigable in his requisitions for the proximity of his vinous Achates, whose advice and co-operation he deemed no less necessary in the library than in the cellar. Multitudes of packages had arrived, by land and water, from London, and Liverpool, and Chester, and Manchester, and Birmingham, and various parts of the mountains: books, wine, cheese, globes, mathematical instruments, turkeys, telescopes, hams, tongues, microscopes, quadrants, sextants, fiddles, flutes, tea, sugar, electrical machines, figs, spices, air-pumps, soda-water, chemical apparatus, eggs, French-horns, drawing-books, palettes, oils and colours, bottled ale and porter, scenery for a private theatre, pickles and fish-sauce, patent lamps and chandeliers, barrels of oysters, sofas, chairs, tables, carpets, beds, looking-glasses, pictures, fruits and confections, nuts, oranges, lemons, packages of salt salmon, and jars of Portugal grapes. These, arriving with infinite rapidity, and in inexhaustible succession, had been deposited at random, as the convenience of the moment dictated,—sofas in the cellar, chandeliers in the kitchen, hampers of ale in the drawing-room, and fiddles and fish-sauce in the library. The servants, unpacking all these in furious haste, and flying with them from place to place, according to the tumultuous directions of Squire Headlong and the little fat butler who fumed at his heels, chafed, and crossed, and clashed, and tumbled over one another, upstairs and down. All was bustle, uproar, and confusion; yet nothing seemed to advance: while the rage and impetuosity of the Squire continued fermenting to the highest degree of exasperation, which he signified, from time to time, by converting some newly unpacked article, such as a book, a bottle, a ham, or a fiddle, into a missile against the head of some unfortunate servant who did not seem to move in a ratio of velocity corresponding to the intensity of his master's desires.

In this state of eager preparation we shall leave the happy inhabitants of Headlong Hall, and return to the three philosophers and the unfortunate divine, whom we left limping with a sprained ankle into the breakfast-room of the inn; where his two supporters deposited him safely in a large armchair, with his wounded leg comfortably stretched out on another. The morning being extremely cold, he contrived to be seated as near the fire as was consistent with his other object of having a perfect command of the table and its apparatus; which consisted not only of the ordinary comforts of tea and toast, but of a delicious supply of new-laid eggs, and a magnificent round of beef; against which Mr. Escot immediately pointed all the artillery of his eloquence, declaring the use of animal food, conjointly with that of fire, to be one of the principal causes of the present degeneracy of mankind. "The natural and original man," said he, "lived in the woods: the roots and fruits of the earth supplied his simple nutriment: he had few desires and no diseases. But, when he began to sacrifice victims on the altar of superstition, to pursue the goat and the deer, and, by the pernicious invention of fire, to pervert their flesh into food, luxury, disease, and premature death, were let loose upon the world. Such is clearly the correct interpretation of the fable of Prometheus, which is a symbolical portraiture of that disastrous epoch, when man first applied fire to culinary purposes, and thereby surrendered his liver to the vulture of disease. From that period the stature of mankind has been in a state of gradual diminution, and I have not the least doubt that it will continue to grow small by degrees and lamentably less, till the whole race will vanish imperceptibly from the face of the earth."

"I cannot agree," said Mr. Foster, "in the consequences being so very disastrous. I admit, that in some respects the use of animal food retards, though it cannot materially inhibit, the perfectibility of the species. But the use of fire was indispensably necessary, as Æschylus and Virgil expressly assert, to give being to the various arts of life, which, in their rapid and interminable progress, will finally conduct every individual of the race to the philosophic pinnacle of pure and perfect felicity."

"In the controversy concerning animal and vegetable food," said Mr. Jenkison, "there is much to be said on both sides; and, the question being in equipoise, I content myself with a mixed diet, and make a point of eating whatever is placed before me, provided it be good in its kind."

In this opinion his two brother philosophers practically coincided, though they both ran down the theory as highly detrimental to the best interests of man.

"I am really astonished," said the Reverend Doctor Gaster, gracefully picking off the supernal fragments of an egg he had just cracked, and clearing away a space at the top for the reception of a small piece of butter—"I am really astonished, gentlemen, at the very heterodox opinions I have heard you deliver: since nothing can be more obvious than that all animals were created solely and exclusively for the use of man."

"Even the tiger that devours him?" said Mr. Escot.

"Certainly," said Doctor Gaster.

"How do you prove it?" said Mr. Escot.

"It requires no proof," said Doctor Gaster: "it is a point of doctrine. It is written, therefore it is so."

"Nothing can be more logical," said Mr. Jenkison. "It has been said," continued he, "that the ox was expressly made to be eaten by man: it may be said, by a parity of reasoning, that man was expressly made to be eaten by the tiger: but as wild oxen exist where there are no men, and men where there are no tigers, it would seem that in these instances they do not properly answer the ends of their creation."

"It is a mystery," said Dr. Gaster.

"Not to launch into the question of final causes," said Mr. Escot, helping himself at the same time to a slice of beef, "concerning which I will candidly acknowledge I am as profoundly ignorant as the most dogmatical theologian possibly can be, I just wish to observe that the pure and peaceful manners which Homer ascribes to the Lotophagi, and which at this day characterize many nations (the Hindoos, for example, who subsist exclusively on the fruits of the earth), depose very strongly in favour of a vegetable regimen."

"It may be said, on the contrary," said Mr. Foster, "that animal food acts on the mind as manure does on flowers, forcing them into a degree of expansion they would not otherwise have attained. If we can imagine a philosophical auricula falling into a train of theoretical meditation on its original and natural nutriment, till it should work itself up into a profound abomination of bullock's blood, sugar-bakers' scum, and other unnatural ingredients of that rich composition of soil which had brought it to perfection, and insist on being planted in common earth, it would have all the advantage of natural theory on its side that the most strenuous advocate of the vegetable system could desire; but it would soon discover the practical error of its retrograde experiment by its lamentable inferiority in strength and beauty to all the auriculas around it. I am afraid, in some instances at least, this analogy holds true with respect to mind. No one will make a comparison, in point of mental power, between the Hindoos and the ancient Greeks."

"The anatomy of the human stomach," said Mr. Escot, "and the formation of the teeth, clearly place man in the class of frugivorous animals."

"Many anatomists," said Mr. Foster, "are of a different opinion, and agree in discerning the characteristics of the carnivorous classes."

"I am no anatomist," said Mr. Jenkison, "and cannot decide, where doctors disagree; in the meantime I conclude that man is omnivorous, and on that conclusion I act."

"Your conclusion is truly orthodox," said the Reverend Doctor Gaster: "indeed the loaves and fishes are typical of a mixed diet; and the practice of the Church in all ages shows——"

"That it never loses sight of the loaves and fishes," said Mr. Escot.

"It never loses sight of any point of sound doctrine," said the reverend doctor.

The coachman now informed them that their time was elapsed; nor could all the pathetic remonstrances of the reverend divine, who declared that he had not half breakfasted, succeed in gaining one minute from the inexorable Jehu.

"You will allow," said Mr. Foster, as soon as they were again in motion, "that the wild man of the woods could not transport himself over two hundred miles of forest with as much facility as one of these vehicles transports you and me through the heart of this cultivated country."

"I am certain," said Mr. Escot, "that a wild man can travel an immense distance without fatigue; but what is the advantage of locomotion? The wild man is happy in one spot, and there he remains: the civilized man is wretched in every place he happens to be in, and then congratulates himself on being accommodated with a machine, that will whirl him to another, where he will be just as miserable as ever."

We shall now leave the mail-coach to find its way to Capel Cerig, the nearest point of the Holyhead road to the dwelling of Squire Headlong.

[Amid preparations at Headlong Hall, the Squire's lovely sister, Caprioletta, arrives to do the honours of the house. She is in time to set all in order and to greet the first visitor, Marmaduke Milestone, Esquire, "a picturesque landscape gardener of the first celebrity." Milestone is followed by other arriving guests in rapid succession: the Reverend Doctor Gaster; the three philosophers; Mr. Cranium and his lovely daughter, Cephalis; two profound critics, Mr. Gall and Mr. Treacle, accompanied by two "very multitudinous versifiers," Mr. Nightshade and Mr. MacLaurel; Mr. Chromatic with his two daughters, Tenorino and Graziosa; Sir Patrick O'Prism, a dilettante painter, with his maiden aunt, Miss Philomela Poppyseed, "an indefatigable compounder of novels, written for the express purpose of supporting every species of superstition and prejudice;" and, finally, Mr. Panscope, "who had run through the whole circle of the sciences, and understood them all equally well."

Mr. Milestone is eager to see the grounds, and the Squire is eager to show them, so they set out at the head of a small party.]

THE GROUNDS

"I PERCEIVE," said Mr. Milestone, after they had walked a few paces, "these grounds have never been touched by the finger of taste."

"The place is quite a wilderness," said Squire Headlong, "for, during the latter part of my father's life, while I was finishing my education, he troubled himself about nothing but the cellar, and suffered everything else to go to rack and ruin. A mere wilderness, as you see, even now in December; but in summer a complete nursery of briers, a forest of thistles, a plantation of nettles, without any live stock but goats that have eaten up all the bark of the trees. Here you see is the pedestal of a statue, with only half a leg and four toes remaining: there were many here once. When I was a boy, I used to sit every day on the shoulders of Hercules: what became of *him* I have never been able to ascertain. Neptune has been lying these seven years in the dust-hole; Atlas had his head knocked off to make him prop a shed; and only the day before yesterday we fished Bacchus out of the horse-pond."

"My dear sir," said Mr. Milestone, "accord me your permission to wave the wand of enchantment over your grounds. The rocks shall be blown up, the trees shall be cut down, the wilderness and all its goats shall vanish like mist. Pagodas and Chinese bridges, gravel walks and shrubberies, bowling-greens, canals, and clumps of larch, shall rise upon its ruins. One age, sir, has brought to light the treasures of ancient learning; a second has penetrated into the depths of metaphysics; a third has brought to perfection the science of astronomy; but it was reserved for the exclusive genius of the present times, to invent the noble art of picturesque gardening, which has given, as it were, a new tint to the complexion of nature, and a new outline to the physiognomy of the universe!"

"Give me leave," said Sir Patrick O'Prism, "to take an exception to that same. Your system of levelling, and trimming, and clipping, and docking, and clumping, and polishing, and cropping, and shaving, destroys all the beautiful intricacies of natural luxuriance, and all the graduated harmonies of light and shade, melting into one another, as you see them on that rock over yonder. I never saw one of your improved places, as you call them, and which are nothing but big bowling-greens, like sheets of green paper, with a parcel of round clumps scattered over them, like so many spots of ink, flicked at random out of a pen, and a solitary animal here and there looking as if it were lost, that I did not think it was for all the world like Hounslow Heath, thinly sprinkled over with bushes and highwaymen."

"Sir," said Mr. Milestone, "you will have the goodness to make a distinction between the picturesque and the beautiful."

"Will I?" said Sir Patrick, "och! but I won't. For what is beautiful? That which pleases the eye. And what pleases the eye? Tints variously broken and blended. Now, tints variously broken and blended constitute the picturesque."

"Allow me," said Mr. Gall. "I distinguish the picturesque and the beautiful, and I add to them, in the laying out of grounds, a third and distinct character, which I call *unexpectedness*."

"Pray sir," said Mr. Milestone, "by what name do you distinguish this character, when a person walks round the grounds for the second time?"

Mr. Gall bit his lips, and inwardly vowed to revenge himself on Milestone, by cutting up his next publication.

A long controversy now ensued concerning the picturesque and the beautiful, highly edifying to Squire Headlong.

The three philosophers stopped, as they wound round a projecting point of rock, to contemplate a little boat which was gliding over the tranquil surface of the lake below.

"The blessings of civilization," said Mr. Foster, "extend themselves to the meanest individuals of the community. That boatman, singing as he sails along, is, I have no doubt, a very happy, and, comparatively to the men of his class some centuries back, a very enlightened and intelligent man."

"As a partisan of the system of the moral perfectibility of the human race," said Mr. Escot,—who was always for considering things on a large scale, and whose thoughts immediately wandered from the lake to the ocean, from the little boat to a ship of the line,—"you will probably be able to point out to me the degree of improvement that you suppose to have taken place in the character of a sailor, from the days when Jason sailed through the Cyanean Symplegades, or Noah moored his ark on the summit of Ararat."

"If you talk to me," said Mr. Foster, "of mythological personages, of course I cannot meet you on fair grounds."

"We will begin, if you please, then," said Mr. Escot, "no further back than the battle of Salamis; and I will ask you if you think the mariners of England are, in any one respect, morally or intellectually, superior to those who then preserved the liberties of Greece, under the direction of Themistocles?"

"I will venture to assert," said Mr. Foster, "that, considered merely as sailors, which is the only fair mode of judging them, they are as far superior to the Athenians as the structure of our ships is superior to that of theirs. Would not one English seventy-four, think you, have been sufficient to have sunk, burned, and put to flight, all the Persian and Grecian vessels in that memorable bay? Contemplate the progress of naval architecture, and the slow, but immense, succession of concatenated intelligence, by which it has gradually attained its present stage of perfectibility. In this, as in all other branches of art and science, every generation possesses all the knowledge of the preceding, and adds to it its own discoveries in a progression to which there seems no limit. The skill requisite to direct these immense machines is proportionate to their magnitude and complicated mechanism; and, therefore, the English sailor, considered merely as a sailor, is vastly superior to the ancient Greek."

"You make a distinction, of course," said Mr. Escot, "between scientific and moral perfectibility?"

"I conceive," said Mr. Foster, "that men are virtuous in proportion as they are enlightened; and that, as every generation increases in knowledge, it also increases in virtue."

"I wish it were so," said Mr. Escot; "but to me the very reverse appears to be the fact. The progress of knowledge is not general: it is confined to a chosen few of every age. How far these are better than their neighbours, we may examine by-and-by. The mass of mankind is composed of beasts of burden, mere clods, and tools of their superiors. By enlarging and complicating your machines, you degrade, not exalt the human animals you employ to direct them. When the boatswain of a seventy-four pipes all hands to the main tack, and flourishes his rope's end over the shoulders of the poor fellows who are tugging at the ropes, do you perceive so dignified, so gratifying a picture, as Ulysses exhorting his dear friends, his ΕΡΙΗΡΕΣ 'ΕΤΑΙΡΟΙ,[1] to ply their oars with energy? You will say, Ulysses was a fabulous character. But the economy of his vessel is drawn from nature. Every man on board has a character and a will of his own. He talks to them, argues with them, convinces them; and they obey him, because they love him, and know the reason of his orders. Now, as I have said before, all singleness of character is lost. We divide men into herds like cattle: an individual man, if you strip him of all that is extraneous to himself, is the most wretched and contemptible creature on the face of the earth. The sciences advance. True. A few

[1 Faithful companions.]

years of study puts a modern mathematician in possession of more than Newton knew, and leaves him at leisure to add new discoveries of his own. Agreed. But does this make him a Newton? Does it put him in possession of that range of intellect, that grasp of mind, from which the discoveries of Newton sprang? It is mental power that I look for: if you can demonstrate the increase of that, I will give up the field. Energy—independence—individuality—disinterested virtue —active benevolence—self-oblivion—universal philanthropy—these are the qualities I desire to find, and of which I contend that every succeeding age produces fewer examples. I repeat it; there is scarcely such a thing to be found as a single individual man: a few classes compose the whole frame of society, and when you know one of a class you know the whole of it. Give me the wild man of the woods; the original, unthinking, unscientific, unlogical savage: in him there is at least some good; but, in a civilized, sophisticated, cold-blooded, mechanical, calculating slave of Mammon and the world, there is none—absolutely none. Sir, if I fall into a river, an unsophisticated man will jump in and bring me out; but a philosopher will look on with the utmost calmness, and consider me in the light of a projectile, and, making a calculation of the degree of force with which I have impinged the surface, the resistance of the fluid, the velocity of the current, and the depth of the water in that particular place, he will ascertain with the greatest nicety in what part of the mud at the bottom I may probably be found, at any given distance of time from the moment of my first immersion."

Mr. Foster was preparing to reply, when the first dinner-bell rang, and he immediately commenced a precipitate return towards the house; followed by his two companions, who both admitted that he was now leading the way to at least a temporary period of physical amelioration: "but, alas!" added Mr. Escot, after a moment's reflection, "Epulæ NOCUÊRE repostæ!" [1]

THE DINNER

THE sun was now terminating his diurnal course, and the lights were glittering on the festal board. When the ladies had retired, and

[1] Protracted banquets have been copious sources of evil.

the Burgundy had taken two or three tours of the table, the following
conversation took place:—

Squire Headlong.—Push about the bottle: Mr. Escot, it stands
with you. No heeltaps. As to skylight, liberty-hall.

Mr. Mac Laurel.—Really, Squire Headlong, this is the vara nactar
itsel. Ye hae saretainly descovered the tarrestrial paradise, but it flows
wi' a better leecor than milk an' honey.

The Rev. Doctor Gaster.—Hem! Mr. Mac Laurel! there is a degree of profaneness in that observation, which I should not have
looked for in so stanch a supporter of Church and State. Milk and
honey was the pure food of the antediluvian patriarchs, who knew
not the use of the grape, happily for them.—(*Tossing off a bumper of
Burgundy.*)

Mr. Escot.—Happily, indeed! The first inhabitants of the world
knew not the use either of wine or animal food; it is, therefore, by
no means incredible that they lived to the age of several centuries,
free from war, and commerce, and arbitrary government, and every
other species of desolating wickedness. But man was then a very different animal to what he now is: he had not the faculty of speech;
he was not encumbered with clothes; he lived in the open air; his
first step out of which, as Hamlet truly observes, is *into his grave.*[1]
His first dwellings, of course, were the hollows of trees and rocks.
In process of time he began to build: thence grew villages; thence
grew cities. Luxury, oppression, poverty, misery, and disease kept pace
with the progress of his pretended improvements, till, from a free,
strong, healthy, peaceful animal, he has become a weak, distempered,
cruel, carnivorous slave.

The Rev. Doctor Gaster.—Your doctrine is orthodox, in so far as
you assert that the original man was not encumbered with clothes,
and that he lived in the open air; but, as to the faculty of speech,
that, it is certain, he had, for the authority of Moses——

Mr. Escot.—Of course, sir, I do not presume to dissent from the
very exalted authority of that most enlightened astronomer and profound cosmogonist, who had, moreover, the advantage of being inspired; but when I indulge myself with a ramble in the fields of
speculation, and attempt to deduce what is probable and rational
from the sources of analysis, experience, and comparison, I confess

[1] See Lord Monboddo's "Ancient Metaphysics."

I am too often apt to lose sight of the doctrines of that great fountain of theological and geological philosophy.

Squire Headlong.—Push about the bottle.

Mr. Foster.—Do you suppose the mere animal life of a wild man, living on acorns, and sleeping on the ground, comparable in felicity to that of Newton, ranging through unlimited space, and penetrating into the arcana of universal motion—to that of a Locke, unravelling the labyrinth of minds—to that of a Lavoisier, detecting the minutest combinations of matter, and reducing all nature to its elements—to that of a Shakespeare, piercing and developing the springs of passion—or of a Milton, identifying himself, as it were, with the beings of an invisible world?

Mr. Escot.—You suppose extreme cases: but, on the score of happiness, what comparison can you make between the tranquil being of the wild man of the woods and the wretched and turbulent existence of Milton, the victim of persecution, poverty, blindness, and neglect? The records of literature demonstrate that Happiness and Intelligence are seldom sisters. Even if it were otherwise, it would prove nothing. The many are always sacrificed to the few. Where one man advances, hundreds retrograde; and the balance is always in favour of universal deterioration.

Mr. Foster.—Virtue is independent of external circumstances. The exalted understanding looks into the truth of things, and in its own peaceful contemplations, rises superior to the world. No philosopher would resign his mental acquisitions for the purchase of any terrestrial good.

Mr. Escot.—In other words, no man whatever would resign his identity, which is nothing more than the consciousness of his perceptions, as the price of any acquisition. But every man, without exception, would willingly effect a very material change in his relative situation to other individuals. Unluckily for the rest of your argument, the understanding of literary people is for the most part *exalted*, as you express it, not so much by the love of truth and virtue, as by arrogance and self-sufficiency; and there is, perhaps, less disinterestedness, less liberality, less general benevolence, and more envy, hatred, and uncharitableness among them, than among any other description of men.

(*The eye of Mr. Escot, as he pronounced these words, rested very innocently and unintentionally on Mr. Gall.*)

Mr. Gall.—You allude, sir, I presume, to my review.

Mr. Escot.—Pardon me, sir. You will be convinced it is impossible I can allude to your review, when I assure you that I have never read a single page of it.

Mr. Gall, Mr. Treacle, Mr. Nightshade, and Mr. Mac Laurel.—Never read our review!!!!

Mr. Escot.—Never. I look on periodical criticism in general to be a species of shop where panegyric and defamation are sold wholesale, retail, and for exportation. I am not inclined to be a purchaser of these commodities, or to encourage a trade which I consider pregnant with mischief.

Mr. Mac Laurel.—I can readily conceive, sir, ye wou'd na wullinly encoorage ony dealer in panegeeric: but, frae the manner in which ye speak o' the first creetics an' scholars o' the age, I shou'd think you wou'd hae a lettle mair predilaction for deefamation.

Mr. Escot.—I have no predilection, sir, for defamation. I make a point of speaking the truth on all occasions; and it seldom happens that the truth can be spoken without some stricken deer pronouncing it a libel.

Mr. Nightshade.—You are, perhaps, sir, an enemy to literature in general?

Mr. Escot.—If I were, sir, I should be a better friend to periodical critics.

Squire Headlong.—Buz!

Mr. Treacle.—May I simply take the liberty to inquire into the basis of your objection?

Mr. Escot.—I conceive that periodical criticism disseminates superficial knowledge, and its perpetual adjunct, vanity; that it checks in the youthful mind the habit of thinking for itself; that it delivers partial opinions, and thereby misleads the judgment; that it is never conducted with a view to the general interests of literature, but to serve the interested ends of individuals, and the miserable purposes of party.

Mr. Mac Laurel.—Ye ken, sir, a mon mun leeve.

Mr. Escot.—While he can live honourably, naturally, justly, certainly: no longer.

Mr. Mac Laurel.—Every mon, sir, leeves according to his ain notions of honour an' justice: there is a wee deference amang the learned wi' respact to the defineetion o' the terms.

Mr. Escot.—I believe it is generally admitted that one of the ingredients of justice is disinterestedness.

Mr. Mac Laurel.—It is na admetted, sir, amang the pheelosophers of Edinbroo' that there is ony sic thing as desenterestedness in the warld, or that a mon can care for onything sae much as his ain sel: for ye mun observe, sir, every mon has his ain parteecular feelings of what is gude, an' beautifu', an' consentaneous to his ain indiveedual nature, an' desires to see everything aboot him in that parteecular state which is maist conformable to his ain notions o' the moral an' poleetical fetness o' things. Twa men, sir, shall purchase a piece o' grund atween 'em, and ae mon shall cover his half wi' a park——

Mr. Milestone.—Beautifully laid out in lawns and clumps, with a belt of trees at the circumference, and an artificial lake in the centre.

Mr. Mac Laurel.—Exactly, sir: and shall keep it a' for his ain sel: an' the other mon shall divide his half into leetle farms of twa or three acres——

Mr. Escot.—Like those of the Roman republic, and build a cottage on each of them, and cover his land with a simple, innocent, and smiling population, who shall owe, not only their happiness, but their existence, to his benevolence.

Mr. Mac Laurel.—Exactly, sir: an' ye will ca' the first mon selfish, an' the second desenterested; but the pheelosophical truth is semply this, that the ane is pleased wi' looking at trees, an' the other wi' seeing people happy an' comfortable. It is aunly a matter of indiveedual feeling. A paisant saves a mon's life for the same reason that a hero or a footpad cuts his thrapple: an' a pheelosopher delevers a mon frae a preson, for the same reason that a tailor or a prime menester puts him into it: because it is conformable to his ain particular feelings o' the moral an' poleetical fetness o' things.

Squire Headlong.—Wake the Reverend Doctor. Doctor, the bottle stands with you.

The Rev. Doctor Gaster.—It is an error of which I am seldom guilty.

Mr. Mac Laurel.—Noo, ye ken, sir, every mon is the centre of his ain system, and endaivours as much as possible to adapt everything aroond him to his ain parteecular views.

Mr. Escot.—Thus, sir, I presume, it suits the particular views of a poet, at one time to take the part of the people against their oppressors, and at another to take the part of the oppressors against the people.

Mr. Mac Laurel.—Ye mun alloo, sir, that poetry is a sort of ware or commodity that is brought into the public market wi' a' other descreptions of merchandise, an' that a mon is pairfectly justified in getting the best price he can for his article. Noo, there are three reasons for taking the part o' the people: the first is, when general leeberty an' public happiness are conformable to your ain parteecular feelings o' the moral an' poleetical fetness o' things: the second is, when they happen to be, as it were, in a state of exceetabeelity, an' ye think ye can get a gude price for your commodity by flingin' in a leetle seasoning o' pheelanthropy an' republican speerit: the third is, when ye think ye can bully the menestry into gieing ye a place or a pansion to haud your din, an' in that case, ye point an attack against them within the pale o' the law; an', if they tak nae heed o' ye, ye open a stronger fire; an' the less heed they tak, the mair ye bawl; an' the mair factious ye grow, always within the pale o' the law, till they send a plenipotentiary to treat wi' ye for yoursel, an' then the mair popular ye happen to be, the better price ye fetch.

Squire Headlong.—Off with your heeltaps.

Mr. Cranium.—I perfectly agree with Mr. Mac Laurel in his definition of self-love and disinterestedness: every man's actions are determined by his peculiar views, and those views are determined by the organization of his skull. A man in whom the organ of benevolence is not developed, cannot be benevolent: he in whom it is so, cannot be otherwise. The organ of self-love is prodigiously developed in the greater number of subjects that have fallen under my observation.

Mr. Escot.—Much less, I presume, among savage than civilized men, who, *constant only to the love of self, and consistent only in their aim to deceive, are always actuated by the hope of personal advantage, or by the dread of personal punishment.*

Mr. Cranium.—Very probably.

Mr. Escot.—You have, of course, found very copious specimens of the organs of hypocrisy, destruction, and avarice.

Mr. Cranium.—Secretiveness, destructiveness, and covetiveness. You may add, if you please, that of constructiveness.

Mr. Escot.—Meaning, I presume, the organ of building; which I contend to be not the natural organ of the featherless biped.

Mr. Cranium.—Pardon me: it is here.—(*As he said these words he produced a skull from his pocket, and placed it on the table, to the great surprise of the company.*)—This was the skull of Sir Christopher Wren. You observe this protuberance—(*the skull was handed round the table*).

Mr. Escot.—I contend that the original unsophisticated man was by no means constructive. He lived in the open air, under a tree.

The Reverend Doctor Gaster.—The tree of life. Unquestionably. Till he had tasted the forbidden fruit.

Mr. Jenkison.—At which period, probably, the organ of constructiveness was added to his anatomy, as a punishment for his transgression.

Mr. Escot.—There could not have been a more severe one, since the propensity which has led him to building cities has proved the greatest curse of his existence.

Squire Headlong.—(*Taking the skull*)—Memento mori. Come, a bumper of Burgundy.

Mr. Nightshade.—A very classical application, Squire Headlong. The Romans were in the practice of adhibiting skulls at their banquets, and sometimes little skeletons of silver, as a silent admonition to the guests to enjoy life while it lasted.

The Reverend Doctor Gaster.—Sound doctrine, Mr. Nightshade.

Mr. Escot.—I question its soundness. The use of vinous spirit has a tremendous influence in the deterioration of the human race.

Mr. Foster.—I fear, indeed, it operates as a considerable check to the progress of the species towards moral and intellectual perfection. Yet many great men have been of opinion that it exalts the imagination, fires the genius, accelerates the flow of ideas, and imparts to dispositions naturally cold and deliberative, that enthusiastic sublimation which is the source of greatness and energy.

Mr. Nightshade.—Laudibus arguitur vini vinosus Homerus.[1]

[1] Homer is proved to have been a lover of wine by the praises he bestows upon it.

Mr. Jenkison.—I conceive the use of wine to be always pernicious in excess, but often useful in moderation: it certainly kills some, but it saves the lives of others: I find that an occasional glass, taken with judgment and caution, has a very salutary effect in maintaining that equilibrium of the system, which it is always my aim to preserve; and this calm and temperate use of wine was, no doubt, what Homer meant to inculcate when he said:

Παρ δε δεπας οινοιο, πιειν ὀτε βυμός ανωγοι.[1]

Squire Headlong.—Good. Pass the bottle.

(*Un morne silence.*)

Sir Christopher does not seem to have raised our spirits. Chromatic, favour us with a specimen of your vocal powers. Something in point.

Mr. Chromatic, without further preface, immediately struck up the following

SONG.

In his last binn SIR PETER lies,
    Who knew not what it was to frown:
Death took him mellow, by surprise,
    And in his cellar stopped him down,
Through all our land we could not boast
    A knight more gay, more prompt than he,
To rise and fill a bumper toast,
    And pass it round with THREE TIMES THREE.

None better knew the feast to sway,
    Or keep Mirth's boat in better trim;
For Nature had but little clay
    Like that of which she moulded him.
The meanest guest that graced his board
    Was there the freest of the free,
His bumper toast when PETER poured,
    And passed it round with THREE TIMES THREE.

He kept at true good humour's mark
    The social flow of pleasure's tide:
He never made a brow look dark,
    Nor caused a tear, but when he died.
No sorrow round his tomb should dwell:
    More pleased his gay old ghost would be,
For funeral song, and passing bell,
    To hear no sound but THREE TIMES THREE.

[1] A cup of wine at hand, to drink as inclination prompts.

(Hammering of knuckles and glasses, and shouts of Bravo!)

Mr. Panscope *(suddenly emerging from a deep reverie).*—I have heard, with the most profound attention, everything which the gentleman on the other side of the table has thought proper to advance on the subject of human deterioration; and I must take the liberty to remark, that it augurs a very considerable degree of presumption in any individual to set himself up against the *authority* of so many great men, as may be marshalled in metaphysical phalanx under the opposite banners of the controversy; such as Aristotle, Plato, the scholiast on Aristophanes, St. Chrysostom, St. Jerome, St. Athanasius, Orpheus, Pindar, Simonides, Gronovius, Hemsterhusius, Longinus, Sir Isaac Newton, Thomas Paine, Doctor Paley, the King of Prussia, the King of Poland, Cicero, Monsieur Gautier, Hippocrates, Machiavelli, Milton, Colley Cibber, Bojardo, Gregory Nazianzenus, Locke, D'Alembert, Boccaccio, Daniel Defoe, Erasmus, Doctor Smollett, Zimmermann, Solomon, Confucius, Zoroaster, and Thomas-à-Kempis.

Mr. Escot.—I presume, sir, you are one of those who value an *authority* more than a reason.

Mr. Panscope.—The *authority*, sir, of all these great men, whose works, as well as the whole of the Encyclopædia Britannica, the entire series of the Monthly Review, the complete set of the Variorum Classics, and the Memoirs of the Academy of Inscriptions, I have read through from beginning to end, deposes, with irrefragable refutation, against your ratiocinative speculations, wherein you seem desirous, by the futile process of analytical dialectics, to subvert the pyramidal structure of synthetically deduced opinions, which have withstood the secular revolutions of physiological disquisition, and which I maintain to be transcendentally self-evident, categorically certain, and syllogistically demonstrable.

Squire Headlong.—Bravo! Pass the bottle. The very best speech that ever was made.

Mr. Escot.—It has only the slight disadvantage of being unintelligible.

Mr. Panscope.—I am not obliged, sir, as Dr. Johnson observed on a similar occasion, to furnish you with an understanding.

Mr. Escot.—I fear, sir, you would have some difficulty in furnishing me with such an article from your own stock.

Mr. Panscope.—'Sdeath, sir, do you question my understand-ing?

Mr. Escot.—I only question, sir, where I expect a reply; which, from things that have no existence, I am not visionary enough to anticipate.

Mr. Panscope.—I beg leave to observe, sir, that my language was perfectly perspicuous, and etymologically correct; and, I conceive, I have demonstrated what I shall now take the liberty to say in plain terms, that all your opinions are extremely absurd.

Mr. Escot.—I should be sorry, sir, to advance any opinion that you would not think absurd.

Mr. Panscope.—Death and fury, sir——

Mr. Escot.—Say no more, sir. That apology is quite sufficient.

Mr. Panscope.—Apology, sir?

Mr. Escot.—Even so, sir. You have lost your temper, which I consider equivalent to a confession that you have the worst of the argument.

Mr. Panscope.—Lightning and devils! sir——

Squire Headlong.—No civil war!—Temperance in the name of Bacchus!—A glee! a glee! *Music has charms to bend the knotted oak.* Sir Patrick, you'll join?

Sir Patrick O'Prism.—Troth, with all my heart: for, by my soul, I'm bothered completely.

Squire Headlong.—Agreed, then: you, and I, and Chromatic. Bumpers!—bumpers! Come, strike up.

Squire Headlong, Mr. Chromatic, and Sir Patrick O'Prism, each holding a bumper, immediately vociferated the following

GLEE.

A heeltap! a heeltap! I never could bear it!
So fill me a bumper, a bumper of claret!
Let the bottle pass freely, don't shirk it nor spare it,
For a heeltap! a heeltap! I never could bear it!

No skylight! no twilight! while Bacchus rules o'er us:
No thinking! no shrinking! all drinking in chorus:
Let us moisten our clay, since 't is thirsty and porous:
No thinking! no shrinking! all drinking in chorus!

GRAND CHORUS

By Squire Headlong, Mr. Chromatic, Sir Patrick O'Prism, Mr. Pan-
scope, Mr. Jenkison, Mr. Gall, Mr. Treacle, Mr. Nightshade, Mr.
Mac Laurel, Mr. Cranium, Mr. Milestone, and the Reverend
Doctor Gaster.

A heeltap! a heeltap! I never could bear it!
So fill me a bumper, a bumper of claret!
Let the bottle pass freely, don't shirk it nor spare it,
For a heeltap! a heeltap! I never could bear it!

The little butler now waddled in with a summons from the ladies
to tea and coffee. The squire was unwilling to leave his Burgundy.
Mr. Escot strenuously urged the necessity of immediate adjournment, observing, that the longer they continued drinking the worse
they should be. Mr. Foster seconded the motion, declaring the transition from the bottle to female society to be an indisputable amelioration of the state of the sensitive man. Mr. Jenkison allowed the
squire and his two brother philosophers to settle the point between
them, concluding that was just as well in one place as another. The
question of adjournment was then put, and carried by a large majority.

[Dinner ended, Mr. Panscope determines to revenge himself upon
the contemptuous Mr. Escot by winning the favour of the fair
Cephalis. While the universal scientist broods, Mr. Cranium retires to work on the lecture with which he proposes to edify the
company, and the other members of the house party divert themselves according to their several tastes.]

THE WALK

IT WAS an old custom in Headlong Hall to have breakfast ready
at eight, and continue it till two; that the various guests might rise
at their own hour, breakfast when they came down, and employ the
morning as they thought proper; the Squire only expecting that they

should punctually assemble at dinner. During the whole of this period, the little butler stood sentinel at a side-table near the fire, copiously furnished with all the apparatus of tea, coffee, chocolate, milk, cream, eggs, rolls, toast, muffins, bread, butter, potted beef, cold fowl and partridge, ham, tongue, and anchovy. The Reverend Doctor Gaster found himself rather queasy in the morning, therefore preferred breakfasting in bed, on a mug of buttered ale and an anchovy toast. The three philosophers made their appearance at eight, and enjoyed *les prémices des dépouilles*. Mr. Foster proposed, that, as it was a fine frosty morning, and they were all good pedestrians, they should take a walk to Tremadoc, to see the improvements carrying on in that vicinity. This being readily acceded to, they began their walk.

After their departure, appeared Squire Headlong and Mr. Milestone, who agreed, over their muffin and partridge, to walk together to a ruined tower, within the precincts of the squire's grounds, which Mr. Milestone thought he could improve.

The other guests dropped in by ones and twos, and made their respective arrangements for the morning. Mr. Panscope took a little ramble with Mr. Cranium, in the course of which, the former professed a great enthusiasm for the science of craniology, and a great deal of love for the beautiful Cephalis, adding a few words about his expectations: the old gentleman was unable to withstand this triple battery, and it was accordingly determined—after the manner of the heroic age, in which it was deemed superfluous to consult the opinions and feelings of the lady, as to the manner in which she should be disposed of—that the lovely Miss Cranium should be made the happy bride of the accomplished Mr. Panscope. We shall leave them for the present to settle preliminaries, while we accompany the three philosophers in their walk to Tremadoc.

The vale contracted as they advanced, and, when they had passed the termination of the lake, their road wound along a narrow and romantic pass, through the middle of which an impetuous torrent dashed over vast fragments of stone. The pass was bordered on both sides by perpendicular rocks, broken into the wildest forms of fantastic magnificence.

"These are, indeed," said Mr. Escot, "*confracti mundi rudera.*" [1]

[1] Fragments of a demolished world.

yet they must be feeble images of the valleys of the Andes, where the philosophic eye may contemplate, in their utmost extent, the effects of that tremendous convulsion which destroyed the perpendicularity of the poles, and inundated this globe with that torrent of physical evil, from which the greater torrent of moral evil has issued, that will continue to roll on, with an expansive power and an accelerated impetus, till the whole human race shall be swept away in its vortex."

"The precession of the equinoxes," said Mr. Foster, "will gradually ameliorate the physical state of our planet, till the ecliptic shall again coincide with the equator, and the equal diffusion of light and heat over the whole surface of the earth typify the equal and happy existence of man, who will then have attained the final step of pure and perfect intelligence."

"It is by no means clear," said Mr. Jenkison, "that the axis of the earth was ever perpendicular to the plane of its orbit, or that it ever will be so. Explosion and convulsion are necessary to the maintenance of either hypothesis: for La Place has demonstrated, that the precession of the equinoxes is only a secular equation of a very long period, which, of course, proves nothing either on one side or the other."

They now emerged, by a winding ascent, from the vale of Llanberris, and after some little time arrived at Bedd Gelert. Proceeding through the sublimely romantic pass of Aberglaslynn, their road led along the edge of Traeth Mawr, a vast arm of the sea, which they then beheld in all the magnificence of the flowing tide. Another five miles brought them to the embankment, which has since been completed, and which, by connecting the two counties of Meirionnydd and Caernarvon, excludes the sea from an extensive tract. The embankment, which was carried on at the same time from both the opposite coasts, was then very nearly meeting in the centre. They walked to the extremity of that part of it which was thrown out from the Caernarvonshire shore. The tide was now ebbing: it had filled the vast basin within, forming a lake about five miles in length and more than one in breadth. As they looked upwards with their backs to the open sea, they beheld a scene which no other in this country can parallel, and which the admirers of the magnificence of nature will ever remember with regret, whatever consolation may be de-

rived from the probable utility of the works which have excluded the
waters from their ancient receptacle. Vast rocks and precipices, inter-
sected with little torrents, formed the barrier on the left: on the
right, the triple summit of Moëlwyn reared its majestic boundary: in
the depth was that sea of mountains, the wild and stormy outline of
the Snowdonian chain, with the giant Wyddfa towering in the
midst. The mountain-frame remains unchanged, unchangeable; but
the liquid mirror it enclosed is gone.

The tide ebbed with rapidity: the waters within, retained by the
embankment, poured through its two points an impetuous cataract,
curling and boiling in innumerable eddies, and making a tumultuous
melody admirably in unison with the surrounding scene. The three
philosophers looked on in silence; and at length unwillingly turned
away and proceeded to the little town of Tremadoc, which is built on
land recovered in a similar manner from the sea. After inspecting
the manufactories, and refreshing themselves at the inn on a cold
saddle of mutton and a bottle of sherry, they retraced their steps
towards Headlong Hall, commenting as they went on the various
subjects they had seen.

Mr. Escot.—I regret that time did not allow us to see the caves
on the sea-shore. There is one of which the depth is said to be unknown. There is a tradition in the country, that an adventurous
fiddler once resolved to explore it; that he entered and never returned; but that the subterranean sound of a fiddle was heard at a
farm-house seven miles inland. It is, therefore, concluded that he lost
his way in the labyrinth of caverns, supposed to exist under the rocky
soil of this part of the country.

Mr. Jenkison.—A supposition that must always remain in force,
unless a second fiddler, equally adventurous and more successful,
should return with an accurate report of the true state of the fact.

Mr. Foster.—What think you of the little colony we have just
been inspecting; a city, as it were, in its cradle?

Mr. Escot.—With all the weakness of infancy, and all the vices
of maturer age. I confess, the sight of those manufactories, which
have suddenly sprung up, like fungous excrescences, in the bosom of
these wild and desolate scenes, impressed me with as much horror
and amazement as the sudden appearance of the stocking-manufac-
tory struck into the mind of Rousseau, when, in a lonely valley of

the Alps, he had just congratulated himself on finding a spot where man had never been.

Mr. Foster.—The manufacturing system is not yet purified from some evils which necessarily attend it, but which I conceive are greatly overbalanced by their concomitant advantages. Contemplate the vast sum of human industry to which this system so essentially contributes: seas covered with vessels, ports resounding with life, profound researches, scientific inventions, complicated mechanism, canals carried over deep valleys and through the bosoms of hills: employment and existence thus given to innumerable families, and the multiplied comforts and conveniences of life diffused over the whole community.

Mr. Escot.—You present to me a complicated picture of artificial life, and require me to admire it. Seas covered with vessels: every one of which contains two or three tyrants, and from fifty to a thousand slaves, ignorant, gross, perverted, and active only in mischief. Ports resounding with life: in other words, with noise and drunkenness, the mingled din of avarice, intemperance, and prostitution. Profound researches, scientific inventions: to what end? To contract the sum of human wants? to teach the art of living on a little? to disseminate independence, liberty, and health? No; to multiply factitious desires, to stimulate depraved appetites, to invent unnatural wants, to heap up incense on the shrine of luxury, and accumulate expedients of selfish and ruinous profusion. Complicated machinery: behold its blessings. Twenty years ago, at the door of every cottage sate the good woman with her spinning-wheel: the children, if not more profitably employed than in gathering heath and sticks, at least laid in a stock of health and strength to sustain the labours of maturer years. Where is the spinning-wheel now, and every simple and insulated occupation of the industrious cottager? Wherever this boasted machinery is established, the children of the poor are death doomed from their cradles. Look for one moment at midnight into a cotton-mill, amidst the smell of oil, the smoke of lamps, the rattling of wheels, the dizzy and complicated motions of diabolical mechanism: contemplate the little human machines that keep play with the revolutions of the iron work, robbed at that hour of their natural rest, as of air and exercise by day: observe their pale and ghastly features, more ghastly in that baleful and malignant light, and tell me if you do not fancy yourself on the threshold of Virgil's hell, where

> Continuo auditæ voces, vagitus et ingens,
> Infantumque animæ flentes, in limine primo,
> Quos dulcis vitæ exsortes, et ab ubere raptos,
> Abstulit atra dies, et FUNERE MERSIT ACERBO! [1]

As Mr. Escot said this, a little rosy-cheeked girl, with a basket of heath on her head, came tripping down the side of one of the rocks on the left. The force of contrast struck even on the phlegmatic spirit of Mr. Jenkison, and he almost inclined for a moment to the doctrine of deterioration. Mr. Escot continued:

"Nor is the lot of the parents more enviable. Sedentary victims of unhealthy toil, they have neither the corporeal energy of the savage, nor the mental acquisitions of the civilized man. Mind, indeed, they have none, and scarcely animal life. They are mere automata, component parts of the enormous machines which administer to the pampered appetites of the few, who consider themselves the most valuable portion of a state, because they consume in indolence the fruits of the earth, and contribute nothing to the benefit of the community.

Mr. Jenkison.—That these are evils cannot be denied; but they have their counterbalancing advantages. That a man should pass the day in a furnace and the night in a cellar, is bad for the individual, but good for others who enjoy the benefit of his labour.

Mr. Escot.—By what right do they so?

Mr. Jenkison.—By the right of all property and all possession: le droit du plus fort.

Mr. Escot.—Do you justify that principle?

Mr. Jenkison.—I neither justify nor condemn it. It is practically recognized in all societies; and, though it is certainly the source of enormous evil, I conceive it is also the source of abundant good, or it would not have so many supporters.

Mr. Escot.—That is by no means a consequence. Do we not

[1 Loud shrieks are heard, and wails of the distrest,
The souls of babes, those on the threshold cry,
Rapt of sweet life, and ravished from the breast,
And early plunged in bitter death.
Aeneid VI 426.]

every day see men supporting the most enormous evils, which they know to be so with respect to others, and which in reality are so with respect to themselves, though an erroneous view of their own miserable self-interest induces them to think otherwise?

Mr. Jenkison.—Good and evil exist only as they are perceived. I cannot therefore understand, how that which a man perceives to be good can be in reality an evil to him: indeed, the word *reality* only signifies *strong belief*.

Mr. Escot.—The views of such a man I contend are false. If he could be made to see the truth——

Mr. Jenkison.—He sees his own truth. Truth is that which a man *troweth*. Where there is no man there is no truth. Thus the truth of one is not the truth of another.

Mr. Escot.—I am aware of the etymology; but I contend that there is an universal and immutable truth, deducible from the nature of things.

Mr. Jenkison.—By whom deducible? Philosophers have investigated the nature of things for centuries, yet no two of them will agree in *trowing* the same conclusion.

Mr. Foster.—The progress of philosophical investigation, and the rapidly increasing accuracy of human knowledge, approximate by degrees the diversities of opinion; so that, in process of time, moral science will be susceptible of mathematical demonstration; and, clear and indisputable principles being universally recognized, the coincidence of deduction will necessarily follow.

Mr. Escot.—Possibly, when the inroads of luxury and disease shall have exterminated nine hundred and ninety-nine thousand nine hundred and ninety-nine of every million of the human race, the remaining fractional units may congregate into one point, and come to something like the same conclusion.

Mr. Jenkison.—I doubt it much. I conceive, if only we three were survivors of the whole system of terrestrial being, we should never agree in our decisions as to the cause of the calamity.

Mr. Escot.—Be that as it may, I think you must at least assent to the following positions: that the many are sacrificed to the few; that ninety-nine in a hundred are occupied in a perpetual struggle for the preservation of a perilous and precarious existence, while the remaining one wallows in all the redundancies of luxury that can be wrung from their labours and privations; that luxury and liberty are incompatible; and that every new want you invent for civilized man is a new instrument of torture for him who cannot indulge it.

They had now regained the shores of the lake, when the conversation was suddenly interrupted by a tremendous explosion, followed by a violent splashing of water, and various sounds of tumult and confusion, which induced them to quicken their pace towards the spot whence they proceeded.

THE TOWER

In ALL the thoughts, words, and actions of Squire Headlong, there was a remarkable alacrity of progression, which almost annihilated the interval between conception and execution. He was utterly regardless of obstacles, and seemed to have expunged their very name from his vocabulary. His designs were never nipped in their infancy by the contemplation of those trivial difficulties which often turn awry the current of enterprise; and, though the rapidity of his movements was sometimes arrested by a more formidable barrier, either naturally existing in the pursuit he had undertaken, or created by his own impetuosity, he seldom failed to succeed either in knocking it down or cutting his way through it. He had little idea of gradation: he saw no interval between the first step and the last, but pounced upon his object with the impetus of a mountain cataract. This rapidity of movement, indeed, subjected him to some disasters which cooler spirits would have escaped. He was an excellent sportsman, and almost always killed his game; but now and then he killed his dog. Rocks, streams, hedges, gates, and ditches, were objects of no account in his estimation; though a dislocated shoulder, several severe bruises, and two or three narrow escapes for his neck, might have been expected to teach him a certain degree of caution in effecting his transitions. He was so singularly alert in climbing precipices and traversing torrents, that, when he went out on a shooting party, he was very soon left to continue his sport alone, for he was sure to dash up or down some nearly perpendicular path, where no one else had either ability or inclination to follow. He had a pleasure boat on the lake, which he steered with amazing dexterity; but as he always indulged himself in the utmost possible latitude of sail, he was occasionally upset by a sudden gust, and was indebted to his skill in the art of swimming for the opportunity of tempering with a copious libation of wine the unnatural frigidity introduced into his stomach by the extraordinary intrusion of water, an element which he had religiously determined should never pass his lips, but of which, on these occasions, he was sometimes compelled to swallow no inconsiderable quantity. This circumstance alone, of the various disasters that befell him, occasioned him any permanent affliction, and he accordingly noted the day in his pocket-book as a *dies nefastus*,[1] with this simple abstract, and brief chronicle of the calamity: *Mem. Swallowed two or three pints of water*: without any notice whatever of the concomitant circumstances. These days, of which there were several, were set apart in Headlong Hall for the purpose of anniversary expiation; and, as often as the day returned on which the squire had swallowed water, he not only made a point of swallowing a treble allowance of wine himself, but imposed a heavy mulct on every one of his servants who should be detected in a state of sobriety after sunset: but their conduct on these occasions was so uniformly exemplary, that no instance of the infliction of the penalty appears on record.

The Squire and Mr. Milestone, as we have already said, had set out immediately after breakfast to examine the capabilities of the scenery. The object that most attracted Mr. Milestone's admiration was a ruined tower on a projecting point of rock, almost totally overgrown with ivy. This ivy, Mr. Milestone observed, required trimming and clearing in various parts: a little pointing and polishing was also necessary for the dilapidated walls: and the whole effect would be materially increased by a plantation of spruce fir, interspersed with cypress and juniper, the present rugged and broken ascent from the land side being first converted into a beautiful slope, which might be easily effected by blowing up a part of the rock with gunpowder, laying on a quantity of fine mould, and covering the whole with an elegant stratum of turf.

Squire Headlong caught with avidity at this suggestion; and, as he had always a store of gunpowder in the house, for the accommodation of himself and his shooting visitors, and for the supply of a

[1 evil day.]

small battery of cannon, which he kept for his private amusement, he insisted on commencing operations immediately. Accordingly, he bounded back to the house, and very speedily returned, accompanied by the little butler, and half a dozen servants and labourers, with pickaxes and gunpowder, a hanging stove and a poker, together with a basket of cold meat and two or three bottles of Madeira: for the Squire thought, with many others, that a copious supply of provision is a very necessary ingredient in all rural amusements.

Mr. Milestone superintended the proceedings. The rock was excavated, the powder introduced, the apertures strongly blockaded with fragments of stone: a long train was laid to a spot which Mr. Milestone fixed on as sufficiently remote from the possibility of harm: the Squire seized the poker, and, after flourishing it in the air with a degree of dexterity which induced the rest of the party to leave him in solitary possession of an extensive circumference, applied the end of it to the train; and the rapidly communicated ignition ran hissing along the surface of the soil.

At this critical moment, Mr. Cranium and Mr. Panscope appeared at the top of the tower, which, unseeing and unseen, they had ascended on the opposite side to that where the Squire and Mr. Milestone were conducting their operations. Their sudden appearance a little dismayed the Squire, who, however, comforted himself with the reflection, that the tower was perfectly safe, or at least was intended to be so, and that his friends were in no probable danger but of a knock on the head from a flying fragment of stone.

The succession of these thoughts in the mind of the Squire was commensurate in rapidity to the progress of the ignition, which having reached its extremity, the explosion took place, and the shattered rock was hurled into the air in the midst of fire and smoke.

Mr. Milestone had properly calculated the force of the explosion; for the tower remained untouched: but the Squire, in his consolatory reflections, had omitted the consideration of the influence of sudden fear, which had so violent an effect on Mr. Cranium, who was just commencing a speech concerning the very fine prospect from the top of the tower, that, cutting short the thread of his observations, he bounded, under the elastic influence of terror, several feet into the air. His ascent being unluckily a little out of the perpendicular, he descended with a proportionate curve from the apex of his projection, and alighted, not on the wall of the tower, but in an ivy-bush by its side, which, giving way beneath him, transferred him to a tuft of hazel at its base, which, after upholding him an instant, consigned him to the boughs of an ash that had rooted itself in a fissure about half way down the rock, which finally transmitted him to the waters below.

Squire Headlong anxiously watched the tower as the smoke which at first enveloped it rolled away; but when the shadowy curtain was withdrawn, and Mr. Panscope was discovered, *solus*, in a tragical attitude, his apprehensions became boundless, and he concluded that the unlucky collision of a flying fragment of rock had indeed emancipated the spirit of the craniologist from its terrestrial bondage.

Mr. Escot had considerably outstripped his companions and arrived at the scene of the disaster just as Mr. Cranium, being utterly destitute of natatorial skill, was in imminent danger of final submersion. The deteriorationist, who had cultivated this valuable art with great success, immediately plunged in to his assistance, and brought him alive and in safety to a shelving part of the shore. Their landing was hailed with a view-holla from the delighted Squire, who, shaking them both heartily by the hand, and making ten thousand lame apologies to Mr. Cranium, concluded by asking, in a pathetic tone, *How much water he had swallowed?* and without waiting for his answer, filled a large tumbler with Madeira, and insisted on his tossing it off, which was no sooner said than done. Mr. Jenkison and Mr. Foster now made their appearance. Mr. Panscope descended the tower, which he vowed never again to approach within a quarter of a mile. The tumbler of Madeira was replenished, and handed round to recruit the spirits of the party, which now began to move towards Headlong Hall, the Squire capering for joy in the van, and the little fat butler waddling in the rear.

The Squire took care that Mr. Cranium should be seated next to him at dinner, and plied him so hard with Madeira to prevent him, as he said, from taking cold, that long before the ladies sent in their summons to coffee, every organ in his brain was in a complete state of revolution, and the Squire was under the necessity of ringing for three or four servants to carry him to bed, observing, with a smile of great satisfaction, that he was in a very excellent way for escaping any ill consequences that might have resulted from his accident.

The beautiful Cephalis, being thus freed from his *surveillance*, was enabled, during the course of the evening, to develop to his preserver the full extent of her gratitude.

[Mr. Escot passes a night made sleepless by thoughts of love, sets out for a dawn walk, encounters a garrulous sexton, and acquires a skull of "very extraordinary magnitude," which the sexton swears is that of the great Cadwallader himself.]

THE SKULL

WHEN Mr. Escot entered the breakfast-room he found the majority of the party assembled, and the little butler very active at his station. Several of the ladies shrieked at the sight of the skull; and Miss Tenorina, starting up in great haste and terror, caused the subversion of a cup of chocolate, which a servant was handing to the Reverend Doctor Gaster, into the nape of the neck of Sir Patrick O'Prism. Sir Patrick, rising impetuously, *to clap an extinguisher, as he expressed himself, on the farthing rushlight of the rascal's life*, pushed over the chair of Marmaduke Milestone, Esquire, who, catching for support at the first thing that came in his way, which happened unluckily to be the corner of the table-cloth, drew it instantaneously with him to the floor, involving plates, cups and saucers, in one promiscuous ruin. But, as the principal *matériel* of the breakfast apparatus was on the little butler's side-table, the confusion occasioned by this accident was happily greater than the damage. Miss Tenorina was so agitated that she was obliged to retire: Miss Graziosa accompanied her through pure sisterly affection and sympathy, not without a lingering look at Sir Patrick, who likewise retired to change his coat, but was very expeditious in returning to resume his attack on the cold partridge. The broken cups were cleared away, the cloth re-laid, and the array of the table restored with wonderful celerity.

Mr. Escot was a little surprised at the scene of confusion which signalized his entrance; but, perfectly unconscious that it originated with the skull of Cadwallader, he advanced to seat himself at the table by the side of the beautiful Cephalis, first placing the skull in a corner, out of the reach of Mr. Cranium, who sate eyeing it with lively curiosity, and after several efforts to restrain his impatience, exclaimed, "You seem to have found a rarity."

"A rarity indeed," said Mr. Escot, cracking an egg as he spoke; "no less than the genuine and indubitable skull of Cadwallader."

"The skull of Cadwallader!" vociferated Mr. Cranium: "O treasure of treasures!"

Mr. Escot then detailed by what means he had become possessed of it, which gave birth to various remarks from the other individuals of the party: after which, rising from table, and taking the skull again in his hand:

"This skull," he said, "is the skull of a hero, παλαι κατατεθνειωτος,[1] and sufficiently demonstrates a point, concerning which I never myself entertained a doubt, that the human race is undergoing a gradual process of diminution in length, breadth, and thickness. Observe this skull. Even the skull of our reverend friend, which is the largest and thickest in the company, is not more than half its size. The frame this skull belonged to could scarcely have been less than nine feet high. Such is the lamentable progress of degeneracy and decay. In the course of ages, a boot of the present generation would form an ample château for a large family of our remote posterity. The mind, too, participates in the contraction of the body. Poets and philosophers of all ages and nations have lamented this too visible process of physical and moral deterioration. 'The sons of little men,' says Ossian.'Οιοι νυν βροτοι εισιν,'says Homer: 'such men as live in these degenerate days.' 'All things,' says Virgil, 'have a retrocessive tendency, and grow worse and worse by the inevitable doom of fate.' 'We live in the ninth age,' says Juvenal, 'an age worse than the age of iron; nature has no metal sufficiently pernicious to give a denomination to its wickedness.' 'Our fathers,' says Horace, 'worse than our grandfathers, have given birth to us, their more vicious progeny, who, in our turn, shall become the parents of a still viler generation.' You all know the fable of the buried Pict, who bit off the end of a pickaxe, with which sacrilegious hands were breaking open his grave, and called out with a voice like subterranean thunder, *I perceive the degeneracy of your race by the smallness of your little finger!* videlicet,

[1] Long since dead.

the pickaxe. This, to be sure, is a fiction; but it shows the prevalent opinion, the feeling, the conviction, of absolute, universal, irreme-diable deterioration."

"I should be sorry," said Mr. Foster, "that such an opinion should become universal, independently of my conviction of its fallacy. Its general admission would tend, in a great measure, to produce the very evils it appears to lament. What could be its effect, but to check the ardour of investigation, to extinguish the zeal of philanthropy, to freeze the current of enterprising hope, to bury in the torpor of scepticism and in the stagnation of despair, every better faculty of the human mind, which will necessarily become retrograde in ceasing to be progressive?"

"I am inclined to think, on the contrary," said Mr. Escot, "that the deterioration of man is accelerated by his blindness—in many respects wilful blindness—to the truth of the fact itself, and to the causes which produce it; that there is no hope whatever of amelio-rating his condition but in a total and radical change of the whole scheme of human life, and that the advocates of his indefinite perfectibility are in reality the greatest enemies to the practical possibility of their own system, by so strenuously labouring to im-press on his attention that he is going on in a good way, while he is really in a deplorably bad one."

"I admit," said Mr. Foster, "there are many things that may, and therefore will, be changed for the better."

"Not on the present system," said Mr. Escot, "in which every change is for the worse."

"In matters of taste I am sure it is," said Mr. Gall: "there is, in fact, no such thing as good taste left in the world."

"O, Mr. Gall!" said Miss Philomela Poppyseed, "I thought my novel——"

"My paintings," said Sir Patrick O'Prism——

"My ode," said Mr. Mac Laurel——

"My ballad," said Mr. Nightshade——

"My plan for Lord Littlebrain's park," said Marmaduke Mile-stone, Esquire——

"My essay," said Mr. Treacle——

"My sonata," said Mr. Chromatic——

"My claret," said Squire Headlong——

"My lectures," said Mr. Cranium——

"Vanity of vanities," said the Reverend Doctor Gaster, turning down an empty egg-shell; "all is vanity and vexation of spirit."

[The beau-monde of the Cambrian mountains assembles at Headlong Hall for the annual Christmas ball which the Headlongs have given from time immemorial. The distinguished company dines well and rapidly, but is not permitted to dance until Mr. Cranium has delivered himself of his lecture.]

THE LECTURE

"Physiologists have been much puzzled to account for the varieties of moral character in men, as well as for the remarkable similarity of habit and disposition in all the individual animals of every other respective species. A few brief sentences, perspicuously worded, and scientifically arranged, will enumerate all the characteristics of a lion, or a tiger, or a wolf, or a bear, or a squirrel, or a goat, or a horse, or an ass, or a rat, or a cat, or a hog, or a dog; and whatever is physiologically predicted of any individual lion, tiger, wolf, bear, squirrel, goat, horse, ass, hog, or dog, will be found to hold true of all lions, tigers, wolves, bears, squirrels, goats, horses, asses, hogs, and dogs, whatsoever. Now, in man, the very reverse of this appears to be the case; for he has so few distinct and characteristic marks which hold true of all his species, that philosophers in all ages have found it a task of infinite difficulty to give him a definition. Hence one has defined him to be a *featherless biped*, a definition which is equally applicable to an unfledged fowl: another, to be *an animal which forms opinions*, than which nothing can be more inaccurate, for a very small number of the species form opinions, and the remainder take them upon trust, without investigation or inquiry.

"Again, man has been defined to be *an animal that carries a stick:* an attribute which undoubtedly belongs to man only, but not to all men always; though it uniformly characterizes some of the graver and more imposing varieties, such as physicians, oran-outangs, and lords in waiting.

"We cannot define man to be a reasoning animal, for we do not dispute that idiots are men; to say nothing of that very numerous description of persons who consider themselves reasoning animals, and are so denominated by the ironical courtesy of the world, who labour, nevertheless, under a very gross delusion in that essential particular.

"It appears to me that man may be correctly defined an animal which, without any peculiar or distinguishing faculty of its own, is, as it were, a bundle or compound of faculties of other animals, by a distinct enumeration of which any individual of the species may be satisfactorily described. This is manifest even in the ordinary language of conversation, when in summing up, for example, the qualities of an accomplished courtier, we say he has the vanity of a peacock, the cunning of a fox, the treachery of an hyæna, the cold-heartedness of a cat, and the servility of a jackal. That this is perfectly consentaneous to scientific truth will appear in the further progress of these observations.

"Every particular faculty of the mind has its corresponding organ in the brain. In proportion as any particular faculty or propensity acquires paramount activity in any individual, these organs develop themselves, and their development becomes externally obvious by corresponding lumps and bumps, exuberances and protuberances, on the osseous compages of the occiput and sinciput. In all animals but man the same organ is equally developed in every individual of the species: for instance, that of migration in the swallow, that of destruction in the tiger, that of architecture in the beaver, and that of paternal affection in the bear. The human brain, however, consists, as I have said, of a bundle or compound of all the faculties of all other animals; and, from the greater development of one or more of these, in the infinite varieties of combination, result all the peculiarities of individual character.

"Here is the skull of a beaver, and that of Sir Christopher Wren. You observe, in both these specimens, the prodigious development of the organ of constructiveness.

"Here is the skull of a bullfinch, and that of an eminent fiddler. You may compare the organ of music.

"Here is the skull of a tiger. You observe the organ of carnage. Here is the skull of a fox. You observe the organ of plunder. Here is the skull of a peacock. You observe the organ of vanity. Here is the skull of an illustrious robber, who, after a long and triumphant process of depredation and murder, was suddenly checked in his career by means of a certain quality inherent in preparations of hemp, which, for the sake of perspicuity, I shall call *suspensiveness*. Here is the skull of a conqueror, who, after overrunning several kingdoms, burning a number of cities, and causing the deaths of two or three millions of men, women, and children, was entombed with all the pageantry of public lamentation, and figured as the hero of several thousand odes and a round dozen of epics; while the poor highwayman was twice executed—

At the gallows first, and after in a ballad,
Sung to a villanous tune.

You observe, in both these skulls, the combined development of the organs of carnage, plunder, and vanity, which I have separately pointed out in the tiger, the fox, and the peacock. The greater enlargement of the organ of vanity in the hero is the only criterion by which I can distinguish them from each other. Born with the same faculties and the same propensities, these two men were formed by nature to run the same career: the different combinations of external circumstances decided the differences of their destinies.

"Here is the skull of a Newfoundland dog. You observe the organ of benevolence, and that of attachment. Here is a human skull, in which you may observe a very striking negation of both these organs; and an equally striking development of those of destruction, cunning, avarice, and self-love. This was one of the most illustrious statesmen that ever flourished in the page of history.

"Here is the skull of a turnspit, which, after a wretched life of dirty work, was turned out of doors to die on a dunghill. I have been induced to preserve it in consequence of its remarkable similarity to this, which belonged to a courtly poet, who having grown gray in flattering the great, was cast off in the same manner to perish by the same catastrophe."

After these, and several other illustrations, during which the

skulls were handed round for the inspection of the company, Mr.
Cranium proceeded thus:—

"It is obvious from what I have said that no man can hope for
worldly honour or advancement, who is not placed in such a relation to external circumstances, as may be consentaneous to his
peculiar cerebral organs; and I would advise every parent who has
the welfare of his son at heart, to procure as extensive a collection
as possible of the skulls of animals, and, before determining on the
choice of a profession, to compare with the utmost nicety their
bumps and protuberances with those of the skull of his son. If the
development of the organ of destruction point out a similarity between the youth and the tiger, let him be brought to some profession (whether that of a butcher, a soldier, or a physician, may be
regulated by circumstances) in which he may be furnished with a
licence to kill: as, without such licence the indulgence of his natural propensity may lead to the untimely rescission of his vital thread,
'with edge of penny cord and vile reproach.' If he show an analogy
with the jackal, let all possible influence be used to procure him
a place at court, where he will infallibly thrive. If his skull bear a
marked resemblance to that of a magpie, it cannot be doubted that
he will prove an admirable lawyer; and if with this advantageous
conformation be combined any similitude to that of an owl, very
confident hopes may be formed of his becoming a judge."

A furious flourish of music was now heard from the ballroom,
the Squire having secretly despatched the little butler to order it
to strike up, by way of a hint to Mr. Cranium to finish his harangue.
The company took the hint, and adjourned tumultuously, having
just understood as much of the lecture as furnished them with
amusement for the ensuing twelvemonth, in feeling the skulls of
all their acquaintance.

THE BALL

The ball-room was adorned with great taste and elegance, under
the direction of Miss Caprioletta and her friend Miss Cephalis, who

were themselves its most beautiful ornaments, even though romantic Meirion, the pre-eminent in loveliness, sent many of its loveliest daughters to grace the festive scene. Numberless were the solicitations of the dazzled swains of Cambria for the honour of the two first dances with the one or the other of these fascinating friends; but little availed, on this occasion, the pedigree lineally traced from Caractacus or King Arthur: their two philosophical lovers, neither of whom could have given the least account of his great-great-grandfather, had engaged them many days before. Mr. Panscope chafed and fretted like Llugwy in his bed of rocks, when the object of his adoration stood up with his rival: but he consoled himself with a lively damsel from the vale of Edeirnion, having first compelled Miss Cephalis to promise him her hand for the fourth set.

The ball was accordingly opened by Miss Caprioletta and Mr. Foster, which gave rise to much speculation among the Welsh gentry, as to who this Mr. Foster could be; some of the more learned among them secretly resolving to investigate most profoundly the antiquity of the name of Foster, and ascertain what right a person so denominated could have to open the most illustrious of all possible balls with the lovely Caprioletta Headlong, the only sister of Harry Headlong, Esquire, of Headlong Hall, in the Vale of Llanberris, the only surviving male representative of the antediluvian family of Headlong Ap-Rhaiader.

When the two first dances were ended, Mr. Escot, who did not choose to dance with any one but his adorable Cephalis, looking round for a convenient seat, discovered Mr. Jenkison in a corner by the side of the Reverend Doctor Gaster, who was keeping excellent time with his nose to the lively melody of the harp and fiddle. Mr. Escot seated himself by the side of Mr. Jenkison, and inquired if he took no part in the amusement of the night.

Mr. Jenkison.—No. The universal cheerfulness of the company induces me to rise; the trouble of such violent exercise induces me to sit still. Did I see a young lady in want of a partner, gallantry would incite me to offer myself as her devoted knight for half an hour: but, as I perceive there are enough without me, that motive is null. I have been weighing these points pro and con, and remain in statu quo.

Mr. Escot.—I have danced, contrary to my system, as I have

done many other things since I have been here, from a motive that you will easily guess. (*Mr. Jenkison smiled.*) I have great objections to dancing. The wild and original man is a calm and contemplative animal. The stings of natural appetite alone rouse him to action. He satisfies his hunger with roots and fruits, unvitiated by the malignant adhibition of fire, and all its diabolical processes of elixion and assation: he slakes his thirst in the mountain-stream, and returns to his peaceful state of meditative repose.

Mr. Jenkison.—Like the metaphysical statue of Condillac.

Mr. Escot.—With all its senses and purely natural faculties developed, certainly. Imagine this tranquil and passionless being, occupied in his first meditation on the simple question of *Where am I? Whence do I come? And what is the end of my existence?* Then suddenly place before him a chandelier, a fiddler, and a magnificent beau in silk stockings and pumps, bounding, skipping, swinging, capering, and throwing himself into ten thousand attitudes, till his face glows with fever, and distils with perspiration: the first impulse excited in his mind by such an apparition will be that of violent fear, which, by the reiterated perception of its harmlessness, will subside into simple astonishment. Then let any genius, sufficiently powerful to impress on his mind all the terms of the communication, impart to him, that after a long process of ages, when his race shall have attained what some people think proper to denominate a very advanced stage of perfectibility, the most favoured and distinguished of the community shall meet by hundreds, to grin, and labour, and gesticulate, like the phantasma before him, from sunset to sunrise, while all nature is at rest, and that they shall consider this a happy and pleasurable mode of existence, and furnishing the most delightful of all possible contrasts to what they will call his vegetative state: would he not groan from his inmost soul for the lamentable condition of his posterity?

Mr. Jenkison.—I know not what your wild and original man might think of the matter in the abstract; but comparatively, I conceive, he would be better pleased with the vision of such a scene as this, than with that of a party of Indians (who would have all the advantage of being nearly as wild as himself) dancing their infernal war-dance round a midnight fire in a North American forest.

Mr. Escot.—Not if you should impart to him the true nature of both, by laying open to his view the springs of action in both parties.

Mr. Jenkison.—To do this with effect, you must make him a profound metaphysician, and thus transfer him at once from his wild and original state to a very advanced stage of intellectual progression; whether that progression be towards good or evil, I leave you and our friend Foster to settle between you.

Mr. Escot.—I wish to make no change in his habits and feelings, but to give him, hypothetically, so much mental illumination, as will enable him to take a clear view of two distinct stages of the deterioration of his posterity, that he may be enabled to compare them with each other, and with his own more happy condition. The Indian, dancing round the midnight fire, is very far deteriorated; but the magnificent beau, dancing to the light of chandeliers, is infinitely more so. The Indian is a hunter: he makes great use of fire, and subsists almost entirely on animal food. The malevolent passions that spring from these pernicious habits involve him in perpetual war. He is, therefore, necessitated, for his own preservation, to keep all the energies of his nature in constant activity: to this end his midnight war-dance is very powerfully subservient, and though in itself a frightful spectacle, is at least justifiable on the iron plea of necessity.

Mr. Jenkison.—On the same iron plea, the modern system of dancing is more justifiable. The Indian dances to prepare himself for killing his enemy: but while the beaus and belles of our assemblies dance, they are in the very act of killing theirs—TIME! a more inveterate and formidable foe than any the Indian has to contend with; for, however completely and ingeniously killed, he is sure to rise again, "with twenty mortal murders on his crown," leading his army of blue devils, with ennui in the van, and vapours in the rear.

Mr. Escot.—Your observation militates on my side of the question; and it is a strong argument in favour of the Indian, that he has no such enemy to kill.

Mr. Jenkison.—There is certainly a great deal to be said against dancing: there is also a great deal to be said in its favour. The first side of the question I leave for the present to you: on the latter, I may venture to allege that no amusement seems more natural and more congenial to youth than this. It has the advantage of bringing young persons of both sexes together, in a manner which its publicity renders perfectly unexceptionable, enabling them to see and know each other better than, perhaps, any other mode of general association. *Tête-à-têtes* are dangerous things. Small family parties are too much under mutual observation. A ball-room appears to me almost the only scene uniting that degree of rational and innocent liberty of intercourse, which it is desirable to promote as much as possible between young persons, with that scrupulous attention to the delicacy and propriety of female conduct, which I consider the fundamental basis of all our most valuable social relations.

Mr. Escot.—There would be some plausibility in your argument, if it were not the very essence of this species of intercourse to exhibit them to each other under false colours. Here all is show, and varnish, and hypocrisy, and coquetry; they dress up their moral character for the evening at the same toilet where they manufacture their shapes and faces. Ill-temper lies buried under a studied accumulation of smiles. Envy, hatred, and malice retreat from the countenance, to entrench themselves more deeply in the heart. Treachery lurks under the flowers of courtesy. Ignorance and folly take refuge in that unmeaning gabble which it would be profanation to call language, and which even those whom long experience in "the dreary intercourse of daily life" has screwed up to such a pitch of stoical endurance that they can listen to it by the hour, have branded with the ignominious appellation of "*small talk.*" Small indeed!—the absolute minimum of the infinitely little.

Mr. Jenkison.—Go on. I have said all I intended to say on the favourable side. I shall have great pleasure in hearing you balance the argument.

Mr. Escot.—I expect you to confess that I shall have more than balanced it. A ball-room is an epitome of all that is most worthless and unamiable in the great sphere of human life. Every petty and malignant passion is called into play. Coquetry is perpetually on the alert to captivate, caprice to mortify, and vanity to take offence. One amiable female is rendered miserable for the evening by seeing another, whom she intended to outshine, in a more attractive dress than her own; while the other omits no method of giving stings to her triumph, which she enjoys with all the secret arrogance of an oriental sultana. Another is compelled to dance with a monster she abhors. A third has set her heart on dancing with a particular partner, perhaps for the amiable motive of annoying one of her dear friends; not only he does not ask her, but she sees him dancing with that identical dear friend, whom from that moment she hates more cordially than ever. Perhaps, what is worse than all, she has set her heart on refusing some impertinent fop, who does not give her the opportunity.—As to the men, the case is very nearly the same with them. To be sure, they have the privilege of making the first advances, and are, therefore, less liable to have an odious partner forced upon them; though this sometimes happens, as I know by woful experience: but it is seldom they can procure the very partner they prefer; and when they do, the absurd necessity of changing every two dances forces them away, and leaves them only the miserable alternative of taking up with something disagreeable perhaps in itself, and at all events rendered so by contrast, or of retreating into some solitary corner, to vent their spleen on the first idle coxcomb they can find.

Mr. Jenkison.—I hope that is not the motive which brings you to me.

Mr. Escot.—Clearly not. But the most afflicting consideration of all is, that these malignant and miserable feelings are masked under that uniform disguise of pretended benevolence, that fine and delicate irony, called politeness, which gives so much ease and pliability to the mutual intercourse of civilized man, and enables him to assume the appearance of every virtue, without the reality of one.[1]

The second set of dances was now terminated, and Mr. Escot flew off to reclaim the hand of the beautiful Cephalis, with whom he figured away with surprising alacrity, and probably felt at least as happy among the chandeliers and silk stockings, at which he had just been railing, as he would have been in an American forest, making one in an Indian ring, by the light of a blazing fire, even though his hand had been locked in that of the most beautiful squaw that ever listened to the roar of Niagara.

Squire Headlong was now beset by his maiden aunt, Miss Brindle-

[1] Rousseau, Discours sur les Sciences.

mew Grimalkin Phœbe Tabitha Ap-Headlong, on one side, and Sir Patrick O'Prism on the other; the former insisting that he should immediately procure her a partner; the latter earnestly requesting the same interference in behalf of Miss Philomela Poppyseed. The Squire thought to emancipate himself from his two petitioners by making them dance with each other; but Sir Patrick vehemently pleading a prior engagement, the Squire threw his eyes around till they alighted on Mr. Jenkison and the Reverend Doctor Gaster; both of whom, after waking the latter, he pressed into the service. The doctor, arising with a strange kind of guttural sound, which was half a yawn and half a groan, was handed by the officious Squire to Miss Philomela, who received him with sullen dignity: she had not yet forgotten his falling asleep during the first chapter of her novel, while she was condescending to detail to him the outlines of four superlative volumes. The doctor, on his part, had most completely forgotten it; and though he thought there was something in her physiognomy rather more forbidding than usual, he gave himself no concern about the cause, and had not the least suspicion that it was at all connected with himself. Miss Brindle-mew was very well contented with Mr. Jenkison, and gave him two or three ogles, accompanied by a most risible distortion of the countenance which she intended for a captivating smile. As to Mr. Jenkison, it was all one to him with whom he danced, or whether he danced or not: he was therefore just as well pleased as if he had been left alone in his corner; which is probably more than could have been said of any other human being under similar circumstances.

At the end of the third set, supper was announced; and the party, pairing off like turtles, adjourned to the supper-room. The Squire was now the happiest of mortal men, and the little butler the most laborious. The centre of the largest table was decorated with a model of Snowdon, surmounted with an enormous artificial leek, the leaves of angelica, and the bulb of blanc-mange. A little way from the summit was a tarn, or mountain-pool, supplied through concealed tubes with an inexhaustible flow of milk-punch, which, dashing in cascades down the miniature rocks, fell into the more capacious lake below, washing the mimic foundations of Headlong Hall. The reverend doctor handed Miss Philomela to the chair most conveniently situated for enjoying this interesting scene, protesting he had never before been sufficiently impresssed with the magnificence of that mountain, which he now perceived to be well worthy of all the fame it had obtained.

[Supper is followed by singing, the final chorus celebrating the ancient and glorious lineage of the illustrious family of Headlong Ap-Headlong; after which the company returns to the ball-room, "where they kept it up till sun-rise, when the little butler summoned them to breakfast."]

THE PROPOSALS

THE chorus, which celebrated the antiquity of her lineage, had been ringing all night in the ears of Miss Brindle-mew Grimalkin Phœbe Tabitha Ap-Headlong, when taking the Squire aside, while the visitors were sipping their tea and coffee, "Nephew Harry," said she, "I have been noting your behaviour, during the several stages of the ball and supper; and, though I cannot tax you with any want of gallantry, for you are a very gallant young man, nephew Harry, very gallant—I wish I could say as much for every one" (added she, throwing a spiteful look towards a distant corner, where Mr. Jenkison was sitting with great nonchalance, and at the moment dipping a rusk in a cup of chocolate); "but I lament to perceive that you were at least as pleased with your lakes of milk-punch, and your bottles of Champagne and Burgundy, as with any of your delightful partners. Now, though I can readily excuse this degree of incombustibility in the descendant of a family so remarkable in all ages for personal beauty as ours, yet I lament it exceedingly, when I consider that, in conjunction with your present predilection for the easy life of a bachelor, it may possibly prove the means of causing our ancient genealogical tree, which has its roots, if I may so speak, in the foundations of the world, to terminate suddenly in a point: unless you feel yourself moved by my exhortations to follow the example of all your ancestors, by choosing yourself a fitting and suitable helpmate to immortalize the pedigree of Headlong Ap-Rhaiader."

"Egad!" said Squire Headlong, "that is very true. I'll marry directly. A good opportunity to fix on some one, now they are all here; and I'll pop the question without further ceremony."

"What think you," said the old lady, "of Miss Nanny Glyn-Du, the lineal descendant of Llewelyn Ap-Yorwerth?"

"She won't do," said Squire Headlong.

"What say you, then," said the lady, "to Miss Williams, of Pontyglasrhydyrallt, the descendant of the ancient family of——?"

"I don't like her," said Squire Headlong; "and as to her ancient family, that is a matter of no consequence. I have antiquity enough for two. They are all moderns, people of yesterday, in comparison with us. What signify six or seven centuries, which are the most they can make up?"

"Why, to be sure," said the aunt, "on that view of the question, it is of no consequence. What think you, then, of Miss Owen, of Nidd-y-Gygfraen? She will have six thousand a year."

"I would not have her," said Squire Headlong, "if she had fifty. I'll think of somebody presently. I should like to be married on the same day with Caprioletta."

"Caprioletta!" said Miss Brindle-mew; "without my being consulted!"

"Consulted!" said the Squire: "I was commissioned to tell you, but somehow or other I let it slip. However, she is going to be married to my friend Mr. Foster, the philosopher."

"Oh!" said the maiden aunt, "that a daughter of our ancient family should marry a philosopher! It is enough to make the bones of all the Ap-Rhaiaders turn in their graves!"

"I happen to be more enlightened," said Squire Headlong, "than any of my ancestors were. Besides, it is Caprioletta's affair, not mine. I tell you, the matter is settled, fixed, determined; and so am I, to be married on the same day. I don't know, now I think of it, whom I can choose better than one of the daughters of my friend Chromatic."

"A Saxon!" said the aunt, turning up her nose, and was commencing a vehement remonstrance; but the Squire, exclaiming "Music has charms!" flew over to Mr. Chromatic, and, with a hearty slap on the shoulder, asked him "how he should like him for a son-in-law?" Mr. Chromatic, rubbing his shoulder, and highly delighted with the proposal, answered, "Very much indeed:" but, proceeding to ascertain which of his daughters had captivated the Squire, the Squire demurred, and was unable to satisfy his curiosity. "I hope," said Mr. Chromatic, "it may be Tenorina; for I imagine Graziosa has conceived a *penchant* for Sir Patrick O'Prism."— "Tenorina, exactly," said Squire Headlong; and became so impatient to bring the matter to a conclusion, that Mr. Chromatic undertook to communicate with his daughter immediately. The young lady proved to be as ready as the Squire, and the preliminaries were arranged in little more than five minutes.

Mr. Chromatic's words, that he imagined his daughter Graziosa had conceived a *penchant* for Sir Patrick O'Prism, were not lost on the Squire, who at once determined to have as many companions in the scrape as possible, and who, as soon as he could tear himself from Mrs. Headlong elect, took three flying bounds across the room to the baronet, and said, "So, Sir Patrick, I find you and I are going to be married?"

"Are we?" said Sir Patrick: "then sure won't I wish you joy, and myself too? for this is the first I have heard of it."

"Well," said Squire Headlong, "I have made up my mind to it, and you must not disappoint me."

"To be sure I won't, if I can help it," said Sir Patrick; "and I am very much obliged to you for taking so much trouble off my hands. And pray, now, who is it that I am to be metamorphosing into Lady O'Prism?"

"Miss Graziosa Chromatic," said the Squire.

"Och violet and vermilion!" said Sir Patrick; "though I never thought of it before, I dare say she will suit me as well as another: but then you must persuade the ould Orpheus to draw out a few notes of rather a more magical description than those he is so fond of scraping on his crazy violin."

"To be sure he shall," said the Squire; and, immediately returning to Mr. Chromatic, concluded the negotiation for Sir Patrick as expeditiously as he had done for himself.

The Squire next addressed himself to Mr. Escot: "Here are three couple of us going to throw off together, with the Reverend Doctor Gaster for whipper-in: now, I think you cannot do better than make the fourth with Miss Cephalis; and then, as my father-in-law that is to be would say, we shall compose a very harmonious octave."

"Indeed," said Mr. Escot, "nothing would be more agreeable to both of us than such an arrangement: but the old gentleman, since I first knew him, has changed, like the rest of the world, very lamentably for the worse: now, we wish to bring him to reason, if possible, though we mean to dispense with his consent, if he should prove much longer refractory."

"I'll settle him," said Squire Headlong; and immediately posted up to Mr. Cranium, informing him that four marriages were about to take place by way of a merry winding up of the Christmas festivities.

"Indeed!" said Mr. Cranium; "and who are the parties?"

"In the first place," said the Squire, "my sister and Mr. Foster: in the second, Miss Graziosa Chromatic and Sir Patrick O'Prism: in the third, Miss Tenorina Chromatic and your humble servant: and in the fourth—to which, by-the-by, your consent is wanted——"

"Oho!" said Mr. Cranium.

"Your daughter," said Squire Headlong.

"And Mr. Panscope?" said Mr. Cranium.

"And Mr. Escot," said Squire Headlong. "What would you have better? He has ten thousand virtues."

"So has Mr. Panscope," said Mr. Cranium; "he has ten thousand a year."

"Virtues?" said Squire Headlong.

"Pounds," said Mr. Cranium.

"I have set my mind on Mr. Escot," said the Squire.

"I am much obliged to you," said Mr. Cranium, "for dethroning me from my paternal authority."

"Who fished you out of the water?" said Squire Headlong.

"What is that to the purpose?" said Mr. Cranium. "The whole process of the action was mechanical and necessary. The application of the poker necessitated the ignition of the powder: the ignition necessitated the explosion: the explosion necessitated my sudden fright, which necessitated· my sudden jump, which, from a necessity equally powerful, was in a curvilinear ascent: the descent, being in a corresponding curve, and commencing at a point perpendicular to the extreme line of the edge of the tower, I was, by the necessity of gravitation, attracted, first, through the ivy, and secondly through the hazel, and thirdly through the ash, into the water beneath. The motive or impulse thus adhibited in the person of a drowning man, was as powerful on his material compages as the force of gravitation on mine; and he could no more help jumping into the water than I could help falling into it."

"All perfectly true," said Squire Headlong; "and, on the same principle, you make no distinction between the man who knocks you down and him who picks you up."

"I make this distinction," said Mr. Cranium, "that I avoid the former as a machine containing a peculiar *cataballitive* quality, which I have found to be not consentaneous to my mode of pleasurable existence; but I attach no moral merit or demerit to either of them, as these terms are usually employed, seeing that they are equally creatures of necessity, and must act as they do from the nature of their organization. I no more blame or praise a man for what is called vice or virtue, than I tax a tuft of hemlock with malevolence or discover great philanthropy in a field of potatoes, seeing that the men and the plants are equally incapacitated, by their original internal organization, and the combinations and modifications of external circumstances, from being anything but what they are. *Quod victus fateare necesse est.*" [1]

"Yet you destroy the hemlock," said Squire Headlong, "and cultivate the potato: that is my way, at least."

"I do," said Mr. Cranium; "because I know that the farinaceous qualities of the potato will tend to preserve the great requisites of unity and coalescence in the various constituent portions of my animal republic; and that the hemlock, if gathered by mistake for parsley, chopped up small with butter, and eaten with a boiled chicken, would necessitate a great derangement, and perhaps a total decomposition, of my corporeal mechanism."

"Very well," said the Squire; "then you are necessitated to like Mr. Escot better than Mr. Panscope?"

"That is a *non sequitur*," said Mr. Cranium.

"Then this is a *sequitur*," said the Squire: "your daughter and Mr. Escot are necessitated to love one another: and, unless you

[1 You must confess what has been proved.]

feel necessitated to adhibit your consent, they will feel necessitated
to dispense with it; since it does appear to moral and political economists to be essentially inherent in the eternal fitness of things."

Mr. Cranium fell into a profound reverie: emerging from which,
he said, looking Squire Headlong full in the face, "Do you think Mr.
Escot would give me that skull?"

"Skull!" said Squire Headlong.

"Yes," said Mr. Cranium, "the skull of Cadwallader."

"To be sure he will," said the Squire.

"Ascertain the point," said Mr. Cranium.

"How can you doubt it?" said the Squire.

"I simply know," said Mr. Cranium, "that if it were once in my
possession, I would not part with it for any acquisition on earth,
much less for a wife. I have had one: and, as marriage has been
compared to a pill, I can very safely assert that one is a dose; and
my reason for thinking that he will not part with it is, that its
extraordinary magnitude tends to support his system, as much as its
very marked protuberances tend to support mine; and you know
his own system is of all things the dearest to every man of liberal
thinking and a philosophical tendency."

The Squire flew over to Mr. Escot. "I told you," said he, "I
would settle him: but there is a very hard condition attached to his
compliance."

"I submit to it," said Mr. Escot, "be it what it may."

"Nothing less," said Squire Headlong, "than the absolute and un-
conditional surrender of the skull of Cadwallader."

"I resign it," said Mr. Escot.

"The skull is yours," said the Squire, skipping over to Mr.
Cranium.

"I am perfectly satisfied," said Mr. Cranium.

"The lady is yours," said the Squire, skipping back to Mr.
Escot.

"I am the happiest man alive," said Mr. Escot.

"Come," said the Squire, "then there is an amelioration in the
state of the sensitive man."

"A slight oscillation of good in the instance of a solitary individual," answered Mr. Escot, "by no means affects the solidity of my

opinions concerning the general deterioration of the civilized world; which when I can be induced to contemplate with feelings of satisfaction, I doubt not but that I may be persuaded *to be in love with tortures, and to think charitably of the rack.*" [1]

Saying these words, he flew off as nimbly as Squire Headlong himself, to impart the happy intelligence to his beautiful Cephalis.

Mr. Cranium now walked up to Mr. Panscope, to condole with him on the disappointment of their mutual hopes. Mr. Panscope begged him not to distress himself on the subject, observing, that the monotonous system of female education brought every individual of the sex to so remarkable an approximation of similarity, that no wise man would suffer himself to be annoyed by a loss so easily repaired; and that there was much truth, though not much elegance, in a remark which he had heard made on a similar occasion by a post-captain of his acquaintance, "that there never was a fish taken out of the sea, but left another as good behind."

Mr. Cranium replied, that no two individuals having all the organs of the skull similarly developed, the universal resemblance of which Mr Panscope had spoken could not possibly exist. Mr. Panscope rejoined; and a long discussion ensued, concerning the comparative influence of natural organization and artificial education, in which the beautiful Cephalis was totally lost sight of, and which ended, as most controversies do, by each party continuing firm in his own opinion, and professing his profound astonishment at the blindness and prejudices of the other.

In the meanwhile, a great confusion had arisen at the outer doors, the departure of the ball-visitors being impeded by a circumstance which the experience of ages had discovered no means to obviate. The grooms, coachmen, and postilions, were all drunk. It was proposed that the gentlemen should officiate in their places: but the gentlemen were almost all in the same condition. This was a fearful dilemma: but a very diligent investigation brought to light a few servants and a few gentlemen not above *half-seas over;* and by an equitable distribution of these rarities, the greater part of the guests were enabled to set forward, with very nearly an even chance of not having their necks broken before they reached home.

[1] Jeremy Taylor.

THE CONCLUSION

THE Squire and his select party of philosophers and dilettanti were again left in peaceful possession of Headlong Hall: and, as the former made a point of never losing a moment in the accomplishment of a favorite object, he did not suffer many days to elapse, before the spiritual metamorphosis of eight into four was effected by the clerical dexterity of the Reverend Doctor Gaster.

Immediately after the ceremony, the whole party dispersed, the Squire having first extracted from every one of his chosen guests a positive promise to re-assemble in August, when they would be better enabled, in its most appropriate season, to form a correct judgment of Cambrian hospitality.

Mr. Jenkison shook hands at parting with his two brother philosophers. "According to your respective systems," said he, "I ought to congratulate you on a change for the better, which I do most cordially: and to condole with you on a change for the worse, though, when I consider whom you have chosen, I should violate every principle of probability in doing so."

"You will do well," said Mr. Foster, "to follow our example. The extensive circle of general philanthropy, which, in the present advanced stage of human nature, comprehends in its circumference the destinies of the whole species, originated, and still proceeds, from that narrower circle of domestic affection, which first set limits to the empire of selfishness, and, by purifying the passions and enlarging the affections of mankind, has given to the views of benevolence an increasing and illimitable expansion, which will finally diffuse happiness and peace over the whole surface of the world."

"The affection," said Mr. Escot, "of two congenial spirits, united, not by legal bondage and superstitious imposture, but by mutual confidence and reciprocal virtues, is the only counterbalancing consolation in this scene of mischief and misery. But how rarely is this the case according to the present system of marriage! So far from being a central point of expansion to the great circle of universal benevolence, it serves only to concentrate the feelings of natural sympathy in the reflected selfishness of family interest, and to substitute for the *humani nihil alienum puto* [1] of youthful philanthropy, the *charity begins at home* of maturer years. And what accession of individual happiness is acquired by this oblivion of the general good? Luxury, despotism, and avarice have so seized and entangled nine hundred and ninety-nine out of every thousand of the human race, that the matrimonial compact, which ought to be the most easy, the most free, and the most simple of all engagements, is become the most slavish and complicated,—a mere question of finance,— a system of bargain, and barter, and commerce, and trick, and chicanery, and dissimulation, and fraud. Is there one instance in ten thousand, in which the buds of first affection are not most cruelly and hopelessly blasted, by avarice, or ambition, or arbitrary power? Females, condemned during the whole flower of their youth to a worse than monastic celibacy, irrevocably debarred from the hope to which their first affections pointed, will, at a certain period of life, as the natural delicacy of taste and feeling is gradually worn away by the attrition of society, become willing to take up with any coxcomb or scoundrel, whom that merciless and mercenary gang of cold-blooded slaves and assassins, called, in the ordinary prostitution of language, *friends*, may agree in designating as a *prudent choice*.—Young men, on the other hand, are driven by the same vile superstitions from the company of the most amiable and modest of the opposite sex, to that of those miserable victims and outcasts of a world which dares to call itself virtuous, whom that very society whose pernicious institutions first caused their aberrations,— consigning them, without one tear of pity or one struggle of remorse, to penury, infamy, and disease,—condemns to bear the burden of its own atrocious absurdities! Thus, the youth of one sex is consumed in slavery, disappointment, and spleen; that of the other, in frantic folly and selfish intemperance: till at length, on the necks of a couple so enfeebled, so perverted, so distempered both in body and soul, society throws the yoke of marriage: that yoke which, once riveted on the necks of its victims, clings to them like the poisoned garments of Nessus or Medea. What can be expected from these ill-assorted yoke-fellows, but that, like two ill-tempered hounds, coupled by a tyrannical sportsman, they should drag on their in-

[1 Nothing human is alien to me.]

dissoluble fetter, snarling and growling, and pulling in different directions? What can be expected for their wretched offspring, but sickness and suffering, premature decrepitude, and untimely death? In this, as in every other institution of civilized society, avarice, luxury, and disease constitute the TRIANGULAR HARMONY of the life of man. Avarice conducts him to the abyss of toil and crime; luxury seizes on his ill-gotten spoil; and, while he revels in her enchantments, or groans beneath her tyranny, disease bursts upon him, and sweeps him from the earth."

"Your theory," said Mr. Jenkison, "forms an admirable counterpoise to your example. As far as I am attracted by the one, I am repelled by the other. Thus, the scales of my philosophical balance remain eternally equiponderant, and I see no reason to say of either of them, ΟΙΧΕΤΑΙ ΕΙΣ ΑΪΔ ΑΟ."[1]

[1] It descends to the shades: or, in other words, it goes to the devil.

Melincourt or Sir Oran Haut-ton

ANTHELIA

ANTHELIA MELINCOURT, at the age of twenty-one, was mistress of herself and of ten thousand a year, and of a very ancient and venerable castle in one of the wildest valleys in Westmoreland. It follows of course, without reference to her personal qualifications, that she had a very numerous list of admirers, and equally of course that there were both Irishmen and clergymen among them. The young lady nevertheless possessed sufficient attractions to kindle the flames of disinterested passion; and accordingly we shall venture to suppose, that there was at least one in the number of her sighing swains with whom her rent-roll and her old castle were secondary considerations; and if the candid reader should esteem this supposition too violent for the probabilities of daily experience in this calculating age, he will at least concede it to that degree of poetical licence which is invariably accorded to a tale founded on facts.

Melincourt Castle had been a place of considerable strength in those golden days of feudal and royal prerogative, when no man was safe in his own house unless he adopted every possible precaution for shutting out all his neighbours. It is, therefore, not surprising, that a rock, of which three sides were perpendicular, and which was only accessible on the fourth by a narrow ledge, forming a natural bridge over a tremendous chasm, was considered a very enviable situation for a gentleman to build on. An impetuous torrent boiled through the depth of the chasm, and after eddying round the base of the castle-rock, which it almost insulated, disappeared in the

59

obscurity of a woody glen, whose mysterious recesses, by popular superstition formerly consecrated to the devil, are now fearlessly explored by the solitary angler, or laid open to view by the more profane hand of the picturesque tourist, who contrives, by the magic of his pencil, to transport their romantic terrors from the depths of mountain-solitude to the gay and crowded, though not very wholesome, atmosphere of a metropolitan exhibition.

The narrow ledge, which formed the only natural access to the castle-rock, had been guarded by every impediment which the genius of fortification could oppose to the progress of the hungry Scot, who might be disposed, in his neighbourly way, to drop in without invitation and carouse at the expense of the owner, rewarding him, as usual, for his extorted hospitality, by cutting his throat and setting fire to his house. A drawbridge over the chasm, backed by a double portcullis, presented the only mode of admission. In this secure retreat thus strongly guarded both by nature and art, and always plentifully victualled for a siege, lived the lords of Melincourt in all the luxury of rural seclusion, throwing open their gates on occasional halcyon days to regale all the peasants and mountaineers of the vicinity with roasted oxen and vats of October.

When these times of danger and turbulence had passed, Melincourt Castle was not, as most of its brother edifices were, utterly deserted. The drawbridge, indeed, became gradually divorced from its chains; the double portcullis disappeared; the turrets and battlements were abandoned to the owl and the ivy; and a very spacious wing was left free to the settlement of a colony of ghosts, which, according to the report of the peasantry and the domestics, very soon took possession, and retained it most pertinaciously, notwithstanding the pious incantations of the neighbouring vicar, the Reverend Mr. Portpipe, who often passed the night in one of the dreaded apartments over a blazing fire with the same invariable exorcising apparatus of a large venison pasty, a little Prayer-book, and three bottles of Madeira: for the reverend gentleman sagaciously observed, that as he had always found the latter an infallible charm against blue devils, he had no doubt of its proving equally efficacious against black, white, and gray. In this opinion experience seemed to confirm him; for though he always maintained a becoming silence as to the mysteries of which he was a witness during his spectral vigils, yet a very correct inference might be drawn from the fact, that he was always found in the morning comfortably asleep in his large arm-chair, with the dish scraped clean, the three bottles empty, and the Prayer-book clasped and folded precisely in the same state and place in which it had lain the preceding night.

But the larger and more commodious part of the castle continued still to be inhabited; and while one half of the edifice was fast improving into a picturesque ruin, the other was as rapidly degenerating, in its interior at least, into a comfortable modern dwelling.

In this romantic seclusion Anthelia was born. Her mother died in giving her birth. Her father, Sir Henry Melincourt, a man of great acquirements, and of a retired disposition, devoted himself in solitude to the cultivation of his daughter's understanding; for he was one of those who maintained the heretical notion that women are, or at least may be, rational beings; though, from the great pains usually taken in what is called education to make them otherwise, there are unfortunately very few examples to warrant the truth of the theory.

The majestic forms and wild energies of Nature that surrounded her from her infancy, impressed their character on her mind, communicating to it all their own wildness, and more than their own beauty. Far removed from the pageantry of courts and cities, her infant attention was awakened to spectacles more interesting and more impressive: the misty mountain-top, the ash-fringed precipice, the gleaming cataract, the deep and shadowy glen, and the fantastic magnificence of the mountain clouds. The murmur of the woods, the rush of the winds, and the tumultuous dashing of the torrents, were the first music of her childhood. A fearless wanderer among these romantic solitudes, the spirit of mountain liberty diffused itself through the whole tenor of her feelings, modelled the symmetry of her form, and illumined the expressive but feminine brilliancy of her features: and when she had attained the age at which the mind expands itself to the fascinations of poetry, the muses of Italy became the chosen companions of her wanderings, and nourished a naturally susceptible imagination by conjuring up the splendid visions of chivalry and enchantment in scenes so congenial to their development.

It was seldom that the presence of a visitor dispelled the solitude

of Melincourt; and the few specimens of the living world with whom
its inmates held occasional intercourse, were of the usual character
of country acquaintance, not calculated to leave behind them any
very lively regret, except for the loss of time during the period of
their stay. One of these was the Reverend Mr. Portpipe, whom we
have already celebrated for his proficiency in the art of exorcising
goblins by dint of venison and Madeira. His business in the ghost
line had, indeed, declined with the progress of the human understanding, and no part of his vocation was in very high favour with
Sir Henry, who, though an unexceptionable moral character, was unhappily not one of the children of grace, in the theological sense of
the word: but the vicar, adopting St. Paul's precept of being all
things to all men, found it on this occasion his interest to be liberal;
and observing that no man could coerce his opinions, repeated with
great complacency the line of Virgil:

Tros Tyriusque mihi nullo discrimine agetur; [1]

though he took especial care that his heterodox concession should
not reach the ears of his bishop, who would infallibly have unfrocked
him for promulgating a doctrine so subversive of the main pillar of
all orthodox establishments.

When Anthelia had attained her sixteenth year, her father
deemed it necessary to introduce her to that human world of which
she had hitherto seen so little, and for this purpose took a journey to
London, where he was received by the surviving portion of his old
acquaintance as a ghost returned from Acheron. The impression
which the gay scenes of the metropolis made on the mind of Anthelia—to what illustrious characters she was introduced—"and all she
thought of all she saw,"—it would be foreign to our present purpose
to detail: suffice it to say, that from this period Sir Henry regularly
passed the winter in London and the summer in Westmoreland, till
his daughter attained the age of twenty, about which period he died.

Anthelia passed twelve months from this time in total seclusion at
Melincourt, notwithstanding many pressing invitations from various
match-making dowagers in London, who were solicitous to dispose of
her according to their views of her advantage; in which how far their
own was lost sight of, it may not be difficult to determine.

[1 Trojan and Tyrian will I treat as one.]

Among the numerous lovers who had hitherto sighed at her shrine, not one had succeeded in making the slightest impression on her heart; and during the twelve months of seclusion which elapsed from the death of her father to the commencement of this authentic history, they had all completely vanished from the tablet of her memory. Her knowledge of love was altogether theoretical; and her theory, being formed by the study of Italian poetry in the bosom of mountain solitude, naturally and necessarily pointed to a visionary model of excellence which it was very little likely the modern world could realize.

The dowagers at length despairing of drawing her from her retirement, respectively came to various resolutions for the accomplishment of their ends; some resolving to go in person to Melincourt, and exert all their powers of oratory to mould her to their wishes, and others instigating their several *protégés* to set boldly forward in search of fortune, and lay siege to the castle and its mistress together.

[Among these dowagers is the Honourable Mrs. Pinmoney, who arrives at Melincourt with her daughter Miss Danaretta Contantina, and announces that her dashing nephew, Sir Telegraph Paxarett, will soon be driving his barouche in the same direction. As Anthelia has had intimations of other male visitors, she invites an old relative of hers, Humphrey Hippy, to stay at Melincourt in the role of lord seneschal. Mr. Hippy, whose manservant, Harry Fell, is a living mirror of his master's changing moods, arises from a slough of melancholia to accept with enthusiasm. In the meantime, Sir Telegraph, on his way to Melincourt, has paused to pass the night with an old friend, Sylvan Forester, who has fitted up Redrose Abbey as his dwelling place, "with the view of carrying on in peace and seclusion some peculiar experiments on the nature and progress of man." Mr. Forester's researches are based on the conviction that the human species "is gradually decreasing in size and strength," but his household boasts at least one member whose strength is beyond question. This is Sir Oran Haut-ton, Baronet, a strange and ugly but fashionable figure, whose social graces and complete silence excite Sir Telegraph's curiosity. This is in no way abated when Sir Oran, having taciturnly collaborated in the consumption of much wine, leaps through the dining-room window and dances off into the woods. Mr. Forester retrieves his friend and explains to Sir Telegraph.]

SIR ORAN HAUT-TON [1]

Mr. Forester.—Sir Oran Haut-ton was caught very young in the woods of Angola.

Sir Telegraph Paxarett.—Caught!

Mr. Forester.—Very young. He is a specimen of the natural and original man—the wild man of the woods; called in the language of the more civilized and sophisticated natives of Angola, *Pongo*, and in that of the Indians of South America, *Oran Outang*.

Sir Telegraph Paxarett.—The devil he is!

Mr. Forester.—Positively. Some presumptuous naturalists have refused his species the honours of humanity; but the most enlightened and illustrious philosophers agree in considering him in his true light as the natural and original man. One French philosopher, indeed, has been guilty of an inaccuracy, in considering him as a degenerated man; degenerated he cannot be; as his prodigious physical strength, his uninterrupted health, and his amiable simplicity of manners demonstrate. He is, as I have said, a specimen of the natural and original man—a genuine fac-simile of the philosophical Adam.

He was caught by an intelligent negro very young, in the woods of Angola; and his gentleness and sweet temper winning the hearts of the negro and negress, they brought him up in their cottage as the playfellow of their little boys and girls, where, with the exception of speech, he acquired the practice of such of the simpler arts of life as the degree of civilization in that part of Africa admits. In this way he lived till he was about seventeen years of age——

Sir Telegraph Paxarett.—By his own reckoning?

Mr. Forester.—By analogical computation. At this period, my old friend Captain Hawltaught of the Tornado frigate, being driven by stress of weather to the coast of Angola, was so much struck with the contemplative cast of Sir Oran's countenance, that he offered the

[1 The account of Sir Oran owes much to Lord Monboddo, a debt acknowledged by Peacock in many footnotes.]

negro an irresistible bribe to surrender him to his possession. The negro brought him on board, and took an opportunity to leave him slily, but with infinite reluctance and sympathetic grief. When the ship weighed anchor, and Sir Oran found himself separated from the friends of his youth, and surrounded with strange faces, he wept bitterly, and fell into such deep grief that his life was despaired of. The surgeon of the ship did what he could for him; and a much better doctor, Time, completed his cure. By degrees a very warm friendship for my friend Captain Hawltaught extinguished his recollection of his negro friends. Three years they cruised together in the Tornado, when a dangerous wound compelled the old captain to renounce his darling element, and lay himself up in ordinary for the rest of his days. He retired on his half-pay and the produce of his prize-money to a little village in the West of England, where he employed himself very assiduously in planting cabbages and watching the changes of the wind. Mr. Oran, as he was then called, was his inseparable companion, and became a very expert practical gardener. The old captain used to observe, he could always say he had an honest man in his house, which was more than could be said of many honourable houses where there was much vapouring about honour.

Mr. Oran had long before shown a taste for music, and, with some little instruction from a marine officer in the Tornado, had become a proficient on the flute and French horn. He could never be brought to understand the notes; but, from hearing any simple tune played or sung two or three times, he never failed to perform it with great exactness and brilliancy of execution. I shall merely observe, en passant, that music appears, from this and several similar circumstances, to be more natural to man than speech. The old captain was fond of his bottle of wine after dinner, and his glass of grog at night. Mr. Oran was easily brought to sympathize in this taste; and they have many times sat up together half the night over a flowing bowl, the old captain singing Rule Britannia, True Courage, or Tom Tough, and Sir Oran accompanying him on the French horn.

During a summer tour in Devonshire, I called on my old friend Captain Hawltaught, and was introduced to Mr. Oran. You, who have not forgotten my old speculations on the origin and progress of man, may judge of my delight at this happy rencontre. I exerted all the eloquence I was master of to persuade Captain Hawltaught

to resign him to me, that I might give him a philosophical education. Finding this point unattainable, I took a house in the neighbourhood, and the intercourse which ensued was equally beneficial
and agreeable to all three.

Sir Telegraph Paxarett.—And what part did you take in their
nocturnal concerts, with Tom Tough and the French horn?

Mr. Forester.—I was seldom present at them, and often remon-
strated, but ineffectually, with the captain, on his corrupting the
amiable simplicity of the natural man by this pernicious celebration
of vinous and spirituous orgies; but the only answer I could ever get
from him was a hearty damn against all water-drinkers, accompanied
with a reflection that he was sure every enemy to wine and grog must
have clapped down the hatches of his conscience on some secret
villany, which he feared good liquor would pipe ahoy: and he usually
concluded by striking up *Nothing like Grog, Saturday Night,* or
Swing the flowing Bowl, his friend Oran's horn ringing in sympathetic symphony.

The old captain used to say that grog was the elixir of life; but
it did not prove so to him; for one night he tossed off his last
bumper, sung his last stave, and heard the last flourish of his Oran's
horn. I thought poor Oran would have broken his heart; and, had
he not been familiarized to me, and conceived a very lively friendship for me before the death of his old friend, I fear the consequences would have been fatal.

Considering that change of scene would divert his melancholy,
I took him with me to London. The theatres delighted him, particularly the opera, which not only accorded admirably with his taste for
music, but where, as he looked round on the ornaments of the fashionable world, he seemed to be particularly comfortable, and to feel
himself completely at home. •

There is, to a stranger, something ludicrous in a first view of his
countenance, which led me to introduce him only into the best society, where politeness would act as a preventive to the propensity to
laugh; for he has so nice a sense of honour (which I shall observe,
by the way, is peculiar to man), that if he were to be treated with
any kind of contumely, he would infallibly die of a broken heart, as
has been seen in some of his species. With a view of ensuring him
the respect of society which always attends on rank and fortune, I

have purchased him a baronetcy, and made over to him an estate. I have also purchased of the Duke of Rottenburgh one half of the elective franchise vested in the body of Mr. Christopher Corporate, the free, fat, and dependent burgess of the ancient and honourable borough of Onevote, who returns two members to Parliament, one of whom will shortly be Sir Oran. (*Sir Telegraph gave a long whistle.*) But before taking this important step, I am desirous that he should finish his education. (*Sir Telegraph whistled again.*) I mean to say that I wish, if possible, to put a few words into his mouth, which I have hitherto found impracticable, though I do not entirely despair of ultimate success. But this circumstance, for reasons which I will give you by-and-by, does not at all militate against the proofs of his being a man.

Sir Telegraph Paxarett.—If he be but half a man, he will be the fitter representative of half an elector; for as that "large body corporate of one," the free, fat, and dependent burgess of Onevote returns two members to the honourable house, Sir Oran can only be considered as the representative of half of him. But, seriously, is not your principal object an irresistible exposure of the universality and omnipotence of corruption by purchasing for an oran outang one of those seats, the sale of which is unblushingly acknowledged to be *as notorious as the sun at noon-day?* or do you really think him one of us?

Mr. Forester.—I really think him a variety of the human species; and this is a point which I have it much at heart to establish in the acknowledgment of the civilized world.

Sir Telegraph Paxarett.—Buffon, whom I dip into now and then in the winter, ranks him, with Linnæus, in the class of *Simiæ.*

Mr. Forester.—Linnæus has given him the curious denominations of *Troglodytes, Homo nocturnus,* and *Homo silvestris:* [1] but he evidently thought him a man; he describes him as having a hissing speech, thinking, reasoning, believing that the earth was made for him, and that he will one day be its sovereign.

Sir Telegraph Paxarett.—God save King Oran! By-the-by, you put me very much in mind of Valentine and Orson. This wild man of yours will turn out some day to be the son of a king, lost in the

[1 Cave-dweller, nocturnal man, and man of the woods.]

woods, and suckled by a lioness:—"No waiter, but a knight templar:"
—no Oran, but a true prince.

Mr. Forester.—As to Buffon, it is astonishing how that great naturalist could have placed him among the *singes*, when the very words of his description give him all the characteristics of human nature. It is still more curious to think that modern travellers should have made beasts, under the names of Pongos, Mandrills, and Oran Outangs, of the very same beings whom the ancients worshipped as divinities under the names of Fauns and Satyrs, Silenus and Pan.

Sir Telegraph Paxarett.—Your Oran rises rapidly in the scale of being:—from a baronet and M.P. to a king of the world, and now to a god of the woods.

Mr. Forester.—When I was in London last winter, I became acquainted with a learned mythologist, who has long laboured to rebuild the fallen temple of Jupiter. I introduced him to Sir Oran, for whom he immediately conceived a high veneration, and would never call him by any name but Pan. His usual saluation to him was in the following words:

Ἐλθέ, μακαρ, σκιρτητα, φιλενθεος, αντροδιαιτε,
'Ἁρμονιην κοσμοιο κρεκων φιλοπαιγμονι μολπη,
Κοσμοκρατωρ, βακχευτα![1]

Which he thus translated:

King of the world! enthusiast free,
Who dwell'st in caves of liberty!
And on thy wild pipe's notes of glee
Respondest Nature's harmony!
Leading beneath the spreading tree
The Bacchanalian revelry!

"This," said he, "is part of the Orphic invocation of Pan. It alludes to the happy existence of the dancing Pans, Fauns, Orans, *et id genus omne*, whose dwellings are the caves of rocks and the hollows of trees, such as undoubtedly was, or would have been, the natural mode of life of our friend Pan among the woods of Angola. It alludes, too, to their musical powers, which in our friend Pan it gives me indescribable pleasure to find so happily exemplified. The epithet *Bacchic*,

[1] Orphica, Hymn. XI. (X. Gesn).

our friend Pan's attachment to the bottle demonstrates to be very appropriate; and the epithet κοσμοκρατωρ, king of the world, points out a striking similarity between the Orphic Pan and the Troglodyte of Linnæus, who believes that the earth was made for him, and that he will again be its sovereign." He laid great stress on the word AGAIN, and observed, if he were to develop all the ideas to which this word gave rise in his mind, he should find ample matter for a volume. Then repeating several times, Παν κοσμοκρατωρ, and interum fore telluris imperantem,[1] he concluded by saying he had known many profound philosophical and mythological systems founded on much slighter analogies.

Sir Telegraph Paxarett.—Your learned mythologist appears to be *non compos*.

Mr. Forester.—By no means. He has a system of his own, which only appears in the present day more absurd than other systems, because it has fewer followers. The manner in which the spirit of system twists everything to its own views is truly wonderful. I believe that in every nation of the earth the system which has most followers will be found the most absurd in the eye of an enlightened philosophy.

Sir Telegraph Paxarett.—But if your Oran be a man, how is it that his long intercourse with other varieties of the human species has not taught him to speak?

Mr. Forester.—Speech is a highly artificial faculty. Civilized man is a highly artificial animal. The change from the wild to the civilized state, affects not only his moral, but his physical nature, and this not rapidly and instantly, but in a long process of generations. The same change is obvious in domestic animals, and in cultivated plants. You know not where to look for the origin of the common dog, or the common fowl. The wild and tame hog, and the wild and tame cat, are marked by more essential differences than the oran and the civilized man. The origin of corn is as much a mystery to us as the source of the Nile was to the ancients. Innumerable flowers have been so changed from their original simplicity, that the art of horticulture may almost lay claim to the magic of a new creation. Is it then wonderful that the civilized man should have acquired some physical faculties which the natural man has not? It is demonstrable

[1 He will again be king of the earth.]

that speech is one. I do not, however, despair of seeing him make some progress in this art. Comparative anatomy shows that he has all the organs of articulation. Indeed he has, in every essential particular, the human form, and the human anatomy. *Now I will only observe that if an animal who walks upright—is of the human form, both outside and inside—uses a weapon for defence and attack—associates with his kind—makes huts to defend himself from the weather, better I believe than those of the New Hollanders—is tame and gentle —and instead of killing men and women, as he could easily do, takes them prisoners and makes servants of them—who has, what I think essential to the human kind, a sense of honour; which is shown by breaking his heart, if laughed at, or made a show, or treated with any kind of contumely—who, when he is brought into the company of civilized men, behaves (as you have seen) with dignity and composure, altogether unlike a monkey; from whom he differs likewise in this material respect, that he is capable of great attachment to particular persons, of which the monkey is altogether incapable; and also in this respect, that a monkey never can be so tamed that we may depend on his not doing mischief when left alone, by breaking glasses or china within his reach; whereas the oran outang is altogether harmless;—who has so much of the docility of a man that he learns not only to do the common offices of life, but also to play on the flute and French horn; which shows that he must have an idea of melody and concord of sounds, which no brute animal has;—and lastly, if joined to all these qualities he has the organ of pronunciation, and consequently the capacity of speech, though not the actual use of it; if, I say, such an animal be not a man, I should desire to know in what the essence of a man consists, and what it is that distinguishes a natural man from the man of art.*[1] That he understands many words, though he does not yet speak any, I think you may have observed, when you asked him to take wine, and applied to him for fish and partridge.

Sir Telegraph Paxarett.—The gestures, however slight, that accompany the expression of the ordinary forms of intercourse, may possibly explain that.

Mr. Forester.—You will find that he understands many things addressed to him on occasions of very unfrequent occurrence. With re-

[1] The words in italics are from Lord Monboddo.

gard to his moral character, he is undoubtedly a man, and a much better man than many that are to be found in civilized countries, as, when you are better acquainted with him, I feel very confident you will readily acknowledge.

Sir Telegraph Paxarett.—I shall be very happy, when his election comes on for Onevote, to drive him down in my barouche to the honourable and ancient borough.

Mr. Forester promised to avail himself of this proposal; when the iron tongue of midnight tolling twelve induced them to separate for the night.

THE PRINCIPLE OF POPULATION

The next morning, while Sir Telegraph, Sir Oran, and Mr. Forester were sitting down to their breakfast, a post-chaise rattled up to the door; the glass was let down, and a tall, thin, pale, grave-looking personage peeped from the aperture. "This is Mr. Fax," said Mr. Forester, "the champion of calm reason, the indefatigable explorer of the cold clear springs of knowledge, the bearer of the torch of dispassionate truth, that gives more light than warmth. He looks on the human world, the world of mind, the conflict of interests, the collision of feelings, the infinitely diversified developments of energy and intelligence, as a mathematician looks on his diagrams, or a mechanist on his wheels and pulleys, as if they were foreign to his own nature, and were nothing more than subjects of curious speculation."

Mr. Forester had not time to say more; for Mr. Fax entered, and shook hands with him, was introduced in due form to Sir Telegraph, and sat down to assist in the demolition of the *matériel* of breakfast.

Mr. Fax.—Your Redrose Abbey is a beautiful metamorphosis.— I can scarcely believe that these are the mouldering walls of the pious fraternity of Rednose, which I contemplated two years ago.

Mr. Forester.—The picturesque tourists will owe me no good-will for the metamorphosis, though I have endeavoured to leave them as much mould, mildew, and weather-stain as possible.

Mr. Fax.—The exterior has suffered little; it still retains a truly venerable monastic character.

Sir Telegraph Paxarett.—Something monastic in the interior too. —Very orthodox old wine in the cellar, I can tell you. And the Reverend Father Abbot there, as determined a bachelor as the Pope.

Mr. Forester.—If I am so, it is because, like the Squire of Dames, I seek and cannot find. I see in my mind's eye the woman I would choose, but I very much fear that is the only mode of optics in which she will ever be visible.

Mr. Fax.—No matter. Bachelors and spinsters I decidedly venerate. The world is overstocked with featherless bipeds. More men than corn is a fearful pre-eminence, the sole and fruitful cause of penury, disease, and war, plague, pestilence, and famine.

Sir Telegraph Paxarett.—I hope you will not long have cause to venerate me. What is life without love? A rosebush in winter, all thorns, and no flowers.

Mr. Fax.—And what is it with love? A double-blossomed cherry, flowers without fruit; if the blossoms last a month, it is as much as can be expected: they fall, and what comes in their place? Vanity, and vexation of spirit.

Sir Telegraph Paxarett.—Better vexation, than stagnation: marriage may often be a stormy lake, but celibacy is almost always a muddy horsepond.

Mr. Fax.—Rather a calm clear river——

Mr. Forester.—Flowing through a desert, where it moves in loneliness, and reflects no forms of beauty.

Mr. Fax.—That is not the way to consider the case. Feelings and poetical images are equally out of place in a calm philosophical view of human society. Some must marry, that the world may be peopled: many must abstain, that it may not be overstocked. *Little and good*, is very applicable in this case. It is better that the world should have a smaller number of peaceable and rational inhabitants, living in universal harmony and social intercourse, than the disproportionate mass of fools, slaves, coxcombs, thieves, rascals, liars, and cut-throats, with which its surface is at present encumbered. It is in vain to declaim about the preponderance of physical and moral evil, and attribute it, with the Manicheans, to a mythological principle, or, with some modern philosophers, to the physical constitution of the globe. The cause of all the evils of human society is single, obvious, reducible to the most exact mathematical calculation; and of course susceptible not only of remedy but even of utter annihilation. The cause is the tendency of population to increase beyond the means of subsistence. The remedy is an universal social compact, binding both sexes to equally rigid celibacy, till the prospect of maintaining the average number of six children be as clear as the arithmetic of futurity can make it.

Mr. Forester.—The arithmetic of futurity has ·been found in a more than equal number of instances to baffle human skill. The rapid and sudden mutations of fortune are the inexhaustible theme of history, poetry, and romance; and they are found in forms as various and surprising, in the scenes of daily life, as on the stage of Drury Lane.

Mr. Fax.—That the best prospects are often overshadowed, is most certainly true; but there are degrees and modes of well-grounded reliance on futurity, sufficient to justify the enterprises of prudence, and equally well-grounded prospiciencies of hopelessness and helplessness, that should check the steps of rashness and passion, in their headlong progress to perdition.

Mr. Forester.—You have little cause to complain of the present age. It is calculating enough to gratify the most determined votary of moral and political arithmetic. This certainly is not the time,

When unrevenged stalks Cocker's injured ghost.

What is friendship—except in some most rare and miraculous instances—but the fictitious bond of interest, or the heartless intercourse of idleness and vanity? What is love, but the most venal of all venal commodities? What is marriage, but the most sordid of bargains, the most cold and slavish of all the forms of commerce? We want no philosophical ice-rock, towed into the Dead Sea of modern society, to freeze that which is too cold already. We want rather the torch of Prometheus to revivify our frozen spirits. We are a degenerate race, half-reasoning developments of the principle of infinite littleness, "with hearts in our bodies no bigger than pins' heads." We are in no danger of forgetting that two and two make four. There is no fear that the warm impulses of feeling will ever overpower, with us, the tangible eloquence of the pocket.

Mr. Fax.—With relation to the middle and higher classes, you are right in a great measure as to fact, but wrong, as I think, in the asperity of your censure. But among the lower orders the case is quite different. The baleful influence of the poor laws has utterly destroyed the principle of calculation in them. They marry by whole-sale, without scruple or compunction, and commit the future care of their family to Providence and the overseer. They marry even in the workhouse, and convert the intended asylum of age and infirm-ity into a flourishing manufactory of young beggars and vagabonds.

Sir Telegraph's barouche rolled up gracefully to the door. Mr. Forester pressed him to stay another day, but Sir Telegraph's plea of urgency was not to be overcome. He promised very shortly to revisit Redrose Abbey, shook hands with Mr. Forester and Sir Oran, bowed politely to Mr. Fax, mounted his box, and disappeared among the trees.

"Those four horses," said Mr. Fax, as the carriage rolled away, "consume the subsistence of eight human beings, for the foolish amusement of one. As Solomon observes: 'This is vanity, and a great evil.'"

"Sir Telegraph is thoughtless," said Mr. Forester, "but he has a good heart and a good natural capacity. I have great hopes of him. He had some learning, when he went to college; but he was cured of it before he came away. Great, indeed, must be the zeal for im-provement which an academical education cannot extinguish."

[Sir Telegraph is welcomed to Melincourt, where a distinguished company is soon assembled, its most eminent personage being Lord Anophel Achthar, son and heir of the Marquis of Agaric, who is accompanied by his tutor, Mr. Grovelgrub, and a celebrated poet, Mr. Feathernest, "to whom the Marquis had recently given a place in exchange for his conscience." Mr. Harum O'Scarum, proprietor of a vast bog in Kerry, and Mr. Derrydown, who has abandoned metaphysics for the study of old ballads, are two other suitors who have found *logement* in Anthelia's neighbourhood, and found further that Mr. Hippy's hospitality sometimes enables them to pass several successive days at the Castle. Anthelia, pur-sued by many Strephons, encourages none. But time flows pleas-antly at Melincourt.]

THE PHILOSOPHY OF BALLADS

Music and conversation consumed the evenings. Mr. Feathernest and Mr. Derrydown were both zealous admirers of old English literature; but the former was chiefly enraptured with the ecclesiastical writers and the translation of the Bible; the latter admired nothing but ballads, which he maintained to be, whether ancient or modern, the only manifestations of feeling and thought containing any vestige of truth and nature.

"Surely," said Mr. Feathernest one evening, "you will not maintain that Chevy Chase is a finer poem than Paradise Lost?"

Mr. Derrydown.—I do not know what you mean by a fine poem; but I will maintain that it gives a much deeper insight into the truth of things.

Mr. Feathernest.—I do not know what you mean by the truth of things.

The Rev. Mr. Grovelgrub.—Define, gentlemen, define: let the one explain what he means by a fine poem, and the other what he means by the truth of things.

Mr. Feathernest.—A fine poem is a luminous development of the complicated machinery of action and passion, exalted by sublimity, softened by pathos, irradiated with scenes of magnificence, figures of loveliness and characters of energy, and harmonized with infinite variety of melodious combination.

Lord Anophel Achthar.—Admirable!

Miss Danaretta Contantina Pinmoney.—Admirable, indeed, my lord! (*With a sweet smile at his lordship, which unluckily missed fire.*)

The Rev. Mr. Grovelgrub.—Now, Sir, for the truth of things.

Mr. O'Scarum.—Troth, Sir, that is the last point about which I should expect a gentleman of your cloth to be very solicitous.

The Rev. Mr. Grovelgrub.—I must say, Sir, that is a very uncalled-for and very illiberal observation.

Mr. O'Scarum.—Your coat is your protection, Sir.

The Rev. Mr. Grovelgrub.—I will appeal to his lordship if——

Mr. O'Scarum.—I shall be glad to know his lordship's opinion.

Lord Anophel Achthar.—Really, Sir, I have no opinion on the subject.

Mr. O'Scarum.—I am sorry for it, my lord.

Mr. Derrydown.—The truth of things is nothing more than an exact view of the necessary relations between object and subject, in all the modes of reflection and sentiment which constitute the reciprocities of human association.

The Rev. Mr. Grovelgrub.—I must confess I do not exactly comprehend——

Mr. Derrydown.—I will illustrate. You all know the ballad of Old Robin Gray.

> Young Jamie loved me well, and asked me for his bride;
> But saving a crown, he had nothing else beside.
> To make the crown a pound my Jamie went to sea,
> And the crown and the pound they were both for me.
>
> He had not been gone a twelvemonth and a day,
> When my father broke his arm, and our cow was stolen away;
> My mother she fell sick, and Jamie at the sea,
> And old Robin Gray came a-courting to me.

In consequence whereof, as you all very well know, old Robin being rich, the damsel married the aforesaid old Robin.

The Rev. Mr. Grovelgrub.—In the heterodox kirk of the north?

Mr. Derrydown.—Precisely. Now, in this short space, you have a more profound view than the deepest metaphysical treatise or the most elaborate history can give you of the counteracting power of opposite affections, the conflict of duties and inclinations, the omnipotence of interest, tried by the test of extremity, and the supreme and irresistible dominion of universal moral necessity.

> Young Jamie loved me well, and ask'd me for his bride;

and would have had her, it is clear, though she does not explicitly say so, if there had not been a necessary moral motive counteracting what would have been otherwise the plain free will of both. "Young Jamie loved me well." She does not say that she loved young Jamie; and here is a striking illustration of that female decorum which forbids young ladies to speak as they think on any subject whatever:

an admirable political institution, which has been found by experience to be most happily conducive to that ingenuousness of mind
and simplicity of manner which constitute so striking a charm in the
generality of the fair sex.

But saving a crown, he had nothing else beside.

Here is the quintessence of all that has been said and written on the
subject of love and prudence, a decisive refutation of the stoical
doctrine that poverty is no evil, a very clear and deep insight into the
nature of the preventive or prudential check to population, and a
particularly luminous view of the respective conduct of the two sexes
on similar occasions. The poor love-stricken swain, it seems, is ready
to sacrifice all for love. He comes with a crown in his pocket, and
asks for his bride. The damsel is a better arithmetician. She is fully
impressed with the truth of the old proverb about poverty coming
in at the door, and immediately stops him short, with "What can
you settle on me, Master Jamie?" or, as Captain Bobadil would express it, "How much money ha' you about you, Master Matthew?"
Poor Jamie looks very foolish—fumbles in his pocket—produces his
crown-piece— and answers like Master Matthew, with a remarkable
elongation of visage, " 'Faith, I ha'n't past a five shillings or so."
"Then," says the young lady, in the words of another very admirable
ballad—where you will observe it is also the damsel who asks the
question:

> Will the love that you're so rich in,
> Make a fire in the kitchen?

On which the poor lover shakes his head, and the lady gives him
leave of absence. Hereupon Jamie falls into a train of reflections.

Mr. O'Scarum.—Never mind his reflections.

Mr. Derrydown.—The result of which is, that he goes to seek
his fortune at sea; intending, with the most perfect and disinterested
affection, to give all he can get to his mistress, who seems much
pleased with the idea of having it. But when he comes back, as you
will see in the sequel, he finds his mistress married to a rich old man.
The detail of the circumstances abounds with vast and luminous

views of human nature and society, and striking illustrations of the truth of things.

Mr. Feathernest.—I do not yet see that the illustration throws any light on the definition, or that we are at all advanced in the answer to the question concerning Chevy Chase and Paradise Lost.

Mr. Derrydown.—We will examine Chevy Chase, then, with a view to the truth of things, instead of Old Robin Gray:

> God prosper long our noble king,
> Our lives and safeties all.

Mr. O'Scarum.—God prosper us all, indeed! if you are going through Chevy Chase at the same rate as you were through Old Robin Gray, there is an end of us all for a month. The truth of things, now!—is it that you're looking for? Ask Miss Melincourt to touch the harp. The harp is the great key to the truth of things: and in the hand of Miss Melincourt it will teach you the music of the spheres, the concord of creation, and the harmony of the universe.

Anthelia.—You are a libeller of our sex, Mr. Derrydown, if you think the truth of things consists in showing it to be more governed by the meanest species of self-interest than yours. Few, indeed, are the individuals of either in whom the spirit of the age of chivalry survives.

Mr. Derrydown.—And yet, a man distinguished by that spirit would not be in society what Miss Melincourt is—a phœnix. Many knights can wield the sword of Orlando, but only one nymph can wear the girdle of Florimel.

The Hon. Mrs. Pinmoney.—That would be a very pretty compliment, Mr. Derrydown, if there were no other ladies in the room.

Poor Mr. Derrydown looked a little disconcerted: he felt conscious that he had on this occasion lost sight of his usual politeness by too close an adherence to the truth of things.

Anthelia.—Both sexes, I am afraid, are too much influenced by the spirit of mercenary calculation. The desire of competence is prudence; but the desire of more than competence is avarice: it is against the latter only that moral censure should be directed: but I fear that in ninety-nine cases out of a hundred in which the course of true love is thwarted by considerations of fortune, it will be found that avarice rather than prudence is to be considered as the cause. Love in the age of chivalry, and love in the age of commerce, are certainly two very different deities; so much so, that the former may almost be regarded as a departed power; and, perhaps, the little ballad I am about to sing does not contain too severe an allegory in placing the tomb of chivalric love among the ruins of the castles of romance.

THE TOMB OF LOVE

By the mossy weed-flowr'd column,
   Where the setting moonbeam's glance
Streams a radiance cold and solemn
   On the haunts of old romance:
Know'st thou what those shafts betoken,
   Scatter'd on that tablet lone,
Where the ivory bow lies broken
   By the monumental stone!

When true knighthood's shield, neglected,
   Moulder'd in the empty hall;
When the charms that shield protected
   Slept in death's eternal thrall;
When chivalric glory perish'd
   Like the pageant of a dream,
Love in vain its memory cherish'd,
   Fired in vain the minstrel's theme.

Falsehood to an elfish minion
   Did the form of Love impart;
Cunning plumed its vampire pinion;
   Avarice tipp'd its golden dart.
Love, the hideous phantom flying,
   Hither came, no more to rove:
There his broken bow is lying
   On that stone—the tomb of Love!

THE TORRENT

ANTHELIA did not wish to condemn herself to celibacy, but in none of her present suitors could she discover any trace of the character she had drawn in her mind for the companion of her life: yet she was aware of the rashness of precipitate judgments, and willing to avail herself of this opportunity of studying the kind of beings that constitute modern society. She was happy in the long interval between breakfast and dinner, to retire to the seclusion of her favourite apartment; whence she sometimes wandered into the shades of her shrubbery: sometimes passing onward through a little postern door, she descended a flight of rugged steps, which had been cut in the solid stone, into the gloomy glen of the torrent that dashed round the base of the castle rock; and following a lonely path through the woods that fringed its sides, wandered into the deepest recesses of mountain solitude. The sunshine of a fine autumnal day, the solemn beauty of the fading woods, the thin gray mist, that spread waveless over the mountains, the silence of the air, the deep stillness of nature, broken only by the sound of the eternal streams, tempted her on one occasion beyond her usual limits.

Passing over the steep and wood-fringed hills of rock that formed the boundary of the valley of Melincourt, she descended through a grove of pines, into a romantic chasm, where a foaming stream was crossed by a rude and ancient bridge, consisting of two distinct parts, each of which rested against a columnar rock, that formed an island in the roaring waters. An ash had fixed its roots in the fissures of the rock, and the knotted base of its aged trunk offered to the passenger a natural seat, over-canopied with its beautiful branches, and leaves, now tinged with their autumnal yellow. Anthelia rested awhile in this delightful solitude. There was no breath of wind, no song of birds, no humming of insects, only the dashing of the waters beneath. She felt the presence of the genius of the scene. She sat absorbed in a train of contemplations, dimly defined, but infinitely delightful: emotions rather than thoughts, which attention would have utterly dissipated, if it had paused to seize their images.

She was roused from her reverie by sounds of music, issuing from the grove of pines, through which she had just passed, and which skirted the hollow. The notes were wild and irregular, but their effect was singular and pleasing. They ceased. Anthelia looked to the spot from whence they had proceeded, and saw, or thought she saw, a face peeping at her through the trees; but the glimpse was momentary. There was in the expression of the countenance something so extraordinary, that she almost felt convinced her imagination had created it; yet her imagination was not in the habit of creating such physiognomies. She could not, however, apprehend that this remarkable vision portended any evil to her; for, if so, alone and defenceless as she was, why should it be deferred? She rose, therefore, to pursue her walk, and ascended, by a narrow winding path, the brow of a lofty hill, which sunk precipitously on the other side, to the margin of a lake, that seemed to slumber in the same eternal stillness as the rocks that bordered it. The murmur of the torrent was inaudible at that elevation. There was an almost oppressive silence in the air. The motion and life of nature seemed suspended. The gray mist that hung on the mountains spreading its thin transparent uniform veil over the whole surrounding scene, gave a deeper impression to the mystery of loneliness, the predominant feeling that pressed on the mind of Anthelia, to seem the only thing that lived and moved in all that wide and awful scene of beauty.

Suddenly the gray mist fled before the rising wind, and a deep black line of clouds appeared in the west, that rising rapidly, volume on volume, obscured in a few minutes the whole face of the heavens. There was no interval of preparation, no notice for retreat. The rain burst down in a sheeted cataract, comparable only to the bursting of a water-spout. The sides of the mountains gleamed at once with a thousand torrents. Every little hollow and rain-worn channel, which but a few minutes before was dry, became instantaneously the bed of a foaming stream. Every half-visible rivulet swelled to a powerful and turbid river. Anthelia glided down the hill like an Oread, but the wet and slippery footing of the steep descent necessarily retarded her progress. When she regained the bridge, the swollen torrent had filled the chasm beneath, and was still rising like a rapid and impetuous tide, rushing and roaring along with boiling tumult and inconceivable swiftness. She had passed one half of the bridge—she had gained the insular rock—a few steps would have placed her on the other side of the chasm—when a large trunk of an oak, which months, perhaps years, before had baffled the woodman's skill, and fallen into the dingle above, now disengaged by the flood, and hurled onward with irresistible strength, with large and projecting boughs towering high above the surface, struck the arch she had yet to pass, which, shattered into instant ruin, seemed to melt like snow into the torrent, leaving scarcely a vestige of its place.

Anthelia followed the trunk with her eyes till it disappeared among the rocks, and stood gazing on the torrent with feelings of awful delight. The contemplation of the mighty energies of nature, energies of liberty and power which nothing could resist or impede, absorbed, for a time, all considerations of the difficulty of regaining her home. The water continued to rise, but still she stood rivetted to the spot, watching with breathless interest its tumultuous revolutions. She dreamed not, that its increasing pressure was mining the foundation of the arch she had passed. She was roused from her reverie only by the sound of its dissolution. She looked back, and found herself on the solitary rock insulated by the swelling flood.

Would the flood rise above the level of the rock? The ash must in that case be her refuge. Could the force of the torrent rend its massy roots from the rocky fissures which grasped them with giant strength? Nothing could seem less likely: yet it was not impossible. But she had always looked with calmness on the course of necessity: she felt that she was always in the order of nature. Though her life had been a series of uniform prosperity, she had considered deeply the changes of things, and *the nearness of the paths of night and day* in every pursuit and circumstance of human life. She sate on the stem of the ash. The torrent rolled almost at her feet. Could this be the calm sweet scene of the morning, the ivied bridges, the romantic chasm, the stream far below, bright in its bed of rocks, chequered by the pale sunbeams through the leaves of the ash?

She looked towards the pine-grove, through which she had descended in the morning; she thought of the wild music she had heard, and of the strange face that had appeared among the trees. Suddenly it appeared again: and shortly after a stranger issuing from the wood, ran with surprising speed to the edge of the chasm.

Anthelia had never seen so singular a physiognomy; but there was nothing in it to cause alarm. The stranger seemed interested for her situation, and made gestures expressive of a design to assist her. He paused a moment, as if measuring with his eyes the breadth of the chasm, and then, returning to the grove, proceeded very deliberately to pull up a pine. Anthelia thought him mad; but infinite was her astonishment to see the tree sway and bend beneath the efforts of his incredible strength, till at length he tore it from the soil, and bore it on his shoulders to the chasm: where placing one end on a high point of the bank, and lowering the other on the insulated rock, he ran like a flash of lightning along the stem, caught Anthelia in his arms, and carried her safely over in an instant: not that we should wish the reader to suppose our heroine, a mountaineer from her infancy, could not have crossed a pine-bridge without such assistance; but the stranger gave her no time to try the experiment.

The remarkable physiognomy and unparalleled strength of the stranger caused much of surprise, and something of apprehension to mingle with Anthelia's gratitude: but the air of high fashion which characterized his whole deportment, diminished her apprehension, while it increased her surprise at the exploit he had performed.

Shouts were now heard in the wood, from which shortly emerged Mr. Hippy, Lord Anophel Achthar, and the Reverend Mr. Grovelgrub. Anthelia had been missed at Melincourt at the commencement of the storm, and Mr. Hippy had been half distracted on the occasion. The whole party had in consequence dispersed in various directions in search of her, and accident had directed these three gentlemen to the spot where Anthelia was just set down by her polite deliverer, Sir Oran Haut-ton, Baronet.

Mr. Hippy ran up with great alacrity to Anthelia, assuring her that at the time when Miss Danaretta Constantina Pinmoney informed him his dear niece was missing, he was suffering under a complete paralysis of his right leg, and was on the point of swallowing a potion sent to him by Dr. Killquick, which, on receiving the alarming intelligence, he had thrown out of the window, and he believed it had alighted on the doctor's head as he was crossing the court. Anthelia communicated to him the particulars of the signal service she had received from the stranger, whom Mr. Hippy stared at heartily, and shook hands with cordially.

Lord Anophel now came up, and surveyed Sir Oran through his quizzing-glass, who making him a polite bow, took his quizzing-glass from him, and examined him through it in the same manner. Lord Anophel flew into a furious passion; but receiving a gentle hint from Mr. Hippy, that the gentleman to whom he was talking had just pulled up a pine, he deemed it prudent to restrain his anger within due bounds.

The Reverend Mr. Grovelgrub now rolled up to the party, muffled in a ponderous greatcoat, and surmounted with an enormous umbrella, humbly soliciting Miss Melincourt to take shelter. Anthelia assured him that she was so completely wet through, as to render all shelter superfluous, till she could change her clothes. On this, Mr. Hippy, who was wet through himself, but had not till that moment been aware that he was so, voted for returning to Melincourt with all possible expedition; adding, that he feared it would be necessary, immediately on their arrival, to send off an express for Dr. Killquick, for his dear Anthelia's sake, as well as his own. Anthelia disclaimed any intention or necessity on her part of calling in the services of the learned doctor, and, turning to Sir Oran, requested the favour of his company to dinner at Melincourt. This invitation was warmly seconded by Mr. Hippy, with gestures as well as words. Sir Oran bowed acknowledgment, but pointing in a direction different from that of Melincourt, shook his head, and took a respectful farewell.

"I wonder who he is," said Mr. Hippy, as they walked rapidly homewards: "manifestly dumb, poor fellow! a man of consequence, no doubt: no great beauty, by-the-by; but as strong as Hercules—quite an Orlando Furioso. He pulled up a pine, my lord, as you would a mushroom."

"Sir," said Lord Anophel, "I have nothing to do with mushrooms; and as to this gentleman, whoever he is, I must say, notwithstanding his fashionable air, his taking my quizzing-glass was a piece of impertinence, for which I shall feel necessitated to require gentlemanly satisfaction."

A long, toilsome, and slippery walk brought the party to the castle-gate.

THE LAW

SIR ORAN HAUT-TON, as we conjecture, had taken a very long ramble beyond the limits of Redrose Abbey, and had sat down in the pine-grove to solace himself with his flute, when Anthelia, bursting upon him like a beautiful vision, rivetted him in silent admiration to the spot whence she departed, about which he lingered in hopes of her re-appearance, till the accident which occurred on her return enabled him to exert his extraordinary physical strength in a manner so remarkably advantageous to her. On parting from her and her companions, he ran back all the way to the Abbey, a formidable distance, and relieved the anxious apprehensions which his friend Mr. Forester entertained respecting him.

A few mornings after this occurrence, as Mr. Forester, Mr. Fax, and Sir Oran were sitting at breakfast, a letter was brought in, addressed to *Sir Oran Haut-ton, Baronet, Redrose Abbey*; a circumstance which very much surprised Mr. Forester, as he could not imagine how Sir Oran had obtained a correspondent, seeing that he could neither write nor read. He accordingly took the liberty of opening the letter himself.

It proved to be from a limb of the law, signing himself Richard Ratstail, and purporting to be a notice to Sir Oran to defend himself in an action brought against him by the said Richard Ratstail, solicitor, in behalf of his client, Lawrence Litigate, Esquire, lord of the manor of Muckwormsby, for that he, the said Oran Haut-ton, did, with force and arms, videlicet, sword, pistols, daggers, bludgeons, and staves, break into the manor of the said Lawrence Litigate, Esquire, and did then and there, with malice aforethought, and against the peace of our sovereign lord the King, his crown and dignity, cut down, root up, hew, hack, and cut in pieces, sundry and several pine-trees, of various sizes and dimensions, to the utter ruin, havoc, waste, and devastation of a large tract of pine-land; and that he had wilfully, maliciously, and with intent to injure the said Lawrence Litigate, Esquire, carried off with force and arms, namely, swords, pistols, bludgeons, daggers, and staves, fifty cartloads of trunks, fifty cartloads of bark, fifty cartloads of loppings, and fifty cartloads of toppings.

This was a complete enigma to Mr. Forester; and his surprise was increased when, on reading further, he found that Miss Melincourt, of Melincourt Castle, was implicated in the affair, as having aided and abetted Sir Oran in devastating the pine-grove, and carrying it off by cartloads with force and arms.

It immediately occurred to him that the best mode he could adopt of elucidating the mystery would be to call on Miss Melincourt, whom, besides, Sir Telegraph's enthusiastic description had given him some curiosity to see; and the present appeared a favourable opportunity to indulge it.

He therefore asked Mr. Fax if he were disposed for a very long walk. Mr. Fax expressed a cordial assent to the proposal, and no time was lost in preparation.

Mr. Forester, though he had built stables for the accommodation of his occasional visitors, kept no horses himself, for reasons which will appear hereafter.

They set forth accordingly, accompanied by Sir Oran, who joined them without waiting for an invitation.

THE LIBRARY

MR. FORESTER, Mr. Fax, and Sir Oran Haut-ton arrived at Melincourt Castle. They were shown into a parlour, where they were left alone a few minutes; when Mr. Hippy made his appearance, and recognizing Sir Oran, shook hands with him very cordially. Mr. Forester produced the letter he had received from Mr. Ratstail, which Mr. Hippy having read, vented a string of invectives against the impudent rascal, and explained the mystery of the adventure, though he seemed to think it strange that Sir Oran could not have explained it himself. Mr. Forester shook his head significantly; and Mr. Hippy, affecting to understand the gesture, exclaimed, "Ah! poor gentleman!" He then invited them to stay to dinner. "I won't be refused," said he; "I am lord and master of this castle at present, and here you shall stay till to-morrow. Anthy will be delighted to see her friend here" (bowing to Sir Oran, who returned it with great politeness), "and we will hold a council of war, how to deal with this pair of puppies, Lawrence Litigate, Esquire, and Richard Ratstail, solicitor. I have several visitors here already: lords, baronets, and squires, all Corydons, sighing for Anthy; but it seems *Love's Labour Lost* with all of them. However, love and wine, you know! Anthy won't give them the first, so I drench them with the second: there will be more bottles than hearts cracked in the business, for all Anthy's beauty. *Men die and worms eat them, as usual, but not for love.*

Mr. Forester inquired for Sir Telegraph Paxarett. "An excellent fellow after dinner!" exclaimed Mr. Hippy. "I never see him in the morning; nor any one else, but my rascal, Harry Fell, and now and then Harry Killquick. The moment breakfast is over, one goes one way, and another another. Anthy locks herself up in the library."

"Locks herself up in the library!" said Mr. Fax: "a young lady, a beauty, and an heiress, in the nineteenth century, think of cultivating her understanding!"

"Strange, but true," said Mr. Hippy; "and here am I, a poor invalid, left alone all the morning to prowl about the castle like a ghost; that is, when I am well enough to move, which is not always the case. But the library is opened at four, and the party assembles there before dinner; and as it is now about the time, come with me, and I will introduce you."

They followed Mr. Hippy to the library, where they found Anthelia alone.

"Anthy," said Mr. Hippy, after the forms of introduction, "do you know you are accused of laying waste a pine-grove, and carrying it off by cartloads, with force and arms?"

Anthelia read Mr. Ratstail's letter. "This is a very strange piece of folly," she said: "I hope it will not be a mischievous one." She then renewed the expressions of her gratitude to Sir Oran, and bade him welcome to Melincourt. Sir Oran bowed in silence.

"Folly and mischief," said Mr. Fax, "are very nearly allied; and nowhere more conspicuously than in the forms of the law."

Mr. Forester.—You have an admirable library, Miss Melincourt: and I judge from the great number of Italian books, you are justly partial to the poets of that exquisite language. The apartment itself seems singularly adapted to the genius of their poetry, which combines the magnificent simplicity of ancient Greece with the mysterious grandeur of the feudal ages. Those windows of stained glass would recall to an enthusiastic mind the attendant spirit of Tasso; and the waving of the cedars beyond, when the wind makes music in their boughs, with the birds singing in their shades and the softened dash of the torrent from the dingle below, might, with little aid from fancy, be modulated into that exquisite combination of melody which flowed from the enchanted wood at the entrance of Rinaldo, and which Tasso has painted with a degree of harmony not less magical than the music he describes. Italian poetry is all fairyland: I know not any description of literature so congenial to the tenderness and delicacy of the female mind, which, however opposite may be the tendency of modern education, Nature has most pre-eminently adapted to be "a mansion for all lovely forms: a dwelling-place for all sweet sounds and harmonies." Of these, Italian poetry is a most inexhaustible fountain; and for that reason I could wish it to be generally acknowledged a point of the very first importance in female education.

Anthelia.—You have a better opinion of the understandings of women, sir, than the generality of your lordly sex seems disposed to entertain.

Mr. Forester.—The conduct of men, in this respect, is much like that of a gardener who should plant a plot of ground with merely ornamental flowers, and then pass sentence on the soil for not bearing substantial fruit. If women are treated only as pretty dolls, and dressed in all the fripperies of irrational education; if the vanity of personal adornment and superficial accomplishments be made from their very earliest years to suppress all mental aspirations, and to supersede all thoughts of intellectual beauty, is it to be inferred that they are incapable of better things? But such is the usual logic of tyranny, which first places its extinguisher on the flame, and then argues that it cannot burn.

Mr. Fax.—Your remark is not totally just: for though custom, how justly I will not say, banishes women from the fields of classical literature, yet the study of Italian poetry, of which you think so highly, is very much encouraged among them.

Mr. Forester.—You should rather say it is not discouraged. They are permitted to know it: but in very few instances is the permission accompanied by any practical aid. The only points practically enforced in female education are sound, colour, and form,—music, dress, drawing, and dancing. The mind is left to take care of itself.

Mr. Fax.—And has as much chance of doing so as a horse in a pound, circumscribed in the narrowest limits, and studiously deprived of nourishment.

Anthelia.—The simile is, I fear, too just. To think is one of the most unpardonable errors a woman can commit in the eyes of society. In our sex a taste for intellectual pleasures is almost equivalent to taking the veil; and though not absolutely a vow of perpetual celibacy, it has almost always the same practical tendency. In that universal system of superficial education which so studiously depresses the mind of women, a female who aspires to mental improvement will scarcely find in her own sex a congenial associate; and the other will regard her as an intruder on its prescriptive authority, its legitimate and divine right over the dominion of thought and reason: and the general consequence is, that she remains insulated between both, in more than cloistered loneliness. Even in its effect on herself, the ideal beauty which she studies will make her fastidious, too fastidious, perhaps, to the world of realities, and deprive her of the happiness that might be her portion, by fixing her imagination on chimæras of unattainable excellence.

Mr. Forester.—I can answer for men, Miss Melincourt, that there are some, many I hope, who can appreciate justly that most heavenly of earthly things, an enlightened female mind; whatever may be thought by the pedantry that envies, the foppery that fears, the folly that ridicules, or the wilful blindness that will not see its loveliness. I am afraid your last observation approaches most nearly to the truth, and that it is owing more to their own fastidiousness than to the want of friends and admirers, that intelligent women are so often alone in the world. But were it otherwise, the objection will not apply to Italian poetry, a field of luxuriant beauty, from which women are not interdicted even by the most intolerant prejudice of masculine usurpation.

Anthelia.—They are not interdicted, certainly; but they are seldom encouraged to enter it. Perhaps it is feared, that, having gone thus far, they might be tempted to go farther: that the friend of Tasso might aspire to the acquaintance of Virgil, or even to an introduction to Homer and Sophocles.

Mr. Forester.—And why should she not? Far from desiring to suppress such a noble ambition, how delightful should I think the task of conducting the lovely aspirant through the treasures of Grecian genius!—to wander hand-in-hand with such a companion among the valleys and fountains of Ida, and by the banks of the eddying Scamander; through the island of Calypso, and the gardens of Alcinous; to the rocks of the Scythian desert; to the caverned shores of the solitary Lemnos and to the fatal sands of Trœzene: to kindle in such scenes the enthusiasm of such a mind, and to see the eyes of love and beauty beaming with their reflected inspiration! Miserably perverted, indeed, must be the selfishness of him who, having such happiness in his power, would,

> Like the base Indian, throw a pearl away,
> Richer than all his tribe.

Mr. Fax.—My friend's enthusiasm, Miss Melincourt, usually runs away with him when any allusion is made to ancient Greece.

Mr. Forester had spoken with ardour and animation; for the scenes of which he spoke rose upon his mind as depicted in the incomparable poetry to which he had alluded; the figurative idea of wandering among them with a young and beautiful female aspirant, assumed for a moment a visionary reality; and when he subsequently reflected on it, it appeared to him very singular that the female figure in the mental picture had assumed the form and features of Anthelia Melincourt.

Anthelia, too, saw in the animated countenance of Sylvan Forester traces of more than common feeling, generosity, and intelligence: his imaginary wanderings through the classic scenes of antiquity assumed in her congenial mind the brightest colours of intellectual beauty; and she could not help thinking that if he were what he appeared, such wanderings, with such a guide, would not be the most unenviable of earthly destinies.

The other guests dropped in by ones and twos. Sir Telegraph was agreeably surprised to see Mr. Forester: "By-the-by," said he, "have you heard that a general election is to take place immediately?"

"I have," said Mr. Forester, "and was thinking of putting you and your barouche in requisition very shortly."

"As soon as you please," said Sir Telegraph.

The Honourable Mrs. Pinmoney took Sir Telegraph aside, to make inquiry concerning the new-comers.

The Hon. Mrs. Pinmoney.—Who is that very bright-eyed wild-looking young man?

Sir Telegraph Paxarett.—That is my old acquaintance and fellow-collegian, Sylvan Forester, now of Redrose Abbey, in this county.

The Hon. Mrs. Pinmoney.—Is he respectable?

Sir Telegraph Paxarett.—He has a good estate, if you mean that.

The Hon. Mrs. Pinmoney.—To be sure I mean that. And who is that tall thin saturnine personage?

Sir Telegraph Paxarett.—I know nothing of him but that his name is Fax, and that he is now on a visit to Mr. Forester at Redrose Abbey.

The Hon Mrs. Pinmoney.—And who is that very tall and remarkably ugly gentleman?

Sir Telegraph Paxarett.—That is Sir Oran Haut-ton, Baronet; to which designation you may shortly add M.P. for the ancient and honourable borough of Onevote.

The Hon. Mrs. Pinmoney.—A Baronet! and M.P.! Well, now I look at him again, I certainly do not think him so very plain: he has a very fashionable air. Haut-ton! French extraction, no doubt. And now I think of it, there is something very French in his physiognomy.

Dinner was announced, and the party adjourned to the diningroom. Mr. Forester offered his hand to Anthelia; and Sir Oran Haut-ton, following the example, presented his to the Honourable Mrs. Pinmoney.

THE SYMPOSIUM

THE dinner passed off with great harmony. The ladies withdrew. The bottle revolved with celerity, under the presidency of Mr. Hippy, and the vice-presidency of Sir Telegraph Paxarett. The Reverend Mr. Portpipe, who was that day of the party, pronounced an eulogium on the wine, which was echoed by the Reverend Mr. Grovelgrub, Mr. O'Scarum, Lord Anophel Achthar, Mr. Feathernest, and Mr. Derrydown. Mr. Forester and Mr. Fax showed no disposition to destroy the unanimity of opinion on this interesting subject. Sir Oran Haut-ton maintained a grave and dignified silence, but demonstrated by his practice that his taste was orthodox. Mr. O'Scarum sat between Sir Oran and the Reverend Mr. Portpipe, and kept a sharp look-out on both sides of him; but did not, during the whole course of the sitting, detect either of his supporters in the heinous fact of a heeltap.

Mr. Hippy.—Doctor Killquick may say what he pleases

Of mithridate, cordials, and elixirs;
But from my youth this was my only physic.—
Here's a colour! what lady's cheek comes near it?
It sparkles, hangs out diamonds! O my sweet heart!
Mistress of merry hearts! they are not worth thy favours
Who number thy moist kisses in these crystals!

The Rev. Mr. Portpipe.—An excellent text!—sound doctrine, plain and practical. When I open the bottle, I shut the book of Numbers. There are two reasons for drinking: one is, when you are thirsty, to cure it; the other, when you are not thirsty, to prevent it. The first is obvious, mechanical, and plebeian; the second is most refined, abstract, prospicient, and canonical. I drink by anticipation of thirst that may be. Prevention is better than cure. Wine is the elixir of life. "The soul," says St. Augustine, "cannot live in drought." What is death? Dust and ashes. There is nothing so dry. What is life? Spirit. What is spirit? Wine.

Mr. O'Scarum.—And whisky.

The Rev. Mr. Portpipe.—Whisky is hepatic, phlogistic, and exanthematous. Wine is the hierarchical and archiepiscopal fluid. Bacchus is said to have conquered the East, and to have returned loaded with its spoils. "Marry how? tropically." The conquests of Bacchus are the victories of imagination, which, sublimated by wine, puts to rout care, fear, and poverty, and revels in the treasures of Utopia.

Mr. Feathernest.—The juice of the grape is the liquid quintessence of concentrated sunbeams. Man is an exotic, in this northern climate, and must be nourished like a hothouse plant, by the perpetual adhibition of artificial heat.

Lord Anophel Achthar.—You were not always so fond of wine, Feathernest?

Mr. Feathernest.—Oh, my lord! no allusion, I beseech you, to my youthful errors. Demosthenes being asked what wine he liked best, answered, that which he drank at the expense of others.

The Rev. Mr. Portpipe.—Demosthenes was right. His circumstance, or qualification, is an accompaniment of better relish than a devilled biscuit or an anchovy toast.

Mr. Feathernest.—In former days, my lord, I had no experience that way; therefore I drank water against my will.

Lord Anophel Achthar.—And wrote Odes upon it, to Truth and Liberty.

Mr. Feathernest.—"Ah, no more of that, an' thou lovest me." Now that I can get it for a song, I take my pipe of wine a year: and what is the effect? Not cold phlegmatic lamentations over the sufferings of the poor, but high-flown, jovial, reeling dithyrambics "to all the crowned heads in Europe." I had then a vague notion that all was wrong. Persuasion has since appeared to me in a tangible shape, and convinced me that all is right, especially at court.—Then I saw darkly through a glass—of water. Now I see clearly through a glass of wine.

The Rev. Mr. Portpipe (looking through his glass at the light). —An infallible telescope!

Mr. Forester.—I am unfortunately one of those, sir, who very much admired your Odes to Truth and Liberty, and read your royal lyrics with very different sensations.

Mr. Feathernest.—I presume, sir, every man has a right to change his opinions.

Mr. Forester.—From disinterested conviction undoubtedly: but when it is obviously from mercenary motives, the apostacy of a public man is a public calamity. It is not his single loss to the cause he supported, that is alone to be lamented: the deep shade of mistrust which his conduct throws on that of all others who embark in the same career, tends to destroy all sympathy with the enthusiasm of genius, all admiration for the intrepidity of truth, all belief in the sincerity of zeal for public liberty: if their advocates drop one by one into the vortex of courtly patronage, every new one that arises will be more and more regarded as a hollow-hearted hypocrite, a false and venal angler for pension and place; for there is in these cases no criterion by which the world can distinguish the baying of a noble dog that will defend his trust till death, from the yelping of a political cur, that only infests the heels of power to be silenced with the offals of corruption.

Lord Anophel Achthar.—Cursed severe, Feathernest, 'pon honour.

Mr. Fax.—*The gradual falling off of prudent men from unprofitable virtues, is perhaps too common an occurrence to deserve much notice, or justify much reprobation.*[1]

---

[1] Edinburgh Review, No. liii. p. 10.

Mr. Forester.—If it were not common, it would not need reprobation. Vices of unfrequent occurrence stand sufficiently self-exposed in the insulation of their own deformity. The vices that call for the scourge of satire, are those which pervade the whole frame of society, and which, under some specious pretence of private duty, or the sanction of custom and precedent, are almost permitted to assume the semblance of virtue, or at least to pass unstigmatized in the crowd of congenial transgressions.

Mr. Feathernest.—You may say what you please, sir. I am accustomed to this language, and am quite callous to it, I assure you. I am in good odour at court, sir; and you know, *Non cuivis homini contingit adire Corinthum.*[1] While I was out, sir, I made a great noise till I was let in. There was a pack of us, sir, to keep up your canine metaphor: two or three others got in at the same time: we knew very well that those who were shut out, would raise a hue and cry after us: it was perfectly natural: we should have done the same in their place: mere envy and malice, nothing more. Let them bark on: when they are either wanted or troublesome, they will be let in, in their turn. If there be any man, who prefers a crust and water, to venison and sack, I am not of his mind. It is pretty and politic to make a virtue of necessity: but when there is an end of the necessity I am very willing that there should be an end of the virtue. *If you could live on roots, said Diogenes to Aristippus, you would have nothing to do with kings.*—If you could live on kings, replied Aristippus, you would have nothing to do with roots.—Every man for himself, sir, and God for us all.

Mr. Derrydown.—The truth of things on this subject is contained in the following stave:

> This world is a well-furnish'd table,
> Where guests are promiscuously set:
> We all fare as well as we're able,
> And scramble for what we can get.

Sir Telegraph Paxarett.—Buz the bottle.
Mr. O'Scarum.—Over, by Jupiter!
Sir Telegraph Paxarett.—No.
Mr. O'Scarum.—Yes.

[1 It is not everyone who can get to Corinth.]

The Rev. Mr. Portpipe.—No. The baronet has a most mathematical eye. Buzzed to a drop!

Mr. Forester.—Fortunately, sir, for the hopes of mankind, every man does not bring his honour and conscience to market, though I admit the majority do: there are some who dare to be honest in the worst of times.

Mr. Feathernest.—Perhaps, sir, you are one of those who can afford to have a conscience, and are therefore under no necessity of bringing it to market. If so, you should "give God thanks, and make no boast of it." It is a great luxury certainly, and well worth keeping, *cœteris paribus.* But it is neither meat, clothes, nor fire. It becomes a good coat well; but it will never make one. Poets are verbal musicians, and, like other musicians, they have a right to sing and play, where they can be best paid for their music.

Mr. Forester.—There could be no objection to that, if they would be content to announce themselves as dealers and chapmen: but the poetical character is too frequently a combination of the most arrogant and exclusive assumption of freedom and independence in theory, with the most abject and unqualified venality, servility, and sycophancy in practice.

Mr. Feathernest.—It is as notorious, sir, as the sun at noonday, that theory and practice are never expected to coincide. If a West Indian planter declaims against the Algerines, do you expect him to lose any favourable opportunity of increasing the number of his own slaves? If an invaded country cries out against spoliation, do you suppose, if the tables were turned, it would show its weaker neighbours the forbearance it required? If an Opposition orator clamours for a reform in Parliament, does any one dream that, if he gets into office, he will ever say another word about it? If one of your reverend friends should display his touching eloquence on the subject of temperance, would you therefore have the barbarity to curtail him of one drop of his three bottles? Truth and liberty, sir, are pretty words, very pretty words—a few years ago they were the gods of the day—they superseded in poetry the agency of mythology and magic: they were the only passports into the poetical market: I acted accordingly the part of a prudent man: I took my station, became my own crier, and vociferated Truth and Liberty, till the noise I made brought people about me, to bid for me: and to the highest bidder

I knocked myself down, at less than I am worth certainly; but when an article is not likely to keep, it is by no means prudent to postpone the sale.

> What makes all doctrines plain and clear?
> About two hundred pounds a year.—
> And that which was proved true before,
> Prove false again?—Two hundred more.

Mr. Hippy.—A dry discussion! Pass the bottle, and moisten it.

Mr. O'Scarum.—Here's half of us fast asleep. Let us make a little noise to wake us. A glee now: I'll be one; who'll join?

Sir Telegraph Paxarett.—I.

The Rev. Mr. Portpipe.—And I.

Mr. Hippy.—Strike up then. Silence!

Glee—THE GHOSTS

> In life three ghostly friars were we,
> And now three friarly ghosts we be.
> Around our shadowy table placed,
> The spectral bowl before us floats:
> With wine that none but ghosts can taste,
> We wash our unsubstantial throats.
> Three merry ghosts—three merry ghosts—three merry
> ghosts are we:
> Let the ocean be Port, and we'll think it good sport
> To be laid in that Red Sea.

> With songs that jovial spectres chaunt,
> Our old refectory still we haunt.
> The traveller hears our midnight mirth:
> "O list!" he cries, "the haunted choir!
> The merriest ghost that walks the earth,
> Is sure the ghost of a ghostly friar."
> Three merry ghosts—three merry ghosts—three merry
> ghosts are we:
> Let the ocean be Port, and we'll think it good sport
> To be laid in that Red Sea.

Mr. Hippy.—Bravo! I should like to have my house so haunted. The deuce is in it, if three such ghosts would not keep the blue devils at bay. Come, we'll lay them in a bumper of claret.

(*Sir Oran Haut-ton took his flute from his pocket, and played over the air of the glee. The company was at first extremely surprised, and then joined in applauding his performance. Sir Oran bowed acknowledgment, and returned his flute to his pocket.*)

Mr. Forester.—It is, perhaps, happy for yourself, Mr. Feathernest, that you can treat with so much levity a subject that fills me with the deepest grief. Man under the influence of civilization has fearfully diminished in size and deteriorated in strength. The intellectual are confessedly nourished at the expense of the physical faculties. Air, the great source and fountain of health and life, can scarcely find access to civilized man, muffled as he is in clothes, pent in houses, smoke-dried in cities, half-roasted by artificial fire, and parboiled in the hydrogen of crowded apartments. Diseases multiply upon him in compound proportion. Even if the prosperous among us enjoy some comforts unknown to the natural man, yet what is the poverty of the savage, compared with that of the lowest classes in civilized nations? The specious aspect of luxury and abundance in one is counter-balanced by the abject penury and circumscription of hundreds. Commercial prosperity is a golden surface, but all beneath it is rags and wretchedness. It is not in the splendid bustle of our principal streets—in the villas and mansions that sprinkle our valleys—for those who enjoy these things (even if they did enjoy them —even if they had health and happiness—and the rich have seldom either), bear but a small proportion to the whole population:—but it is in the mud hovel of the labourer—in the cellar of the artisan— in our crowded prisons—our swarming hospitals—our overcharged workhouses—in those narrow districts of our overgrown cities, which the affluent never see—where thousands and thousands of families are compressed within limits not sufficient for the pleasure-ground of a simple squire,—that we must study the true mechanism of political society. When the philosopher turns away in despair from this dreadful accumulation of moral and physical evil, where is he to look for consolation, if not in the progress of science, in the enlargement of mind, in the diffusion of philosophical truth? But if truth is a chimæra—if virtue is a name—if science is not the handmaid of moral improvement, but the obsequious minister of recondite luxury, the specious appendage of vanity and power— then indeed, *that man has fallen never to rise again*, is as much the cry of nature as the dream of superstition.

The Rev. Mr. Portpipe.—Man has fallen, certainly, by the fruit of the tree of knowledge: which shows that human learning is vanity and a great evil, and therefore very properly discountenanced by all bishops, priests, and deacons.

Mr. Fax.—The picture which you have drawn of poverty is not very tempting; and you must acknowledge that it is most galling to the most refined feelings. You must not, therefore, wonder that it is peculiarly obnoxious to the practical notions of poets. If the radiance of gold and silver gleam not through the foliage of the Pierian laurel, there is something to be said in their excuse if they carry their chaplet to those who will gild its leaves; and in that case they will find their best customers and patrons among those who are ambitious of acquiring panegyric by a more compendious method than the troublesome practice of the virtues that deserve it.

Mr. Forester.—You have quoted Juvenal, but you should have completed the sentence: "If you see no glimpse of coin in the Pierian shade, you will prefer the name and occupation of a barber or an auctioneer." This is most just: if the pursuits of literature conscientiously conducted, condemn their votary to famine, let him live by more humble, but at least by honest, and therefore honourable occupations: he may still devote his leisure to his favourite pursuits. If he produce but a single volume consecrated to moral truth, its effect must be good as far as it goes; but if he purchase leisure and luxury by the prostitution of talent to the cause of superstition and tyranny, every new exertion of his powers is a new outrage to reason and virtue, and in precise proportion to those powers is he a curse to his country, and a traitor to mankind.

Mr. Feathernest.—A barber, sir!—a man of genius turn barber!

Mr. O'Scarum.—Troth, sir, and I think it is better he should be in the suds himself, than help to bring his country into that situation.

Mr. Forester.—I can perceive, sir, in your exclamation the principle that has caused so enormous a superabundance in the number of bad books over that of good ones. The objects of the majority of men of talent seem to be exclusively two: the first, to convince the world of their transcendent abilities; the second, to convert that conviction into a source of the greatest possible pecuniary benefit to themselves. But there is no class of men more resolutely indifferent to the moral tendency of the means by which their ends are accomplished. Yet this is the most extensively pernicious of all modes of dishonesty; for that of a private man can only injure the pockets of a few individuals (a great evil, certainly, but light in comparison); while that of a public writer, who has previously taught the multitude to respect his talents, perverts what is much more valuable, the mental progress of thousands; misleading, on the one hand, the shallow believers in his sincerity; and on the other, stigmatizing the whole literary character in the opinions of all who see through the veil of his venality.

Mr. Feathernest.—All this is no reason, sir, why a man of genius should condescend to be a barber.

Mr. Forester.—He condescends much more in being a sycophant. The poorest barber in the poorest borough in England, who will not sell his vote, is a much more honourable character in the estimate of moral comparison than the most self-satisfied dealer in courtly poetry, whose well-paid eulogiums of licentiousness and corruption were ever re-echoed by the "most sweet voices" of hireling gazetteers and pensioned reviewers.

The summons to tea and coffee put a stop to the conversation.

[Lord Anophel, failing to breach the walls of Anthelia's indifference, attempts to kidnap the lady, on the advice of Grovelgrub, and is foiled by Sir Oran. The culprits, however, escape unrecognized, to try again. Anthelia and Sylvan begin to discover that they are remarkably sympathetic; and the great day of Sir Oran's election as member for the ancient borough of Onevote draws near.]

THE CITY OF NOVOTE

On the evening of the tenth day, the barouche rattled triumphantly into the large and populous city of Novote, which was situated at a short distance from the ancient and honourable borough of Onevote. The city contained fifty thousand inhabitants, and had no representative in the Honourable House, the deficiency being virtually supplied by the two members for Onevote: who, having no affairs to attend to for the borough, or rather the burgess, that did return them, were supposed to have more leisure for those of the city which did not: a system somewhat analogous to that which the learned author of *Hermes* calls a *method of supply by negation.*

Sir Oran signalized his own entrance by playing on his French horn, *See the conquering hero comes!* Bells were ringing, ale was flowing, mobs were huzzaing, and it seemed as if the inhabitants of the large and populous city were satisfied of the truth of the admirable doctrine, that the positive representation of one individual is a virtual representation of fifty thousand. They found afterwards, that all this festivity had been set in motion by Sir Oran's brother candidate, Simon Sarcastic, Esq., to whom we shall shortly introduce our readers.

The barouche stopped at the door of a magnificent inn, and the party was welcomed with some scores of bows from the whole *corps d'hôtel,* with the fat landlady in the van, and Boots in the rear. They were shown into a splendid apartment, a glorious fire was kindled in a minute, and while Mr. Hippy looked over the bill of fare, and followed mine hostess to inspect the state of the larder, Sir Telegraph proceeded to *peel,* and emerged from his four *benjamins,* like a butterfly from its chrysalis.

After dinner they formed, as usual, a semicircle round the fire, with the table in front supported by Mr. Hippy and Sir Telegraph Paxarett.

"Now this," said Sir Telegraph, rubbing his hands, "is what I call devilish comfortable after a cold day's drive—an excellent inn, a superb fire, charming company, and better wine than has fallen to our lot since we left Melincourt Castle."

The waiter had picked up from the conversation at dinner, that one of the destined members for Onevote was in company; and communicated this intelligence to Mr. Sarcastic, who was taking his solitary bottle in another apartment. Mr. Sarcastic sent his compliments to Sir Oran Haut-ton, and hoped he would allow his future colleague the honour of being admitted to join his party. Mr. Hippy, Mr. Forester, and Sir Telegraph, undertook to answer for Sir Oran, who was silent on the occasion: Mr. Sarcastic was introduced, and took his seat in the semicircle.

Sir Telegraph Paxarett.—Your future colleague, Mr. Sarcastic, is a man of few words; but he will join in a bumper to your better acquaintance.—(The collision of glasses ensued between Sir Oran and Mr. Sarcastic.)

Mr. Sarcastic.—I am proud of the opportunity of this introduction. The day after to-morrow is fixed for the election. I have made some preparations to give a little éclat to the affair, and have begun by intoxicating half the city of Novote, so that we shall have a great crowd at the scene of election, whom I intend to harangue from the hustings, on the great benefits and blessings of virtual representation.

Mr. Forester.—I shall, perhaps, take the opportunity of addressing them also, but with a different view of the subject.

Mr. Sarcastic.—Perhaps our views of the subject are not radically different, and the variety is in the mode of treatment. In my ordinary intercourse with the world, I reduce practice to theory: it is a habit, I believe, peculiar to myself, and a source of inexhaustible amusement.

Sir Telegraph Paxarett.—Fill and explain.

Mr. Sarcastic.—Nothing, you well know, is so rare as the coincidence of theory and practice. A man who "will go through fire and water to serve a friend" in words, will not give five guineas to save him from famine. A poet will write Odes to Independence, and become the obsequious parasite of any great man who will hire him. A burgess will hold up one hand for purity of election, while the price of his own vote is slily dropped into the other. I need not accumulate instances.

Mr. Forester.—You would find it difficult, I fear, to adduce many to the contrary.

Mr. Sarcastic.—This then is my system. I ascertain the practice of those I talk to, and present it to them as from myself, in the shape of theory: the consequence of which is, that I am universally stigmatized as a promulgator of rascally doctrines. Thus I said to Sir Oliver Oilcake, "When I get into Parliament I intend to make the sale of my vote as notorious as the sun at noonday. I will have no rule of right, but my own pocket. I will support every measure of every administration, even if they ruin half the nation for the purpose of restoring the Great Lama, or of subjecting twenty millions of people to be hanged, drawn, and quartered at the pleasure of the man-milliner of Mahomet's mother. I will have ship-loads of turtle and rivers of Madeira for myself, if I send the whole swinish multitude to draff and husks." Sir Oliver flew into a rage, and swore he would hold no further intercourse with a man who maintained such infamous principles.

Mr. Hippy.—Pleasant enough, to show a man his own picture, and make him damn the ugly rascal.

Mr. Sarcastic.—I said to Miss Pennylove, whom I knew to be *laying herself out for a good match,* "When my daughter becomes of marriageable age, I shall commission Christie to put her up to auction, 'the highest bidder to be the buyer; and if any dispute arise between two or more bidders, the lot to be put up again and resold.' " Miss Pennylove professed herself utterly amazed and indignant, that any man, and a father especially, should imagine a scheme so outrageous to the dignity and delicacy of the female mind.

The Honourable Mrs. Pinmoney, and Miss Danaretta.—A most horrid idea certainly.

Mr. Sarcastic.—The fact, my dear ladies, the fact: how stands the fact? Miss Pennylove afterwards married a man old enough to be her grandfather, for no other reason but because he was rich; and broke the heart of a very worthy friend of mine, to whom she had been previously engaged, who had no fault but the folly of loving her, and was quite rich enough for all purposes of matrimonial happiness. How the dignity and delicacy of such a person could have been affected, if the preliminary negotiation with her hobbling Strephon had been conducted through the instrumentality of honest Christie's hammer, I cannot possibly imagine.

Mr. Hippy.—Nor I, I must say. All the difference is in the form, and not in the fact. It is a pity that form does not come into fashion: it would save a world of trouble.

Mr. Sarcastic.—I irreparably offended the Reverend Doctor Vorax by telling him, that having a nephew, whom I wished to shine in the church, I was on the look-out for a luminous butler, and a cook of solid capacity, under whose joint tuition he might graduate. "Who knows," said I, "but he may immortalize himself at the University, by giving his name to a pudding?"—I lost the acquaintance of Mrs. Cullender, by saying to her, when she had told me a piece of gossip

as a very particular secret, that there was nothing so agreeable to me
as to be in possession of a secret, for I made a point of telling it to
all my acquaintance;

> Intrusted under solemn vows,
> Of Mum, and Silence, and the Rose,
> To be retailed again in whispers,
> For the easy credulous to disperse.

Mrs. Cullender left me in great wrath, protesting she would never
again throw away her confidence on so leaky a vessel.

Sir Telegraph Paxarett.—Ha! ha! ha! Bravo! Come, a bumper to
Mrs. Cullender.

Mr. Sarcastic.—With all my heart; and another if you please to
Mr. Christopher Corporate, the free, fat, and dependent burgess of
Onevote, of which "plural unit" the Honourable Baronet and my-
self are to be the joint representatives.—(*Sir Oran Haut-ton bowed.*)

Mr. Hippy.—And a third, by all means, to his Grace the Duke of
Rottenburgh.

Mr. Sarcastic.—And a fourth, to crown all, to the blessings of
virtual representation, which I shall endeavour to impress on as many
of the worthy citizens of Novote, as shall think fit to be present, the
day after to-morrow, at the proceedings of the borough of Onevote.

Sir Telegraph Paxarett.—And now for tea and coffee. Touch the
bell for the waiter.

The bottles and glasses vanished, and the beautiful array of urns
and cups succeeded. Sir Telegraph and Mr. Hippy seceded from the
table, and resigned their stations to Mrs. and Miss Pinmoney.

Mr. Forester.—Your system is sufficiently amusing, but I much
question its utility. The object of moral censure is reformation, and
its proper vehicle is plain and fearless sincerity.

Mr. Sarcastic.—I tried that in my youth, when I was troubled
with the *passion for reforming the world;* of which I have been long
cured, by the conviction of the inefficacy of moral theory with respect
to producing a practical change in the mass of mankind. Custom is
the pillar round which opinion twines, and interest is the tie that
binds it. It is not by reason that practical change can be effected,
but by making a puncture to the quick in the feelings of personal
hope and personal fear. The Reformation in England is one of the

supposed triumphs of reason. But if the passions of Henry the Eighth had not been interested in that measure, he would as soon have built mosques as pulled down abbeys: and you will observe that, in all cases, reformation never goes as far as reason requires, but just as far as suits the personal interest of those who conduct it. Place Temperance and Bacchus side by side, in an assembly of jolly fellows, and endow the first with the most powerful eloquence that mere reason can give, with the absolute moral force of mathematical demonstration, Bacchus need not take the trouble of refuting one of her arguments; he will only have to say, "Come, my boys, here's *Damn Temperance in a bumper*," and you may rely on the toast being drank with an unanimous three times three.

(*At the sound of the word bumper, with which Captain Hawltaught had made him very familiar, Sir Oran Haut-ton looked round for his glass, but, finding it vanished, comforted himself with a dish of tea from the fair hand of Miss Danaretta, which, as his friend Mr. Forester had interdicted him from the use of sugar, he sweetened as well as he could with a copious infusion of cream.*)

Sir Telegraph Paxarett.—As an Opposition orator in the Honourable House will bring forward a long detail of unanswerable arguments, without even expecting that they will have the slightest influence on the vote of the majority.

Mr. Sarcastic.—A reform of that honourable body, if ever it should take place, will be one of the "*triumphs of reason.*" But reason will have little to do with it. All that reason can say on the subject has been said for years, by men of all parties—while they were out: but the moment they were *in*, the moment their own interest came in contact with their own reason, the victory of interest was never for a moment doubtful. While the great fountain of interest, rising in the caverns of borough patronage and ministerial influence, flowed through the whole body of the kingdom in channels of paper-money, and loans, and contracts, and jobs, and places either found or made for the useful dealers in secret services, so long the predominant interests of corruption overpowered the true and permanent interests of the country: but as those channels become dry, and they are becoming so with fearful rapidity, the crew of every boat that is left aground are convinced, not by reason—that they had long heard and despised—but by the unexpected pressure of personal suffering, that they had been going on in the wrong way. Thus the reaction of interest takes place; and when the concentrated interests of thousands, combined by the same pressure of personal suffering, shall have created an independent power, greater than the power of the interest of corruption, then, and not till then, the latter will give way, and this will be called the triumph of reason; though, in truth, like all the changes in human society that have ever taken place from the birthday of the world, it will be only the triumph of one mode of interest over another: but as the triumph in this case will be of the interest of the many over that of the few, it is certainly a consummation devoutly to be wished.

Mr. Forester.—If I should admit that "the hope of personal advantage, and the dread of personal punishment," are the only springs that set the mass of mankind in action, the inefficacy of reason, and the inutility of moral theory, will by no means follow from the admission. The progress of truth is slow, but its ultimate triumph is secure; though its immediate effects may be rendered almost imperceptible, by the power of habit and interest. If the philosopher cannot reform his own times, he may lay the foundation of amendment in those that follow. Give currency to reason, improve the moral code of society, and the theory of one generation will be the practice of the next. After a certain period of life, and that no very advanced one, men in general become perfectly unpersuadable to all practical purposes. Few philosophers, therefore, I believe, expect to produce much change in the habits of their contemporaries, as Plato proposed to banish from his republic all above the age of ten, and give a good education to the rest.

Mr. Sarcastic.—Or, as Heraclitus the Ephesian proposed to his countrymen, that all above the age of fourteen should hang themselves, before he would consent to give laws to the remainder.

THE BOROUGH OF ONEVOTE

THE day of election arrived. Mr. Sarcastic's rumoured preparations, and the excellence of the ale which he had broached in the city of Novote, had given a degree of *éclat* to the election for the borough of Onevote, which it had never before possessed; the representatives usually sliding into their nomination with the same silence and decorum with which a solitary spinster slides into her pew at Wednesday's or Friday's prayers in a country church. The resemblance holds good also in this respect, that, as the curate addresses the solitary maiden with the appellation of *dearly beloved brethren,* so the representatives always pluralized their solitary elector, by conferring on him the appellation of *a respectable body of constituents.* Mr. Sarcastic, however, being determined to amuse himself at the expense of this most "venerable *feature*" in our old constitution, as Lord C. calls a rotten borough, had brought Mr. Christopher Corporate into his views, by the adhibition of *persuasion in a tangible shape.* It was generally known in Novote, that something would be going forward at Onevote, though nobody could tell precisely what, except that a long train of brewer's drays had left the city for the borough, in grand procession, on the preceding day, under the escort of a sworn band of special constables, who were to keep guard over the ale all night. This detachment was soon followed by another, under a similar escort, and with similar injunctions: and it was understood that this second expedition of *frothy rhetoric* was sent forth under the auspices of Sir Oran Haut-ton, Baronet, the brother candidate of Simon Sarcastic, Esquire, for the representation of the ancient and honourable borough.

The borough of Onevote stood in the middle of a heath, and consisted of a solitary farm, of which the land was so poor and untractable, that it would not have been worth the while of any human being to cultivate it, had not the Duke of Rottenburgh found it very well worth his to pay his tenant for living there, to keep the honourable borough in existence.

Mr. Sarcastic left the city of Novote some hours before his new acquaintance, to superintend his preparations, followed by crowds of persons of all descriptions, pedestrians and equestrians; old ladies in chariots, and young ladies on donkeys; the farmer on his hunter, and the tailor on his hack; the grocer and his family six in a chaise; the dancing-master in his tilbury; the banker in his tandem; mantua-makers and servant-maids twenty-four in the waggon, fitted up for the occasion with a canopy of evergreens; pastry-cooks, men-milliners, and journeymen tailors, by the stage, running for that day only, six inside and fourteen out; the sallow artisan emerging from the cellar or the furnace, to freshen himself with the pure breezes of Onevote Heath; the bumpkin in his laced boots and Sunday coat, trudging through the dust with his cherry-cheeked lass on his elbow; the gentleman coachman on his box, with his painted charmer by his side; the lean curate on his half-starved Rosinante; the plump bishop setting an example of Christian humility in his carriage and six; the doctor on his white horse, like Death in the Revelations; and the lawyer on his black one, like the devil in the Wild Huntsmen.

Almost in the rear of this motley cavalcade went the barouche of Sir Telegraph Paxarett, and rolled up to the scene of action amidst the shouts of the multitude.

The heath had very much the appearance of a race ground; with booths and stalls, the voices of pie-men and apple-women, the grinding of barrel organs, the scraping of fiddles, the squeaking of ballad-singers, the chirping of corkscrews, the vociferations of ale-drinkers, the cries of the "last dying speeches of desperate malefactors," and of "The History and Antiquities of the honourable Borough of One-vote, a full and circumstantial account, all in half a sheet, for the price of one halfpenny!"

The hustings were erected in proper form, and immediately opposite to them was an enormous marquee with a small opening in front, in which was seated the important person of Mr. Christopher Corporate, with a tankard of ale and a pipe. The ladies remained in the barouche under the care of Sir Telegraph and Mr. Hippy. Mr. Forester, Mr. Fox, and Sir Oran Haut-ton joined Mr. Sarcastic on the hustings.

Mr. Sarcastic stepped forward amidst the shouts of the assembled crowd, and addressed Mr. Christopher Corporate:

"Free, fat, and dependent burgess of this ancient and honourable borough! I stand forward an unworthy candidate, to be the representative of so important a personage, who comprises in himself a three hundredth part of the whole elective capacity of this extensive empire. For if the whole population be estimated at eleven millions, with what awe and veneration must I look on one, who is, as it were, the abstract and quintessence of thirty-three thousand six hundred and sixty-six people! The voice of Stentor was like the voice of fifty, and the voice of Harry Gill [1] was like the voice of three; but what

---

[1] See Mr. Wordsworth's Lyrical Ballads.

are these to the voice of Mr. Christopher Corporate, which gives utterance in one breath to the concentrated power of thirty-three thousand six hundred and sixty-six voices? Of such an one it may indeed be said, that *he is himself an host*, and that *none but himself can be his parallel*.

"Most potent, grave, and reverend signor! it is usual on these occasions to make a great vapouring about honour and conscience: but as those words are now generally acknowledged to be utterly destitute of meaning, I have too much respect for your understanding to say anything about them. The *monied interest*, Mr. Corporate, for which you are as illustrious *as the sun at noon-day*, is the great point of connection and sympathy between us: and no circumstances can throw a *wet blanket* on the ardour of our reciprocal esteem, while the *fundamental feature* of our mutual interests presents itself to us in so *tangible a shape*.[2] How high a value I set upon your voice, you may judge by the price I have paid for half of it: which, indeed, deeply lodged as my feelings are in my pocket, I yet see no reason to regret, since you will thus confer on mine, a transmutable and marketable value, which I trust by proper management will leave me no loser by the bargain."

"Huzza!" said Mr. Corporate.

"People of the city of Novote!" proceeded Mr. Sarcastic, "some of you, I am informed, consider yourselves aggrieved, that, while your large and populous city has no share whatever in the formation of the Honourable House, the *plural unity* of Mr. Christopher Corporate should be invested with the privilege of double representation. But, gentlemen, representation is of two kinds, actual and virtual: an important distinction, and of great political consequence.

"The Honourable Baronet and myself being the actual representatives of the fat burgess of Onevote, shall be the virtual representatives of the worthy citizens of Novote; and you may rely on it, gentlemen (*with his hand on his heart*), we shall always be deeply attentive to your interests, when they happen, as no doubt they sometimes will, to be perfectly compatible with our own.

"A member of Parliament, gentlemen, to speak to you in your own phrase, is a sort of staple commodity, manufactured for home

[2] The figures of speech marked in Italics are familiar to the admirers of parliamentary rhetoric.

consumption. Much has been said of the improvement of machinery in the present age, by which one man may do the work of a dozen. If this be admirable, and admirable it is acknowledged to be by all the civilized world, how much more admirable is the improvement of political machinery, by which one man does the work of thirty thousand! I am sure, I need not say another word to a great manufacturing population like the inhabitants of the city of Novote, to convince them of the beauty and utility of this most luminous arrangement.

"The duty of a representative of the people, whether actual or virtual, is simply to tax. Now this important branch of public business is much more easily and expeditiously transacted by the means of virtual, than it possibly could be by that of actual representation. For when the minister draws up his scheme of ways and means, he will do it with much more celerity and confidence, when he knows that the propitious countenance of virtual representation will never cease to smile upon him as long as he continues in place, than if he had to encounter the doubtful aspect of actual representation, which might, perhaps, look black on some of his favourite projects, thereby greatly impeding the distribution of secret service money at home, and placing foreign legitimacy in a very awkward predicament. The carriage of the state would then be like a chariot in a forest, turning to the left for a troublesome thorn, and to the right for a sturdy oak; whereas it now rolls forward like the car of Juggernaut over the plain, crushing whatever offers to impede its way.

"The constitution says that no man shall be taxed but by his own consent: a very plausible theory, gentlemen, but not reducible to practice. Who will apply a lancet to his own arm, and bleed himself? Very few, you acknowledge. Who then, à fortiori, would apply a lancet to his own pocket, and draw off what is dearer to him than his blood—his money? Fewer still, of course: I humbly opine, none. —What then remains but to appoint a royal college of state surgeons, who may operate on the patient according to their views of his case? Taxation is political phlebotomy: the Honourable House is, figuratively speaking, a royal college of state surgeons. A good surgeon must have firm nerves and a steady hand; and, perhaps, the less feeling the better. Now, it is manifest, that, as all feeling is founded on sympathy, the fewer constituents a representative has, the less must be his sympathy with the public, and the less, of course as is desirable, his feeling for his patient—the people:—who, therefore, with so much *sang froid*, can phlebotomize the nation, as the representative of half an elector?

"Gentlemen, as long as a *full Gazette* is pleasant to the *quidnunc*; as long as an empty purse is delightful to the spendthrift; as long as the cry of *Question* is a satisfactory answer to an argument, and to outvote reason is to refute it; as long as the way to pay old debts is to incur new ones of five times the amount; as long as the grand recipes of political health and longevity are *bleeding* and *hot water*— so long must you rejoice in the privileges of Mr. Christopher Corporate, so long must you acknowledge from the very bottom of your pockets, the benefits and blessings of *virtual representation.*"

This harangue was received with great applause, acclamations rent the air, and ale flowed in torrents. Mr. Forester declined speaking, and the party on the hustings proceeded to business. Sir Oran Haut-ton, Baronet, and Simon Sarcastic, Esquire, were nominated in form. Mr. Christopher Corporate held up both his hands, with his tankard in one, and his pipe in the other: and neither poll nor scrutiny being demanded, the two candidates were pronounced duly elected as representatives of the ancient and honourable borough of Onevote.

The shouts were renewed: the ale flowed rapidly: the pipe and tankard of Mr. Corporate were replenished. Sir Oran Haut-ton, Baronet, M.P., bowed gracefully to the people with his hand on his heart.

A cry was now raised of "Chair 'em! chair 'em!" when Mr. Sarcastic again stepped forward.

"Gentlemen," said he, "a slight difficulty opposes itself to the honour you would confer on us. The members should, according to form, be chaired by their electors; and how can one elector, great man as he is, chair two representatives? But to obviate this dilemma as well as circumstances admit, I move that the 'large body corporate of one' whom the Honourable Baronet and myself have the honour to represent, do resolve himself into a committee."

He had no sooner spoken, than the marquee opened, and a number of bulky personages, all in dress, aspect, size, and figure, very exact resemblances of Mr. Christopher Corporate, each with his pipe and his tankard, emerged into daylight, who encircling their venerable prototype, lifted their tankards high in air, and pronounced with Stentorian symphony, "HAIL, PLURAL UNIT!" Then, after a simultaneous·draught, throwing away their pipes and tankards, for which the mob immediately scrambled, they raised on high two magnificent chairs, and prepared to carry into effect the last ceremony of the election. The party on the hustings descended. Mr. Sarcastic stepped into his chair; and his part of the procession, headed by Mr. Christopher Corporate, and surrounded by a multiform and many-coloured crowd, moved slowly off towards the city of Novote, amidst the undistinguishable clamour of multitudinous voices.

Sir Oran Haut-ton watched the progress of his precursor, as his chair rolled and swayed over the sea of heads, like a boat with one mast on a stormy ocean; and the more he watched the agitation of its movements, the more his countenance gave indications of strong dislike to the process: so that when his seat in the second chair was offered to him, he with a very polite bow declined the honour. The party that was to carry him, thinking that his repugnance arose entirely from diffidence, proceeded with gentle force to overcome his scruples, when not precisely penetrating their motives, and indignant at this attempt to violate the freedom of the natural man, he seized a stick from a sturdy farmer at his elbow, and began to lay about him with great vigour and effect. Those who escaped being knocked down by the first sweep of his weapon, ran away with all their might, but were soon checked by the pressure of the crowd, who hearing the noise of conflict, and impatient to ascertain the cause, bore down from all points upon a common centre, and formed a circumferential pressure that effectually prohibited the egress of those within; and they, in their turn, in their eagerness to escape from Sir Oran (who like Artegall's Iron Man, or like Ajax among the Trojans, or like Rhodomont in Paris, or like Orlando among the soldiers of Agramant, kept clearing for himself an ample space in the midst of the encircling crowd), waged desperate conflict with those without; so that from the equal and opposite action of the centripetal and centrifugal forces, resulted a stationary combat, raging between the circumferences of two concentric circles, with barbaric dissonance of deadly feud, and infinite variety of oath and execration, till Sir Oran, charging desperately along one of the radii, fought a free passage through all opposition; and rushing to the barouche of Sir Telegraph Paxarett, sprung to his old station on the box, from whence he shook his sapling at the foe with looks of mortal defiance. Mr. Forester, who had been forcibly parted from him at the commencement of the strife, and had been all anxiety on his account, mounted with great alacrity to his station on the roof: the rest of the party was already seated: the Honourable Mrs. Pinmoney, half-fainting with terror, earnestly entreated Sir Telegraph to fly: Sir Telegraph cracked his whip, the horses sprang forward like racers, the wheels went round like the wheels of a firework. The tumult of battle lessening as they receded, came wafted to them on the wings of the wind: for the flame of discord having been once kindled, was not extinguished by the departure of its first flambeau —Sir Oran; but war raged wide and far, here in the thickest mass of central fight, there in the light skirmishing of flying detachments. The hustings were demolished, and the beams and planks turned into offensive weapons: the booths were torn to pieces, and the canvas converted into flags floating over the heads of magnanimous heroes that rushed to revenge they knew not what, in deadly battle with they knew not whom. The stalls and barrows were upset; and the pears, apples, oranges, mutton-pies, and masses of gingerbread, flew like missiles of fate in all directions. The *sanctum sanctorum* of the ale was broken into, and the guardians of the Hesperian liquor were put to ignominious rout. Hats and wigs were hurled into the air, never to return to the heads from which they had suffered violent divorce. The collision of sticks, the ringing of empty ale-casks, the shrieks of women, and the vociferations of combatants, mingled in one deepening and indescribable tumult: till at length, everything else being levelled with the heath, they turned the mingled torrent of their wrath on the cottage of Mr. Corporate, to which they triumphantly set fire, and danced round the blaze like a rabble of village boys round the effigy of the immortal Guy. In a few minutes the ancient and honourable borough of Onevote was reduced to ashes: but we have the satisfaction to state that it was rebuilt a few days afterwards, at the joint expense of its two representatives, and His Grace the Duke of Rottenburgh.

[Sir Oran goes to Parliament, but not before he has again worsted
    Lord Anophel and delivered Anthelia Melincourt into the arms
    of Sylvan Forester, so that they may live happily ever after.]

Nightmare Abbey

CHAPTER I

NIGHTMARE ABBEY, a venerable family-mansion, in a highly picturesque state of semi-dilapidation, pleasantly situated on a strip of dry land between the sea and the fens at the verge of the county of Lincoln, had the honour to be the seat of Christopher Glowry, Esquire. This gentleman was naturally of an atrabilarious temperament, and much troubled with those phantoms of indigestion which are commonly called blue devils. He had been deceived in an early friendship: he had been crossed in love; and had offered his hand, from pique, to a lady, who accepted it from interest, and who, in so doing, violently tore asunder the bonds of a tried and youthful attachment. Her vanity was gratified by being the mistress of a very extensive, if not very lively establishment; but all the springs of her sympathies were frozen. Riches she possessed, but that which enriches them, the participation of affection, was wanting. All that they could purchase for her became indifferent to her, because that which they could not purchase, and which was more valuable than themselves, she had, for their sake, thrown away. She discovered, when it was too late, that she had mistaken the means for the end—that riches, rightly used, are instruments of happiness, but are not in themselves happiness. In this wilful blight of her affections, she found them valueless as means: they had been the end to which she had immolated all her affections, and were now the only end that remained to her. She did not confess this to herself as a principle of action, but it operated through the medium of unconscious self-deception, and terminated in inveterate avarice. She laid on external things the blame of her mind's internal disorder, and thus became by degrees an accomplished scold. She often went her daily rounds through a series of deserted apartments, every creature in the house vanishing at the creak of her shoe, much more at the sound of her voice, to which the nature of things affords no simile; for, as far as the voice of woman, when attuned by gentleness and love, transcends all other sounds in harmony, so far does it surpass all others in discord when stretched into unnatural shrillness by anger and impatience.

Mr. Glowry used to say that his house was no better than a spacious kennel, for every one in it led the life of a dog. Disappointed both in love and in friendship, and looking upon human learning as vanity, he had come to a conclusion that there was but one good thing in the world, videlicet, a good dinner; and this his parsimonious lady seldom suffered him to enjoy: but one morning, like Sir Leoline, in "Christabel," "he woke and found his lady dead," and remained a very consolate widower, with one small child.

This only son and heir Mr. Glowry had christened Scythrop, from the name of a maternal ancestor, who had hanged himself one rainy day in a fit of tædium vitæ, and had been eulogized by a coroner's jury in the comprehensive phrase of felo de se; on which account Mr. Glowry held his memory in high honour, and made a punchbowl of his skull.

When Scythrop grew up, he was sent, as usual, to a public school, where a little learning was painfully beaten into him, and thence to the University, where it was carefully taken out of him; and he was sent home, like a well-threshed ear of corn, with nothing in his head: having finished his education to the high satisfaction of the master and fellows of his college, who had, in testimony of their approbation, presented him with a silver fish-slice, on which his name figured at the head of a laudatory inscription in some semi-barbarous dialect of Anglo-Saxonized Latin.

His fellow-students, however, who drove tandem and random in great perfection, and were connoisseurs in good inns, had taught him to drink deep ere he departed. He had passed much of his time with these choice spirits, and had seen the rays of the midnight lamp tremble on many a lengthening file of empty bottles. He passed his vacations sometimes at Nightmare Abbey, sometimes in London, at the house of his uncle, Mr. Hilary, a very cheerful and elastic gentleman, who had married the sister of the melancholy Mr. Glowry. The company that frequented his house was the gayest of the gay. Scythrop danced with the ladies and drank with the gentlemen, and was pronounced by both a very accomplished, charming fellow and an honour to the University.

At the house of Mr. Hilary, Scythrop first saw the beautiful Miss Emily Girouette. He fell in love; which is nothing new. He was favourably received; which is nothing strange. Mr. Glowry and Mr. Girouette had a meeting on the occasion, and quarrelled about the terms of the bargain; which is neither new nor strange. The lovers were torn asunder, weeping and vowing everlasting constancy; and, in three weeks after this tragical event, the lady was led a smiling bride to the altar, by the Honourable Mr. Lackwit; which is neither strange nor new.

Scythrop received this intelligence at Nightmare Abbey, and was half distracted on the occasion. It was his first disappointment, and preyed deeply on his sensitive spirit. His father, to comfort him, read him a Commentary on Ecclesiastes, which he had himself composed, and which demonstrated incontrovertibly that all is vanity. He insisted particularly on the text, "One man among a thousand have I found, but a woman amongst all those have I not found."

"How would he expect it," said Scythrop, "when the whole thousand were locked up in his seraglio? His experience is no precedent for a free state of society like that in which we live."

"Locked up or at large," said Mr. Glowry, "the result is the same: their minds are always locked up, and vanity and interest keep the key. I speak feelingly, Scythrop."

"I am sorry for it, sir," said Scythrop. "But how is it that their minds are locked up? The fault is in their artificial education, which studiously models them into mere musical dolls, to be set out for sale in the great toy-shop of society."

"To be sure," said Mr. Glowry, "their education is not so well finished as yours has been; and your idea of a musical doll is good. I bought one myself, but it was confoundedly out of tune; but, whatever be the cause, Scythrop, the effect is certainly this, that one is pretty nearly as good as another, as far as any judgment can be formed of them before marriage. It is only after marriage that they show their true qualities, as I know by bitter experience. Marriage is, therefore, a lottery, and the less choice and selection a man bestows on his ticket the better; for if he has incurred considerable pains and expense to obtain a lucky number, and his lucky number proves a blank, he experiences not a simple, but a complicated disappointment; the loss of labour and money being superadded to the disappointment of drawing a blank, which, constituting simply and entirely the grievance of him who has chosen his ticket at random, is, from its simplicity, the more endurable." This very excellent reasoning was thrown away upon Scythrop, who retired to his tower as dismal and disconsolate as before.

The tower which Scythrop inhabited stood at the south-eastern angle of the Abbey; and, on the southern side, the foot of the tower opened on a terrace, which was called the garden, though nothing grew on it but ivy, and a few amphibious weeds. The south-western tower, which was ruinous and full of owls, might, with equal propriety, have been called the aviary. This terrace or garden, or terrace-garden, or garden-terrace (the reader may name it *ad libitum*), took in an oblique view of the open sea, and fronted a long tract of level sea-coast, and a fine monotony of fens and windmills.

The reader will judge, from what we have said, that this building was a sort of castellated, abbey; and it will, probably, occur to him to inquire if it had been one of the strongholds of the ancient church militant. Whether this was the case, or how far it had been indebted to the taste of Mr. Glowry's ancestors for any transmutations from its original taste, are, unfortunately, circumstances not within the pale of our knowledge.

The north-western tower contained the apartments of Mr. Glowry. The moat at its base, and the fens beyond, comprised the whole of his prospect. The moat surrounded the Abbey, and was in immediate contact with the walls on every side but the south.

The north-eastern tower was appropriated to the domestics, whom Mr. Glowry always chose by one of two criterions,—a long face or a dismal name. His butler was Raven; his steward was Crow; his valet was Skellet. Mr. Glowry maintained that the valet was of French extraction, and that his name was Squelette. His grooms were Mattocks and Graves. On one occasion, being in want of a footman, he received a letter from a person signing himself Diggory Deathshead, and lost no time in securing this acquisition; but on Diggory's arrival, Mr. Glowry was horror-struck by the sight of a round ruddy face, and a pair of laughing eyes. Deathshead was always grinning,—not a ghastly smile, but the grin of a comic mask; and disturbed the echoes of the hall with so much unhallowed laughter, that Mr. Glowry gave him his discharge. Diggory, however, had stayed long enough to make conquests of all the old gentleman's maids, and left him a flourishing colony of young Deathsheads to join chorus with the owls, that had before been the exclusive choristers of Nightmare Abbey.

The main body of the building was divided into rooms of state, spacious apartments for feasting, and numerous bedrooms for visitors, who, however, were few and far between.

Family interests compelled Mr. Glowry to receive occasional visits from Mr. and Mrs. Hilary, who paid them from the same motive; and, as the lively gentleman on these occasions found few conductors for his exuberant gaiety, he became like a double-charged electric jar, which often exploded in some burst of outrageous merriment to the signal discomposure of Mr. Glowry's nerves.

Another occasional visitor, much more to Mr. Glowry's taste, was Mr. Flosky, [1] a very lachrymose and morbid gentleman, of some note in the literary world, but in his own estimation of much more merit than name. The part of his character which recommended him to Mr. Glowry, was his very fine sense of the grim and the tearful. No one could relate a dismal story with so many minutiæ of supererogatory wretchedness. No one could call up a *rawhead and bloody bones* with so many adjuncts and circumstances of ghastliness. Mystery was his mental element. He lived in the midst of that visionary world in which nothing is but what is not. He dreamed with his eyes open, and saw ghosts dancing round him at noontide. He had been in his youth an enthusiast for liberty, and had hailed the dawn of the French Revolution as the promise of a day that was to banish war and slavery, and every form of vice and misery, from the face of the earth. Because all this was not done, he deduced that nothing was done; and from this deduction, according to his system of logic, he drew a conclusion that worse than nothing was done; that the overthrow of the feudal fortresses of

[1] A corruption of Filosky, quasi φιλοσκιος, a lover, or sectator, of shadows.

tyranny and superstition was the greatest calamity that had ever
befallen mankind; and that their only hope now was to rake the
rubbish together, and rebuild it without any of those loopholes by
which the light had originally crept in. To qualify himself for a
coadjutor in this laudable task, he plunged into the central opacity
of Kantian metaphysics, and lay *perdu* several years in transcendental darkness, till the common daylight of common sense became
intolerable to his eyes. He called the sun an *ignis fatuus;* and ex-
horted all who would listen to his friendly voice, which were about
as many as called "God save King Richard," to shelter themselves,
from its delusive radiance in the obscure haunt of Old Philosophy.
This word Old had great charms for him. The good old times were
always on his lips; meaning the days when polemic theology was
in its prime, and rival prelates beat the drum ecclesiastic with Her-
culean vigour, till the one wound up his series of syllogisms with
the very orthodox conclusion of roasting the other.

But the dearest friend of Mr. Glowry, and his most welcome
guest, was Mr. Toobad, the Manichæan Millenarian. The twelfth
verse of the twelfth chapter of Revelations was always in his mouth:
"Woe to the inhabiters of the earth and of the sea! for the devil is
come among you, having great wrath, because he knoweth that he
hath but a short time." He maintained that the supreme dominion
of the world was, for wise purposes, given over for a while to the
Evil Principle; and that this precise period of time, commonly
called the enlightened age, was the point of his plenitude of power.
He used to add that by-and-by he would be cast down, and a high
and happy order of things succeed; but he never omitted the saving
clause, "Not in our time:" which last words were always echoed in
doleful response by the sympathetic Mr. Glowry.

Another and very frequent visitor, was the Reverend Mr. Larynx,
the vicar of Claydyke, a village about ten miles distant;—a good-
natured accommodating divine, who was always most obligingly
ready to take a dinner and a bed at the house of any country gentleman in distress for a companion. Nothing came amiss to him,—
a game at billiards, at chess, at draughts, at backgammon, at piquet,
or at all-fours in a *tête-à-tête,*—or any game on the cards, round,
square, or triangular, in a party of any number exceeding two. He
would even dance among friends, rather than that a lady, even if

she were on the wrong side of thirty, should sit still for want of
a partner. For a ride, a walk, or a sail, in the morning,—a song after
dinner, a ghost story after supper,—a bottle of port with the squire,
or a cup of green tea with his lady,—for all or any of these, or for
anything else that was agreeable to any one else, consistently with
the dye of his coat, the Reverend Mr. Larynx was at all times equally
ready. When at Nightmare Abbey, he would condole with Mr.
Glowry,—drink Madeira with Scythrop,—crack jokes with Mr.
Hilary,—hand Mrs. Hilary to the piano, take charge of her fan and
gloves, and turn over her music with surprising dexterity,—quote
Revelations with Mr. Toobad,—and lament the good old times of
feudal darkness with the transcendental Mr. Flosky.

CHAPTER II

SHORTLY after the disastrous termination of Scythrop's passion
for Miss Emily Girouette, Mr. Glowry found himself, much against
his will, involved in a lawsuit, which compelled him to dance
attendance on the High Court of Chancery. Scythrop was left alone
at Nightmare Abbey. He was a burnt child, and dreaded the fire
of female eyes. He wandered about the ample pile, or along the
garden terrace, with "his cogitative faculties immersed in cogi-
bundity of cogitation." The terrace terminated at the south-western
tower, which, as we have said, was ruinous and full of owls. Here
would Scythrop take his evening seat, on a fallen fragment of mossy
stone, with his back resting against the ruined wall,—a thick canopy
of ivy, with an owl in it, over his head,—and the Sorrows of Werter
in his hand. He had some taste for romance reading before he went
to the University, where, we must confess, in justice to his college,
he was cured of the love of reading in all its shapes; and the cure
would have been radical, if disappointment in love, and total solitude, had not conspired to bring on a relapse. He began to devour
romances and German tragedies, and, by the recommendation of
Mr. Flosky, to pore over ponderous tomes of transcendental philosophy, which reconciled him to the labour of studying them by their

mystical jargon and necromantic imagery. In the congenial solitude
of Nightmare Abbey, the distempered ideas of metaphysical romance and romantic metaphysics had ample time and space to
germinate into a fertile crop of chimeras, which rapidly shot up into
vigorous and abundant vegetation.

He now became troubled with the *passion for reforming the
world*.[1] He built many castles in the air, and peopled them with
secret tribunals, and bands of illuminati, who were always the imaginary instruments of his projected regeneration of the human species. As he intended to institute a perfect republic, he invested
himself with absolute sovereignty over these mystical dispensers of
liberty. He slept with Horrid Mysteries under his pillow, and
dreamed of venerable eleutherarchs and ghastly confederates holding midnight conventions in subterranean caves. He passed whole
mornings in his study, immersed in gloomy reverie, stalking about
the room in his night-cap, which he pulled over his eyes like a cowl,
and folding his striped calico dressing-gown about him like the
mantle of a conspirator.

"Action," thus he soliloquized, "is the result of opinion, and to
new-model opinion would be to new-model society. Knowledge is
power; it is in the hands of a few, who employ it to mislead the
many, for their own selfish purposes of aggrandisement and
appropriation. What if it were in the hands of a few who should
employ it to lead the many? What if it were universal, and the
multitude were enlightened? No. The many must be always in
leading-strings; but let them have wise and honest conductors.
A few to think, and many to act; that is the only basis of perfect
society. So thought the ancient philosophers: they had their esoterical and exoterical doctrines. So thinks the sublime Kant, who
delivers his oracles in language which none but the initiated can
comprehend. Such were the views of those secret associations of
illuminati, which were the terror of superstition and tyranny, and
which, carefully selecting wisdom and genius from the great wilderness of society, as the bee selects honey from the flowers of the
thorn and the nettle, bound all human excellence in a chain, which,
if it had not been prematurely broken, would have commanded
opinion, and regenerated the world."

[1] See Forsyth's Principles of Moral Science.

Scythrop proceeded to meditate on the practicability of reviving a confederation of regenerators. To get a clear view of his own ideas, and to feel the pulse of the wisdom and genius of the age, he wrote and published a treatise, in which his meanings were carefully wrapt up in the monk's hood of transcendental technology, but filled with hints of matter deep and dangerous, which he thought would set the whole nation in a ferment; and he awaited the result in awful expectation, as a miner who has fired a train awaits the explosion of a rock. However, he listened and heard nothing; for the explosion, if any ensued, was not sufficiently loud to shake a single leaf of the ivy on the towers of Nightmare Abbey; and some months afterwards he received a letter from his bookseller, informing him that only seven copies had been sold, and concluding with a polite request for the balance.

Scythrop did not despair. "Seven copies," he thought, "have been sold. Seven is a mystical number, and the omen is good. Let me find the seven purchasers of my seven copies, and they shall be the seven golden cantlesticks with which I will illuminate the world."

Scythrop had a certain portion of mechanical genius, which his romantic projects tended to develop. He constructed models of cells and recesses, sliding panels and secret passages, that would have baffled the skill of the Parisian police. He took the opportunity of his father's absence to smuggle a dumb carpenter into the Abbey, and between them they gave reality to one of these models in Scythrop's tower. Scythrop foresaw that a great leader of human regeneration would be involved in fearful dilemmas, and determined, for the benefit of mankind in general, to adopt all possible precautions for the preservation of himself.

The servants, even the women, had been tutored into silence. Profound stillness reigned throughout and around the Abbey, except when the occasional shutting of a door would peal in long reverberations through the galleries, or the heavy tread of the pensive butler would wake the hollow echoes of the hall. Scythrop stalked about like the grand inquisitor, and the servants flitted past him like familiars. In his evening meditations on the terrace, under the ivy of the ruined tower, the only sounds that came to his ear were the rustling of the wind in the ivy, the plaintive voices of the feathered choristers, the owls, the occasional striking of the Abbey clock, and the monotonous dash of the sea on its low and level shore. In the meantime, he drank Madeira, and laid deep schemes for a thorough repair of the crazy fabric of human nature.

CHAPTER III

MR. GLOWRY returned from London with the loss of his lawsuit. Justice was with him, but the law was against him. He found Scythrop in a mood most sympathetically tragic; and they vied with each other in enlivening their cups by lamenting the depravity of this degenerate age, and occasionally interspersing divers grim jokes about graves, worms, and epitaphs. Mr. Glowry's friends, whom we have mentioned in the first chapter, availed themselves of his return to pay him a simultaneous visit. At the same time arrived Scythrop's friend and fellow-collegian, the Honourable Mr. Listless. Mr. Glowry had discovered this fashionable young gentleman in London, "stretched on the rack of a too easy chair," and devoured with a gloomy and misanthropical *nil curo*, and had pressed him so earnestly to take the benefit of the pure country air at Nightmare Abbey, that Mr. Listless, finding it would give him more trouble to refuse than to comply, summoned his French valet, Fatout, and told him he was going to Lincolnshire. On this simple hint, Fatout went to work, and the imperials were packed, and the post-chariot was at the door, without the Honourable Mr. Listless having said or thought another syllable on the subject.

Mr. and Mrs. Hilary brought with them an orphan niece, a daughter of Mr. Glowry's youngest sister, who had made a runaway love-match with an Irish officer. The lady's fortune disappeared in the first year: love, by a natural consequence, disappeared in the second: the Irishman himself, by a still more natural consequence, disappeared in the third. Mr. Glowry had allowed his sister an annuity, and she had lived in retirement with her only daughter, whom, at her death, which had recently happened, she commended to the care of Mrs. Hilary.

Miss Marionetta Celestina O'Carroll was a very blooming and

accomplished young lady. Being a compound of the *Allegro Vivace* of the O'Carrolls, and of the *Andante Doloroso* of the Glowries, she exhibited in her own character all the diversities of an April sky. Her hair was light-brown; her eyes hazel, and sparkling with a mild but fluctuating light; her features regular; her lips full, and of equal size; and her person surpassingly graceful. She was a proficient in music. Her conversation was sprightly, but always on subjects light in their nature and limited in their interest: for moral sympathies, in any general sense, had no place in her mind. She had some coquetry, and more caprice, liking and disliking almost in the same moment; pursuing an object with earnestness while it seemed unattainable, and rejecting it when in her power as not worth the trouble of possession.

Whether she was touched with a *penchant* for her cousin Scythrop, or was merely curious to see what effect the tender passion would have on so *outré* a person, she had not been three days in the Abbey before she threw out all the lures of her beauty and accomplishments to make a prize of his heart. Scythrop proved an easy conquest. The image of Miss Emily Girouette was already sufficiently dimmed by the power of philosophy and the exercise of reason: for to these influences, or to any influence but the true one, are usually ascribed the mental cures performed by the great physician Time. Scythrop's romantic dreams had indeed given him many pure anticipated cognitions of combinations of beauty and intelligence, which, he had some misgivings, were not exactly realized in his cousin Marionetta; but, in spite of these misgivings, he soon became distractedly in love; which, when the young lady clearly perceived, she altered her tactics, and assumed as much coldness and reserve as she had before shown ardent and ingenuous attachment. Scythrop was confounded at the sudden change; but, instead of falling at her feet and requesting an explanation, he retreated to his tower, muffled himself in his night-cap, seated himself in the president's chair of his imaginary secret tribunal, summoned Marionetta with all terrible formalities, frightened her out of her wits, disclosed himself, and clasped the beautiful penitent to his bosom.

While he was acting this reverie—in the moment in which the awful president of the secret tribunal was throwing back his cowl and his mantle, and discovering himself to the lovely culprit, as her adoring and magnanimous lover, the door of the study opened, and the real Marionetta appeared.

The motives which had led her to the tower were, a little penitence, a little concern, a little affection, and a little fear as to what the sudden secession of Scythrop, occasioned by her sudden change of manner, might portend. She had tapped several times unheard, and of course unanswered; and at length, timidly and cautiously opening the door, she discovered him standing before a black velvet chair, which was mounted on an old oak table, in the act of throwing open his striped calico dressing gown, and flinging away his night-cap, which is what the French call an imposing attitude.

Each stood a few moments fixed in their respective places—the lady in astonishment, and the gentleman in confusion. Marionetta was the first to break silence. "For heaven's sake," said she, "my dear Scythrop, what is the matter?"

"For heaven's sake, indeed!" said Scythrop, springing from the table; "for your sake, Marionetta, and you are my heaven,— distraction is the matter. I adore you, Marionetta, and your cruelty drives me mad." He threw himself at her knees, devoured her hand with kisses, and breathed a thousand vows in the most passionate language of romance.

Marionetta listened a long time in silence, till her lover had exhausted his eloquence and paused for a reply. She then said, with a very arch look, "I prithee deliver thyself like a man of this world." The levity of this quotation, and of the manner in which it was delivered, jarred so discordantly on the high-wrought enthusiasm of the romantic innamorato, that he sprang upon his feet, and beat his forehead with his clenched fists. The young lady was terrified; and deeming it expedient to soothe him, took one of his hands in hers, placed the other hand on his shoulder, looked up in his face with a winning seriousness, and said, in the tenderest possible tone, "What would you have, Scythrop?"

Scythrop was in heaven again. "What would I have? What but you, Marionetta? You, for the companion of my studies, the partner of my thoughts, the auxiliary of my great designs for the emancipation of mankind."

"I am afraid I should be but a poor auxiliary, Scythrop, what would you have me do?"

"Do as Rosalie does with Carlos, divine Marionetta. Let us each open a vein in the other's arm, mix our blood in a bowl, and drink it as a sacrament of love. Then we shall see visions of transcendental illumination, and soar on the wings of ideas into the space of pure intelligence."

Marionetta could not reply; she had not so strong a stomach as Rosalie, and turned sick at the proposition. She disengaged herself suddenly from Scythrop, sprang through the door of the tower, and fled with precipitation along the corridors. Scythrop pursued her, crying, "Stop, stop, Marionetta—my life, my love!" and was gaining rapidly on her flight, when, at an ill-omened corner, where two corridors ended in an angle, at the head of a staircase, he came into sudden and violent contact with Mr. Toobad, and they both plunged together to the foot of the stairs, like two billiard-balls into one pocket. This gave the young lady time to escape, and enclose herself in her chamber; while Mr. Toobad, rising slowly, and rubbing his knees and shoulders, said, "You see, my dear Scythrop, in this little incident, one of the innumerable proofs of the temporary supremacy of the devil; for what but a systematic design and concurrent contrivance of evil could have made the angles of time and place coincide in our unfortunate persons at the head of this accursed staircase?"

"Nothing else, certainly," said Scythrop: "you are perfectly in the right, Mr. Toobad. Evil, and mischief, and misery, and confusion, and vanity, and vexation of spirit, and death, and disease, and assassination, and war, and poverty, and pestilence, and famine, and avarice, and selfishness, and rancour, and jealousy, and spleen, and malevolence, and the disappointments of philanthropy, and the faithlessness of friendship, and the crosses of love—all prove the accuracy of your views, and the truth of your system; and it is not impossible that the infernal interruption of this fall down stairs may throw a colour of evil on the whole of my future existence."

"My dear boy," said Mr. Toobad, "you have a fine eye for consequences."

So saying, he embraced Scythrop, who retired with a disconsolate step, to dress for dinner; while Mr. Toobad stalked across the hall, repeating, "Woe to the inhabiters of the earth, and of the sea, for the devil is come among you, having great wrath."

CHAPTER IV

THE flight of Marionetta, and the pursuit of Scythrop, had been witnessed by Mr. Glowry, who, in consequence, narrowly observed his son and his niece in the evening; and, concluding from their manner, that there was a better understanding between them than he wished to see, he determined on obtaining the next morning from Scythrop a full and satisfactory explanation. He, therefore, shortly after breakfast, entered Scythrop's tower, with a very grave face, and said, without ceremony or preface, "So, sir, you are in love with your cousin."

Scythrop, with a little hesitation, answered, "Yes, sir."

"That is candid, at least; and she is in love with you?"

"I wish she were, sir."

"You know she is, sir."

"Indeed, sir, I do not."

"But you hope she is."

"I do, from my soul."

"Now that is very provoking, Scythrop, and very disappointing: I could not have supposed that you, Scythrop Glowry, of Nightmare Abbey, would have been infatuated with such a dancing, laughing, singing, thoughtless, careless, merry-hearted thing as Marionetta, in all respects the reverse of you and me. It is very disappointing, Scythrop. And do you know, sir, that Marionetta has no fortune?"

"It is the more, reason, sir, that her husband should have one."

"The more reason for her; but not for you. My wife had no fortune, and I had no consolation in my calamity. And do you reflect, sir, what an enormous slice this lawsuit has cut out of our family estate? we who used to be the greatest landed proprietors in Lincolnshire."

"To be sure, sir, we had more acres of fen than any man on this coast: but what are fens to love? What are dykes and windmills to Marionetta?"

"And what, sir, is love to a windmill? Not grist, I am certain: besides, sir, I have made a choice for you. I have made a choice for you, Scythrop. Beauty, genius, accomplishments, and a great fortune into the bargain. Such a lovely, serious creature, in a fine state of high dissatisfaction with the world, and everything in it. Such a delightful surprise I had prepared for you. Sir, I have pledged my honour to the contract—the honour of the Glowries of Nightmare Abbey: and now, sir, what is to be done?"

"Indeed, sir, I cannot say. I claim, on this occasion, that liberty of action which is the co-natal prerogative of every rational being."

"Liberty of action, sir? There is no such thing as liberty of action. We are all slaves and puppets of a blind and unpathetic necessity."

"Very true, sir; but liberty of action, between individuals, consists in their being differently influenced, or modified, by the same universal necessity; so that the results are unconsentaneous, and their respective necessitated volitions clash and fly off in a tangent."

"Your logic is good, sir: but you are aware, too, that one individual may be a medium of adhibiting to another a mode or form of necessity, which may have more or less influence in the production of consentaneity; and therefore, sir, if you do not comply with my wishes in this instance (you have had your own way in everything else), I shall be under the necessity of disinheriting you, though I shall do it with tears in my eyes." Having said these words, he vanished suddenly, in the dread of Scythrop's logic.

Mr. Glowry immediately sought Mrs. Hilary, and communicated to her his views of the case in point. Mrs. Hilary, as the phrase is, was as fond of Marionetta as if she had been her own child: but— there is always a but on these occasions—she could do nothing for her in the way of fortune, as she had two hopeful sons, who were finishing their education at Brazen-nose, and who would not like to encounter any diminution of their prospects, when they should be brought out of the house of mental bondage—i.e., the University —to the land flowing with milk and honey—i.e., the west end of London.

Mrs. Hilary hinted to Marionetta that propriety, and delicacy, and decorum, and dignity, etc., etc., etc.,[1] would require them to leave the Abbey immediately. Marionetta listened in silent submis-

---

[1] We are not masters of the whole vocabulary. See any novel by any literary lady.

sion, for she knew that her inheritance was passive obedience; but when Scythrop, who had watched the opportunity of Mrs. Hilary's departure, entered, and, without speaking a word, threw himself at her feet in a paroxysm of grief, the young lady, in equal silence and sorrow, threw her arms round his neck and burst into tears. A very tender scene ensued, which the sympathetic susceptibilities of the soft-hearted reader can more accurately imagine than we can delineate. But when Marionetta hinted that she was to leave the Abbey immediately, Scythrop snatched from its repository his ancestor's skull, filled it with Madeira, and presenting himself before Mr. Glowry, threatened to drink off the contents, if Mr. Glowry did not immediately promise that Marionetta should not be taken from the Abbey without her own consent. Mr. Glowry, who took the Madeira to be some deadly brewage, gave the required promise in dismal panic. Scythrop returned to Marionetta with a joyful heart, and drank the Madeira by the way.

Mr. Glowry, during his residence in London, had come to an agreement with his friend, Mr. Toobad, that a match between Scythrop and Mr. Toobad's daughter would be a very desirable occurrence. She was finishing her education in a German convent, but Mr. Toobad described her as being fully impressed with the truth of his Ahrimanic philosophy,[1] and being altogether as gloomy and anti-Thalian a young lady as Mr. Glowry himself could desire for the future mistress of Nightmare Abbey. She had a great fortune in her own right, which was not, as we have seen, without its weight in inducing Mr. Glowry to set his heart upon her as his daughter-in-law that was to be; he was therefore very much disturbed by Scythrop's untoward attachment to Marionetta. He condoled on

[1] Ahrimanes, in the Persian mythology, is the evil power, the prince of the kingdom of darkness. He is the rival of Oromazes, the prince of the kingdom of light. These two powers have divided and equal dominion. Sometimes one of the two has a temporary supremacy.—According to Mr. Toobad, the present period would be the reign of Ahrimanes. Lord Byron seems to be of the same opinion, by the use he has made of Ahrimanes in "Manfred;" where the great Alastor of Persia, is hailed king of the world by the Nemesis of Greece, in concert with three of the Scandinavian Valkyræ, under the name of the Destinies; the astrological spirits of the alchemists of the middle ages; an elemental witch, transplanted from Denmark to the Alps; and a chorus of Dr. Faustus's devils, who come in the last act for a soul. It is difficult to conceive where this heterogeneous mythological company could have originally met, except at a table d'hôte, like the six kings in "Candide."

the occasion with Mr. Toobad; who said that he had been too long accustomed to the intermeddling of the devil in all his affairs to be astonished at this new trace of his cloven claw; but that he hoped to outwit him yet, for he was sure there could be no comparison between his daughter and Marionetta, in the mind of any one who had a proper perception of the fact that, the world being a great theatre of evil, seriousness and solemnity are the characteristics of wisdom, and laughter and merriment make a human being no better than a baboon. Mr. Glowry comforted himself with this view of the subject, and urged Mr. Toobad to expedite his daughter's return from Germany. Mr. Toobad said he was in daily expectation of her arrival in London, and would set off immediately to meet her, that he might lose no time in bringing her to Nightmare Abbey. "Then," he added, "we shall see whether Thalia or Melpomene—whether the Allegra or the Penserosa—will carry off the symbol of victory."

"There can be no doubt," said Mr. Glowry, "which way the scale will incline, or Scythrop is no true scion of the venerable stem of the Glowries."

CHAPTER V

Marionetta felt secure of Scythrop's heart; and, notwithstanding the difficulties that surrounded her, she could not debar herself from the pleasure of tormenting her lover, whom she kept in a perpetual fever. Sometimes she would meet him with the most unqualified affection: sometimes with the most chilling indifference; rousing him to anger by artificial coldness—softening him to love by eloquent tenderness—or inflaming him to jealousy by coquetting with the Honourable Mr. Listless, who seemed, under her magical influence, to burst into sudden life, like the bud of the evening primrose. Sometimes she would sit by the piano, and listen with becoming attention to Scythrop's pathetic remonstrances; but, in the most impassioned part of his oratory, she would convert all his ideas into a chaos, by striking up some Rondo Allegro, and saying, "Is it not pretty?" Scythrop would begin to storm, and she would answer him with,

"Zitti, zitti, piano, piano,
Non facciamo confusione." [1]

or some similar *facezia*, till he would start away from her, and enclose himself in his tower, in an agony of agitation, vowing to renounce her, and her whole sex, for ever; and returning to her presence at the summons of the billet, which she never failed to send with many expressions of penitence, and promises of amendment. Scythrop's schemes for regenerating the world, and detecting his seven golden candlesticks, went on very slowly in this fever of his spirit.

Things proceeded in this train for several days; and Mr. Glowry began to be uneasy at receiving no intelligence from Mr. Toobad; when one evening the latter rushed into the library, where the family and the visitors were assembled, vociferating, "The devil is come among you, having great wrath!" He then drew Mr. Glowry aside into another apartment, and after remaining some time together, they re-entered the library with faces of great dismay, but did not condescend to explain to any one the cause of their discomfiture.

The next morning, early, Mr. Toobad departed. Mr. Glowry sighed and groaned all day, and said not a word to any one. Scythrop had quarrelled, as usual, with Marionetta, and was enclosed in his tower, in a fit of morbid sensibility. Marionetta was comforting herself at the piano, with singing the airs of *Nina pazza per amore*; and the Honourable Mr. Listless was listening to the harmony, as he lay supine on the sofa, with a book in his hand, into which he peeped at intervals. The Reverend Mr. Larynx approached the sofa, and proposed a game at billiards.

The Honourable Mr. Listless.—Billiards! Really I should be very happy; but, in my present exhausted state, the exertion is too much for me. I do not know when I have been equal to such an effort. *(He rang the bell for his valet. Fatout entered.)* Fatout, when did I play at billiards last?

Fatout.—De fourteen December de last year, Monsieur. *(Fatout bowed and retired.)*

The Honourable Mr. Listless.—So it was. Seven months ago. You see, Mr. Larynx; you see, sir. My nerves, Miss O'Carroll, my nerves

[1 Quiet, quiet, softly, softly; let us have no confusion.]

are shattered. I have been advised to try Bath. Some of the faculty recommend Cheltenham. I think of trying both, as the seasons don't clash. The season, you know, Mr. Larynx—the season, Miss O'Carroll —the season is everything.

Marionetta.—And health is something. *N'est-ce pas,* Mr. Larynx?

The Reverend Mr. Larynx.—Most assuredly, Miss O'Carroll. For, however reasoners may dispute about the *summum bonum,* none of them will deny that a very good dinner is a very good thing: and what is a good dinner without a good appetite? and whence is a good appetite but from good health? Now, Cheltenham, Mr. Listless, is famous for good appetites.

The Honourable Mr. Listless.—The best piece of logic I ever heard, Mr. Larynx; the very best I assure you. I have thought very seriously of Cheltenham: very seriously and profoundly. I thought of it—let me see—when did I think of it? *(He rang again, and Fatout re-appeared.)* Fatout, when did I think of going to Cheltenham, and did not go?

Fatout.—De Juillet twenty-von, de last summer, Monsieur. *(Fatout retired.)*

The Honourable Mr. Listless.—So it was. An invaluable fellow that, Mr. Larynx—invaluable, Miss O'Carroll.

Marionette.—So I should judge, indeed. He seems to serve you as a walking memory, and to be a living chronicle, not of your actions only, but of your thoughts.

The Honourable Mr. Listless.—An excellent definition of the fellow, Miss O'Carroll, excellent, upon my honour. Ha! ha! he! Heigho! Laughter is pleasant, but the exertion is too much for me.

A parcel was brought in for Mr. Listless; it had been sent express. Fatout was summoned to unpack it; and it proved to contain a new novel, and a new poem, both of which had long been anxiously expected by a whole host of fashionable readers; and the last number of a popular Review, of which the editor and his coadjutors were in high favour at court, and enjoyed ample pensions [1] for their services to church and state. As Fatout left the room, Mr. Flosky entered, and curiously inspected the literary arrivals.

[1] "PENSION. Pay given to a slave of state for treason to his country."— JOHNSON's *Dictionary.*

Mr. Flosky.—(Turning over the leaves.) "Devilman, a novel." Hm. Hatred—revenge—misanthropy—and quotations from the Bible. Hm. This is the morbid anatomy of black bile.—"Paul Jones, a poem." Hm. I see how it is. Paul Jones, an amiable enthusiast—disappointed in his affections—turns pirate from ennui and magnanimity—cuts various masculine throats, wins various feminine hearts—is hanged at the yard-arm! The catastrophe is very awkward, and very unpoetical.—"The Downing Street Review." Hm. First article—An Ode to the Red Book, by Roderick Sackbut, Esquire. Hm. His own poem reviewed by himself. Hm-m-m.

(Mr. Flosky proceeded in silence to look over the other articles of the Review; Marionetta inspected the novel, and Mr. Listless the poem.)

The Reverend Mr. Larynx.—For a young man of fashion and family, Mr. Listless, you seem to be of a very studious turn.

The Honourable Mr. Listless.—Studious! You are pleased to be facetious, Mr. Larynx. I hope you do not suspect me of being studious. I have finished my education. But there are some fashionable books that one must read, because they are ingredients of the talk of the day: otherwise I am no fonder of books than I dare say you yourself are, Mr. Larynx.

The Reverend Mr. Larynx.—Why, sir, I cannot say that I am indeed particularly fond of books; yet neither can I say that I never do read. A tale or a poem, now and then, to a circle of ladies over their work, is no very heterodox employment of the vocal energy. And I must say, for myself, that few men have a more Job-like endurance of the eternally recurring questions and answers that interweave themselves, on these occasions, with the crisis of an adventure, and heighten the distress of a tragedy.

The Honourable Mr. Listless.—And very often make the distress when the author has omitted it.

Marionetta.—I shall try your patience some rainy morning, Mr. Larynx; and Mr. Listless shall recommend us the very newest book, that everybody reads.

The Honourable Mr. Listless.—You shall receive it, Miss O'Carroll, with all the gloss of novelty; fresh as a ripe green-gage in all the downiness of its bloom. A mail-coach copy from Edinburgh, forwarded express from London.

Mr. Flosky.—This rage for novelty is the bane of literature. Except my works and those of my particular friends, nothing is good that is not as old as Jeremy Taylor: and *entre nous*, the best parts of my friends' books were either written or suggested by myself.

The Honourable Mr. Listless.—Sir, I reverence you. But I must say, modern books are very consolatory and congenial to my feelings. There is, as it were, a delightful north-east wind, an intellectual blight breathing through them; a delicious misanthropy and discontent, that demonstrates the nullity of virtue and energy, and puts me in good humour with myself and my sofa.

Mr. Flosky.—Very true, sir. Modern literature is a north-east wind —a blight of the human soul. I take credit to myself for having helped to make it so. The way to produce fine fruit is to blight the flower. You call this a paradox. Marry, so be it. Ponder thereon.

The conversation was interrupted by the re-appearance of Mr. Toobad, covered with mud. He just showed himself at the door, muttered "The devil is come among you!" and vanished. The road which connected Nightmare Abbey with the civilized world was artificially raised above the level of the fens, and ran through them in a straight line as far as the eye could reach, with a ditch on each side, of which the water was rendered invisible by the aquatic vegetation that covered the surface. Into one of these ditches the sudden action of a shy horse which took fright at a windmill, had precipitated the travelling chariot of Mr. Toobad, who had been reduced to the necessity of scrambling in dismal plight through the window. One of the wheels was found to be broken; and Mr. Toobad, leaving the postilion to get the chariot as well as he could to Claydyke for the purpose of cleaning and repairing, had walked back to Nightmare Abbey, followed by his servant with the imperial, and repeating all the way his favourite quotation from the Revelations.

CHAPTER VI

MR. TOOBAD had found his daughter Celinda in London, and after the first joy of meeting was over, told her he had a husband ready for her. The young lady replied, very gravely, that she should take the liberty to choose for herself. Mr. Toobad said he saw the devil was determined to interfere with all his projects, but he was resolved on his own part, not to nave on his conscience the crime of passive obedience and non-resistance to Lucifer, and therefore she should marry the person he had chosen for her. Miss Toobad replied, *très posément*, she assuredly would not. "Celinda, Celinda," said Mr. Toobad, "you most assuredly shall."—"Have I not a fortune in my own right, sir?" said Celinda. "The more is the pity," said Mr. Toobad: "but I can find means, miss; I can find means. There are more ways than one of breaking in obstinate girls." They parted for the night with the expression of opposite resolutions, and in the morning the young lady's chamber was found empty, and what was become of her Mr. Toobad had no clue to conjecture. He continued to investigate town and country in search of her; visiting and revisiting Nightmare Abbey at intervals, to consult with his friend, Mr. Glowry. Mr. Glowry agreed with Mr. Toobad that this was a very flagrant instance of filial disobedience and rebellion; and Mr. Toobad declared, that when he discovered the fugitive, she should find that "the devil was come unto her, having great wrath."

In the evening, the whole party met, as usual, in the library. Marionetta sat at the harp; the Honourable Mr. Listless sat by her and turned over her music, though the exertion was almost too much for him. The Reverend Mr. Larynx relieved him occasionally in this delightful labour. Scythrop, tormented by the demon Jealousy, sat in the corner biting his lips and fingers. Marionetta looked at him every now and then with a smile of most provoking good humor, which he pretended not to see, and which only the more exasperated his troubled spirit. He took down a volume of Dante, and pretended to be deeply interested in the Purgatorio, though he knew not a word he was reading, as Marionetta was well aware; who, tripping across the room, peeped into his book, and said to him, "I see you are in the middle of Purgatory."—"I am in the middle of hell," said Scythrop furiously. "Are you?" said she; "then come across the room, and I will sing you the finale of Don Giovanni."

"Let me alone," said Scythrop. Marionetta looked at him with a deprecating smile, and said, "You unjust, cross creature, you."—

"Let me alone," said Scythrop, but much less emphatically than at first, and by no means wishing to be taken at his word. Marionetta left him immediately, and returning to the harp, said, just loud enough for Scythrop to hear—"Did you ever read Dante, Mr. Listless? Scythrop is reading Dante, and is just now in Purgatory."—"And I," said the Honourable Mr. Listless, "am not reading Dante, and am just now in Paradise," bowing to Marionetta.

Marionetta.—You are very gallant, Mr. Listless; and I dare say you are very fond of reading Dante.

The Honourable Mr. Listless.—I don't know how it is, but Dante never came in my way till lately. I never had him in my collection, and if I had had him I should not have read him. But I find he is growing fashionable, and I am afraid I must read him some wet morning.

Marionetta.—No, read him some evening, by all means. Were you ever in love, Mr. Listless?

The Honourable Mr. Listless.—I assure you, Miss O'Carroll, never —till I came to Nightmare Abbey. I dare say it is very pleasant; but it seems to give so much trouble that I fear the exertion would be too much for me.

Marionetta.—Shall I teach you a compendious method of courtship, that will give you no trouble whatever?

The Honourable Mr. Listless.—You will confer on me an inexpressible obligation. I am all impatience to learn it.

Marionetta.—Sit with your back to the lady and read Dante; only be sure to begin in the middle, and turn over three or four pages at once—backwards as well as forwards, and she will immediately perceive that you are desperately in love with her—desperately.

(*The Honourable Mr. Listless, sitting between Scythrop and Marionetta, and fixing all his attention on the beautiful speaker, did not observe Scythrop, who was doing as she described*).

The Honourable Mr. Listless.—You are pleased to be facetious, Miss O'Carroll. The lady would infallibly conclude that I was the greatest brute in town.

Marionetta.—Far from it. She would say, perhaps, some people have odd methods of showing their affection.

The Honourable Mr. Listless.—But I should think, with submission——

Mr. Flosky.—(Joining them from another part of the room.) Did I not hear Mr. Listless observe that Dante is becoming fashionable?

*The Honourable Mr. Listless.—*I did hazard a remark to that effect, Mr. Flosky, though I speak on such subjects with a consciousness of my own nothingness, in the presence of so great a man as Mr. Flosky. I know not what is the colour of Dante's devils, but as he is certainly becoming fashionable I conclude they are blue; for the blue devils, as it seems to me, Mr. Flosky, constitute the fundamental feature of fashionable literature.

*Mr. Flosky.—*The blue are, indeed, the staple commodity; but as they will not always be commanded, the black, red, and gray may be admitted as substitutes. Tea, late dinners, and the French Revolution have played the devil, Mr. Listless, and brought the devil into play.

*Mr. Toobad (starting up).—*Having great wrath.

*Mr. Flosky.—*This is no play upon words, but the sober sadness of veritable fact.

*The Honourable Mr. Listless.—*Tea, late dinners, and the French Revolution. I cannot exactly see the connection of ideas.

*Mr. Flosky.—*I should be sorry if you could; I pity the man who can see the connection of his own ideas. Still more do I pity him, the connection of whose ideas any other person can see. Sir, the great evil is, that there is too much commonplace light in our moral and political literature; and light is a great enemy to mystery, and mystery is a great friend to enthusiasm. Now the enthusiasm for abstract truth is an exceedingly fine thing, as long as the truth, which is the object of the enthusiasm, is so completely abstract as to be altogether out of the reach of the human faculties; and, in that sense, I have myself an enthusiasm for truth, but in no other, for the pleasure of metaphysical investigation lies in the means, not in the end; and if the end could be found, the pleasure of the means would cease. The mind, to be kept in health, must be kept in exercise. The proper exercise of the mind is elaborate reasoning. Analytical reasoning is a base and mechanical process, which takes to pieces and examines, bit by bit, the rude material of knowledge, and extracts therefrom a few hard and obstinate things called facts, everything in the shape of which I cordially hate. But synthetical reasoning, setting up as its goal some unattainable abstraction, like an imaginary quantity in algebra, and commencing its course with taking for granted some two assertions which cannot be proved, from the union of these two assumed truths produces a third assumption, and so on in infinite series, to the unspeakable benefit of the human intellect. The beauty of this process is, that at every step it strikes out into two branches, in a compound ratio of ramification; so that you are perfectly sure of losing your way, and keeping your mind in perfect health, by the perpetual exercise of an interminable quest; and for these reasons I have christened my eldest son Emanuel Kant Flosky.

The Reverend Mr. Larynx.—Nothing can be more luminous.

The Honourable Mr. Listless.—And what has all that to do with Dante, and the blue devils?

Mr. Hilary.—Not much, I should think, with Dante, but a great deal with the blue devils.

Mr. Flosky.—It is very certain, and much to be rejoiced at, that our literature is hag-ridden. Tea has shattered our nerves; late dinners make us slaves of indigestion; the French Revolution has made us shrink from the name of philosophy, and has destroyed, in the more refined part of the community (of which number I am one), all enthusiasm for political liberty. That part of the reading public which shuns the solid food of reason for the light diet of fiction, requires a perpetual adhibition of sauce piquante to the palate of its depraved imagination. It lived upon ghosts, goblins, and skeletons (I and my friend Mr. Sackbut served up a few of the best), till even the devil himself, though magnified to the size of Mount Athos, became too base, common, and popular for its surfeited appetite. The ghosts have therefore been laid, and the devil has been cast into outer darkness, and now the delight of our spirits is to dwell on all the vices and blackest passions of our nature, tricked out in a masquerade dress of heroism and disappointed benevolence; the whole secret of which lies in forming combinations that contradict all our experience, and affixing the purple shred of some particular virtue to that precise character, in which we should be most certain not to find it in the living world; and making this single virtue not only redeem all the real and manifest vices of the character, but make them actually pass for necessary adjuncts, and indispensable accompaniments and characteristics of the said virtue.

Mr. Toobad.—That is, because the devil is come among us, and finds it for his interest to destroy all our perceptions of the distinctions of right and wrong.

Marionetta.—I do not precisely enter into your meaning, Mr. Flosky, and should be glad if you would make it a little more plain to me.

Mr. Flosky.—One or two examples will do it, Miss O'Carroll. If I were to take all the mean and sordid qualities of a money-dealing Jew, and tack on to them, as with a nail, the quality of extreme benevolence, I should have a very decent hero for a modern novel; and should contribute my quota to the fashionable method of administering a mass of vice, under a thin and unnatural covering of virtue, like a spider wrapt in a bit of gold leaf, and administered as a wholesome pill. On the same principle, if a man knocks me down, and takes my purse and watch by main force, I turn him to account, and set him forth in a tragedy as a dashing young fellow, disinherited for his romantic generosity, and full of a most amiable hatred of the world in general, and his own country in particular, and of a most enlightened and chivalrous affection for himself: then, with the addition of a wild girl to fall in love with him, and a series of adventures in which they break all the Ten Commandments in succession (always, you will observe, for some sublime motive, which must be carefully analyzed in its progress), I have as amiable a pair of tragic characters as ever issued from that new region of the belles lettres, which I have called the Morbid Anatomy of Black Bile, and which is greatly to be admired and rejoiced at, as affording a fine scope for the exhibition of mental power.

Mr. Hilary.—Which is about as well employed as the power of a hothouse would be in forcing up a nettle to the size of an elm. If we go on in this way, we shall have a new art of poetry, of which one of the first rules will be: To remember to forget that there are any such things as sunshine and music in the world.

The Honourable Mr. Listless.—It seems to be the case with us at present, or we should not have interrupted Miss O'Carroll's music with this exceedingly dry conversation.

Mr. Flosky.—I should be most happy if Miss O'Carroll would remind us that there are yet both music and sunshine——

The Honourable Mr. Listless.—In the voice and the smile of beauty. May I entreat the favour of—(*turning over the pages of music.*)

All were silent, and Marionetta sung:—

> Why are thy looks so blank, gray friar?
> Why are thy looks so blue?
> Thou seem'st more pale and lank, gray friar,
> Than thou wast used to do:—
> Say, what has made thee rue?
>
> Thy form was plump, and a light did shine
> In thy round and ruby face,
> Which showed an outward visible sign
> Of an inward spiritual grace:—
> Say, what has changed thy case?
>
> Yet will I tell thee true, gray friar,
> I very well can see,
> That, if thy looks are blue, gray friar,
> 'Tis all for love of me,—
> 'Tis all for love of me.
>
> But breathe not thy vows to me, gray friar,
> Oh! breathe them not, I pray;
> For ill beseems in a reverend friar,
> The love of a mortal may;
> And I needs must say thee nay.
>
> But, could'st thou think my heart to move
> With that pale and silent scowl?
> Know, he who would win a maiden's love,
> Whether clad in cap or cowl,
> Must be more of a lark than an owl.

Scythrop immediately replaced Dante on the shelf, and joined the circle round the beautiful singer. Marionetta gave him a smile of approbation that fully restored his complacency, and they continued on the best possible terms during the remainder of the evening. The Honourable Mr. Listless turned over the leaves with double alacrity, saying, "You are severe upon invalids, Miss O'Carroll: to escape your satire, I must try to be sprightly, though the exertion is too much for me."

CHAPTER VII

A NEW visitor arrived at the Abbey, in the person of Mr. Asterias, the ichthyologist. This gentleman had passed his life in seeking the living wonders of the deep through the four quarters of the world; he had a cabinet of stuffed and dried fishes, of shells, sea-weeds, corals, and madrepores, that was the admiration and envy of the Royal Society. He had penetrated into the watery den of the Sepia Octopus, disturbed the conjugal happiness of that turtle-dove of the ocean, and come off victorious in a sanguinary conflict. He had been becalmed in the tropical seas, and had watched, in eager expectation, though unhappily always in vain, to see the colossal polypus rise from the water, and entwine its enormous arms round the masts and the rigging. He maintained the origin of all things from water, and insisted that the polypodes were the first of animated things, and that, from their round bodies and many-shooting arms, the Hindoos had taken their gods, the most ancient of deities. But the chief object of his ambition, the end and aim of his researches, was to discover a triton and a mermaid, the existence of which he most potently and implicitly believed, and was prepared to demonstrate, à priori, à posteriori, à fortiori, synthetically and analytically, syllogistically and inductively, by arguments deduced both from acknowledged facts and plausible hypotheses. A report that a mermaid had been seen "sleeking her soft alluring locks" on the sea-coast of Lincolnshire, had brought him in great haste from London, to pay a long-promised and often-postponed visit to his old acquaintance, Mr. Glowry.

Mr. Asterias was accompanied by his son, to whom he had given the name of Aquarius—flattering himself that he would, in the process of time, become a constellation among the stars of ichthyological science. What charitable female had lent him the mould in which this son was cast, no one pretended to know; and, as he never dropped the most distant allusion to Aquarius's mother, some of the wags of London maintained that he had received the favours of a mermaid, and that the scientific perquisitions which kept him always prowling about the sea-shore, were directed by the less philosophical motive of regaining his lost love.

Mr. Asterias perlustrated the sea-coast for several days, and reaped disappointment, but not despair. One night, shortly after his arrival, he was sitting in one of the windows of the library, looking towards the sea, when his attention was attracted by a figure which was moving near the edge of the surf, and which was dimly visible through the moonless summer night. Its motions were irregular, like those of a person in a state of indecision. It had extremely long hair, which floated in the wind. Whatever else it might be, it certainly was not a fisherman. It might be a lady; but it was neither Mrs. Hilary nor Miss O'Carroll, for they were both in the library. It might be one of the female servants; but it had too much grace, and too striking an air of habitual liberty to render it probable. Besides, what should one of the female servants be doing there at this hour, moving to and fro, as it seemed, without any visible purpose? It could scarcely be a stranger, for Claydyke, the nearest village was ten miles distant; and what female would come ten miles across the fens, for no purpose but to hover over the surf, under the walls of Nightmare Abbey? Might it not be a mermaid? It was possibly a mermaid. It was probably a mermaid. It was very probably a mermaid. Nay, what else could it be but a mermaid? It certainly was a mermaid. Mr. Asterias stole out of the library on tip-toe, with his finger on his lips, having beckoned Aquarius to follow him.

The rest of the party was in great surprise at Mr. Asterias's movement, and some of them approached the window to see if the locality would tend to elucidate the mystery. Presently they saw him and Aquarius cautiously stealing along on the other side of the moat, but they saw nothing more; and Mr. Asterias, returning, told them, with accents of great disappointment, that he had had a glimpse of a mermaid, but she had eluded him in the darkness, and was gone, he presumed, to sup with some enamoured triton, in a submarine grotto.

"But, seriously, Mr. Asterias," said the Honourable Mr. Listless, "do you positively believe there are such things as mermaids?"

Mr. Asterias.—Most assuredly; and tritons too.

The Honourable Mr. Listless.—What! things that are half human and half fish?

Mr. Asterias.—Precisely. They are the oran outangs of the sea. But I am persuaded that there are also complete sea men, differing in no respect from us, but that they are stupid and covered with scales; for, though our organization seems to exclude us essentially from the class of amphibious animals, yet anatomists well know that the foramen ovale may remain open in an adult, and that respiration is, in that case, not necessary to life: and how can it be otherwise explained that the Indian divers, employed in the pearl fishery, pass whole hours under the water; and that the famous Swedish gardener of Troningholm lived a day and a half under the ice without being drowned? A Nereid, or mermaid, was taken in the year 1403 in a Dutch lake, and was in every respect like a Frenchwoman except that she did not speak. Towards the end of the seventeenth century, an English ship a hundred and fifty leagues from land, in the Greenland seas, discovered a flotilla of sixty or seventy little skiffs, in each of which was a triton, or sea man: at the approach of the English vessel, the whole of them, seized with simultaneous fear, disappeared, skiffs and all, under the water, as if they had been a human variety of the nautilus. The illustrious Don Feijoo has preserved an authentic and well-attested story of a young Spaniard, named Francis de la Vega, who, bathing with some of his friends in June, 1674, suddenly dived under the sea and rose no more. His friends thought him drowned: they were plebeians and pious Catholics; but a philosopher might very legitimately have drawn the same conclusion.

The Reverend Mr. Larynx.—Nothing could be more logical.

Mr. Asterias.—Five years afterwards, some fishermen near Cadiz found in their nets a triton, or sea man; they spoke to him in several languages——

The Reverend Mr. Larynx.—They were very learned fishermen.

Mr. Hilary.—They had the gift of tongues by especial favour of their brother fisherman, St. Peter.

The Honourable Mr. Listless.—Is Saint Peter the tutelar saint of Cadiz? (*None of the company could answer this question, and Mr. Asterias proceeded.*)

They spoke to him in several languages, but he was as mute as a fish. They handed him over to some holy friars, who exorcised him;

but the devil was mute too. After some days he pronounced the name Lierganes. A monk took him to that village. His mother and brothers recognized and embraced him; but he was as insensible to their caresses as any other fish would have been. He had some scales on his body, which dropped off by degrees; but his skin was as hard and rough as shagreen. He stayed at home nine years, without recovering his speech or his reason: he then disappeared again; and one of his old acquaintance, some years after, saw him pop his head out of the water, near the coast of the Asturias. These facts were certified by his brothers, and by Don Gaspardo de la Riba Aguero, Knight of Saint James, who lived near Lierganes, and often had the pleasure of our triton's company to dinner. Pliny mentions an embassy of the Olyssiponians to Tiberius, to give him intelligence of a triton which had been heard playing on its shell in a certain cave; with several other authenticated facts on the subject of Tritons and Nereids.

The Honourable Mr. Listless.—You astonish me. I have been much on the sea-shore, in the season, but I do not think I ever saw a mermaid. (*He rang, and summoned Fatout, who made his appearance half-seas-over.*) Fatout, did I ever see a mermaid?

Fatout.—Mermaid! mer-r-m-m-maid! Ah! merry maid! Oui, monsieur. Yes, sir, very many. I vish dere vas one or two here in de kitchen—ma foi! Dey be all as melancholic as so many tombstone!

The Honourable Mr. Listless.—I mean, Fatout, an odd kind of human fish.

Fatout.—De odd fish! Ah, oui! I understand the phrase: ve have seen nothing else since ve left town—ma foi!

The Honourable Mr. Listless.—You seem to have a cup too much, sir.

Fatout.—Non, monsieur: de cup too little. De fen be very unwholesome, and I drink-a-de ponch vid Raven de butler, to keep out de bad air.

The Honourable Mr. Listless.—Fatout! I insist on your being sober.

Fatout.—Oui, monsieur; I vil be as sober as de révérendissime père Jean. I should be ver glad of de merry maid; but de butler be de odd fish, and he swim in de bowl de ponch. Ah! ah! I do recollect de little-a song:—"About fair maids, and about fair maids, and about my merry maids all." (*Fatout reeled out, singing.*)

The Honourable Mr. Listless.—I am overwhelmed: I never saw the rascal in such a condition before. But will you allow me, Mr. Asterias, to inquire into the *cui bono* of all the pains and expense you have incurred to discover a mermaid? The *cui bono*, sir, is the question I always take the liberty to ask when I see any one taking much trouble for any object. I am myself a sort of Signor Pococurante, and should like to know if there be anything better or pleasanter, than the state of existing and doing nothing?

Mr. Asterias.—I have made many voyages, Mr. Listless, to remote and barren shores: I have travelled over desert and inhospitable lands: I have defied danger—I have endured fatigue—I have submitted to privation. In the midst of these I have experienced pleasures which I would not at any time have exchanged for that of existing and doing nothing. I have known many evils, but I have never known the worst of all, which, as it seems to me, are those which are comprehended in the inexhaustible varieties of *ennui:* spleen, chagrin, vapours, blue devils, time-killing, discontent, misanthropy, and all their interminable train of fretfulness, querulousness, suspicions, jealousies, and fears, which have alike infected society, and the literature of society; and which would make an arctic ocean of the human mind, if the more humane pursuits of philosophy and science did not keep alive the better feelings and more valuable energies of our nature.

The Honourable Mr. Listless.—You are pleased to be severe upon our fashionable belles lettres.

Mr. Asterias.—Surely not without reason, when pirates, highwaymen, and other varieties of the extensive genus Marauder, are the only *beau idéal* of the active, as splenetic and railing misanthropy is of the speculative energy. A gloomy brow and a tragical voice seem to have been of late the characteristics of fashionable manners: and a morbid, withering, deadly, antisocial sirocco, loaded with moral and political despair, breathes through all the groves and valleys of the modern Parnassus; while science moves on in the calm dignity of its course, affording to youth delights equally pure and vivid—to maturity, calm and grateful occupation—to old age, the most pleasing recollections and inexhaustible materials of agreeable and salutary reflection; and, while its votary enjoys the disinterested pleasure of enlarging the intellect and increasing the comforts of society, he is himself independent of the caprices of human intercourse and the accidents of human fortune. Nature is his great and inexhaustible treasure. His days are always too short for his enjoyment: ennui is a stranger to his door. At peace with the world and with his own mind, he suffices to himself, makes all around him happy, and the close of his pleasing and beneficial existence is the evening of a beautiful day.[1]

The Honourable Mr. Listless.—Really I should like very well to lead such a life myself, but the exertion would be too much for me. Besides, I have been at college. I contrive to get through my day by sinking my morning in bed, and killing the evening in company; dressing and dining in the intermediate space, and stopping the chinks and crevices of the few vacant moments that remain with a little easy reading. And that amiable discontent and antisociality which you reprobate in our present drawing-room table literature, I find, I do assure you, a very fine mental tonic, which reconciles me to my favourite pursuit of doing nothing, by showing me that nobody is worth doing anything for.

Marionetta.—But is there not in such compositions a kind of unconscious self-detection, which seems to carry their own antidote with them? For surely no one who cordially and truly either hates or despises the world will publish a volume every three months to say so.

Mr. Flosky.—There is a secret in all this, which I will elucidate with a dusky remark. According to Berkeley, the esse of things is percipi. They exist as they are perceived. But, leaving for the present, as far as relates to the material world, the materialists, hyloists, and antihyloists, to settle this point among them, which is indeed

> A subtle question, raised among
> Those out o' their wits, and those i' the wrong,

for only we transcendentalists are in the right: we may very safely assert that the esse of happiness is percipi. It exists as it is perceived. "It is the mind that maketh well or ill." The elements of pleasure and pain are everywhere. The degree of happiness that any circum-

[1] See Denys Montfort: *Histoire Naturelle des Mollusques; Vues Générales,* pp. 37, 38.

stances or objects can confer on us depends on the mental disposition with which we approach them. If you consider what is meant by the common phrases, a happy disposition and a discontented temper, you will perceive that the truth for which I am contending is universally admitted. (*Mr. Flosky suddenly stopped; he found himself unintentionally trespassing within the limits of common sense.*)

Mr. Hilary.—It is very true; a happy disposition finds materials of enjoyment everywhere. In the city, or the country—in society, or in solitude—in the theatre, or the forest—in the hum of the multitude, or in the silence of the mountains, are alike materials of reflection and elements of pleasure. It is one mode of pleasure to listen to the music of "Don Giovanni," in a theatre glittering with light, and crowded with elegance and beauty: it is another to glide at sunset over the bosom of a lonely lake, where no sound disturbs the silence but the motion of the boat through the waters. A happy disposition derives pleasure from both, a discontented temper from neither, but is always busy in detecting deficiencies, and feeding dissatisfaction with comparisons. The one gathers all the flowers, the other all the nettles, in its path. The one has the faculty of enjoying everything, the other of enjoying nothing. The one realizes all the pleasure of the present good; the other converts it into pain, by pining after something better, which is only better because it is not present, and which, if it were present, would not be enjoyed. These morbid spirits are in life what professed critics are in literature; they see nothing but faults, because they are predetermined to shut their eyes to beauties. The critic does his utmost to blight genius in its infancy; that which rises in spite of him he will not see; and then he complains of the decline of literature. In like manner, these cankers of society complain of human nature and society, when they have wilfully debarred themselves from all the good they contain, and done their utmost to blight their own happiness and that of all around them. Misanthropy is sometimes the product of disappointed benevolence; but it is more frequently the offspring of overweening and mortified vanity, quarrelling with the world for not being better treated than it deserves.

Scythrop (*to Marionetta*).—These remarks are rather uncharitable. There is great good in human nature, but it is at present ill-conditioned. Ardent spirits cannot but be dissatisfied with things as they are; and, according to their views of the probabilities of amelio ration, they will rush into the extremes of either hope or despair—of which the first is enthusiasm, and the second misanthropy; but their sources in this case are the same, as the Severn and the Wye run in different directions, and both rise in Plinlimmon.

Marionetta.—"And there is salmon in both;" for the resemblance is about as close as that between Macedon and Monmouth.

CHAPTER VIII

MARIONETTA observed the next day a remarkable perturbation in Scythrop, for which she could not imagine any probable cause. She was willing to believe at first that it had some transient and trifling source, and would pass off in a day or two; but, contrary to this ex- pectation, it daily increased. She was well aware that Scythrop had a strong tendency to the love of mystery, for its own sake; that is to say, he would employ mystery to serve a purpose, but would first choose his purpose by its capability of mystery. He seemed now to have more mystery on his hands than the laws of the system allowed, and to wear his coat of darkness with an air of great discomfort. All her little playful arts lost by degrees much of their power, either to irritate or to soothe; and the first perception of her diminished influ- ence produced in her an immediate depression of spirits, and a con- sequent sadness of demeanour, that rendered her very interesting to Mr. Clowry; who, duly considering the improbability of accomplish- ing his wishes with respect to Miss Toobad (which improbability naturally increased in the diurnal ratio of that young lady's absence), began to reconcile himself by degrees to the idea of Marionetta being his daughter.

Marionetta made many ineffectual attempts to extract from Scythrop the secret of his mystery; and, in despair of drawing it from himself, began to form hopes that she might find a clue to it from Mr. Flosky, who was Scythrop's dearest friend, and was more fre- quently than any other person admitted to his solitary tower. Mr. Flosky, however, had ceased to be visible in a morning. He was engaged in the composition of a dismal ballad; and Marionetta's uneasiness overcoming her scruples of decorum, she determined to seek him in the apartment which he had chosen for his study. She tapped at the door, and at the sound "Come in," entered the apartment. It was noon, and the sun was shining in full splendour, much to the annoyance of Mr. Flosky, who had obviated the inconvenience by closing the shutters, and drawing the window-curtains. He was sitting at his table by the light of a solitary candle, with a pen in one hand, and a muffineer in the other, with which he occasionally sprinkled salt on the wick to make it burn blue. He sate with "his eye in a fine frenzy rolling," and turned his inspired gaze on Marionetta as if she had been the ghastly ladie of a magical vision; then placed his hand before his eyes, with an appearance of manifest pain—shook his head —withdrew his hand—rubbed his eyes, like a waking man—and said, in a tone of ruefulness most jeremitalorically pathetic, "To what am I to attribute this very unexpected pleasure, my dear Miss O'Carroll?"

Marionetta.—I must apologise for intruding on you, Mr. Flosky; but the interest which I—you—take in my cousin Scythrop——

Mr. Flosky.—Pardon me, Miss O'Carroll; I do not take any interest in any person or thing on the face of the earth; which sentiment, if you analyse it, you will find to be the quintessence of the most refined philanthropy.

Marionetta.—I will take it for granted that it is so, Mr. Flosky; I am not conversant with metaphysical subtleties, but——

Mr. Flosky.—Subtleties! my dear Miss O'Carroll. I am sorry to find you participating in the vulgar error of the *reading public*, to whom an unusual collocation of words, involving a juxtaposition of antiperistatical ideas, immediately suggests the notion of hyperoxysophistical paradoxology.

Marionetta.—Indeed, Mr. Flosky, it suggests no such notion to me. I have sought you for the purpose of obtaining information.

Mr. Flosky (shaking his head).—No one ever sought me for such a purpose before.

Marionetta.—I think, Mr. Flosky—that is, I believe—that is, I fancy—that is, I imagine——

Mr. Flosky.—The τουτεστι, the *id est*, the *cioè*, the *c'est à dire*,[1]

[1 "that is," in four languages.]

the *that is*, my dear Miss O'Carroll, is not applicable in this case—if you will permit me to take the liberty of saying so. Think is not synonymous with believe—for belief, in many most important particulars, results from the total absence, the absolute negation of thought, and is thereby the sane and orthodox condition of mind; and thought and belief are both essentially different from fancy, and fancy, again, is distinct from imagination. This distinction between fancy and imagination is one of the most abstruse and important points of metaphysics. I have written seven hundred pages of promise to elucidate it, which promise I shall keep as faithfully as the bank will its promise to pay.

Marionetta.—I assure you, Mr. Flosky, I care no more about metaphysics than I do about the bank; and, if you will condescend to talk to a simple girl in intelligible terms——

Mr. Flosky.—Say not condescend! Know you not that you talk to the most humble of men, to one who has buckled on the armour of sanctity, and clothed himself with humility as with a garment?

Marionetta.—My cousin Scythrop has of late had an air of mystery about him, which gives me great uneasiness.

Mr. Flosky.—That is strange: nothing is so becoming to a man as an air of mystery. Mystery is the very key-stone of all that is beautiful in poetry, all that is sacred in faith, and all that is recondite in transcendental psychology. I am writing a ballad which is all mystery; it is "such stuff as dreams are made of," and is, indeed, stuff made of a dream; for, last night I fell asleep as usual over my book, and had a vision of pure reason. I composed five hundred lines in my sleep; so that, having had a dream of a ballad, I am now officiating as my own Peter Quince, and making a ballad of my dream, and it shall be called Bottom's Dream, because it has no bottom.

Marionetta.—I see, Mr. Flosky, you think my intrusion unseasonable, and are inclined to punish it, by talking nonsense to me. (*Mr. Flosky gave a start at the word nonsense, which almost overturned the table.*) I assure you, I would not have intruded if I had not been very much interested in the question I wish to ask you.—(*Mr. Flosky listened in sullen dignity.*)—My cousin Scythrop seems to have some secret preying on his mind.—(*Mr. Flosky was silent.*)—He seems very unhappy—Mr. Flosky.—Perhaps you are acquainted with the cause.—(*Mr. Flosky was still silent.*)—I only wish to know—Mr.

Flosky—if it is anything—that could be remedied by anything—that any one—of whom I know anything—could do.

Mr. Flosky (after a pause).—There are various ways of getting at secrets. The most approved methods, as recommended both theoretically and practically in philosophical novels, are eaves-dropping at key-holes, picking the locks of chests and desks, peeping into letters, steaming wafers, and insinuating hot wire under sealing-wax; none of which methods I hold it lawful to practise.

Marionetta.—Surely, Mr. Flosky, you cannot suspect me of wishing to adopt or encourage such base and contemptible arts.

Mr. Flosky.—Yet are they recommended, and with well-strung reasons, by writers of gravity and note, as simple and easy methods of studying character, and gratifying that laudable curiosity which aims at the knowledge of man.

Marionetta.—I am as ignorant of this morality which you do not approve, as of the metaphysics which you do: I should be glad to know by your means, what is the matter with my cousin; I do not like to see him unhappy, and I suppose there is some reason for it.

Mr. Flosky.—Now I should rather suppose there is no reason for it: it is the fashion to be unhappy. To have a reason for being so would be exceedingly commonplace: to be so without any is the province of genius: the art of being miserable for misery's sake, has been brought to great perfection in our days; and the ancient Odyssey, which held forth a shining example of the endurance of real misfortune, will give place to a modern one, setting out a more instructive picture of querulous impatience under imaginary evils.

Marionetta.—Will you oblige me, Mr. Flosky, by giving me a plain answer to a plain question?

Mr. Flosky.—It is impossible, my dear Miss O'Carroll. I never gave a plain answer to a question in my life.

Marionetta.—Do you, or do you not, know what is the matter with my cousin?

Mr. Flosky.—To say that I do not know, would be to say that I am ignorant of something; and God forbid that a transcendental metaphysician, who has pure anticipated cognitions of everything, and carries the whole science of geometry in his head without ever having looked into Euclid, should fall into so empirical an error as to declare himself ignorant of anything: to say that I do know, would be to pretend to positive and circumstantial knowledge touching present matter of fact, which, when you consider the nature of evidence, and the various lights in which the same thing may be seen——

Marionetta.—I see, Mr. Flosky, that either you have no information, or are determined not to impart it; and I beg your pardon for having given you this unnecessary trouble.

Mr. Flosky.—My dear Miss O'Carroll, it would have given me great pleasure to have said anything that would have given you pleasure; but if any person living could make report of having obtained any information on any subject from Ferdinando Flosky, my transcendental reputation would be ruined for ever.

CHAPTER IX

SCYTHROP grew every day more reserved, mysterious, and *distrait*; and gradually lengthened the duration of his diurnal seclusions in his tower. Marionetta thought she perceived in all this very manifest symptoms of a warm love cooling.

It was seldom that she found herself alone with him in the morning, and, on these occasions, if she was silent in the hope of his speaking first, not a syllable would he utter; if she spoke to him indirectly, he assented monosyllabically; if she questioned him, his answers were brief, constrained, and evasive. Still, though her spirits were depressed, her playfulness had not so totally forsaken her, but that it illuminated at intervals the gloom of Nightmare Abbey; and if, on any occasion, she observed in Scythrop tokens of unextinguished or returning passion, her love of tormenting her lover immediately got the better both of her grief and her sympathy, though not of her curiosity, which Scythrop seemed determined not to satisfy. This playfulness, however, was in a great measure artificial, and usually vanished with the irritable Strephon, to whose annoyance it had been exerted. The Genius Loci, the *tutela* [1] of Nightmare Abbey, the spirit of black melancholy, began to set his seal on her pallescent countenance. Scythrop perceived the change, found his tender sym-

[1 guardian.]

pathies awakened, and did his utmost to comfort the afflicted damsel, assuring her that his seeming inattention had only proceeded from his being involved in a profound meditation on a very hopeful scheme for the regeneration of human society. Marionetta called him ungrateful, cruel, cold-hearted, and accompanied her reproaches with many sobs and tears: poor Scythrop growing every moment more soft and submissive—till, at length, he threw himself at her feet, and declared that no competition of beauty, however dazzling, genius, however transcendent, talents, however cultivated, or philosophy, however enlightened, should ever make him renounce his divine Marionetta.

"Competition!" thought Marionetta, and suddenly, with an air of the most freezing indifference, she said, "You are perfectly at liberty, sir, to do as you please; I beg you will follow your own plans, without any reference to me."

Scythrop was confounded. What was become of all her passion and her tears? Still kneeling, he kissed her hand with rueful timidity, and said, in most pathetic accents, "Do you not love me, Marionetta?"

"No," said Marionetta, with a look of cold composure: "No." Scythrop still looked up incredulously. "No I tell you."

"Oh! very well, madam," said Scythrop, rising, "if that is the case, there are those in the world——"

"To be sure there are, sir;—and do you suppose that I do not see through your designs, you ungenerous monster?"

"My designs, Marionetta!"

"Yes, your designs, Scythrop. You have come here to cast me off, and artfully contrive that it should appear to be my doing, and not yours, thinking to quiet your tender conscience with this pitiful stratagem. But do not suppose that you are of so much consequence to me; do not suppose it: you are of no consequence to me at all— not at all, therefore, leave me: I renounce you: leave me: why do you not leave me?"

Scythrop endeavoured to remonstrate, but without success. She reiterated her injunctions to him to leave her, till, in the simplicity of his spirit, he was preparing to comply. When he had nearly reached the door, Marionetta said, "Farewell." Scythrop looked back. "Farewell, Scythrop," she repeated, "you will never see me again."

"Never see you again, Marionetta?"

"I shall go from hence to morrow, perhaps to-day; and before we meet again, one of us will be married, and we might as well be dead, you know, Scythrop."

The sudden change of her voice in the last few words, and the burst of tears that accompanied them, acted like electricity on the tender-hearted youth; and, in another instant, a complete reconciliation was accomplished without the intervention of words.

There are, indeed, some learned casuists, who maintain that love has no language, and that all the misunderstandings and dissensions of lovers arise from the fatal habit of employing words on a subject to which words are inapplicable; that love, beginning with looks, that is to say, with the physiognomical expression of congenial mental dispositions, tends through a regular gradation of signs and symbols of affection, to that consummation which is most devoutly to be wished; and that it neither is necessary that there should be, nor probable that there would be, a single word spoken from first to last between two sympathetic spirits, were it not that the arbitrary institutions of society have raised, at every step of this very simple process, so many complicaed impediments and barriers in the shape of settlements and ceremonies, parents and guardians, lawyers, Jew-brokers, and parsons, that many an adventurous knight (who, in order to obtain the conquest of a Hesperian fruit, is obliged to fight his way through all these monsters) is either repulsed at the onset, or vanquished before the achievement of his enterprise: and such a quantity of unnatural talking is rendered inevitably necessary through all the stages of the progression, that the tender and volatile spirit of love often takes flight on the pinions of some of the ἐνεα πτεροεντα, or winged words, which are pressed into his service in despite of himself.

At this conjunction, Mr. Glowry entered, and sitting down near them, said, "I see how it is: and, as we are all sure to be miserable do what we may, there is no need of taking pains to make one another more so; therefore, with God's blessing and mine, there"—joining their hands as he spoke.

Scythrop was not exactly prepared for this decisive step; but he could only stammer out, "Really, sir, you are too good;" and Mr. Glowry departed to bring Mr. Hilary to ratify the act.

Now, whatever truth there may ·be in the theory of love and language, of which we have so recently spoken, certain it is, that during Mr. Glowry's absence, which lasted half an hour, not a single word was said by either Scythrop or Marionetta.

Mr. Glowry returned with Mr. Hilary, who was delighted at the prospect of so advantageous an establishment for his orphan niece, of whom he considered himself in some manner the guardian, and nothing remained, as Mr. Glowry observed, but to fix the day.

Marionetta blushed, and was silent. Scythrop was also silent for a time, and at length hesitatingly said, "My dear sir, your goodness overpowers me; but really you are so precipitate."

Now, this remark, if the young lady had made it, would, whether she thought it or not—for sincerity is a thing of no account on these occasions, nor indeed on any other, according to Mr. Flosky—this remark, if the young lady had made it, would have been perfectly comme il faut; but, being made by the young gentleman, it was toute autre chose, and was, indeed, in the eyes of his mistress, a most heinous and irremissible offence. Marionetta was angry, very angry, but she concealed her anger, and said, calmly and coldly, "Certainly, you are much too precipitate, Mr. Glowry. I assure you, sir, I have by no means made up my mind; and, indeed, as far as I know it, it inclines the other way; but it will be quite time enough to think of these matters seven years hence." Before surprise permitted reply, the young lady had locked herself up in her own apartment.

"Why, Scythrop," said Mr. Glowry, elongating his face exceedingly, "the devil is come among us sure enough, as Mr. Toobad observes: I thought you and Marionetta were both of a mind."

"So we are, I believe, sir," said Scythrop, gloomily, and stalked away to his tower.

"Mr. Glowry," said Mr. Hilary, "I do not very well understand all this."

"Whims, brother Hilary," said Mr. Glowry; "some little foolish love quarrel, nothing more. Whims, freaks, April showers. They will be blown over by to-morrow."

"If not," said Mr. Hilary, "these April showers have made us April fools."

"Ah!" said Mr. Glowry, "you are a happy man, and in all your afflictions you can console yourself with a joke, let it be ever so bad, provided you crack it yourself. I should be very happy to laugh with you, if it would give you any satisfaction; but, really at present, my heart is so sad, that I find it impossible to levy a contribution on my muscles."

CHAPTER X

On the evening on which Mr. Asterias had caught a glimpse of a female figure on the sea-shore, which he had translated into the visual sign of his interior cognition of a mermaid, Scythrop, retiring to his tower, found his study pre-occupied. A stranger, muffled in a cloak, was sitting at his table. Scythrop paused in surprise. The stranger rose at his entrance, and looked at him intently a few moments, in silence. The eyes of the stranger alone were visible. All the rest of his figure was muffled and mantled in the folds of a black cloak, which was raised, by the right hand, to the level of the eyes. This scrutiny being completed, the stranger, dropping the cloak, said, "I see, by your physiognomy, that you may be trusted;" and revealed to the astonished Scythrop a female form and countenance of dazzling grace and beauty, with long flowing hair of raven blackness, and large black eyes of almost oppressive brilliancy, which strikingly contrasted with a complexion of snowy whiteness. Her dress was extremely elegant, but had an appearance of foreign fashion, as if both the lady and the mantuamaker were of "far countree."

> "I guess 't was frightful there to see
> A lady so richly clad as she,
> Beautiful exceedingly."

For, if it be terrible for one young lady to find another under a tree at midnight, it must, à fortiori, be much more terrible to a young gentleman to find a young lady in his study at that hour. If the logical consecutiveness of this conclusion be not manifest to my readers, I am sorry for their dulness, and must refer them, for more ample elucidation, to a treatise which Mr. Flosky intends to write, on the Categories of Relation, which comprehend Substance and Accident, Cause and Effect, Action and Re-action.

Scythrop, therefore, either was or ought to have been, frightened; at all events, he was astonished; and astonishment, though not in itself fear, is nevertheless a good stage towards it, and is, indeed, as it were the half-way house between respect and terror, according to Mr. Burke's graduated scale of the sublime.

"You are surprised," said the lady; "yet why should you be surprised? If you had met me in a drawing-room, and I had been introduced to you by an old woman, it would have been a matter of course: can the division of two or three walls, and the absence of an unimportant personage, make the same object essentially different in the perception of a philosopher?"

"Certainly not," said Scythrop; "but when any class of objects has habitually presented itself to our perceptions in invariable conjunction with particular relations, then, on the sudden appearance of one object of the class divested of those accompaniments, the essential difference of the relation is, by an involuntary process transferred to the object itself, which thus offers itself to our perceptions with all the strangeness of novelty."

"You are a philosopher," said the lady, "and a lover of liberty. You are the author of a treatise, called 'Philosophical Gas; or, a Project for a General Illumination of the Human Mind.'"

"I am," said Scythrop, delighted at this first blossom of his renown.

"I am a stranger in this country," said the lady; "I have been but a few days in it, yet I find myself immediately under the necessity of seeking refuge from an atrocious persecution. I had no friend to whom I could apply; and, in the midst of my difficulties, accident threw your pamphlet in my way, I saw that I had, at least, one kindred mind in this nation, and determined to apply to you."

"And what would you have me do?" said Scythrop, more and more amazed, and not a little perplexed.

"I would have you," said the young lady, "assist me in finding some place of retreat, where I can remain concealed from the indefatigable search that is being made for me. I have been so nearly caught once or twice already, that I cannot confide any longer in my own ingenuity."

Doubtless, thought Scythrop, this is one of my golden candlesticks. "I have constructed," said he, "in this tower, an entrance to a small suite of unknown apartments in the main building, which I defy any creature living to detect. If you would like to remain there a day or two, till I can find you a more suitable concealment, you may rely on the honour of a transcendental eleutherarch."

"I rely on myself," said the lady. "I act as I please, go where I please, and let the world say what it will. I am rich enough to set it at defiance. It is the tyrant of the poor and the feeble, but the slave of those who are above the reach of its injury."

Scythrop ventured to inquire the name of his fair protégée. "What is a name?" said the lady: "any name will serve the purpose of distinction. Call me Stella. I see by your looks," she added, "that you think all this very strange. When you know me better, your surprise will cease. I submit not to be an accomplice in my sex's slavery. I am, like yourself, a lover of freedom, and I carry my theory into practice. *They alone are subject to blind authority who have no reliance on their own strength.*"

Stella took possession of the recondite apartments. Scythrop intended to find her another asylum; but from day to day he postponed his intention, and by degrees forgot it. The young lady reminded him of it from day to day, till she also forgot it. Scythrop was anxious to learn her history; but she would add nothing to what she had already communicated, that she was shunning an atrocious persecution. Scythrop thought of Lord C. and the Alien Act, and said, "As you will not tell your name, I suppose it is in the green bag." Stella, not understanding what he meant, was silent; and Scythrop, translating silence into acquiescence, concluded that he was sheltering an *illuminée* whom Lord S. suspected of an intention to take the Tower, and set fire to the Bank: exploits, at least, as likely to be accomplished by the hands and eyes of a young beauty, as by a drunken cobbler and doctor, armed with a pamphlet and an old stocking.

Stella, in her conversations with Scythrop displayed a highly cultivated and energetic mind, full of impassioned schemes of liberty, and impatience of masculine usurpation. She had a lively sense of all the oppressions that are done under the sun; and the vivid pictures which her imagination presented to her of the numberless scenes of injustice and misery which are being acted at every moment in every part of the inhabited world, gave an habitual seriousness to her physiognomy, that made it seem as if a smile had never once hovered on her lips. She was intimately conversant with the German language and literature; and Scythrop listened with delight to her repetitions of her favourite passages from Schiller and Göthe, and to her encomiums on the sublime Spartacus Weishaupt, the immortal founder of the sect of the Illuminati. Scythrop found that his soul had a greater capacity of love than the image of Marionetta had filled. The form of Stella took possession of every vacant corner of the cavity, and by degrees displaced that of Marionetta from many of the outworks of the citadel; though the latter still held possession of the keep. He judged, from his new friend calling herself Stella, that, if it were not her real name, she was an admirer of the principles of the German play from which she had taken it, and took an opportunity of leading the conversation to that subject; but to his great surprise, the lady spoke very ardently of the singleness and exclusiveness of love, and declared that the reign of affection was one and indivisible; that it might be transferred, but could not be participated. "If I ever love," said she, "I shall do so without limit or restriction. I shall hold all difficulties light, all sacrifices cheap, all obstacles gossamer. But for love so total, I shall claim a return as absolute. I will have no rival: whether more or less favoured will be of little moment. I will be neither first nor second—I will be alone. The heart which I shall possess I will possess entirely, or entirely renounce."

Scythrop did not dare to mention the name of Marionetta; he trembled lest some unlucky accident should reveal it to Stella, though he scarcely knew what result to wish or anticipate, and lived in the double fever of a perpetual dilemma. He could not dissemble to himself that he was not in love, at the same time, with two damsels of minds and habits as remote as the antipodes. The scale of predilection always inclined to the fair one who happened to be present; but the absent was never effectually outweighed, though the degrees of exaltation and depression varied according to accidental variations in the outward and visible signs of the inward and spiritual graces of his respective charmers. Passing and repassing several times a day from the company of the one to that of the other, he was like a shuttlecock between two battledores, changing its direction as rapidly as the oscillations of a pendulum, receiving many a hard knock on the cork of a sensitive heart, and flying from point to point on the feathers of a super-sublimated head. This was an awful state of things. He had now as much mystery about him as any romantic transcendentalist or transcendental romancer could desire. He had his esoterical and his exoterical love. He could not endure the thought of losing either of them, but he trembled when he imagined the possibility that some fatal discovery might deprive him of both. The old proverb concerning two strings in a bow gave him some gleams of comfort; but that concerning two stools occurred to him more frequently, and covered his forehead with a cold perspiration. With Stella, he would indulge freely in all his romantic and philosophical visions. He could build castles in the air, and she would pile towers and turrets on the imaginary edifices. With Marionetta it was otherwise: she knew nothing of the world and society beyond the sphere of her own experience. Her life was all music and sunshine, and she wondered what any one could see to complain of in such a pleasant state of things. She loved Scythrop, she hardly knew why; indeed, she was not always sure that she loved him at all: she felt her fondness increase or diminish in an inverse ratio to his. When she had manœuvred him into a fever of passionate love, she often felt and always assumed indifference: if she found that her coldness was contagious, and that Scythrop either was, or pretended to be, as indifferent as herself, she would become doubly kind, and raise him again to that elevation from which she had previously thrown him down. Thus, when his love was flowing, hers was ebbing: when his was ebbing hers was flowing. Now and then there were moments of level tide, when reciprocal affection seemed to promise imperturbable harmony, but Scythrop could scarcely resign his spirit to the pleasing illusion, before the pinnace of the lover's affections was caught in some eddy of the lady's caprice, and he was whirled away from the shore of his hopes, without rudder or compass, into an ocean of mists and storms. It resulted, from this system of conduct, that all that passed between Scythrop and Marionetta consisted in making and unmaking love. He had no opportunity to take measure of her understanding by conversations on general subjects, and on his favourite designs; and being left in this respect to the exercise of indefinite conjecture, he took it for granted, as most lovers would do in similar circumstances, that she had great natural talents, which she wasted at present on trifles: but coquetry would end with marriage, and leave room for philosophy to exert its influence on her mind. Stella had no coquetry, no disguise: she was an enthusiast in subjects of general interest; and her conduct to Scythrop was always uniform, or rather showed a regular progression of partiality which seemed fast ripening into love.

CHAPTER XI

SCYTHROP, attending one day the summons to dinner, found in the drawing-room his friend Mr. Cypress, the poet, whom he had known at college, and who was a great favourite of Mr. Glowry. Mr. Cypress said, he was on the point of leaving England, but could not think of doing so without a farewell-look at Nightmare Abbey and his respected friends, the moody Mr. Glowry and the mysterious Mr. Scythrop, the sublime Mr. Flosky and the pathetic Mr. Listless; to all of whom, and the morbid hospitality of the melancholy dwelling in which they were then assembled, he assured them he should always look back with as much affection as his lacerated spirit could feel for anything. The sympathetic condolence of their respective replies were cut short by Raven's announcement of "dinner on table."

The conversation that took place when the wine was in circulation, and the ladies were withdrawn, we shall report with our usual scrupulous fidelity.

Mr. Glowry.—You are leaving England, Mr. Cypress. There is a delightful melancholy in saying farewell to an old acquaintance, when the chances are twenty to one against ever meeting again. A smiling bumper to sad parting, and let us all be unhappy together.

Mr. Cypress (filling a bumper).—This is the only social habit that the disappointed spirit never unlearns.

The Reverend Mr. Larynx (filling).—It is the only piece of academical learning that the finished educatee retains.

Mr. Flosky (filling).—It is the only objective fact which the sceptic can realize.

Scythrop (filling).—It is the only styptic for a bleeding heart.

The Honourable Mr. Listless (filling).—It is the only trouble that is very well worth taking.

Mr. Asterias (filling).—It is the only key of conversational truth.

Mr. Toobad (filling).—It is the only antidote to the great wrath of the devil.

Mr. Hilary (filling).—It is the only symbol of perfect life. The inscription "HIC NON BIBITUR" [1] will suit nothing but a tombstone.

Mr. Glowry.—You will see many fine old ruins, Mr. Cypress; crumbling pillars and mossy walls—many a one-legged Venus and headless Minerva—many a Neptune buried in sand—many a Jupiter turned topsy-turvy—many a perforated Bacchus doing duty as a water-pipe—many reminiscences of the ancient world, which I hope was better worth living in than the modern; though, for myself, I care not a straw more for one than the other, and would not go twenty miles to see anything that either could show.

Mr. Cypress.—It is something to seek, Mr. Glowry. The mind is restless, and must persist in seeking, though to find is to be disappointed. Do you feel no aspirations towards the countries of Socrates and Cicero? No wish to wander among the venerable remains of the greatness that has passed for ever.

Mr. Glowry.—Not a grain.

Scythrop.—It is, indeed, much the same as if a lover should dig up the buried form of his mistress, and gaze upon relics which are anything but herself, to wander among a few mouldy ruins, that are only imperfect indexes to lost volumes of glory, and meet at every step the more melancholy ruins of human nature—a degenerate race of stupid and shrivelled slaves, grovelling in the lowest depths of servility and superstition.

The Honourable Mr. Listless.—It is the fashion to go abroad. I have thought of it myself, but am hardly equal to the exertion. To be sure, a little eccentricity and originality are allowable in some cases; and the most eccentric and original of all characters is an Englishman who stays at home.

Scythrop.—I should have no pleasure in visiting countries that are past all hope of regeneration. There is great hope of our own; and it seems to me that an Englishman, who, either by his station in society, or by his genius, or (as in your instance, Mr. Cypress) by both, has the power of essentially serving his country in its arduous struggle with its domestic enemies, yet forsakes his country,

[1 No drinking here.]

which is still so rich in hope, to dwell in others which are only fertile in the ruins of memory, does what none of those ancients, whose fragmentary memorials you venerate, would have done in similar circumstances.

Mr. Cypress.—Sir, I have quarrelled with my wife; and a man who has quarrelled with his wife is absolved from all duty to his country. I have written an ode to tell the people as much, and they may take it as they list.

Scythrop.—Do you suppose, if Brutus had quarrelled with his wife, he would have given it as a reason to Cassius for having nothing to do with his enterprise? Or would Cassius have been satisfied with such an excuse?

Mr. Plosky.—Brutus was a senator: so is our dear friend: but the cases are different. Brutus had some hope of political good: Mr. Cypress has none. How should he, after what we have seen in France?

Scythrop.—A Frenchman is born in harness, ready saddled, bitted, and bridled, for any tyrant to ride. He will fawn under his rider one moment, and throw him and kick him to death the next; but another adventurer springs on his back, and by dint of whip and spur, on he goes as before. We may, without much vanity, hope better of ourselves.

Mr. Cypress.—I have no hope for myself or for others. Our life is a false nature; it is not in the harmony of things; it is an all-blasting upas, whose root is earth, and whose leaves are the skies which rain their poison-dews upon mankind. We wither from our youth; we gasp with unslaked thirst for unattainable good; lured from the first to the last by phantoms—love, fame, ambition, avarice—all idle, and all ill—one meteor of many names, that vanishes in the smoke of death. [1]

.. Mr. Flosky.—A most delightful speech, Mr. Cypress. A most amiable and instructive philosophy. You have only to impress its truth on the minds of all living men, and life will then, indeed, be the desert and the solitude; and I must do you, myself, and our mutual friends the justice to observe that let society only give fair play, at one and the same time, as I flatter myself it is inclined to do, to your system of morals, and my system of metaphysics, and

[1] Childe Harold, canto 4, cxxiv. cxxvi.

Scythrop's system of politics, and Mr. Listless's system of manners, and Mr. Toobad's system of religion, and the result will be as fine a mental chaos as even the immortal Kant himself could ever have hoped to see; in the prospect of which I rejoice.

Mr. Hilary.—"Certainly, ancient, it is not a thing to rejoice at:" I am one of those who cannot see the good that is to result from all this mystifying and blue-devilling of society. The contrast it presents to the cheerful and solid wisdom of antiquity is too forcible not to strike any one who has the least knowledge of classical literature. To represent vice and misery as the necessary accompaniments of genius, is as mischievous as it is false, and the feeling is as unclassical as the language in which it is usually expressed.

Mr. Toobad.—It is our calamity. The devil has come among us, and has begun by taking possession of all the cleverest fellows. Yet, forsooth, this is the enlightened age. Marry, how? Did our ancestors go peeping about with dark lanterns, and do we walk at our ease in broad sunshine? Where is the manifestation of our light? By what symptoms do you recognize it? What are its signs, its tokens, its symptoms, its symbols, its categories, its conditions? What is it, and why? How, where, when is it to be seen, felt, and understood? What do we see by it which our ancestors saw not, and which at the same time is worth seeing? We see a hundred men hanged, where they saw one. We see five hundred transported, where they saw one. We see five thousand in the workhouse, where they saw one. We see scores of Bible societies, where they saw none. We see paper, where they saw gold. We see men in stays, where they saw men in armour. We see painted faces, where they saw healthy ones. We see children perishing in manufactories, where they saw them flourishing in the fields. We see prisons, where they saw castles. We see masters, where they saw representatives. In short, they saw true men, where we see false knaves. They saw Milton, and we see Mr. Sackbut.

Mr. Flosky.—The false knave, sir, is my honest friend; therefore, I beseech you, let him be countenanced. God forbid but a knave should have some countenance at his friend's request.

Mr. Toobad.—"Good men and true" was their common term, like the καλος κάγαϑος [1] of the Athenians. It is so long since men

[1 the beautiful and the good.]

have been either good or true, that it is to be questioned which is most obsolete, the fact or the phraseology.

Mr. Cypress.—There is no worth nor beauty but in the mind's idea. Love sows the wind and reaps the whirlwind.[1] Confusion, thrice confounded, is the portion of him who rests even for an instant on that most brittle of reeds—the affection of a human being. The sum of our social destiny is to inflict or to endure.[2]

Mr. Hilary.—Rather to bear and forbear, Mr. Cypress—a maxim which you perhaps despise. Ideal beauty is not the mind's creation: it is real beauty, refined and purified in the mind's alembic, from the alloy which always more or less accompanies it in our mixed and imperfect nature. But still the gold exists in a very ample degree. To expect too much is a disease in the expectant, for which human nature is not responsible; and, in the common name of humanity, I protest against these false and mischievous ravings. To rail against humanity for not being abstract perfection, and against human love for not realizing all the splendid visions of the poets of chivalry, is to rail at the summer for not being all sunshine, and at the rose for not being always in bloom.

Mr. Cypress.—Human love! Love is not an inhabitant of the earth. We worship him as the Athenians did their unknown God: but broken hearts are the martyrs of his faith, and the eye shall never see the form which phantasy paints, and which passion pursues through paths of delusive beauty, among flowers whose odours are agonies, and trees whose gums are poison.[3]

Mr. Hilary.—You talk like a Rosicrusian, who will love nothing but a sylph, who does not believe in the existence of a sylph, and who yet quarrels with the whole universe for not containing a sylph.

Mr. Cypress.—The mind is diseased of its own beauty, and fevers into false creation. The forms which the sculptor's soul has seized exist only in himself.[4]

Mr. Flosky.—Permit me to discept. They are the mediums of common forms combined and arranged into a common standard.

[1] Childe Harold, canto 4, cxxiii.
[2] Ibid., canto 3, lxxi.
[3] Ibid., canto 4, cxxi. cxxxvi.
[4] Ibid., canto 4, cxxii.

The ideal beauty of the Helen of Zeuxis was the combined medium of the real beauty of the virgins of Crotona.

Mr. Hilary.—But to make ideal beauty the shadow in the water, and like the dog in the fable, to throw away the substance in catching at the shadow, is scarcely the characteristic of wisdom, whatever it may be of genius. To reconcile man as he is to the world as it is, to preserve and improve all that is good, and destroy or alleviate all that is evil, in physical and moral nature—have been the hope and aim of the greatest teachers and ornaments of our species. I will say, too, that the highest wisdom and the highest genius have been invariably accompanied with cheerfulness. We have sufficient proofs on record that Shakespeare and Socrates were the most festive companions. But now the little wisdom and genius we have seem to be entering into a conspiracy against cheerfulness.

Mr. Toobad.—How can we be cheerful with the devil among us?

The Honourable Mr. Listless.—How can we be cheerful when our nerves are shattered?

Mr. Flosky.—How can we be cheerful when we are surrounded by a reading public, that is growing too wise for its betters?

Scythrop.—How can we be cheerful when our great general designs are crossed every moment by our little particular passions?

Mr. Cypress.—How can we be cheerful in the midst of disappointment and despair?

Mr. Glowry.—Let us all be unhappy together.

Mr. Hilary.—Let us sing a catch.

Mr. Glowry.—No: a nice tragical ballad. The Norfolk Tragedy to the tune of the Hundredth Psalm.

Mr. Hilary.—I say a catch.

Mr. Glowry.—I say no. A song from Mr. Cypress.

All.—A song from Mr. Cypress.

Mr. Cypress sung—

> There is a fever of the spirit,
>   The brand of Cain's unresting doom,
> Which in the lone dark souls that bear it
>   Glows like the lamp in Tullia's tomb:
> Unlike that lamp, its subtle fire
>   Burns, blasts, consumes its cell, the heart,

Till, one by one hope, joy, desire,
    Like dreams of shadowy smoke depart.

When hope, love, life itself, are only
    Dust—spectral memories—dead and cold—
The unfed fire burns bright and lonely,
    Like that undying lamp of old:
And by that dreary illumination,
    Till time its clay-built home has rent,
Thought broods on feeling's desolation—
    The soul is its own monument.

Mr. Glowry.—Admirable. Let us all be unhappy together.

Mr. Hilary.—Now, I say again, a catch.

The Reverend Mr. Larynx.—I am for you.

Mr. Hilary.—"Seamen three."

The Reverend Mr. Larynx.—Agreed. I'll be Harry Gill, with the voice of three. Begin.

Mr. Hilary and the Reverend Mr. Larynx—

Seamen three! What men be ye?
Gotham's three wise men we be.
Whither in your bowl so free?
To rake the moon from out the sea.
The bowl goes trim. The moon doth shine.
And our ballast is old wine;
And your ballast is old wine.

Who art thou, so fast adrift?
I am he they call Old Care.
Here on board we will thee lift.
No: I may not enter there.
Wherefore so? 'Tis Jove's degree,
In a bowl Care may not be;
In a bowl Care may not be.

Fear ye not the waves that roll?
No: in charmed bowl we swim.
What the charm that floats the bowl?
Water may not pass the brim.
The bowl goes trim. The moon doth shine.
And our ballast is old wine;
And your ballast is old wine.

This catch was so well executed by the spirit and science of Mr. Hilary, and the deep tri-une voice of the reverend gentleman, that the whole party, in spite of themselves, caught the contagion, and joined in chorus at the conclusion, each raising a bumper to his lips:

> The bowl goes trim: the moon doth shine:
> And our ballast is old wine.

Mr. Cypress, having his ballast on board, stepped, the same evening, into his bowl, or travelling chariot, and departed to rake seas and rivers, lakes and canals, for the moon of ideal beauty.

CHAPTER XII

It was the custom of the Honourable Mr. Listless, on adjourning from the bottle to the ladies, to retire for a few moments to make a second toilette, that he might present himself in becoming taste. Fatout, attending as usual, appeared with a countenance of great dismay, and informed his master that he had just ascertained that the abbey was haunted. Mrs. Hilary's *gentlewoman*, for whom Fatout had lately conceived a *tendresse*, had been, as she expressed it, "fritted out of her seventeen senses" the preceding night as she was retiring to her bedchamber, by a ghostly figure she had met stalking along one of the galleries, wrapped in a white shroud, with a bloody turban on its head. She had fainted away with fear; and, when she recovered, she found herself in the dark, and the figure was gone. "*Sacré—cochon—bleu!*" exclaimed Fatout, giving very deliberate emphasis to every portion of his terrible oath—"I vould not meet de *revenant*, de ghost—non—not for all de *bowl-de-ponch* in de vorld."

"Fatout," said the Honourable Mr. Listless, "did I ever see a ghost?"

"*Jamais*, monsieur, never."

"Then I hope I never shall, for, in the present shattered state of my nerves, I am afraid it would be too much for me. There— loosen the lace of my stays a little, for really this plebeian practice of eating—Not too loose—consider my shape. That will do. And I desire that you bring me no more stories of ghosts; for, though I do not believe in such things, yet, when one is awake in the night, one is apt, if one thinks of them, to have fancies that give one a kind of a chill, particularly if one opens one's eyes suddenly on one's dressing gown hanging in the moonlight, between the bed and the window."

The Honourable Mr. Listless, though he had prohibited Fatout from bringing him any more stories of ghosts, could not help thinking of that which Fatout had already brought; and, as it was uppermost in his mind, when he descended to the tea and coffee cups, and the rest of the company in the library, he almost involuntarily asked Mr. Flosky, whom he looked up to as a most oraculous personage, whether any story of any ghost that had ever appeared to any one, was entitled to any degree of belief?

Mr. Flosky.—By far the greater number to a very great degree.

The Honourable Mr. Listless.—Really, that is very alarming!

Mr. Flosky.—*Sunt geminæ somni portæ.* [1] There are two gates through which ghosts find their way to the upper air: fraud and self-delusion. In the latter case a ghost is a *deceptio visûs*, an ocular spectrum, an idea with the force of a sensation. I have seen many ghosts myself. I dare say there are few in this company who have not seen a ghost.

The Honourable Mr. Listless.—I am happy to say, I never have, for one.

The Reverend Mr. Larynx.—We have such high authority for ghosts, that it is rank scepticism to disbelieve them. Job saw a ghost, which came for the express purpose of asking a question, but did not wait for an answer.

The Honourable Mr. Listless.—Because Job was too frightened to give one.

The Reverend Mr. Larynx.—Spectres appeared to the Egyptians during the darkness with which Moses covered Egypt. The witch of Endor raised the ghost of Samuel. Moses and Elias appeared on Mount Tabor. An evil spirit was sent into the army of Sennacherib, and exterminated it in a single night.

[1 There are two gates of sleep.]

Mr. Toobad.—Saying, The devil has come among you, having great wrath.

Mr. Flosky.—Saint Macarius interrogated a skull, which was found in the desert, and made it relate, in presence of several witnesses, what was going forward in hell. Saint Martin of Tours, being jealous of a pretended martyr, who was the rival saint of his neighbourhood, called up his ghost, and made him confess that he was damned. Saint Germain, being on his travels, turned out of an inn a large party of ghosts, who had every night taken possession of the *table d'hôte*, and consumed a copious supper.

Mr. Hilary.—Jolly ghosts, and no doubt all friars. A similar party took possession of the cellar of M. Swebach, the painter, in Paris, drank his wine, and threw the empty bottles at his head.

The Reverend Mr. Larynx.—An atrocious act.

Mr. Flosky.—Pausanias relates, that the neighing of horses and the tumult of combatants were heard every night on the field of Marathon: but those who went purposely to hear these sounds suffered severely for their curiosity; but those who heard them by accident passed with impunity.

The Reverend Mr. Larynx.—I once saw a ghost myself in my study, which is the last place where any one but a ghost would look for me. I had not been into it for three months, and was going to consult Tillotson, when on opening the door, I saw a venerable figure in a flannel dressing gown, sitting in my arm-chair, and reading my Jeremy Taylor. It vanished in a moment, and so did I; and what it was or what it wanted I have never been able to ascertain.

Mr. Plosky.—It was an idea with the force of a sensation. It is seldom that ghosts appeal to two senses at once; but, when I was in Devonshire, the following story was well attested to me. A young woman, whose lover was at sea, returning one evening over some solitary fields, saw her lover sitting on a stile over which she was to pass. Her first emotions were surprise and joy, but there was a paleness and seriousness in his face that made them give place to alarm. She advanced towards him, and he said to her, in a solemn voice, "The eye that hath seen me shall see me no more. Thine eye is upon me, but I am not." And with these words he vanished; and on that very day and hour, as it afterwards appeared, he had perished by shipwreck.

The whole party now drew round in a circle, and each related
some ghostly anecdote, heedless of the flight of time, till, in a pause
of the conversation, they heard the hollow tongue of midnight sounding twelve.

Mr. Hilary.—All these anecdotes admit of solution on psychological principles. It is more easy for a soldier, a philosopher, or
even a saint, to be frightened at his own shadow, than for a dead
man to come out of his grave. Medical writers cite a thousand singular examples of the force of imagination. Persons of feeble, nervous,
melancholy temperament, exhausted by fever, by labour, or by spare
diet, will readily conjure up, in the magic ring of their old phantasy, spectres, gorgons, chimæras, and all the objects of their hatred
and their love. We are most of us like Don Quixote, to whom a
windmill was a giant, and Dulcinea was a magnificent princess: all
more or less the dupes of our own imagination, though we do not
all go so far as to see ghosts, or to fancy ourselves pipkins and tea-
pots.

Mr. Flosky.—I can safely say, I have seen too many ghosts myself to believe in their external existence. I have seen all kinds of
ghosts: black spirits and white, red spirits and gray. Some in the
shape of venerable old men, who have met me in my rambles at
noon; some of beautiful young women, who have peeped through
my curtains at midnight.

The Honourable Mr. Listless.—And have proved, I doubt not,
"palpable to feeling as to sight."

Mr. Plosky.—By no means, sir. You reflect upon my purity. Myself and my friends, particularly my friend Mr. Sackbut, are famous
for our purity. No, sir, genuine untangible ghosts. I live in a world
of ghosts. I see a ghost at this moment.

Mr. Flosky fixed his eyes on the door at the further end of the
library. The company looked in the same direction. The door silently
opened, and a ghastly figure, shrouded in white drapery, with the
semblance of a bloody turban on its head, entered and stalked slowly
up the apartment. Mr. Flosky, familiar as he was with ghosts, was
not prepared for this apparition, and made the best of his way out
at the opposite door. Mrs. Hilary and Marionetta followed, scream-
ing. The Honourable Mr. Listless, by two turns of his body, rolled
first off the sofa and then under it. The Reverend Mr. Larynx

leaped up and fled with so much precipitation, that he overturned the table on the foot of Mr. Glowry. Mr. Glowry roared with pain in the ear of Mr. Toobad. Mr. Toobad's alarm so bewildered his senses, that, missing the door, he threw up one of the windows, jumped out in his panic, and plunged over head and ears in the moat. Mr. Asterias and his son, who were on the watch for their mermaid, were attracted by the splashing, threw a net over him, and dragged him to land.

Scythrop and Mr. Hilary meanwhile had hastened to his assistance, and, on arriving at the edge of the moat, followed by several servants with ropes and torches, found Mr. Asterias and Aquarius busy in endeavouring to extricate Mr. Toobad from the net, who was entangled in the meshes, and floundering with rage. Scythrop was lost in amazement; but Mr. Hilary saw, at one view, all the circumstances of the adventure, and burst into an immoderate fit of laughter; on recovering from which, he said to Mr. Asterias, "You have caught an odd fish, indeed." Mr. Toobad was highly exasperated at this unseasonable pleasantry; but Mr. Hilary softened his anger, by producing a knife, and cutting the Gordian knot of his reticular envelopment. "You see," said Mr. Toobad—"you see, gentlemen, in my unfortunate person proof upon proof of the present dominion of the devil in the affairs of this world; and I have no doubt but that the apparition of this night was Apollyon himself in disguise, sent for the express purpose of terrifying me into this complication of misadventures. The devil is come among you, having great wrath, because he knoweth that he hath but a short time."

CHAPTER XIII

MR. GLOWRY was much surprised, on occasionally visiting Scythrop's tower, to find the door always locked, and to be kept sometimes waiting many minutes for admission: during which he invariably heard a heavy rolling sound like that of a ponderous mangle, or of a waggon on a weighing-bridge, or of theatrical thunder.

He took little notice of this for some time: at length his curiosity was excited, and, one day, instead of knocking at the door, as usual, the instant he reached it, he applied his ear to the key-hole, and like Bottom, in the Midsummer Night's Dream, "spied a voice," which he guessed to be of the feminine gender, and knew to be not Scythrop's, whose deeper tones he distinguished at intervals. Having attempted in vain to catch a syllable of the discourse, he knocked violently at the door, and roared for immediate admission. The voices ceased, and Scythrop was discovered alone. Mr. Glowry looked round to every corner of the apartment, and then said, "Where is the lady?"

"The lady, sir?" said Scythrop.

"Yes, sir, the lady."

"Sir, I do not understand you."

"You don't, sir?"

"No, indeed, sir. There is no lady here."

"But, sir, this is not the only apartment in the tower, and I make no doubt there is a lady upstairs."

"You are welcome to search, sir."

"Yes, and while I am searching, she will slip out from some lurking-place, and make her escape."

"You may lock this door, sir, and take the key with you."

"But there is the terrace door: she has escaped by the terrace."

"The terrace, sir, has no other outlet, and the walls are too high for a lady to jump down."

"Well, sir, give me the key."

Mr. Glowry took the key, searched every nook of the tower, and returned.

"You are a fox, Scythrop; you are an exceedingly cunning fox, with that demure visage of yours. What was that lumbering sound I heard before you opened the door?"

"Sound, sir?"

"Yes, sir, sound."

"My dear sir, I am not aware of any sound, except my great table, which I moved on rising to let you in."

"The table!—let me see that. No, sir; not a tenth part heavy enough, not a tenth part."

"But, sir, you do not consider the laws of acoustics: a whisper becomes a peal of thunder in the focus of reverberation. Allow me to explain this: sounds striking on concave surfaces are reflected from them, and, after reflection, converge to points which are the foci of these surfaces. It follows, therefore, that the ear may be so placed in one, as that it shall hear a sound better than when situated nearer to the point of the first impulse: again, in the case of two concave surfaces placed opposite to each other——"

"Nonsense, sir. Don't tell me of foci. Pray, sir, will concave surfaces produce two voices when nobody speaks? I heard two voices, and one was feminine; feminine, sir: what say you to that?"

"Oh, sir, I perceive your mistake: I am writing a tragedy, and was acting over a scene to myself. To convince you, I will give you a specimen; but you must first understand the plot. It is a tragedy on the German model. The Great Mogul is in exile, and has taken lodgings at Kensington, with his only daughter, the Princess Rantrorina, who takes in needlework, and keeps a day-school. *The princess is discovered hemming a set of shirts for the parson of the parish: they are to be marked with a large R. Enter to her the Great Mogul. A pause, during which they look at each other expressively. The princess changes colour several times. The Mogul takes snuff in great agitation. Several grains are heard to fall on the stage. His heart is seen to beat through his upper benjamin.*—THE MOGUL (with a mournful look at his left shoe). "My shoestring is broken."—THE PRINCESS (after an interval of melancholy reflection). "I know it."—THE MOGUL. "My second shoe-string! The first broke when I lost my empire: the second has broken to-day. When will my poor heart break!"—THE PRINCESS. "Shoe-strings, hearts, and empires! Mysterious sympathy!"

"Nonsense, sir," interrupted Mr. Glowry. "That is not at all like the voice I heard."

"But, sir," said Scythrop, "a key-hole may be so constructed as to act like an acoustic tube, and an acoustic tube, sir, will modify sound in a very remarkable manner. Consider the construction of the ear, and the nature and causes of sound. The external part of the ear is a cartilaginous funnel."

"It won't do, Scythrop. There is a girl concealed in this tower, and find her I will. There are such things as sliding panels and secret closets."—He sounded round the room with his cane, but detected no hollowness.—"I have heard, sir," he continued, "that during my absence, two years ago, you had a dumb carpenter closeted with you, day after day. I did not dream that you were laying contrivances for carrying on secret intrigues. Young men will have their way: I had my way when I was a young man: but, sir, when your cousin Marionetta——"

Scythrop now saw that the affair was growing serious. To have clapped his hand upon his father's mouth, to have entreated him to be silent, would, in the first place, not have made him so; and, in the second, would have shown a dread of being overheard by somebody. His only resource, therefore, was to try and drown Mr. Glowry's voice; and, having no other subject, he continued his description of the ear, raising his voice continually as Mr. Glowry raised his.

"When your cousin Marionetta," said Mr. Glowry, "whom you profess to love—whom you profess to love, sir——"

"The internal canal of the ear," said Scythrop, "is partly bony and partly cartilaginous. This internal canal is—"

"Is actually in the house, sir; and, when you are so shortly to be —as I expect——"

"Closed at the further end by the *membrana tympani*—"

"Joined together in holy matrimony—"

"Under which is carried a branch of the fifth pair of nerves—"

"I say, sir, when you are so shortly to be married to your cousin Marionetta—"

"The *cavitas tympani*—"

A loud noise was heard behind the book-case, which, to the astonishment of Mr. Glowry, opened in the middle, and the massy compartments, with all their weight of books, receding from each other in the manner of a theatrical scene, with a heavy rolling sound (which Mr. Glowry immediately recognized to be the same which had excited his curiosity) disclosed an interior apartment, in the entrance of which stood the beautiful Stella, who, stepping forward, exclaimed, "Married! Is he going to be married? The profligate!"

"Really, madam," said Mr. Glowry, "I do not know what he is going to do, or what I am going to do, or what any one is going to do; for all this is incomprehensible."

"I can explain it all," said Scythrop, "in a most satisfactory manner, if you will but have the goodness to leave us alone."

"Pray, sir, to which act of the tragedy of the Great Mogul does this incident belong?"

"I entreat you, my dear sir, leave us alone."

Stella threw herself into a chair, and burst into a tempest of tears. Scythrop sat down by her, and took her hand. She snatched her hand away, and turned her back upon him. He rose, sat down on the other side, and took her other hand. She snatched it away, and turned from him again. Scythrop continued entreating Mr. Glowry to leave them alone; but the old gentleman was obstinate, and would not go.

"I suppose, after all," said Mr. Glowry maliciously, "it is only a phænomenon in acoustics, and this young lady is a reflection of sound from concave surfaces."

Some one tapped at the door: Mr. Glowry opened it, and Mr. Hilary entered. He had been seeking Mr. Glowry, and had traced him to Scythrop's tower. He stood a few moments in silent surprise, and then addressed himself to Mr. Glowry for an explanation.

"The explanation," said Mr. Glowry, "is very satisfactory. The Great Mogul has taken lodgings at Kensington, and the external part of the ear is a cartilaginous funnel."

"Mr. Glowry, that is no explanation."

"Mr. Hilary, it is all I know about the matter."

"Sir, this pleasantry is very unseasonable. I perceive that my niece is sported with in a most unjustifiable manner, and I shall see if she will be more successful in obtaining an intelligible answer." And he departed in search of Marionetta.

Scythrop was now in a hopeful predicament. Mr. Hilary made a hue and cry in the abbey, and summoned his wife and Marionetta to Scythrop's apartment. The ladies, not knowing what was the matter, hastened in great consternation. Mr. Toobad saw them sweeping along the corridor, and judging from their manner that the devil had manifested his wrath in some new shape, followed from pure curiosity.

Scythrop, meanwhile, vainly endeavoured to get rid of Mr. Glowry and to pacify Stella. The latter attempted to escape from the tower, declaring she would leave the abbey immediately, and he should never see or hear of her more. Scythrop held her hand, and detained her by force, till Mr. Hilary reappeared with Mrs. Hilary and Marionetta. Marionetta, seeing Scythrop grasping the hand of a strange beauty, fainted away in the arms of her aunt. Scythrop flew to her assistance; and Stella, with redoubled anger, sprang towards the door, but was intercepted in her intended flight by being caught in the arms of Mr. Toobad, who exclaimed—"Celinda!"

"Papa!" said the young lady disconsolately.

"The devil is come among you," said Mr. Toobad, "how came my daughter here?"

"Your daughter!" exclaimed Mr. Glowry.

"Your daughter!" exclaimed Scythrop, and Mr. and Mrs. Hilary.

"Yes," said Mr. Toobad, "my daughter Celinda."

Marionetta opened her eyes and fixed them on Celinda; Celinda, in return, fixed hers on Marionetta. They were at remote points of the apartment. Scythrop was equidistant from both of them, central and motionless, like Mahomet's coffin.

"Mr. Glowry," said Mr. Toobad, "can you tell by what means my daughter came here?"

"I know no more," said Mr. Glowry, "than the Great Mogul."

"Mr. Scythrop," said Mr. Toobad, "how came my daughter here?"

"I did not know, sir, that the lady was your daughter."

"But how came she here?"

"By spontaneous locomotion," said Scythrop, sullenly.

"Celinda," said Mr. Toobad, "what does all this mean?"

"I really do not know, sir."

"This is most unaccountable. When I told you in London that I had chosen a husband for you, you thought proper to run away from him; and now, to all appearance, you have run away to him."

"How, sir! was that your choice?"

"Precisely; and if he is yours too we shall be both of a mind, for the first time in our lives."

"He is not my choice, sir. This lady has a prior claim: I renounce him."

"And I renounce him," said Marionetta.

Scythrop knew not what to do. He could not attempt to conciliate the one without irreparably offending the other; and he was so fond of both, that the idea of depriving himself for ever of the society of either was intolerable to him; he therefore retreated into his stronghold, mystery; maintained an impenetrable silence; and contented himself with stealing occasionally a deprecating glance at each of the objects of his idolatry. Mr. Toobad and Mr. Hilary, in the meantime, were each insisting on an explanation from Mr. Glowry, who they thought had been playing a double game on this occasion. Mr. Glowry was vainly endeavouring to persuade them of his innocence in the whole transaction. Mrs. Hilary was endeavouring to mediate between her husband and brother. The Honourable Mr. Listless, the Reverend Mr. Larynx, Mr. Flosky, Mr. Asterias, and Aquarius, were attracted by the tumult to the scene of action, and were appealed to severally and conjointly by the respective disputants. Multitudinous questions, and answers en masse, composed a charivari, to which the genius of Rossini alone could have given a suitable accompaniment, and which was only terminated by Mrs Hilary and Mr. Toobad retreating with the captive damsels. The whole party followed, with the exception of Scythrop, who threw himself into his armchair, crossed his left foot over his right knee, placed the hollow of his left hand on the interior ankle of his left leg, rested his right elbow on the elbow of the chair, placed the ball of his right thumb against his right temple, curved the fore-finger along the upper part of his forehead, rested the point of the middle finger on the bridge of his nose, and the points of the two others on the lower part of the palm, fixed his eyes intently on the veins in the back of his left hand, and sat in this position like the immovable Theseus, who, as is well known to many who have not been at college, and to some few who have, *sedet, æternumque sedebit*.[1] We hope the admirers of the *minutiæ* in poetry and romance will appreciate this accurate description of a pensive attitude.

[1] Sits, and will sit for ever.

CHAPTER XIV

SCYTHROP was still in this position when Raven entered to announce that dinner was on table.

"I cannot come," said Scythrop.

Raven sighed. "Something is the matter," said Raven: "but man is born to trouble."

"Leave me," said Scythrop; "go, and croak elsewhere."

"Thus it is," said Raven. "Five-and-twenty years have I lived in Nightmare Abbey, and now all the reward of my affection is—Go, and croak elsewhere. I have danced you on my knee, and fed you with marrow."

"Good Raven," said Scythrop, "I entreat you to leave me."

"Shall I bring your dinner here?" said Raven. "A boiled fowl and a glass of Madeira are prescribed by the faculty in cases of low spirits. But you had better join the party: it is very much reduced already."

"Reduced! How?"

"The Honourable Mr. Listless is gone. He declared that, what with family quarrels in the morning, and ghosts at night, he could get neither sleep nor peace; and that the agitation was too much for his nerves: though Mr. Glowry assured him that the ghost was only poor Crow walking in his sleep, and that the shroud and bloody turban were a sheet and a red night-cap."

"Well, sir?"

"The Reverend Mr. Larynx has been called off on duty, to marry or bury (I don't know which) some unfortunate person or persons, at Claydyke: but man is born to trouble!"

"Is that all?"

"No. Mr. Toobad is gone too, and a strange lady with him."

"Gone!"

"Gone. And Mr. and Mrs. Hilary, and Miss O'Carroll: they are all gone. There is nobody left but Mr. Asterias and his son, and they are going to-night."

"Then I have lost them both!"

"Won't you come to dinner?"

"No."

"Shall I bring your dinner here?"

"Yes."

"What will you have?"

"A pint of port and a pistol." [1]

"A pistol!"

"And a pint of port. I will make my exit like Werter. Go. Stay. Did Miss O'Carroll say anything?"

"No."

"Did Miss Toobad say anything?"

"The strange lady? No."

"Did either of them cry?"

"No."

"What did they do?"

"Nothing."

"What did Mr. Toobad say?"

"He said, fifty times over, the devil was come among us."

"And they are gone?"

"Yes; and the dinner is getting cold. There is a time for everything under the sun. You may as well dine first, and be miserable afterwards."

"True, Raven. There is something in that. I will take your advice: therefore bring me——"

"The port and the pistol?"

"No; the boiled fowl and Madeira."

Scythrop had dined, and was sipping his Madeira alone, immersed in melancholy musing, when Mr. Glowry entered, followed by Raven, who, having placed an additional glass, and set a chair for Mr. Glowry, withdrew. Mr. Glowry sat down opposite Scythrop. After a pause, during which each filled and drank in silence, Mr. Glowry said, "So, sir, you have played your cards well. I proposed Miss Toobad to you: you refused her. Mr. Toobad proposed you to her: she refused you. You fell in love with Marionetta, and were going to poison yourself, because, from pure fatherly regard to your temporal interests, I withheld my consent. When, at length, I offered you my consent, you told me I was too precipitate. And, after all, I find you and Miss Toobad living together in the same tower, and behaving in every respect like two plighted lovers. Now,

[1] See "The Sorrows of Werter," Letter 93.

sir, if there be any rational solution of all this absurdity, I shall be very much obliged to you for a small glimmering of information."

"The solution, sir, is of little moment; but I will leave it in writing for your satisfaction. The crisis of my fate is come: the world is a stage, and my direction is *exit*."

"Do not talk so, sir;—do not talk so, Scythrop. What would you have?"

"I would have my love."

"And pray, sir, who is your love?"

"Celinda—Marionetta—either—both."

"Both! That may do very well in a German tragedy; and the Great Mogul might have found it very feasible in his lodgings at Kensington; but it will not do in Lincolnshire. Will you have Miss Toobad?"

"Yes."

"And renounce Marionetta?"

"No."

"But you must renounce one."

"I cannot."

"And you cannot have both. What is to be done?"

"I must shoot myself."

"Don't talk so, Scythrop. Be rational, my dear Scythrop. Consider, and make a cool, calm choice, and I will exert myself in your behalf."

"Why should I choose, sir? Both have renounced me: I have no hope of either."

"Tell me which you would have, and I will plead your cause irresistibly."

"Well, sir,—I will have—no, sir, I cannot renounce either. I cannot choose either. I am doomed to be the victim of eternal disappointments; and I have no resource but a pistol."

"Scythrop—Scythrop;—if one of them should come to you— what then?"

"That, sir, might alter the case: but that cannot be."

"It can be, Scythrop; it will be: I promise you it will be. Have but a little patience—but a week's patience; and it shall be."

"A week, sir, is an age: but, to oblige you, as a last act of filial duty, I will live another week. It is now Thursday evening, twenty-five minutes past seven. At this hour and minute, on Thursday next, love and fate shall smile on me, or I will drink my last pint of port in this world."

Mr. Glowry ordered his travelling-chariot, and departed from the abbey.

CHAPTER XV

THE day after Mr. Glowry's departure was one of incessant rain, and Scythrop repented of the promise he had given. The next day was one of bright sunshine: he sat on the terrace, read a tragedy of Sophocles, and was not sorry, when Raven announced dinner, to find himself alive. On the third evening, the wind blew, and the rain beat, and the owl flapped against his windows; and he put a new flint in his pistol. On the fourth day, the sun shone again; and he locked the pistol up in a drawer, where he left it undisturbed till the morning of the eventful Thursday, when he ascended the turret with a telescope, and spied anxiously along the road that crossed the fens from Claydyke: but nothing appeared on it. He watched in this manner from ten a.m. till Raven summoned him to dinner at five; when he stationed Crow at the telescope, and descended to his own funeral-feast. He left open the communications between the tower and the turret, and called aloud at intervals to Crow,—"Crow, Crow, is anything coming?" Crow answered, "The wind blows, and the windmills turn, but I see nothing coming;" and, at every answer, Scythrop found the necessity of raising his spirits with a bumper. After dinner, he gave Raven his watch to set by the abbey clock. Raven brought it, Scythrop placed it on the table, and Raven departed. Scythrop called again to Crow; and Crow, who had fallen asleep, answered mechanically, "I see nothing coming." Scythrop laid his pistol between his watch and his bottle. The hour-hand passed the VII.—the minute-hand moved on;—it was within three minutes of the appointed time. Scythrop called again to Crow. Crow answered as before. Scythrop rang the bell: Raven appeared.

"Raven," said Scythrop, "the clock is too fast."

"No, indeed," said Raven, who knew nothing of Scythrop's intentions; "if anything, it is too slow."

"Villain!" said Scythrop, pointing the pistol at him; "it is too fast!"

"Yes—yes—too fast, I meant," said Raven, in manifest fear.

"How much too fast?" said Scythrop.

"As much as you please," said Raven.

"How much, I say?" said Scythrop, pointing the pistol again.

"An hour, a full hour, sir," said the terrified butler.

"Put back my watch," said Scythrop.

Raven, with trembling hand, was putting back the watch, when the rattle of wheels was heard in the court; and Scythrop, springing downstairs by three steps together, was at the door in sufficient time to have handed either of the young ladies from the carriage, if she had happened to be in it; but Mr. Glowry was alone.

"I rejoice to see you," said Mr. Glowry; "I was fearful of being too late, for I waited till the last moment, in the hope of accomplishing my promise; but all my endeavours have been vain, as these letters will show."

Scythrop impatiently broke the seals. The contents were these:—

"Almost a stranger in England, I fled from parental tyranny, and the dread of an arbitrary marriage, to the protection of a stranger and a philosopher, whom I expected to find something better than, or at least something different from, the rest of his worthless species. Could I, after what has occurred, have expected nothing more from you than the commonplace impertinence of sending your father to treat with me, and with mine, for me? I should be a little moved in your favour, if I could believe you capable of carrying into effect the resolutions which your father says you have taken, in the event of my proving inflexible; though I doubt not you will execute them as far as relates to the pint of wine, twice over, at least. I wish you much happiness with Miss O'Carroll. I shall always cherish a grateful recollection of Nightmare Abbey, for having been the means of introducing me to a true transcendentalist; and, though he is a little older than myself, which is all one in Germany, I shall very soon have the pleasure of subscribing myself

                                        CELINDA FLOSKY."

"I hope, my dear cousin, that you will not be angry with me, but that you will always think of me as a sincere friend, who will always feel interested in your welfare; I am sure you love Miss Toobad much better than me, and I wish you much happiness with her. Mr. Listless assures me that people do not kill themselves for love nowadays, though it is still the fashion to talk about it. I shall, in a very short time, change my name and situation, and shall always be happy to see you in Berkeley Square, when, to the unalterable designation of your affectionate cousin, I shall subjoin the signature of

MARIONETTA LISTLESS."

Scythrop tore both the letters to atoms, and railed in good set terms against the fickleness of women.

"Calm yourself, my dear Scythrop," said Mr. Glowry; "there are yet maidens in England."

"Very true, sir," said Scythrop.

"And the next time," said Mr. Glowry, "have but one string to your bow."

"Very good advice," said Scythrop.

"And, besides," said Mr. Glowry, "the fatal time is past, for it is now almost eight."

"Then that villain Raven," said Scythrop, "deceived me, when he said that the clock was too fast; but, as you observe very justly, the time has gone by, and I have just reflected that these repeated crosses in love qualify me to take a very advanced degree in misanthropy; and there is, therefore, good hope that I may make a figure in the world. But I shall ring for the rascal Raven, and admonish him."

Raven appeared. Scythrop looked at him very fiercely two or three minutes; and Raven, still remembering the pistol, stood quaking in mute apprehension, till Scythrop, pointing significantly towards the dining-room, said, "Bring some Madeira."

Maid Marian

[I]

"THE ABBOT, in his alb arrayed," stood at the altar in the abbey-chapel of Rubygill, with all his plump, sleek, rosy friars, in goodly lines disposed, to solemnize the nuptials of the beautiful Matilda Fitzwater, daughter of the Baron of Arlingford, with the noble Robert Fitz-Ooth, Earl of Locksley and Huntingdon. The abbey of Rubygill stood in a picturesque valley, at a little distance from the western boundary of Sherwood Forest, in a spot which seemed adapted by nature to be the retreat of monastic mortification, being on the banks of a fine trout-stream, and in the midst of woodland coverts, abounding with excellent game. The bride, with her father and attendant maidens, entered the chapel; but the earl had not arrived. The baron was amazed, and the bridemaidens were disconcerted. Matilda feared that some evil had befallen her lover, but felt no diminution of her confidence in his honour and love. Through the open gates of the chapel she looked down the narrow road that wound along the side of the hill; and her ear was the first that heard the distant trampling of horses, and her eye was the first that caught the glitter of snowy plumes, and the light of polished spears. "It is strange," thought the baron, "that the earl should come in this martial array to his wedding;" but he had not long to meditate on the phenomenon, for the foaming steeds swept up to the gate like a whirlwind, and the earl, breathless with speed, and followed by a few of his yeomen, advanced to his smiling bride. It was then no time to ask questions, for the organ was in full peal, and the choristers were in full voice.

The abbot began to intone the ceremony in a style of modula-

184

tion impressively exalted, his voice issuing most canonically from the roof of his mouth, through the medium of a very musical nose, newly tuned for the occasion. But he had not proceeded far enough to exhibit all the variety and compass of this melodious instrument, when a noise was heard at the gate, and a party of armed men entered the chapel. The song of the choristers died away in a shake of demisemi-quavers, contrary to all the rules of psalmody. The organ-blower, who was working his musical air-pump with one hand, and with two fingers and a thumb of the other insinuating a peeping-place through the curtain of the organ-gallery, was struck motionless by the double operation of curiosity and fear; while the organist, intent only on his performance, and spreading all his fingers to strike a swell of magnificent chords, felt his harmonic spirit ready to desert his body on being answered by the ghastly rattle of empty keys, and in the consequent *agitato furioso* of the internal movements of his feelings, was prepared to restore harmony by the *segue subito* of an *appogiatura con foco* with a corner of a book of anthems on the head of his neglectful assistant, when his hand and his attention together were arrested by the scene below. The voice of the abbot subsided into silence through a descending scale of long-drawn melody, like the sound of the ebbing sea to the explorers of a cave. In a few moments all was silence, interrupted only by the iron tread of the armed intruders, as it rang on the marble floor and echoed from the vaulted aisles.

The leader strode up to the altar; and placing himself opposite to the abbot, and between the earl and Matilda, in such a manner that the four together seemed to stand on the four points of a diamond, exclaimed, "In the name of King Henry, I forbid the ceremony, and attach Robert Earl of Huntingdon as a traitor!" and, at the same time, he held his drawn sword between the lovers, as if to emblem that royal authority which laid its temporal ban upon their contract. The earl drew his own sword instantly, and struck down the interposing weapon; then clasped his left arm round Matilda, who sprang into his embrace, and held his sword before her with his right hand. His yeomen ranged themselves at his side, and stood with their swords drawn, still and prepared, like men determined to die in his defence. The soldiers, confident in superiority of numbers, paused. The abbot took advantage of the pause to introduce a word of exhortation. "My children," said he, "if you are going to cut each other's throats, I entreat you, in the name of peace and charity, to do it out of the chapel."

"Sweet Matilda," said the earl, "did you give your love to the Earl of Huntingdon, whose lands touch the Ouse and the Trent, or to Robert Fitz-Ooth, the son of his mother?"

"Neither to the earl nor his earldom," answered Matilda firmly, "but to Robert Fitz-Ooth and his love."

"That I well knew," said the earl; "and though the ceremony be incomplete, we are not the less married in the eye of my only saint, our Lady, who will yet bring us together. Lord Fitzwater, to your care, for the present, I commit your daughter.—Nay, sweet Matilda, part we must for a while; but we will soon meet under brighter skies, and be this the seal of our faith."

He kissed Matilda's lips, and consigned her to the baron, who glowered about him with an expression of countenance that showed he was mortally wroth with somebody; but whatever he thought or felt he kept to himself. The earl, with a sign to his followers, made a sudden charge on the soldiers, with the intention of cutting his way through. The soldiers were prepared for such an occurrence, and a desperate skirmish succeeded. Some of the women screamed, but none of them fainted; for fainting was not so much the fashion in those days, when the ladies breakfasted on brawn and ale at sunrise, as in our more refined age of green tea and muffins at noon. Matilda seemed disposed to fly again to her lover, but the baron forced her from the chapel. The earl's bowmen at the door sent in among the assailants a volley of arrows, one of which whizzed past the ear of the abbot, who, in mortal fear of being suddenly translated from a ghostly friar into a friarly ghost, began to roll out of the chapel as fast as his bulk and his holy robes would permit, roaring "Sacrilege!" with all his monks at his heels, who were, like himself, more intent to go at once than to stand upon the order of their going. The abbot, thus pressed from behind, and stumbling over his own drapery before, fell suddenly prostrate in the door-way that connected the chapel with the abbey, and was instantaneously buried under a pyramid of ghostly carcasses, that fell over him and each other, and lay a rolling chaos of animated rotundities, sprawling and bawling in unseemly disarray, and sending forth the names of all the saints in and out of heaven, amidst the clashing of swords, the ringing of bucklers, the clattering of helmets, the twanging of bow strings, the whizzing of arrows, the screams of women, the shouts of the warriors, and the vociferations of the peasantry, who had been assembled to the intended nuptials, and who, seeing a fair set-to, contrived to pick a quarrel among themselves on the occasion, and proceeded, with staff and cudgel, to crack each other's skulls for the good of the king and the earl. One tall friar alone was untouched by the panic of his brethren, and stood steadfastly watching the combat with his arms akimbo, the colossal emblem of an unarmed neutrality.

At length, through the midst of the internal confusion, the earl, by the help of his good sword, the staunch valour of his men, and the blessing of the Virgin, fought his way to the chapel-gate—his bowmen closed him in—he vaulted into his saddle, clapped spurs to his horse, rallied his men on the first eminence, and exchanged his sword for a bow and arrow, with which he did bold execution among the pursuers, who at last thought it most expedient to desist from offensive warfare, and to retreat into the abbey, where, in the king's name, they broached a pipe of the best wine, and attached all the venison in the larder, having first carefully unpacked the tuft of friars, and set the fallen abbot on his legs.

The friars, it may be well supposed, and such of the king's men as escaped unhurt from the affray, found their spirits a cup too low, and kept the flask moving from noon till night. The peaceful brethren, unused to the tumult of war, had undergone, from fear and discomposure, an exhaustion of animal spirits that required extraordinary refection. During the repast, they interrogated Sir Ralph Montfaucon, the leader of the soldiers, respecting the nature of the earl's offence.

"A complication of offences," replied Sir Ralph, "superinduced on the original basis of forest-treason. He began with hunting the king's deer, in despite of all remonstrance; followed it up by contempt of the king's mandates, and by armed resistance to his power, in defiance of all authority; and combined with it the resolute withholding of payment of certain moneys to the abbot of Doncaster, in denial of all law; and has thus made himself the declared enemy of church and state, and all for being too fond of venison." And the knight helped himself to half a pasty.

"A heinous offender," said a little round oily friar, appropriating the portion of pasty which Sir Ralph had left.

"The earl is a worthy peer," said the tall friar whom we have already mentioned in the chapel scene, "and the best marksman in England."

"Why this is flat treason, Brother Michael," said the little round friar, "to call an attainted traitor a worthy peer."

"I pledge you," said Brother Michael. The little friar smiled and filled his cup. "He will draw the long-bow," pursued Brother Michael, "with any bold yeoman among them all."

"Don't talk of the long-bow," said the abbot, who had the sound of the arrow still whizzing in his ear: "what have we pillars of the faith to do with the long-bow?"

"Be that as it may," said Sir Ralph, "he is an outlaw from this moment."

"So much the worse for the law then," said Brother Michael. "The law will have a heavier miss of him than he will have of the law. He will strike as much venison as ever, and more of other game. I know what I say; but *basta*: Let us drink."

"What other game?" said the little friar. "I hope he won't poach among our partridges."

"Poach! not he," said Brother Michael: "if he wants your partridges, he will strike them under your nose (here's to you), and drag your trout-stream for you on a Thursday evening."

"Monstrous! and starve us on fast-day," said the little friar.

"But that is not the game I mean," said Brother Michael.

"Surely, son Michael," said the abbot, "you do not mean to insinuate that the noble earl will turn freebooter?"

"A man must live," said Brother Michael, "earl or no. If the law takes his rents and beeves without his consent, he must take beeves and rents where he can get them without the consent of the law. This is the *lex talionis*."

"Truly," said Sir Ralph, "I am sorry for the damsel: she seems fond of this wild runagate."

"A mad girl, a mad girl," said the little friar.

"How a mad girl?" said Brother Michael. "Has she not beauty, grace, wit, sense, discretion, dexterity, learning, and valour?"

"Learning!" exclaimed the little friar; "what has a woman to do with learning? And valour! who ever heard a woman commended for valour? Meekness, and mildness, and softness, and gentleness, and tenderness, and humility, and obedience to her husband, and faith in her confessor, and domesticity, or, as learned doctors call it, the faculty of stayathomeitiveness, and embroidery, and music, and pickling, and preserving, and the whole complex and multiplex detail of the noble science of dinner, as well in preparation for the table, as in arrangement over it, and in distribution around it to knights, and squires, and ghostly friars,—these are female virtues: but valour— why who ever heard——?"

"She is the all in all," said Brother Michael, "gentle as a ring-dove, yet high-soaring as a falcon: humble below her deserving, yet deserving beyond the estimate of panegyric: an exact economist in all superfluity, yet a most bountiful dispenser in all liberality: the chief regulator of her household, the fairest pillar of her hall, and the sweetest blossom of her bower: having, in all opposite proposings, sense to understand, judgment to weigh, discretion to choose, firmness to undertake, diligence to conduct, perseverance to accomplish, and resolution to maintain. For obedience to her husband, that is not to be tried till she has one: for faith in her confessor, she has as much as the law prescribes: for embroidery an Arachne: for music a Siren: and for pickling and preserving, did not one of her jars of sugared apricots give you your last surfeit at Arlingford Castle?"

"Call you that preserving?" said the little friar; "I call it destroying. Call you it pickling? Truly it pickled me. My life was saved by miracle."

"By canary," said Brother Michael. "Canary is the only life preserver, the true aurum potabile, the universal panacea for all diseases, thirst, and short life. Your life was saved by canary."

"Indeed, reverend father," said Sir Ralph, "if the young lady be half what you describe, she must be a paragon: but your commending her for valour does somewhat amaze me."

"She can fence," said the little friar, "and draw the long-bow, and play at single-stick and quarter-staff."

"Yet mark you," said Brother Michael, "not like a virago or a hoyden, or one that would crack a serving-man's head for spilling gravy on her ruff, but with such womanly grace and temperate self-command as if those manly exercises belonged to her only, and were become for her sake feminine."

"You incite me," said Sir Ralph, "to view her more nearly. That madcap earl found me other employment than to remark her in the chapel."

"The earl is a worthy peer," said Brother Michael; "he is worth any fourteen earls on this side Trent, and any seven on the other." (The reader will please to remember that Rubygill Abbey was *north* of Trent.)

"His mettle will be tried," said Sir Ralph. "There is many a courtier will swear to King Henry to bring him in dead or alive."

"They must look to the brambles then," said Brother Michael.

> "The bramble, the bramble, the bonny forest bramble,
>   Doth make a jest
>   Of silken vest,
>   That will through greenwood scramble:
>   The bramble, the bramble, the bonny forest bramble."

"Plague on your lungs, son Michael," said the abbot; "this is your old coil: always roaring in your cups."

"I know what I say," said Brother Michael; "there is often more sense in an old song than in a new homily.

> "The courtly pad doth amble,
>   When his gay lord would ramble:
>   But both may catch
>   An awkward scratch,
>   If they ride among the bramble:
>   The bramble, the bramble, the bonny forest bramble."

"Tall friar," said Sir Ralph, "either you shoot the shafts of your merriment at random, or you know more of the earl's designs than beseems your frock."

"Let my frock," said Brother Michael, "answer for its own sins. It is worn past covering mine. It is too weak for a shield, too transparent for a screen, too thin for a shelter, too light for gravity, and too threadbare for a jest. The wearer would be naught indeed who should mis-beseem such a wedding garment.

"But wherefore does the sheep wear wool?
That he in season sheared may be,
And the shepherd be warm though his flock be cool:
So I'll have a new cloak about me."

[II]

THE Earl of Huntingdon, living in the vicinity of a royal forest, and passionately attached to the chase from his infancy, had long made as free with the king's deer as Lord Percy proposed to do with those of Lord Douglas in the memorable hunting of Cheviot. It is sufficiently well known how severe were the forest laws in those days, and with what jealousy the kings of England maintained this branch of their prerogative; but menaces and remonstrances were thrown away on the earl, who declared that he would not thank Saint Peter for admission into Paradise, if he were obliged to leave his bow and hounds at the gate. King Henry (the Second) swore by Saint Botolph to make him rue his sport, and, having caused him to be duly and formally accused, summoned him to London to answer the charge. The earl, deeming himself safer among his own vassals than among King Henry's courtiers, took no notice of the mandate. King Henry sent a force to bring him, vi et armis, to court. The earl made a resolute resistance, and put the king's forces to flight under a shower of arrows: an act which the courtiers declared to be treason. At the same time the abbot of Doncaster sued up the payment of certain moneys, which the earl, whose revenue ran a losing race with his hospitality, had borrowed at sundry times of the said abbot: for the abbots and the bishops were the chief usurers of those days, and, as the end sanctifies the means, were not in the least scrupulous of employing what would have been extortion in the profane, to accomplish the pious purpose of bringing a blessing on the land by rescuing it from the frail hold of carnal and temporal into the firmer grasp of ghostly and spiritual possessors. But the earl, confident in the number and attachment of his retainers, stoutly refused either to repay the money, which he could not, or to yield the forfeiture, which he would not: a refusal which in those days was an act of outlawry in a gentleman, as it is now of bankruptcy in a base mechanic; the gentleman having in our wiser times a more liberal privilege of gentility, which enables him to keep his lands, and laugh at his creditor. Thus the mutual resentments and interests of the king and the abbot concurred to subject the earl to the penalties of outlawry, by which the abbot would gain his due upon the lands of Locksley, and the rest would be confiscate to the king. Still the king did not think it advisable to assail the earl in his own stronghold, but caused a diligent watch to be kept over his motions, till at length his rumoured marriage with the heiress of Arlingford seemed to point out an easy method of laying violent hands on the offender. Sir Ralph Montfaucon, a young man of good lineage and of an aspiring temper, who readily seized the first opportunity that offered of recommending himself to King Henry's favour by manifesting his zeal in his service, undertook the charge: and how he succeeded we have seen.

Sir Ralph's curiosity was strongly excited by the friar's description of the young lady of Arlingford, and he prepared in the morning to visit the castle, under the very plausible pretext of giving the baron an explanation of his intervention at the nuptials. Brother Michael and the little fat friar proposed to be his guides. The proposal was courteously accepted, and they set out together, leaving Sir Ralph's followers at the abbey. The knight was mounted on a spirited charger; Brother Michael on a large, heavy-trotting horse; and the little fat friar on a plump, soft-paced galloway, so correspondent with himself in size, rotundity, and sleekness, that if they had been amalgamated into a centaur, there would have been nothing to alter in their proportions.

"Do you know," said the little friar, as they wound along the banks of the stream, "the reason why lake-trout is better than river-trout and shyer withal?"

"I was not aware of the fact," said Sir Ralph.

"A most heterodox remark," said Brother Michael; "know you not, that in all nice matters you should take the implication for absolute, and, without looking into the fact *whether*, seek only the *reason why?* But the fact is so, on the word of a friar; which what layman will venture to gainsay who prefers a down bed to a gridiron?"

"The fact being so," said the knight, "I am still at a loss for the reason; nor would I undertake to opine in a matter of that magnitude: since, in all that appertains to the good things either of this world or the next, my reverend spiritual guides are kind enough to take the trouble of thinking off my hands."

"Spoken," said Brother Michael, "with a sound Catholic conscience. My little brother here is most profound in the matter of trout. He has marked, learned, and inwardly digested the subject, twice a week at least for five-and-thirty years. I yield to him in this. My strong points are venison and canary."

"The good qualities of a trout," said the little friar, "are firmness and redness, redness, indeed, being the visible sign of all other virtues."

"Whence," said Brother Michael, "we choose our abbot by his nose:

"The rose on the nose does all virtues disclose:
For the outward grace shows
That the inward o'erflows
When it glows in the rose of a red, red nose."

"Now," said the little friar, "as is the firmness, so is the redness, and as is the redness, so is the shyness."

"Marry why?" said Brother Michael. "The solution is not physical-natural, but physical-historical, or natural super-inductive. And thereby hangs a tale, which may be either said or sung:

"The damsel stood to watch the fight
By the banks of Kingslea Mere,
And they brought to her feet her own true knight
Sore wounded on a bier.

"She knelt by him his wounds to bind,
She washed them with many a tear;
And shouts rose fast upon the wind,
Which told that the foe was near.

" 'Oh! let not,' he said, 'while yet I live,
The cruel foe me take:
But with thy sweet lips a last kiss give,
And cast me in the lake.'

"Around his neck she wound her arms,
And she kissed his lips so pale:

And evermore the war's alarms
Came louder up the vale.

"She drew him to the lake's steep side,
    Where the red heath fringed the shore;
She plunged with him beneath the tide,
    And they were seen no more.

"Their true blood mingled in Kingslea Mere,
    That to mingle on earth was fain:
And the trout that swims in the crystal clear
    Is tinged with the crimson stain.

"Thus, you see how good comes of evil, and how a holy friar may fare better on fast-day for the violent death of two lovers two hundred years ago. The inference is most consecutive, that wherever you catch a red-fleshed trout, love lies bleeding under the water: an occult quality, which can only act in the stationary waters of a lake, being neutralized by the rapid transition of those of a stream."

"And why is the trout shyer for that?" asked Sir Ralph.

"Do you not see?" said Brother Michael. "The virtues of both lovers diffuse themselves through the lake. The infusion of masculine valour makes the fish active and sanguineous: the infusion of maiden modesty makes him coy and hard to win: and you shall find through life, the fish which is most easily hooked is not the best worth dishing. But yonder are the towers of Arlingford."

The little friar stopped. He seemed suddenly struck with an awful thought, which caused a momentary palescence in his rosy complexion; and after a brief hesitation, he turned his galloway, and told his companions he should bid them good-day.

"Why, what is in the wind now, Brother Peter?" said Friar Michael.

"The Lady Matilda," said the little friar, "can draw the long-bow. She must bear no goodwill to Sir Ralph; and if she should espy him from her tower, she may testify her recognition with cloth-yard shaft. She is not so infallible a markswoman, but that she might shoot at a crow, and kill a pigeon. She might peradventure miss the knight, and hit me, who never did her any harm."

"Tut, tut, man," said Brother Michael, "there is no such fear."

"Mass," said the little friar, "but there is such a fear, and very strong too. You who have it not may keep your way, and I who have it shall take mine. I am not just now in the vein for being picked off at a long shot." And saying these words, he spurred up his four-footed better-half, and galloped off as nimbly as if he heard an arrow singing behind him.

"Is this Lady Matilda, then, so very terrible a damsel?" said Sir Ralph to Brother Michael.

"By no means," said the friar. "She has certainly a high spirit; but it is the wing of the eagle, without his beak or his claw. She is as gentle as magnanimous; but it is the gentleness of the summer wind, which, however lightly it wave the tuft of the pine, carries with it the intimation of a power, that, if roused to its extremity, could make it bend to the dust."

"From the warmth of your panegyric, ghostly father," said the knight, "I should almost suspect you were in love with the damsel."

"So I am," said the friar, "and I care not who knows it; but all in the way of honesty, master soldier. I am, as it were, her spiritual lover; and were she a damsel errant, I would be her ghostly esquire, her friar militant. I would buckle me in armour of proof, and the devil might thresh me black with an iron flail before I would knock under in her cause. Though they be not yet one canonically, thanks to your soldiership, the earl is her liege lord, and she is his liege lady. I am her father confessor and ghostly director: I have taken on me to show her the way to the next world; and how can I do that if I lose sight of her in this? seeing that this is but the road to the other, and has so many circumvolutions and ramifications of by-ways and beaten paths (all more thickly set than the true one with finger-posts and milestones, not one of which tells truth), that a traveller has need of some one who knows the way, or the odds go hard against him that he will ever see the face of Saint Peter."

"But there must surely be some reason," said Sir Ralph, "for Father Peter's apprehension."

"None," said Brother Michael, "but the apprehension itself; fear being its own father, and most prolific in self-propagation. The lady did, it is true, once signalize her displeasure against our little brother, for reprimanding her in that she would go hunting a-mornings instead of attending matins. She cut short the thread of his eloquence by sportively drawing her bow-string, and loosing an arrow over his

head; he waddled off with singular speed, and was in much awe of
her for many months. I thought he had forgotten it: but let that
pass. In truth, she would have had little of her lover's company, if
she had liked the chaunt of the choristers better than the cry of the
hounds: yet I know not; for they were companions from the cradle,
and reciprocally fashioned each other to the love of the fern and the
foxglove. Had either been less sylvan, the other might have been
more saintly: but they will now never hear matins but those of the
lark, nor reverence vaulted aisle but that of the greenwood canopy.
They are twin plants of the forest and are identified with its growth.

"For the tender beech and the sapling oak,
    That grow by the shadowy rill,
You may cut down both at a single stroke,
    You may cut down which you will.

"But this you must know, that as long as they grow,
    Whatever change may be,
You never can teach either oak or beech
    To be aught but a greenwood tree."

[III]

THE knight and the friar arrived at Arlingford Castle, and leaving
their horses in the care of Lady Matilda's groom, with whom the
friar was in great favour, were ushered into a stately apartment, where
they found the baron alone, flourishing an enormous carving-knive
over a brother baron—of beef—with as much vehemence of action as
if he were cutting down an enemy. The baron was a gentleman of a
fierce and choleric temperament: he was lineally descended from the
redoubtable Fireabras of Normandy, who came over to England with
the Conqueror, and who, in the battle of Hastings, killed with his
own hand four-and-twenty Saxon cavaliers all on a row. The very
excess of the baron's internal rage on the preceding day had smothered its external manifestation: he was so equally angry with both
parties, that he knew not on which to vent his wrath. He was enraged with the earl for having brought himself into such a dilemma
without his privity; and he was no less enraged with the king's men

for their very unseasonable intrusion. He could willingly have fallen on both parties, but he must necessarily have begun with one; and he felt that on whichever side he should strike the first blow, his retainers would immediately join battle. He had therefore contented himself with forcing away his daughter from the scene of action. In the course of the evening he had received intelligence that the earl's castle was in possession of a party of the king's men, who had been detached by Sir Ralph Montfaucon to seize on it during the earl's absence. The baron inferred from this that the earl's case was desperate; and those who have had the opportunity of seeing a rich friend fall suddenly into poverty, may easily judge by their own feelings how quickly and completely the whole moral being of the earl was changed in the baron's estimation. The baron immediately proceeded to require in his daughter's mind the same summary revolution that had taken place in his own, and considered himself exceedingly ill-used by her non-complance. The lady had retired to her chamber, and the baron had passed a supperless and sleepless night, stalking about his apartments till an advanced hour of the morning, when hunger compelled him to summon into his presence the spoils of the buttery, which, being the intended array of an uneaten wedding feast, were more than usually abundant, and on which, when the knight and the friar entered, he was falling with desperate valour. He looked up at them fiercely, with his mouth full of beef and his eyes full of flame, and rising, as ceremony required, made an awful bow to the knight, inclining himself forward over the table, and presenting his carving-knife en militaire, in a manner that seemed to leave it doubtful whether he meant to show respect to his visitor, or to defend his provision: but the doubt was soon cleared up by his politely motioning the knight to be seated; on which the friar advanced to the table, saying, "For what we are going to receive," and commenced operations without further prelude by filling and drinking a goblet of wine. The baron at the same time offered one to Sir Ralph, with the look of a man in whom habitual hospitality and courtesy were struggling with the ebullitions of natural anger. They pledged each other in silence, and the baron, having completed a copious draught, continued working his lips and his throat, as if trying to swallow his wrath as he had done his wine. Sir Ralph, not knowing well what to make of these ambiguous signs, looked for instructions to the friar, who by significant looks and gestures seemed to advise him to follow his example and partake of the good cheer before him, without speaking till the baron should be more intelligible in his demeanour. The knight and the friar, accordingly, proceeded to refect themselves after their ride; the baron looking first at the one and then at the other, scrutinizing alternately the serious looks of the knight and the merry face of the friar, till at length, having calmed himself sufficiently to speak, he said, "Courteous knight and ghostly father, I presume you have some other business with me than to eat my beef and drink my canary; and if so, I patiently await your leisure to enter on the topic."

"Lord Fitzwater," said Sir Ralph, "in obedience to my royal master, King Henry, I have been the unwilling instrument of frustrating the intended nuptials of your fair daughter; yet will you, I trust, owe me no displeasure for my agency herein, seeing that the noble maiden might otherwise by this time have been the bride of an outlaw."

"I am very much obliged to you, sir," said the baron; "very exceedingly obliged. Your solicitude for my daughter is truly paternal, and for a young man and a stranger very singular and exemplary: and it is very kind withal to come to the relief of my insufficiency and inexperience, and concern yourself so much in that which concerns you not."

"You misconceive the knight, noble baron," said the friar. "He urges not his reason in the shape of a preconceived intent, but in that of a subsequent extenuation. True, he has done the Lady Matilda great wrong——"

"How great wrong?" said the baron. "What do you mean by great wrong? Would you have had her married to a wild fly-by-night, that accident made an earl and nature a deer-stealer? that has not wit enough to eat venison without picking a quarrel with monarchy? that flings away his own lands into the clutches of rascally friars, for the sake of hunting in other men's grounds, and feasting vagabonds that wear Lincoln green, and would have flung away mine into the bargain if he had had my daughter? What do you mean by great wrong?"

"True," said the friar: "great right, I meant."

"Right!" exclaimed the baron: "what right has any man to do my daughter right but myself? What right has any man to drive my daughter's bridegroom out of the chapel in the middle of the marriage ceremony, and turn all our merry faces into green wounds and bloody cockscombs, and then come and tell me he has done us great right?"

"True," said the friar: "he has done neither right nor wrong."

"But he has," said the baron, "he has done both, and I will maintain it with my glove."

"It shall not need," said Sir Ralph; "I will concede anything in honour."

"And I," said the baron, "will concede nothing in honour: I will concede nothing in honour to any man."

"Neither will I, Lord Fitzwater," said Sir Ralph, "in that sense: but hear me. I was commissioned by the king to apprehend the Earl of Huntingdon. I brought with me a party of soldiers, picked and tried men, knowing that he would not lightly yield. I sent my lieutenant with a detachment to surprise the earl's castle in his absence, and laid my measures for intercepting him on the way to his intended nuptials; but he seems to have had intimation of this part of my plan, for he brought with him a large armed retinue, and took a circuitous route, which made him, I believe, somewhat later than his appointed hour. When the lapse of time showed me that he had taken another track, I pursued him to the chapel; and I would have awaited the close of the ceremony, if I had thought that either yourself or your daughter would have felt desirous that she should have been the bride of an outlaw."

"Who said, sir," cried the baron, "that we were desirous of any such thing? But truly, sir, if I had a mind to the devil for a son-in-law, I would fain see the man that should venture to interfere."

"That would I," said the friar; "for I have undertaken to make her renounce the devil."

"She shall not renounce the devil," said the baron, "unless I please. You are very ready with your undertakings. Will you undertake to make her renounce the earl, who, I believe, is the devil incarnate? Will you undertake that?"

"Will I undertake," said the friar, "to make Trent run westward, or to make flame burn downward, or to make a tree grow with its head in the earth, and its root in the air?"

"So then," said the baron, "a girl's mind is as hard to change as nature and the elements, and it is easier to make her renounce the devil than a lover. Are you a match for the devil, and no match for a man?"

"My warfare," said the friar, "is not of this world. I am a militant, not against man, but the devil, who goes about seeking what he may devour."

"Oh! does he so?" said the baron: "then I take it that makes you look for him so often in my buttery. Will you cast out the devil whose name is Legion, when you cannot cast out the imp whose name is Love?"

"Marriages," said the friar, "are made in heaven. Love is God's work, and therewith I meddle not."

"God's work, indeed!" said the baron, "when the ceremony was cut short in the church. Could men have put them asunder if God had joined them together? And the earl is now no earl, but plain Robert Fitz-Ooth: therefore, I'll none of him."

"He may atone," said the friar, "and the king may mollify. The earl is a worthy peer, and the king is a courteous king."

"He cannot atone," said Sir Ralph. "He has killed the king's men; and if the baron should aid and abet, he will lose his castle and land."

"Will I?" said the baron. "Not while I have a drop of blood in my veins. He that comes to take them shall first serve me as the friar serves my flasks of canary: he shall drain me dry as hay. Am I not disparaged? Am I not outraged? Is not my daughter vilified and made a mockery? A girl half-married? There was my butler brought home with a broken head. My butler, friar: there is that may move your sympathy. Friar, the earl-no-earl shall come no more to my daughter."

"Very good," said the friar.

"It is not very good," said the baron, "for I cannot get her to say so."

"I fear," said Sir Ralph, "the young lady must be much distressed and discomposed."

"Not a whit, sir," said the baron. "She is, as usual, in a most provoking imperturbability, and contradicts me so smilingly that it would enrage you to see her."

"I had hoped," said Sir Ralph, "that I might have seen her, to make my excuse in person for the hard necessity of my duty."

He had scarcely spoken, when the door opened, and the lady made her appearance.

[IV]

MATILDA, not dreaming of visitors, tripped into the apartment, in a dress of forest green, with a small quiver by her side, and a bow and arrow in her hand. Her hair, black and glossy as the raven's wing, curled like wandering clusters of dark ripe grapes under the edge of her round bonnet; and a plume of black feathers fell back negligently above it, with an almost horizontal inclination, that seemed the habitual effect of rapid motion against the wind. Her black eyes sparkled like sunbeams on a river: a clear, deep, liquid radiance, the reflection of ethereal fire,—tempered, not subdued, in the medium of its living and gentle mirror. Her lips were half-opened to speak as she entered the apartment; and with a smile of recognition to the friar, and a courtesy to the stranger knight, she approached the baron, and said, "You are late at your breakfast, father."

"I am not at breakfast," said the baron. "I have been at supper: my last night's supper; for I had none."

"I am sorry," said Matilda, "you should have gone to bed supperless."

"I did not go to bed supperless," said the baron; "I did not go to bed at all: and what are you doing with that green dress and that bow and arrow?"

"I am going a-hunting," said Matilda.

"A-hunting!" said the baron. "What, I warrant you, to meet with the earl, and slip your neck into the same noose?"

"No," said Matilda, "I am not going out of our own woods to-day."

"How do I know that?" said the baron. "What surety have I of that?"

"Here is the friar," said Matilda. "He will be surety."

"Not he," said the baron: "he will undertake nothing but where the devil is a party concerned."

"Yes, I will," said the friar: "I will undertake anything for the Lady Matilda."

"No matter for that" said the baron: "she shall not go hunting to-day."

"Why, father," said Matilda, "if you coop me up here in this odious castle, I shall pine and die like a lonely swan on a pool."

"No," said the baron, "the lonely swan does not die on the pool. If there be a river at hand, she flies to the river, and finds her a mate; and so shall not you."

"But," said Matilda, "you may send with me any, or as many, of your grooms as you will."

"My grooms," said the baron, "are all false knaves. There is not a rascal among them but loves you better than me. Villains that I feed and clothe."

"Surely," said Matilda, "it is not villany to love me: if it be, I should be sorry my father were an honest man." The baron relaxed his muscles into a smile. "Or my lover either," added Matilda. The baron looked grim again.

"For your lover," said the baron, "you may give God thanks of him. He is as arrant a knave as ever poached."

"What, for hunting the king's deer?" said Matilda. "Have I not heard you rail at the forest laws by the hour?"

"Did you ever hear me," said the baron, "rail myself out of house and land? If I had done that, then were I a knave."

"My lover," said Matilda, "is a brave man, and a true man, and a generous man, and a young man, and a handsome man; ay, and an honest man too."

"How can he be an honest man," said the baron, "when he has neither house nor land, which are the better part of a man?"

"They are but the husk of a man," said Matilda, "the worthless coat of the chestnut; the man himself is the kernel."

"The man is the grape stone," said the baron, "and the pulp of the melon. The house and land are the true substantial fruit, and all that give him savour and value."

"He will never want house or land," said Matilda, "while the meeting boughs weave a green roof in the wood, and the free range of the hart marks out the bounds of the forest."

"Vert and venison! vert and venison!" exclaimed the baron.

"Treason and flat rebellion. Confound your smiling face! what makes you look so good-humoured? What! you think I can't look at you, and be in a passion? You think so, do you? We shall see. Have you no fear in talking thus, when here is the king's liegeman come to take us all into custody, and confiscate our goods and chattels?"

"Nay, Lord Fitzwater," said Sir Ralph, "you wrong me in your report. My visit is one of courtesy and excuse, not of menace and authority."

"There it is," said the baron: "every one takes a pleasure in contradicting me. Here is this courteous knight, who has not opened his mouth three times since he has been in my house except to take in provision, cuts me short in my story with a flat denial."

"Oh! I cry you mercy, sir knight," said Matilda; "I did not mark you before. I am your debtor for no slight favour, and so is my liege lord."

"Her liege lord!" exclaimed the baron, taking large strides across the chamber.

"Pardon me, gentle lady," said Sir Ralph. "Had I known you before yesterday, I would have cut off my right hand ere it should have been raised to do you displeasure."

"Oh, sir," said Matilda, "a good man may be forced on an ill office: but I can distinguish the man from his duty." She presented to him her hand, which he kissed respectfully, and simultaneously with the contact thirty-two invisible arrows plunged at once into his heart, one from every point of the compass of his pericardia.

"Well, father," added Matilda, "I must go to the woods."

"Must you?" said the baron; "I say you must not."

"But I am going," said Matilda.

"But I will have up the drawbridge," said the baron.

"But I will swim the moat," said Matilda.

"But I will secure the gates," said the baron.

"But I will leap from the battlement," said Matilda.

"But I will lock you in an upper chamber," said the baron.

"But I will shred the tapestry," said Matilda, "and let myself down."

"But I will lock you in a turret," said the baron, "where you shall only see light through a loophole."

"But through that loophole," said Matilda, "will I take my flight, like a young eagle from its eyrie; and, father, while I go out freely, I will return willingly: but if once I slip out through a loop-hole——" She paused a moment, and then added, singing,—

"The love that follows fain
Will never its faith betray:
But the faith that is held in a chain
Will never be found again,
If a single link give way."

The melody acted irresistibly on the harmonious propensities of the friar, who accordingly sang in his turn,—

"For hark! hark! hark!
The dog doth bark,
That watches the wild deer's lair.
The hunter awakes at the peep of the dawn,
But the lair it is empty, the deer it is gone,
And the hunter knows not where."

Matilda and the friar then sang together,—

"Then follow, oh follow! the hounds do cry:
The red sun flames in the eastern sky;
The stag bounds over the hollow.
He that lingers in spirit, or loiters in hall,
Shall see us no more till the evening fall,
And no voice but the echo shall answer his call:
Then follow, oh follow, follow:
Follow, oh follow, follow!"

During the process of this harmony, the baron's eyes wandered from his daughter to the friar, and from the friar to his daughter again, with an alternate expression of anger differently modified: when he looked on the friar, it was anger without qualification; when he looked on his daughter it was still anger, but tempered by an expression of involuntary admiration and pleasure. These rapid fluctuations of the baron's physiognomy—the habitual, reckless, resolute merriment in the jovial face of the friar,—and the cheerful, elastic spirits that played on the lips and sparkled in the eyes of Matilda,—would have presented a very amusing combination to Sir Ralph, if one of the three images in the group had not absorbed his total attention with feelings of intense delight very nearly allied to pain. The baron's wrath was somewhat counteracted by the reflection that his daughter's good spirits seemed to show that they would naturally rise triumphant over all disappointments; and he had had sufficient experience of her humour to know that she might sometimes be led, but never could be driven. Then, too, he was always delighted to hear her sing, though he was not at all pleased in this instance with the subject of her song. Still he would have endured the subject for the sake of the melody of the treble, but his mind was not sufficiently attuned to unison to relish the harmony of the bass. The friar's accompaniment put him out of all patience, and—"So," he exclaimed, "this is the way you teach my daughter to renounce the devil, is it? A hunting friar, truly! Who ever heard before of a hunting friar? A profane, roaring, bawling, bumper-bibbing, neck-breaking, catch-singing friar?"

"Under favour, bold baron," said the friar; but the friar was warm with canary, and in his singing vein; and he could not go on in plain unmusical prose. He therefore sang in a new tune,—

"Though I be now a gray, gray friar,
  Yet I was once a hale young knight:
The cry of my dogs was the only choir
  In which my spirit did take delight.

"Little I recked of matin bell,
  But drowned its toll with my clanging horn:
And the only beads I loved to tell
  Were the beads of dew on the spangled thorn."

The baron was going to storm, but the friar paused, and Matilda sang in repetition,—

"Little I reck of matin bell,
  But drown its toll with my clanging horn:
And the only beads I love to tell
  Are the beads of dew on the spangled thorn."

And then she and the friar sang the four lines together, and rang the changes upon them alternately.

"Little I reck of matin bell,"
sang the friar.

"A precious friar," said the baron.

"But drown its toll with my clanging horn,"

sang Matilda.
"More shame for you," said the baron.

"And the only beads I love to tell
    Are the beads of dew on the spangled thorn,"

sang Matilda and the friar together.
"Penitent and confessor," said the baron: "a hopeful pair truly."
The friar went on,—

"An archer keen I was withal,
    As ever did lean on greenwood tree,
And could make the fleetest roebuck fall,
    A good three hundred yards from me.
Though changeful time, with hand severe,
    Has made me now these joys forego,
Yet my heart bounds whene'er I hear
    Yoicks! hark away! and tally ho!"

Matilda chimed in as before.
"Are you mad?" said the baron. "Are you insane? Are you possessed? What do you mean? What in the devil's name do you both mean?"

"Yoicks! hark away! and tally ho!"

roared the friar.
The baron's pent-up wrath had accumulated like the waters above the dam of an overshot mill. The pond-head of his passion being now filled to the utmost limit of its capacity, and beginning to overflow in the quivering of his lips and the flashing of his eyes, he pulled up all the flash-boards at once, and gave loose to the full torrent of his indignation, by seizing, like furious Ajax, not a massy stone more than two modern men could raise, but a vast dish of beef more than fifty ancient yeomen could eat, and whirled it like a quoit, *in*

terrorem, over the head of the friar, to the extremity of the apartment,

> Where it on oaken floor did settle,
> With mighty din of ponderous metal.

"Nay, father," said Matilda, taking the baron's hand, "do not harm the friar: he means not to offend you. My gaiety never before displeased you. Least of all should it do so now, when I have need of all my spirits to outweigh the severity of my fortune."

As she spoke the last words, tears started into her eyes, which, as if ashamed of the involuntary betraying of her feelings, she turned away to conceal. The baron was subdued at once. He kissed his daughter, held out his hand to the friar, and said, "Sing on, in God's name, and crack away the flasks till your voice swims in canary." Then turning to Sir Ralph, he said, "You see how it is, sir knight. Matilda is my daughter; but she has me in leading-strings, that is the truth of it."

[Matilda, having received her father's permission to range at liberty, under promise to return home, meets up with her outlaw lover and assists him in a vigorous skirmish with Sir Ralph Montfaucon and the Sheriff of Nottingham, in which the forces of the law are routed. Whereupon, ministers of justice arrive before Arlingford Castle with orders to apprehend the person of Matilda Fitzwater, but they are rudely sent about their business by the baron. The king's men, however, succeed in seizing another of Robin Hood's friends, young William Gamwell, of Gamwell Hall, who is condemned to be hanged at Nottingham, but who is snatched from the scaffold by the Sherwood foresters, and taken into their company under the name of Scarlet. King Henry dies, Richard Cœur-de-Lion goes crusading, and the usurper John, busy with military operations round Nottingham, is smitten with the charms of Matilda. Repulsed, he swears that arms will succeed where persuasion has failed.]

[V]

PRINCE JOHN sat down impatiently before Arlingford Castle in the hope of starving out the besieged; but finding the duration of their supplies extend itself in an equal ratio with the prolongation of his hope, he made vigorous preparations for carrying the place by storm. He constructed an immense machine on wheels, which, being advanced to the edge of the moat, would lower a temporary bridge, of which one end would rest on the bank and the other on the battlements, and which, being well furnished with stepping boards, would enable his men to ascend the inclined plane with speed and facility. Matilda received intimation of this design by the usual friendly channel of a blunt arrow, which must either have been sent from some secret friend in the prince's camp, or from some vigorous archer beyond it: the latter will not appear improbable, when we consider that Robin Hood and Little John could shoot two English miles and an inch point blank.

Come scrive Turpino, che non erra.[1]

The machine was completed, and the ensuing morning fixed for the assault. Six men, relieved at intervals, kept watch over it during the night. Prince John retired to sleep, congratulating himself in the expectation that another day would place the fair culprit at his princely mercy. His anticipations mingled with the visions of his slumber, and he dreamed of wounds and drums, and sacking and firing the castle, and bearing off in his arms the beautiful prize through the midst of fire and smoke. In the height of this imaginary turmoil, he awoke, and conceived for a few moments that certain sounds which rang in his ears, were the continuation of those of his dream, in that sort of half-consciousness between sleeping and waking when reality and phantasy meet and mingle in dim and confused resemblance. He was, however, very soon fully awake to the fact of his guards calling on him to arm, which he did in haste, and beheld the machine in flames, and a furious conflict raging around it. He hurried to the spot, and found that his camp had been suddenly assailed from one side by a party of foresters, and that the baron's

[1] [As Turpin writes who never errs.]

people had made a sortie on the other, and that they had killed the guards, and set fire to the machine, before the rest of the camp could come to the assistance of their fellows.

The night was in itself intensely dark, and the fire-light shed around it a vivid and unnatural radiance. On one side, the crimson light quivered by its own agitation on the waveless moat, and on the bastions and buttresses of the castle, and their shadows lay in massy blackness on the illuminated walls: on the other, it shone upon the woods, streaming far within among the open trunks, or resting on the closer foliage. The circumference of darkness bounded the scene on all sides: and in the centre raged the war; shields, helmets, and bucklers gleaming and glittering as they rang and clashed against each other; plumes confusedly tossing in the crimson light, and the massy light and shade that fell on the faces of the combatants, giving additional energy to their ferocious expression.

John, drawing nearer to the scene of action, observed two young warriors fighting side by side, one of whom wore the habit of a forester, the other that of a retainer of Arlingford. He looked intently on them both: their position towards the fire favoured the scrutiny: and the hawk's eye of love very speedily discovered that the latter was the fair Matilda. The forester he did not know: but he had sufficient tact to discern that his success would be very much facilitated by separating her from this companion, above all others. He therefore formed a party of men into a wedge, only taking especial care not to be the point of it himself, and drove it between them with so much precision, that they were in a moment far asunder.

"Lady Matilda," said John, "yield yourself my prisoner."

"If you would wear me, prince," said Matilda, "you must win me:" and without giving him time to deliberate on the courtesy of fighting with the lady of his love, she raised her sword in the air, and lowered it on his head with an impetus that would have gone nigh to fathom even that extraordinary depth of brain which always by divine grace furnishes the interior of a head-royal, if he had not very dexterously parried the blow. Prince John wished to disarm and take captive, not in any way to wound or injure, least of all to kill, his fair opponent. Matilda was only intent to get rid of her antagonist at any rate: the edge of her weapon painted his complexion with streaks of very unloverlike crimson, and she would probably have marred John's hand for ever signing Magna Charta, but that he was backed by the advantage of numbers, and that her sword broke short on the boss of his buckler. John was following up his advantage to make a captive of the lady, when he was suddenly felled to the earth by an unseen antagonist. Some of his men picked him carefully up and conveyed him to his tent, stunned and stupefied.

When he recovered, he found Harpiton diligently assisting in his recovery, more in the fear of losing his place than in that of losing his master: the prince's first inquiry was for the prisoner he had been on the point of taking at the moment when his *habeas corpus* was so unseasonably suspended. He was told that his people had been on the point of securing the said prisoner, when the devil suddenly appeared among them in the likeness of a tall friar, having his gray frock cinctured with a sword-belt, and his crown, which whether it were shaven or no they could not see, surmounted with a helmet, and flourishing an eight-foot staff, with which he laid about him to the right and to the left, knocking down the prince and his men as if they had been so many nine-pins: in fine, he had rescued the prisoner, and made a clear passage through friend and foe, and in conjunction with a chosen party of archers, had covered the retreat of the baron's men and the foresters, who had all gone off in a body towards Sherwood Forest.

Harpiton suggested that it would be desirable to sack the castle, and volunteered to lead the van on the occasion, as the defenders were withdrawn, and the exploit seemed to promise much profit and little danger: John considered that the castle would in itself be a great acquisition to him, as a stronghold in furtherance of his design on his brother's throne; and was determining to take possession with the first light of morning, when he had the mortification to see the castle burst into flames in several places at once. A piteous cry was heard from within, and while the prince was proclaiming a reward to any one who would enter into the burning pile, and elucidate the mystery of the doleful voice, forth waddled the little fat friar in an agony of fear, out of the fire into the frying-pan; for he was instantly taken into custody and carried before Prince John, wringing his hands and tearing his hair.

"Are you the friar," said Prince John, in a terrible voice, "that laid me prostrate in battle, mowed down my men like grass, rescued my captive, and covered the retreat of my enemies? And, not content with this, have you now set fire to the castle in which I intended to take up my royal quarters?"

The little friar quaked like a jelly: he fell on his knees, and attempted to speak; but in his eagerness to vindicate himself from this accumulation of alarming charges, he knew not where to begin; his ideas rolled round upon each other like the radii of a wheel; the words he desired to utter, instead of issuing, as it were, in a right line from his lips, seemed to conglobate themselves into a sphere turning on its own axis in his throat: after several ineffectual efforts, his utterance totally failed him, and he remained gasping, with his mouth open, his lips quivering, his hands clasped together, and the whites of his eyes turned up towards the prince with an expression most ruefully imploring.

"Are you that friar?" repeated the prince.

Several of the bystanders declared that he was not that friar. The little friar, encouraged by this patronage, found his voice, and pleaded for mercy. The prince questioned him closely concerning the burning of the castle. The little friar declared, that he had been in too great fear during the siege to know much of what was going forward, except that he had been conscious during the last few days of a lamentable deficiency of provisions, and had been present that very morning at the broaching of the last butt of sack. Harpiton groaned in sympathy. The little friar added, that he knew nothing of what had passed since, till he heard the flames roaring at his elbow.

"Take him away, Harpiton," said the prince, "fill him with sack, and turn him out."

"Never mind the sack," said the little friar, "turn me out at once."

"A sad chance," said Harpiton, "to be turned out without sack."

But what Harpiton thought a sad chance the little friar thought a merry one, and went bounding like a fat buck towards the abbey of Rubygill.

An arrow, with a letter attached to it, was shot into the camp, and carried to the prince. The contents were these:—

"PRINCE JOHN,—I do not consider myself to have resisted lawful authority in defending my castle against you, seeing that you are at present in a state of active rebellion against your liege sovereign Richard: and if my provisions had not failed me, I would have maintained it till doomsday. As it is, I have so well disposed my combustibles that it shall not serve you as a stronghold in your rebellion. If you hunt in the chases of Nottinghamshire, you may catch other game than my daughter. Both she and I are content to be houseless for a time, in the reflection that we have deserved your enmity, and the friendship of Cœur-de-Lion.

"Fitzwater."

[VI]

The baron, with some of his retainers and all the foresters, halted at daybreak in Sherwood Forest. The foresters quickly erected tents, and prepared an abundant breakfast of venison and ale.

"Now, Lord Fitzwater," said the chief forester, "recognize your son-in-law that was to have been, in the outlaw Robin Hood."

"Ay, ay," said the baron, "I have recognized you long ago."

"And recognize your young friend Gamwell," said the second, "in the outlaw Scarlet."

"And Little John, the page," said the third, "in Little John the outlaw."

"And Father Michael, of Rubygill Abbey," said the friar, "in Friar Tuck, of Sherwood Forest. Truly, I have a chapel here hard by, in the shape of a hollow tree, where I put up my prayers for travellers, and Little John holds the plate at the door, for good praying deserves good paying."

"I am in fine company," said the baron.

"In the very best of company," said the friar, "in the high court of Nature, and in the midst of her own nobility. Is it not so? This goodly grove is our palace: the oak and the beech are its colonnade and its canopy: the sun and the moon and the stars are its everlasting lamps: the grass, and the daisy, and the primrose, and the violet, are its many-coloured floor of green, white, yellow, and blue; the May-flower, and the woodbine, and the eglantine, and the ivy, are its decorations, its curtains, and its tapestry: the lark, and the thrush, and the linnet, and the nightingale, are its unhired minstrels and musicians. Robin Hood is king of the forest both by dignity of birth and by virtue of his standing army: to say nothing of the free choice of his people, which he has indeed, but I pass it by as an illegitimate basis of power. He holds his dominion over the forest, and its horned multitude of citizen-deer, and its swinish multitude or peasantry of wild boars, by right of conquest and force of arms. He levies contributions among them by the free consent of his archers, their virtual representatives. If they should find a voice to complain that we are 'tyrants and usurpers to kill and cook them up in their assigned and native dwelling-place,' we should most convincingly admonish them, with point of arrow, that they have nothing to do with our laws but to obey them. Is it not written that the fat ribs of the herd shall be fed upon by the mighty in the land? And have not they withal my blessing?—my orthodox, canonical, and archiepiscopal blessing? Do I not give thanks for them when they are well roasted and smoking under my nose? What title had William of Normandy to England, that Robin of Locksley has not to merry Sherwood? William fought for his claim. So does Robin. With whom, both? With any that would, or will dispute it. William raised contributions. So does Robin. From whom, both? From all that they could or can make pay them. Why did any pay them to William? Why do any pay them to Robin? For the same reason to both: because they could not, or cannot help it. They differ, indeed, in this, that William took from the poor and gave to the rich, and Robin takes from the rich and gives to the poor: and therein is Robin illegitimate: though in all else he is true prince. Scarlet and John, are they not peers of the forest? lords temporal of Sherwood? And am not I lord spiritual? Am I not archbishop? Am I not pope? Do I not consecrate their banner and absolve their sins? Are not they state, and am not I Church? Are not they state monarchical, and am not I Church militant? Do I not excommunicate our enemies from venison and brawn, and by 'r Lady, when need calls, beat them down under my feet? The state levies tax, and the Church levies tithe. Even so do we. Mass, we take all at once. What then? It is tax by redemption, and tithe by commutation. Your William and Richard can cut and come again, but our Robin deals with slippery subjects that come not twice to his exchequer. What need we then to constitute a court, except a fool and a laureate? For the fool, his only use is to make false knaves merry by art, and we are true men, and are merry by nature. For the laureate, his only office is to find virtues in those who have none, and to drink sack for his pains. We have quite virtue enough to need him not, and can drink our sack for ourselves."

"Well preached, friar," said Robin Hood: "yet there is one thing wanting to constitute a court, and that is a queen. And now, lovely Matilda, look round upon these sylvan shades where we have so often roused the stag from his ferny covert. The rising sun smiles upon us through the stems of that beechen knoll. Shall I take your hand, Matilda, in the presence of this my court? Shall I crown you with our wild-wood coronal, and hail you Queen of the Forest? Will you be the Queen Matilda of your own true King Robin?"

Matilda smiled assent.

"Not Matilda," said the friar: "the rules of our holy alliance re- quire new birth. We have excepted in favour of Little John, because he is great John, and his name is a misnomer. I sprinkle, not thy forehead with water, but thy lips with wine, and baptize thee MARIAN."

"Here is a pretty conspiracy," exclaimed the baron. "Why, you villanous friar, think you to nickname and marry my daughter before my face with impunity?"

"Even so, bold baron," said the friar; "we are strongest here. Say you, might overcomes right? I say no. There is no right but might: and to say that might overcomes right is to say that right overcomes itself: an absurdity most palpable. Your right was the stronger in Arlingford, and ours is the stronger in Sherwood. Your right was right as long as you could maintain it; so is ours. So is King Richard's, with all deference be it spoken; and so is King Saladin's; and their two mights are now committed in bloody fray, and that which over- comes will be right, just as long as it lasts, and as far as it reaches. And now, if any of you know any just impediment——"

"Fire and fury!" said the baron.

"Fire and fury," said the friar, "are modes of that might which constitutes right, and are just impediments to anything against which they can be brought to bear. They are our allies upon occasion, and would declare for us now, if you should put them to the test."

"Father," said Matilda, "you know the terms of our compact:

from the moment you restrained my liberty, you renounced your claim to all but compulsory obedience. The friar argues well. Right ends with might. Thick walls, dreary galleries, and tapestried chambers, were indifferent to me while I could leave them at pleasure, but have ever been hateful to me since they held me by force. May I never again have roof but the blue sky, nor canopy but the green leaves, nor barrier but the forest-bounds; with the foresters to my train, Little John to my page, Friar Tuck to my ghostly adviser, and Robin Hood to my liege lord. I am no longer Lady Matilda Fitzwater, of Arlingford Castle, but plain Maid Marian, of Sherwood Forest."

"Long live Maid Marian!" re-echoed the foresters.

"Oh, false girl!" said the baron, "do you renounce your name and parentage?"

"Not my parentage," said Marian, "but my name indeed: do not all maids renounce it at the altar?"

"The altar!" said the baron: "grant me patience! what do you mean by the altar?"

"Pile green turf," said the friar; "wreathe it with flowers, and crown it with fruit, and we will show the noble baron what we mean by the altar."

The foresters did as the friar directed.

"Now, Little John," said the friar, "on with the cloak of the Abbot of Doubleflask. I appoint thee my clerk: thou art here duly elected in full mote."

"I wish you were all in full mote together," said the baron, "and smooth wall on both sides."

"Punnest thou?" said the friar. "A heinous, anti-Christian offence. Why anti-Christian? Because anti-Catholic. Why anti-Catholic?Because anti-Roman. Why anti-Roman? Because Carthaginian. Is not pun from Punic? punica fides: the very quint-essential quiddity of bad faith: double-visaged: double-tongued. He that will make a pun will—— I say no more. Fie on it. Stand forth, clerk. Who is the bride's father?"

"There is no bride's father," said the baron. "I am the father of Matilda Fitzwater."

"There is none such," said the friar. "This is the fair Maid Marian. Will you make a virtue of necessity, or will you give laws to the flowing tide? Will you give her, or shall Robin take her? Will you be her true natural father, or shall I commute paternity? Stand forth, Scarlet."

"Stand back, Sirrah Scarlet," said the baron. "My daughter shall have no father but me. Needs must when the devil drives."

"No matter who drives," said the friar, "so that, like a well-disposed subject, you yield cheerful obedience to those who can enforce it."

"Mawd, sweet Mawd," said the baron, "will you then forsake your poor old father in his distress, with his castle in ashes, and his enemy in power?"

"Not so, father," said Marian; "I will always be your true daughter: I will always love, and serve, and watch, and defend you: but neither will I forsake my plighted love, and my own liege lord, who was your choice before he was mine, for you made him my associate in infancy; and that he continued to be mine when he ceased to be yours, does not in any way show remissness in my duties, or falling off in my affections. And though I here plight my troth at the altar to Robin, in the presence of this holy priest and pious clerk, yet . . . . Father, when Richard returns from Palestine, he will restore you to your barony, and perhaps, for your sake, your daughter's husband to the earldom of Huntingdon: should that never be, should it be the will of fate that we must live and die in the greenwood, I will live and die MAID MARIAN." [1]

"A pretty resolution," said the baron, "if Robin will let you keep it."

"I have sworn it," said Robin. "Should I expose her tenderness to the perils of maternity, when life and death may hang on shifting at a moment's notice from Sherwood to Barnsdale, and from Barnsdale to the sea-shore? And why should I banquet when my merry men starve? Chastity is our forest law, and even the friar has kept it since he has been here."

"Truly so," said the friar; "for temptation dwells with ease and luxury: but the hunter is Hippolytus, and the huntress is Dian. And now, dearly beloved——"

[1] And therefore is she called Maid Marian,
Because she leads a spotless maiden life,
And shall till Robin's outlaw life have end.—*Old Play.*

The friar went through the ceremony with great unction, and Little John was most clerical in the intonation of his responses. After which, the friar sang, and Little John fiddled, and the foresters danced, Robin with Marian, and Scarlet with the baron; and the venison smoked, and the ale frothed, and the wine sparkled, and the sun went down on their unwearied festivity; which they wound up with the following song, the friar leading, and the foresters joining chorus:—

Oh! bold Robin Hood is a forester good,
As ever drew bow in the merry greenwood:
At his bugle's shrill singing the echoes are ringing,
The wild deer are springing for many a rood:
Its summons we follow, through brake, over hollow,
The thrice-blown shrill summons of bold Robin Hood.

And what eye hath ere seen such a sweet Maiden Queen
As Marian the pride of the forester's green?
A sweet garden-flower, she blooms in the bower,
Where alone to this hour the wild rose has been
We hail her in duty the queen of all beauty:
We will live, we will die by our sweet Maiden Queen.

And here's a gray friar, good as heart can desire,
To absolve all our sins as the case may require:
Who with courage so stout, lays his oak-plant about,
And puts to the rout all the foes of his choir:
For we are his choristers, we merry foresters,
Chorusing thus with our militant friar.

And Scarlet doth bring his good yew-bough and string,
Prime minister is he of Robin our king:
No mark is too narrow for Little John's arrow,
That hits a cock-sparrow a mile on the wing;
Robin and Marian. Scarlet and Little John,
Long with their glory old Sherwood shall ring.

Each a good liver, for well-feathered quiver
Doth furnish brawn, venison, and fowl of the river:
But the best game we dish-up, it is a fat bishop:
When his angels we fish up, he proves a free giver:
For a prelate so lowly has angels more holy,
And should this world's false angels to sinners deliver.

Robin and Marion, Scarlet and Little John,
Drink to them one by one, drink as ye sing:
Robin and Marion, Scarlet and Little John,
Echo to echo through Sherwood shall fling:
Robin and Marion, Scarlet and Little John,
Long with their glory old Sherwood shall ring.

[VII]

THE next morning Robin Hood convened his foresters, and desired Little John, for the baron's edification, to read over the laws
of their forest society. Little John read aloud with a stentorophonic
voice:—

"At a high court of foresters, held under the greenwood tree,
an hour after sunrise, Robin Hood president, William Scarlet vice-
president, Little John secretary: the following articles, moved by
Friar Tuck, in his capacity of Peer Spiritual, and seconded by
Much the Miller, were unanimously agreed to.

"The principles of our society are six: Legitimacy, Equity,
Hospitality, Chivalry, Chastity, and Courtesy.

"The articles of Legitimacy are four:

"I. Our government is legitimate, and our society is founded on
the one golden rule of right, consecrated by the universal consent
of mankind, and by the practice of all ages, individuals, and nations: namely, To keep what we have, and to catch what we can.

"II. Our government being legitimate, all our proceedings shall
be legitimate: wherefore we declare war against the whole world,
and every forester is by this legitimate declaration legitimately invested with a roving commission, to make lawful prize of everything that comes in his way.

"III. All forest laws but our own we declare to be null and
void.

"IV. All such of the old laws of England as do not in any way
interfere with, or militate against, the views of this honourable
assembly, we will loyally adhere to and maintain. The rest we declare null and void as far as relates to ourselves, in all cases wherein

a vigour beyond the law may be conducive to our own interest
and preservation.

"The articles of Equity are three:

"I. The balance of power among the people being very much
deranged, by one having too much and another nothing, we hereby
resolve ourselves into a congress or court of equity, to restore as far
as in us lies the said natural balance of power, by taking from all
who have too much as much of the said too much as we can lay
our hands on; and giving to those who have nothing such a portion thereof as it may seem to us expedient to part with.

"II. In all cases a quorum of foresters shall constitute a court
of equity, and as many as may be strong enough to manage the
matter in hand shall constitute a quorum.

"III. All usurers, monks, courtiers, and other drones of the great
hive of society, who shall be found laden with any portion of the
honey whereof they have wrongfully despoiled the industrious bee,
shall be rightfully despoiled thereof in turn; and all bishops and
abbots shall be bound and beaten,[1] especially the Abbot of Doncaster; as shall also all sheriffs, especially the Sheriff of Nottingham.

"The articles of Hospitality are two:

"I. Postmen, carriers, and market-folk, peasants and mechanics,
farmers and millers, shall pass through our forest dominions without let or molestation.

"II. All other travellers through the forest shall be graciously
invited to partake of Robin's hospitality; and if they come not willingly they shall be compelled; and the rich man shall pay well for
his fare; and the poor man shall feast scot free, and peradventure
receive bounty in proportion to his desert and necessity.

"The article of Chivalry is one:

---

[1] "These byshoppes and these archbyshoppes
      Ye shall them bete and bynde,"

says Robin Hood, in an old ballad. Perhaps, however, this is to be taken not in
a literal, but in a figurative sense, from the binding and beating of wheat: for
as all rich men were Robin's harvest, the bishops and archbishops must have
been the finest and fattest ears among them, from which Robin merely proposes
to thresh the grain when he directs them to be bound and beaten: and as
Pharoah's fat kine were typical of fat ears of wheat, so may fat ears of wheat,
mutatis mutandis, be typical of fat kine.

"I. Every forester shall, to the extent of his power, aid and protect maids, widows, and orphans, and all weak and distressed persons whomsoever: and no woman shall be impeded or molested in any way; nor shall any company receive harm which any woman is in.

"The article of Chastity is one:

"I. Every forester, being Diana's forester and minion of the moon, shall commend himself to the grace of the Virgin, and shall have the gift of continency on pain of expulsion: that the article of chivalry may be secure from infringement, and maids, wives, and widows pass without fear through the forest.

"The article of Courtesy is one:

"I. No one shall miscall a forester. He who calls Robin Robert of Huntingdon, or salutes him by any other title or designation whatsoever except plain Robin Hood; or who calls Marian Matilda Fitzwater, or salutes her by any other title or designation whatsoever except plain Maid Marian; and so of all others; shall for every such offence forfeit a mark, to be paid to the friar.

"And these articles we swear to keep as we are good men and true. Carried by acclamation. God save King Richard.

"LITTLE JOHN, Secretary."

"Excellent laws," said the baron: "excellent, by the holy rood. William of Normandy, with my great-great-grandfather Fierabras at his elbow, could not have made better. And now, sweet Mawd——"

"A fine, a fine," cried the friar, "a fine, by the article of courtesy."

"Od's life," said the baron, "shall I not call my own daughter Mawd? Methinks there should be a special exception in my favour."

"It must not be," said Robin Hood: "our constitution admits no privilege."

"But I will commute," said the friar; "for twenty marks a year duly paid into my ghostly pocket you shall call your daughter Mawd two hundred times a day."

"Gramercy," said the baron, "and I agree, honest friar, when I can get twenty marks to pay: for till Prince John be beaten from Nottingham, my rents are like to prove but scanty."

"I will trust," said the friar, "and thus let us ratify the stipulation; so shall our laws and your infringement run together in an amicable parallel."

"But," said Little John, "this is a bad precedent, master friar. It is turning discipline into profit, penalty into perquisite, public justice into private revenue. It is rank corruption, master friar."

"Why are laws made?" said the friar. "For the profit of somebody. Of whom? Of him who makes them first, and of others as it may happen. Was not I legislator in the last article, and shall I not thrive by my own law?"

"Well then, sweet Mawd," said the baron, "I must leave you, Mawd; your life is very well for the young and the hearty, but it squares not with my age or my humour. I must house, Mawd. I must find refuge: but where? That is the question."

"Where Sir Guy of Gamwell has found it," said Robin Hood, "near the borders of Barnsdale. There you may dwell in safety with him and fair Alice, till King Richard return, and Little John shall give you safe conduct. You will have need to travel with caution, in disguise and without attendants, for Prince John commands all this vicinity, and will doubtless lay the country for you and Marian. Now it is first expedient to dismiss your retainers. If there be any among them who like our life, they may stay with us in the greenwood; the rest may return to their homes."

Some of the baron's men resolved to remain with Robin and Marian, and were furnished accordingly with suits of green, of which Robin always kept good store.

Marian now declared that as there was danger in the way to Barnsdale, she would accompany Little John and the baron, as she would not be happy unless she herself saw her father placed in security. Robin was very unwilling to consent to this, and assured her that there was more danger for her than the baron: but Marian was absolute.

"If so, then," said Robin, "I shall be your guide instead of Little John, and I shall leave him and Scarlet joint-regents of Sherwood during my absence, and the voice of Friar Tuck shall be decisive between them if they differ in nice questions of state policy."

[Robin and Marian lead her father to safe refuge with Sir Guy of
    Gamwell, again beating Montfaucon and his men along the way.

On the homeward journey to Sherwood, they unexpectedly encounter Friar Tuck in circumstances that might lead uncharitable persons to suspect that the pious friar leaves "his good vow" of chastity "in the forest behind," when he retires to his "devotions" beyond the forest's bounds. But the king and queen of the greenwood are not, of course, lacking in charity.]

[VIII]

So Robin and Marian dwelt and reigned in the forest, ranging the glades and the greenwoods from the matins of the lark to the vespers of the nightingale, and administering natural justice according to Robin's ideas of rectifying the inequalities of human condition: raising genial dews from the bags of the rich and idle, and returning them in fertilizing showers on the poor and industrious; an operation which more enlightened statesmen have happily reversed, to the unspeakable benefit of the community at large. The light footsteps of Marian were impressed on the morning dew beside the firmer step of her lover, and they shook its large drops about them as they cleared themselves a passage through the thick tall fern, without any fear of catching cold, which was not much in fashion in the twelfth century. Robin was as hospitable as Cathmor; for seven men stood on seven paths to call the stranger to his feast. It is true, he super-added the small improvement of making the stranger pay for it: than which what could be more generous? For Cathmor was himself the prime giver of his feast, whereas Robin was only the agent to a series of strangers, who provided in turn for the entertainment of their successors; which is carrying the disinterestedness of hospitality to its acme. Marian often killed the deer,

> Which Scarlet dressed, and Friar Tuck blessed,
> While Little John wandered in search of a guest.

Robin was very devout, though there was great unity in his religion: it was exclusively given to our Lady the Virgin, and he never set forth in a morning till he had said three prayers, and had heard the sweet voice of his Marian singing a hymn to their mutual patroness. Each of his men had, as usual, a patron saint according to his name or taste. The friar chose a saint for himself, and fixed on Saint Botolph, whom he euphonized into Saint Bottle, and maintained that he was that very Panomphic Pantagruelian saint, well known in ancient France as a female divinity, by the name of La Dive Bouteille, whose oracular monosyllable "Trincq," is celebrated and understood by all nations, and is expounded by the learned doctor Alcofribas, [1] who has treated at large on the subject, to signify "drink." Saint Bottle, then, was the saint of Friar Tuck, who did not yield even to Robin and Marian in the assiduity of his devotions to his chosen patron. Such was their summer life, and in their winter caves they had sufficient furniture, ample provender, store of old wine, and assuredly no lack of fuel, with joyous music and pleasant discourse to charm away the season of darkness and storms.

Many moons had waxed and waned, when on the afternoon of a lovely summer day a lusty broad-boned knight was riding through the forest of Sherwood. The sun shone brilliantly on the full green foliage, and afforded the knight a fine opportunity of observing picturesque effects, of which it is to be feared he did not avail himself. But he had not proceeded far, before he had an opportunity of observing something much more interesting; namely, a fine young outlaw leaning, in the true Sherwood fashion, with his back against a tree. The knight was preparing to ask the stranger a question, the answer to which, if correctly given, would have relieved him from a doubt that pressed heavily on his mind, as to whether he was in the right road or the wrong, when the youth prevented the inquiry by saying: "In God's name, sir knight, you are late to your meals. My master has tarried dinner for you these three hours."

"I doubt," said the knight, "I am not he you wot of. I am nowhere bidden to-day, and I know none in this vicinage."

"We feared," said the youth, "your memory would be treacherous: therefore I am stationed here to refresh it."

[1] Alcofribas Nasier: an anagram of François Rabelais, and his assumed appellation. The reader who desires to know more about this oracular divinity, may consult the said doctor Alcofribas Nasier, who will usher him into the adytum through the medium of the high priestess Bacbuc.

"Who is your master?" said the knight; "and where does he abide?"

"My master," said the youth, "is called Robin Hood, and he abides hard by."

"And what knows he of me?" said the night.

"He knows you," answered the youth, "as he does every way-faring knight and friar, by instinct."

"Gramercy," said the knight; "then I understand his bidding: but how if I say I will not come?"

"I am enjoined to bring you," said the youth. "If persuasion avail not, I must use other argument."

"Say'st thou so?" said the knight; "I doubt if thy stripling rhetoric would convince me."

"That," said the young forester, "we will see."

"We are not equally matched, boy," said the knight. "I should get less honour by thy conquest, than grief by thy injury."

"Perhaps," said the youth, "my strength is more than my seeming, and my cunning more than my strength. Therefore let it please your knighthood to dismount."

"It shall please my knighthood to chastise thy presumption," said the knight, springing from his saddle.

Hereupon, which in those days was usually the result of a meeting between any two persons anywhere, they proceeded to fight.

The knight had in an uncommon degree both strength and skill: the forester had less strength, but not less skill than the knight, and showed such a mastery of his weapon as reduced the latter to great admiration.

They had not fought many minutes by the forest clock, the sun; and had as yet done each other no worse injury than that the knight had wounded the forester's jerkin, and the forester had disabled the knight's plume; when they were interrupted by a voice from a thicket, exclaiming, "Well fought, girl: well fought. Mass, that had nigh been a shrewd hit. Thou owest him for that, lass. Mary, stand by, I'll pay him for thee."

The knight turning to the voice, beheld a tall friar issuing from the thicket, brandishing a ponderous cudgel.

"Who art thou?" said the knight.

"I am the church militant of Sherwood," answered the friar. "Why art thou in arms against our lady queen?"

"What meanest thou?" said the knight.

"Truly this," said the friar, "is our liege lady of the forest, against whom I do apprehend thee in overt act of treason. What sayest thou for thyself?"

"I say," answered the knight, "that if this be indeed a lady, man never yet held me so long."

"Spoken," said the friar, "like one who hath done execution. Hast thou thy stomach full of steel? Wilt thou diversify thy repast with a taste of my oak-graff? Or wilt thou incline thine heart to our venison, which truly is cooling? Wilt thou fight? or wilt thou dine? or wilt thou fight and dine? or wilt thou dine and fight? I am for thee, choose as thou mayest."

"I will dine," said the knight; "for with lady I never fought before, and with friar I never fought yet, and with neither will I ever fight knowingly: and if this be the queen of the forest, I will not, being in her own dominions, be backward to do her homage."

So saying, he kissed the hand of Marian, who was pleased most graciously to express her approbation.

"Gramercy, sir knight," said the friar, "I laud thee for thy courtesy, which I deem to be no less than thy valour. Now do thou follow me, while I follow my nose, which scents the pleasant odour of roast from the depth of the forest recesses. I will lead thy horse, and do thou lead my lady."

The knight took Marian's hand, and followed the friar, who walked before them, singing:

> "When the wind blows, when the wind blows,
> From where under buck the dry log glows,
> What guide can you follow,
> O'er brake and o'er hollow,
> So true as a ghostly, ghostly nose?"

[IX]

THEY proceeded, following their infallible guide, first along a light elastic greensward under the shade of lofty and wide-spreading

trees that skirted a sunny opening of the forest, then along labyrin-
thine paths, which the deer, the outlaw, or the woodman had made,
through the close shoots of the young coppices, through the thick
undergrowth of the ancient woods, through beds of gigantic fern
that filled the narrow glades and waved their green feathery heads
above the plume of the knight. Along these sylvan alleys they
walked in single file; the friar singing and pioneering in the van,
the horse plunging and floundering behind the friar, the lady following "in maiden meditation, fancy free," and the knight bringing up
the rear, much marvelling at the strange company into which his
stars had thrown him. Their path had expanded sufficiently to allow
the knight to take Marian's hand again, when they arrived in the
august presence of Robin Hood and his court.

Robin's table was spread under a high overarching canopy of
living boughs, on the edge of a natural lawn of verdure starred with
flowers, through which a swift transparent rivulet ran sparkling in
the sun. The board was covered with abundance of choice food
and excellent liquor, not without the comeliness of snow-white
linen and the splendour of costly plate, which the Sheriff of Nottingham had unwillingly contributed to supply, at the same time with
an excellent cook, whom Little John's art had spirited away to the
forest with the contents of his master's silver scullery.

An hundred foresters were here assembled over-ready for their
dinner, some seated at the table and some lying in groups under
the trees.

Robin bade courteous welcome to the knight, who took his seat
between Robin and Marian at the festal board; at which was already placed one strange guest in the person of a portly monk,
sitting between Little John and Scarlet, with his rotund physiognomy
elongated into an unnatural oval by the conjoint influence of sorrow and fear: sorrow for the departed contents of his travelling
treasury, a good-looking valise which was hanging empty on a
bough; and fear for his personal safety, of which all the flasks and
pasties before him could not give him assurance. The appearance
of the knight, however, cheered him up with a semblance of protection, and gave him just sufficient courage to demolish a cygnet and
a numble-pie, which he diluted with the contents of two flasks of
canary sack.

But wine, which sometimes creates and often increases joy, doth also, upon occasion, heighten sorrow: and so it fared now with our portly monk, who had no sooner explained away his portion of provender, than he began to weep and bewail himself bitterly.

"Why dost thou weep, man?" said Robin Hood. "Thou hast done thine embassy justly, and shalt have thy Lady's grace."

"Alack! alack!" said the monk: "no embassy had I, luckless sinner, as well thou wottest, but to take to my abbey in safety the treasure whereof thou hast despoiled me."

"Propound me his case," said Friar Tuck, "and I will give him ghostly counsel."

"You well remember," said Robin Hood, "the sorrowful knight who dined with us here twelve months and a day gone by."

"Well do I," said Friar Tuck. "His lands were in jeopardy with a certain abbot, who would allow him no longer day for their redemption. Whereupon you lent to him the four hundred pounds which he needed, and which he was to repay this day, though he had no better security to give than our Lady the Virgin."

"I never desired better," said Robin, "for she never yet failed to send me my pay; and here is one of her own flock, this faithful and well-favoured monk of St. Mary's hath brought it me duly, principal and interest to a penny, as Little John can testify, who told it forth. To be sure, he denied having it, but that was to prove our faith. We sought and found it."

"I know nothing of your knight," said the monk: "and the money was our own, as the Virgin shall bless me."

"She shall bless thee," said Friar Tuck, "for a faithful messenger."

The monk resumed his wailing. Little John brought him his horse. Robin gave him leave to depart. He sprang with singular nimbleness into the saddle, and vanished without saying, God give you good day.

The stranger knight laughed heartily as the monk rode off.

"They say, sir knight," said Friar Tuck, "they should laugh who win: but thou laughest who art likely to lose."

"I have won," said the knight, "a good dinner, some mirth, and some knowledge: and I cannot lose by paying for them."

"Bravely said," answered Robin. "Still it becomes thee to pay:

for it is not meet that a poor forester should treat a rich knight. How much money hast thou with thee?"

"Troth, I know not," said the knight. "Sometimes much, sometimes little, sometimes none. But search, and what thou findest, keep: and for the sake of thy kind heart and open hand, be it what it may, I shall wish it were more."

"Then, since thou sayest so," said Robin, "not a penny will I touch. Many a false churl comes hither, and disburses against his will: and till there is lack of these, I prey not on true men."

"Thou art thyself a true man, right well I judge, Robin," said the stranger knight, "and seemest more like one bred in court than to thy present outlaw life."

"Our life," said the friar, "is a craft, an art, and a mystery. How much of it, think you, could be learned at court?"

"Indeed, I cannot say," said the stranger knight; "but I should apprehend very little."

"And so should I," said the friar: "for we should find very little of our bold open practice, but should bear abundance of praise of our principles. To live in seeming fellowship and secret rivalry; to have a hand for all, and a heart for none; to be everybody's acquaintance, and nobody's friend; to meditate the ruin of all on whom we smile, and to dread the secret stratagems of all who smile on us; to pilfer honours and despoil fortunes, not by fighting in daylight, but by sapping in darkness: these are arts which the court can teach, but which we, by 'r Lady, have not learned. But let your court-minstrel tune up his throat to the praise of your court-hero, then come our principles into play: then is our practice extolled: not by the same name, for their Richard is a hero, and our Robin is a thief: marry, your hero guts an exchequer, while your thief disembowels a portmanteau; your hero sacks a city, while your thief sacks a cellar: your hero marauds on a larger scale, and that is all the difference, for the principle and the virtue are one: but two of a trade cannot agree: therefore your hero makes laws to get rid of your thief, and gives him an ill name that he may hang him: for might is right, and the strong make laws for the weak, and they that make laws to serve their own turn do also make morals to give colour to their laws."

"Your comparison, friar," said the stranger, "fails in this: that your thief fights for profit, and your hero for honour. I have fought under the banners of Richard, and if, as you phrase it, he guts exchequers, and sacks cities, it is not to win treasure for himself, but to furnish forth the means of his greater and more glorious aim."

"Misconceive me not, sir knight," said the friar. "We all love and honour King Richard, and here is a deep draught to his health: but I would show you, that we foresters are miscalled by opprobrious names, and that our virtues, though they follow at humble distance, are yet truly akin to those of Cœur-de-Lion. I say not that Richard is a thief, but I say that Robin is a hero: and for honour, did ever yet man, miscalled thief, win greater honour than Robin? Do not all men grace him with some honourable epithet? The most gentle thief, the most courteous thief, the most bountiful thief, yea, and the most honest thief? Richard is courteous, bountiful, honest, and valiant: but so also is Robin: it is the false word that makes the unjust distinction. They are twin-spirits, and should be friends, but that fortune hath differently cast their lot: but their names shall descend together to the latest days, as the flower of their age and of England: for in the pure principles of freebootery have they excelled all men; and to the principles of freebootery, diversely developed, belong all the qualities to which song and story concede renown."

"And you may add, friar," said Marian, "that Robin, no less than Richard, is king in his own dominion; and that if his subjects be fewer, yet are they more uniformly loyal."

"I would, fair lady," said the stranger, "that thy latter observation were not so true. But I nothing doubt, Robin, that if Richard could hear your friar, and see you and your lady, as I now do, there is not a man in England whom he would take by the hand more cordially than yourself."

"Gramercy, sir knight," said Robin——But his speech was cut short by Little John calling, "Hark!"

All listened. A distant trampling of horses was heard. The sounds approached rapidly, and at length a group of horsemen glittering in holyday dresses was visible among the trees.

"God's my life!" said Robin, "what means this? To arms, my merry men all."

"No arms, Robin," said the foremost horseman, riding up and springing from his saddle: "have you forgotten Sir William of the Lee?"

"No, by my fay," said Robin; "and right welcome again to Sherwood."

Little John bustled to re-array the disorganized economy of the table, and replace the dilapidations of the provender.

"I come late, Robin," said Sir William, "but I came by a wrestling, where I found a good yeoman wrongfully beset by a crowd of sturdy varlets, and I stayed to do him right."

"I thank thee for that, in God's name," said Robin, "as if thy good service had been to myself."

"And here," said the knight, "is thy four hundred pound; and my men have brought thee an hundred bows and as many well-furnished quivers; which I beseech thee to receive and to use as a poor token of my grateful kindness to thee: for me and my wife and children didst thou redeemed from beggary."

"Thy bows and arrows," said Robin, "will I joyfully receive: but of thy money, not a penny. It is paid already. My Lady, who was thy security, hath sent it me for thee."

Sir William pressed, but Robin was inflexible.

"It is paid," said Robin, "as this good knight can testify, who saw my Lady's messenger depart but now."

Sir William looked round to the stranger knight, and instantly fell on his knee, saying, "God save King Richard."

The foresters, friar and all, dropped on their knees together, and repeated in chorus: "God save King Richard."

"Rise, rise," said Richard, smiling: "Robin is king here, as his lady hath shown. I have heard much of thee, Robin, both of thy present and thy former state. And this, thy fair forest-queen, is, if tales say true, the lady Matilda Fitzwater."

Marian signed acknowledgment.

"Your father," said the king, "has approved his fidelity to me, by the loss of his lands, which the newness of my return, and many public cares, have not yet given me time to restore: but this justice shall be done to him, and to thee also, Robin, if thou wilt leave thy forest-life and resume thy earldom, and be a peer of

Cœur-de-Lion: for braver heart and juster hand I never yet found."

Robin looked round on his men.

"Your followers," said the king, "shall have free pardon, and such of them as thou wilt part with shall have maintenance from me; and if ever I confess to priest, it shall be to thy friar."

"Gramercy to your majesty," said the friar; "and my inflictions shall be flasks of canary; and if the number be (as in grave cases I may, peradventure, make it) too great for one frail mortality, I will relieve you by vicarious penance, and pour down my own throat the redundancy of the burden."

Robin and his followers embraced the king's proposal. A joyful meeting soon followed with the baron and Sir Guy of Gamwell: and Richard himself honoured with his own presence a formal solemnization of the nuptials of our lovers, whom he constantly distinguished with his peculiar regard.

The friar could not say, Farewell to the forest, without something of a heavy heart: and he sang as he turned his back upon its bounds, occasionally reverting his head:

"Ye woods, that oft at sultry noon
    Have o'er me spread your massy shade:
Ye gushing streams, whose murmured tune
    Has in my ear sweet music made,
While, where the dancing pebbles show
    Deep in the restless fountain-pool,
The gelid water's upward flow,
    My second flask was laid to cool:

"Ye pleasant sights of leaf and flower:
    Ye pleasant sounds of bird and bee:
Ye sports of deer in sylvan bower:
    Ye feasts beneath the greenwood tree:
Ye baskings in the vernal sun:
    Ye slumbers in the summer dell:
Ye trophies that this arm has won:
    And must ye hear your friar's farewell?"

But the friar's farewell was not destined to be eternal. He was domiciled as the family confessor of the Earl and Countess of Huntingdon, who led a discreet and courtly life, and kept up old hospitality in all its munificence, till the death of King Richard and the usurpation of John, by placing their enemy in power, compelled them to return to their greenwood sovereignty; which, it is probable, they would have before done from choice, if their love of sylvan liberty had not been counteracted by their desire to retain the friendship of Cœur-de-Lion. Their old and tried adherents, the friar among the foremost, flocked again round their forest-banner; and in merry Sherwood they long lived together, the lady still retaining her former name of Maid Marian, though the appellation was then as much a misnomer as that of Little John.

The Misfortunes of Elphin

THE PROSPERITY OF GWAELOD

IN the beginning of the sixth century, when Uther Pendragon held the nominal sovereignty of Britain over a number of petty kings, Gwythno Garanhir was king of Caredigion. The most valuable portion of his dominions was the Great Plain of Gwaelod, an extensive tract of level land, stretching along that part of the sea coast which now belongs to the counties of Merioneth and Cardigan. This district was populous and highly cultivated. It contained sixteen fortified towns, superior to all the towns and cities of the Cymry, excepting Caer Lleon upon Usk; and, like Caer Lleon, they bore in their architecture, their language, and their manners, vestiges of past intercourse with the Roman lords of the world. It contained also one of the three privileged ports of the isle of Britain, which was called the Port of Gwythno. This port, we may believe, if we please, had not been unknown to the Phœnicians and Carthaginians, when they visited the island for metal, accommodating the inhabitants, in return, with luxuries which they would not otherwise have dreamed of, and which they could very well have done without; of course, in arranging the exchange of what they denominated equivalents, imposing on their simplicity, and taking advantage of their ignorance, according to the approved practice of civilized nations; which they called imparting the blessings of Phœnician and Carthaginian light.

An embankment of massy stone protected this lowland country from the sea, which was said, in the traditions older than the embankment, to have, in occasional spring-tides, paid short but unwelcome visits to the interior inhabitants, and to have, by slow

233

aggressions, encroached considerably on the land. To prevent the repetition of the first of these inconveniences, and to check the progress of the second, the people of Gwaelod had built the stony rampart, which had withstood the shock of the waves for centuries, when Gwythno began his reign.

Gwythno, like other kings, found the business of governing too light a matter to fill up the vacancy of either his time or his head, and took to the more solid pursuits of harping and singing; not forgetting feasting, in which he was glorious; nor hunting, wherein he was mighty. His several pursuits composed a very harmonious triad. The chace conduced to the good cheer of the feast, and to the good appetite which consumed it; the feast inspired the song; and the song gladdened the feast, and celebrated the chace.

Gwythno and his subjects went on together very happily. They had little to do with him but to pay him revenue, and he had little to do with them but to receive it. Now and then they were called on to fight for the protection of his sacred person, and for the privilege of paying revenue to him rather than to any of the kings in his vicinity, a privilege of which they were particularly tenacious. His lands being far more fertile, and his people, consequently, far more numerous, than those of the rocky dwellers on his borders, he was always victorious in the defensive warfare to which he restricted his military achievements; and, after the invaders of his dominions had received two or three inflictions of signal chastisement, they limited their aggressions to coming quietly in the night, and vanishing, before morning, with cattle: an heroic operation, in which the preeminent glory of Scotland renders the similar exploits of other nations not worth recording.

Gwythno was not fond of the sea: a moonstruck bard had warned him to beware of the oppression of Gwenhidwy;[1] and he thought he could best do so by keeping as far as possible out of her way. He had a palace built of choice slate stone on the rocky banks of the Mawddach, just above the point where it quitted its native mountains, and entered the plain of Gwaelod. Here, among green woods and sparkling waters, he lived in festal munificence, and ex-

[1] *Gwen-hudiw,* "the white alluring one:" the name of a mermaid. Used figuratively for the elemental power of the sea.

pended his revenue in encouraging agriculture, by consuming a large quantity of produce.

Watch-towers were erected along the embankment, and watchmen were appointed to guard against the first approaches of damage or decay. The whole of these towers, and their companies of guards, were subordinate to a central castle, which commanded the seaport already mentioned, and wherein dwelt Prince Seithenyn ap Seithyn Saidi, who held the office of Arglwyd Gorwarcheidwad yr Argae Breninawl, which signifies, in English, Lord High Commissioner of Royal Embankment; and he executed it as a personage so denominated might be expected to do: he drank the profits, and he left the embankment to his deputies, who left it to their assistants, who left it to itself.

The condition of the head, in a composite, as in a simple body, affects the entire organization to the extremity of the tail, excepting that, as the tail in the figurative body usually receives the largest share in the distribution of punishment, and the smallest in the distribution of reward, it has the stronger stimulus to ward off evil, and the smaller supply of means to indulge in diversion; and it sometimes happens that one of the least regarded of the component parts of the said tail will, from a pure sense of duty, or an inveterate love of business, or an oppressive sense of ennui, or a development of the organ of order, or some other equally cogent reason, cheerfully undergo all the care and labour, of which the honour and profit will redound to higher quarters.

Such a component portion of the Gwaelod High Commission of Royal Embankment was Teithren ap Tathral, who had the charge of a watch-tower where the embankment terminated at the point of Mochres, in the high land of Ardudwy. Teithrin kept his portion of the embankment in exemplary condition, and paced with daily care the limits of his charge; but one day, by some accident, he strayed beyond them, and observed symptoms of neglect that filled him with dismay. This circumstance induced him to proceed till his wanderings brought him round to the embankment's southern termination in the high land of Caredigion. He met with abundant hospitality at the towers of his colleagues, and at the castle of Seithenyn: he was supposed to be walking for his amusement; he was asked no questions, and he carefully abstained from asking any. He examined and observed in silence; and, when he had completed his observations, he hastened to the palace of Gwythno.

Preparations were making for a high festival, and Gwythno was composing an ode. Teithrin knew better than to interrupt him in his awen. [1]

Gwythno had a son named Elphin, who is celebrated in history as the most expert of fishers. Teithrin, finding the king impracticable, went in search of the young prince.

Elphin had been all the morning fishing in the Mawddach, in a spot where the river, having quitted the mountains and not yet entered the plain, ran in alternate streams and pools sparkling through a pastoral valley. Elphin sat under an ancient ash, enjoying the calm brightness of an autumnal noon, and the melody and beauty of the flying stream, on which the shifting sunbeams fell chequering through the leaves. The monotonous music of the river, and the profound stillness of the air, had contributed to the deep abstraction of a meditation into which Elphin had fallen. He was startled into attention by a sudden rush of the wind through the trees, and during the brief interval of transition from the state of reverie to that of perfect consciousness, he heard, or seemed to hear, in the gust that hurried by him, the repetition of the words, "Beware of the oppression of Gwenhidwy." The gust was momentary: the leaves ceased to rustle, and the deep silence of nature returned.

The prophecy, which had long haunted the memory and imagination of his father, had been often repeated to Elphin, and had sometimes occupied his thoughts, but it had formed no part of his recent meditation, and he could not persuade himself that the words had not been actually spoken near him. He emerged from the shade of the trees that fringed the river, and looked round him from the rocky bank.

At this moment Teithrin ap Tathral discovered and approached him.

Elphin knew him not, and inquired his name. He answered, "Teithrin ap Tathral."

"And what seek you here?" said Elphin.

"I seek," answered Teithrin, "the Prince of Gwaelod, Elphin ap Gwythno Garanhir."

[1] The rapturous and abstracted state of poetical inspiration.

"You spoke," said Elphin, "as you approached." Teithrin answered in the negative.

"Assuredly you did," said Elphin. "You repeated the words, 'Beware of the oppression of Gwenhidwy.'"

Teithrin denied having spoken the words; but their mysterious impression made Elphin listen readily to his information and advice; and the result of their conference was a determination, on the part of the prince, to accompany Teithren ap Tathral on a visit of remonstrance to the Lord High Commissioner.

They crossed the centre of the enclosed country to the privileged port of Gwythno, near which stood the castle of Seithenyn. They walked towards the castle along a portion of the embankment, and Teithrin pointed out to the prince its dilapidated condition. The sea shone with the glory of the setting sun; the air was calm; and the white surf, tinged with the crimson of sunset, broke lightly on the sands below. Elphin turned his eyes from the dazzling splendour of the Plain of Gwaelod; the trees, that in the distance thickened into woods; the wreaths of smoke rising from among them, marking the solitary cottages, or the populous towns; the massy barrier of mountains beyond, with the forest rising from their base; the precipices frowning over the forest; and the clouds resting on their summits, reddened with the reflection of the west. Elphin gazed earnestly on the peopled plain, reposing in the calm of evening between the mountains and the sea, and thought, with deep feelings of secret pain, how much of life and human happiness was entrusted to the ruinous mound on which he stood.

THE DRUNKENNESS OF SEITHENYN

The sun had sunk beneath the waves when they reached the castle of Seithenyn. The sound of the harp and the song saluted them as they approached it. As they entered the great hall, which was already blazing with torchlight, they found his highness, and his highness's household, convincing themselves and each other, with wine and wassail, of the excellence of their system of virtual superintendence; and the following jovial chorus broke on the ears of the visitors:

THE CIRCLING OF THE MEAD HORNS

Fill the blue horn, the blue buffalo horn:
Natural is mead in the buffalo horn:
As the cuckoo in spring, as the lark in the morn,
So natural is mead in the buffalo horn.

As the cup of the flower to the bee when he sips,
Is the full cup of mead to the true Briton's lips:
From the flower-cups of summer, on field and on tree,
Our mead cups are filled by the vintager bee.

Seithenyn [1] ap Seithyn, the generous, the bold,
Drinks the wine of the stranger from vessels of gold; [2]
But we from the horn, the blue silver-rimmed horn,
Drink the ale and the mead in our fields that were born.

The ale-froth is white, and the mead sparkles bright;
They both smile apart, and with smiles they unite: [3]
The mead from the flower, and the ale from the corn,
Smile, sparkle, and sing in the buffalo horn.

The horn, the blue horn, cannot stand on its tip;
Its path is right on from the hand to the lip:
Though the bowl and the wine-cup our tables adorn,
More natural the draught from the buffalo horn.

But Seithenyn ap Seithyn, the generous, the bold,
Drinks the bright-flowing wine from the far-gleaming gold:
The wine, in the bowl by his lip that is worn,
Shall be glorious as mead in the buffalo horn.

The horns circle fast, but their fountains will last,
As the stream passes ever, and never is past:
Exhausted so quickly, replenished so soon,
They wax and they wane like the horns of the moon.

Fill high the blue horn, the blue buffalo horn;
Fill high the long silver-rimmed buffalo horn:
While the roof of the hall by our chorus is torn,
Fill, fill to the brim the deep silver-rimmed horn.

[1] The accent is on the second syllable: Seithényn.
[2] Gwin . . . . o eur . . . . ANEURIN.
[3] The mixture of ale and mead made bradawd, a favourite drink of the Ancient Britons.

Elphin and Teithrin stood some time on the floor of the hall before they attracted the attention of Seithenyn, who, during the chorus, was flourishing his golden goblet. The chorus had scarcely ended when he noticed them, and immediately roared aloud, "You are welcome all four."

Elphin answered, "We thank you: we are but two."

"Two or four," said Seithenyn, "all is one. You are welcome all. When a stranger enters, the custom in other places is to begin by washing his feet. My custom is, to begin by washing his throat. Seithenyn ap Seithyn Saidi bids you welcome."

Elphin, taking the wine-cup, answered, "Elphin ap Gwythno Garanhir thanks you."

Seithenyn started up. He endeavoured to straighten himself into perpendicularity, and to stand steadily on his legs. He accomplished half his object by stiffening all his joints but those of his ankles, and from these the rest of his body vibrated upwards with the inflexibility of a bar. After thus oscillating for a time, like an inverted pendulum, finding that the attention requisite to preserve his rigidity absorbed all he could collect of his dissipated energy, and that he required a portion of them for the management of his voice, which he felt a dizzy desire to wield with peculiar steadiness in the presence of the son of the king, he suddenly relaxed the muscles that perform the operation of sitting, and dropped into his chair like a plummet. He then, with a gracious gesticulation, invited Prince Elphin to take his seat on his right hand, and proceeded to compose himself into a dignified attitude, throwing his body back into the left corner of his chair, resting his left elbow on its arm and his left cheekbone on the middle of the back of his left hand, placing his left foot on a footstool, and stretching out his right leg as straight and as far as his position allowed. He had thus his right hand at liberty, for the ornament of his eloquence and the conduct of his liquor.

Elphin seated himself at the right hand of Seithenyn. Teithrin remained at the end of the hall: on which Seithenyn exclaimed, "Come on, man, come on. What if you be not the son of a king, you are the guest of Seithenyn ap Seithyn Saidi. The most honourable place to the most honourable guest, and the next most honourable place to the next most honourable guest; the least honourable guest above the most honourable inmate; and, where there are but two guests, be the most honourable who he may, the least honourable of the two is next in honour to the most honourable of the two, because there are no more but two; and, where there are only two, there can be nothing between. Therefore, sit, and drink. GWIN O EUR: wine from gold."

Elphin motioned Teithrin to approach, and sit next to him.

Prince Seithenyn, whose liquor was "his eating and his drinking solely," seemed to measure the gastronomy of his guests by his own; but his groom of the pantry thought the strangers might be disposed to eat, and placed before them a choice of provision, on which Teithrin ap Tathral did vigorous execution.

"I pray your excuses," said Seithenyn, "my stomach is weak, and I am subject to dizziness in the head, and my memory is not so good as it was, and my faculties of attention are somewhat impaired, and I would dilate more upon the topic, whereby you should hold me excused, but I am troubled with a feverishness and parching of the mouth, that very much injures my speech, and impedes my saying all I would say, and will say before I have done, in token of my loyalty and fealty to your highness and your highness's house. I must just moisten my lips, and I will then proceed with my observations. Cupbearer, fill."

"Prince Seithenyn," said Elphin, "I have visited you on a subject of deep moment. Reports have been brought to me, that the embankment, which has been so long entrusted to your care, is in a state of dangerous decay."

"Decay," said Seithenyn, "is one thing, and danger is another. Everything that is old must decay. That the embankment is old, I am free to confess; that it is somewhat rotten in parts, I will not altogether deny; that it is any the worse for that, I do most sturdily gainsay. It does its business well: it works well: it keeps out the water from the land, and it lets in the wine upon the High Commission of Embankment. Cupbearer, fill. Our ancestors were wiser than we: they built it in their wisdom; and, if we should be so rash as to try to mend it, we should only mar it."

"The stonework," said Teithrin, "is sapped and mined: the piles are rotten, broken, and dislocated: the floodgates and sluices are leaky and creaky."

"That is the beauty of it," said Seithenyn. "Some parts of it are rotten, and some parts of it are sound."

"It is well," said Elphin, "that some parts are sound: it were better that all were so."

"So I have heard some people say before," said Seithenyn; "perverse people, blind to venerable antiquity: that very unamiable sort of people, who are in the habit of indulging their reason. But I say, the parts that are rotten give elasticity to those that are sound: they give them elasticity, elasticity, elasticity. If it were all sound, it would break by its own obstinate stiffness: the soundness is checked by the rottenness, and the stiffness is balanced by the elasticity. There is nothing so dangerous as innovation. See the waves in the equinoctial storms, dashing and clashing, roaring and pouring, spattering and battering, rattling and battling against it. I would not be so presumptuous as to say, I could build anything that would stand against them half an hour; and here this immortal old work, which God forbid the finger of modern mason should bring into jeopardy, this immortal work has stood for centuries, and will stand for centuries more, if we let it alone. It is well: it works well: let well alone. Cupbearer, fill. It was half rotten when I was born, and that is a conclusive reason why it should be three parts rotten when I die."

The whole body of the High Commission roared approbation.

"And after all," said Seithenyn, "the worst that could happen would be the overflow of a spring-tide, for that was the worst that happened before the embankment was thought of; and, if the high water should come in, as it did before, the low water would go out again, as it did before. We should be no deeper in it than our ancestors were, and we could mend as easily as they could make."

"The level of the sea," said Teithrin, "is materially altered."

"The level of the sea!" exclaimed Seithenyn. "Who ever heard of such a thing as altering the level of the sea? Alter the level of that bowl of wine before you, in which, as I sit here, I see a very ugly reflection of your very good-looking face. Alter the level of that: drink up the reflection: let me see the face without the reflection, and leave the sea to level itself."

"Not to level the embankment," said Teithrin.

"Good, very good," said Seithenyn. "I love a smart saying, though it hits at me. But whether yours is a smart saying or no, I do not very clearly see; and, whether it hits at me or no, I do not very sensibly feel. But all is one. Cupbearer, fill."

"I think," pursued Seithenyn, looking as intently as he could at Teithrin ap Tathral, "I have seen something very like you before. There was a fellow here the other day very like you: he stayed here some time: he would not talk: he did nothing but drink: he used to drink till he could not stand, and then he went walking about the embankment. I suppose he thought it wanted mending; but he did not say anything. If he had, I should have told him to embank his own throat, to keep the liquor out of that. That would have posed him: he could not have answered that: he would not have had a word to say for himself after that."

"He must have been a miraculous person," said Teithrin, "to walk when he could not stand."

"All is one for that," said Seithenyn. "Cupbearer, fill."

"Prince Seithenyn," said Elphin, "if I was not aware that wine speaks in the silence of reason, I should be astonished at your strange vindication of your neglect of duty, which I take shame to myself for not having sooner known and remedied. The wise bard has well observed, 'Nothing is done without the eye of the king.'"

"I am very sorry," said Seithenyn, "that you see things in a wrong light: but we will not quarrel, for three reasons: first, because you are the son of the king, and may do and say what you please without any one having a right to be displeased: second, because I never quarrel with a guest, even if he grows riotous in his cups: third, because there is nothing to quarrel about; and perhaps that is the best reason of the three; or, rather, the first is the best, because you are the son of the king; and the third is the second, that is, the second best, because there is nothing to quarrel about: and the second is nothing to the purpose, because, though guests will grow riotous in their cups, in spite of my good orderly example, God forbid I should say that is the case with you. And I completely agree in the truth of your remark, that reason speaks in the silence of wine."

Seithenyn accompanied his speech with a vehement swinging of his right hand: in so doing, at this point, he dropped his cup: a sudden impulse of rash volition to pick it dexterously up, before he resumed his discourse, ruined all his devices for maintaining dignity;

in stooping forward from his chair he lost his balance, and fell prostrate on the floor.

The whole body of the High Commission arose in simultaneous confusion, each zealous to be the foremost in uplifting his fallen chief. In the vehemence of their uprise, they hurled the benches backward, and the tables forward; the crash of cups and bowls accompanied their overthrow; and rivulets of liquor ran gurgling through the hall. The household wished to redeem the credit of their leader in the eyes of the prince; but the only service they could render him was to participate in his discomfiture; for Seithenyn, as he was first in dignity, was also, as was fitting, hardest in skull; and that which had impaired his equilibrium had utterly destroyed theirs. Some fell, in the first impulse, with the tables and benches; others were tripped up by the rolling bowls; and the remainder fell at different points of progression, by jostling against each other, or stumbling over those who had fallen before them.

THE OPPRESSION OF GWENHIDWY

A SIDE door, at the upper end of the hall, to the left of Seithenyn's chair, opened, and a beautiful young girl entered the hall, with her domestic bard, and her attendant maidens.

It was Angharad, the daughter of Seithenyn. The tumult had drawn her from the solitude of her chamber, apprehensive that some evil might befall her father in that incapability of self-protection to which he made a point of bringing himself by set of sun. She gracefully saluted Prince Elphin, and directed the cupbearers (who were bound by their office to remain half-sober till the rest of the company were finished off, after which they indemnified themselves at leisure)—she directed the cupbearers to lift up Prince Seithenyn, and bear him from the hall. The cupbearers reeled off with their lord, who had already fallen asleep, and who now began to play them a pleasant march with his nose, to inspirit their progression.

Elphin gazed with delight on the beautiful apparition, whose gentle and serious loveliness contrasted so strikingly with the broken trophies and fallen heroes of revelry that lay scattered at her feet.

"Stranger," she said, "this seems an unfitting place for you: let me conduct you where you will be more agreeably lodged."

"Still less should I deem it fitting for you, fair maiden," said Elphin.

She answered, "The pleasure of her father is the duty of Angharad."

Elphin was desirous to protract the conversation, and this very desire took from him the power of speaking to the purpose. He paused for a moment to collect his ideas, and Angharad stood still, in apparent expectation that he would show symptoms of following, in compliance with her invitation.

In this interval of silence, he heard the loud dashing of the sea, and the blustering of the wind through the apertures of the walls.

This supplied him with what has been, since Britain was Britain, the alpha and omega of British conversation. He said, "It seems a stormy night."

She answered, "We are used to storms: we are far from the mountains, between the lowlands and the sea, and the winds blow round us from all quarters."

There was another pause of deep silence. The noise of the sea was louder, and the gusts pealed like thunder through the apertures. Amidst the fallen and sleeping revellers, the confused and littered hall, the low and wavering torches, Angharad, lovely always, shone with single and surpassing loveliness. The gust died away in murmurs, and swelled again into thunder, and died away in murmurs again; and, as it died away, mixed with the murmurs of ocean, a voice, that seemed one of the many voices of the wind, pronounced the ominous words, "Beware of the oppression of Gwenhidwy."

They looked at each other, as if questioning whether all had heard alike.

"Did you not hear a voice?" said Angharad, after a pause.

"The same," said Elphin, "which has once before seemed to say to me, 'Beware of the oppression of Gwenhidwy.'"

Teithrin hurried forth on the rampart: Angharad turned pale, and leaned against a pillar of the hall. Elphin was amazed and awed, absorbed as his feelings were in her. The sleepers on the floor made an uneasy movement, and uttered an inarticulate cry.

Teithrin returned. "What saw you?" said Elphin.

Teithrin answered, "A tempest is coming from the west. The

moon has waned three days, and is half hidden in clouds, just visible above the mountains: the bank of clouds is black in the west; the scud is flying before them; and the white waves are rolling to the shore."

"This is the highest of the spring-tides," said Angharad, "and they are very terrible in the storms from the west, when the spray flies over the embankment, and the breakers shake the tower which has its foot in the surf."

"Whence was the voice," said Elphin, "which we heard erewhile? Was it the cry of a sleeper in his drink, or an error of the fancy, or a warning voice from the elements?"

"It was surely nothing earthly," said Angharad, "nor was it an error of the fancy, for we all heard the words, 'Beware of the oppression of Gwenhidwy.' Often and often, in the storms of the spring-tides, have I feared to see her roll her power over the fields of Gwaelod."

"Pray heaven she do not to-night," said Teithrin.

"Can there be such a danger?" said Elphin.

"I think," said Teithrin, "of the decay I have seen, and I fear the voice I have heard."

A long pause of deep silence ensued, during which they heard the intermitting peals of the wind, and the increasing sound of the rising sea swelling progressively into wilder and more menacing tumult, till, with one terrific impulse, the whole violence of the equinoctial tempest seemed to burst upon the shore. It was one of those tempests which occur once in several centuries, and which, by their extensive devastations, are chronicled to eternity; for a storm that signalizes its course with extraordinary destruction, becomes as worthy of celebration as a hero for the same reason. The old bard seemed to be of this opinion; for the turmoil which appalled Elphin, and terrified Angharad, fell upon his ears as the sound of inspiration: the awen came upon him; and, seizing his harp, he mingled his voice and his music with the uproar of the elements:

THE SONG OF THE FOUR WINDS [1]

Wind from the north: the young spring day
Is pleasant on the sunny mead;
The merry harps at evening play;

[1] This poem is a specimen of a numerous class of ancient Welsh poems, in which each stanza begins with a repetition of the predominant idea, and ter-

The dance gay youths and maidens lead:
The thrush makes chorus from the thorn:
The mighty drinker fills his horn.

Wind from the east: the shore is still;
The mountain-clouds fly tow'rds the sea;
The ice is on the winter-rill;
The great hall fire is blazing free:
The prince's circling feast is spread:
Drink fills with fumes the brainless head.

Wind from the south: in summer shade
'Tis sweet to hear the loud harp ring;
Sweet is the step of comely maid,
Who to the bard a cup doth bring:
The black crow flies where carrion lies:
Where pignuts lurk, the swine will work.

Wind from the west: the autumnal deep
Rolls on the shore its billowy pride:
He, who the rampart's watch must keep,
Will mark with awe the rising tide:
The high spring-tide that bursts its mound,
May roll o'er miles of level ground.

Wind from the west: the mighty wave
Of ocean bounds o'er rock and sand;
The foaming surges roar and rave
Against the bulwarks of the land:
When waves are rough, and winds are high,
Good is the land that's high and dry.

Wind from the west: the storm-clouds rise;
The breakers rave: the whirlblasts roar;
The mingled rage of seas and skies
Bursts on the low and lonely shore:
When safety's far, and danger nigh,
Swift feet the readiest aid supply.

Wind from the west—

minates with a proverb, more or less applicable to the subject. In some poems, the sequency of the main images is regular and connected, and the proverbial terminations strictly appropriate: in others, the sequency of the main images is loose and incoherent, and the proverbial termination has little or nothing to do with the subject of the stanza. The basis of the poem in the text is in the Englynion of Llwyarch Hên.

His song was cut short by a tremendous crash. The tower, which had its foot in the sea, had long been sapped by the waves; the storm had prematurely perfected the operation, and the tower fell into the surf, carrying with it a portion of the wall of the main building, and revealing through the chasm the white raging of the breakers beneath the blackness of the midnight storm. The wind rushed into the hall, extinguishing the torches within the line of its course, tossing the gray locks and loose mantle of the bard, and the light white drapery and long black tresses of Angharad. With the crash of the falling tower, and the simultaneous shriek of the women, the sleepers started from the floor, staring with drunken amazement; and, shortly after, reeling like an Indian from the wine-rolling Hydaspes,[1] in staggered Seithenyn ap Seithyn.

Seithenyn leaned against a pillar, and stared at the sea through the rifted wall with wild and vacant surprise. He perceived that there was an innovation, and he felt that he was injured: how, and by whom, he did not quite so clearly discern. He looked at Elphin and Teithrin, at his daughter, and at the members of his household, with a long and dismal aspect of blank and mute interrogation, modified by the struggling consciousness of puzzled self-importance, which seemed to require from his chiefship some word of command in this incomprehensible emergency. But the longer he looked, the less clearly he saw; and the longer he pondered, the less he understood. He felt the rush of the wind; he saw the white foam of the sea; his ears were dizzy with their mingled roar. He remained at length motionless, leaning against the pillar, and gazing on the breakers with fixed and glaring vacancy.

"The sleepers of Gwaelod," said Elphin, "they who sleep in peace and security, trusting to the vigilance of Seithenyn, what will become of them?"

"Warn them with the beacon fire," said Teithrin, "if there be fuel on the summit of the landward tower."

"That, of course, has been neglected too," said Elphin.

[1] In the fourteenth and fifteenth books of the Dionysiaca of Nonnus, Bacchus changes the river Astacis into wine; and the multitudinous army of water-drinking Indians proceeding to quench their thirst in the stream, become franticly drunk, and fall an easy prey to the Bacchic invaders. In the thirty-fifth book, the experiment is repeated on the Hydaspes. "Ainsi conquesta Bacchus l'Inde," as Rabelais has it.

"Not so," said Angharad; "that has been my charge."

Teithrin seized a torch, and ascended the eastern tower, and in a few minutes, the party in the hall beheld the breakers reddening with the reflected fire, and deeper, and yet deeper crimson tinging the whirling foam, and sheeting the massy darkness of the bursting waves.

Seithenyn turned his eyes on Elphin. His recollection of him was extremely faint, and the longer he looked on him he remembered him the less. He was conscious of the presence of strangers, and of the occurrence of some signal mischief, and associated the two circumstances in his dizzy perceptions with a confused, but close connection. He said at length, looking sternly at Elphin, "I do not know what right the wind has to blow upon me here; nor what business the sea has to show itself here; nor what business you have here: but one thing is very evident, that either my castle or the sea is on fire; and I shall be glad to know who has done it, for terrible shall be the vengeance of Seithenyn ap Seithyn. Show me the enemy," he pursued, drawing his sword furiously, and flourishing it over his head, "Show me the enemy; show me the enemy!"

An unusual tumult mingled with the roar of the waves; a sound, the same in kind, but greater in degree, with that produced by the loose stones of the beach, which are rolled to and fro by the surf.

Teithrin rushed into the hall, exclaiming, "All is over! the mound is broken; and the spring-tide is rolling through the breach!"

Another portion of the castle wall fell into the mining waves, and, by the dim and thickly-clouded moonlight, and the red blaze of the beacon fire, they beheld a torrent pouring in from the sea upon the plain, and rushing immediately beneath the castle walls, which, as well as the points of the embankment that formed the sides of the breach, continued to crumble away into the waters.

"Who has done this?" vociferated Seithenyn. "Show me the enemy."

"There is no enemy but the sea," said Elphin, "to which you, in your drunken madness, have abandoned the land. Think, if you can think, of what is passing in the plain. The storm drowns the cries of your victims; but the curses of the perishing are upon you."

"Show me the enemy," vociferated Seithenyn, flourishing his sword more furiously.

Angharad looked deprecatingly at Elphin, who abstained from further reply.

"There is no enemy but the sea," said Teithrin, "against which your sword avails not."

"Who dares to say so?" said Seithenyn. "Who dares to say that there is an enemy on earth against whom the sword of Seithenyn ap Seithyn is unavailing? Thus, thus I prove the falsehood."

And, springing suddenly forward, he leaped into the torrent, flourishing his sword as he descended.

"Oh, my unhappy father!" sobbed Angharad, veiling her face with her arm on the shoulder of one of her female attendants, whom Elphin dexterously put aside, and substituted himself as the supporter of the desolate beauty.

"We must quit the castle," said Teithrin, "or we shall be buried in its ruins. We have but one path of safety, along the summit of the embankment, if there be not another breach between us and the high land, and if we can keep our footing in this hurricane. But there is no alternative. The walls are melting away like snow."

The bard, who was now recovered from his awen, and beginning to be perfectly alive to his own personal safety, conscious at the same time that the first duty of his privileged order was to animate the less-gifted multitude by examples of right conduct in trying emergencies, was the first to profit by Teithrin's admonition, and to make the best of his way through the door that opened to the embankment, on which he had no sooner set his foot than he was blown down by the wind; his harp-strings ringing as he fell. He was indebted to the impediment of his harp for not being rolled down the mound into the waters which were rising within.

Teithrin picked him up, and admonished him to abandon his harp to its fate, and fortify his steps with a spear. The bard murmured objections: and even the reflection that he could more easily get another harp than another life, did not reconcile him to parting with his beloved companion. He got over the difficulty by slinging his harp, cumbrous as it was, to his left side, and taking a spear in his right hand.

Angharad, recovering from the first shock of Seithenyn's catastrophe, became awake to the imminent danger. The spirit of the Cymric female, vigilant and energetic in peril, disposed her and her attendant maidens to use their best exertions for their own preservation. Following the advice and example of Elphin and Teithrin, they armed themselves with spears, which they took down from the walls.

Teithrin led the way, striking the point of his spear firmly into the earth, and leaning from it on the wind: Angharad followed in the same manner: Elphin followed Angharad, looking as earnestly to her safety as was compatible with moderate care of his own: the attendant maidens followed Elphin; and the bard, whom the result of his first experiment had rendered unambitious of the van, followed the female train. Behind them went the cupbearers, whom the accident of sobriety had qualified to march: and behind them reeled and roared those of the bacchanal rout who were able and willing to move; those more especially who had wives or daughters to support their tottering steps. Some were incapable of locomotion, and others, in the heroic madness of liquor, sat down to await their destiny, as they finished the half-drained vessels.

The bard, who had somewhat of a picturesque eye, could not help sparing a little leisure from the care of his body, to observe the effects before him: the volumed blackness of the storm; the white bursting of the breakers in the faint and scarcely-perceptible moonlight; the rushing and rising of the waters within the mound; the long floating hair and waving drapery of the young women; the red light of the beacon fire falling on them from behind; the surf rolling up the side of the embankment, and breaking almost at their feet; the spray flying above their heads; and the resolution with which they impinged the stony ground with their spears, and bore themselves up against the wind.

Thus they began their march. They had not proceeded far, when the tide began to recede, the wind to abate somewhat of its violence, and the moon to look on them at intervals through the rifted clouds, disclosing the desolation of the inundated plain, silvering the tumultuous surf, gleaming on the distant mountains, and revealing a lengthened prospect of their solitary path, that lay in its irregular line like a ribbon on the deep.

THE LAMENTATIONS OF GWYTHNO

KING GWYTHNO had feasted joyously, and had sung his new ode to a chosen party of his admiring subjects, amidst their, of course, enthusiastic applause. He heard the storm raging without, as he laid himself down to rest: he thought it a very hard case for those who were out in it, especially on the sea; congratulated himself on his own much more comfortable condition; and went to sleep with a pious reflection on the goodness of Providence to himself.

He was roused from a pleasant dream by a confused and tumultuous dissonance that mingled with the roar of the tempest. Rising with much reluctance, and looking forth from his window, he beheld in the moonlight a half-naked multitude, larger than his palace thrice multiplied could have contained, pressing round the gates, and clamouring for admission and shelter: while beyond them his eye fell on the phenomenon of stormy waters, rolling in the place of the fertile fields from which he derived his revenue.

Gwythno, though a king and his own laureate, was not without sympathy for the people who had the honour and happiness of victualling his royal house, and he issued forth on his balcony full of perplexities and alarms, stunned by the sudden sense of the half-understood calamity, and his head still dizzy from the effects of abruptly-broken sleep, and the vapours of the overnight's glorious festival.

Gwythno was altogether a reasonably good sort of person, and a poet of some note. His people were somewhat proud of him on the latter score, and very fond of him on the former; for even the tenth part of those homely virtues, that decorate the memories of "husbands kind and fathers dear" in every churchyard, are matters of plebeian admiration in the persons of royalty; and every tangible point in every such virtue so located, becomes a convenient peg for the suspension of love and loyalty. While, therefore, they were unanimous in consigning the soul of Seithenyn to a place that no well-bred divine will name to a polite congregation, they overflowed, in the abundance of their own griefs, with a portion of sympathy for Gwythno, and saluted him, as he issued forth on his balcony, with a hearty *Duw cadw y Brenin*, or God save the King, which he returned with a benevolent wave of the hand; but they followed it up by an intense vociferation for food and lodging, which he received with a pitiful shake of the head.

Meanwhile the morning dawned: the green spots, that peered with the ebbing tide above the waste of waters, only served to indicate the irremediableness of the general desolation.

Gwythno proceeded to hold a conference with his people, as deliberately as the stormy state of the weather and their minds, and the confusion of his own, would permit. The result of the conference was, that they should use their best exertions to catch some stray beeves, which had escaped the inundation, and were lowing about the rocks in search of new pastures. This measure was carried into immediate effect: the victims were killed and roasted, carved, distributed, and eaten, in a very Homeric fashion, and washed down with a large portion of the contents of the royal cellars; after which, having more leisure to dwell on their losses, the fugitives of Gwaelod proceeded to make loud lamentation, all collectively for home and for country, and severally for wife or husband, parent or child, whom the flood had made its victims.

In the midst of these lamentations arrived Elphin and Angharad, with her bard and attendant maidens, and Teithrin ap Tathral. Gwythno, after a consultation, despatched Teithrin and Angharad's domestic bard on an embassy to the court of Uther Pendragon, and to such of the smaller kings as lay in the way, to solicit such relief as their several majesties might be able and willing to afford to a king in distress. It is said that the bard, finding a royal bardship vacant in a more prosperous court, made the most of himself in the market, and stayed where he was better fed and lodged than he could except to be in Caredigion; but that Teithrin returned, with many valuable gifts, and most especially one from Merlin, being a hamper, which multiplied an hundred-fold by morning whatever was put into it overnight, so that, for a ham and a flask put by in the evening, an hundred hams and an hundred flasks were taken out in the morning. It is at least certain that such a hamper is enumerated among the thirteen wonders of Merlin's art, and, in the authentic catalogue thereof, is called the hamper of Gwythno.

Be this as it may, Gwythno, though shorn of the beams of his revenue, kept possession of his palace. Elphin married Angharad, and built a salmon-weir on the Mawddach, the produce of which, with that of a series of beehives, of which his princess and her maidens made mead, constituted for some time the principal wealth and subsistence of the royal family of Caredigion.

King Gwythno, while his son was delving or fishing, and his daughter spinning or making mead, sat all day on the rocks, with his harp between his knees, watching the rolling of ocean over the locality of his past dominion, and pouring forth his soul in pathetic song on the change of his own condition, and the mutability of human things.

* * * * * *

Thus the kingdom of Caredigion fell into ruin: its people were destroyed, or turned out of house and home; and its royal family were brought to a condition in which they found it difficult to get loaves to their fishes. We, who live in more enlightened times, amidst the "gigantic strides of intellect," when offices of public trust are so conscientiously and zealously discharged, and so vigilantly checked and superintended, may wonder at the wicked negligence of Seithenyn; at the sophisms with which, in his liquor, he vindicated his system, and pronounced the eulogium of his old dilapidations, and at the blind confidence of Gwythno and his people in this virtual guardian of their lives and property: happy that our own public guardians are too virtuous to act or talk like Seithenyn, and that we ourselves are too wise not to perceive, and too free not to prevent it, if they should be so disposed.

[One night Angharad dreams that the weir has caught "a miraculous draught of fish." Hastening to test the dream's truth, she and Elphin find no fish, but they do find a small boat of basketwork, which holds a sleeping infant boy whose smiling beauty is so great that they at once name him Taliesin, or Radiant Brow, and take him to their bosoms. Two years later a daughter of their own is born, and named Melanghel. The weir prospers, while cultivation of the uplands brings the old king some revenue.]

THE EDUCATION OF TALIESIN

As Taliesin grew up, Gwythno instructed him in all the knowledge of the age, which was of course not much, in comparison with ours. The science of political economy was sleeping in the womb of time. The advantage of growing rich by getting into debt and paying interest was altogether unknown: the safe and economical currency, which is produced by a man writing his name on a bit of paper, for which other men give him their property, and which he is always ready to exchange for another bit of paper, of an equally safe and economical manufacture, being also equally ready to render his own person, at a moment's notice, as impalpable as the metal which he promises to pay, is a stretch of wisdom to which the people of those days had nothing to compare. They had no steam-engines, with fires as eternal as those of the nether world, wherein the squalid many, from infancy to age, might be turned into component portions of machinery for the benefit of the purple-faced few. They could neither poison the air with gas, nor the waters with its dregs: in short, they made their money of metal, and breathed pure air, and drank pure water, like unscientific barbarians.

Of moral science they had little; but morals, without science, they had about the same as we have. They had a number of fine precepts, partly from their religion, partly from their bards, which they remembered in their liquor, and forgot in their business.

Political science they had none. The blessings of virtual representation were not even dreamed of; so that, when any of their barbarous metallic currency got into their pockets or coffers, it had a chance to remain there, subjecting them to the inconvenience of unemployed capital. Still they went to work politically much as we do. The powerful took all they could get from their subjects and neighbors; and called something or other sacred and glorious, when they wanted the people to fight for them. They repressed disaffection by force, when it showed itself in an overt act; but they encouraged freedom of speech, when it was, like Hamlet's reading, "words, words, words."

There was no liberty of the press, because there was no press;

but there was liberty of speech to the bards, whose persons were inviolable, and the general motto of their order was y Gwir yn erbyn y Byd: the Truth against the World. If many of them, instead of acting up to this splendid profession, chose to advance their personal fortunes by appealing to the selfishness, the passions, and the prejudices of kings, factions, and the rabble, our free press gentry may afford them a little charity out of the excess of their own virtue.

In physical science, they supplied the place of knowledge by converting conjectures into dogmas; an art which is not yet lost. They held that the earth was the centre of the universe; that an immense ocean surrounded the earth; that the sky was a vast frame resting on the ocean; that the circle of their contact was a mystery of infinite mist; with a great deal more of cosmogony and astronomy, equally correct and profound, which answered the same purpose as our more correct and profound astronomy answers now, that of elevating the mind, as the eidouranion lectures have it, to sublime contemplations.

Medicine was cultivated by the Druids, and it was just as much a science with them as with us; but they had not the wit or the means to make it a flourishing trade; the principal means to that end being women with nothing to do, articles which especially belong to a high state of civilization.

The laws lay in a small compass: every bard had those of his own community by heart. The king, or chief, was the judge; the plaintiff and defendant told their own story; and the cause was disposed of in one hearing. We may well boast of the progress of light, when we turn from this picture to the statutes at large, and the Court of Chancery; and we may indulge in a pathetic reflection on our sweet-faced myriads of "learned friends," who would be under the unpleasant necessity of suspending themselves by the neck, if this barbaric "Practice of the Courts" were suddenly revived.

The religion of the time was Christianity grafted on Druidism. The Christian faith had been very early preached in Britain. Some of the Welsh historians are of opinion that it was first preached by some of the apostles: most probably by St. John. They think the evidence inconclusive with respect to St. Paul. But, at any rate, the faith had made considerable progress among the Britons at the period of the arrival of Hengist; for many goodly churches, and, what was still better, richly-endowed abbeys, were flourishing in many places. The British clergy were, however, very contumacious towards the See of Rome, and would only acknowledge the spiritual authority of the Archbishopric of Caer Lleon, which was, during many centuries, the primacy of Britain. St. Augustin, when he came over, at a period not long subsequent to that of the present authentic history, to preach Christianity to the Saxons, who had, for the most part, held fast to their Odinism, had also the secondary purpose of making them instruments for teaching the British clergy submission to Rome: as a means to which end, the newly-converted Saxons set upon the monastery of Bangor Iscoed, and put its twelve hundred monks to the sword. This was the first overt act in which the Saxons set forth their new sense of a religion of peace. It is alleged, indeed, that these twelve hundred monks supported themselves by the la-bour of their own hands. If they did so, it was, no doubt, a gross heresy; but whether it deserved the castigation it received from St. Augustin's proselytes, may be a question in polemics.

As the people did not read the Bible, and had no religious tracts, their religion, it may be assumed, was not very pure. The rabble of Britons must have seen little more than the superficial facts that the lands, revenues, privileges, and so forth, which once belonged to Druids and so forth, now belonged to abbots, bishops, and so forth, who, like their extruded precursors, walked occasionally in a row, chanting unintelligible words, and never speaking in common lan-guage but to exhort the people to fight; having, indeed, better no-tions than their predecessors of building, apparel, aud cookery; and a better knowledge of the means of obtaining good wine, and of the final purpose for which it was made.

They were observant of all matters of outward form, and tradition even places among them personages who were worthy to have founded a society for the suppression of vice. It is recorded in the Triads that "Gwrgi Garwlwyd killed a male and female of the Cymry daily, and devoured them; and on the Saturday he killed two of each, that he might not kill on the Sunday." This can only be a type of some sanctimonious hero who made a cloak of piety for oppressing the poor.

But, even among the Britons, in many of the least populous and most mountainous districts, Druidism was still struggling with Christianity. The lamb had driven the wolf from the rich pastures of the valleys to the high places of the wilderness, where the rites and mysteries of the old religion flourished in secrecy, and where a stray proselyte of the new light was occasionally caught and roasted for the glory of Andraste.

Taliesin, worshipping Nature in her wildest solitudes, often strayed away for days from the dwelling of Elphin, and penetrated the recesses of Eryri,[1] where one especial spot on the banks of Lake Ceirionydd became the favourite haunt of his youth. In these lonely recesses he became familiar with Druids, who initiated him in their mysteries, which, like all other mysteries, consisted of a quantity of allegorical mummery, pretending to be symbolical of the immortality of the soul, and of its progress through various stages of being; interspersed with a little, too literal, ducking and singeing of the aspirant, by way of trying his metal, just enough to put him in fear, but not in risk, of his life.

That Taliesin was thoroughly initiated in these mysteries is evident from several of his poems, which have neither head nor tail, and which, having no sense in any other point of view, must necessarily, as a learned mythologist has demonstrated, be assigned to the class of theology in which an occult sense can be found or made for them, according to the views of the expounder. One of them, a shade less obscure than its companions, unquestionably adumbrates the Druidical doctrine of transmigration. According to this poem, Taliesin had been with the cherubim at the fall of Lucifer, in Paradise at the fall of man, and with Alexander at the fall of Babylon; in the ark with Noah, and in the milky way with Tetragrammaton; and in many other equally marvellous or memorable conditions: showing that, though the names and histories of the new religion were adopted, its doctrines had still to be learned; and, indeed, in all cases of this description, names are changed more readily than doctrines, and doctrines more readily than ceremonies.

When any of the Romans or Saxons, who invaded the island, fell into the hands of the Britons, before the introduction of Christianity, they were handed over to the Druids, who sacrificed them, with pious ceremonies, to their goddess Andraste. These human sacrifices have done much injury to the Druidical character amongst us, who

[1] Snowdon.

never practise them in the same way. They lacked, it must be confessed, some of our light, and also some of our prisons. They lacked some of our light, to enable them to perceive that the act of coming, in great multitudes, with fire and sword, to the remote dwellings of peaceable men, with the premeditated design of cutting their throats, ravishing their wives and daughters, killing their children, and appropriating their worldly goods, belongs, not to the department of murder and robbery, but to that of legitimate war, of which all the practitioners are gentlemen, and entitled to be treated like gentlemen. They lacked some of our prisons, in which our philanthropy has provided accommodation for so large a portion of our own people, wherein, if they had left their prisoners alive, they could have kept them from returning to their countrymen, and being at their old tricks again immediately. They would also, perhaps, have found some difficulty in feeding them, from the lack of the county rates, by which the most sensible and amiable part of our nation, the country squires, contrive to coop up, and feed, at the public charge, all who meddle with the wild animals of which they have given themselves the monopoly. But as the Druids could neither lock up their captives, nor trust them at large, the darkness of their intellect could suggest no alternative to the process they adopted, of putting them out of the way, which they did with all the sanctions of religion and law. If one of these old Druids could have slept, like the seven sleepers of Ephesus, and awaked, in the nineteenth century, some fine morning near Newgate, the exhibition of some half-dozen funipendulous forgers might have shocked the tender bowels of his humanity, as much as one of his wicker baskets of captives in the flames shocked those of Cæsar; and it would, perhaps, have been difficult to convince him that paper credit was not an idol, and one of a more sanguinary character than his Andraste. The Druids had their view of these matters, and we have ours; and it does not comport with the steam-engine speed of our march of mind to look at more than one side of a question.

The people lived in darkness and vassalage. They were lost in the grossness of beef and ale. They had no pamphleteering societies to demonstrate that reading and writing are better than meat and drink; and they were utterly destitute of the blessings of those "schools for all," the house of correction, and the treadmill, wherein the autochthonal justice of our agrestic kakistocracy now castigates the heinous sins which were then committed with impunity, of treading on old footpaths, picking up dead wood, and moving on the face of the earth within the sound of the whirr of a partridge.

The learning of the time was confined to the bards. It consisted in a somewhat complicated art of versification; in a great number of pithy apophthegms, many of which have been handed down to posterity under the title of the Wisdom of Catog; in an interminable accumulation of Triads, in which form they bound up all their knowledge, physical, traditional, and mythological; and in a mighty condensation of mysticism, being the still-cherished relics of the Druidical rites and doctrines.

The Druids were the sacred class of the bardic order. Before the change of religion, it was by far the most numerous class; for the very simple reason, that there was most to be got by it: all ages and nations having been sufficiently enlightened to make the trade of priest more profitable than that of poet. During this period, therefore, it was the only class that much attracted the notice of foreigners. After the change of religion, the denomination was retained as that of the second class of the order. The Bardd Braint, or Bard of Presidency, was of the ruling order, and wore a robe of sky-blue. The Derwydd, or Druid, wore a robe of white. The Ovydd, or Ovate, was of the class of initiation, and wore a robe of green. The Awenyddion, or disciples, the candidates for admission into the Bardic order, wore a variegated dress of the three colours, and were passed through a very severe moral and intellectual probation.

Gwythno was a Bardd Braint, or Bard of Presidency, and as such he had full power in his own person, without the intervention of a Bardic Congress, to make his Awenydd, or disciple, Taliesin, an Ovydd, or Ovate, which he did accordingly. Angharad, under the old king's instructions, prepared the green robe of the young aspirant's investiture. He afterwards acquired the white robe amongst the Druids of Eryri.

In all Bardic learning, Gwythno was profound. All that he knew he taught to Taliesin. The youth drew in the draughts of inspiration among the mountain forests and the mountain streams, and grew up under the roof of Elphin, in the perfection of genius and beauty.

[Elphin succeeds his father as king; Uther Pendragon dies, and
Arthur reigns in Caer Lleon over the minor kings of Britain. One
of these is Maelgon, a mighty hunter, who plunders Elphin's
dwelling and carries Elphin himself off to his Castle of Dikanwy
to enjoy enforced hospitality. During this period of entertainment
there is some argument regarding the virtue of wives, and Maelgon's son, Rhûn, undertakes to seduce Angharad during her husband's absence. Deceived by an old trick, in which maid substitutes
for mistress, he returns in triumph to Diganwy; but Elphin refuses
to credit his proofs, and for his refusal is promptly imprisoned.
During Elphin's absence, his household is hard pressed to provide
for itself and repair the havoc done by Maelgon's visitation, but
young blood still has its way and Taliesin declares his love for
Melanghel. What can he do to win hers in return? He must free
her father, he declares. With this end in view he goes straight to
Diganwy, where he first charms Maelgon with a mead song, and
then learns that Elphin is not to be freed until he admits the
unchastity of Angharad. That he will never do, says Taliesin, and
explains the hoax by which Rhûn was deceived. Furious, the latter
determines on a second attempt. Then Taliesin sings a second
song, in which he warns Maelgon of Arthur's vengeance; but
Maelgon sneers, saying that Arthur has his hands full searching
for his queen who has been carried off by some unknown marauder. After a third song, of dire prophecy, Taliesin takes his leave
and returns home, where he awaits Rhûn's coming, springs a trap,
and imprisons the unhappy prince in a mountain cave, behind a
boulder that only Elphin can remove.]

THE HEROES OF DINAS VAWR

Prince rhun being safe in schistous bastile, Taliesin commenced
his journey to the court of King Arthur. On his way to Caer Lleon,
he was received with all hospitality, entertained with all admiration,
and dismissed with all honour, at the castles of several petty kings,
and, amongst the rest, at the castle of Dinas Vawr, on the Towy,
which was then garrisoned by King Melvas, who had marched with

a great force out of his own kingdom, on the eastern shores of the Severn, to levy contributions in the country to the westward, where, as the pleasure of his company had been altogether unlooked for, he had got possession of a good portion of movable property. The castle of Dinas Vawr presenting itself to him as a convenient hold, he had taken it by storm; and having cut the throats of the former occupants, thrown their bodies into the Towy, and caused a mass to be sung for the good of their souls, he was now sitting over his bowl with the comfort of a good conscience, enjoying the fruits of the skill and courage with which he had planned and accomplished his scheme of ways and means for the year.

The hall of Melvas was full of magnanimous heroes, who were celebrating their own exploits in sundry choruses, especially in that which follows, which is here put upon record as being the quintessence of all the war-songs that ever were written, and the sum and substance of all the appetencies, tendencies, and consequences of military glory:

THE WAR-SONG OF DINAS VAWR

The mountain sheep are sweeter,
But the valley sheep are fatter;
We therefore deemed it meeter
To carry off the latter.
We made an expedition;
We met an host and quelled it;
We forced a strong position,
And killed the men who held it.

On Dyfed's richest valley,
Where herds of kine were browsing,
We made a mighty sally,
To furnish our carousing.
Fierce warriors rushed to meet us;
We met them, and o'erthrew them:
They struggled hard to beat us;
But we conquered them, and slew them.

As we drove our prize at leisure,
The king marched forth to catch us:
His rage surpassed all measure,
But his people could not match us.
He fled to his hall-pillars;

And, ere our force we led off,
Some sacked his house and cellars,
While others cut his head off.

We there, in strife bewildering,
Spilt blood enough to swim in:
We orphaned many children,
And widowed many women.
The eagles and the ravens
We glutted with our foemen:
The heroes and the cravens,
The spearmen and the bowmen.

We brought away from battle,
And much their land bemoaned them,
Two thousand head of cattle,
And the head of him who owned them:
Ednyfed, King of Dyfed,
His head was borne before us;
His wine and beasts supplied our feasts,
And his overthrow, our chorus.

As the doughty followers of Melvas, having sung themselves
hoarse with their own praises, subsided one by one into drunken
sleep, Taliesin, sitting near the great central fire, and throwing
around a scrutinizing glance on all the objects in the hall, noticed a
portly and somewhat elderly personage, of an aspect that would have
been venerable, if it had been less rubicund and Bacchic, who continued plying his potations with undiminished energy, while the
heroes of the festival dropped round him, like the leaves of autumn.
This figure excited Taliesin's curiosity. The features struck him with
a sense of resemblance to objects which had been somewhere familiar
to him; but he perplexed himself in vain, with attempts at definite
recollections. At length, when these two were almost the sole survivors of the evening, the stranger approached him with a golden
goblet, which he had just replenished with the choicest wine of the
vaults of Dinas Vawr, and pronounced the oracular monosyllable,
"Drink!" to which he subjoined emphatically, "Gwin o eur: Wine
from gold. That is my taste. Ale is well; mead is better; wine is best.
Horn is well; silver is better; gold is best."

Taliesin, who had been very abstemious during the evening, took
a golden goblet and drank, to please the inviter, in the hope that he

would become communicative, and satify the curiosity his appearance had raised.

The stranger sat down near him, evidently in that amiable state of semi-intoxication which inflates the head, warms the heart, lifts up the veil of the inward man, and sets the tongue flying, or rather tripping, in the double sense of nimbleness and titubancy.

The stranger repeated, taking a copious draught, "My taste is wine from gold."

"I have heard those words," said Taliesin, "GWIN O EUR, repeated as having been the favourite saying of a person whose memory is fondly cherished by one as dear to me as a mother, though his name, with all others, is the by-word of all that is disreputable."

"I cannot believe," said the stranger, "that a man whose favourite saying was GWIN O EUR could possibly be a disreputable person, or deserve any other than that honourable remembrance which you say only one person is honest enough to entertain for him."

"His name," said Taliesin, "is too unhappily notorious throughout Britain by the terrible catastrophe of which his 'Gwin o eur' was the cause."

"And what might that be?" said the stranger.

"The inundation of Gwaelod," said Taliesin.

"You speak, then," said the stranger, taking an enormous potation, "of Seithenyn, Prince Seithenyn, Seithenyn ap Seithin Saidi, Arglwyd Gorwarcheidwad yr Argae Breninawl."

"I seldom hear his name," said Taliesin, "with any of those sounding additions; he is usually called Seithenyn the Drunkard."

The stranger goggled about his eyes in an attempt to fix them steadily on Taliesin, screwed up the corners of his mouth, stuck out his nether lip, pursed up his chin, thrust forward his right foot, and elevated his golden goblet in his right hand; then, in a tone which he intended to be strongly becoming of his impressive accent and imposing attitude, he muttered, "Look at me!"

Taliesin looked at him accordingly, with as much gravity as he could preserve.

After a silence, which he designed to be very dignified and solemn, the stranger spoke again: "I am the man."

"What man?" said Taliesin.

"The man," replied his entertainer, "of whom you have spoken so disparagingly; Seithenyn ap Seithyn Saidi."

"Seithenyn," said Taliesin, "has slept twenty years under the waters of the western sea, as King Gwythno's Lamentations have made known to all Britain."

"They have not made it known to me," said Seithenyn, "for the best of all reasons, that one can only know the truth; for, if that which we think we know is not truth, it is something which we do not know. A man cannot know his own death; for, while he knows anything he is alive; at least, I never heard of a dead man who knew anything, or pretended to know anything: if he had so pretended, I should have told him to his face he was no dead man."

"Your mode of reasoning," said Taliesin, "unquestionably corresponds with what I have heard of Seithenyn's: but how is it possible Seithenyn can be living?"

"Everything that is, is possible, says Catog the Wise," answered Seithenyn, with a look of great sapience. "I will give you proof that I am not a dead man; for, they say dead men tell no tales: now, I will tell you a tale, and a very interesting one it is. When I saw the sea sapping the tower, I jumped into the water, and just in the nick of time. It was well for me that I had been so provident as to empty so many barrels, and that somebody, I don't know who, but I suppose it was my daughter, had been so provident as to put the bungs into them, to keep them sweet; for the beauty of it was that, when there was so much water in the case, it kept them empty; and when I jumped into the sea, the sea was just making a great hole in the cellar, and they were floating out by dozens. I don't know how I managed it, but I got one arm over one, and the other arm over another: I nipped them pretty tight; and though my legs were under water, the good liquor I had in me kept me warm. I could not help thinking—as I had nothing else to think of just then that touched me so nearly—that if I had left them full, and myself empty, as a sober man would have done, we should all three—that is, I and the two barrels, have gone to the bottom together, that is to say, separately; for we should never have come together, except at the bottom, perhaps, when no one of us could have done the other any good; whereas they have done me much good, and I have requited it; for, first, I did them the service of emptying them; and then they did me the service of floating me with the tide, whether the ebb, or the flow, or both, is more than I can tell, down to the coast of Dyfed, where I was picked up by fishermen; and such was my sense of gratitude that, though I had always before detested any empty barrel, except as a trophy, I swore I would not budge from the water unless my two barrels went with me; so we were all marched inland together, and were taken into the service of King Ednyfed, where I stayed till his castle was sacked, and his head cut off, and his beeves marched away with, by the followers of King Melvas, of whom I killed two or three; but they were too many for us: therefore, to make the best of a bad bargain, I followed leisurely in the train of the beeves, and presented myself to King Melvas, with this golden goblet, saying, 'Gwin o eur.' He was struck with my deportment, and made me his chief butler; and now my two barrels are the two pillars of his cellar, where I regularly fill them from affection, and as regularly empty them from gratitude, taking care to put the bungs in them, to keep them sweet."

"But all this while," said Taliesin, "did you never look back to the Plain of Gwaelod, to your old king, and, above all, to your daughter?"

"Why yes," said Seithenyn, "I did in a way! But as to the Plain of Gwaelod, that was gone, buried under the sea, along with many good barrels, which I had been improvident enough to leave full: then, as to the old king, though I had a great regard for him, I thought he might be less likely to feast me in his hall, than to set up my head on a spike over his gate; then, as to my daughter—"

Here he shook his head, and looked maudlin; and dashing two or three drops from his eye, he put a great many into his mouth.

"Your daughter," said Taliesin, "is the wife of King Elphin, and has a daughter, who is now as beautiful as her mother was."

"Very likely," said Seithenyn, "and I should be very glad to see them all; but I am afraid King Elphin, as you call him (what he is king of, you shall tell me at leisure), would do me a mischief. At any rate, he would stint me in liquor. No! If they will visit me, here I am. Fish, and water, will not agree with me. I am growing old, and need cordial nutriment. King Melvas will never want for beeves and wine; nor, indeed, for anything else that is good. I can tell you what," he added, in a very low voice, cocking his eye, and putting his finger on his lips, "he has got in this very castle the finest woman in Britain."

"That I doubt," said Taliesin.

"She is the greatest, at any rate," said Seithenyn, "and ought to be the finest."

"How the greatest?" said Taliesin.

Seithenyn looked round, to observe if there were any listener near, and fixed a very suspicious gaze on a rotund figure of a fallen hero, who lay coiled up like a maggot in a filbert, and snoring with an energy that, to the muddy apprehensions of Seithenyn, seemed to be counterfeit. He determined, by a gentle experiment, to ascertain if his suspicions were well founded; and proceeded, with what he thought great caution, to apply the point of his foot to the most bulging portion of the fat sleeper's circumference. But he greatly miscalculated his intended impetus, for he impinged his foot with a force that overbalanced himself, and hurled him headlong over his man, who instantly sprang on his legs, shouting "To arms!" Numbers started up at the cry; the hall rang with the din of arms, and with the vociferation of questions, which there were many to ask, and none to answer. Some stared about for the enemy; some rushed to the gates; others to the walls. Two or three, reeling in the tumult and the darkness, were jostled over the parapet, and went rolling down the precipitous slope of the castle hill, crashing through the bushes, and bellowing for some one to stop them, till their clamours were cut short by a plunge into the Towy, where the conjoint weight of their armour and their liquor carried them at once to the bottom. The rage which would have fallen on the enemy, if there had been one, was turned against the author of the false alarm; but, as none could point him out, the tumult subsided by degrees, through a descending scale of imprecations, into the last murmured malediction of him whom the intensity of his generous anger kept longest awake. By this time, the rotund hero had again coiled himself up into his ring; and Seithenyn was stretched in a right line, as a tangent to the circle, in a state of utter incapacity to elucidate the mystery of King Melvas's possession of the finest woman in Britain.

THE SPLENDOUR OF CAER LLEON

THE sunset of a bright December day was glittering on the waves of the Usk, and on the innumerable roofs, which, being composed chiefly of the glazed tiles of the Romans, reflected the light almost as vividly as the river; when Taliesin descended one of the hills that border the beautiful valley in which then stood Caer Lleon, the metropolis of Britain, and in which now stands, on a small portion of the selfsame space, a little insignificant town, possessing nothing of its ancient glory but the unaltered name of Caer Lleon.

The rapid Usk flowed then, as now, under the walls: the high wooden bridge, with its slender piles, was then much the same as it is at this day: it seems to have been never regularly rebuilt, but to have been repaired, from time to time, on the original Roman model. The same green and fertile meadows, the same gently-sloping wood-covered hills, that now meet the eye of the tourist, then met the eye of Taliesin; except that the woods on one side of the valley, were then only the skirts of an extensive forest, which the nobility and beauty of Caer Lleon made frequently re-echo to the clamours of the chase.

The city, which had been so long the centre of the Roman supremacy, which was now the seat of the most illustrious sovereign that had yet held the sceptre of Britain, could not be approached by the youthful bard, whose genius was destined to eclipse that of all his countrymen, without feelings and reflections of deep interest. The sentimental tourist, who, perching himself on an old wall, works himself up into a soliloquy of philosophical pathos, on the vicissitudes of empire and the mutability of all sublunary things, interrupted only by an occasional peep at his watch, to ensure his not overstaying the minute at which his fowl, comfortably roasting at the nearest inn, has been promised to be ready, has, no doubt, many fine thoughts well worth recording in a dapper volume; but Taliesin had an interest in the objects before him too deep to have a thought to spare, even for his dinner. The monuments of Roman magnificence, and of Roman domination, still existing in comparative freshness; the arduous struggle, in which his countrymen were then engaged with the Saxons, and which, notwithstanding the actual triumphs of Arthur, Taliesin's prophetic spirit told him would end in their being dispossessed of all the land of Britain, except the wild region of Wales, (a result which political sagacity might have apprehended from their disunion, but which, as he told it to his countrymen in that memorable prophecy which every child of the Cymry knows, has established for him, among them, the fame of a prophet;) the importance to himself and his benefactors of the objects of his visit to the city, on the result of which depended the liberation of Elphin, and the success of his love for Melanghel; the degree in which these objects might be promoted by the construction he had put on Seithenyn's imperfect communication respecting the lady in Dinas Vawr; furnished, altogether, more materials for absorbing thought, than the most zealous peregrinator, even if he be at once poet, antiquary, and philosopher, is likely to have at once in his mind, on the top of the finest old wall on the face of the earth.

Taliesin passed, in deep musing, through the gates of Caer Lleon; but his attention was speedily drawn to the objects around him. From the wild solitudes in which he had passed his earlier years, the transition to the castles and cities he had already visited, furnished much food to curiosity: but the ideas of them sunk into comparative nothingness before the magnificence of Caer Lleon.

He did not stop in the gateway to consider the knotty question, which has since puzzled so many antiquaries, whether the name of Caer Lleon signifies the City of Streams, the City of Legions, or the City of King Lleon? He saw a river filled with ships, flowing through fine meadows, bordered by hills and forests; walls of brick, as well as of stone; a castle, of impregnable strength; stately houses, of the most admirable architecture; palaces with gilded roofs; Roman temples, and Christian churches; a theatre, and an amphitheatre. The public and private buildings of the departed Romans were in excellent preservation; though the buildings, and especially the temples, were no longer appropriated to their original purposes. The king's butler, Bedwyr, had taken possession of the Temple of Diana, as a cool place of deposit for wine: he had recently effected a stowage of vast quantities therein, and had made a most luminous arrangement of the several kinds; under the judicious and experienced superintendence of Dyvrig, the Ex-Archbishop of Caer Lleon; who had just then nothing else to do, having recently resigned his see in favour of King Arthur's uncle, David, who is, to this day, illustrious as the St. David in whose honour the Welshmen annually adorn their hats with a leek. This David was a very respectable character in his way: he was a man of great sanctity and simplicity; and, in order to eschew the vanities of the world, which were continually present to him in Caer Lleon, he removed the metropolitan see, from Caer Lleon, to the rocky, barren, woodless, streamless, meadowless, tempest-beaten point of Mynyw, which was afterwards called St. David's. He was the mirror and pattern of a godly life; teaching by example, as by precept; admirable in words, and excellent in deeds; tall in stature, handsome in aspect, noble in deportment, affable in address, eloquent and learned, a model to his followers, the life of the poor, the protector of widows, and the father of orphans. This makes altogether a very respectable saint; and it cannot be said, that the honourable leek is unworthily consecrated. A long series of his Catholic successors maintained, in great magnificence, a cathedral, a college, and a palace; keeping them all in repair, and feeding the poor into the bargain, from the archiepiscopal, or, when the primacy of Caer Lleon had merged in that of Canterbury, from the episcopal, revenues: but these things were reformed altogether by one of the first Protestant bishops, who, having a lady that longed for the gay world, and wanting more than all the revenues for himself and his family, first raised the wind by selling off the lead from the roof of his palace, and then obtained permission to remove from it, on the plea that it was not water-tight. The immediate successors of this bishop, whose name was Barlow, were in every way worthy of him; the palace and college have, consequently, fallen into incurable dilapidation, and the cathedral has fallen partially into ruins, and, most impartially, into neglect and defacement.

To return to Taliesin, in the streets of Caer Lleon. Plautus and Terence were not heard in the theatre, nor to be heard of in its neighbourhood; but it was thought an excellent place for an Eisteddfod, or Bardic Congress, and was made the principal place of assembly of the bards of the island of Britain. This is what Ross of Warwick means, when he says there was a noble university of students in Caer Lleon.

The mild precepts of the new religion had banished the ferocious sports to which the Romans had dedicated the amphitheatre, and, as Taliesin passed, it was pouring forth an improved and humanized multitude, who had been enjoying the pure British pleasure of baiting a bear.

The hot baths and aqueducts, the stoves of "wonderful artifice," as Giraldus has it, which diffused hot air through narrow spiracles, and many other wonders of the place, did not all present themselves to a first observation. The streets were thronged with people, especially of the fighting order, of whom a greater number flocked about Arthur than he always found it convenient to pay. Horsemen, with hawks and hounds, were returning from the neighbouring forest, accompanied by beautiful huntresses in scarlet and gold.

Taliesin, having perlustrated the city, proceeded to the palace of Arthur. At the gates he was challenged by a formidable guard, but passed by his bardic privilege. It was now very near Christmas, and when Taliesin entered the great hall it was blazing with artificial light, and glowing with the heat of the Roman stoves.

Arthur had returned victorious from the great battle of Badon Hill, in which he had slain with his own hand four hundred and forty Saxons; and was feasting as merrily as an honest man can be supposed to do while his wife is away. Kings, princes, and soldiers of fortune, bards and prelates, ladies superbly apparelled, and many of them surpassingly beautiful; and a most gallant array of handsome young cupbearers, marshalled and well drilled by the king's butler, Bedwyr, who was himself a petty king, were the chief components of the illustrious assembly.

Amongst the ladies were the beautiful Tegau Eurvron; Dywir, the Golden-haired; Enid, the daughter of Yniwl; Garwen, the daughter of Henyn; Gwyl, the daughter of Enddaud; and Indeg, the daughter of Avarwy Hir, of Maelienydd. Of these, Tegau Eurvron, or Tegau of the Golden Bosom, was the wife of Caradoc, and one of the Three Chaste Wives of the island of Britain. She is the heroine who, as the lady of Sir Cradock, is distinguished above all the ladies of Arthur's court in the ballad of the Boy and the Mantle.

Amongst the bards were Prince Llywarch, then in his youth, afterwards called Llywarch Hên, or Llywarch the Aged; Aneurin, the British Homer, who sang the fatal battle of Cattraëth, which laid the foundation of the Saxon ascendency, in heroic numbers, which the gods have preserved to us, and who was called the Monarch of the Bards, before the days of the glory of Taliesin; and Merddin Gwillt, or Merlin the Wild, who was so deep in the secrets of nature, that he obtained the fame of a magician, to which he had at least as good a title as either Friar Bacon or Cornelius Agrippa.

Amongst the petty kings, princes, and soldiers of fortune, were twenty-four marchawg, or cavaliers, who were the counsellors and champions of Arthur's court. This was the heroic band, illustrious, in the songs of chivalry, as the Knights of the Round Table. Their names and pedigrees would make a very instructive and entertaining chapter; and would include the interesting characters of Gwalchmai ap Gwyar the Courteous, the nephew of Arthur; Caradoc, "Colofn Cymry," the Pillar of Cambria, whose lady, as above noticed, was the mirror of chastity; and Trystan ap Tallwch, the lover of the beautiful Essyllt, the daughter, or, according to some, the wife of his uncle March ap Meirchion; persons known to all the world, as Sir Gawain, Sir Cradock, and Sir Tristram.

On the right of King Arthur sate the beautiful Indeg, and on his left the lovely Garwen. Taliesin advanced, along the tesselated floor, towards the upper end of the hall, and kneeling before King Arthur, said, "What boon will King Arthur grant to him who brings tidings of his wife?"

"Any boon," said Arthur, "that a king can give."

"Queen Gwenyvar," said Taliesin, "is the prisoner of King Melvas, in the castle of Dinas Vawr."

The mien and countenance of his informant satisfied the king that he knew what he was saying; therefore, without further parlance, he broke up the banquet, to make preparations for assailing Dinas Vawr.

But, before he began his march, King Melvas had shifted his quarters, and passed beyond the Severn to the isle of Avallon, where the marshes and winter floods assured him some months of tranquillity and impunity.

King Arthur was highly exasperated, on receiving the intelligence of Melvas's movement; but he had no remedy, and was reduced to the alternative of making the best of his Christmas with the ladies, princes, and bards who crowded his court.

The period of the winter solstice had been always a great festival with the northern nations, the commencement of the lengthening

of the days being, indeed, of all points in the circle of the year, that
in which the inhabitants of cold countries have most cause to rejoice. This great festival was anciently called Yule; whether derived
from the Gothic *Iola*, to make merry; or from the Celtic *Hiaul*, the
sun: or from the Danish and Swedish *Hiaul*, signifying wheel or
revolution, December being *Hiul-month*, or the month of
return; or from the Cimbric word *Ol*, which has the important
signification of ALE, is too knotty a controversy to be settled here:
but Yule had been long a great festival, with both Celts and Saxons;
and, with the change of religion, became the great festival of Christmas, retaining most of its ancient characteristics while England was
Merry England; a phrase which must be a mirifical puzzle to any
one who looks for the first time on its present most lugubrious
inhabitants.

The mistletoe of the oak was gathered by the Druids with great
ceremonies, as a symbol of the season. The mistletoe continued to
be so gathered, and to be suspended in halls and kitchens, if not
in temples, implying an unlimited privilege of kissing; which circumstance, probably, led a learned antiquary to opine that it was the
forbidden fruit.

The Druids, at this festival, made, in a capacious cauldron, a
mystical brewage of carefully selected ingredients, full of occult virtues, which they kept from the profane, and which was typical of
the new year and of the transmigration of the soul. The profane,
in humble imitation, brewed a bowl of spiced ale, or wine, throwing therein roasted crabs; the hissing of which, as they plunged
piping hot into the liquor, was heard with much unction at mid-
winter, as typical of the conjunct benignant influences of fire and
strong drink. The Saxons called this the Wassail-bowl, and the
brewage of it is reported to have been one of the charms with which
Rowena fascinated Voltigern.

King Arthur kept his Christmas so merrily, that the memory of it
passed into a proverb: "As merry as Christmas in Caer Lleon."

Caer Lleon was the merriest of places, and was commonly known
by the name of Merry Caer Lleon; which the English ballad-makers,
for the sake of the smoother sound, and confounding Cambria with
Cumbria, most ignorantly or audaciously turned into Merry Carlisle; thereby emboldening a northern antiquary to set about proving

that King Arthur was a Scotchman; according to the old principles of harry and foray, which gave Scotchmen a right to whatever they could find on the English border; though the English never admitted their title to anything there, excepting a halter in Carlisle.

The chase, in the neighboring forest: tilting in the amphitheatre; trials of skill in archery, in throwing the lance and riding at the quintain, and similar amusements of the morning, created good appetites for the evening feasts; in which Prince Cei, who is well known as Sir Kay, the seneschal, superintended the viands, as King Bedwyr did the liquor: having each a thousand men at command, for their provision, arrangement, and distribution; and music worthy of the banquet was provided and superintended by the king's chief harper, Geraint, of whom a contemporary poet observes, that, when he died, the gates of heaven were thrown wide open, to welcome the ingress of so divine a musician.

THE GHOSTLINESS OF AVALLON

"WHERE is the young bard," said King Arthur, after some nights of Christmas had passed by, "who brought me the news of my queen, and to whom I promised a boon, which he has not yet claimed?"

None could satisfy the king's curiosity. Taliesin had disappeared from Caer Lleon. He knew the power and influence of Maelgon Gwyneth; and he was aware that King Arthur, however favourably he might receive his petition, would not find leisure to compel the liberation of Elphin, till he had enforced from Melvas the surrender of his queen. It occurred to him that her restoration might be effected by peaceable means; and he knew that, if he could be in any degree instrumental to this result, it would greatly strengthen his claims on the king. He engaged a small fishing-vessel, which had just landed a cargo for the Christmas feasts of Caer Lleon, and set sail for the isle of Avallon. At that period, the spring-tides of the sea rolled round a cluster of islands, of which Avallon was one, over the extensive fens, which wiser generations have embanked and reclaimed.

The abbey of Avallon, afterwards called Glastonbury, was, even then, a comely and commodious pile, though not possessing any of that magnificence which the accumulated wealth of ages subsequently gave to it. A large and strongly fortified castle, almost adjoining the abbey, gave to the entire place the air of a stronghold of the church militant. King Melvas was one of the pillars of the orthodoxy of those days: he was called the Scourge of the Pelagians; and extended the shield of his temporal might over the spiritual brotherhood of Avallon, who, in return, made it a point of conscience not to stint him in absolutions.

Some historians pretend that a comfortable nunnery was erected at a convenient distance from the abbey, that is to say, close to it; but this involves a nice question in monastic antiquity, which the curious may settle for themselves.

It was about midway between nones and vespers when Taliesin sounded, on the gate of the abbey, a notice of his wish for admission. A small trapdoor in the gate was cautiously opened, and a face, as round and as red as the setting sun in November, shone forth in the aperture.

The topographers who have perplexed themselves about the origin of the name of Ynys Avallon, "the island of apples," had not the advantage of this piece of meteoroscopy: if they could have looked on this archetype of a Norfolk beefin, with the knowledge that it was only a sample of a numerous fraternity, they would at once have perceived the fitness of the appellation. The brethren of Avallon were the apples of the church. It was the oldest monastic establishment in Britain; and consequently, as of reason, the most plump, succulent, and rosy. It had, even in the sixth century, put forth the fruits of good living, in a manner that would have done honour to a more enlightened age. It went on steadily improving in this line till the days of its last abbot, Richard Whiting, who built the stupendous kitchen, which has withstood the ravages of time and the Reformation; and who, as appears by authentic documents, and, amongst others, by a letter signed with the honoured name of Russell, was found guilty, by a right worshipful jury, of being suspected of great riches, and of an inclination to keep them; and was accordingly sentenced to be hanged forthwith, along with his treasurer and subtreasurer, who were charged with aiding and abetting him in the safe custody of his cash and plate; at the same time that the Abbot of Peterborough was specially reprieved from the gallows, on the ground that he was the said Russell's particular friend. This was a compendium of justice and mercy according to the new light of King Henry the Eighth. The abbot's kitchen is the most interesting and perfect portion of the existing ruins. These ruins were overgrown with the finest ivy in England, till it was, not long since, pulled down by some Vandal, whom the Society of Antiquaries had sent down to make drawings of the walls, which he executed literally, by stripping them bare, that he might draw the walls, and nothing else. Its shade no longer waves over the musing moralist, who, with folded arms, and his back against a wall, dreams of the days that are gone; or the sentimental cockney, who, seating himself with much gravity on a fallen column, produces a flute from his pocket, and strikes up "I'd be a butterfly."

From the phænomenon of a blushing fruit that was put forth in the abbey gate of Avallon issued a deep, fat, gurgling voice, which demanded of Taliesin his name and business.

"I seek the Abbot of Avallon," said Taliesin.

"He is confessing a penitent," said the ghostly brother, who was officiating in turn as porter.

"I can await his leisure," said Taliesin, "but I must see him."

"Are you alone?" said the brother.

"I am," said Taliesin.

The gate unclosed slowly, just wide enough to give him admittance. It was then again barred and barricaded.

The ghostly brother, of whom Taliesin had now a full view, had a figure corresponding with his face, and wanted nothing but a pair of horns and a beard in ringlets to look like an avatar of Bacchus. He maintained, however, great gravity of face, and decorum of gesture, as he said to Taliesin, "Hospitality is the rule of our house; but we are obliged to be cautious in these times, though we live under powerful protection. Those bloody Nimrods, the Saxons, are athirst for the blood of the righteous. Monsters that are born with tails."

Taliesin had not before heard of this feature of Saxon conformation, and expressed his astonishment accordingly.

"How?" said the monk. "Did not a rabble of them fasten goats' tails to the robe of the blessed preacher in Riw, and did he not, therefore, pray that their posterity might be born with tails? And it is so. But let that pass. Have they not sacked monasteries, plundered churches, and put holy brethren to the sword? The blood of the saints calls for vengeance."

"And will have it," said Taliesin, "from the hand of Arthur."

The name of Arthur evidently discomposed the monk, who, desiring Taliesin to follow him, led the way across the hall of the abbey, and along a short wide passage, at the end of which was a portly door.

The monk disappeared through this door, and, presently returning, said, "The abbot requires your name and quality."

"Taliesin, the bard of Elphin ap Gwythno Garanhir," was the reply.

The monk disappeared again, and returning, after a longer pause than before, said, "You may enter."

The abbot was a plump and comely man, of middle age, having three roses in his complexion; one in full blossom on each cheek, and one in bud on the tip of his nose.

He was sitting at a small table, on which stood an enormous vase, and a golden goblet; and opposite to him sat the penitent of whom the round-faced brother had spoken, and in whom Taliesin recognized his acquaintance of Dinas Vawr, who called himself Seithenyn ap Seithyn.

The abbot and Seithenyn sat with their arms folded on the table, leaning forward towards each other, as if in momentous discussion.

The abbot said to Taliesin, "Sit;" and to his conductor, "Retire, and be silent."

"Will it not be better," said the monk, "that I cross my lips with the sign of secrecy?"

"It is permitted," said the abbot.

Seithenyn held forth the goblet to the monk, who swallowed the contents with much devotion. He then withdrew, and closed the door.

"I bid you most heartily welcome," said Seithenyn to Taliesin. "Drink off this, and I will tell you more. You are admitted to this special sitting at my special instance. I told the abbot I knew you well. Now I will tell you what I know. You have told King Arthur that King Melvas has possession of Queen Gwenyvar, and, in consequence, King Arthur is coming here, to sack and raze the castle and abbey, and cut every throat in the isle of Avallon. I have just brought the abbot this pleasant intelligence, and, as I knew it would take him down a cup or two, I have also brought what I call my little jug, to have the benefit of his judgment on a piece of rare wine which I have broached this morning: there is no better in Caer Lleon. And now we are holding council on the emergency. But I must say you abuse your bardic privilege, to enjoy people's hospitality, worm out their secrets, and carry the news to the enemy. It was partly to give you this candid opinion, that I have prevailed on the abbot to admit you to this special sitting. Therefore drink. GWIN O EUR: Wine from gold."

"King Arthur is not a Saxon, at any rate," sighed the abbot, winding up his fainting spirits with a draught. "Think not, young stranger, that I am transgressing the laws of temperance: my blood runs so cold when I think of the bloodthirsty Saxons, that I take a little wine medicinally, in the hope of warming it; but it is a slow and tedious remedy."

"Take a little more," said Seithenyn. "That is the true quantity. Wine is my medicine; and my quantity is a little more. A little more."

"King Arthur," said Taliesin, "is not a Saxon; but he does not brook injuries lightly. It were better for your abbey that he came not here in arms. The aiders and abettors of Melvas, even though they be spiritual, may not carry off the matter without some share of his punishment, which is infallible."

"That is just what I've been thinking," said Seithenyn.

"God knows," said the abbot, "we are not abettors of Melvas, though we need his temporal power to protect us from the Saxons."

"How can it be otherwise," said Taliesin, "than that these Saxon despoilers should be insolent and triumphant, while the princes of Britain are distracted with domestic broils: and for what?"

"Ay," said Seithenyn, "that is the point. For what? For a woman, or some such rubbish."

"Rubbish, most verily," said the abbot. "Women are the flesh which we renounce with the devil."

"Holy father," said Taliesin, "have you not spiritual influence with Melvas, to persuade him to surrender the queen without bloodshed, and, renewing his allegiance to Arthur, assist him in his most sacred war against the Saxon invaders?"

"A righteous work," said the abbot; "but Melvas is headstrong and difficult."

"Screw yourself up with another goblet," said Seithenyn; "you will find the difficulty smooth itself off wonderfully. Wine from gold has a sort of double light, that illuminates a dark path miraculously."

The abbot sighed deeply, but adopted Seithenyn's method of throwing light on the subject.

"The anger of King Arthur," said Taliesin, "is certain, and its consequences infallible. The anger of King Melvas is doubtful, and its consequences to you cannot be formidable."

"That is nearly true," said the abbot, beginning to look resolute, as the rosebud at his nose-tip deepened into damask.

"A little more," said Seithenyn, "and it will become quite true."

By degrees the proposition ripened into absolute truth. The abbot suddenly inflated his cheeks, started on his legs, and stalked bolt upright out of the apartment, and forthwith out of the abbey, followed by Seithenyn, tossing his goblet in the air, and catching it in his hand, as he went.

The round-faced brother made his appearance almost immediately. "The abbot," he said, "commends you to the hospitality of the brotherhood. They will presently assemble to supper. In the meanwhile, as I am thirsty, and content with whatever falls in my way, I will take a simple and single draught of whatever happens to be here."

His draught was a model of simplicity and singleness; for, having uplifted the ponderous vase, he held it to his lips till he had drained it of the very copious remnant which the abrupt departure of the abbot had caused Seithenyn to leave in it.

Taliesin proceeded to enjoy the hospitality of the brethren, who set before him a very comfortable hot supper, at which he quickly perceived, that, however dexterous King Elphin might be at catching fish, the monks of Avallon were very far his masters in the three great arts of cooking it, serving it up, and washing it down; but he had not time to profit by their skill and experience in these matters, for he received a pressing invitation to the castle of Melvas, which he obeyed immediately.

THE RIGHT OF MIGHT

"Friend seithenyn," said the abbot, when, having passed the castle gates, and solicited an audience, he was proceeding to the presence of Melvas, "this task to which I have accinged myself, is arduous, and in some degree awful; being, in truth, no less than to persuade a king to surrender a possession, which he has inclination to keep for ever, and power to keep, at any rate, for an indefinite time."

"Not so very indefinite," said Seithenyn; "for with the first song of the cuckoo (whom I mention on this occasion as a party concerned), King Arthur will batter his castle about his ears, and, in all likelihood, the abbey about yours."

The abbot sighed heavily.

"If your heart fail you," said Seithenyn, "another cup of wine will set all to rights."

"Nay, nay, friend Seithenyn," said the abbot, "that which I have already taken has just brought me to the point at which the heart is inspirited and the wit sharpened, without any infraction of the wisdom and gravity which become my character, and best suit my present business."

Seithenyn, however, took an opportunity of making signs to some cupbearers, and, when they entered the apartment of Melvas they were followed by vessels of wine and goblets of gold.

King Melvas was a man of middle age, with a somewhat round, large, regular-featured face, and an habitual smile of extreme self-satisfaction, which he could occasionally convert into a look of terrific ferocity, the more fearful for being rare. His manners were, for the most part, pleasant. He did much mischief, not for mischief's sake, nor yet for the sake of excitement, but for the sake of something tangible. He had a total and most complacent indifference to everything but his own will and pleasure. He took what he wanted wherever he could find it, by the most direct process, and without any false pretence. He would have disdained the trick which the chroniclers ascribed to Hengist, of begging as much land as a bull's hide would surround, and then shaving it into threads, which surrounded a goodly space. If he wanted a piece of land, he encamped upon it, saying, "This is mine." If the former possessor could eject him, so; it was not his: if not, so; it remained his. Cattle, wine, furniture, another man's wife, whatever he took a fancy to, he pounced upon and appropriated. He was intolerant of resistance, and, as the shortest way of getting rid of it, and not from any blood-thirstiness of disposition, or, as the phrenologists have it, development of the organ of destructiveness, he always cut through the resisting body, longitudinally, horizontally, or diagonally, as he found most convenient. He was the arch-marauder of West Britain. The abbey of Avallon shared largely in the spoil, and they made up together a most harmonious church and state. He had some respect for King Arthur; wished him success against the Saxons; knew the superiority of his power to his own; but he had heard that Queen Gwenyvar was the most beautiful woman in Britain; was, therefore, satisfied of his own title to her, and, as she was hunting in the forest, while King Arthur was absent from Caer Lleon, he seized her, and carried her off.

"Be seated, holy father," said Melvas; "and you also, Seithenyn, unless the abbot wishes you away."

But the abbot's heart misgave him, and he assented readily to Seithenyn's stay.

Melvas.—Now, holy father, to your important matter of private conference.

Seithenyn.—He is tongue-tied, and a cup too low.

The Abbot.—Set the goblet before me, and I will sip in moderation.

Melvas.—Sip, or not sip, tell me your business.

The Abbot.—My business, of a truth, touches the lady your prisoner, King Arthur's queen.

Melvas.—She is my queen, while I have her, and no prisoner. Drink, man, and be not afraid. Speak your mind: I will listen, and weigh your words.

The Abbot.—This queen—

Seithenyn.—Obey the king: first drink, then speak.

The Abbot.—I drink to please the king.

Melvas.—Proceed.

The Abbot.—This queen, Gwenyvar, is as beautiful as Helen, who caused the fatal war that expelled our forefathers from Troy: and I fear she will be a second Helen, and expel their posterity from Britain. [1] The infidel Saxons, to whom the cowardly and perfidious Vortigern gave footing in Britain, have prospered even more by the disunion of her princes than either by his villany or their own valour. And now there is no human hope against them but in the arms of Arthur. And how shall his arms prosper against the common enemy, if he be forced to turn them on the children of his own land for the recovery of his own wife?

Melvas.—What do you mean by his own? That which he has is his own: but that which I have is mine. I have the wife in question, and some of the land. Therefore, they are mine.

The Abbot.—Not so. The land is yours under fealty to him.

Melvas.—As much fealty as I please, or he can force me to give him.

The Abbot.—His wife, at least, is most lawfully his.

Melvas.—The winner makes the law, and his law is always against the loser. I am so far the winner, and, by my own law, she is lawfully mine.

The Abbot.—There is a law above all human law, by which she is his.

Melvas.—From that it is for you to absolve me; and I dispense my bounty according to your indulgence.

The Abbot.—There are limits we must not pass.

Melvas.—You set up your landmark, and I set up mine. They are both movable.

The Abbot.—The Church has not been niggardly in its indulgences to King Melvas.

Melvas.—Nor King Melvas in his gifts to the Church.

The Abbot.—But, setting aside this consideration, I would treat it as a question of policy.

Seithenyn.—Now you talk sense. Right without might is the lees of an old barrel, without a drop of the original liquor.

---

[1] According to the "British Chronicles," Brutus, the great grandson of Æneas, having killed his father, Silvius, to fulfil a prophecy, went to Greece, where he found the posterity of Helenus, the son of Priam; collected all of the Trojan race within the limits of Greece; and, after some adventures by land and sea, settled them in Britain, which was before uninhabited, "except by a few giants."

The Abbot.—I would appeal to you, King Melvas, by your love to your common country, by your love of the name of Britain, by your hatred of the infidel Saxons, by your respect for the character of Arthur; will you let your passion for a woman, even though she be a second Helen, frustrate, or even impede, the great cause of driving these spoilers from a land in which they have no right even to breathe?

Melvas.—They have a right to do all they do, and to have all they have. If we can drive them out, they will then have no right here. Have not you and I a right to this good wine, which seems to trip very merrily over your ghostly palate? I got it by seizing a good ship, and throwing the crew overboard, just to remove them out of the way, because they were troublesome. They disputed my right, but I taught them better. I taught them a great moral lesson, though they had not much time to profit by it. If they had had the might to throw me overboard, I should not have troubled myself about their right, any more, or at any rate, any longer, than they did about mine.

Seithenyn.—The wine was lawful spoil of war.

The Abbot.—But, if King Arthur brings his might to bear upon yours, I fear neither you nor I shall have a right to this wine, nor to anything else that is here.

Seithenyn.—Then make the most of it while you have it.

The Abbot.—Now, while you have some months of security before you, you may gain great glory by surrendering the lady; and, if you be so disposed, you may, no doubt, claim from the gratitude of King Arthur, the fairest princess of his court to wife, and an ample dower withal.

Melvas.—That offers something tangible.

Seithenyn.—Another ray from the golden goblet will set it in a most luminous view.

The Abbot.—Though I should advise the not making it a condition, but asking it as a matter of friendship, after the first victory that you have helped him to gain over the Saxons.

Melvas.—The worst of those Saxons is, that they offer nothing tangible, except hard knocks. They bring nothing with them. They come to take; and lately they have not taken much. But I will muse on your advice; and, as it seems I may get more by following than rejecting it, I shall very probably take it, provided that you now attend me to the banquet in the hall.

Seithenyn.—Now you talk of the hall and the banquet, I will just intimate that the finest of all youths, and the best of all bards, is a guest in the neighbouring abbey.

Melvas.—If so, I have a clear right to him, as a guest for myself.

The abbot was not disposed to gainsay King Melvas's right. Taliesin was invited accordingly, and seated at the left hand of the king, the abbot being on the right. Taliesin summoned all the energies of his genius to turn the passions of Melvas into the channels of anti-Saxonism, and succeeded so perfectly that the king and his whole retinue of magnanimous heroes were inflamed with intense ardour to join the standard of Arthur; and Melvas vowed most solemnly to Taliesin that another sun should not set before Queen Gwenyvar should be under the most honourable guidance on her return to Caer Lleon.

[Taliesin competes in the great Bardic Congress held at Caer Lleon at Christmastime, and vanquishes the principal bards of Britain to win "the highest honours of the sitting."]

THE JUDGMENTS OF ARTHUR

KING ARTHUR had not long returned to his hall, when Queen Gwenyvar arrived, escorted by the Abbot of Avallon and Seithenyn ap Seithyn Saidi, who had brought his golden goblet, to gain a new harvest of glory from the cellars of Caer Lleon.

Seithenyn assured King Arthur, in the name of King Melvas, and on the word of a king, backed by that of his butler, which, truth being in wine, is good warranty even for a king, that the queen returned as pure as on the day King Melvas had carried her off.

"None here will doubt that," said Gwenvach, the wife of Modred. Gwenyvar was not pleased with the compliment, and, almost before she had saluted King Arthur, she turned suddenly round, and slapped Gwenvach on the face, with a force that brought more crimson into one cheek than blushing had ever done into both. This slap is recorded in the Bardic Triads as one of the Three Fatal Slaps of the Island of Britain. A terrible effect is ascribed to this small cause; for it is said to have been the basis of that enmity between Arthur and Modred, which terminated in the battle of Camlan, wherein all the flower of Britain perished on both sides: a catastrophe more calamitous than any that ever before or since happened in Christendom, not even excepting that of the battle of Roncesvalles; for, in the battle of Camlan, the Britons exhausted their own strength, and could no longer resist the progress of the Saxon supremacy. This, however, was a later result, and comes not within the scope of the present veridicous narrative.

Gwenvach having flounced out of the hall, and the tumult occasioned by this little incident having subsided, Queen Gwenyvar took her ancient seat by the side of King Arthur, who proceeded to inquire into the circumstances of her restoration. The Abbot of Avallon began an oration, in praise of his own eloquence, and its miraculous effects on King Melvas; but he was interrupted by Seithenyn, who said, "The abbot's eloquence was good and well timed; but the chief merit belongs to this young bard, who prompted him with good counsel, and to me, who inspirited him with good liquor. If he had not opened his mouth pretty widely when I handed him this golden goblet, exclaiming Gwin o eur, he would never have had the heart to open it to any other good purpose. But the most deserving person is this very promising youth, in whom I can see no fault, but that he has not the same keen perception as my friend the abbot has of the excellent relish of wine from gold. To be sure, he plied me very hard with strong drink in the hall of Dinas Vawr, and thereby wormed out of me the secret of Queen Gwenyvar's captivity; and, afterwards, he pursued us to Avallon, where he persuaded me and the abbot, and the abbot persuaded King Melvas, that it would be better for all parties to restore the queen peaceably: and then he clenched the matter with the very best song I ever heard in my life. And, as my young friend has a boon to ask, I freely give him all my share of the merit, and the abbot's into the bargain."

"Allow me, friend of GWIN O EUR," said the abbot, "to dispose of my own share of merit in my own way. But, such as it is, I freely give it to this youth, in whom, as you say, I can see no fault, but that his head is brimfull of Pagan knowledge."

Arthur paid great honour to Taliesin, and placed him on his left hand at the banquet. He then said to him, "I judge, from your song of this morning, that the boon you require from me concerns Maelgon Gwyneth. What is his transgression, and what is the justice you require?"

Taliesin narrated the adventures of Elphin in such a manner as gave Arthur an insight into his affection for Melanghel; and he supplicated King Arthur to command and enforce the liberation of Elphin from the Stone Tower of Diganwy.

Before King Arthur could signify his assent, Maelgon Gwyneth stalked into the hall, followed by a splendid retinue. He had been alarmed by the absence of Rhûn, had sought him in vain on the banks of the Mawddach, had endeavoured to get at the secret by pouncing upon Angharad and Melanghel, and had been baffled in his project by the vigilance of Teithrin ap Tathral. He had, therefore, as a last resort, followed Taliesin to Caer Lleon, conceiving that he might have had some share in the mysterious disappearance of Rhûn.

Arthur informed him that he was in possession of all the circumstance, and that Rhûn, who was in safe custody, would be liberated on the restoration of Elphin.

Maelgon boiled with rage and shame, but had no alternative but submission to the will of Arthur.

King Arthur commanded that all the parties should be brought before him. Caradoc was charged with the execution of this order, and, having received the necessary communications and powers from Maelgon and Taliesin, he went first to Diganwy, where he liberated Elphin, and then proceeded to give effect to Teithrin's declaration, that "no hand but Elphin's should raise the stone of Rhûn's captivity." Rhûn, while his pleasant adventure had all the gloss of novelty upon it, and his old renown as a gay deceiver was consequently in such dim eclipse, was very unwilling to present himself before the ladies of Caer Lleon; but Caradoc was peremptory, and carried off the crest-fallen prince, together with his bard of all work, who was always willing to go to any court, with any character, or none.

Accordingly, after a moderate lapse of time, Caradoc re-appeared in the hall of Arthur, with the liberated captives, accompanied by Angharad and Melanghel, and Teithrin ap Tathral.

King Arthur welcomed the new comers with a magnificent festival, at which all the beauties of his court were present, and, addressing himself to Elphin, said, "We are all debtors to this young bard: my queen and myself for her restoration to me; you for your liberation from the Stone Tower of Diganwy. Now, if there be, amongst all these ladies, one whom he would choose for his bride, and in whose eyes he may find favour, I will give the bride a dowry worthy of the noblest princess in Britain."

Taliesin, thus encouraged, took the hand of Melanghel, who did not attempt to withdraw it, but turned to her father a blushing face. in which he read her satisfaction and her wishes. Elphin immediately said, "I have nothing to give him but my daughter; but her I most cordially give him."

Taliesin said, "I owe to Elphin more than I can ever repay: life, honour, and happiness."

Arthur said, "You have not paid him ill; but you owe nothing to Maelgon and Rhûn, who are your debtors for a lesson of justice, which I hope they will profit by during the rest of their lives. Therefore Maelgon shall defray the charge of your wedding, which shall be the most splendid that has been seen in Caer Lleon."

Maelgon looked exceedingly grim, and wished himself well back in Diganwy.

There was a very pathetic meeting of recognition between Seithenyn and his daughter; at the end of which he requested her husband's interest to obtain for him the vacant post of second butler to King Arthur. He obtained this honourable office; and was so zealous in the fulfilment of its duties, that, unless on actual service with a detachment of liquor, he never was a minute absent from the Temple of Diana.

At a subsequent Bardic Congress, Taliesin was unanimously elected Pen Beirdd, or Chief of the Bards of Britain. The kingdom of Caredigion flourished under the protection of Arthur, and, in the ripeness of time, passed into the hands of Avaon, the son of Taliesin and Melanghel.

Crotchet Castle

THE VILLA

IN one of those beautiful valleys, through which the Thames (not yet polluted by the tide, the scouring of cities, or even the minor defilement of the sandy streams of Surrey), rolls a clear flood through flowery meadows, under the shade of old beech woods, and the smooth glossy greensward of the chalk hills (which pour into it their tributary rivulets, as pure and pellucid as the fountain of Bandusium, or the wells of Scamander, by which the wives and daughters of the Trojans washed their splendid garments in the days of peace, before the coming of the Greeks); in one of those beautiful valleys, on a bold round-surfaced lawn, spotted with juniper, that opened itself in the bosom of an old wood, which rose with a steep, but not precipitous ascent, from the river to the summit of the hill, stood the castellated villa of a retired citizen. Ebenezer Mac Crotchet, Esquire, was the London-born offspring of a worthy native of the "north countrie," who had walked up to London on a commercial adventure, with all his surplus capital, not very neatly tied up in a not very clean handkerchief, suspended over his shoulder from the end of a hooked stick, extracted from the first hedge on his pilgrimage; and who, after having worked himself a step or two up the ladder of life, had won the virgin heart of the only daughter of a highly respectable merchant of Duke's Place, with whom he inherited the honest fruits of a long series of ingenuous dealings.

Mr. Mac Crotchet had derived from his mother the instinct, and from his father the rational principle, of enriching himself at the expense of the rest of mankind, by all the recognized modes of accumulation on the windy side of the law. After passing many years in the alley, watching the turn of the market, and playing many games almost as desperate as that of the soldier of Lucullus, [1] the fear of losing what he had so righteously gained predominated over the sacred thirst of paper-money; his caution got the better of his instinct, or rather transferred it from the department of acquisition to that of conservation. His friend, Mr. Ramsbottom, the zodiacal mythologist, told him that he had done well to withdraw from the region of Uranus or Brahma, the maker, to that of Saturn or Veeshnu, the preserver, before he fell under the eye of Jupiter or Seva, the destroyer, who might have struck him down at a blow.

It is said that a Scotchman returning home, after some years' residence in England, being asked what he thought of the English, answered: "They hanna ower muckle sense, but they are an unco braw people to live amang;" which would be a very good story, if it were not rendered apocryphal, by the incredible circumstance of the Scotchman going back.

Mr. Mac Crotchet's experience had given him a just title to make, in his own person, the last-quoted observation, but he would have known better than to go back, even if himself, and not his father, had been the first comer of his line from the north. He had married an English Christian, and, having none of the Scotch accent, was ungracious enough to be ashamed of his blood. He was desirous to obliterate alike the Hebrew and Caledonian vestiges in his name, and signed himself E. M. Crotchet, which by degrees induced the majority of his neighbours to think that his name was Edward Matthew. The more effectually to sink the Mac, he christened his villa Crotchet Castle, and determined to hand down to posterity the honours of Crotchet of Crotchet. He found it essential to his dignity to furnish himself with a coat of arms, which, after the proper ceremonies (payment being the principal), he obtained, videlicet: Crest, a crotchet rampant in A sharp: Arms, three empty bladders, turgescent, to show how opinions are formed; three bags of gold, pendent, to show why they are maintained; three naked swords, tranchant, to show how they are administered; and three barbers' blocks, gaspant, to show how they are swallowed.

Mr. Crotchet was left a widower, with two children; and, after

[1] Luculli miles, &c.—HOR., Ep. ii. 2, 26. "In Anna's wars, a soldier poor and bold," &c.—POPE's Imitation.

the death of his wife, so strong was his sense of the blessed comfort she had been to him, that he determined never to give any other woman an opportunity of obliterating the happy recollection.

He was not without a plausible pretence for styling his villa a castle, for, in its immediate vicinity, and within his own enclosed domain, were the manifest traces, on the brow of the hill, of a Roman station, or *castellum*, which was still called the castle by the country people. The primitive mounds and trenches, merely overgrown with greensward, with a few patches of juniper and box on the vallum, and a solitary ancient beech surmounting the place of the prætorium, presented nearly the same depths, heights, slopes, and forms, which the Roman soldiers had originally given them. From this *castellum* Mr. Crotchet christened his villa. With his rustic neighbours he was of course immediately and necessarily a squire—Squire Crotchet of the castle; and he seemed to himself to settle down as naturally into an English country gentleman, as if his parentage had been as innocent of both Scotland and Jerusalem, as his education was of Rome and Athens.

But as, though you expel nature with a pitchfork, she will yet always come back;[1] he could not become, like a true-born English squire, part and parcel of the barley-giving earth; he could not find in game-bagging, poacher-shooting, trespasser-pounding, footpath-stopping, common-enclosing, rack-renting, and all the other liberal pursuits and pastimes which make a country gentleman an ornament to the world and a blessing to the poor; he could not find in these valuable and amiable occupations, and in a corresponding range of ideas, nearly commensurate with that of the great King Nebuchadnezzar, when he was turned out to grass; he could not find in this great variety of useful action, and vast field of comprehensive thought, modes of filling up his time that accorded with his Caledonian instinct. The inborn love of disputation, which the excitements and engagements of a life of business had smothered, burst forth through the calmer surface of a rural life. He grew as fain as Captain Jamy, "to hear some airgument betwixt ony tway;" and being very hospitable in his establishment, and liberal in his invitations, a numerous detachment from the advanced guard of the "march of intellect," often marched down to Crotchet Castle.

[1] Naturam expellas furcâ, tamen usque recurret.—Hor., Ep. i. 10, 24.

When the fashionable season filled London with exhibitors of all descriptions, lecturers, and else, Mr. Crotchet was in his glory; for, in addition to the perennial literati of the metropolis, he had the advantage of the visits of a number of hardy annuals, chiefly from the north, who, as the interval of their metropolitan flowering allowed, occasionally accompanied their London brethren in excursions to Crotchet Castle.

Amongst other things, he took very naturally to political economy, read all the books on the subject which were put forth by his own countrymen, attended all lectures thereon, and boxed the technology of the sublime science as expertly as an able seaman boxes the compass.

With this agreeable mania he had the satisfaction of biting his son, the hope of his name and race, who had borne off from Oxford the highest academical honours; and who, treading in his father's footsteps to honour and fortune, had, by means of a portion of the old gentleman's surplus capital, made himself a junior partner in the eminent loan-jobbing firm of Catchflat and Company. Here, in the days of paper-prosperity, he applied his science-illumined genius to the blowing of bubbles, the bursting of which sent many a poor devil to the jail, the workhouse, or the bottom of the river, but left young Crotchet rolling in riches.

These riches he had been on the point of doubling, by a marriage with the daughter of Mr. Touchandgo, the great banker, when, one foggy morning, Mr. Touchandgo and the contents of his till were suddenly reported absent; and as the fortune which the young gentleman had intended to marry was not forthcoming, this tender affair of the heart was nipped in the bud.

Miss Touchandgo did not meet the shock of separation quite so complacently as the young gentleman; for he lost only the lady, whereas she lost a fortune as well as a lover. Some jewels, which had glittered on her beautiful person as brilliantly as the bubble of her father's wealth had done in the eyes of his gudgeons, furnished her with a small portion of paper currency; and this, added to the contents of a fairy purse of gold, which she found in her shoe on the eventful morning when Mr. Touchandgo melted into thin air, enabled her to retreat into North Wales, where she took up her lodging in a farm-house in Merionethshire, and boarded very

comfortably for a trifling payment, and the additional consideration
of teaching English, French, and music to the little Ap-Llymry's.
In the course of this occupation, she acquired sufficient knowledge
of Welsh to converse with the country people.

She climbed the mountains and descended the dingles, with a
foot which daily habit made by degrees almost as steady as a native's. She became the nymph of the scene; and if she sometimes.
pined in thought for her faithless Strephon, her melancholy was
anything but green and yellow; it was as genuine white and red as
occupation, mountain air, thyme-fed mutton, thick cream, and fat
bacon, could make it: to say nothing of an occasional glass of
double X, which Ap-Llymry, [1] who yielded to no man west of
the Wrekin in brewage, never failed to press upon her at dinner
and supper. He was also earnest, and sometimes successful, in the
recommendation of his mead, and most pertinacious on winter nights.
in enforcing a trial of the virtues of his elder wine. The young lady's
personal appearance, consequently, formed a very advantageous contrast to that of her quondam lover, whose physiognomy the intense
anxieties of his bubble-blowing days, notwithstanding their triumphant result, had left blighted, sallowed, and crow's-footed, to a
degree not far below that of the fallen spirit who, in the expressive
language of German romance, is described as "scathed by the in-
eradicable traces of the thunderbolts of Heaven;" so that, contem-
plating their relative geological positions, the poor deserted damsel
was flourishing on slate, while her rich and false young knight was
pining on chalk.

Squire Crotchet had also one daughter, whom he had christened
Lemma, and who, as likely to be endowed with a very ample fortune, was, of course, an object very tempting to many young soldiers
of fortune, who were marching with the march of mind, in a good
condition for taking castles, as far as not having a groat is a qualification for such exploits.[2] She was also a glittering bait to divers young
squires expectant (whose fathers were too well acquainted with the
occult signification of mortgage), and even to one or two sprigs of
nobility, who thought that the lining of a civic purse would super-
induce a very passable factitious nap upon a threadbare title. The

[1] Llymry—Anglicè, flummery.
[2] "Let him take castles who has ne'er a groat."—POPE, ubi suprà.

young lady had received an expensive and complicated education; complete in all the elements of superficial display. She was thus eminently qualified to be the companion of any masculine luminary who had kept due pace with the "astounding progress" of intelligence. It must be confessed, that a man who has not kept due pace with it is not very easily found; this march being one of that "astounding" character in which it seems impossible that the rear can be behind the van. The young lady was also tolerably good-looking: north of the Tweed, or in Palestine, she would probably have been a beauty; but, for the valleys of the Thames, she was perhaps a little too much to the taste of Solomon, and had a nose which rather too prominently suggested the idea of the tower of Lebanon, which looked towards Damascus.

In a village in the vicinity of the castle was the vicarage of the Reverend Doctor Folliott, a gentleman endowed with a tolerable stock of learning, an interminable swallow, and an indefatigable pair of lungs. His pre-eminence in the latter faculty gave occasion to some etymologists to ring changes on his name, and to decide that it was derived from Follis Optimus, softened through an Italian medium into Folle Ottimo, contracted poetically into Folleotto, and elided Anglicè into Folliott, signifying a first-rate pair of bellows. He claimed to be descended lineally from the illustrious Gilbert Folliott, the eminent theologian, who was a bishop of London in the twelfth century, whose studies were interrupted in the dead of night by the devil; when a couple of epigrams passed between them; and the devil, of course, proved the smaller wit of the two.[1]

---

[1] The devil began (he had caught the bishop musing on politics):

> Oh Gilberte Folliott!
> Dum revolvis tot et tot,
> Deus tuus est Astarot.

> Oh Gilbert Folliott!
> While thus you muse and plot,
> Your God is Astarot.

The bishop answered:

> Tace, dæmon: qui est deus
> Sabbaot, est ille meus.

> Peace, fiend; the power I own
> Is Sabbaoth's Lord alone.

This reverend gentleman, being both learned and jolly, became by degrees an indispensable ornament to the new squire's table. Mr. Crotchet himself was eminently jolly, though by no means eminently learned. In the latter respect he took after the great majority of the sons of his father's land; had a smattering of many things, and a knowledge of none; but possessed the true northern art of making the most of his intellectual harlequin's jacket, by keeping the best patches always bright and prominent.

THE MARCH OF MIND

"God bless my soul, sir!" exclaimed the Reverend Doctor Folliott, bursting, one fine May morning, into the breakfast-room at Crotchet Castle, "I am out of all patience with this march of mind. Here has my house been nearly burned down, by my cook taking it into her head to study hydrostatics in a sixpenny tract, published by the Steam Intellect Society, and written by a learned friend who is for doing all the world's business as well as his own, and is equally well qualified to handle every branch of human knowledge. I have a great abomination of this learned friend; as author, lawyer, and politician, he is triformis, like Hecate: and in every one of his three forms he is bifrons, like Janus; the true Mr. Facing-both-ways of Vanity Fair. My cook must read his rubbish in bed; and, as might naturally be expected, she dropped suddenly fast asleep, overturned the candle, and set the curtains in a blaze. Luckily, the footman went into the room at the moment in time to tear down the curtains and throw them into the chimney, and a pitcher of water on her nightcap extinguished her wick: she is a greasy subject, and would have burned like a short mould."

It must be confessed, the devil was easily posed in the twelfth century. He was a sturdier disputant in the sixteenth.

> Did not the devil appear to Martin
> Luther in Germany for certain?

when the "heroic student," as Mr. Coleridge calls him, was forced to proceed to "voies de fait." The curious may see at this day, on the wall of Luther's study, the traces of the ink-bottle which he threw at the devil's head.

The reverend gentleman exhaled his grievance without looking to the right or to the left; at length, turning on his pivot, he perceived that the room was full of company, consisting of young Crotchet and some visitors whom he had brought from London. The Reverend Doctor Folliott was introduced to Mr. Mac Quedy, [1] the economist; Mr. Skionar, [2] the transcendental poet; Mr. Firedamp, the meteorologist; and Lord Bossnowl, son of the Earl of Foolincourt, and member for the borough of Rogueingrain.

The divine took his seat at the breakfast-table, and began to compose his spirits by the gentle sedative of a large cup of tea, the demulcent of a well-buttered muffin, and the tonic of a small lobster.

The Rev. Dr. Folliott.—You are a man of taste, Mr. Crotchet. A man of taste is seen at once in the array of his breakfast-table. It is the foot of Hercules, the far-shining face of the great work, according to Pindar's doctrine: ἀρχομένου ἔργου πρόσωπον χρή θέμεν τηλαυγές.[3] The breakfast is the πρόσωπον of the great work of the day. Chocolate, coffee, tea, cream, eggs, ham, tongue, cold fowl,—all these are good, and bespeak good knowledge in him who sets them forth: but the touchstone is fish: anchovy is the first step, prawns and shrimps the second; and I laud him who reaches to these: potted char and lampreys are the third, and a fine stretch of progression; but lobster is, indeed, matter for a May morning, and demands a rare combination of knowledge and virtue in him who sets it forth.

Mr. Mac Quedy.—Well, sir, and what say you to a fine fresh trout, hot and dry, in a napkin? or a herring out of the water into the frying-pan, on the shore of Loch Fyne?

The Rev. Dr. Folliott.—Sir, I say every nation has some eximious virtue; and your country is pre-eminent in the glory of fish for breakfast. We have much to learn from you in that line at any rate.

Mr. Mac Quedy.—And in many others, sir, I believe. Morals and metaphysics, politics and political economy, the way to make the

---

[1] Quasi Mac Q. E. D., son of a demonstration.
[2] ΣΚΙᾶς ΟΝΑΡ. *Umbræ somnium.*
[3] Far-shining be the face
Of a great work begun.—PIND., Ol. vi.

most of all the modifications of smoke; steam, gas, and paper currency; you have all these to learn from us; in short, all the arts and sciences. We are the modern Athenians.

The Rev. Dr. Folliott.—I, for one, sir, am content to learn nothing from you but the art and science of fish for breakfast. Be content, sir, to rival the Bœotians, whose redeeming virtue was in fish, touching which point you may consult Aristophanes and his scholiast, in the passage of Lysistrata, ἀλλ' ἄφελε τὰς ἐγχέλεις,[1] and leave the name of Athenians to those who have a sense of the beautiful, and a perception of metrical quantity.

Mr. Mac Quedy.—Then, sir, I presume you set no value on the right principles of rent, profit, wages, and currency?

The Rev. Dr. Folliott.—My principles, sir, in these things are, to take as much as I can get, and to pay no more than I can help. These are every man's principles, whether they be the right principles or no. There, sir, is political economy in a nutshell.

Mr. Mac Quedy.—The principles, sir, which regulate production and consumption are independent of the will of any individual as to giving or taking, and do not lie in a nutshell by any means.

The Rev. Dr. Folliott.—Sir, I will thank you for a leg of that capon.

Lord Bossnowl.—But, sir, by-the-by, how came your footman to be going into your cook's room? It was very providential to be sure, but——

The Rev. Dr. Folliott.—Sir, as good came of it, I shut my eyes, and asked no questions. I suppose he was going to study hydrostatics, and he found himself under the necessity of practising hydraulics.

Mr. Firedamp.—Sir, you seem to make very light of science.

The Rev. Dr. Folliott.—Yes, sir, such science as the learned friend deals in: everything for everybody, science for all, schools for all, rhetoric for all, law for all, physic for all, words for all, and sense for none. I say, sir, law for lawyers, and cookery for cooks: and I wish the learned friend, for all his life, a cook that will pass her time in studying his works; then every dinner he sits down to at home, he will sit on the stool of repentance.

[1] Calonice wishes destruction to all Bœotians. Lysistrata answers, "Except the eels."—Lysistrata, 36.

Lord Bossnowl.—Now really that would be too severe: my cook should read nothing but Ude.

The Rev. Dr. Folliott.—No, sir! let Ude and the learned friend singe fowls together; let both avaunt from my kitchen. Θύρας δ' ἐπίθεσθε βεβήλοις.[1] Ude says an elegant supper may be given with sandwiches. *Horresco referens.* An elegant supper! *Di meliora piis.* No Ude for me. Conviviality went out with punch and suppers. I cherish their memory. I sup when I can, but not upon sandwiches. To offer me a sandwich, when I am looking for a supper, is to add insult to injury. Let the learned friend, and the modern Athenians, sup upon sandwiches.

Mr. Mac Quedy.—Nay, sir; the modern Athenians know better than that. A literary supper in sweet Edinbroo' would cure you of the prejudice you seem to cherish against us.

The Rev. Dr. Folliott.—Well, sir, well; there is cogency in a good supper; a good supper, in these degenerate days, bespeaks a good man; but much more is wanted to make up an Athenian. Athenians, indeed! where is your theatre? who among you has written a comedy? where is your Attic salt? which of you can tell who was Jupiter's great grandfather? or what metres will successively remain, if you take off the three first syllables, one by one, from a pure antispastic acatalectic tetrameter? Now, sir, there are three questions for you; theatrical, mythological, and metrical; to every one of which an Athenian would give an answer that would lay me prostrate in my own nothingness.

Mr. Mac Quedy.—Well, sir, as to your metre and your mythology, they may e'en wait a wee. For your comedy, there is the Gentle Shepherd of the divine Allan Ramsay.

The Rev. Dr. Folliott.—The Gentle Shepherd? It is just as much a comedy as the book of Job.

Mr. Mac Quedy.—Well, sir, if none of us have written a comedy, I cannot see that it is any such great matter, any more than I can conjecture what business a man can have at this time of day with Jupiter's great grandfather.

The Rev. Dr. Folliott.—The great business is, sir, that you call yourselves Athenians, while you know nothing that the Athenians thought worth knowing, and dare not show your noses before the

[1] "Shut the doors against the profane."—ORPHICA, *passim.*

civilized world in the practice of any one art in which they were excellent. Modern Athens, sir! the assumption is a personal affront to every man who has a Sophocles in his library. I will thank you for an anchovy.

Mr. Mac Quedy.—Metaphysics, sir; metaphysics. Logic and moral philosophy. There we are at home. The Athenians only sought the way, and we have found it; and to all this we have added political economy, the science of sciences.

The Rev. Dr. Folliott.—A hyperbarbarous technology, that no Athenian ear could have borne. Premises assumed without evidence, or in spite of it; and conclusions drawn from them so logically, that they must necessarily be erroneous.

Mr. Skionar.—I cannot agree with you, Mr. Mac Quedy, that you have found the true road of metaphysics, which the Athenians only sought. The Germans have found it, sir: the sublime Kant, and his disciples.

Mr. Mac Quedy.—I have read the sublime Kant, sir, with an anxious desire to understand him; and I confess I have not succeeded.

The Rev. Dr. Folliott.—He wants the two great requisites of head and tail.

Mr. Skionar.—Transcendentalism is the philosophy of intuition, the development of universal convictions; truths which are inherent in the organization of mind, which cannot be obliterated, though they may be obscured, by superstitious prejudice on the one hand, and by the Aristotelian logic on the other.

Mr. Mac Quedy.—Well, sir, I have no notion of logic obscuring a question.

Mr. Skionar.—There is only one true logic, which is the transcendental; and this can prove only the one true philosophy, which is also the transcendental. The logic of your modern Athens can prove everything equally; and that is, in my opinion, tantamount to proving nothing at all.

Mr. Crotchet.—The sentimental against the rational, the intuitive against the inductive, the ornamental against the useful, the intense against the tranquil, the romantic against the classical; these are great and interesting controversies, which I should like, before I die, to see satisfactorily settled.

Mr. Firedamp.—There is another great question, greater than all these, seeing that it is necessary to be alive in order to settle any question; and this is the question of water against human woe. Wherever there is water, there is *malaria*, and wherever there is *malaria* there are the elements of death. The great object of a wise man should be to live on a gravelly hill, without so much as a duck-pond within ten miles of him, eschewing cisterns and water-butts, and taking care that there be no gravel-pits for lodging the rain. The sun sucks up infection from water, wherever it exists on the face of the earth.

The Rev. Dr. Folliott.—Well, sir, you have for you the authority of the ancient mystagogue, who said: "Ἐστιν ὕδωρ ψυχῇ θάνατος.[1] For my part, I care not a rush (or any other aquatic and inesculent vegetable) who or what sucks up either the water or the infection. I think the proximity of wine a matter of much more importance than the longinquity of water. You are here within a quarter of a mile of the Thames; but, in the cellar of my friend Mr. Crotchet, there is the talismanic antidote of a thousand dozen of old wine; a beautiful spectacle, I assure you, and a model of arrangement.

Mr. Firedamp.—Sir, I feel the malignant influence of the river in every part of my system. Nothing but my great friendship for Mr. Crotchet would have brought me so nearly within the jaws of the lion.

The Rev. Dr. Folliott.—After dinner, sir, after dinner, I will meet you on this question. I shall then be armed for the strife. You may fight like Hercules against Achelous, but I shall flourish the Bacchic thyrsus, which changed rivers into wine: as Nonnus sweetly sings: Οἴνῳ κυματόεντι μέλας κελάρυζεν Ὑδάσπης.[2]

Mr. Crotchet, jun.—I hope, Mr. Firedamp, you will let your friendship carry you a little closer into the jaws of the lion. I am fitting up a flotilla of pleasure-boats, with spacious cabins and a good cellar, to carry a choice philosophical party up the Thames and Severn, into the Ellesmere canal, where we shall be among the mountains of North Wales; which we may climb or not, as we think proper; but we will, at any rate, keep our floating hotel well provi-

[1] Literally, which is sufficient for the present purpose, "Water is death to the soul."—ORPHICA: *Fr.* XIX.

[2] Hydaspes gurgled, dark with billowy wine.—DIONYSIACA, XXV. 280.

sioned; and we will try to settle all the questions over which a shadow of doubt yet hangs in the world of philosophy.

Mr. Firedamp.—Out of my great friendship for you, I will certainly go; but I do not expect to survive the experiment.

The Rev. Dr. Folliott.—*Alter erit tum Tiphys, et altera quæ vehat Argo Delectos Heroas.*[2] I will be of the party, though I must hire an officiating curate, and deprive poor Mrs. Folliott, for several weeks, of the pleasure of combing my wig.

Lord Bossnowl.—I hope, if I am to be of the party, our ship is not to be the ship of fools! He! he!

The Rev. Dr. Folliott.—If you are one of the party, sir, it most assuredly will not: ha! ha!

Lord Bossnowl.—Pray, sir, what do you mean by ha! ha?

The Rev. Dr. Folliott.—Precisely, sir, what you mean by he! he!

Mr. Mac Quedy.—You need not dispute about terms; they are two modes of expressing merriment, with or without reason; reason being in no way essential to mirth. No man should ask another why he laughs, or at what, seeing that he does not always know, and that, if he does, he is not a responsible agent. Laughter is an involuntary action of certain muscles, developed, in the human species, by the progress of civilization. The savage never laughs.

The Rev. Dr. Folliott.—No, sir; he has nothing to laugh at. Give him Modern Athens, the "learned friend," and the Steam Intellect Society. They will develop his muscles.

THE ROMAN CAMP

THE Rev. Dr. Folliott, having promised to return to dinner, walked back to his vicarage, meditating whether he should pass the morning in writing his next sermon, or in angling for trout, and had nearly decided in favour of the latter proposition, repeating to himself with great unction, the lines of Chaucer:—

2 "Another Typhys on the waves shall float,
And chosen heroes freight his glorious boat."
VIRG., *Ecl.* IV.

> And as for me, though I can but lite,
> On bokis for to read I me delite,
> And to 'hem yeve I faithe and full credence,
> And in mine herte have 'hem in reverence,
> So hertily that there is game none,
> That fro my bokis makith me to gone,
> But it be seldome, on the holie daie;
> Save certainly whan that the month of Maie,
> Is comin, and I hear the foulis sing,
> And that the flouris ginnin for to spring,
> Farewell my boke and my devocion:

when his attention was attracted by a young gentleman who was sitting on a camp-stool, with a portfolio on his knee, taking a sketch of the Roman Camp, which, as has been already said, was within the enclosed domain of Mr. Crotchet. The young stranger, who had climbed over the fence, espying the portly divine, rose up, and hoped that he was not trespassing. "By no means, sir," said the divine; "all the arts and sciences are welcome here: music, painting, and poetry; hydrostatics and political economy; meteorology, transcendentalism, and fish for breakfast."

The Stranger.—A pleasant association, sir, and a liberal and discriminating hospitality. This is an old British camp, I believe, sir?

The Rev. Dr. Folliott.—Roman, sir; Roman: undeniably Roman. The vallum is past controversy. It was not a camp, sir, a *castrum*, but a *castellum*, a little camp, or watch-station, to which was attached, on the peak of the adjacent hill, a beacon for transmitting alarms. You will find such here and there, all along the range of chalk hills, which traverses the country from north-east to south-west, and along the base of which runs the ancient Ikenild road, whereof you may descry a portion in that long straight white line.

The Stranger.—I beg your pardon, sir: do I understand this place to be your property?

The Rev. Dr. Folliott.—It is not mine, sir: the more is the pity; yet is it so far well, that the owner is my good friend, and a highly respectable gentleman.

The Stranger.—Good and respectable, sir, I take it, mean rich?

The Rev. Dr. Folliott.—That is their meaning, sir.

The Stranger.—I understand the owner to be a Mr. Crotchet. He has a handsome daughter, I am told.

The Rev. Dr. Folliott.—He has, sir. Her eyes are like the fishpools of Heshbon, by the gate of Bethrabbim; and she is to have a handsome fortune, to which divers disinterested gentlemen are paying their addresses. Perhaps you design to be one of them.

The Stranger.—No, sir; I beg pardon if my questions seem impertinent; I have no such design. There is a son, too, I believe, sir, a great and successful blower of bubbles.

The Rev. Dr. Folliott.—A hero, sir, in his line. Never did angler in September hook more gudgeons.

The Stranger.—To say the truth, two very amiable young people, with whom I have some little acquaintance, Lord Bossnowl, and his sister, Lady Clarinda, are reported to be on the point of concluding a double marriage with Miss Crotchet and her brother, by way of putting a new varnish on old nobility. Lord Foolincourt, their father, is terribly poor for a lord who owns a borough.

The Rev. Dr. Folliott.—Well, sir, the Crotchets have plenty of money, and the old gentleman's weak point is a hankering after high blood. I saw your acquaintance Lord Bossnowl this morning; but I did not see his sister. She may be there, nevertheless, and doing fashionable justice to this fine May morning, by lying in bed till noon.

The Stranger.—Young Mr. Crotchet, sir, has been, like his father, the architect of his own fortune, has he not? An illustrious example of the reward of honesty and industry?

The Rev. Dr. Folliott.—As to honesty, sir, he made his fortune in the city of London; and if that commodity be of any value there, you will find it in the price current. I believe it is below par, like the shares of young Crotchet's fifty companies. But his progress has not been exactly like his father's: it has been more rapid, and he started with more advantages. He began with a fine capital from his father. The old gentleman divided his fortune into three not exactly equal portions: one for himself, one for his daughter, and one for his son, which he handed over to him, saying, "Take it once for all, and make the most of it; if you lose it where I won it, not another stiver do you get from me during my life." But, sir, young Crotchet doubled, and trebled, and quadrupled it, and is, as you say, a striking example of the reward of industry; not that I think his labour has been so great as his luck.

The Stranger.—But, sir, is all this solid? is there no danger of reaction? no day of reckoning, to cut down in an hour prosperity that has grown up like a mushroom?

The Rev. Dr. Folliott.—Nay, sir, I know not. I do not pry into these matters. I am, for my own part, very well satisfied with the young gentleman. Let those who are not so look to themselves. It is quite enough for me that he came down last night from London, and that he had the good sense to bring with him a basket of lobsters. Sir, I wish you a good-morning.

The stranger, having returned the reverend gentleman's good morning, resumed his sketch, and was intently employed on it when Mr. Crotchet made his appearance, with Mr. Mac Quedy and Mr. Skionar, whom he was escorting round his grounds, according to his custom with new visitors; the principal pleasure of possessing an extensive domain being that of showing it to other people. Mr. Mac Quedy, according also to the laudable custom of his countrymen, had been appraising everything that fell under his observation; but, on arriving at the Roman Camp, of which the value was purely imaginary, he contented himself with exclaiming, "Eh! this is just a curiosity, and very pleasant to sit in on a summer day."

Mr. Skionar.—And call up the days of old, when the Roman eagle spread its wings in the place of that beechen foliage. It gives a fine idea of duration, to think that that fine old tree must have sprung from the earth ages after this camp was formed.

Mr. Mac Quedy.—How old, think you, may the tree be?

Mr. Crotchet.—I have records which show it to be three hundred years old.

Mr. Mac Quedy.—That is a great age for a beech in good condition. But you see the camp is some fifteen hundred years, or so, older; and three times six being eighteen, I think you get a clearer idea of duration out of the simple arithmetic than out of your eagle and foliage.

Mr. Skionar.—That is a very unpoetical, if not unphilosophical, mode of viewing antiquities. Your philosophy is too literal for our imperfect vision. We cannot look directly into the nature of things; we can only catch glimpses of the mighty shadow in the camera obscura of transcendental intelligence. These six and eighteen are only words to which we give conventional meanings. We can reason, but we cannot feel, by help of them. The tree and the eagle, contemplated in the ideality of space and time, become subjective realities, that rise up as landmarks in the mystery of the past.

Mr. Mac Quedy.—Well, sir, if you understand that, I wish you joy. But I must be excused for holding that my proposition, three times six are eighteen, is more intelligible than yours. A worthy friend of mine, who is a sort of amateur in philosophy, criticism, politics, and a wee bit of many things more, says, "Men never begin to study antiquities till they are saturated with civilization." [1]

Mr. Skionar.—What is civilization?

Mr. Mac Quedy.—It is just respect for property: a state in which no man takes wrongfully what belongs to another, is a perfectly civilized state.

Mr. Skionar.—Your friend's antiquaries must have lived in El Dorado, to have had an opportunity of being saturated with such a state.

Mr. Mac Quedy.—It is a question of degree. There is more respect for property here than in Angola.

Mr. Skionar.—That depends on the light in which things are viewed.

Mr. Crotchet was rubbing his hands, in hopes of a fine discussion, when they came round to the side of the camp where the picturesque gentleman was sketching. The stranger was rising up, whn Mr. Crotchet begged him not to disturb himself, and presently walked away with his two guests.

Shortly after Miss Crotchet and Lady Clarinda, who had breakfasted by themselves, made their appearance at the same spot, hanging each on an arm of Lord Bossnowl, who very much preferred their company to that of the philosophers, though he would have preferred the company of the latter, or any company, to his own. He thought it very singular that so agreeable a person as he held himself to be to others, should be so exceedingly tiresome to himself: he did not attempt to investigate the cause of this phenomenon, but was contented with acting on his knowledge of the fact, and giving himself as little of his own private society as possible.

The stranger rose as they approached, and was immediately recognized by the Bossnowls as an old acquaintance, and saluted with the exclamation of "Captain Fitzchrome!" The interchange of saluta-

[1] *Edinburgh Review,* somewhere.

tion between Lady Clarinda and the captain, was accompanied with an amiable confusion on both sides, in which the observant eyes of Miss Crotchet seemed to read the recollection of an affair of the heart.

Lord Bossnowl was either unconscious of any such affair, or indifferent to its existence. He introduced the captain very cordially to Miss Crotchet, and the young lady invited him, as the friend of their guests, to partake of her father's hospitality; an offer which was readily accepted.

The captain took his portfolio under his right arm, his campstool in his right hand, offered his left arm to Lady Clarinda, and followed at a reasonable distance behind Miss Crotchet and Lord Bossnowl, contriving, in the most natural manner possible, to drop more and more into the rear.

Lady Clarinda.—I am glad to see you can make yourself so happy with drawing old trees and mounds of grass.

Captain Fitzchrome.—Happy, Lady Clarinda! oh, no! How can I be happy when I see the idol of my heart about to be sacrificed on the shrine of mammon?

Lady Clarinda.—Do you know, though Mammon has a sort of ill name, I really think he is a very popular character; there must be at the bottom something amiable about him. He is certainly one of those pleasant creatures whom everybody abuses, but without whom no evening party is endurable. I dare say love in a cottage is very pleasant; but then it positively must be a cottage ornée: but would not the same love be a great deal safer in a castle, even if Mammon furnished the fortification?

Captain Fitzchrome.—Oh, Lady Clarinda! there is a heartlessness in that language that chills me to the soul.

Lady Clarinda.—Heartlessness! No: my heart is on my lips. I speak just what I think. You used to like it, and say it was as delightful as it was rare.

Captain Fitzchrome.—True, but you did not then talk as you do now, of love in a castle.

Lady Clarinda.—Well, but only consider: a dun is a horridly vulgar creature; it is a creature I cannot endure the thought of: and a cottage lets him in so easily. Now a castle keeps him at bay. You are a half-pay officer, and are at leisure to command the garrison: but where is the castle? and who is to furnish the commissariat?

Captain Fitzchrome.—Is it come to this, that you make a jest of my poverty? Yet is my poverty only comparative. Many decent families are maintained on smaller means.

Lady Clarinda.—Decent families: ay, decent is the distinction from respectable. Respectable means rich, and decent means poor. I should die if I heard my family called decent. And then your decent family always live in a snug little place: I hate a little place; I like large rooms and large looking-glasses, and large parties, and a fine large butler, with a tinge of smooth red in his face; an outward and visible sign that the family which he serves is respectable; if not noble, highly respectable.

Captain Fitzchrome.—I cannot believe that you say all this in earnest. No man is less disposed than I am to deny the importance of the substantial comforts of life. I once flattered myself that in our estimate of these things we were nearly of a mind.

Lady Clarinda.—Do you know, I think an opera-box a very substantial comfort, and a carriage. You will tell me that many decent people walk arm-in-arm through the snow, and sit in clogs and bonnets in the pit at the English theatre. No doubt it is very pleasant to those who are used to it; but it is not to my taste.

Captain Fitzchrome.—You always delighted in trying to provoke me; but I cannot believe that you have not a heart.

Lady Clarinda.—You do not like to believe that I have a heart, you mean. You wish to think I have lost it, and you know to whom; and when I tell you that it is still safe in my own keeping, and that I do not mean to give it away, the unreasonable creature grows angry.

Captain Fitzchrome.—Angry! far from it: I am perfectly cool.

Lady Clarinda.—Why you are pursing your brows, biting your lips, and lifting up your foot as if you would stamp it into the earth. I must say anger becomes you; you would make a charming Hotspur. Your every-day-dining-out face is rather insipid: but I assure you my heart is in danger when you are in the heroics. It is so rare, too, in these days of smooth manners, to see anything like natural expression in a man's face. There is one set form for every man's face in female society; a sort of serious comedy, walking gentleman's face: but the moment the creature falls in love, he begins to give himself airs, and plays off all the varieties of his physiognomy, from the Master Slender to the Petruchio; and then he is actually very amusing.

Captain Fitzchrome.—Well, Lady Clarinda, I will not be angry, amusing as it may be to you: I listen more in sorrow than in anger. I half believe you in earnest, and mourn as over a fallen angel.

Lady Clarinda.—What, because I have made up my mind not to give away my heart when I can sell it? I will introduce you to my new acquaintance, Mr. Mac Quedy: he will talk to you by the hour about exchangeable value, and show you that no rational being will part with anything, except to the highest bidder.

Captain Fitzchrome.—Now, I am sure you are not in earnest. You cannot adopt such sentiments in their naked deformity.

Lady Clarinda.—Naked deformity: why Mr. Mac Quedy will prove to you that they are the cream of the most refined philosophy. You live a very pleasant life as a bachelor, roving about the country with your portfolio under your arm. I am not fit to be a poor man's wife. I cannot take any kind of trouble, or do any one thing that is of any use. Many decent families roast a bit of mutton on a string; but if I displease my father I shall not have as much as will buy the string, to say nothing of the meat; and the bare idea of such cookery gives me the horrors.

By this time they were near the castle, and met Miss Crotchet and her companion, who had turned back to meet them. Captain Fitzchrome was shortly after heartily welcomed by Mr. Crotchet, and the party separated to dress for dinner, the captain being by no means in an enviable state of mind, and full of misgivings as to the extent of belief that he was bound to accord to the words of the lady of his heart.

THE PARTY

"If I were sketching a bandit who had just shot his last pursuer, having outrun all the rest, that is the very face I would give him," soliloquized the captain, as he studied the features of his rival in the drawing-room, during the miserable half-hour before dinner, when dulness reigns predominant over the expectant company, especially when they are waiting for some one last comer, whom they all heartily curse in their hearts, and whom, nevertheless, or indeed therefore-the-more, they welcome as a sinner, more heartily than all the just persons who had been punctual to their engagement. Some new visitors had arrived in the morning, and, as the company dropped in one by one, the captain anxiously watched the unclosing door for the form of his beloved; but she was the last to make her appearance, and on her entry gave him a malicious glance, which he construed into a telegraphic communication that she had stayed away to torment him. Young Crotchet escorted her with marked attention to the upper end of the drawing-room, where a great portion of the company was congregated around Miss Crotchet. These being the only ladies in the company, it was evident that old Mr. Crotchet would give his arm to Lady Clarinda, an arrangement with which the captain could not interfere. He therefore took his station near the door, studying his rival from a distance, and determined to take advantage of his present position, to secure the seat next to his charmer. He was meditating on the best mode of operation for securing this important post with due regard to *bienséance*, when he was twitched by the button by Mr. Mac Quedy, who said to him: "Lady Clarinda tells me, sir, that you are anxious to talk with me on the subject of exchangeable value, from which I infer that you have studied political economy; and as a great deal depends on the definition of value, I shall be glad to set you right on that point."— "I am much obliged to you, sir," said the captain, and was about to express his utter disqualification for the proposed instruction, when Mr. Skionar walked up, and said: "Lady Clarinda informs me that you wish to talk over with me the question of subjective reality. I am delighted to fall in with a gentleman who duly appreciates the transcendental philosophy."—"Lady Clarinda is too good," said the captain; and was about to protest that he had never heard the word transcendental before, when the butler announced dinner. Mr. Crotchet led the way with Lady Clarinda: Lord Bossnowl followed with Miss Crotchet: the economist and transcendentalist pinned in the captain, and held him, one by each arm, as he impatiently descended the stairs in the rear of several others of the company, whom they had forced him to let pass; but the moment he entered the dining-room he broke loose from them, and at the expense of a little *brusquerie*, secured his position.

"Well, captain," said Lady Clarinda, "I perceive you can still manœuvre."

"What could possess you," said the captain, "to send two unendurable and inconceivable bores to intercept me with rubbish about which I neither know nor care any more than the moon?"

"Perhaps," said Lady Clarinda, "I saw your design, and wished to put your generalship to the test. But do not contradict any thing I have said about you, and see if the learned will find you out."

"There is fine music, as Rabelais observes, in the *cliquetis d'assiettes*, a refreshing shade in the *ombre de salle à manger*, and an elegant fragrance in the *fumée de rôti*," said a voice at the captain's elbow. The captain, turning round, recognized his clerical friend of the morning, who knew him again immediately, and said he was extremely glad to meet him there; more especially as Lady Clarinda had assured him that he was an enthusiastic lover of Greek poetry.

"Lady Clarinda," said the captain, "is a very pleasant young lady."

The Rev. Dr. Folliott.—So she is, sir: and I understand she has all the wit of the family to herself, whatever that *totum* may be. But a glass of wine after soup is, as the French say, the *verre de santé*. The current of opinion sets in favour of Hock: but I am for Madeira; I do not fancy Hock till I have laid a substratum of Madeira. Will you join me?

Captain Fitzchrome.—With pleasure.

The Rev. Dr. Folliott.—Here is a very fine salmon before me: and May is the very *point nommé* to have salmon in perfection. There is a fine turbot close by, and there is much to be said in his behalf; but salmon in May is the king of fish.

Mr. Crotchet.—That salmon before you, doctor, was caught in the Thames this morning.

The Rev. Dr. Folliott.—Παπαπαῖ![1] Rarity of rarities! A Thames salmon caught this morning. Now, Mr. Mac Quedy, even in fish your modern Athens must yield. *Cedite Graii.*[2]

Mr. Mac Quedy.—Eh! sir, on its own ground, your Thames salmon has two virtues over all others: first, that it is fresh; and second,

[1 Exclamation. 2 Give place, you Greeks!]

that it is rare; for I understand you do not take half a dozen in a year.

The Rev. Dr. Folliott.—In some years, sir, not one. Mud, filth, gas dregs, lock-weirs, and the march of mind, developed in the form of poaching, have ruined the fishery. But when we do catch a salmon, happy the man to whom he falls.

Mr. Mac Quedy.—I confess, sir, this is excellent; but I cannot see why it should be better than a Twaed salmon at Kelso.

The Rev. Dr. Folliott.—Sir, I will take a glass of hock with you.

Mr. Mac Quedy.—With all my heart, sir. There are several varieties of the salmon genus: but the common salmon, the *salmo salar,* is only one species, one and the same everywhere, just like the human mind. Locality and education make all the difference.

The Rev. Dr. Folliott.—Education! Well, sir, I have no doubt schools for all are just as fit for the species *salmo salar* as for the genus *homo.* But you must allow that the specimen before us has finished his education in a manner that does honour to his college. However, I doubt that the *salmo salar* is only one species, that is to say, precisely alike in all localities. I hold that every river has its own breed, with essential differences, in flavour especially. And as for the human mind, I deny that it is the same in all men. I hold that there is every variety of natural capacity, from the idiot to Newton and Shakspeare; the mass of mankind midway between these extremes, being blockheads of different degrees; education leaving them pretty nearly as it found them, with this single difference, that it gives a fixed direction to their stupidity, a sort of incurable wry-neck to the thing they call their understanding. So one nose points always east, and another always west, and each is ready to swear that it points due north.

Mr. Crotchet.—If that be the point of truth, very few intellectual noses point due north.

Mr. Mac Quedy.—Only those that point to the Modern Athens.

The Rev. Dr. Folliott.—Where all native noses point southward.

Mr. Mac Quedy.—Eh, sir, northward for wisdom, and southward for profit.

Mr. Crotchet, jun.—Champagne, doctor?

The Rev. Dr. Folliott.—Most willingly. But you will permit my drinking it while it sparkles. I hold it a heresy to let it deaden in my hand while the glass of my compotator is being filled on the opposite side of the table. By-the-by, captain, you remember a passage in Athenæus, where he cites Menander on the subject of fish-sauce: ὀψάριος ἐπὶ ἰχθύος.[1] (The captain was aghast for an answer that would satisfy both his neighbours, when he was relieved by the divine continuing.) The science of fish-sauce, Mr. Mac Quedy, is by no means brought to perfection; a fine field of discovery still lies open in that line.

Mr. Mac Quedy.—Nay, sir, beyond lobster-sauce, I take it, ye cannot go.

The Rev. Dr. Folliott.—In their line, I grant you, oyster and lobster sauce are the pillars of Hercules. But I speak of the cruet sauces, where the quintessence of the sapid is condensed in a phial. I can taste, in my mind's palate, a combination which, if I could give it reality, I would christen with the name of my college, and hand it down to posterity as the seat of learning indeed.

Mr. Mac Quedy.—Well, sir, I wish you success, but I cannot let slip the question we started just now. I say, cutting off idiots, who have no minds at all, all minds are by nature alike. Education (which begins from their birth) makes them what they are.

The Rev. Dr. Folliott.—No, sir, it makes their tendencies, not their power. Cæsar would have been the first wrestler on the village common. Education might have made him a Nadir Shah; it might also have made him a Washington; it could not have made him a merry-andrew, for our newspapers to extol as a model of eloquence.

Mr. Mac Quedy.—Now, sir, I think education would have made him just anything, and fit for any station, from the throne to the stocks; saint or sinner, aristocrat or democrat; judge, counsel, or prisoner at the bar.

The Rev. Dr. Folliott.—I will thank you for a slice of lamb, with lemon and pepper. Before I proceed with this discussion—Vin de Grave, Mr. Skionar—I must interpose one remark. There is a set of persons in your city, Mr. Mac Quedy, who concoct every three or four months a thing which they call a review: a sort of sugar-plum manufacturers to the Whig aristocracy.

Mr. Mac Quedy.—I cannot tell, sir, exactly what you mean by

[1 sauce for fish.]

that; but I hope you will speak of those gentlemen with respect, seeing that I am one of them.

The Rev. Dr. Folliott.—Sir, I must drown my inadvertence in a glass of Sauterne with you. There is a set of gentlemen in your city——

Mr. Mac Quedy.—Not in our city, exactly; neither are they a set. There is an editor, who forages for articles in all quarters, from John O'Groat's house to the Land's End. It is not a board, or a society: it is a mere intellectual bazaar, where A, B, and C bring their wares to market.

The Rev. Dr. Folliott.—Well, sir, these gentlemen among them, the present company excepted, have practised as much dishonesty as, in any other department than literature, would have brought the practitioner under the cognizance of the police. In politics, they have run with the hare and hunted with the hound. In criticism they have, knowingly and unblushingly, given false characters, both for good and for evil: sticking at no art of misrepresentation to clear out of the field of literature all who stood in the way of the interests of their own clique. They have never allowed their own profound ignorance of anything (Greek, for instance) to throw even an air of hesitation into their oracular decision on the matter. They set an example of profligate contempt for truth, of which the success was in proportion to the effrontery; and when their prosperity had filled the market with competitors, they cried out against their own reflected sin, as if they had never committed it, or were entitled to a monopoly of it. The latter, I rather think, was what they wanted.

Mr. Crotchet.—Hermitage, doctor?

The Rev. Dr. Folliott.—Nothing better, sir. The father who first chose the solitude of that vineyard, knew well how to cultivate his spirit in retirement. Now, Mr. Mac Quedy, Achilles was distinguished above all the Greeks for his inflexible love of truth: could education have made Achilles one of your reviewers?

Mr. Mac Quedy.—No doubt of it, even if your character of them were true to the letter.

The Rev. Dr. Folliott.—And I say, sir—chicken and asparagus— Titan had made him of better clay.[1] I hold with Pindar: "All that is most excellent is so by nature." Education can give purposes, but not

[1] Juv., xiv. 35.

powers; and whatever purposes had been given him, he would have gone straight forward to them; straight forward, Mr. Mac Quedy.

Mr. Mac Quedy.—No, sir, education makes the man, powers, purposes, and all.

The Rev. Dr. Folliott.—There is the point, sir, on which we join issue.

Several others of the company now chimed in with their opinions, which gave the divine an opportunity to degustate one or two side dishes, and to take a glass of wine with each of the young ladies.

CHARACTERS

Lady clarinda (to the Captain).—I declare the creature has been listening to all this rigmarole, instead of attending to me. Do you ever expect forgiveness? But now that they are all talking together, and you cannot make out a word they say, nor they hear a word that we say, I will describe the company to you. First, there is the old gentleman on my left hand, at the head of the table, who is now leaning the other way to talk to my brother. He is a good-tempered, half-informed person, very unreasonably fond of reasoning, and of reasoning people; people that talk nonsense logically: he is fond of disputation himself, when there are only one or two, but seldom does more than listen in a large company of illuminés. He made a great fortune in the city, and has the comfort of a good conscience. He is very hospitable, and is generous in dinners; though nothing would induce him to give sixpence to the poor, because he holds that all misfortune is from imprudence, that none but the rich ought to marry, and that all ought to thrive by honest industry, as he did. He is ambitious of founding a family, and of allying himself with nobility; and is thus as willing as other grown children, to throw away thousands for a gew-gaw, though he would not part with a penny for charity. Next to him is my brother, whom you know as well as I do. He has finished his education with credit, and as he never ventures to oppose me in anything, I have no doubt he is very sensible. He has good manners, is a model of dress, and is reckoned ornamental in all societies. Next to him is Miss Crotchet, my sister-in-law that is to be. You see, she is rather pretty, and very genteel. She is tolerably accomplished, has her table always covered with new novels, thinks Mr. Mac Quedy an oracle, and is extremely desirous to be called "my lady." Next to her is Mr. Firedamp, a very absurd person, who thinks that water is the evil principle. Next to him is Mr. Eavesdrop, a man who, by dint of a certain something like smartness, has got into good society. He is a sort of bookseller's tool, and coins all his acquaintance in reminiscences and sketches of character. I am very shy of him, for fear he should print me.

Captain Fitzchrome.—If he print you in your own likeness, which is that of an angel, you need not fear him. If he print you in any other, I will cut his throat. But proceed—

Lady Clarinda.—Next to him is Mr. Henbane, the toxicologist, I think he calls himself. He has passed half his life in studying poisons and antidotes. The first thing he did on his arrival here, was to kill the cat; and while Miss Crotchet was crying over her, he brought her to life again. I am more shy of him than the other.

Captain Fitzchrome.—They are two very dangerous fellows, and I shall take care to keep them both at a respectful distance. Let us hope that Eavesdrop will sketch off Henbane, and that Henbane will poison him for his trouble.

Lady Clarinda.—Well, next to him sits Mr. Mac Quedy, the Modern Athenian, who lays down the law about everything, and therefore may be taken to understand everything. He turns all the affairs of this world into questions of buying and selling. He is the Spirit of the Frozen Ocean to everything like romance and sentiment. He condenses their volume of steam into a drop of cold water in a moment. He has satisfied me that I am a commodity in the market, and that I ought to set myself at a high price. So you see he who would have me must bid for me.

Captain Fitzchrome.—I shall discuss that point with Mr. Mac Quedy.

Lady Clarinda.—Not a word for your life. Our flirtation is our own secret. Let it remain so.

Captain Fitzchrome.—Flirtation, Clarinda! Is that all that the most ardent——

Lady Clarinda.—Now, don't be rhapsodical here. Next to Mr. Mac Quedy is Mr. Skionar, a sort of poetical philosopher, a curious compound of the intense and the mystical. He abominates all the ideas of Mr. Mac Quedy, and settles everything by sentiment and intuition.

Captain Fitzchrome.—Then, I say, he is the wiser man.

Lady Clarinda.—They are two oddities; but a little of them is amusing, and I like to hear them dispute. So you see I am in training for a philosopher myself.

Captain Fitzchrome.—Any philosophy, for heaven's sake, but the pound-shilling-and-pence philosophy of Mr. Mac Quedy.

Lady Clarinda.—Why, they say that even Mr. Skionar, though he is a great dreamer, always dreams with his eyes open, or with one eye at any rate, which is an eye to his gain: but I believe that in this respect the poor man has got an ill name by keeping bad company. He has two dear friends, Mr. Wilful Wontsee, and Mr. Rumblesack Shantsee, poets of some note, who used to see visions of Utopia, and pure republics beyond the Western deep: but finding that these El Dorados brought them no revenue, they turned their vision-seeing faculty into the more profitable channel of espying all sorts of virtues in the high and the mighty who were able and willing to pay for the discovery.

Captain Fitzchrome.—I do not fancy these virtue-spyers.

Lady Clarinda.—Next to Mr. Skionar, sits Mr. Chainmail, a good-looking young gentleman, as you see, with very antiquated tastes. He is fond of old poetry, and is something of a poet himself. He is deep in monkish literature, and holds that the best state of society was that of the twelfth century, when nothing was going forward but fighting, feasting, and praying, which he says are the three great purposes for which man was made. He laments bitterly over the inventions of gunpowder, steam, and gas, which he says have ruined the world. He lives within two or three miles, and has a large hall, adorned with rusty pikes, shields, helmets, swords, and tattered banners, and furnished with yew-tree chairs, and two long, old, worm-eaten oak tables, where he dines with all his household, after the fashion of his favourite age. He wants us all to dine with him, and I believe we shall go.

Captain Fitzchrome.—That will be something new at any rate.

Lady Clarinda.—Next to him is Mr. Toogood, the cooperationist, who will have neither fighting nor praying; but wants to parcel out the world into squares like a chess-board, with a community on each, raising everything for one another, with a great steam-engine to serve them in common for tailor and hosier, kitchen and cook.

Captain Fitzchrome.—He is the strangest of the set so far.

Lady Clarinda.—This brings us to the bottom of the table, where sits my humble servant, Mr. Crotchet the younger. I ought not to describe him.

Captain Fitzchrome.—I entreat you do.

Lady Clarinda.—Well, I really have very little to say in his favour.

Captain Fitzchrome.—I do not wish to hear anything in his favour; and I rejoice to hear you say so, because——

Lady Clarinda.—Do not flatter yourself. If I take him, it will be to please my father, and to have a town and country-house, and plenty of servants, and a carriage and an opera-box, and make some of my acquaintance who have married for love, or for rank, or for anything but money, die for envy of my jewels. You do not think I would take him for himself. Why he is very smooth and spruce, as far as his dress goes; but as to his face, he looks as if he had tumbled headlong into a volcano, and been thrown up again among the cinders.

Captain Fitzchrome.—I cannot believe that, speaking thus of him, you mean to take him at all.

Lady Clarinda.—Oh! I am out of my teens. I have been very much in love; but now I am come to years of discretion, and must think, like other people, of settling myself advantageously. He was in love with a banker's daughter, and cast her off on her father's bankruptcy, and the poor girl has gone to hide herself in some wild place.

Captain Fitzchrome.—She must have a strange taste, if she pines for the loss of him.

Lady Clarinda.—They say he was good-looking, till his bubble-schemes, as they call them, stamped him with the physiognomy of a desperate gambler. I suspect he has still a *penchant* towards his first flame. If he takes me, it will be for my rank and connection, and the second seat of the borough of Rogueingrain. So we shall meet on equal terms, and shall enjoy all the blessedness of expecting nothing from each other.

Captain Fitzchrome.—You can expect no security with such an adventurer.

Lady Clarinda.—I shall have the security of a good settlement, and then if *andare al diavolo* be his destiny, he may go, you know, by himself. He is almost always dreaming and *distrait*. It is very likely that some great reverse is in store for him: but that will not concern me, you perceive.

Captain Fitzchrome.—You torture me, Clarinda, with the bare possibility.

Lady Clarinda.—Hush! Here is music to soothe your troubled spirit. Next to him, on this side, sits the dilettante composer, Mr. Trillo; they say his name was O'Trill, and he has taken the O from the beginning, and put it at the end. I do not know how this may be. He plays well on the violoncello, and better on the piano: sings agreeably; has a talent at verse-making, and improvises a song with some felicity. He is very agreeable company in the evening, with his instruments and music-books. He maintains that the sole end of all enlightened society is to get up a good opera, and laments that wealth, genius, and energy are squandered upon other pursuits, to the neglect of this one great matter.

Captain Fitzchrome.—That is a very pleasant fancy at any rate.

Lady Clarinda.—I assure you he has a great deal to say for it. Well, next to him again, is Dr. Morbific, who has been all over the world to prove that there is no such thing as contagion; and has inoculated himself with plague, yellow fever, and every variety of pestilence, and is still alive to tell the story. I am very shy of him, too; for I look on him as a walking phial of wrath, corked full of all infections, and not to be touched without extreme hazard.

Captain Fitzchrome.—This is the strangest fellow of all.

Lady Clarinda.—Next to him sits Mr. Philpot,[1] the geographer, who thinks of nothing but the heads and tails of rivers, and lays down the streams of Terra Incognita as accurately as if he had been there. He is a person of pleasant fancy, and makes a sort of fairy land of every country he touches, from the frozen ocean to the Deserts of Sahara.

Captain Fitzchrome.—How does he settle matters with Mr. Fire-damp?

[1] ΦΙΛοΠΟΤαμος. *Fluvorium amans.*

Lady Clarinda.—You see Mr. Firedamp has got as far as possible out of his way. Next to him is Sir Simon Steeltrap, of Steeltrap Lodge, Member for Crouching-Curtown, Justice of Peace for the county, and Lord of the United Manors of Springgun and Tread-mill; a great preserver of game and public morals. By administering the laws which he assists in making, he disposes, at his leisure, of the land and its live stock, including all the two-legged varieties, with and without feathers, in a circumference of several miles round Steeltrap Lodge. He has enclosed commons and woodlands; abolished cottage-gardens; taken the village cricket-ground into his own park, out of pure regard to the sanctity of Sunday; shut up footpaths and ale-houses (all but those which belong to his electioneering friend, Mr. Quassia, the brewer); put down fairs and fiddlers; committed many poachers; shot a few; convicted one-third of the peasantry; suspected the rest; and passed nearly the whole of them through a wholesome course of prison discipline, which has finished their education at the expense of the county.

Captain Fitzchrome.—He is somewhat out of his element here: among such a diversity of opinions he will hear some he will not like.

Lady Clarinda.—It was rather ill-judged in Mr. Crotchet to invite him to-day. But the art of assorting company is above these parvenus. They invite a certain number of persons without considering how they harmonize with each other. Between Sir Simon and you is the Reverend Doctor Folliott. He is said to be an excellent scholar, and is fonder of books than the majority of his cloth; he is very fond, also, of the good things of this world. He is of an admirable temper, and says rude things in a pleasant half-earnest manner, that nobody can take offence with. And next to him, again, is one Captain Fitzchrome, who is very much in love with a certain person that does not mean to have anything to say to him, because she can better her fortune by taking somebody else.

Captain Fitzchrome.—And next to him, again, is the beautiful, the accomplished, the witty, the fascinating, the tormenting, Lady Clarinda, who traduces herself to the said captain by assertions which it would drive him crazy to believe.

Lady Clarinda.—Time will show, sir. And now we have gone the round of the table.

Captain Fitzchrome.—But I must say, though I know you had

always a turn for sketching characters, you surprise me by your observation, and especially by your attention to opinions.

Lady Clarinda.—Well, I will tell you a secret: I am writing a novel.

Captain Fitzchrome.—A novel!

Lady Clarinda.—Yes, a novel. And I shall get a little finery by it: trinkets and fal-lals, which I cannot get from papa. You must know I have been reading several fashionable novels, the fashionable this, and the fashionable that; and I thought to myself, why I can do better than any of these myself. So I wrote a chapter or two, and sent them as a specimen to Mr. Puffall, the bookseller, telling him they were to be a part of the fashionable something or other, and he offered me, I will not say how much, to finish it in three volumes, and let him pay all the newspapers for recommending it as the work of a lady of quality, who had made very free with the characters of her acquaintance.

Captain Fitzchrome.—Surely you have not done so?

Lady Clarinda.—Oh, no; I leave that to Mr. Eavesdrop. But Mr. Puffall made it a condition that I should let him say so.

Captain Fitzchrome.—A strange recommendation.

Lady Clarinda.—Oh, nothing else will do. And it seems you may give yourself any character you like, and the newspapers will print it as if it came from themselves. I have commended you to three of our friends here, as an economist, a transcendentalist, and a classical scholar; and if you wish to be renowned through the world for these, or any other accomplishments, the newspapers will confirm you in their possession for half-a-guinea a piece.

Captain Fitzchrome.—Truly, the praise of such gentry must be a feather in any one's cap.

Lady Clarinda.—So you will see, some morning, that my novel is "the most popular production of the day." This is Mr. Puffall's favourite phrase. He makes the newspapers say it of every thing he publishes. But "the day," you know, is a very convenient phrase; it allows of three hundred and sixty-five "most popular productions" in a year. And in leap-year one more.

THEORIES

MEANWHILE, the last course, and the dessert, passed by. When the ladies had withdrawn, young Crotchet addressed the company.

Mr. Crotchet, jun.—There is one point in which philosophers of all classes seem to be agreed; that they only want money to regenerate the world.

Mr. Mac Quedy.—No doubt of it. Nothing is so easy as to lay down the outlines of perfect society. There wants nothing but money to set it going. I will explain myself clearly and fully by reading a paper. (*Producing a large scroll.*) "In the infancy of society—"

The Rev. Dr. Folliott.—Pray, Mr. Mac Quedy, how is it that all gentlemen of your nation begin everything they write with the "infancy of society?"

Mr. Mac Quedy.—Eh, sir, it is the simplest way to begin at the beginning. "In the infancy of society, when government was invented to save a percentage; say two and a half per cent.—"

The Rev. Dr. Folliott.—I will not say any such thing.

Mr. Mac Quedy.—Well, say any percentage you please.

The Rev. Dr. Folliott.—I will not say any percentage at all.

Mr. Mac Quedy.—"On the principle of the division of labour—"

The Rev. Dr. Folliott.—Government was invented to spend a percentage.

Mr. Mac Quedy.—To save a percentage.

The Rev. Dr. Folliott.—No, sir, to spend a percentage; and a good deal more than two and a half per cent. Two hundred and fifty per cent.; that is intelligible.

Mr. Mac Quedy.—"In the infancy of society"—

Mr. Toogood.—Never mind the infancy of society. The question is of society in its maturity. Here is what it should be. (*Producing a paper.*) I have laid it down in a diagram.

Mr. Skionar.—Before we proceed to the question of government, we must nicely discriminate the boundaries of sense, understanding, and reason. Sense is a receptivity.—

Mr. Crotchet, jun.—We are proceeding too fast. Money being all that is wanted to regenerate society, I will put into the hands of this company a large sum for the purpose. Now let us see how to dispose of it.

Mr. Mac Quedy.—We will begin by taking a committee-room in London, where we will dine together once a week, to deliberate.

The Rev. Dr. Folliott.—If the money is to go in deliberative dinners, you may set me down for a committee man and honorary caterer.

Mr. Mac Quedy.—Next, you must all learn political economy, which I will teach you, very compendiously, in lectures over the bottle.

The Rev. Dr. Folliott.—I hate lectures over the bottle. But pray, sir, what is political economy?

Mr. Mac Quedy.—Political economy is to the state what domestic economy is to the family.

The Rev. Dr. Folliott.—No such thing, sir. In the family there is a *paterfamilias*, who regulates the distribution, and takes care that there shall be no such thing in the household as one dying of hunger while another dies of surfeit. In the state, it is all hunger at one end, and all surfeit at the other. Matchless claret, Mr. Crotchet.

Mr. Crotchet.—Vintage of fifteen, doctor.

Mr. Mac Quedy.—The family consumes, and so does the state.

The Rev. Dr. Folliott.—Consumes, sir! Yes: but the mode, the proportions; there is the essential difference between the state and the family. Sir, I hate false analogies.

Mr. Mac Quedy.—Well, sir, the analogy is not essential. Distribution will come under its proper head.

The Rev. Dr. Folliott.—Come where it will, the distribution of the state is in no respect analogous to the distribution of the family. ·
The *paterfamilias*, sir: the *paterfamilias*.

Mr. Mac Quedy.—Well, sir, let that pass. The family consumes, and in order to consume, it must have supply.

The Rev. Dr. Folliott.—Well, sir, Adam and Eve knew that when they delved and span.

Mr. Mac Quedy.—Very true, sir (*reproducing his scroll*). In the infancy of society——"

Mr. Toogood.—The reverend gentleman has hit the nail on the head. It is the distribution that must be looked to: it is the *pater-*

familias that is wanting in the state. Now, here I have provided him. (*Reproducing his diagram.*)

Mr. Trillo.—Apply the money, sir, to building and endowing an opera-house, where the ancient altar of Bacchus may flourish, and justice may be done to sublime compositions. (*Producing a part of a manuscript opera.*)

Mr. Skionar.—No, sir, build *sacella* [1] for transcendental oracles to teach the world how to see through a glass darkly. (*Producing a scroll.*)

Mr. Trillo.—See through an opera-glass brightly.

The Rev. Dr. Folliott.—See through a wine-glass, full of claret: then you see both darkly and brightly. But, gentlemen, if you are all in the humour for reading papers, I will read you the first half of my next Sunday's sermon. (*Producing a paper.*)

Omnes.—No sermon! No sermon!

The Rev. Dr. Folliott.—Then I move that our respective papers be committed to our respective pockets.

Mr. Mac Quedy.—Political economy is divided into two great branches, production and consumption.

The Rev. Dr. Folliott.—Yes, sir; there are two great classes of men: those who produce much, and consume little; and those who consume much, and produce nothing. The *fruges consumere nati* [2] have the best of it. Eh, captain! you remember the characteristics of a great man according to Aristophanes: ὅστις γε πίνειν οἶδε καὶ βίνειν μόνον.[3] Ha! ha! ha! Well, captain, even in these tight-laced days, the obscurity of a learned language allows a little pleasantry.

Captain Fitzchrome.—Very true, sir: the pleasantry and the obscurity go together: they are all one, as it were;—to me, at any rate (aside).

Mr. Mac Quedy.—Now, sir—

The Rev. Dr. Folliott.—Pray, sir, let your science alone, or you will put me under the painful necessity of demolishing it bit by bit, as I have done your exordium. I will undertake it any morning; but it is too hard exercise after dinner.

Mr. Mac Quedy.—Well, sir, in the meantime I hold my science established.

[1 shrines.]
[2 born consumers. 3 But he is all for wine and women.]

The Rev. Dr. Folliott.—And I hold it demolished.

Mr. Crotchet, jun.—Pray, gentlemen, pocket your manuscripts; fill your glasses, and consider what we shall do with our money.

Mr. Mac Quedy.—Build lecture-rooms and schools for all.

Mr. Trillo.—Revive the Athenian theatre: regenerate the lyrical drama.

Mr. Toogood.—Build a grand co-operative parallelogram, with a steam-engine in the middle for a maid of all-work.

Mr. Firedamp.—Drain the country, and get rid of *malaria,* by abolishing duck-ponds.

Dr. Morbific.—Found a philanthropic college of anti-contagionists, where all the members shall be inoculated with the virus of all known diseases. Try the experiment on a grand scale.

Mr. Chainmail.—Build a great dining-hall: endow it with beef and ale, and hang the hall round with arms to defend the provisions.

Mr. Henbane.—Found a toxicological institution, for trying all poisons and antidotes. I myself have killed a frog twelve times, and brought him to life eleven; but the twelfth time he died. I have a phial of the drug which killed him, in my pocket, and shall not rest till I have discovered its antidote.

The Rev. Dr. Folliott.—I move that the last speaker be dispossessed of his phial, and that it be forthwith thrown into the Thames.

Mr. Henbane.—How, sir? my invaluable, and, in the present state of human knowledge, infallible poison?

The Rev. Dr. Folliott.—Let the frogs have all the advantage of it.

Mr. Crotchet.—Consider, doctor, the fish might participate. Think of the salmon!

The Rev. Dr. Folliott.—Then let the owner's right-hand neighbour swallow it.

Mr. Eavesdrop.—Me, sir? What have I done, sir, that I am to be poisoned, sir!

The Rev. Dr. Folliott.—Sir, you have published a character of your facetious friend, the Reverend Doctor F., wherein you have sketched off me; me, sir, even to my nose and wig. What business have the public with my nose and wig?

Mr. Eavesdrop.—Sir, it is all good-humoured: all in *bonhommie:* all friendly and complimentary.

The Rev. Dr. Folliott.—Sir, the bottle, *la Dive Bouteille,* is a recondite oracle which makes an Eleusinian temple of the circle in which it moves. He who reveals its mysteries must die. Therefore, let the dose be administered. *Fiat experimentum in animâ vili.*[1]

Mr. Eavesdrop.—Sir, you are very facetious at my expense.

The Rev. Dr. Folliott.—Sir, you have been very unfacetious, very inficete at mine. You have dished me up, like a savory omelette, to gratify the appetite of the reading rabble for gossip. The next time, sir, I will respond with the *argumentum baculinum.*[2] Print that, sir; put it on record as a promise of the Rev. Doctor F., which shall be most faithfully kept, with an exemplary bamboo.

Mr. Eavesdrop.—Your cloth protects you, sir.

The Rev. Dr. Folliott.—My bamboo shall protect me, sir.

Mr. Crotchet.—Doctor! doctor, you are growing too polemical.

The Rev. Dr. Folliott.—Sir, my blood boils. What business have the public with my nose and wig?

Mr. Crotchet.—Doctor! doctor!

Mr. Crotchet, jun.—Pray, gentlemen, return to the point. How shall we employ our fund?

Mr. Philpot.—Surely in no way so beneficial as in exploring rivers. Send a fleet of steam-boats down the Niger, and another up the Nile. So shall you civilize Africa, and establish stocking factories in Abyssinia and Bambo.

The Rev. Dr. Folliott.—With all submission, breeches and petticoats must precede stockings. Send out a crew of tailors. Try if the King of Bambo will invest in inexpressibles.

Mr. Crotchet, jun.—Gentlemen, it is not for partial, but for general benefit, that this fund is proposed: a grand and universally applicable scheme for the amelioration of the condition of man.

Several Voices.—That is my scheme. I have not heard a scheme but my own that has a grain of common sense.

Mr. Trillo.—Gentlemen, you inspire me. Your last exclamation runs itself into a chorus, and sets itself to music. Allow me to lead, and to hope for your voices in harmony.

> After careful meditation,
> And profound deliberation,
> On the various pretty projects which have just been shown,

[1 Let experiment be made on a worthless soul.]
[2 argument of the club: i.e. force.]

Not a scheme in agitation,
For the world's amelioration,
Has a grain of common sense in it, except my own.

Several Voices.—We are not disposed to join in any such chorus.

The Rev. Dr. Folliott.—Well, of all these schemes, I am for Mr. Trillo's. Regenerate the Athenian theatre. My classical friend here, the captain, will vote with me.

Captain Fitzchrome.—I, sir? oh! of course, sir.

Mr. Mac Quedy.—Surely, captain, I rely on you to uphold political economy.

Captain Fitzchrome.—Me, sir? oh! to be sure, sir.

The Rev. Dr. Folliott.—Pray, sir, will political economy uphold the Athenian theatre?

Mr. Mac Quedy.—Surely not. It would be a very unproductive investment.

The Rev. Dr. Folliott.—Then the captain votes against you. What, sir, did not the Athenians, the wisest of nations, appropriate to their theatre their most sacred and intangible fund? Did not they give to melopœia, choreography, and the sundry forms of didascalics, the precedence of all other matters, civil and military? Was it not their law, that even the proposal to divert this fund to any other purpose should be punished with death? But, sir, I further propose that the Athenian theatre being resuscitated, the admission shall be free to all who can expound the Greek choruses, constructively, mythologically, and metrically, and to none others. So shall all the world learn Greek: Greek, the Alpha and Omega of all knowledge. At him who sits not in the theatre, shall be pointed the finger of scorn: he shall be called in the highway of the city, "a fellow without Greek."

Mr. Trillo.—But the ladies, sir, the ladies.

The Rev. Dr. Folliott.—Every man may take in a lady: and she who can construe and metricise a chorus, shall, if she so please, pass in by herself.

Mr. Trillo.—But, sir, you will shut me out of my own theatre. Let there at least be a double passport, Greek and Italian.

The Rev. Dr. Folliott.—No, sir; I am inexorable. No Greek, no theatre.

Mr. Trillo.—Sir, I cannot consent to be shut out from my own theatre.

The Rev. Dr. Folliott.—You see how it is, Squire Crotchet the younger; you can scarcely find two to agree on a scheme, and no two of those can agree on the details. Keep your money in your pocket. And so ends the fund for regenerating the world.

Mr. Mac Quedy.—Nay, by no means. We are all agreed on deliberative dinners.

The Rev. Dr. Folliott.—Very true; we will dine and discuss. We will sing with Robin Hood, "If I drink water while this doth last;" and while it lasts we will have no adjournment, if not to the Athenian theatre.

Mr. Trillo.—Well, gentlemen, I hope this chorus at least will please you:

> If I drink water while this doth last,
> May I never again drink wine:
> For how can a man, in his life of a span,
> Do anything better than dine?
> We'll dine and drink, and say if we think
> That anything better can be;
> And when we have dined, wish all mankind
> May dine as well as we.
>
> And though a good wish will fill no dish,
> And brim no cup with sack,
> Yet thoughts will spring, as the glasses ring,
> To illume our studious track.
> On the brilliant dreams of our hopeful schemes
> The light of the flask shall shine;
> And we'll sit till day, but we'll find the way
> To drench the world with wine.

The schemes for the world's regeneration evaporated in a tumult of voices.

THE SLEEPING VENUS

THE library of Crotchet Castle was a large and well-furnished apartment, opening on one side into an ante-room, on the other into a music-room. It had several tables stationed at convenient distances; one consecrated to the novelties of literature, another to the novelties of embellishment; others unoccupied, and at the disposal of the company. The walls were covered with a copious collection of ancient and modern books; the ancient having been selected and arranged by the Reverend Doctor Folliott. In the ante-room were card-tables; in the music-room were various instruments, all popular operas, and all fashionable music. In this suite of apartments, and not in the drawing-room, were the evenings of Crotchet Castle usually passed.

The young ladies were in the music-room; Miss Crotchet at the piano, Lady Clarinda, at the harp, playing and occasionally singing, at the suggestion of Mr. Trillo, portions of *Matilde di Shabran*. Lord Bossnowl was turning over the leaves for Miss Crotchet; the captain was performing the same office for Lady Clarinda, but with so much more attention to the lady than the book, that he often made sad work with the harmony, by turning over two leaves together. On these occasions Miss Crotchet paused, Lady Clarinda laughed, Mr. Trillo scolded, Lord Bossnowl yawned, the captain apologised, and the performance proceeded.

In the library, Mr. Mac Quedy was expounding political economy to the Reverend Doctor Folliott, who was *pro more* demolishing its doctrines *seriatim*.

Mr. Chainmail was in hot dispute with Mr. Skionar, touching the physical and moral well-being of man. Mr. Skionar was enforcing his friend Mr. Shantsee's views of moral discipline; maintaining that the sole thing needful for man in this world, was loyal and pious education; the giving men good books to read, and enough of the hornbook to read them; with a judicious interspersion of the lessons of Old Restraint, which was his poetic name for the parish stocks. Mr. Chainmail, on the other hand, stood up for the exclusive necessity of beef and ale, lodging and raiment, wife and chil-

dren, courage to fight for them all, and armour wherewith to
do so.

Mr. Henbane had got his face scratched, and his finger bitten,
by the cat, in trying to catch her for a second experiment in killing
and bringing to life; and Doctor Morbific was comforting him with
a disquisition, to prove that there were only four animals having
the power to communicate hydrophobia, of which the cat was one;
and that it was not necessary that the animal should be in a rabid
state, the nature of the wound being everything, and the idea of
contagion a delusion. Mr. Henbane was listening very lugubriously
to this dissertation.

Mr. Philpot had seized on Mr. Firedamp, and pinned him down
to a map of Africa, on which he was tracing imaginary courses of
mighty inland rivers, terminating in lakes and marshes, where they
were finally evaporated by the heat of the sun; and Mr. Firedamp's
hair was standing on end at the bare imagination of the mass of
malaria that must be engendered by the operation. Mr. Toogood
had begun explaining his diagrams to Sir Simon Steeltrap; but Sir
Simon grew testy, and told Mr. Toogood that the promulgators of
such doctrines ought to be consigned to the tread-mill. The philan-
thropist walked off from the country gentleman, and proceeded to
hold forth to young Crotchet, who stood silent, as one who listens,
but in reality without hearing a syllable. Mr. Crotchet, senior, as
the master of the house, was left to entertain himself with his own
meditations, till the Reverend Doctor Folliott tore himself from
Mr. Mac Quedy, and proceeded to expostulate with Mr. Crotchet
on a delicate topic.

There was an Italian painter, who obtained the name of
Il Bragatore, by the superinduction of inexpressibles on the naked
Apollos and Bacchuses of his betters. The fame of this worthy remained one and indivisible, till a set of heads, which had been,
by a too common mistake of nature's journeymen, stuck upon
magisterial shoulders, as the Corinthian capitals of "fair round
bellies with fat capon lined," but which nature herself had intended
for the noddles of porcelain mandarins, promulgated simultaneously
from the east and the west of London, an order that no plaster-of-
Paris Venus should appear in the streets without petticoats. Mr.
Crotchet, on reading this order in the evening paper, which, by

the postman's early arrival, was always laid on his breakfast-table, determined to fill his house with Venuses of all sizes and kinds. In pursuance of this resolution, came packages by water-carriage, containing an infinite variety of Venuses. There were the Medicean Venus, and the Bathing Venus; the Uranian Venus, and the Pandemian Venus; the Crouching Venus, and the Sleeping Venus; the Venus rising from the sea, the Venus with the apple of Paris, and the Venus with the armour of Mars.

The Rev. Dr. Folliott had been very much astonished at this unexpected display. Disposed, as he was, to hold that whatever had been in Greece was right, he was more than doubtful of the propriety of throwing open the classical *adytum* to the illiterate profane. Whether, in his interior mind, he was at all influenced either by the consideration that it would be for the credit of his cloth with some of his vice-suppressing neighbours, to be able to say that he had expostulated; or by curiosity, to try what sort of defence his city-bred friend, who knew the classics only by translations, and whose reason was always a little a-head of his knowledge, would make for his somewhat ostentatious display of liberality in matters of taste, is a question on which the learned may differ: but after having duly deliberated on two full-sized casts of the Uranian and Pandemian Venus, in niches on each side of the chimney, and on three alabaster figures in glass cases, on the mantelpiece, he proceeded, peirastically, to open his fire.

The Rev. Dr. Folliott.—These little alabaster figures on the mantelpiece, Mr. Crotchet, and those large figures in the niches —may I take the liberty to ask you what they are intended to represent?

Mr. Crotchet.—Venus, sir; nothing more, sir; just Venus.

The Rev. Dr. Folliott.—May I ask you, sir, why they are there?

Mr. Crotchet.—To be looked at, sir; just to be looked at: the reason for most things in a gentleman's house being in it at all; from the paper on the walls, and the drapery of the curtains, even to the books in the library, of which the most essential part is the appearance of the back.

The Rev. Dr. Folliott.—Very true, sir. As great philosophers hold that the esse of things is *percipi*, so a gentleman's furniture exists to be looked at. Nevertheless, sir, there are some things more fit to be looked at than others; for instance, there is nothing more fit to be looked at than the outside of a book. It is, as I may say from repeated experience, a pure and unmixed pleasure to have a goodly volume lying before you, and to know that you may open it if you please, and need not open it unless you please. It is a resource against *ennui*, if *ennui* should come upon you. To have the resource and not to feel the *ennui*, to enjoy your bottle in the present, and your book in the indefinite future, is a delightful condition of human existence. There is no place, in which a man can move or sit, in which the outside of a book can be otherwise than an innocent and becoming spectacle. Touching this matter, there cannot, I think, be two opinions. But with respect to your Venuses there can be, and indeed there are, two very distinct opinions. Now, sir, that little figure in the centre of the mantelpiece—as a grave *paterfamilias*, Mr. Crotchet, with a fair nubile daughter, whose eyes are like the fishpools of Heshbon—I would ask you if you hold that figure to be altogether delicate?

Mr. Crotchet.—The Sleeping Venus, sir? Nothing can be more delicate than the entire contour of the figure, the flow of the hair on the shoulders and neck, the form of the feet and fingers. It is altogether a most delicate morsel.

The Rev. Dr. Folliott.—Why, in that sense, perhaps, it is as delicate as whitebait in July. But the attitude, sir, the attitude.

Mr. Crotchet.—Nothing can be more natural, sir.

The Rev. Dr. Folliott.—That is the very thing, sir. It is too natural: too natural, sir. it lies for all the world like—— I make no doubt the pious cheesemonger, who recently broke its plaster facsimile over the head of the itinerant vendor, was struck by a certain similitude to the position of his own sleeping beauty, and felt his noble wrath thereby justly aroused.

Mr. Crotchet.—Very likely, sir. In my opinion, the cheesemonger was a fool, and the justice who sided with him was a greater.

The Rev. Dr. Folliott.—Fool, sir, is a harsh term: call not thy brother a fool?

Mr. Crotchet.—Sir, neither the cheesemonger nor the justice is a brother of mine.

The Rev. Dr. Folliott.—Sir, we are all brethren.

Mr. Crotchet.—Yes, sir, as the hangman is of the thief; the 'squire of the poacher; the judge of the libeller; the lawyer of his client; the statesman of his colleague; the bubble-blower of the bubble-buyer; the slave-driver of the negro; as these are brethren, so am I and the worthies in question.

The Rev. Dr. Folliott.—To be sure, sir, in these instances, and in many others, the term brother must be taken in its utmost latitude of interpretation: we are all brothers, nevertheless. But to return to the point. Now, these two large figures: one with drapery on the lower half of the body, and the other with no drapery at all: upon my word, sir, it matters not what godfathers and godmothers may have promised and vowed for the children of this world, touching the devil and other things to be renounced, if such figures as those are to be put before their eyes.

Mr. Crotchet.—Sir, the naked figure is the Pandemian Venus, and the half-draped figure is the Uranian Venus; and I say, sir, that figure realizes the finest imaginings of Plato, and is the personification of the most refined and exalted feeling of which the human mind is susceptible; the love of pure, ideal, intellectual beauty.

The Rev. Dr. Folliott.—I am aware, sir, that Plato, in his Symposium, discourseth very eloquently touching the Uranian and Pandemian Venus: but you must remember that, in our Universities, Plato is held to be little better than a misleader of youth; and they have shown their contempt for him, not only by never reading him (a mode of contempt in which they deal very largely), but even by never printing a complete edition of him; although they have printed many ancient books which nobody suspects to have been ever read on the spot, except by a person attached to the press, who is therefore emphatically called "the reader."

Mr. Crotchet.—Well, sir?

The Rev. Dr. Folliott.—Why, sir, to "the reader" aforesaid (supposing either of our Universities to have printed an edition of Plato), or to any one else who can be supposed to have read Plato, or indeed to be ever likely to do so, I would very willingly show these figures; because to such they would, I grant you, be the outward and visible signs of poetical and philosophical ideas: but, to the multitude, the gross carnal multitude, they are but two beautiful women—one half undressed, and the other quite so.

Mr. Crotchet.—Then, sir, let the multitude look upon them and learn modesty.

The Rev. Dr. Folliott.—I must say that, if I wished my footman to learn modesty, I should not dream of sending him to school to a naked Venus.

Mr. Crotchet.—Sir, ancient sculpture is the true school of modesty. But where the Greeks had modesty, we have cant; where they had poetry, we have cant; where they had patriotism, we have cant; where they had anything that exalts, delights, or adorns humanity, we have nothing but cant, cant, cant. And, sir, to show my contempt for cant in all its shapes, I have adorned my house with the Greek Venus, in all her shapes, and am ready to fight her battle against all the societies that were ever instituted for the suppression of truth and beauty.

The Rev. Dr. Folliott.—My dear sir, I am afraid you are growing warm. Pray be cool. Nothing contributes so much to good digestion as to be perfectly cool after dinner.

Mr. Crotchet.—Sir, the Lacedæmonian virgins wrestled naked with young men: and they grew up, as the wise Lycurgus had foreseen, into the most modest of women, and the most exemplary of wives and mothers.

The Rev. Dr. Folliott.—Very likely, sir, but the Athenian virgins did no such thing, and they grew up into wives who stayed at home —stayed at home, sir; and looked after the husband's dinner—his dinner, sir, you will please to observe.

Mr. Crotchet.—And what was the consequence of that, sir? that they were such very insipid persons that the husband would not go home to eat his dinner, but preferred the company of some Aspasia, or Lais.

The Rev. Dr. Folliott.—Two very different persons, sir, give me leave to remark.

Mr. Crotchet.—Very likely, sir; but both too good to be married in Athens.

The Rev. Dr. Folliott.—Sir, Lais was a Corinthian.

Mr. Crotchet.—'Od's vengeance, sir, some Aspasia and any other Athenian name of the same sort of person you like——

The Rev. Dr. Folliott.—I do not like the sort of person at all:

the sort of person I like, as I have already implied, is a modest woman, who stays at home and looks after her husband's dinner.

Mr. Crotchet.—Well, sir, that was not the taste of the Athenians. They preferred the society of women who would not have made any scruple about sitting as models to Praxiteles; as you know, sir, very modest women in Italy did to Canova: one of whom, an Italian countess, being asked by an English lady, "How she could bear it?" answered, "Very well; there was a good fire in the room."

The Rev. Dr. Folliott.—Sir, the English lady should have asked how the Italian lady's husband could bear it. The phials of my wrath would overflow if poor dear Mrs. Folliott——: sir, in return for your story, I will tell you a story of my ancestor, Gilbert Folliott. The devil haunted him, as he did Saint Francis, in the likeness of a beautiful damsel; but all he could get from the exemplary Gilbert was an admonition to wear a stomacher and long petticoats.

Mr. Crotchet.—Sir, your story makes for my side of the question. It proves that the devil, in the likeness of a fair damsel, with short petticoats and no stomacher, was almost too much for Gilbert Folliott. The force of the spell was in the drapery.

The Rev. Dr. Folliott.—Bless my soul, sir!

Mr. Crotchet.—Give me leave, sir. Diderot——

The Rev. Dr. Folliott.—Who was he, sir?

Mr. Crotchet.—Who was he, sir? The sublime philosopher, the father of the encyclopædia, of all the encyclopædias that have ever been printed.

The Rev. Dr. Folliott.—Bless me, sir, a terrible progeny! they belong to the tribe of *Incubi.*

Mr. Crotchet.—The great philosopher, Diderot——

The Rev. Dr. Folliott.—Sir, Diderot is not a man after my heart. Keep to the Greeks, if you please; albeit this Sleeping Venus is not an antique.

Mr. Crotchet.—Well, sir, the Greeks: why do we call the Elgin marbles inestimable? Simply because they are true to nature. And why are they so superior in that point to all modern works, with all our greater knowledge of anatomy? Why, sir, but because the Greeks, having no cant, had better opportunities of studying models?

The Rev. Dr. Folliott.—Sir, I deny our greater knowledge of anatomy. But I shall take the liberty to employ, on this occasion, the *argumentum ad hominem.* [1] Would you have allowed Miss Crotchet to sit for a model to Canova?

Mr. Crotchet.—Yes, sir.

"God bless my soul, sir!" exclaimed the Reverend Doctor Folliott, throwing himself back into a chair, and flinging up his heels, with the premeditated design of giving emphasis to his exclamation: but, by miscalculating his *impetus,* he overbalanced his chair, and laid himself on the carpet in a right angle, of which his back was the base.

SCIENCE AND CHARITY

The Reverend Dr. Folliott took his departure about ten o'clock, to walk home to his vicarage. There was no moon; but the night was bright and clear, and afforded him as much light as he needed. He paused a moment by the Roman Camp, to listen to the nightingale; repeated to himself a passage of Sophocles; proceeded through the park-gate, and entered the narrow lane that led to the village. He walked on in a very pleasant mood of the state called reverie; in which fish and wine, Greek and political economy, the Sleeping Venus he had left behind and poor dear Mrs. Folliott, to whose fond arms he was returning, passed as in a camera obscura over the tablets of his imagination. Presently, the image of Mr. Eavesdrop, with a printed sketch of the Reverend Doctor F., presented itself before him, and he began mechanically to flourish his bamboo. The movement was prompted by his good genius, for the uplifted bamboo received the blow of a ponderous cudgel, which was intended for his head. The reverend gentleman recoiled two or three paces, and saw before him a couple of ruffians, who were preparing to renew the attack, but whom, with two swings of his bamboo, he laid with cracked sconces on the earth, where he proceeded to deal with them like corn beneath the flail of the thresher. One of them drew a pistol, which went off in the very act of being

[1 directly personal argument.]

struck aside by the bamboo, and lodged a bullet in the brain of the other. There was then only one enemy, who vainly struggled to rise, every effort being attended with a new and more signal prostration. The fellow roared for mercy. "Mercy, rascal!" cried the divine; "what mercy were you going to show me, villain? What! I warrant me, you thought it would be an easy matter, and no sin, to rob and murder a parson on his way home from dinner. You said to yourself, doubtless, 'We'll waylay the fat parson' (you irreverent knave) 'as he waddles home' (you disparaging ruffian), 'half-seas-over' (you calumnious vagabond)." And with every dyslogistic term, which he supposed had been applied to himself, he inflicted a new bruise on his rolling and roaring antagonist. "Ah, rogue!" he proceeded; "you can roar now, marauder; you were silent enough when you devoted my brains to dispersion under your cudgel. But seeing that I cannot bind you, and that I intend you not to escape, and that it would be dangerous to let you rise, I will disable you in all your members; I will contund you as Thestylis did strong-smelling herbs in the quality whereof you do most gravely partake, as my nose beareth testimony, ill weed that you are. I will beat you to a jelly, and I will then roll you into the ditch, to lie till the constable comes for you, thief."

"Hold! hold! reverend sir," exclaimed the penitent culprit, "I am disabled already in every finger, and in every joint. I will roll myself into the ditch, reverend sir."

"Stir not, rascal," returned the divine, "stir not so much as the quietest leaf above you, or my bamboo rebounds on your body like hail in a thunder-storm. Confess speedily, villain; are you simple thief, or would you have manufactured me into a subject, for the benefit of science? Ay, miscreant caitiff, you would have made me a subject for science, would you? You are a schoolmaster abroad, are you? You are marching with a detachment of the march of mind, are you? You are a member of the Steam Intellect Society, are you? You swear by the learned friend, do you?

"Oh, no! reverend sir," answered the criminal, "I am innocent of all these offences, whatever they are, reverend sir. The only friend I had in the world is lying dead beside me, reverend sir."

The reverend gentleman paused a moment, and leaned on his bamboo. The culprit, bruised as he was, sprang on his legs, and went off in double quick time. The doctor gave him chase, and had nearly brought him within arm's length, when the fellow turned at right angles, and sprang clean over a deep dry ditch. The divine, following with equal ardour, and less dexterity, went down over head and ears into a thicket of nettles. Emerging with much discomposure, he proceeded to the village, and roused the constable; but the constable found, on reaching the scene of action, that the dead man was gone, as well as his living accomplice.

"Oh, the monster!" exclaimed the Reverend Doctor Folliott, "he has made a subject for science of the only friend he had in the world." "Ay, my dear," he resumed, the next morning at breakfast, "if my old reading, and my early gymnastics (for, as the great Hermann says, before I was demulced by the Muses, I was *ferocis ingenii puer, et ad arma quam ad literas paratior* [1]), had not imbued me indelibly with some of the holy rage of *Frère Jean des Entommeures,* [2] I should be, at this moment, lying on the table of some flinty-hearted anatomist, who would have sliced and disjointed me as unscrupulously as I do these remnants of the capon and chine, wherewith you consoled yourself yesterday for my absence at dinner. Phew! I have a noble thirst upon me, which I will quench with floods of tea."

The reverend gentleman was interrupted by a messenger, who informed him that the Charity Commissioners requested his presence at the inn, where they were holding a sitting.

"The Charity Commissioners!" exclaimed the reverend gentleman, "who on earth are they?"

The messenger could not inform him, and the reverend gentleman took his hat and stick, and proceeded to the inn.

On entering the best parlour, he saw three well-dressed and bulky gentlemen sitting at a table, and a fourth officiating as clerk, with an open book before him, and a pen in his hand. The churchwardens, who had been also summoned, were already in attendance.

The chief commissioner politely requested the Reverend Doctor Folliott to be seated; and after the usual meteorological preliminaries

[1] "A boy of fierce disposition, more inclined to arms than to letters."— HERMANN's *Dedication of Homer's Hymns to his Preceptor, Ilgen.*
[2 Friar John of the Funnels.—Rabelais.]

had been settled by a resolution, nem. con., that it was a fine day but very hot, the chief commissioner stated, that in virtue of the comission of Parliament, which they had the honour to hold, they were now to inquire into the state of the public charities of this village.

The Rev. Dr. Folliott.—The state of the public charities, sir, is exceedingly simple. There are none. The charities here are all private, and so private that I for one know nothing of them.

First Commissioner.—We have been informed sir, that there is an annual rent charged on the land of Hautbois, for the endowment and repair of an almshouse.

The Rev. Dr. Folliott.—Hautbois! Hautbois!

First Commissioner.—The manorial farm of Hautbois, now occupied by Farmer Seedling, is charged with the endowment and maintenance of an almshouse.

The Rev. Dr. Folliott (to the churchwarden).—How is this, Mr. Bluenose?

First Churchwarden.—I really do not know, sir. What say you, Mr. Appletwig?

Mr. Appletwig (parish clerk and schoolmaster; an old man).—I do remember, gentlemen, to have been informed, that there did stand at the end of the village a ruined cottage, which had once been an almshouse, which was endowed and maintained, by an annual revenue of a mark and a half, or one pound sterling, charged some centuries ago on the farm of Hautbois; but the means, by the progress of time, having become inadequate to the end, the almshouse tumbled to pieces.

First Commissioner.—But this is a right which cannot be abrogated by desuetude, and the sum of one pound per annum is still chargeable for charitable purposes on the manorial farm of Hautbois.

The Rev. Dr. Folliott.—Very well, sir.

Mr. Appletwig.—But sir, the one pound per annum is still received by the parish, but was long ago, by an unanimous vote in open vestry, given to the minister.

The Three Commissioners (unâ voce).—The minister!

First Commissioner.—This is an unjustifiable proceeding.

Second Commissioner.—A misappropriation of a public fund.

Third Commissioner.—A flagrant perversion of a charitable donation.

The Rev. Dr. Folliott.—God bless my soul, gentlemen! I know nothing of this matter. How is this, Mr. Bluenose? Do I receive this one pound per annum?

First Churchwarden.—Really, sir, I know no more about it than you do.

Mr. Appletwig.—You certainly receive it, sir. It was voted to one of your predecessors. Farmer Seedling lumps it in with his tithes.

First Commissioner.—Lumps it in, sir! Lump in a charitable donation!

Second and Third Commissioner.—Oh-oh-oh-h-h!

First Commissioner.—Reverend sir, and gentlemen, officers of this parish, we are under the necessity of admonishing you that this is a most improper proceeding; and you are hereby duly admonished accordingly. Make a record, Mr. Milky.

Mr. Milky (writing).—The clergyman and churchwardens of the village of Hm-m m-m gravely admonished. Hm-m-m-m.

The Rev. Dr. Folliott.—Is that all, gentlemen?

The Commissioners.—That is all, sir, and we wish you a good-morning.

The Rev. Dr. Folliott.—A very good-morning to you, gentlemen.

"What in the name of all that is wonderful, Mr. Bluenose," said the Rev. Dr. Folliott, as he walked out of the inn—"what in the name of all that is wonderful can those fellows mean? They have come here in a chaise and four, to make a fuss about a pound per annum, which, after all, they leave as it was. I wonder who pays them for their trouble, and how much."

Mr. Appletwig.—The public pay for it, sir. It is a job of the learned friend whom you admire so much. It makes away with public money in salaries, and private money in lawsuits, and does no particle of good to any living soul.

The Rev. Dr. Folliott.—Ay, ay, Mr. Appletwig; that is just the sort of public service to be looked for from the learned friend. Oh, the learned friend! the learned friend! He is the evil genius of everything that falls in his way.

The reverend doctor walked off to Crotchet Castle, to narrate his misadventures, and exhale his budget of grievances on Mr. Mac Quedy, whom he considered a ringleader of the march of the mind.

THE VOYAGE

Four beautiful cabined pinnaces, one for the ladies, one for the gentlemen, one for kitchen and servants, one for a dining-room and band of music, weighed anchor, on a fine July morning, from below Crotchet Castle, and were towed merrily, by strong trotting horses, against the stream of the Thames. They passed from the district of chalk, successively into the districts of clay, of sand-rock, of oolite, and so forth. Sometimes they dined in their floating dining-room, sometimes in tents, which they pitched on the dry, smooth-shaven green of a newly mown meadow; sometimes they left their vessels to see sights in the vicinity; sometimes they passed a day or two in a comfortable inn.

At Oxford, they walked about to see the curiosities of architecture, painted windows, and undisturbed libraries. The Reverend Doctor Folliott laid a wager with Mr. Crotchet "that in all their perlustrations they would not find a man reading," and won it. "Ay, sir," said the reverend gentleman, "this is still a seat of learning, on the principle of—once a captain always a captain. We may well ask, in these great reservoirs of books whereof no man ever draws a sluice, *Quorsum pertinuit stipare Platona Menandro?* [1] What is done here for the classics? Reprinting German editions on better paper! A great boast, verily! What for mathematics? What for metaphysics? What for history? What for anything worth knowing? This was a seat of learning in the days of Friar Bacon. But the friar is gone, and his learning with him. Nothing of him is left but the immortal nose, which, when his brazen head had tumbled to pieces, crying 'Time's past,' was the only palpable fragment among its minutely pulverized atoms, and which is still resplendent over the portals of its cognominal college. That nose, sir, is the only thing to which I shall take off my hat, in all this Babylon of buried literature."

[1] Wherefore is Plato on Menander piled?—Hor. *Sat.* ii. 3, 11.

Mr. Crotchet.—But, doctor, it is something to have a great reservoir of learning, at which some may draw if they please.

The Rev. Dr. Folliott.—But, here, good care is taken that nobody shall please. If even a small drop from the sacred fountain πίδακος ἐξ ἱερῆς ὀλίγη λιβὰς,[1] as Callimachus has it, were carried off by any one, it would be evidence of something to hope for. But the system of dissuasion from all good learning is brought here to a pitch of perfection that baffles the keenest aspirant. I run over to myself the names of the scholars of Germany, a glorious catalogue! but ask for those of Oxford—Where are they? The echoes of their courts, as vacant as their heads, will answer, Where are they? The tree shall be known by its fruit; and seeing that this great tree, with all its specious seeming, brings forth no fruit, I do denounce it as a barren fig.

Mr. Mac Quedy.—I shall set you right on this point. We do nothing without motives. If learning get nothing but honour, and very little of that; and if the good things of this world, which ought to be the rewards of learning, become the mere gifts of self-interested patronage; you must not wonder if, in the finishing of education, the science which takes precedence of all others should be the science of currying favour.

The Rev. Dr. Folliott.—Very true, sir. Education is well-finished, for all worldly purposes, when the head is brought into the state whereinto I am accustomed to bring a marrow-bone when it has been set before me on a toast, with a white napkin wrapped round it. Nothing trundles along the high road of preferment so trimly as a well-biased sconce, picked clean within, and polished without; totus teres atque rotundus.[2] The perfection of the finishing lies in the bias, which keeps it trundling in the given direction. There is good and sufficient reason for the fig being barren, but it is not therefore the less a barren fig.

At Godstow, they gathered hazel on the grave of Rosamond; and, proceeding on their voyage, fell into a discussion on legendary histories.

Lady Clarinda.—History is but a tiresome thing in itself; it becomes more agreeable the more romance is mixed up with it. The

[1 small trickle from the sacred spring.]
2 All smooth and round.

great enchanter has made me learn many things which I should never have dreamed of studying, if they had not come to me in the form of amusement.

The Rev. Dr. Folliott.—What enchanter is that? There are two enchanters: he of the North, and he of the South.

Mr. Trillo.—Rossini?

The Rev. Dr. Folliott.—Ay, there is another enchanter. But I mean the great enchanter of Covent Garden: he who, for more than a quarter of a century, has produced two pantomimes a year, to the delight of children of all ages, including myself at all ages. That is the enchanter for me. I am for the pantomimes. All the northern enchanter's romances put together would not furnish materials for half the southern enchanter's pantomimes.

Lady Clarinda.—Surely you do not class literature with pantomime?

The Rev. Dr. Folliott.—In these cases I do. They are both one, with a slight difference. The one is the literature of pantomime, the other is the pantomime of literature. There is the same variety of character, the same diversity of story, the same copiousness of incident, the same research into costume, the same display of heraldry, falconry, minstrelsy, scenery, monkery, witchery, devilry, robbery, poachery, piracy, fishery, gipsy-astrology, demonology, architecture, fortification, castrametation, navigation; the same running base of love and battle. The main difference is, that the one set of amusing fictions is told in music and action; the other in all the worst dialects of the English language. As to any sentence worth remembering, any moral or political truth, anything having a tendency, however remote, to make men wiser or better, to make them think, to make them even think of thinking; they are both precisely alike: *nuspiam, nequaquam, nullibi, nullimodis.*

Lady Clarinda.—Very amusing, however.

The Rev. Dr. Folliott.—Very amusing, very amusing.

Mr. Chainmail.—My quarrel with the northern enchanter is, that he has grossly misrepresented the twelfth century.

The Rev. Dr. Folliott.—He has misrepresented everything, or he would not have been very amusing. Sober truth is but dull matter to the reading rabble. The angler, who puts not on his hook the bait that best pleases the fish, may sit all day on the bank without catching a gudgeon. [1]

Mr. Mac Quedy.—But how do you mean that he has misrepresented the twelfth century? By exhibiting some of its knights and ladies in the colours of refinement and virtue, seeing that they were all no better than ruffians, and something else that shall be nameless?

Mr. Chainmail.—By no means. By depicting them as much worse than they were, not, as you suppose, much better. No one would infer from his pictures that theirs was a much better state of society than this which we live in.

Mr. Mac Quedy.—No, nor was it. It was a period of brutality, ignorance, fanaticism, and tyranny; when the land was covered with castles, and every castle contained a gang of banditti, headed by a titled robber, who levied contributions with fire and sword; plundering, torturing, ravishing, burying his captives in loathsome dungeons, and broiling them on gridirons, to force from them the surrender of every particle of treasure which he suspected them of possessing; and fighting every now and then with the neighbouring lords, his conterminal bandits, for the right of marauding on the boundaries. This was the twelfth century, as depicted by all contemporary historians and poets.

Mr. Chainmail.—No, sir. Weigh the evidence of specific facts; you will find more good than evil. Who was England's greatest hero; the mirror of chivalry, the pattern of honour, the fountain of generosity, the model to all succeeding ages of military glory? Richard the First. There is a king of the twelfth century. What was the first step of liberty? Magna Charta. That was the best thing ever done by lords. There are lords of the twelfth century. You must remember, too, that these lords were petty princes, and made war on each other as legitimately as the heads of larger communities did or do. For their system of revenue, it was, to be sure, more rough and summary than that which has succeeded it, but it was certainly less searching and less productive. And as to the people, I content myself with these great points: that every man was armed,

---

[1] Eloquentiæ magister, nisi, tamquam piscator, eam imposuerit hamis escam quam scierit appetituros esse pisciculos, sine spe prædræ moratur in scopulo. —PETRONIUS ARBITER.

every man was a good archer, every man could and would fight effectively with sword or pike, or even with oaken cudgel: no man would live quietly without beef and ale; if he had them not, he fought till he either got them, or was put out of condition to want them. They were not, and could not be, subjected to that powerful pressure of all the other classes of society, combined by gunpowder, steam, and *fiscality*, which has brought them to that dismal degradation in which we see them now. And there are the people of the twelfth century.

Mr. Mac Quedy.—As to your king, the enchanter has done him ample justice, even in your own view. As to your lords and their ladies, he has drawn them too favourably, given them too many of the false colours of chivalry, thrown too attractive a light on their abominable doings. As to the people, he keeps them so much in the background, that he can hardly be said to have represented them at all, much less misrepresented them, which indeed he could scarcely do, seeing that, by your own showing, they were all thieves, ready to knock down any man for what they could not come by honestly.

Mr. Chainmail.—No, sir. They could come honestly by beef and ale, while they were left to their simple industry. When oppression interfered with them in that, then they stood on the defensive, and fought for what they were not permitted to come by quietly.

Mr. Mac Quedy.—If A, being aggrieved by B, knocks down C, do you call that standing on the defensive?

Mr. Chainmail.—That depends on who or what C is.

The Rev. Dr. Folliott.—Gentleman, you will never settle this controversy, till you have first settled what is good for man in this world; the great question, *de finibus*, which has puzzled all philosophers. If the enchanter has represented the twelfth century too brightly for one, and too darkly for the other of you, I should say, as an impartial man, he has represented it fairly. My quarrel with him is, that his works contain nothing worth quoting; and a book that furnishes no quotations, is, *me judice*, no book—it is a plaything. There is no question about the amusement—amusement of multitudes; but if he who amuses us most, is to be our enchanter κατ᾿ ἐξοχήν,[1] then my enchanter is the enchanter of Covent Garden.

[1 par excellence.]

THE VOYAGE, CONTINUED

"There is a beautiful structure," said Mr. Chainmail, as they glided by Lechlade Church; "a subject for the pencil, Captain. It is a question worth asking, Mr. Mac Quedy, whether the religious spirit which reared these edifices, and connected with them everywhere an asylum for misfortune and a provision for poverty, was not better than the commercial spirit, which has turned all the business of modern life into schemes of profit, and processes of fraud and extortion. I do not see, in all your boasted improvements, any compensation for the religious charity of the twelfth century. I do not see any compensation for that kindly feeling which, within their own little communities, bound the several classes of society together, while full scope was left for the development of natural character, wherein individuals differed as conspicuously as in costume. Now, we all wear one conventional dress, one conventional face; we have no bond of union, but pecuniary interest; we talk any thing that comes uppermost, for talking's sake, and without expecting to be believed; we have no nature, no simplicity, no picturesqueness: everything about us is as artificial and as complicated as our steam-machinery: our poetry is a kaleidoscope of false imagery, expressing no real feeling, portraying no real existence. I do not see any compensation for the poetry of the twelfth century."

Mr. Mac Quedy. I wonder to hear you, Mr. Chainmail, talking of the religious charity of a set of lazy monks and beggarly friars, who were much more occupied with taking than giving, of whom, those who were in earnest did nothing but make themselves, and everybody about them, miserable, with fastings, and penances, and other such trash; and those who were not, did nothing but guzzle and royster, and, having no wives of their own, took very unbecoming liberties with those of honester men. And as to your poetry of the twelfth century, it is not good for much.

Mr. Chainmail.—It has, at any rate, what ours wants, truth to nature, and simplicity of diction. The poetry, which was addressed to the people of the dark ages, pleased in proportion to the truth with which it depicted familiar images, and to their natural connection with the time and place to which they were assigned. In the poetry of our enlightened times, the characteristics of all seasons, soils, and climates, may be blended together, with much benefit to the author's fame as an original genius. The cowslip of a civic poet is always in blossom, his fern is always in full feather; he gathers the celandine, the primrose, the heath-flower, the jasmine, and the chrysanthemum, all on the same day, and from the same spot: his nightingale sings all the year round, his moon is always full, his cygnet is as white as his swan, his cedar is as tremulous as his aspen, and his poplar as embowering as his beech. Thus all nature marches with the march of mind; but, among barbarians, instead of mead and wine, and the best seat by the fire, the reward of such a genius would have been, to be summarily turned out of doors in the snow, to meditate on the difference between day and night, and between December and July. It is an age of liberality, indeed, when not to know an oak from a burdock is no disqualification for sylvan minstrelsy. I am for truth and simplicity.

The Rev. Dr. Folliott.—Let him who loves them read Greek: Greek, Greek, Greek.

Mr. Mac Quedy.—If he can, sir.

The Rev. Dr. Folliott.—Very true, sir; if he can. Here is the captain, who can. But I think he must have finished his education at some very rigid college, where a quotation, or any other overt act showing acquaintance with classical literature, was visited with a severe penalty. For my part, I make it my boast that I was not to be so subdued. I could not be abated of a single quotation by all the bumpers in which I was fined.

In this manner they glided over the face of the waters, discussing everything and settling nothing. Mr. Mac Quedy and the Reverend Doctor Folliott had many digladiations on political economy: wherein, each in his own view, Doctor Folliott demolished Mr. Mac Quedy's science, and Mr. Mac Quedy demolished Doctor Folliott's objections.

We would print these dialogues if we thought any one would read them: but the world is not yet ripe for this *haute sagesse Pantagrueline.* We must, therefore, content ourselves with an *échantillon* of one of the Reverend Doctor's perorations.

"You have given the name of a science to what is yet an imperfect inquiry; and the upshot of your so-called science is this, that you increase the wealth of a nation by increasing in it the quantity of things which are produced by labour: no matter what they are, no matter how produced, no matter how distributed. The greater the quantity of labour that has gone to the production of the quantity of things in a community, the richer is the community. That is your doctrine. Now, I say, if this be so, riches are not the object for a community to aim at. I say, the nation is best off, in relation to other nations, which has the greatest quantity of the common necessaries of life distributed among the greatest number of persons; which has the greatest number of honest hearts and stout arms united in a common interest, willing to offend no one, but ready to fight in defence of their own community against all the rest of the world, because they have something in it worth fighting for. The moment you admit that one class of things, without any reference to what they respectively cost, is better worth having than another; that a smaller commercial value, with one mode of distribution, is better than a greater commercial value, with another mode of distribution; the whole of that curious fabric of postulates and dogmas, which you call the science of political economy, and which I call *politicæ æconomiæ inscientia,*[1] tumbles to pieces."

Mr. Toogood agreed with Mr. Chainmail against Mr. Mac Quedy, that the existing state of society was worse than that of the twelfth century; but he agreed with Mr. Mac Quedy against Mr. Chainmail, that it was in progress to something much better than either—to which "something much better" Mr. Toogood and Mr. Mac Quedy attached two very different meanings.

Mr. Chainmail fought with Doctor Folliott the battle of the romantic against the classical in poetry; and Mr. Skionar contended with Mr. Mac Quedy for intuition and synthesis, against analysis and induction in philosophy.

Mr. Philpot would lie along for hours, listening to the gurgling of the water round the prow, and would occasionally edify the company with speculations on the great changes that would be effected in the world by the steam-navigation of rivers: sketching the course of a steam-boat up and down some mighty stream which civilization

[1 Ignorance of political economy.]

had either never visited, or long since deserted; the Missouri and the Columbia, the Oroonoko and the Amazon, the Nile and the Niger, the Euphrates and the Tigris, the Oxus and the Indus, the Ganges and the Hoangho; under the overcanopying forests of the new, or by the long-silent ruins of the ancient world; through the shapeless mounds of Babylon, or the gigantic temples of Thebes.

Mr. Trillo went on with the composition of his opera, and took the opinions of the young ladies on every step in its progress; occasionally regaling the company with specimens, and wondering at the blindness of Mr. Mac Quedy, who could not, or would not see that an opera in perfection, being the union of all the beautiful arts—music, painting, dancing, poetry—exhibiting female beauty in its most attractive aspects, and in its most becoming costume—was, according to the well-known precept, *Ingenuas didicisse*, etc., the most efficient instrument of civilization, and ought to take precedence of all other pursuits in the minds of true philanthropists. The Reverend Doctor Folliott, on these occasions, never failed to say a word or two on Mr. Trillo's side, derived from the practice of the Athenians, and from the combination, in their theatre, of all the beautiful arts, in a degree of perfection unknown to the modern world.

Leaving Lechlade, they entered the canal that connects the Thames with the Severn; ascended by many locks; passed, by a tunnel three miles long, through the bowels of Sapperton Hill; agreed unanimously that the greatest pleasure derivable from visiting a cavern of any sort was that of getting out of it; descended, by many locks again, through the valley of Stroud into the Severn; continued their navigation into the Ellesmere canal; moored their pinnaces in the vale of Llangollen by the aqueduct of Pontycysyllty; and determined to pass some days in inspecting the scenery, before commencing their homeward voyage.

The captain omitted no opportunity of pressing his suit on Lady Clarinda, but could never draw from her any reply but the same doctrines of worldly wisdom, delivered in a tone of *badinage*, mixed with a certain kindness of manner that induced him to hope she was not in earnest.

But the morning after they had anchored under the hills of the Dee—whether the lady had reflected more seriously than usual, or was somewhat less in good-humour than usual, or the captain was more pressing than usual—she said to him, "It must not be, Captain Fitzchrome, 'the course of true love never did run smooth:' my father must keep his borough, and I must have a town house and a country house, and an opera-box and a carriage. It is not well for either of us that we should flirt any longer: 'I must be cruel only to be kind.' Be satisfied with the assurance that you alone, of all men, have ever broken my rest. To be sure, it was only for about three nights in all; but that is too much."

The captain had le cœur navré. He took his portfolio under his arm, made up the little valise of a pedestrian, and, without saying a word to any one, wandered off at random among the mountains.

After the lapse of a day or two, the captain was missed, and every one marvelled what was become of him. Mr. Philpot thought he must have been exploring a river, and fallen in and got drowned in the process. Mr. Firedamp had no doubt he had been crossing a mountain bog, and had been suddenly deprived of life by the exhalations of marsh miasmata. Mr. Henbane deemed it probable that he had been tempted in some wood by the large black brilliant berries of the Atropa Belladonna, or deadly nightshade; and lamented that he had not been by, to administer an infallible antidote. Mr. Eavesdrop hoped the particulars of his fate would be ascertained; and asked if any one present could help him to any authentic anecdotes of their departed friend. The Reverend Doctor Folliott proposed that an inquiry should be instituted, as to whether the march of intellect had reached that neighbourhood; as, if so, the captain had probably been made a subject for science. Mr. Mac Quedy said it was no such great matter to ascertain the precise mode in which the surplus population was diminished by one. Mr. Toogood asseverated that there was no such thing as surplus population, and that the land, properly managed, would maintain twenty times its present inhabitants: and hereupon they fell into a disputation.

Lady Clarinda did not doubt that the captain had gone away designedly: she missed him more than she could have anticipated; and wished she had at least postponed her last piece of cruelty till the completion of their homeward voyage.

CORRESPONDENCE

THE captain was neither drowned nor poisoned, neither miasmatized nor anatomised. But, before we proceed to account for him, we must look back to a young lady, of whom some little notice was taken in the first chapter; and who, though she has since been out of sight, has never with us been out of mind; Miss Susannah Touchandgo, the forsaken of the junior Crotchet, whom we left an inmate of a solitary farm, in one of the deep valleys under the cloudcapt summits of Meirion, comforting her wounded spirit with air and exercise, rustic cheer, music, painting, and poetry, and the prattle of the little Ap Llymrys.

One evening, after an interval of anxious expectation, the farmer, returning from market, brought for her two letters, of which the contents were these:—

> "*Dotandcarryonetown,*
> *State of Apodidraskiana:* [1]
> *April* 1. 18 . .

"MY DEAR CHILD,

"I am anxious to learn what are your present position, intention, and prospects. The fairies who dropped gold in your shoe, on the morning when I ceased to be a respectable man in London, will soon find a talismanic channel for transmitting you a stocking full of dollars, which will fit the shoe, as well as the foot of Cinderella fitted her slipper. I àm happy to say I am again become a respectable man. It was always my ambition to be a respectable man; and I am a very respectable man here, in this new township of a new state, where I have purchased five thousand acres of land, at two dollars an acre, hard cash, and established a very flourishing bank. The notes of Touchandgo and Company, soft cash, are now the exclusive currency of all this vicinity. This is the land in which all men flourish; but there are three classes of men who flourish especially—Methodist-preachers, slave-drivers, and paper-money manufacturers; and as one of the latter, I have just painted the word 'BANK' on a fine slab of maple, which was green and growing when I arrived, and have discounted for the settlers, in my own currency, sundry bills, which

[1 Based on Greek word, "to run away."]

are to be paid when the proceeds of the crop they have just sown shall return from New Orleans; so that my notes are the representatives of vegetation that is to be, and I am accordingly a capitalist of the first magnitude. The people here know very well that I ran away from London, but the most of them have run away from some place or other; and they have a great respect for me, because they think I ran away with something worth taking, which few of them had the luck or the wit to do. This gives them confidence in my resources, at the same time that, as there is nothing portable in the settlement except my own notes, they have no fear that I shall run away with them. They know I am thoroughly conversant with the principles of banking; and as they have plenty of industry, no lack of sharpness, and abundance of land, they wanted nothing but capital to organize a flourishing settlement; and this capital I have manufactured to the extent required, at the expense of a small importation of pens, ink, and paper, and two or three inimitable copper plates. I have abundance here of all good things, a good conscience included; for I really cannot see that I have done any wrong. This was my position: I owed half a million of money; and I had a trifle in my pocket. It was clear that this trifle could never find its way to the right owner. The question was, whether I should keep it, and live like a gentleman; or hand it over to lawyers and commissioners of bankruptcy, and die like a dog on a dunghill. If I could have thought that the said lawyers, etc., had a better title to it than myself, I might have hesitated; but, as such title was not apparent to my satisfaction, I decided the question in my own favour; the right owners, as I have already said, being out of the question altogether. I have always taken scientific views of morals and politics, a habit from which I derive much comfort under existing circumstances.

"I hope you adhere to your music, though I cannot hope again to accompany your harp with my flute. My last *andante* movement was too *forte* for those whom it took by surprise. Let not your *allegro vivace* be damped by young Crotchet's desertion, which, though I have not heard it, I take for granted. He is, like myself, a scientific politician, and has an eye as keen as a needle, to his own interest. He has had good luck so far, and is gorgeous in the spoils of many gulls; but I think the Polar Basin and Walrus Company will be too much for him yet. There has been a splendid outlay on credit; and he is the only man, of the original parties concerned, of whom his majesty's sheriffs could give any account.

"I will not ask you to come here. There is no husband for you. The men smoke, drink, and fight, and break more of their own heads than of girls' hearts. Those among them who are musical sing nothing but psalms. They are excellent fellows in their way, but you would not like them.

"*Au reste*, here are no rents, no taxes, no poor-rates, no tithes, no church-establishment, no routs, no clubs, no rotten boroughs, no operas, no concerts, no theatres, no beggars, no thieves, no king, no lords, no ladies, and only one gentleman, videlicet, your loving father,

"TIMOTHY TOUCHANDGO.

"P.S.—I send you one of my notes; I can afford to part with it. If you are accused of receiving money from me, you may pay it over to my assignees. Robthetill continues to be my factotum; I say no more of him in this place: he will give you an account of himself."

"*Dotandcarryonetown, etc.*

"DEAR MISS,

"Mr. Touchandgo will have told you of our arrival here, of our setting up a bank, and so forth. We came here in a tilted waggon, which served us for parlour, kitchen, and all. We soon got up a log-house; and, unluckily, we as soon got it down again, for the first fire we made in it burnt down house and all. However, our second experiment was more fortunate; and we are pretty well lodged in a house of three rooms on a floor; I should say the floor, for there is but one.

"This new state is free to hold slaves; all the new states have not this privilege: Mr. Touchandgo has bought some, and they are building him a villa. Mr. Touchandgo is in a thriving way, but he is not happy here: he longs for parties and concerts, and a seat in Congress. He thinks it very hard that he cannot buy one with his own coinage, as he used to do in England. Besides, he is afraid of the regulators, who, if they do not like a man's character, wait upon him and flog him, doubling the dose at stated intervals, till he takes himself off. He does not like this system of administering justice: though I think he has nothing to fear from it. He has the character of having money,

which is the best of all characters here, as at home. He lets his old
English prejudices influence his opinions of his new neighbours; but
I assure you they have many virtues. Though they do keep slaves,
they are all ready to fight for their own liberty; and I should not like
to be an enemy within reach of one of their rifles. When I say enemy,
I include bailiff in the term. One was shot not long ago. There was
a trial; the jury gave two dollars damages; the judge said they must
find guilty or not guilty; but the counsel for the defendant (they
would not call him prisoner), offered to fight the judge upon the
point: and as this was said literally, not metaphorically, and the counsel was a stout fellow, the judge gave in. The two dollars damages
were not paid after all; for the defendant challenged the foreman to
box for double or quits, and the foreman was beaten. The folks in
New York made a great outcry about it, but here it was considered
all as it should be. So you see, Miss, justice, liberty, and everything
else of that kind, are different in different places, just as suits the
convenience of those who have the sword in their own hands. Hop-
ing to hear of your health and happiness, I remain,

"Dear Miss, your dutiful servant,
"RODERICK ROBTHETILL."

Miss Touchandgo replied as follows to the first of these letters:—

"MY DEAR FATHER,
"I am sure you have the best of hearts, and I have no doubt
you have acted with the best intentions. My lover, or I should rather
say, my fortune's lover, has indeed forsaken me. I cannot say I did
not feel it; indeed, I cried very much; and the altered looks of people
who used to be so delighted to see me, really annoyed me so that I
determined to change the scene altogether. I have come into Wales,
and am boarding with a farmer and his wife. Their stock of English
is very small, but I managed to agree with them; and they have four
of the sweetest children I ever saw, to whom I teach all I know, and
I manage to pick up some Welsh. I have puzzled out a little song,
which I think very pretty; I have translated it into English, and I
send it you with the original air. You shall play it on your flute at
eight o'clock every Saturday evening, and I will play and sing it at

the same time, and I will fancy that I hear my dear papa accompanying me.

"The people in London said very unkind things of you: they hurt me very much at the time; but now I am out of their way, I do not seem to think their opinion of much consequence. I am sure, when I recollect, at leisure, everything I have seen and heard among them, I cannot make out what they do that is so virtuous as to set them up for judges of morals. And I am sure they never speak the truth about anything, and there is no sincerity in either their love or their friendship. An old Welsh bard here, who wears a waistcoat embroidered with leeks, and is called the Green Bard of Cadair Idris, says the Scotch would be the best people in the world if there was nobody but themselves to give them a character; and so, I think, would the Londoners. I hate the very thought of them, for I do believe they would have broken my heart if I had not got out of their way. Now I shall write you another letter very soon, and describe to you the country, and the people, and the children, and how I amuse myself, and every thing that I think you will like to hear about: and when I seal this letter, I shall drop a kiss on the cover.

"Your loving daughter,
"Susannah Touchandgo.

"P.S.—Tell Mr. Robthetill I will write to him in a day or two. This is the little song I spoke of:—

"Beyond the sea, beyond the sea,
My heart is gone, far, far from me;
And ever on its track will flee
My thoughts, my dreams, beyond the sea.

Beyond the sea, beyond the sea,
The swallow wanders fast and free:
Oh, happy bird, were I like thee,
I, too, would fly beyond the sea.

Beyond the sea, beyond the sea,
Are kindly hearts and social glee:
But here for me they may not be:
My heart is gone beyond the sea."

THE MOUNTAIN INN

THE captain wandered despondingly up and down hill for several days, passing many hours of each in sitting on rocks; making, almost mechanically, sketches of waterfalls, and mountain pools; taking care, nevertheless, to be always before night-fall in a comfortable inn, where, being a temperate man, he wiled away the evening with making a bottle of sherry into negus. His rambles brought him at length into the interior of Merionethshire, the land of all that is beautiful in nature, and all that is lovely in woman.

Here, in a secluded village, he found a little inn, of small pretension and much comfort. He felt so satisfied with his quarters, and discovered every day so much variety in the scenes of the surrounding mountains, that his inclination to proceed farther diminished progressively.

It is one thing to follow the high road through a country, with every principally remarkable object carefully noted down in a book, taking, as therein directed, a guide at particular points, to the more recondite sights: it is another to sit down on one chosen spot, especially when the choice is unpremeditated, and from thence, by a series of explorations, to come day by day on unanticipated scenes. The latter process has many advantages over the former; it is free from the disappointment which attends excited expectation, when imagination has outstripped reality, and from the accidents that mar the scheme of the tourist's single day, when the valleys may be drenched with rain, or the mountains shrouded with mist.

The captain was one morning preparing to sally forth on his usual exploration, when he heard a voice without, inquiring for a guide to the ruined castle. The voice seemed familiar to him, and going forth into the gateway, he recognized Mr. Chainmail. After greetings and inquiries for the absent, "You vanished very abruptly, captain," said Mr. Chainmail, "from our party on the canal."

Captain Fitzchrome.—To tell you the truth, I had a particular reason for trying the effect of absence from a part of that party.

Mr. Chainmail.—I surmised as much: at the same time, the unusual melancholy of an in general most vivacious young lady made me wonder at your having acted so precipitately. The lady's heart is yours, if there be truth in signs.

Captain Fitzchrome.—Hearts are not now what they were in the days of the old song, "Will love be controlled by advice?"

Mr. Chainmail.—Very true, hearts, heads, and arms have all degenerated, most sadly. We can no more feel the high impassioned love of the ages, which some people have the impudence to call dark, than we can wield King Richard's battleaxe, bend Robin Hood's bow, or flourish the oaken graff of the Pinder of Wakefield. Still we have our tastes and feelings, though they deserve not the name of passions; and some of us may pluck up spirit to try to carry a point, when we reflect that we have to contend with men no better than ourselves.

Captain Fitzchrome.—We do not now break lances for ladies.

Mr. Chainmail.—No, nor even bulrushes. We jingle purses for them, flourish paper-money banners, and tilt with scrolls of parchment.

Captain Fitzchrome.—In which sort of tilting I have been thrown from the saddle. I presume it was not love that led you from the flotilla.

Mr. Chainmail.—By no means. I was tempted by the sight of an old tower, not to leave this land of ruined castles, without having collected a few hints for the adornment of my baronial hall.

Captain Fitzchrome.—I understand you live en famille with your domestics. You will have more difficulty in finding a lady who would adopt your fashion of living, than one who would prefer you to a richer man.

Mr. Chainmail.—Very true. I have tried the experiment on several as guests; but once was enough for them: so, I suppose, I shall die a bachelor.

Captain Fitzchrome.—I see, like some others of my friends, you will give up anything except your hobby.

Mr. Chainmail.—I will give up anything but my baronial hall.

Captain Fitzchrome.—You will never find a wife for your purpose, unless in the daughter of some old-fashioned farmer.

Mr. Chainmail.—No, I thank you. I must have a lady of gentle blood; I shall not marry below my own condition: I am too much of a herald; I have too much of the twelfth century in me for that.

Captain Fitzchrome.—Why then your chance is not much better than mine. A well-born beauty would scarcely be better pleased with your baronial hall, than with my more humble offer of love in a cottage. She must have a town-house, and an opera-box, and roll about the streets in a carriage; especially if her father has a rotten borough, for the sake of which he sells his daughter, that he may continue to sell his country. But you were inquiring for a guide to the ruined castle in this vicinity; I know the way, and will conduct you.

The proposal pleased Mr. Chainmail, and they set forth on their expedition.

THE LAKE.—THE RUIN

Mr. CHAINMAIL.—Would it not be a fine thing, captain,—you being picturesque, and I poetical; you being for the lights and shadows of the present, and I for those of the past,—if we were to go together over the ground which was travelled in the twelfth century by Giraldus de Barri, when he accompanied Archbishop Baldwin to preach the crusade?

Captain Fitzchrome.—Nothing, in my present frame of mind, could be more agreeable to me.

Mr. Chainmail.—We would provide ourselves with his *Itinerarium;* compare what has been with what is; contemplate in their decay the castles and abbeys which he saw in their strength and splendour; and, while you were sketching their remains, I would dispassionately inquire what has been gained by the change.

Captain Fitzchrome.—Be it so.

But the scheme was no sooner arranged than the captain was summoned to London by a letter on business, which he did not expect to detain him long. Mr. Chainmail, who, like the captain, was fascinated with the inn and the scenery, determined to await his companion's return; and, having furnished him with a list of books, which he was to bring with him from London, took leave of him, and began to pass his days like the heroes of Ariosto, who

——tutto il giorno, al bel oprar intenti,
Saliron balze, e traversar torrenti.[1]

One day Mr. Chainmail traced upwards the course of a mountain-
stream, to a spot where a small waterfall threw itself over a slab of
perpendicular rock, which seemed to bar his farther progress. On a
nearer view, he discovered a flight of steps, roughly hewn in the rock,
on one side of the fall. Ascending these steps, he entered a narrow
winding pass, between high and naked rocks, that afforded only space
for a rough footpath carved on one side, at some height above the
torrent.

The pass opened on a lake, from which the stream issued, and
which lay like a dark mirror, set in a gigantic frame of mountain
precipices. Fragments of rock lay scattered on the edge of the lake,
some half-buried in the water: Mr. Chainmail scrambled some way
over these fragments, till the base of a rock, sinking abruptly in the
water, effectually barred his progress. He sat down on a large smooth
stone; the faint murmur of the stream he had quitted, the occasional
flapping of the wings of the heron, and at long intervals the solitary
springing of a trout, were the only sounds that came to his ear. The
sun shone brightly half-way down the opposite rocks, presenting, on
their irregular faces, strong masses of light and shade. Suddenly he
heard the dash of a paddle, and, turning his eyes, saw a solitary and
beautiful girl gliding over the lake in a coracle; she was proceeding
from the vicinity of the point he had quitted towards the upper end
of the lake. Her apparel was rustic, but there was in its style something more récherché, in its arrangement something more of elegance
and precision, than was common to the mountain peasant girl. It
had more of the contadina [2] of the opera than of the genuine mountaineer; so at least thought Mr. Chainmail; but she passed so rapidly,
and took him so much by surprise, that he had little opportunity for
accurate observation. He saw her land, at the farther extremity, and
disappear among the rocks: he rose from his seat, returned to the
mouth of the pass, stepped from stone to stone across the stream,
and attempted to pass round by the other side of the lake; but there
again the abruptly sinking precipice closed his way.

[1 —all day, determined on fine deeds,
Leaped cliffs and traversed torrents.]

[2 peasant.]

Day after day he haunted the spot, but never saw again either the damsel or the coracle. At length, marvelling at himself for being so solicitous about the apparition of a peasant girl in a coracle, who could not, by any possibility, be anything to him, he resumed his explorations in another direction. ·

One day he wandered to the ruined castle, on the sea-shore, which was not very distant from his inn; and sitting on the rock, near the base of the ruin, was calling up the forms of past ages on the wall of an ivied tower, when on its summit appeared a female figure, whom he recognized in an instant for his nymph of the coracle. The folds of the blue gown pressed by the sea breeze against one of the most symmetrical of figures, the black feather of the black hat, and the ringleted hair beneath it fluttering in the wind; the apparent peril of her position, on the edge of the mouldering wall, from whose immediate base the rock went down perpendicularly to the sea, presented a singularly interesting combination to the eye of the young antiquary.

Mr. Chainmail had to pass half round the castle, on the land side, before he could reach the entrance: he coasted the dry and bramble-grown moat, crossed the unguarded bridge, passed the unportcullise arch of the gateway, entered the castle court, ascertained the tower, ascended the broken stairs, and stood on the ivied wall. But the nymph of the place was gone. He searched the ruins within and without, but he found not what he sought: he haunted the castle day after day, as he had done the lake, but the damsel appeared no more.

THE DINGLE

MISS SUSANNAH TOUCHANDGO had read the four great poets of Italy, and many of the best writers of France. About the time of her father's downfall, accident threw into her way *Les Rêveries du Promeneur Solitaire*; and from the impression which these made on her, she carried with her into retirement all the works of Rousseau. In the midst of that startling light which the conduct of old friends on a sudden reverse of fortune throws on a young and inexperienced mind, the doctrines of the philosopher of Geneva struck with double force upon her sympathies: she imbibed the sweet poison, as somebody calls it, of his writings, even to a love of truth; which, every wise man knows, ought to be left to those who can get anything by it. The society of children, the beauties of nature, the solitude of the mountains, became her consolation, and, by degrees, her delight. The gay society from which she had been excluded remained on her memory only as a disagreeable dream. She imbibed her new monitor's ideas of simplicity of dress, assimilating her own with that of the peasant girls in the neighbourhood; the black hat, the blue gown, the black stockings, the shoes tied on the instep.

Pride was, perhaps, at the bottom of the change; she was willing to impose in some measure on herself, by marking a contemptuous indifference to the characteristics of the class of society from which she had fallen.

> And with the food of pride sustained her soul
> In solitude.

It is true that she somewhat modified the forms of her rustic dress; to the black hat she added a black feather, to the blue gown she added a tippet, and a waistband fastened in front with a silver buckle; she wore her black stockings very smooth and tight on her ankles, and tied her shoes in tasteful bows, with the nicest possible ribbon. In this apparel, to which, in winter, she added a scarlet cloak, she made dreadful havoc among the rustic mountaineers, many of whom proposed to "keep company" with her in the Cambrian fashion, an honour which, to their great surprise, she always declined. Among these, Harry Ap-Heather, whose father rented an extensive sheepwalk, and had a thousand she-lambs wandering in the mountains, was the most strenuous in his suit, and the most pathetic in his lamentations for her cruelty.

Miss Susannah often wandered among the mountains alone, even to some distance from the farm-house. Sometimes she descended into the bottom of the dingles, to the black rocky beds of the torrents, and dreamed away hours at the feet of the cataracts. One spot in particular, from which she had at first shrunk with terror, became by degrees her favourite haunt. A path turning and returning at acute angles, led down a steep wood-covered slope to the edge of a chasm, where a pool, or resting-place of a torrent, lay far below. A cataract fell in a single sheet into the pool; the pool boiled and bubbled at the base of the fall, but through the greater part of its extent lay calm, deep, and black, as if the cataract had plunged through it to an unimaginable depth without disturbing its eternal repose. At the opposite extremity of the pool, the rocks almost met at their summits, the trees of the opposite banks intermingled their leaves, and another cataract plunged from the pool into a chasm on which the sunbeams never gleamed. High above, on both sides, the steep woody slopes of the dingle soared into the sky; and from a fissure in the rock, on which the little path terminated, a single gnarled and twisted oak stretched itself over the pool, forming a fork with its boughs at a short distance from the rock. Miss Susannah often sat on the rock, with her feet resting on this tree: in time, she made her seat on the tree itself, with her feet hanging over the abyss; and at length she accustomed herself to lie along upon its trunk, with her side on the mossy boll of the fork, and an arm round one of the branches. From this position a portion of the sky and the woods was reflected in the pool, which, from its bank, was but a mass of darkness. The first time she reclined in this manner, her heart beat audibly; in time, she lay down as calmly as on the mountain heather: the perception of the sublime was probably heightened by an intermingled sense of danger; and perhaps that indifference to life, which early disappointment forces upon sensitive minds, was necessary to the first experiment. There was, in the novelty and strangeness of the position, an excitement which never wholly passed away, but which became gradually subordinate to the influence, at once tranquillizing, and elevating, of the mingled eternity of motion, sound, and solitude.

One sultry noon, she descended into this retreat with a mind more than usually disturbed by reflections on the past. She lay in her favourite position, sometimes gazing on the cataract; looking sometimes up the steep sylvan acclivities into the narrow space of the cloudless ether; sometimes down into the abyss of the pool, and the deep bright-blue reflections that opened another immensity below her. The distressing recollections of the morning, the world, and all its littlenesses, faded from her thoughts like a dream; but her wounded and wearied spirit drank in too deeply the tranquillizing power of the place, and she dropped asleep upon the tree like a ship-boy on the mast.

At this moment Mr. Chainmail emerged into daylight, on a pro-jection of the opposite rock, having struck down through the woods in search of unsophisticated scenery. The scene he discovered filled him with delight: he seated himself on the rock, and fell into one of his romantic reveries; when suddenly the semblance of a black hat and feather caught his eye among the foliage of the projecting oak. He started up, shifted his position, and got a glimpse of a blue gown. It was his lady of the lake, his enchantress of the ruined castle, divided from him by a barrier, which, at a few yards below, he could almost overleap, yet unapproachable but by a circuit perhaps of many hours. He watched with intense anxiety. To listen if she breathed was out of the question: the noses of a dean and chapter would have been soundless in the roar of the torrent. From her extreme stillness, she appeared to sleep: yet what creature, not desperate, would go wilfully to sleep in such a place? Was she asleep then? Nay, was she alive? She was as motionless as death. Had she been murdered, thrown from above, and caught in the tree? She lay too regularly and too composedly for such a supposition. She was asleep then, and in all probability her waking would be fatal. He shifted his position. Below the pool two beetle-browed rocks nearly overarched the chasm, leaving just such a space at the summit as was within the possibility of a leap; the torrent roared below in a fearful gulf. He paused some time on the brink, measuring the practicability and the danger, and casting every now and then an anxious glance to his sleeping beauty. In one of these glances he saw a slight movement of the blue gown, and, in a moment after, the black hat and feather dropped into the pool. Reflection was lost for a moment, and, by a sudden impulse, he bounded over the chasm.

He stood above the projecting oak; the unknown beauty lay like the nymph of the scene; her long black hair, which the fall of her hat had disengaged from its fastenings, drooping through the boughs: he saw that the first thing to be done was to prevent her throwing her feet off the trunk, in the first movements of waking. He sat down on the rock, and placed his feet on the stem, securing her ankles between his own: one of her arms was round a branch of the fork, the other lay loosely on her side. The hand of this arm he endeavoured to reach, by leaning forward from his seat; he approximated, but could not touch it: after several tantalizing efforts, he gave up the point in despair. He did not attempt to wake her, because he feared it might have bad consequences, and he resigned himself to expect the moment of her natural waking, determined not to stir from his post, if she should sleep till midnight.

In this period of forced inaction, he could contemplate at leisure the features and form of his charmer. She was not one of the slender beauties of romance; she was as plump as a partridge; her cheeks were two roses, not absolutely damask, yet verging thereupon; her lips twin-cherries of equal size; her nose regular, and almost Grecian; her forehead high, and delicately fair; her eyebrows symmetrically arched; her eye-lashes long, black, and silky, fitly corresponding with the beautiful tresses that hung among the leaves of the oak, like clusters of wandering grapes.[1] Her eyes were yet to be seen; but how could he doubt that their opening would be the rising of the sun, when all that surrounded their fringy portals was radiant as "the forehead of the morning sky?"

THE FARM

At length the young lady awoke. She was startled at the sudden sight of the stranger, and somewhat terrified at the first perception of her position. But she soon recovered her self-possession, and, extending her hand to the offered hand of Mr. Chainmail, she raised herself up on the tree, and stepped on the rocky bank.

Mr. Chainmail solicited permission to attend her to her home, which the young lady graciously conceded. They emerged from the woody dingle, traversed an open heath, wound along a mountain road by the shore of a lake, descended to the deep bed of another stream, crossed it by a series of stepping stones, ascended to some height on the opposite side, and followed upwards the line of the stream, till the banks opened into a spacious amphitheatre, where stood, in its fields and meadows, the farm-house of Ap-Llymry.

[1] Nonnus.

During this walk, they had kept up a pretty animated conversation. The lady had lost her hat; and, as she turned towards Mr. Chainmail, in speaking to him, there was no envious projection of brim to intercept the beams of those radiant eyes he had been so anxious to see unclosed. There was in them a mixture of softness and brilliancy, the perfection of the beauty of female eyes, such as some men have passed through life without seeing, and such as no man ever saw, in any pair of eyes, but once; such as can never be seen and forgotten. Young Crotchet had seen it; he had not forgotten it; but he had trampled on its memory, as the renegade tramples on the emblems of a faith which his interest only, and not his heart or his reason, has rejected.

Her hair streamed over her shoulders; the loss of the black feather had left nothing but the rustic costume, the blue gown, the black stockings, and the ribbon-tied shoes. Her voice had that full soft volume of melody which gives to common speech the fascination of music. Mr. Chainmail could not reconcile the dress of the damsel with her conversation and manners. He threw out a remote question or two, with the hope of solving the riddle; but, receiving no reply, he became satisfied that she was not disposed to be communicative respecting herself, and, fearing to offend her, fell upon other topics. They talked of the scenes of the mountains, of the dingle, the ruined castle, the solitary lake. She told him that lake lay under the mountains behind her home, and the coracle and the pass at the extremity saved a long circuit to the nearest village, whither she sometimes went to inquire for letters.

Mr. Chainmail felt curious to know from whom these letters might be; and he again threw out two or three fishing questions, to which, as before, he obtained no answer.

The only living biped they met in their walk was the unfortunate Harry Ap-Heather, with whom they fell in by the stepping-stones, who, seeing the girl of his heart hanging on another man's arm, and, concluding at once that they were "keeping company," fixed on her a mingled look of surprise, reproach, and tribulation; and, unable to control his feelings under the sudden shock, burst into a flood of tears, and blubbered till the rocks re-echoed.

They felt him mingling his tears with the stream, and his lamentations with its murmurs. Mr. Chainmail inquired who that strange creature might be, and what was the matter with him. The young lady answered, that he was a very worthy young man, to whom she had been the innocent cause of much unhappiness.

"I pity him sincerely," said Mr. Chainmail; and nevertheless, he could scarcely restrain his laughter at the exceedingly original figure which the unfortunate rustic lover had presented by the stepping-stones.

The children ran out to meet their dear Miss Susan, jumped all round her, and asked what was become of her hat. Ap-Llymry came out in great haste, and invited Mr. Chainmail to walk in and dine: Mr. Chainmail did not wait to be asked twice. In a few minutes the whole party, Miss Susan and Mr. Chainmail, Mr. and Mrs. Ap-Llymry, and progeny, were seated over a clean homespun tablecloth, ornamented with fowls and bacon, a pyramid of potatoes, another of cabbage, which Ap-Llymry said "was poiled with the pacon, and as coot as marrow," a bowl of milk for the children, and an immense brown jug of foaming ale, with which Ap-Llymry seemed to delight in filling the horn of his new guest.

Shall we describe the spacious apartment, which was at once kitchen, hall, and dining-room,—the large dark rafters, the pendent bacon and onions, the strong old oaken furniture, the bright and trimly-arranged utensils? Shall we describe the cut of Ap-Llymry's coat, the colour and tie of his neck-cloth, the number of buttons at his knees—the structure of Mrs. Ap Llymry's cap, having lappets over the ears, which were united under the chin, setting forth especially whether the bond of union were a pin or a ribbon? We shall leave this tempting field of interesting expatiation to those whose brains are high-pressure steam-engines for spinning prose by the furlong, to be trumpeted in paid-for paragraphs in the quack's corner of newspapers: modern literature having attained the honourable distinction of sharing with blacking and macassar oil, the space which used to be monopolized by razor-strops and the lottery, whereby that very enlightened community, the reading public, is tricked into the perusal of much exemplary nonsense; though the few who see through the trickery have no reason to complain, since as "good wine needs no bush," so, ex vi oppositi,[1] these bushels of venal panegyric point out very clearly that the things they celebrate are not worth reading.

[1 by force of the opposite.]

The party dined very comfortably in a corner most remote from the fire; and Mr. Chainmail very soon found his head swimming with two or three horns of ale, of a potency to which even he was unaccustomed. After dinner, Ap-Llymry made him finish a bottle of mead, which he willingly accepted, both as an excuse to remain, and as a drink of the dark ages, which he had no doubt was a genuine brewage, from uncorrupted tradition.

In the meantime, as soon as the cloth was removed, the children had brought out Miss Susannah's harp. She began, without affectation, to play and sing to the children, as was her custom of an afternoon, first in their own language, and their national melodies, then in English; but she was soon interrupted by a general call of little voices for "Ouf! di giorno." She complied with the request, and sung the ballad from Paër's Camilla: *Un dì carco il mulinaro.* The children were very familiar with every syllable of this ballad, which had been often fully explained to them. They danced in a circle with the burden of every verse, shouting out the chorus with good articulation and joyous energy; and at the end of the second stanza, where the traveller has his nose pinched by his grandmother's ghost, every nose in the party was nipped by a pair of little fingers. Mr. Chainmail, who was not prepared for the process, came in for a very energetic tweak, from a chubby girl that sprung suddenly on his knees for the purpose, and made the roof ring with her laughter.

So passed the time till evening, when Mr. Chainmail moved to depart. But it turned out on inquiry that he was some miles from his inn, that the way was intricate, and that he must not make any difficulty about accepting the farmer's hospitality until morning. The evening set in with rain: the fire was found agreeable; they drew around it. The young lady made tea; and afterwards, from time to time, at Mr. Chainmail's special request, delighted his ear with passages of ancient music. Then came a supper of lake trout, fried on the spot, and thrown, smoking hot, from the pan to the plate. Then came a brewage, which the farmer called his nightcap, of which he insisted on Mr. Chainmail's taking his full share. After which the gentleman remembered nothing, till he awoke, the next morning, to the pleasant consciousness that he was under the same roof with one of the most fascinating creatures under the canopy of heaven.

THE NEWSPAPER

Mr. CHAINMAIL forgot the captain and the route of Giraldus de Barri. He became suddenly satisfied that the ruined castle in his present neighbourhood was the best possible specimen of its class, and that it was needless to carry his researches further.

He visited the farm daily; found himself always welcome; flattered himself that the young lady saw him with pleasure, and dragged a heavier chain at every new parting from Miss Susan, as the children called his nymph of the mountains. What might be her second name, he had vainly endeavoured to discover.

Mr. Chainmail was in love; but the determination he had long before formed and fixed in his mind, to marry only a lady of gentle blood, without a blot on her escutcheon, repressed the declarations of passion which were often rising to his lips. In the meantime, he left no means untried to pluck out the heart of her mystery.

The young lady soon divined his passion, and penetrated his prejudices. She began to look on him with favourable eyes; but she feared her name and parentage would present an insuperable barrier to his feudal pride.

Things were in this state when the captain returned, and unpacked his maps and books in the parlour of the inn.

Mr. Chainmail.—Really, captain, I find so many objects of attraction in this neighbourhood, that I would gladly postpone our purpose.

Captain Fitzchrome.—Undoubtedly, this neighbourhood has many attractions; but there is something very inviting in the scheme you laid down.

Mr. Chainmail.—No doubt, there is something very tempting in the route of Giraldus de Barri. But there are better things in this vicinity even than that. To tell you the truth, captain, I have fallen in love.

Captain Fitzchrome.—What! while I have been away?

Mr. Chainmail.—Even so.

Captain Fitzchrome.—The plunge must have been very sudden, if you are already over head and ears.

Mr. Chainmail.—As deep as Llyn-y-dreiddiad-vrawd.

Captain Fitzchrome.—And what may that be?

Mr. Chainmail.—A pool not far off: a resting-place of a mountain-stream, which is said to have no bottom. There is a tradition connected with it; and here is a ballad on it, at your service:—

LLYN-Y-DREIDDIAD-VRAWD.

THE POOL OF THE DIVING FRIAR.

GWENWYNWYN withdrew from the feasts of his hall;
He slept very little, he prayed not at all;
He pondered, and wandered, and studied alone;
And sought, night and day, the philosopher's stone.

He found it at length, and he made its first proof
By turning to gold all the lead of his roof:
Then he bought some magnanimous heroes, all fire,
Who lived but to smite and be smitten for hire.

With these, on the plains like a torrent he broke;
He filled the whole country with flame and with smoke;
He killed all the swine, and he broached all the wine;
He drove off the sheep, and the beeves, and the kine;

He took castles and towns; he cut short limbs and lives;
He made orphans and widows of children and wives:
This course many years he triumphantly ran,
And did mischief enough to be called a great man.

When, at last, he had gained all for which he had striven,
He bethought him of buying a passport to heaven;
Good and great as he was, yet he did not well know
How soon, or which way, his great spirit might go.

He sought the gray friars, who, beside a wild stream,
Refected their frames on a primitive scheme;
The gravest and wisest Gwenwynwyn found out,
All lonely and ghostly, and angling for trout.

Below the white dash of a mighty cascade,
Where a pool of the stream a deep resting-place made,
And rock-rooted oaks stretched their branches on high,
The friar stood musing, and throwing his fly.

To him said Gwenwynwyn, "Hold, father, here's store,
For the good of the Church, and the good of the poor;"
Then he gave him the stone; but, ere more he could speak,
Wrath came on the friar, so holy and meek;

He had stretched forth his hand to receive the red gold,
And he thought himself mocked by Gwenwynwyn the Bold;
And in scorn at the gift, and in rage at the giver,
He jerked it immediately into the river.

Gwenwynwyn, aghast, not a syllable spake;
The philosopher's stone made a duck and a drake:
Two systems of circles a moment were seen,
And the stream smoothed them off, as they never had been.

Gwenwynwyn regained, and uplifted his voice:
"Oh friar, gray friar, full rash was thy choice;
The stone, the good stone, which away thou hast thrown,
Was the stone of all stones, the philosopher's stone!"

The friar looked pale, when his error he knew;
The friar looked red, and the friar looked blue;
And heels over head, from the point of a rock,
He plunged, without stopping to pull off his frock.

He dived very deep, but he dived all in vain,
The prize he had slighted he found not again:
Many times did the friar his diving renew,
And deeper and deeper the river still grew.

Gwenwynwyn gazed long, of his senses in doubt,
To see the gray friar a diver so stout:
Then slowly and sadly his castle he sought,
And left the friar diving, like dabchick distraught.

Gwenwynwyn fell sick with alarm and despite,
Died, and went to the devil, the very same night:
The magnanimous heroes he held in his pay
Sacked his castle, and marched with the plunder away.

No knell on the silence of midnight was rolled,
For the flight of the soul of Gwenwynwyn the Bold:
The brethren, unfeed, let the mighty ghost pass,
Without praying a prayer, or intoning a mass.

The friar haunted ever beside the dark stream;
The philosopher's stone was his thought and his dream;
And day after day, ever head under heels,
He dived, all the time he could spare from his meals.

He dived, and he dived, to the end of his days,
As the peasants oft witnessed with fear and amaze:
The mad friar's diving-place long was their theme,
And no plummet can fathom that pool of the stream.

And still, when light clouds on the midnight winds ride,
If by moonlight you stray on the lone river-side,
The ghost of the friar may be seen diving there,
With head in the water, and heels in the air.

Captain Fitzchrome.—Well, your ballad is very pleasant: you shall show me the scene, and I will sketch it; but just now I am more interested about your love. What heroine of the twelfth century has risen from the ruins of the old castle, and looked down on you from the ivied battlements?

Mr. Chainmail.—You are nearer the mark than you suppose. Even from those battlements a heroine of the twelfth century has looked down on me.

Captain Fitzchrome.—Oh! some vision of an ideal beauty. I suppose the whole will end in another tradition and a ballad.

Mr. Chainmail.—Genuine flesh and blood; as genuine as Lady Clarinda. I will tell you the story.

Mr. Chainmail narrated his adventures.

Captain Fitzchrome. —Then you seem to have found what you wished. Chance has thrown in your way what none of the gods would have ventured to promise you.

Mr. Chainmail.—Yes, but I know nothing of her birth and parentage. She tells me nothing of herself, and I have no right to question her directly.

Captain Fitzchrome.—She appears to be expressly destined for the light of your baronial hall. Introduce me: in this case two heads are better than one.

Mr. Chainmail.—No, I thank you. Leave me to manage my chance of a prize, and keep you to your own chance of a——

Captain Fitzchrome.—Blank? As you please. Well, I will pitch my tent here, till I have filled my portfolio, and shall be glad of as much of your company as you can spare from more attractive society.

Matters went on pretty smoothly for several days, when an unlucky newspaper threw all into confusion. Mr. Chainmail received newspapers by the post, which came in three times a week. One morning, over their half-finished breakfast, the captain had read half a newspaper very complacently, when suddenly he started up in a frenzy, hurled over the breakfast table, and, bouncing from the apartment, knocked down Harry Ap-Heather, who was coming in at the door to challenge his supposed rival to a boxing-match.

Harry sprang up in a double rage, and intercepted Mr. Chainmail's pursuit of the captain, placing himself in the doorway in a pugilistic attitude. Mr. Chainmail, not being disposed for this mode of combat, stepped back into the parlour, took the poker in his right hand, and, displacing the loose bottom of a large elbow-chair, threw it over his left arm, as a shield. Harry, not liking the aspect of the enemy in this imposing attitude, retreated with backward steps into the kitchen, and tumbled over a cur, which immediately fastened on his rear.

Mr. Chainmail, half-laughing, half-vexed, anxious to overtake the captain, and curious to know what was the matter with him, pocketed the newspaper, and sallied forth, leaving Harry roaring for a doctor and a tailor, to repair the lacerations of his outward man.

Mr. Chainmail could find no trace of the captain. Indeed, he sought him but in one direction, which was that leading to the farm; where he arrived in due time, and found Miss Susan alone. He laid the newspaper on the table, as was his custom, and proceeded to converse with the young lady: a conversation of many pauses, as much of signs as of words. The young lady took up the paper, and turned it over and over, while she listened to Mr. Chainmail, whom she found every day more and more agreeable, when suddenly her eye glanced on something which made her change colour, and, dropping the paper on the ground, she rose from her seat, exclaiming, "Miserable must she be who trusts any of your faithless sex! Never, never, never, will I endure such misery twice!" And she vanished up the stairs. Mr. Chainmail was petrified. At length, he cried aloud, "Cornelius Agrippa must have laid a spell on this accursed newspaper;" and was turning it over to look for the source of the mischief, when Mrs. Ap-Llymry made her appearance.

Mrs. Ap-Llymry.—What have you done to poor dear Miss Susan? She is crying ready to break her heart.

Mr. Chainmail.—So help me the memory of Richard Cœur-de-Lion, I have not the most distant notion of what is the matter!

Mrs. Ap-Llymry.—Oh, don't tell me, sir; you must have ill-used her. I know how it is. You have been keeping company with her, as if you wanted to marry her; and now, all at once, you have been trying to make her your mistress. I have seen such tricks more than once, and you ought to be ashamed of yourself.

Mr. Chainmail.—My dear madam, you wrong me utterly. I have none but the kindest feelings and the most honourable purposes towards her. She has been disturbed by something she has seen in this rascally paper.

Mrs. Ap-Llymry.—Why, then, the best thing you can do is to go away, and come again to-morrow.

Mr. Chainmail.—Not I, indeed, madam. Out of this house I stir not till I have seen the young lady, and obtained a full explanation.

Mrs. Ap-Llymry.—I will tell Miss Susan what you say. Perhaps she will come down.

Mr. Chainmail sate, with as much patience as he could command, running over the paper, from column to column. At length he lighted on an announcement of the approaching marriage of Lady Clarinda Bossnowl with Mr. Crotchet the younger. This explained the captain's discomposure, but the cause of Miss Susan's was still to be sought; he could not know that it was one and the same.

Presently the sound of the longed-for step was heard on the stairs; the young lady reappeared and resumed her seat: her eyes showed that she had been weeping. The gentleman was now exceedingly puzzled how to begin, but the young lady relieved him by asking, with great simplicity, "What do you wish to have explained, sir?"

Mr. Chainmail.—I wish, if I may be permitted, to explain myself to you. Yet could I first wish to know what it was that disturbed you in this unlucky paper. Happy should I be if I could remove the cause of your inquietude!

Miss Susannah.—The cause is already removed. I saw something that excited painful recollections; nothing that I could now wish otherwise than as it is.

Mr. Chainmail.—Yet, may I ask why it is that I find one so accomplished living in this obscurity, and passing only by the name of Miss Susan?

Miss Susannah.—The world and my name are not friends. I

have left the world, and wish to remain for ever a stranger to all whom I once knew in it.

Mr. Chainmail.—You can have done nothing to dishonour your name.

Miss Susannah.—No, sir. My father has done that of which the world disapproves, in matters of which I pretend not to judge. I have suffered for it as I will never suffer again. My name is my own secret; I have no other, and that is one not worth knowing. You see what I am, and all I am. I live according to the condition of my present fortune; and here, so living, I have found tranquillity.

Mr. Chainmail.—Yet, I entreat you, tell me your name.

Miss Susannah.—Why, sir?

Mr. Chainmail.—Why, but to throw my hand, my heart, my fortune at your feet, if——

Miss Susannah.—If my name be worthy of them.

Mr. Chainmail.—Nay, nay, not so; if your hand and heart are free.

Miss Susannah.—My hand and heart are free; but they must be sought from myself, and not from my name.

She fixed her eyes on him, with a mingled expression of mistrust, of kindness, and of fixed resolution, which the far-gone *innamorato* found irresistible.

Mr. Chainmail.—Then from yourself alone I seek them.

Miss Susannah.—Reflect. You have prejudices on the score of parentage. I have not conversed with you so often, without knowing what they are. Choose between them and me. I too have my own prejudices on the score of personal pride.

Mr. Chainmail.—I would choose you from all the world, were you even the daughter of the *executeur des hautes œuvres*,[1] as the heroine of a romantic story I once read turned out to be.

Miss Susannah.—I am satisfied. You have now a right to know my history; and, if you repent, I absolve you from all obligations.

She told him her history; but he was out of the reach of repentance. "It is true," as at a subsequent period he said to the captain, "she is the daughter of a money-changer; one who, in the days of Richard the First, would have been plucked by the beard in the streets; but she is, according to modern notions, a lady of gentle

[1 public executioner.]

blood. As to her father's running away, that is a minor consideration: I have always understood, from Mr. Mac Quedy, who is a great oracle in this way, that promises to pay ought not to be kept; the essence of a safe and economical currency being an interminable series of broken promises. There seems to be a difference among the learned as to the way in which the promises ought to be broken; but I am not deep enough in their casuistry to enter into such nice distinctions."

In a few days there was a wedding, a pathetic leave-taking of the farmer's family, a hundred kisses from the bride to the children, and promises twenty times reclaimed and renewed, to visit them in the ensuing year.

THE INVITATION

THIS veridicous history began in May, and the occurrences already narrated have carried it on to the middle of autumn. Stepping over the interval to Christmas, we find ourselves in our first locality, among the chalk hills of the Thames; and we discover our old friend, Mr. Crotchet, in the act of accepting an invitation, for himself, and any friends who might be with him, to pass their Christmas-day at Chainmail Hall, after the fashion of the twelfth century. Mr. Crotchet had assembled about him, for his own Christmas-festivities, nearly the same party which was introduced to the reader in the spring. Three of that party were wanting. Dr. Morbific, by inoculating himself once too often with non-contagious matter, had explained himself out of the world. Mr. Henbane had also departed, on the wings of an infallible antidote. Mr. Eavesdrop, having printed in a magazine some of the after-dinner conversations of the castle, had had sentence of exclusion passsed upon him, on the motion of the Reverend Doctor Folliott, as a flagitious violator of the confidences of private life.

Miss Crotchet had become Lady Bossnowl, but Lady Clarinda had not yet changed her name to Crotchet. She had, on one pretence and another, procrastinated the happy event, and the gentleman had not been very pressing; she had, however, accompanied her brother and sister-in-law, to pass Christmas at Crotchet Castle.

With these, Mr. Mac Quedy, Mr. Philpot, Mr. Trillo, Mr. Skionar, Mr. Toogood, and Mr. Firedamp, were sitting at breakfast, when the Reverend Doctor Folliott entered and took his seat at the table.

The Rev. Dr. Folliott.—Well, Mr. Mac Quedy, it is now some weeks since we have met: how goes on the march of mind?

Mr. Mac Quedy.—Nay, sir; I think you may see that with your own eyes.

The Rev. Dr. Folliott.—Sir, I have seen it, much to my discomfiture. It has marched into my rick-yard, and set my stacks on fire, with chemical materials, most scientifically compounded. It has marched up to the door of my vicarage, a hundred and fifty strong; ordered me to surrender half my tithes; consumed all the provisions I had provided for my audit feast, and drunk up my old October. It has marched in through my back-parlour shutters, and out again with my silver spoons, in the dead of the night. The policeman, who was sent down to examine, says my house has been broken open on the most scientific principles. All this comes of education.

Mr. Mac Quedy.—I rather think it comes of poverty.

The Rev. Dr. Folliott.—No, sir. Robbery perhaps comes of poverty, but scientific principles of robbery come of education. I suppose the learned friend has written a sixpenny treatise on mechanics, and the rascals who robbed me have been reading it.

Mr. Crotchet.—Your house would have been very safe, doctor, if they had had no better science than the learned friend's to work with.

The Rev. Dr. Folliott.—Well, sir, that may be. Excellent potted char. The Lord deliver me from the learned friend.

Mr. Crotchet.—Well, doctor, for your comfort, here is a declaration of the learned friend's that he will never take office.

The Rev. Dr. Folliott.—Then, sir, he will be in office next week. Peace be with him! Sugar and cream.

Mr. Crotchet.—But, doctor, are you for Chainmail Hall on Christmas-day?

The Rev. Dr. Folliott.—That am I, for there will be an excellent dinner, though, peradventure, grotesquely served.

Mr. Crotchet.—I have not seen my neighbour since he left us on the canal.

The Rev. Dr. Folliott.—He has married a wife, and brought her home.

Lady Clarinda.—Indeed! If she suits him, she must be an oddity: it will be amusing to see them together.

Lord Bossnowl.—Very amusing. He! he!

Mr. Firedamp.—Is there any water about Chainmail Hall?

Rev. Dr. Folliott.—An old moat.

Mr. Firedamp.—I shall die of malaria.

Mr. Trillo.—Shall we have any music?

The Rev. Dr. Folliott.—An old harper.

Mr. Trillo.—Those fellows are always horridly out of tune. What will he play?

The Rev. Dr. Folliott.—Old songs and marches.

Mr. Skionar.—Amongst so many old things, I hope we shall find Old Philosophy.

The Rev. Dr. Folliott.—An old woman.

Mr. Philpot.—Perhaps an old map of the river in the twelfth century.

The Rev. Dr. Folliott.—No doubt.

Mr. Mac Quedy.—How many more old things?

The Rev. Dr. Folliott.—Old hospitality, old wine, old ale—all the images of old England; an old butler.

Mr. Toogood.—Shall we all be welcome?

The Rev. Dr. Folliott.—Heartily; you will be slapped on the shoulder, and called old boy.

Lord Bossnowl.—I think we should all go in our old clothes. He! he!

The Rev. Dr. Folliott.—You will sit on old chairs, round an old table, by the light of old lamps, suspended from pointed arches, which, Mr. Chainmail says, first came into use in the twelfth century; with old armour on the pillars, and old banners in the roof.

Lady Clarinda.—And what curious piece of antiquity is the lady of the mansion?

The Rev. Dr. Folliott.—No antiquity there; none.

Lady Clarinda.—Who was she?

The Rev. Dr. Folliott.—That I know not.

Lady Clarinda.—Have you seen her?

The Rev. Dr. Folliott.—I have.

Lady Clarinda.—Is she pretty?

The Rev. Dr. Folliott.—More—beautiful. A subject for the pen of Nonnus, or the pencil of Zeuxis. Features of all loveliness, radiant with all virtue and intelligence. A face for Antigone. A form at once plump and symmetrical, that, if it be decorous to divine it by externals, would have been a model for the Venus of Cnidos. Never was anything so goodly to look on, the present company expected, and poor dear Mrs. Folliott. She reads moral philosophy, Mr. Mac Quedy, which indeed she might as well let alone; she reads Italian poetry, Mr. Skionar; she sings Italian music, Mr. Trillo; but, with all this, she has the greatest of female virtues, for she superintends the household, and looks after her husband's dinner. I believe she was a mountaineer: παρθένος οὐρεσίφοιτος ἐρήμαδι σύντροφος ὕλῃ,[1] as Nonnus sweetly sings.

CHAINMAIL HALL

THE party which was assembled on Christmas Day in Chainmail Hall comprised all the guests of Crotchet Castle, some of Mr. Chainmail's other neighbours, all his tenants, and domestics, and Captain Fitzchrome. The hall was spacious and lofty; and with its tall fluted pillars and pointed arches, its windows of stained glass, its display of arms and banners intermingled with holly and mistletoe, its blazing cressets and torches, and a stupendous fire in the centre, on which blocks of pine were flaming and crackling, had a striking effect on eyes unaccustomed to such a dining-room. The fire was open on all sides, and the smoke was caught and carried back, under a funnel-formed canopy, into a hollow central pillar. This fire was the line of demarcation between gentle and simple, on days of high festival. Tables extended from it on two sides, to nearly the end of the hall.

Mrs. Chainmail was introduced to the company. Young Crotchet felt some revulsion of feeling at the unexpected sight of one whom he had forsaken, but not forgotten, in a condition apparently so much happier than his own. The lady held out her hand to him

[1] A mountain-wandering maid,
Twin-nourished with the solitary wood.

with a cordial look of more than forgiveness; it seemed to say that she had much to thank him for. She was the picture of a happy bride, rayonnante de joie et d'amour.

Mr. Crotchet told the Reverend Doctor Folliott the news of the morning. "As you predicted," he said, "your friend, the learned friend, is in office; he has also a title; he is now Sir Guy de Vaux."

The Rev. Dr. Folliott.—Thank heaven for that. He is disarmed from further mischief. It is something, at any rate, to have that hollow and wind-shaken reed rooted up for ever from the field of public delusion.[1]

Mr. Crotchet.—I suppose, doctor, you do not like to see a great reformer in office; you are afraid for your vested interests.

The Rev. Dr. Folliott.—Not I, indeed, sir; my vested interests are very safe from all such reformers as the learned friend. I vaticinate what will be the upshot of all his schemes of reform. He will make

---

[1] I may here insert, as somewhat germane to the matter, some lines which were written by me, in March, 1831, and printed in the Examiner of August 14, 1831. They were then called "An Anticipation:" they may now (1837) be fairly entitled "A Prophecy fulfilled."

THE FATE OF A BROOM: AN ANTICIPATION

Lo! in Corruption's lumber-room,
The remnants of a wondrous broom;
That walking, talking, oft was seen,
Making stout promise to sweep clean;
But evermore, at every push,
Proved but a stump without a brush.
Upon its handle-top, a sconce,
Like Brahma's, looked four ways at once,
Pouring on king, lords, church, and rabble,
Long floods of favour-currying gabble;
From four-fold mouth-piece always spinning
Projects of plausible beginning,
Whereof said sconce did ne'er intend
That any one should have an end;
Yet still, by shifts and quaint inventions,
Got credit for its good intentions,
Adding no trifle to the store,
Wherewith the devil paves his floor.
Worn out at last, found bare and scrubbish,
And thrown aside with other rubbish,
We'll e'en hand o'er the enchanted stick,
As a choice present for old Nick,
To sweep, beyond the Stygian lake,
The pavement it has helped to make.

a speech of seven hours' duration, and this will be its quintessence: that, seeing the exceeding difficulty of putting salt on the bird's tail, it will be expedient to consider the best method of throwing dust in the bird's eyes. All the rest will be

Τιτιτιτιτιμπρό.
Ποποποί, ποποποί.
Τιοτιοτιοτιοτιοτιοτιοτίγξ.
Κικκακαῦ, κικηαϑαῦ.
τοροτοροτοροτοροΛιλιΛίλξ.[2]

as Aristophanes has it; and so I leave him, in Nephelo-coccygia.[3]

Mr. Mac Quedy came up to the divine as Mr. Crotchet left him, and said: "There is one piece of news which the old gentleman has not told you. The great firm of Catchflat and Company, in which young Crotchet is a partner, has stopped payment."

Rev. Dr. Folliott.—Bless me! that accounts for the young gentleman's melancholy. I thought they would over-reach themselves with their own tricks. The day of reckoning, Mr. Mac Quedy, is the point which your paper-money science always leaves out of view.

Mr. Mac Quedy.—I do not see, sir, that the failure of Catchflat and Company has anything to do with my science.

The Rev. Dr. Folliott.—It has this to do with it, sir, that you would turn the whole nation into a great paper-money shop, and take no thought of the day of reckoning. But the dinner is coming. I think you, who are so fond of paper-promises, should dine on the bill of fare.

The harper at the head of the hall struck up an ancient march, and the dishes were brought in, in grand procession.

The boar's head, garnished with rosemary, with a citron in its mouth, led the van. Then came tureens of plum-porridge; then a series of turkeys, and, in the midst of them, an enormous sausage, which required two men to carry. Then came geese and capons, tongues and hams, the ancient glory of the Christmas pie, a gigantic plum-pudding, a pyramid of minced pies, and a baron of beef bringing up the rear.

[2] Sounds without meaning; imitative of the voices of birds. From the 'Ορνιθες [*Birds*] of Aristophanes.
[3] "Cuckoo-city-in-the-clouds." From the same comedy.

"It is something new under the sun," said the divine, as he sat down, "to see a great dinner without fish."

Mr. Chainmail.—Fish was for fasts, in the twelfth century.

The Rev. Dr. Folliott.—Well, sir, I prefer our reformed system of putting fasts and feasts together. Not but there is ample indemnity.

Ale and wine flowed in abundance. The dinner passed off merrily; the old harper playing all the while the oldest music in his repertory. The tables being cleared, he indemnified himself for lost time at the lower end of the hall, in company with the old butler and the other domestics, whose attendance on the banquet had been indispensable.

The scheme of Christmas gambols, which Mr. Chainmail had laid for the evening, was interrupted by a tremendous clamour without.

The Rev. Dr. Folliott.—What have we here? Mummers?

Mr. Chainmail.—Nay, I know not. I expect none.

"Who is there?" he added, approaching the door of the hall.

"Who is there?" vociferated the divine, with the voice of Stentor.

"Captain Swing," replied a chorus of discordant voices.

The Rev. Dr. Folliott.—Ho, ho! here is a piece of the dark ages we did not bargain for. Here is the Jacquerie. Here is the march of mind with a witness.

Mr. Mac Quedy.—Do you not see that you have brought disparates together? the Jacquerie and the march of mind.

The Rev. Dr. Folliott.—Not at all, sir. They are the same thing, under different names. Πολλῶν ὀνομάτων μορφημία.[1] What was Jacquerie in the dark ages, is the march of mind in this very enlightened one—very enlightened one.

Mr. Chainmail.—The cause is the same in both; poverty in despair.

Mr. Mac Quedy.—Very likely; but the effect is extremely disagreeable.

The Rev. Dr. Folliott.—It is the natural result, Mr. Mac Quedy, of that system of state seamanship which your science upholds. Putting the crew on short allowance, and doubling the rations of

[1] "One shape of many names."—ÆSCHYLUS, *Prometheus.*

the officers, is the sure way to make a mutiny on board a ship in distress, Mr. Mac Quedy.

Mr. Mac Quedy.—Eh! sir, I uphold no such system as that. I shall set you right as to cause and effect. Discontent increases with the increase of information.[1] That is all.

The Rev. Dr. Folliott.—I said it was the march of mind. But we have not time for discussing cause and effect now. Let us get rid of the enemy.

And he vociferated at the top of his voice, "What do you want here?"

"Arms, arms," replied a hundred voices. "Give us the arms."

The Rev. Dr. Folliott.—You see, Mr. Chainmail, this is the inconvenience of keeping an armoury, not fortified with sand bags, green bags, and old bags of all kinds.

Mr. Mac Quedy.—Just give them the old spits and toasting irons, and they will go away quietly.

Mr. Chainmail.—My spears and swords! not without my life. These assailants are all aliens to my land and house. My men will fight for me, one and all. This is the fortress of beef and ale.

Mr. Mac Quedy.—Eh! sir, when the rabble is up, it is very indiscriminating. You are e'en suffering for the sins of Sir Simon Steeltrap, and the like, who have pushed the principle of accumulation a little too far.

Mr. Chainmail.—The way to keep the people down is kind and liberal usage.

Mr. Mac Quedy.—That is very well (where it can be afforded), in the way of prevention; but in the way of cure, the operation must be more drastic. (*Taking down a battle-axe.*) I would fain have a good blunderbuss charged with slugs.

Mr. Chainmail.—When I suspended these arms for ornament, I never dreamed of their being called into use.

Mr. Skionar.—Let me address them. I never failed to convince an audience that the best thing they could do was to go away.

[1] This looks so like caricature (a thing abhorrent to our candour), that we must give authority for it. "We ought to look the evil manfully in the face, and not amuse ourselves with the dreams of fancy. The discontent of the labourers in our times is rather a proof of their superior information than of their deterioration."—*Morning Chronicle: December 20,* 1830.

Mr. Mac Quedy.—Eh! sir, I can bring them to that conclusion in less time than you.

Mr. Crotchet.—I have no fancy for fighting. It is a very hard case upon a guest, when the latter end of a feast is the beginning of a fray.

Mr. Mac Quedy.—Give them the old iron.

The Rev. Dr. Folliott.—Give them weapons! *Pessimo medius fidius, exemplo.*[1] Forbid it the spirit of *Frère Jean des Entommeures!*[2] No! let us see what the church militant, in the armour of the twelfth century, will do against the march of mind. Follow me who will, and stay who list. Here goes: *Pro aris et focis!* that is, for tithe pigs and fires to roast them!

He clapped a helmet on his head, seized a long lance, threw open the gates, and tilted out on the rabble, side by side with Mr. Chainmail, followed by the greater portion of the male inmates of the hall, who had armed themselves at random.

The rabble route, being unprepared for such a sortie, fled in all directions, over hedge and ditch.

Mr. Trillo stayed in the hall, playing a march on the harp, to inspirit the rest to sally out. The water-loving Mr. Philpot had diluted himself with so much wine, as to be quite *hors de combat.* Mr. Toogood, intending to equip himself in purely defensive armour, contrived to slip a ponderous coat of mail over his shoulders, which pinioned his arms to his sides; and in this condition, like a chicken trussed for roasting, he was thrown down behind a pillar, in the first rush of the sortie. Mr. Crotchet seized the occurrence as a pretext for staying with him, and passed the whole time of the action in picking him out of his shell.

"Phew!" said the divine, returning; "an inglorious victory: but it deserves a devil and a bowl of punch."

Mr. Chainmail.—A wassail-bowl.

The Rev. Dr. Folliott.—No, sir. No more of the twelfth century for me.

Mr. Chainmail.—Nay, doctor. The twelfth century has backed you well. Its manners and habits, its community of kind feelings

---

[1] A most pernicious example, by Hercules!—Petronius Arbiter.
[2 Friar John of the Funnels.]

between master and man, are the true remedy for these ebullitions.

Mr. Toogood.—Something like it: improved by my diagram: arts for arms.

The Rev. Dr. Folliott.—No wassail-bowl for me. Give me an unsophisticated bowl of punch, which belongs to that blissful middle period, after the Jacquerie was down, and before the march of mind was up. But, see, who is floundering in the water?

Proceeding to the edge of the moat, they fished up Mr. Firedamp, who had missed his way back, and tumbled in. He was drawn out, exclaiming, "that he had taken his last dose of *malaria* in this world."

The Rev. Dr. Folliott.—Tut, man; dry clothes, a turkey's leg and rump, well devilled, and a quart of strong punch, will set all to rights.

"Wood embers," said Mr. Firedamp, when he had been accommodated with a change of clothes, "there is no antidote to *malaria* like the smoke of wood embers; pine embers." And he placed himself, with his mouth open, close by the fire.

The Rev. Dr. Folliott.—Punch, sir, punch: there is no antidote like punch.

Mr. Chainmail.—Well, doctor, you shall be indulged. But I shall have my wassail-bowl nevertheless.

An immense bowl of spiced wine, with roasted apples hissing on its surface, was borne into the hall by four men, followed by an empty bowl of the same dimensions, with all the materials of arrack punch, for the divine's especial brewage. He accinged himself to the task, with his usual heroism; and having finished it to his entire satisfaction, reminded his host to order in the devil.

The Rev. Dr. Folliott.—I think, Mr. Chainmail, we can amuse ourselves very well here all night. The enemy may be still excubant: and we had better not disperse till daylight. I am perfectly satisfied with my quarters. Let the young folks go on with their gambols; let them dance to your old harper's minstrelsy; and if they please to kiss under the mistletoe, whereof I espy a goodly bunch suspended at the end of the hall, let those who like it not, leave it to those who do. Moreover, if among the more sedate portion of the assembly, which, I foresee, will keep me company, there were any to revive the good old custom of singing after supper, so to fill up the intervals of the dances, the steps of night would move more lightly.

Mr. Chainmail.—My Susan will set the example, after she has set that of joining in the rustic dance, according to good customs long departed.

After the first dance, in which all classes of the company mingled, the young lady of the mansion took her harp, and following the reverend gentleman's suggestion, sang a song of the twelfth century.

FLORENCE AND BLANCHFLOR.[1]

Florence and Blanchflor, loveliest maids,
 Within a summer grove,
Amid the flower-enamelled shades
 Together talked of love.

A clerk sweet Blanchflor's heart had gained;
 Fair Florence loved a knight:
And each with ardent voice maintained
 She loved the worthiest wight.

Sweet Blanchflor praised her scholar dear,
 As courteous, kind, and true;
Fair Florence said her chevalier
 Could every foe subdue.

And Florence scorned the bookworm vain,
 Who sword nor spear could raise;
And Blanchflor scorned the unlettered brain
 Could sing no lady's praise.

From dearest love, the maidens bright
 To deadly hatred fell;
Each turned to shun the other's sight,
 And neither said farewell.

The king of birds, who held his court
 Within that flowery grove,
Sang loudly: " 'T will be rare disport
 To judge this suit of love."

[1] Imitated from the Fabliau, *De Florance et de Blanche Flor, alias Jugement d'Amour.*

Before him came the maidens bright,
    With all his birds around,
To judge the cause, if clerk or knight
    In love be worthiest found.

The falcon and the sparrow-hawk
    Stood forward for the fight:
Ready to do, and not to talk,
    They voted for the knight.

And Blanchflor's heart began to fail,
    Till rose the strong-voiced lark,
And, after him, the nightingale,
    And pleaded for the clerk.

The nightingale prevailed at length,
    Her pleading had such charms;
So eloquence can conquer strength,
    And arts can conquer arms.

The lovely Florence tore her hair,
    And died upon the place;
And all the birds assembled there,
    Bewailed the mournful case.

They piled up leaves and flowerets rare,
    Above the maiden bright,
And sang: "Farewell to Florence fair,
    Who too well loved her knight."

Several others of the party sang in the intervals of the dances. Mr. Chainmail handed to Mr. Trillo another ballad of the twelfth century, of a merrier character than the former. Mr. Trillo readily accommodated it with an air, and sang,—

THE PRIEST AND THE MULBERRY TREE.[1]

Did you hear of the curate who mounted his mare,
And merrily trotted along to the fair?
Of creature more tractable none ever heard,
In the height of her speed she would stop at a word;
And again with a word, when the curate said Hey,
She put forth her mettle, and galloped away.

As near to the gates of the city he rode,
While the sun of September all brilliantly glowed,

[1] Imitated from the Fabliau, Du Provoire qui mengea des Môres.

The good priest discovered, with eyes of desire,
A mulberry tree in a hedge of wild briar;
On boughs long and lofty, in many a green shoot,
Hung large, black, and glossy, the beautiful fruit.

The curate was hungry and thirsty to boot;
He shrunk from the thorns, though he longed for the fruit;
With a word he arrested his courser's keen speed,
And he stood up erect on the back of his steed;
On the saddle he stood, while the creature stood still,
And he gathered the fruit, till he took his good fill.

"Sure never," he thought, "was a creature so rare,
So docile, so true, as my excellent mare.
Lo, here, how I stand" (and he gazed all around).
"As safe and as steady as if on the ground.
Yet how had it been, if some traveller this way,
Had, dreaming no mischief, but chanced to cry Hey?"

He stood with his head in the mulberry tree,
And he spoke out aloud in his fond reverie:
At the sound of the word, the good mare made a push,
And down went the priest in the wild-briar bush.
He remembered too late, on his thorny green bed,
Much that well may be thought, cannot wisely be said.

Lady Clarinda, being prevailed on to take the harp in her turn,
sang the following stanzas:—

In the days of old,
Lovers felt true passion,
Deeming years of sorrow
By a smile repaid.
Now the charms of gold,
Spells of pride and fashion,
Bid them say good morrow
To the best-loved maid.

Through the forests wild,
O'er the mountains lonely,
They were never weary
Honour to pursue:
If the damsel smiled
Once in seven years only,
All their wanderings dreary
Ample guerdon knew.

Now one day's caprice
Weighs down years of smiling,
Youthful hearts are rovers,
Love is bought and sold:
Fortune's gifts may cease,
Love is less beguiling;
Wiser were the lovers,
In the days of old.

The glance which she threw at the Captain, as she sang the last verse, awakened his dormant hopes. Looking round for his rival, he saw that he was not in the hall, and, approaching the lady of his heart, he received one of the sweetest smiles of their earlier days.

After a time, the ladies, and all the females of the party, retired. The males remained on duty with punch and wassail, and dropped off one by one into sweet forgetfulness; so that when the rising sun of December looked through the painted windows on mouldering embers and flickering lamps, the vaulted roof was echoing to a mellifluous concert of noses, from the clarionet of the waiting-boy at one end of the hall, to the double bass of the Reverend Doctor, ringing over the empty punch-bowl, at the other.

CONCLUSION

FROM this eventful night, young Crotchet was seen no more on English mould. Whither he had vanished, was a question that could no more be answered in his case than in that of King Arthur, after the battle of Camlan. The great firm of Catchflat and Company figured in the Gazette and paid six-pence in the pound; and it was clear that he had shrunk from exhibiting himself on the scene of his former greatness, shorn of the beams of his paper prosperity. Some supposed him to be sleeping among the undiscoverable secrets of some barbel-pool in the Thames; but those who knew him best were more inclined to the opinion that he had gone across the Atlantic, with his pockets full of surplus capital, to join his old acquaintance, Mr. Touchandgo, in the bank of Dotandcarryone-town.

Lady Clarinda was more sorry for her father's disappointment than her own; but she had too much pride to allow herself to be put up a second time in the money-market; and when the Captain renewed his assiduities, her old partiality for him, combining with a sense of gratitude for a degree of constancy which she knew she scarcely deserved, induced her, with Lord Foolincourt's hard-wrung consent, to share with him a more humble, but less precarious fortune, than that to which she had been destined as the price of a rotten borough.

Gryll Grange

MISNOMERS

"PALESTINE soup!" said the Reverend Doctor Opimian, dining
with his friend Squire Gryll, "a curiously complicated misnomer. We have an excellent old vegetable, the artichoke, of which
we eat the head; we have another of subsequent introduction, of
which we eat the root, and which we also call artichoke, because it
resembles the first in flavour, although, *me judice*, a very inferior
affair. This last is a species of the helianthus, or sunflower genus of
the *Syngenesia frustranea* class of plants. It is therefore a girasol, or
turn-to-the-sun. From this girasol we have made Jerusalem, and
from the Jerusalem artichoke we make Palestine soup."

Mr. Gryll.—A very good thing, doctor.

The Rev. Dr. Opimian.—A very good thing; but a palpable
misnomer.

Mr. Gryll.—I am afraid we live in a world of misnomers, and of
a worse kind than this. In my little experience I have found that a
gang of swindling bankers is a respectable old firm; that men who
sell their votes to the highest bidder, and want only "the protection
of the ballot" to sell the promise of them to both parties, are a free
and independent constituency; that a man who successively betrays everybody that trusts him, and abandons every principle he
ever professed, is a great statesman, and a Conservative, forsooth,
à *nil conservando*; that schemes for breeding pestilence are sanitary
improvements; that the test of intellectual capacity is in swallow,
and not in digestion; that the art of teaching everything, except
what will be of use to the recipient, is national education; and that

387

a change for the worse is reform. Look across the Atlantic. A
Sympathizer would seem to imply a certain degree of benevolent
feeling. Nothing of the kind. It signifies a ready-made accomplice
in any species of political villany. A Know-Nothing would seem to
imply a liberal self-diffidence—on the scriptural principle that the
beginning of knowledge is to know that thou art ignorant. No such
thing. It imples furious political dogmatism, enforced by bludgeons
and revolvers. A Locofoco is the only intelligible term: a fellow
that would set any place on fire to roast his own eggs. A Filibuster
is· a pirate under national colours; but I suppose the word in its
origin implies something virtuous: perhaps a friend of humanity.

   The Rev. Dr. Opimian.—More likely a friend of roaring—
Φιλοβωστρὴς —in the sense in which roaring is used by our old
dramatists; for which see Middleton's *Roaring Girl,* and the
commentators thereon. [1]

   Mr. Gryll.—While we are on the subject of misnomers, what
say you to the wisdom of Parliament?

   The Rev. Dr. Opimian.—Why, sir, I do not call that a misnomer.
The term wisdom is used in a parliamentary sense. The wisdom of
Parliament is a wisdom *sui generis.* It is not like any other wisdom. It is not the wisdom of Socrates, nor the wisdom of Solomon.
It is the wisdom of Parliament. It is not easily analysed or defined;
but it is very easily understood. It has achieved wonderful things by
itself, and still more when Science has come to its aid. Between
them, they have poisoned the Thames, and killed the fish in the
river. A little further development of the same wisdom and science
will complete the poisoning of the air, and kill the dwellers on the
banks. It is pleasant that the precious effluvium has been brought
so efficiently under the Wisdom's own wise nose. Thereat the nose,
like Trinculo's, has been in great indignation. The Wisdom has
ordered the Science to do something. The Wisdom does not know
what, nor the Science either. But the Wisdom has empowered the

---

   [1] "*Roaring boys* was a cant term for the riotous, quarrelsome blades of the
time, who abounded in London, and took pleasure in annoying its quieter
inhabitants. Of *Roaring Girls,* the heroine of the present play was the choicest
specimen. Her real name was *Mary Frith,* but she was most commonly known
by that of *Moll Cutpurse.*"—DYCE. She wore male apparel, smoked, fought,
robbed on the highway, kept all minor thieves in subjection, and compelled the
restitution of stolen goods, when duly paid for her services.

Science to spend some millions of money; and this, no doubt, the Science will do. When the money has been spent, it will be found that the something has been worse than nothing. The Science will want more money to do some other something, and the Wisdom will grant it. *Redit labor actus in orbem.* [1] But you have got on moral and political ground. My remark was merely on a perversion of words, of which we have an inexhaustible catalogue.

Mr. Gryll.—Whatever ground we take, doctor, there is one point common to most of these cases: the word presents an idea which does not belong to the subject, critically considered. Palestine soup is not more remote from the true Jerusalem, than many an honourabl friend from public honesty and honour. However, doctor, what say you to a glass of old Madeira, which I really believe is what it is called?

The Rev. Dr. Opimian.—*In vino veritas,* I accept with pleasure.

Miss Gryll.—You and my uncle, doctor, get up a discussion on everything that presents itself; dealing with your theme like a series of variations in music. You have run half round the world àpropos of the soup. What say you to the fish?

The Rev. Dr. Opimian.—Premising that this is a remarkably fine slice of salmon, there is much to be said about fish: but not in the way of misnomers. Their names are single and simple. Perch, sole, cod, eel, carp, char, skate, tench, trout, brill, bream, pike, and many others, plain monosyllables: salmon, dory, turbot, gudgeon, lobster, whitebait, grayling, haddock, mullet, herring, oyster, sturgeon, flounder, turtle, plain dissyllables: only two trisyllables worth naming, anchovy and mackerel; unless any one should be disposed to stand up for halibut, which, for my part, I have excommunicated.

Mr. Gryll.—I agree with you on that point; but I think you have named one or two that might as well keep it company.

The Rev. Dr. Opimian.—I do not think I have named a single unpresentable fish.

Mr. Gryll.—Bream, doctor: there is not much to be said for bream.

The Rev. Dr. Opimian.—On the contrary, sir, I think there is much to be said for him. In the first place, there is the authority of the monastic brotherhoods, who are universally admitted to have

[1] The labour returns, compelled into a circle.

been connoisseurs in fish, and in the mode of preparing it; and you will find bream pie set down as a prominent item of luxurious living in the indictments prepared against them at the dissolution of the monasteries. The work of destruction was rather too rapid, and I fear the receipt is lost. But he can still be served up as an excellent stew, provided always that he is full-grown, and has swum all his life in clear running water. I call everything fish that seas, lakes, and rivers furnish to cookery; though, scientifically, a turtle is a reptile, and a lobster an insect. Fish, Miss Gryll—I could discourse to you on fish by the hour: but for the present I will forbear: as Lord Curryfin is coming down to Thornback Bay, to lecture the fishermen on fish and fisheries, and to astonish them all with the science of their art. You will, no doubt, be curious to hear him. There will be some reserved seats.

Miss Gryll.—I shall be very curious to hear him, indeed. I have never heard a lecturing lord. The fancy of lords and gentlemen to lecture everybody on everything, everywhere, seems to me something very comical; but perhaps it is something very serious, gracious in the lecturer, and instructive to the audience. I shall be glad to be cured of my unbecoming propensity to laugh whenever I hear of a lecturing lord.

The Rev. Dr. Opimian.—I hope, Miss Gryll, you will not laugh at Lord Curryfin: for you may be assured nothing will be farther from his lordship's intention than to say anything in the slightest degree droll.

Mr. Gryll.—Doctor Johnson was astonished at the mania for lectures, even in his day, when there were no lecturing lords. He thought little was to be learned from lectures, unless where, as in chemistry, the subject required illustration by experiment. Now, if your lord is going to exhibit experiments in the art of cooking fish, with specimens in sufficient number for all his audience to taste, I have no doubt his lecture will be well attended, and a repetition earnestly desired.

The Rev. Dr. Opimian.—I am afraid the lecture will not have the aid of such pleasant adventitious attractions. It will be a pure scientific exposition, carefully classified, under the several divisions and subdivisions of Ichthyology, Entomology, Herpetology, and Conchology. But I agree with Doctor Johnson, that little is to be

learned from lectures. For the most part those who do not already
understand the subject will not understand the lecture, and those
who do will learn nothing from it. The latter will hear many things
they would like to contradict, which the *bienséance* of the lecture-
room does not allow. I do not comprehend how people can find
amusement in lectures. I should much prefer a *tenson* of the twelfth
century, when two or three masters of the Gai Saber discussed questions of love and chivalry.

Miss Gryll.—I am afraid, doctor, our age is too prosy for that
sort of thing. We have neither wit enough, nor poetry enough, to
furnish the disputants. I can conceive a state of society in which
such *tensons* would form a pleasant winter evening amusement: but
that state of society is not ours.

The Rev. Dr. Opimian.—Well, Miss Gryll, I should like, some
winter evening, to challenge you to a *tenson*, and your uncle should
be umpire. I think you have wit enough by nature, and I have poetry
enough by memory, to supply a fair portion of the requisite materials,
without assuming an absolute mastery of the *Gai Saber*.

Miss Gryll.—I shall accept the challenge, doctor. The wit on one
side will, I am afraid, be very shortcoming; but the poetry on the
other will no doubt be abundant.

Mr. Gryll. Suppose, doctor, you were to get up a *tenson* a little
more relative to our own wise days. Spirit-rapping, for example, is
a fine field. *Nec pueri credunt . . . . Sed tu vera puta.*[1] You might
go beyond the limits of a *tenson*. There is ample scope for an
Aristophanic comedy In the contest between the Just and the Unjust in the *Clouds*, and in other scenes of Aristophanes, you have
ancient specimens of something very like *tensons*, except that love
has not much share in them. Let us for a moment suppose this same
spirit-rapping to be true—dramatically so, at least. Let us fit up a
stage for the purpose: make the invoked spirits visible as well as
audible: and calling before us some of the illustrious of former days,
ask them what they think of us and our doings? Of our astounding
progress of intellect? Our march of mind? Our higher tone of morality?
Our vast diffusion of education? Our art of choosing the most unfit
man by competitive examination?

The Rev. Dr. Opimian.—You had better not bring on many of

[1] Not even boys believe it: but suppose it to be true.

them at once, nor ask many similar questions, or the chorus of ghostly laughter will be overwhelming. I imagine the answer would be something like Hamlet's: "You yourselves, sirs, shall be as wise as we were, if, like crabs, you could go backward." It is thought something wonderful that uneducated persons should believe in witchcraft in the nineteenth century: as if educated persons did not believe in grosser follies: such as this same spirit-rapping, unknown tongues, clairvoyance, table-turning, and all sorts of fanatical impositions, having for the present their climax in Mormonism. Herein all times are alike. There is nothing too monstrous for human credulity. I like the notion of the Aristophanic comedy. But it would require a numerous company, especially as the chorus is indispensable. The *tenson* may be carried on by two.

Mr. Gryll.—I do not see why we should not have both.

Miss Gryll.—O pray, doctor! let us have the comedy. We hope to have a houseful at Christmas, and I think we may get it up well, chorus and all. I should so like to hear what my great ancestor, Gryllus, thinks of us: and Homer, and Dante, and Shakespeare, and Richard the First, and Oliver Cromwell.

The Rev. Dr. Opimian.—A very good *dramatis personæ*. With these, and the help of one or two Athenians and Romans, we may arrive at a tolerable judgment on our own immeasurable superiority to everything that has gone before us.

Before we proceed farther, we will give some account of our interlocutors.

THE SQUIRE AND HIS NIECE

GREGORY GRYLL, ESQ., of Gryll Grange in Hampshire, on the borders of the New Forest, in the midst of a park which was a little forest in itself, reaching nearly to the sea, and well stocked with deer, having a large outer tract, where a numerous light-rented and well-conditioned tenantry fattened innumerable pigs, considered himself well located for what he professed to be, *Epicuri de grege porcus*,[1] and held, though he found it difficult to trace the pedi-

---

[1] A pig from the herd of Epicurus. The old philosophers accepted good-humoredly the disparaging terms attached to them by their enemies or rivals.

gree, that he was lineally descended from the ancient and illustrious Gryllus, who maintained against Ulysses the superior happiness of the life of other animals to that of the life of man.

It might seem that, to a man who traced his ancestry from the palace of Circe, the first care would be the continuance of his ancient race; but a wife presented to him the forethought of a perturbation of his equanimity, which he never could bring himself to encounter. He liked to dine well, and withal to dine quietly, and to have quiet friends at his table, with whom he could discuss questions which might afford ample room for pleasant conversation, and none for acrimonious dispute. He feared that a wife would interfere with his dinner, his company, and his after-dinner bottle of port. For the perpetuation of his name, he relied on an orphan niece, whom he had brought up from a child, who superintended his household, and sate at the head of his table. She was to be his heiress, and her husband was to take his name. He left the choice to her, but reserved to himself a veto, if he should think the aspirant unworthy of the honourable appellation.

The young lady had too much taste, feeling, and sense to be likely to make a choice which her uncle would not approve; but time, as it rolled on, foreshadowed a result which the squire had not anticipated. Miss Gryll did not seem likely to make any choice at all. The atmosphere of quiet enjoyment in which she had grown up seemed to have steeped her feelings in its own tranquillity; and still more, the affection which she felt for her uncle, and the conviction that, though he had always premeditated her marriage, her departure from his house would be the severest blow that fate could inflict on him, led her to postpone what she knew must be an evil day to him, and might peradventure not be a good one to her.

"Oh, the ancient name of Gryll!" sighed the squire to himself. "What if it should pass away in the nineteenth century, after having lived from the time of Circe!"

Often, indeed, when he looked at her at the head of his table, the star of his little circle, joyous herself, and the source of joy in others, he thought the actual state of things admitted no change

The Epicureans acquiesced in the pig, the Cynics in the dog, and Cleanthes was content to be called the Ass of Zeno as being alone capable of bearing the burthen of the Stoic philosophy.

for the better, and the perpetuity of the old name became a second- ᵗ ary consideration; but though the purpose was dimmed in the evening, it usually brightened in the morning. In the meantime the young lady had many suitors, who were permitted to plead their cause, though they made little apparent progress.

Several young gentlemen of fair promise, seemingly on the point of being accepted, had been, each in his turn, suddenly and summarily dismissed. Why, was the young lady's secret. If it were known, it would be easy, she said, in these days of artificial manners, to counterfeit the presence of the qualities she liked, and, still more easy, the absence of the qualities she disliked. There was sufficient diversity in the characters of the rejected to place conjecture at fault, and Mr. Gryll began to despair.

The uncle and niece had come to a clear understanding on this subject. He might present to her attention any one whom he might deem worthy to be her suitor, and she might reject the suitor without assigning a reason for so doing. In this way several had appeared and passed away, like bubbles on a stream.

Was the young lady over fastidious, or were none among the presented worthy, or had that which was to touch her heart not yet appeared?

Mr. Gryll was the godfather of his niece, and to please him, she had been called Morgana. He had had some thoughts of calling her Circe, but acquiesced in the name of a sister enchantress, who had worked out her own idea of a beautiful garden, and exercised similar power over the minds and forms of men.

THE DUKE'S FOLLY

WORDSWORTH's question, in his *Poet's Epitaph,*

> Art thou a man of purple cheer,
> A rosy man, right plump to see?

might have been answered in the affirmative by the Reverend Doctor Opimian. The worthy divine dwelt in an agreeably situated vicarage, on the outskirts of the New Forest. A good living, a comfortable patrimony, a moderate dowry with his wife, placed him sufficiently above the cares of the world to enable him to gratify all his tastes without minute calculations of cost. His tastes, in fact, were four: a good library, a good dinner, a pleasant garden, and rural walks. He was an athlete in pedestrianism. He took no pleasure in riding, either on horseback or in a carriage; but he kept a brougham for the service of Mrs. Opimian, and for his own occasional use in dining out.

Mrs. Opimian was domestic. The care of the doctor had supplied her with the best books on cookery, to which his own inventive genius and the kindness of friends had added a large, and always increasing manuscript volume. The lady studied them carefully, and by diligent superintendence left the doctor nothing to desire in the service of his table. His cellar was well stocked with a selection of the best vintages, under his own especial charge. In all its arrangements, his house was a model of order and comfort; and the whole establishment partook of the genial physiognomy of the master. From the master and mistress to the cook, and from the cook to the tom cat, there was about the inhabitants of the vicarage a sleek and purring rotundity of face and figure that denoted community of feelings, habits, and diet; each in its kind, of course, for the doctor had his port, the cook her ale, and the cat his milk, in sufficiently liberal allowance. In the morning, while Mrs. Opimian found ample occupation in the details of her household duties and the care of her little family, the doctor, unless he had predestined the whole day to an excursion, studied in his library. In the afternoon he walked; in the evening he dined; and after dinner read to his wife and family, or heard his children read to him. This was his home life. Now and then he dined out; more frequently than at any other place with his friend and neighbour, Mr. Gryll, who entirely sympathized with him in his taste for a good dinner.

Beyond the limits of his ordinary but within those of his occasional range was a solitary round tower on an eminence backed with wood, which had probably in old days been a landmark for hunters; but having in modern days no very obvious use, was designated, as many such buildings are, by the name of the Folly. The country people called it "The Duke's Folly," though who the Duke in question was nobody could tell. Tradition had dropped his name.

One fine Midsummer day, with a southerly breeze and a cloudless sky, the doctor, having taken an early breakfast, in the process of which he had considerably reduced the altitude of a round of beef, set out with a good stick in his hand and a Newfoundland dog at his heels for one of his longest walks, such as he could only take in the longest days.

Arriving at the Folly, which he had not visited for a long time, he was surprised to find it enclosed, and having at the back the novelty of a covered passage, built of the same gray stone as the tower itself. This passage passed away into the wood at the back, whence was ascending a wreath of smoke which immediately recalled to him the dwelling of Circe. Indeed, the change before him had much the air of enchantment; and the Circean similitude was not a little enhanced by the antique masonry, and the expanse of sea which was visible from the eminence. He leaned over the gate, repeated aloud the lines of the Odyssey, and fell into a brown study, from which he was aroused by the approach of a young gentleman from within the enclosure.

"I beg your pardon, sir," said the doctor, "but my curiosity is excited by what I see here; and if you do not think it impertinent, and would inform me how these changes have come about, I should be greatly obliged."

"Most willingly, sir," said the other; "but if you will walk in, and see what has been done, the obligation will be mine."

The doctor readily accepted the proposal. The stranger led the way, across an open space in the wood, to a circular hall, from each side of which a wide passage led, on the left hand to the tower, and on the right to the new building, which was so masked by the wood, as not to be visible except from within the glade. It was a square structure of plain stone, much in the same style as that of the tower.

The young gentleman took the left-hand passage, and introduced the doctor to the lower floor of the tower.

"I have divided the tower," he observed, "into three rooms: one on each floor. This is the dining-room; above it is my bedroom; above it again is my library. The prospect is good from all the floors, but from the library it is most extensive, as you look over the woods far away into the open sea."

"A noble dining-room," said the doctor. "The height is well proportioned to the diameter. That circular table well becomes the form of the room, and gives promise of a fine prospect in its way."

"I hope you will favour me by forming a practical judgment on the point," said his new acquaintance, as he led the way to the upper floor, the doctor marvelling at the extreme courtesy with which he was treated. "This building," thought he, "might belong to the age of chivalry, and my young host might be Sir Calidore himself." But the library brought him back to other days.

The walls were covered with books, the upper portion accessible by a gallery, running entirely round the apartment. The books of the lower circle were all classical; those of the upper, English, Italian, and French, with a few volumes in Spanish.

The young gentleman took down a Homer, and pointed out to the doctor the passage which, as he leaned over the gate, he had repeated from the *Odyssey*. This accounted to the doctor for the deference shown to him. He saw at once into the Greek sympathy.

"You have a great collection of books," said the doctor.

"I believe," said the young gentleman, "I have all the best books in the languages I cultivate. Horne Tooke says: 'Greek, Latin, Italian, and French, are unfortunately the usual bounds of an English scholar's acquisition.' I think any scholar fortunate whose acquisition extends so far. These languages and our own comprise, I believe, with a few rare exceptions, all the best books in the world. I may add Spanish, for the sake of Cervantes, Lope de Vega, and Calderon. It was a *dictum* of Porson, that 'Life is too short to learn German:' meaning, I apprehend, not that it is too difficult to be acquired within the ordinary space of life, but that there is nothing in it to compensate for the portion of life bestowed on its acquirement, however little that may be."

The doctor was somewhat puzzled what to say. He had come French and more Italian, being fond of romances of chivalry; and in Greek and Latin he thought himself a match for any man; but he was more occupied with speculations on the position and character of his new acquaintance, than on the literary opinions he was enunciating. He marvelled to find a young man, rich enough to do what he here saw done, doing anything of the kind, and fitting up a library in a solitary tower, instead of passing his time in clubs and *réunions*, and other pursuits and pleasures of general society. But he thought it necessary to say something to the point, and rejoined:

"Porson was a great man, and his *dictum* would have weighed with me if I had had a velleity towards German; but I never had any. But I rather wonder you should have placed your library on the upper instead of the middle floor. The prospect, as you have observed, is fine from all the floors; but here you have the sea and the sky to the greatest advantage; and I would assign my best look-out to the hours of dressing and undressing; the first thing in the morning, the last at night, and the half-hour before dinner. You can give greater attention to the views before you, when you are following operations, important certainly, but mechanical from repetition, and uninteresting in themselves, than when you are engaged in some absorbing study, which probably shuts out all perception of the external world."

"What you say is very true, sir," said the other; "but you know the lines of Milton—

> Or let my lamp, at midnight hour,
> Be seen in some high lonely tower,
> Where I may oft outwatch the Bear,
> With thrice great Hermes.

"These lines have haunted me from very early days, and principally influenced me in purchasing this tower, and placing my library on the top of it. And I have another association with such a mode of life."

A French clock in the library struck two, and the young gentleman proposed to his visitor to walk into the house. They accordingly descended the stairs, and crossed the entrance-hall to a large drawing-room, simply but handsomely furnished; having some good pictures on the walls, an organ at one end of the room, a piano and harp at the other, and an elegantly disposed luncheon in the middle.

"At this time of the year," said the young gentleman, "I lunch at two, and dine at eight. This gives me two long divisions of the morning, for any in-door and out-door purposes. I hope you will partake with me. You will not find a precedent in Homer for declining the invitation."

"Really," said the doctor, "that argument is cogent and conclusive. I accept with pleasure: and indeed my long walk has given me an appetite."

"Now you must know," said the young gentleman, "I have none but female domestics. You will see my two waiting-maids."

He rang the bell, and the specified attendants appeared: two young girls about sixteen and seventeen; both pretty, and simply, but very becomingly, dressed.

Of the provision set before him the doctor preferred some cold chicken and tongue. Madeira and sherry were on the table, and the young attendants offered him hock and claret. The doctor took a capacious glass from each of the fair cup-bearers, and pronounced both wines excellent, and deliciously cool. He declined more, not to overheat himself in walking, and not to infringe on his anticipations of dinner. The dog, who had behaved throughout with exemplary propriety, was not forgotten. The doctor rose to depart.

"I think," said his host, "I may now ask you the Homeric question—Τίς; πόθεν εἶς ἀνδρῶν."[1]

"Most justly," said the doctor. "My name is Theophilus Opimian. I am a Doctor of Divinity, and the incumbent of Ashbrook-cum-Ferndale."

"I am simply," said the other, "Algernon Falconer. I have inherited some money, but no land. Therefore having the opportunity, I made this purchase to fit it up in my own fashion, and live in it in my own way."

The doctor preparing to depart, Mr. Falconer proposed to accompany him part of the way, and calling out another Newfoundland dog, who immediately struck up a friendship with his companion, he walked away with the Doctor, the two dogs gambolling before them.

THE FOREST

THE REV. DR. OPIMIAN.—It strikes me as singular that, with such a house, you should have only female domestics.

Mr. Falconer.—It is not less singular perhaps that they are seven sisters, all the children of two old servants of my father and mother. The eldest is about my own age, twenty-six, so that they have all grown up with me in time and place. They live in great harmony to-

[1] Who, and whence, are you?

gether, and divide among them the charge of all the household duties. Those whom you saw are the two youngest.

The Rev. Dr. Opimian.—If the others acquit themselves as well, you have a very efficient staff; but seven young women as the establishment of one young bachelor, for such I presume you to be (*Mr. Falconer assented*), is something new and strange. The world is not over charitable.

Mr. Falconer.—The world will never suppose a good motive, where it can suppose a bad one. I would not willingly offend any of its prejudices. I would not affect eccentricity. At the same time I do not feel disposed to be put out of my way because it is not the way of the world—*Le Chemin du Monde*, as a Frenchman entitled Congreve's comedy—but I assure you these seven young women live here as they might do in the temple of Vesta. It was a singular combination of circumstances that induced and enabled me to form such an establishment; but I would not give it up, nor alter it, nor diminish it, nor increase it, for any earthly consideration.

The Rev. Dr. Opimian.—You hinted that, besides Milton's verses, you had another association of ideas with living in the top of a tower.

Mr. Falconer.—I have read of somebody who lived so, and admitted to his *sanctum* only one young person, a niece or a daughter, I forget which, but on very rare occasions would descend to speak to some visitor who had previously propitiated the young lady to obtain him an interview. At last the young lady introduced one who proposed for her, and gained the consent of the recluse (I am not sure of his name, but I always call him Lord Noirmont) to carry her off. I think this was associated with some affliction that was cured, or some mystery that was solved, and that the hermit returned into the every-day world. I do not know where I read it, but I have always liked the idea of living like Lord Noirmont, when I shall have become a sufficiently disappointed man.

The Rev. Dr. Opimian.—You look as little like a disappointed man as any I have seen; but as you have neither daughter nor niece, you would have seven links instead of one between the top of your tower and the external world.

Mr. Falconer.—We are all born to disappointment. It is as well to be prospective. Our happiness is not in what is, but in what is to be. We may be disappointed in our every-day realities, and if not, we may make an ideality of the unattainable, and quarrel with nature for not giving what she has not to give. It is unreasonable to be so disappointed, but it is disappointment not the less.

The Rev. Dr. Opimian.—It is something like the disappointment of the men of Gotham when they could not fish up the moon from the sea.

Mr. Falconer.—It is very like it, and there are more of us in the predicament of the men of Gotham than are ready to acknowledge the similitude.

The Rev. Dr. Opimian.—I am afraid I am too matter-of-fact to sympathize very clearly with this form of æstheticism; but here is a charming bit of forest scenery. Look at that old oak with the deer under it; the long and deep range of fern running up from it to that beech-grove on the upland, the lights and shadows on the projections and recesses of the wood, and the blaze of foxglove in its foreground. It is a place in which a poet might look for a glimpse of a Hamadryad.

Mr. Falconer.—Very beautiful for the actual present—too beautiful for the probable future. Some day or other the forest will be disforested; the deer will be either banished or destroyed; the wood will be either shut up or cut down. Here is another basis for disappointment. The more we admire it now, the more we shall regret it then. The admiration of sylvan and pastoral scenery is at the mercy of an enclosure act, and instead of the glimpse of a Hamadryad you will some time see a large board warning you off the premises under penalty of rigour of law.

The Rev. Dr. Opimian.—But, my dear young friend, you have yourself enclosed a favourite old resort of mine and of many others. I did not see such a board as you speak of; but there is an effective fence which answers the purpose.

Mr. Falconer.—True; but when the lot of crown land was put up for sale, it was sure to be purchased and shut up by somebody. At any rate, I have not interfered with the external picturesque; and I have been much more influenced by an intense desire of shutting up myself than of shutting up the place, merely because it is my property.

About half way from their respective homes the two new friends separated, the doctor having promised to walk over again soon to dine and pass the night.

[When Mrs. Opimian is told of her husband's adventure, and of Mr. Falconer's idyllic establishment, she declares that she has "no belief in the virtue of young men." The good doctor pays a second visit to the Folly, where the seven sisters entertain him with a musical concert, which concludes with a hymn to St. Catharine, whom their master comes close to worshipping.]

THE VICAR AND HS WIFE.—FAMILIES OF LOVE.— THE NEWSPAPER

"AGAPETUS and Agapêtê," said the Reverend Doctor Opimian, the next morning at breakfast, "in the best sense of the words: that, I am satisfied, is the relation between this young gentleman and his handmaids."

Mrs. Opimian.—Perhaps, doctor, you will have the goodness to make your view of this relation a little more intelligible to me.

The Rev. Dr. Opimian.—Assuredly, my dear. The word signifies "beloved," in its purest sense. And in this sense it was used by Saint Paul in reference to some of his female co-religionists and fellow-labourers in the vineyard, in whose houses he occasionally dwelt. And in this sense it was applied to virgins and holy men, who dwelt under the same roof in spiritual love.

Mrs. Opimian.—Very likely indeed. You are a holy man, doctor, but I think, if you were a bachelor, and I were a maid, I should not trust myself to be your aga—aga—

The Rev. Dr. Opimian.—Agapêtê. But I never pretended to this sort of spiritualism. I followed the advice of Saint Paul, who says it is better to marry.

Mrs. Opimian.—You need not finish the quotation.

The Rev. Dr. Opimian.—Agapêtê is often translated "adoptive sister." A very possible relation, I think, where there are vows of celibacy, and inward spiritual grace.

Mrs. Opimian.—Very possible, indeed: and equally possible where there are none.

The Rev. Dr. Opimian.—But more possible where there are seven adoptive sisters, than where there is only one.

Mrs. Opimian.—Perhaps.

The Rev. Dr. Opimian.—The manners, my dear, of these damsels towards their young master, are infallible indications of the relations between them. Their respectful deference to him is a symptom in which I cannot be mistaken.

Mrs. Opimian.—I hope you are not.

The Rev. Dr. Opimian.—I am sure I am not. I would stake all my credit for observation and experience on the purity of the seven Vestals. I am not strictly accurate in calling them so: for in Rome the number of Vestals was only six. But there were seven Pleiads, till one disappeared. We may fancy she became a seventh Vestal. Or as the planets used to be seven, and are now more than fifty, we may pass a seventh Vestal in the name of modern progress.

Mrs. Opimian.—There used to be seven deadly sins. How many has modern progress added to them?

The Rev. Dr. Opimian.—None, I hope, my dear. But this will be due, not to its own tendencies, but to the comprehensiveness of the old definitions.

Mrs. Opimian.—I think I have heard something like your Greek word before.

The Rev. Dr. Opimian.—Agapêmonê, my dear. You may have heard the word Agapêmonê.

Mrs. Opimian.—That is it. And what may it signify?

The Rev. Dr. Opimian.—It signifies Abode of Love: spiritual love, of course.

Mrs. Opimian.—Spiritual love, which rides in carriages and four, fares sumptuously, like Dives, and protects itself with a high wall from profane observation.

The Rev. Dr. Opimian.—Well, my dear, and there may be no harm in all that.

Mrs. Opimian.—Doctor, you are determined not to see harm in anything.

The Rev. Dr. Opimian.—I am afraid I see more harm in many things than I like to see. But one reason for not seeing harm in this Agapêmonê matter is, that I hear so little about it. The world is ready enough to promulgate scandal; but that which is quietly right may rest in peace.

Mrs. Opimian.—Surely, doctor, you do not think this Agapêmonê right?

The Rev. Dr. Opimian.—I only say I do not know whether it is right or wrong. It is nothing new. Three centuries ago there was a Family of Love, on which Middleton wrote a comedy. Queen Elizabeth persecuted this family; Middleton made it ridiculous; but it outlived them both, and there may have been no harm in it after all.

Mrs. Opimian.—Perhaps, doctor, the world is too good to see any novelty except in something wrong.

The Rev. Dr. Opimian.—Perhaps it is only wrong that arrests attention, because right is common, and wrong is rare. Of the many thousand persons who walk daily through a street you only hear of one who has been robbed or knocked down. If ever Hamlet's news— "that the world has grown honest"—should prove true, there would be an end of our newspaper. For, let us see, what is the epitome of a newspaper? In the first place, specimens of all the deadly sins, and infinite varieties of violence and fraud; a great quantity of talk, called by courtesy legislative wisdom, of which the result is "an incoherent and undigested mass of law, shot down, as from a rubbish-cart, on the heads of the people;" lawyers barking at each other in that peculiar style of hylactic delivery which is called forensic eloquence, and of which the first and most distinguished practitioner was Cerberus; bear-garden meetings of mismanaged companies, in which directors and shareholders abuse each other in choice terms, not all to be found even in Rabelais; burstings of bank bubbles, which, like a touch of harlequin's wand, strip off their masks and dominoes from "highly respectable" gentlemen, and leave them in their true figures of cheats and pickpockets; societies of all sorts, for teaching everybody everything, meddling with everybody's business, and mending everybody's morals; mountebank advertisements promising the beauty of Helen in a bottle of cosmetic, and the age of Old Parr in a box of pills; folly all alive in things called réunions; announcements that some exceedingly stupid fellow has been "entertaining" a select company; matters, however multiform, multifarious, and multitudinous, all brought into family likeness by the varnish of false pretension with which they are all overlaid.

Mrs. Opimian.—I did not like to interrupt you, doctor; but it struck me, while you were speaking, that in reading the newspaper you do not hear the bark of the lawyers.

The Rev. Dr. Opimian.—True; but no one who has once heard the wow-wow can fail to reproduce it in imagination.

Mrs. Opimian.—You have omitted accidents, which occupy a large space in the newspaper. If the world grew ever so honest, there would still be accidents.

The Rev. Dr. Opimian.—But honesty would materially diminish the number. High-pressure steam boilers would not scatter death and destruction around them, if the dishonesty of avarice did not tempt their employment, where the more costly low pressure would ensure absolute safety. Honestly built houses would not come suddenly down and crush their occupants. Ships, faithfully built and efficiently manned, would not so readily strike on a lee shore, nor go instantly to pieces on the first touch of the ground. Honestly made sweetmeats would not poison children; honestly compounded drugs would not poison patients. In short, the larger portion of what we call accidents are crimes.

Mrs. Opimian.—I have often heard you say, of railways and steam vessels, that the primary cause of their disasters is the insane passion of the public for speed. That is not crime, but folly.

The Rev. Dr. Opimian.—It is crime in those who ought to know better than to act in furtherance of the folly. But when the world has grown honest, it will no doubt grow wise. When we have got rid of crime, we may consider how to get rid of folly. So that question is adjourned to the Greek kalends.

Mrs. Opimian.—There are always in a newspaper some things of a creditable character.

The Rev. Dr. Opimian.—When we are at war, naval and military heroism abundantly; but in time of peace, these virtues sleep. They are laid up like ships in ordinary. No doubt, of the recorded facts of civil life some are good, and more are indifferent, neither good nor bad; but good and indifferent together are scarcely more than a twelfth part of the whole. Still, the matters thus presented are all exceptional cases. A hermit reading nothing but a newspaper might find little else than food for misanthropy; but living among friends, and in the bosom of our family, we see the dark side of life in the occasional picture, the bright is its every-day aspect. The occasional is the matter of curiosity, of incident, of adventure, of things that really happen to few, and may possibly happen to any. The interest attendant on any action or event is in just proportion to its rarity; and, happily, quiet virtues are all around us, and obtrusive virtues seldom cross our path. On the whole, I agree in opinion with Theseus, that there is more good than evil in the world.

Mrs. Opimian.—I think, doctor, you would not maintain any opinion if you had not an authority two thousand years old for it.

The Rev. Dr. Opimian.—Well, my dear, I think most opinions worth maintaining have an authority of about that age.

[The doctor cultivates Mr. Falconer's acquaintance, and persuades him to assist with the Aristophanic comedy that is to be produced at the Grange. Shortly afterwards, Mr. Gryll and his niece are forced to take refuge in the Folly, when one of their carriage horses is struck by lightning, Miss Gryll's recovery from a state of shock requires several days, after which time the dedicated bachelor is in love, but determined not to be. However, a few words from Dr. Opimian, regarding a possible rival, bring the young man to Gryll Grange as visitor and theatrical collaborator.]

LORD CURRYFIN.—SIBERIAN DINNERS.—
SOCIAL MONOTONY

A LARGE party was assembled at the Grange. Among them were some of the young ladies who were to form the chorus; one elderly spinster, Miss Ilex, who passed more than half her life in visits, and was everywhere welcome, being always good-humoured, agreeable in conversation, having much knowledge of society, good sense in matters of conduct, good taste and knowledge in music; sound judgment in dress, which alone sufficed to make her valuable to young ladies; a fair amount of reading, old and new; and on most subjects an opinion of her own, for which she had always something to say; Mr. Mac-Borrowdale, an old friend of Mr. Gryll, a gentleman who comprised in himself all that Scotland had ever been supposed to possess of mental, moral, and political philosophy; "And yet he bore it not

about;" not "as being loth to wear it out," [1] but because he held that
there was a time for all things, and that dinner was the time for
joviality, and not for argument; Mr. Minim, the amateur composer
of the music for the comedy; Mr. Pallet, the amateur painter of the
scenery; and last, not least, the newly-made acquaintance, Lord
Curryfin.

Lord Curryfin was a man on the younger side of thirty, with a
good person, handsome features, a powerful voice, and an agreeable
delivery. He had a strong memory, much power of application, and
a facility of learning rapidly whatever he turned his mind to. But
with all this, he valued what he learned less for the pleasure which
he derived from the acquisition, than from the effect which it enabled him to produce on others. He liked to shine in conversation,
and there was scarcely a subject which could be mooted in any society, on which his multifarious attainments did not qualify him to
say something. He was readily taken by novelty in doctrine, and followed a new lead with great pertinacity; and in this way he had been
caught by the science of pantopragmatics, and firmly believed for a
time, that a scientific organization for teaching everybody everything,
would cure all the evils of society. But being one of those "over sharp
wits whose edges are very soon turned," he did not adhere to any
opinion with sufficient earnestness to be on any occasion betrayed
into intemperance in maintaining it. So far from this, if he found any
unfortunate opinion in a hopeless minority of the company he happened to be in, he was often chivalrous enough to come to its aid,
and see what could be said for it. When lecturing became a mania,
he had taken to lecturing; and looking about for an unoccupied subject, he had lighted on the natural history of fish, in which he soon
became sufficiently proficient to amuse the ladies, and astonish the
fishermen in any sea-side place of fashionable resort. Here he always
arranged his lecture-room, so that the gentility of his audience could
sit on a platform, and the natives in a gallery above, and that thus
the fishy and tarry odours which the latter were most likely to bring

[1] 'Tis true, although he had much wit,
  He was very shy of using it,
  As being loth to wear it out;
  And therefore bore it not about,
  Except on holidays or so,
  As men their best apparel do.—HUDIBRAS.

with them, might ascend into the upper air, and not mingle with the more delicate fragrances that surrounded the select company below. He took a summer tour to several watering-places, and was thoroughly satisfied with his success. The fishermen at first did not take cordially to him; but their wives attended from curiosity, and brought their husbands with them on nights not favourable to fishing; and by degrees he won on their attention, and they took pleasure in hearing him, though they learned nothing from him that was of any use in their trade. But he seemed to exalt their art in the eyes of themselves and others, and he told them some pleasant anecdotes of strange fish, and of perilous adventures of some of their own craft, which led in due time to the crowding of his gallery. The ladies went, as they always will go, to lectures, where they fancy they learn something, whether they learn anything or not; and on these occasions, not merely to hear the lecturer, but to be seen by him. To them, however attractive the lecture might have been, the lecturer was more so. He was an irresistible temptation to matrons with marriageable daughters, and wherever he sojourned he was overwhelmed with invitations. It was a contest who should have him to dinner, and in the simplicity of his heart, he ascribed to admiration of his science and eloquence, all the courtesies and compliments with which he was everywhere received. He did not like to receive unreturned favours, and never left a place in which he had accepted many invitations, without giving in return a ball and supper on a scale of great munificence; which filled up the measure of his popularity, and left on all his guests a very enduring impression of a desire to see him again.

So his time passed pleasantly, with a heart untouched by either love or care, till he fell in at a dinner party with the Reverend Doctor Opimian. The doctor spoke of Gryll Grange and the Aristophanic comedy which was to be produced at Christmas, and Lord Curryfin, with his usual desire to have a finger in every pie, expressed an earnest wish to be introduced to the squire. This was no difficult matter. The doctor had quickly brought it about, and Lord Curryfin had gone over in the doctor's company to pass a few days at the Grange. Here, in a very short time, he had made himself completely at home; and had taken on himself the office of architect, to superintend the construction of the theatre, receiving with due deference instructions on the subject from the Reverend Doctor Opimian.

Sufficient progress had been made in the comedy for the painter and musician to begin work on their respective portions; and Lord Curryfin, whose heart was in his work, passed whole mornings in indefatigable attention to the progress of the building. It was near the house, and was to be approached by a covered way. It was a miniature of the Athenian theatre, from which it differed in having a roof, but it resembled it in the arrangements of the stage and orchestra, and in the graduated series of semicircular seats for the audience.

When dinner was announced, Mr. Gryll took in Miss Ilex. Miss Gryll, of course, took the arm of Lord Curryfin. Mr. Falconer took in one of the young ladies and placed her on the left hand of the host. The Reverend Doctor Opimian took in another, and was consequently seated between her and Miss Ilex. Mr. Falconer was thus as far removed as possible from the young lady of the house, and was consequently, though he struggled as much as possible against it, frequently distrait, unconsciously and unwillingly observing Miss Gryll and Lord Curryfin, and making occasional observations very wide of the mark to the fair damsels on his right and left, who set him down in their minds for a very odd young man. The soup and fish were discussed in comparative silence; the entrées not much otherwise; but suddenly a jubilant expression from Mr. MacBorrowdale hailed the disclosure of a large sirloin of beef which figured before Mr. Gryll.

Mr. MacBorrowdale.—You are a man of taste, Mr. Gryll. That is a handsomer ornament of a dinner-table than clusters of nosegays, and all sorts of uneatable decorations. I detest and abominate the idea of a Siberian [1] dinner, where you just look on fiddle-faddles, while your dinner is behind a screen, and you are served with rations like a pauper.

The Rev. Dr. Opimian.—I quite agree with Mr. MacBorrowdale. I like to see my dinner. And herein I rejoice to have Addison on my side; for I remember a paper, in which he objects to having roast beef placed on a sideboard. Even in his day it had been displaced to make way for some incomprehensible French dishes, among which he could find nothing to eat. I do not know what he would have said

[1 Allusion to Russian style of serving, which had recently become fashionable.]

to its being placed altogether out of sight. Still there is something
to be said on the other side. There is hardly one gentleman in twenty
who knows how to carve; and as to ladies, though they did know
once on a time, they do not now. What can be more pitiable than
the right-hand man of the lady of the house, awkward enough in
himself, with the dish twisted round to him in the most awkward
possible position, digging in unutterable mortification for a joint
which he cannot find, and wishing the unanatomisable *volaille* behind a Russian screen with the footmen?

Mr. MacBorrowdale.—I still like to see the *volaille*. It might be
put on table with its joints divided.

Mr. Gryll.—As that turkey-poult is, Mr. MacBorrowdale; which
gives my niece no trouble; but the precaution is not necessary with
such a right-hand man as Lord Curryfin, who carves to perfection.

Mr. MacBorrowdale.—Your arrangements are perfect. At the last
of these Siberian dinners at which I had the misfortune to be present, I had offered me, for two of my rations, the tail of a mullet and
the drum-stick of a fowl. Men who carve behind screens ought to
pass a competitive examination before a jury of gastronomers. Men
who carve at a table are drilled by degrees into something like tolerable operators by the mere shame of the public process.

Mr. Gryll.—I will guarantee you against a Siberian dinner, whenever you dine with me.

The Rev. Dr. Opimian.—Mr. Gryll is a true conservative in
dining.

Mr. Gryll.—A true conservative, I hope. Not what a *soi-disant*
conservative is practically: a man who sails under national colours,
hauls them down, and hoists the enemy's. I like old customs. I like
a glass of wine with a friend. What say you, doctor? Mr. MacBorrowdale will join us?

Mr. MacBorrowdale.—Most willingly.

Miss Gryll.—My uncle and the doctor have got as usual into a
discussion, to the great amusement of the old lady, who sits between
them and says nothing.

Lord Curryfin.—Perhaps their discussion is too recondite for her.

Miss Gryll.—No; they never talk before ladies of any subject in
which ladies cannot join. And she has plenty to say for herself when
she pleases. But when conversation pleases her, she likes to listen and

be silent. It strikes me, by a few words that float this way, that they are discussing the Art of Dining. She ought to be a proficient in it, for she lives much in the world, and has met as many persons whom she is equally willing either to meet to-morrow, or never to meet again, as any regular *dineur en ville*. And indeed that is the price that must be paid for society. Whatever difference of character may lie under the surface, the persons you meet in its circles are externally others yet the same: the same dress, the same manners, the same tastes and opinions, real or assumed. Strongly defined characteristic differences are so few, and artificial general resemblances so many, that in every party you may always make out the same theatrical company. It is like the flowing of a river: it is always different water, but you do not see the difference.

Lord Curryfin.—For my part I do not like these monotonous exteriors. I like visible character. Now, in your party here, there is a good deal of character. Your uncle and Mr. MacBorrowdale are characters. Then the Reverend Doctor Opimian. He is not a man made to pattern. He is simple-minded, learned, tolerant, and the quintessence of *bonhomie*. The young gentleman who arrived to-day, the Hermit of the Folly, is evidently a character. I flatter myself, I am a character (*laughing*).

Miss Gryll (*laughing*).—Indeed you are, or rather many characters in one. I never knew a man of such infinite variety. You seem always to present yourself in the aspect in which those you are with would best wish to see you.

There was some ambiguity in the compliment; but Lord Curryfin took it as implying that his aspect in all its variety was agreeable to the young lady. He did not then dream of a rival in the Hermit of the Folly.

MUSIC AND PAINTING.—JACK OF DOVER

THE dinner and dessert passed away. The ladies retired to the drawing-room: the gentlemen discoursed over their wine. Mr. MacBorrowdale pronounced an eulogium on the port, which was cordially echoed by the divine in regard to the claret.

Mr. Falconer.—Doctor, your tastes and sympathies are very much with the Greeks; but I doubt if you would have liked their wine. Condiments of sea-water and turpentine must have given it an odd flavour; and mixing water with it, in the proportion of three to one, must have reduced the strength of merely fermented liquor to something like the smallest ale of Christophero Sly.

The Rev. Dr. Opimian.—I must say I should not like to put either salt-water or turpentine into this claret: they would not improve its bouquet; nor to dilute it with any portion of water: it has to my mind, as it is, just the strength it ought to have, and no more. But the Greek taste was so exquisite in all matters in which we can bring it to the test, as to justify a strong presumption that in matters in which we cannot test it, it was equally correct. Salt-water and turpentine do not suit our wine: it does not follow that theirs had not in it some basis of contrast, which may have made them pleasant in combination. And it was only a few of their wines that were so treated.

Lord Curryfin.—Then it could not have been much like their drink of the present day. "My master cannot be right in his mind," said Lord Byron's man Fletcher, "or he would not have left Italy, where we had everything, to go to a country of savages; there is nothing to eat in Greece but tough billy-goats, or to drink but spirits of turpentine."

The Rev. Dr. Opimian.—There is an ambiguous present, which somewhat perplexes me, in an epigram of Rhianus, "Here is a vessel of half-wine, half-turpentine, and a singularly lean specimen of kid: the sender, Hippocrates, is worthy of all praise." Perhaps this was a doctor's present to a patient. Alcæus, Anacreon, and Nonnus could not have sung as they did under the inspiration of spirit of turpentine. We learn from Athenæus, and Pliny, and the old comedians, that the Greeks had a vast variety of wine, enough to suit every variety of taste. I infer the unknown from the known. We know little of their music. I have no doubt it was as excellent in its kind as their sculpture.

Mr. Minim.—I can scarcely think that, sir. They seem to have had only the minor key, and to have known no more of counterpoint than they did of perspective.

The Rev. Dr. Opimian.—Their system of painting did not require perspective. Their main subject was on one foreground. Buildings, rocks, trees, served simply to indicate, not to delineate, the scene.

Mr. Falconer.—I must demur to their having only the minor key. The natural ascent of the voice is in the major key, and with their exquisite sensibility to sound they could not have missed the obvious expression of cheerfulness. With their three scales, diatonic, chromatic, and enharmonic, they must have exhausted every possible expression of feeling. Their scales were in true intervals; they had really major and minor tones; we have neither, but a confusion of both. They had both sharps and flats: we have neither, but a mere set of semitones, which serve for both. In their enharmonic scale the fineness of their ear perceived distinctions, which are lost on the coarseness of ours.

Mr. Minim.—With all that they never got beyond melody. They had no harmony, in our sense. They sang only in unisons and octaves.

Mr. Falconer.—It is not clear that they did not sing in fifths. As to harmony in one sense, I will not go so far as to say with Ritson, that the only use of the harmony is to spoil the melody; but I will say, that to my taste a simple accompaniment, in strict subordination to the melody, is far more agreeable than that Niagara of sound under which it is now the fashion to bury it.

Mr. Minim.—In that case, you would prefer a song with a simple pianoforte accompaniment to the same song on the Italian stage.

Mr. Falconer.—A song sung with feeling and expression is good, however accompanied. Otherwise, the pianoforte is not much to my mind. All its intervals are false, and temperament is a poor substitute for natural intonation. Then its incapability of sustaining a note has led, as the only means of producing effect, to those infinitesimal subdivisions of sound, in which all sentiment and expression are twittered and frittered into nothingness.

The Rev. Dr. Opimian.—I quite agree with you. The other day a band passed my gate playing "The Campbells are coming;" but instead of the fine old Scotch lilt, and the emphasis on "Oho! oho!" what they actually played was, "The Ca-a-a-a-ampbells are co-o-o-o-ming, Oh-o-ho-o-o! Oh-o-ho-o-o;" I thought to myself, There is the essence and quintessence of modern music. I like the old organ-music such as it was, when there were no keys but C and F, and every note responded to a syllable. The effect of the prolonged and sustained sound must have been truly magnificent:

> Where, through the long-drawn aisle and fretted vault,
> The pealing anthem swelled the note of praise.

Who cares to hear sacred music on a piano?

Mr. Minim.—Yet I must say that there is a great charm in that brilliancy of execution, which is an exclusively modern and very modern accomplishment.

Mr. Falconer.—To those who perceive it. All things are as they are perceived. To me music has no charm without expression.

LORD CURRYFIN (*who, having observed* MR. MACBORROWDALE's *determination not to be drawn into an argument, amused himself with asking his opinion on all subjects*), What is your opinion, Mr. MacBorrowdale?

Mr. MacBorrowdale.—I hold to the opinion I have already expressed, that this is as good a glass of port as ever I tasted.

Lord Curryfin.—I mean your opinion of modern music and musical instruments.

Mr. MacBorrowdale.—The organ is very good for psalms, which I never sing, and the pianoforte for jigs, which I never dance. And if I were not to hear either of them from January to December, I should not complain of the privation.

Lord Curryfin.—You are an utilitarian, Mr. MacBorrowdale. You are all for utility—public utility—and you see none in music.

Mr. MacBorrowdale.—Nay, not exactly so. If devotion is good, if cheerfulness is good, and if music promotes each of them in proper time and place, music is useful. If I am as devout without the organ, and as cheerful without the piano, as I ever should be with them, that may be the defect of my head or my ear. I am not for forcing my tastes or no-tastes on other people. Let every man enjoy himself in his own way, while he does not annoy others. I would not deprive you of your enjoyment of a brilliant symphony, and I hope you would not deprive me of my enjoyment of a glass of old wine.

The Rev. Dr. Opimian:

> "Tres mihi convivæ prope dissentire videntur,
> Poscentes vario multum diversa palato." [1]

Mr. Falconer.—Nor our reverend friend of the pleasure of a classical quotation.

[1] Three guests dissent most widely in their wishes:
With different taste they call for different dishes.

The Rev. Dr. Opimian.—And the utility, too, sir: for I think I am indebted to one for the pleasure of your acquaintance.

Mr. Falconer.—When you did me the honour to compare my house to the Palace of Circe. The gain was mine.

Mr. Pallet.—You admit, sir, that the Greeks had no knowledge of perspective.

The Rev. Dr. Opimian.—Observing, that they had no need of it. Their subject was a foreground like a relievo. Their background was a symbol, not a representation. "No knowledge" is perhaps too strong. They had it where it was essential. They drew a peristyle, as it appeared to the eye, as accurately as we can do. In short, they gave to each distinct object its own proper perspective, but to separate objects they did not give their relative perspective, for the reason I have given, that they did not need it.

Mr. Falconer.—There is to me one great charm in their painting, as we may judge from the specimens in Pompeii, which, though not their greatest works, indicate their school. They never crowded their canvas with figures. They presented one, two, three, four, or, at most, five persons, preferring one, and rarely exceeding three. These persons were never lost in the profusion of scenery, dress, and decoration. They had clearly defined outlines, and were agreeable objects from any part of the room in which they were placed.

Mr. Pallet.—They must have lost much in beauty of detail.

The Rev. Dr. Opimian.—Therein is the essential difference of ancient and modern taste. Simple beauty—of idea in poetry, of sound in music, of figure in painting—was their great characteristic. Ours is detail in all these matters, overwhelming detail. We have not grand outlines for the imagination of the spectator or hearer to fill up: his imagination has no play of its own: it is overloaded with minutiæ and kaleidoscopical colours.

Lord Curryfin.—Detail has its own beauty. I have admired a Dutch picture of a butcher's shop, where all the charm was in detail.

The Rev. Dr. Opimian.—I cannot admire anything of the kind. I must take pleasure in the thing represented before I can derive any from the representation.

Mr. Pallet.—I am afraid, sir, as our favourite studies all lead us to extreme opinions, you think the Greek painting was the better for not having perspective, and the Greek music for not having harmony.

The Rev. Dr. Opimian.—I think they had as much perspective and as much harmony as was consistent with that simplicity, which characterized their painting and music as much as their music and poetry.

Lord Curryfin.—What is your opinion, Mr. MacBorrowdale?

Mr. MacBorrowdale.—I think you may just buz that bottle before you.

Lord Curryfin.—I mean your opinion of Greek perspective?

Mr. MacBorrowdale.—Troth, I am of opinion that a bottle looks smaller at a distance than when it is close by, and I prefer it as a full-sized object in the foreground.

Lord Curryfin.—I have often wondered that a gentleman so well qualified as you are to discuss all subjects should so carefully avoid discussing any.

Mr. MacBorrowdale.—After dinner, my lord, after dinner. I work hard all the morning at serious things, sometimes till I get a headache, which, however, does not often trouble me. After dinner I like to crack my bottle and chirp and talk nonsense, and fit myself for the company of Jack of Dover.

Lord Curryfin.—Jack of Dover! Who was he?

Mr. MacBorrowdale.—He was a man who travelled in search of a greater fool than himself, and did not find him.

The Rev. Dr. Opimian.—He must have lived in odd times. In our days he would not have gone far without falling in with a teetotaller, or a decimal coinage man, or a school-for-all man, or a competitive examination man, who would not allow a drayman to lower a barrel into a cellar unless he could expound the mathematical principles by which he performed the operation.

Mr. MacBorrowdale.—Nay, that is all pragmatical fooling. The fooling Jack looked for was jovial fooling, fooling to the top of his bent, excellent fooling, which, under the semblance of folly, was both merry and wise. He did not look for mere unmixed folly, of which there never was a deficiency. The fool he looked for was one which it takes a wise man to make—a Shakspearian fool.

The Rev. Dr. Opimian.—In that sense he might travel far, and return, as he did in his own day, without having found the fool he looked for.

Mr. MacBorrowdale.—A teetotaller! Well! He is the true Heautontimorumenos, the self-punisher, with a jug of toast-and-water for his Christmas wassail. So far his folly is merely pitiable, but his intolerance makes it offensive. He cannot enjoy his own tipple unless he can deprive me of mine. A fox that has lost his tail. There is no tyrant like a thorough-paced reformer. I drink to his own reformation.

Mr. Gryll.—He is like Bababec's faquir, who sat in a chair full of nails, *pour avoir de la considération.* But the faquir did not want others to do the same. He wanted all the consideration for himself, and kept all the nails for himself. If these meddlers would do the like by their toast-and-water, nobody would begrudge it them.

The Rev. Dr. Opimian.—Now, sir, if the man who has fooled the greatest number of persons to the top of their bent were to be adjudged the fittest companion for Jack of Dover, you would find him in a distinguished meddler with everything, who has been for half a century the merry-andrew of a vast arena, which he calls moral and political science, but which has in it a dash of everything that has ever occupied human thought.

Lord Curryfin.—I know whom you mean; but he is a great man in his way, and has done much good.

The Rev. Dr. Opimian.—He has helped to introduce much change; whether for good or for ill remains to be seen. I forgot he was your lordship's friend. I apologize, and drink to his health.

Lord Curryfin.—Oh! pray, do not apologize to me. I would not have my friendships, tastes, pursuits, and predilections interfere in the slightest degree with the fullest liberty of speech on all persons and things. There are many who think with you that he is a moral and political Jack of Dover. So be it. Time will bring him to his level.

Mr. MacBorrowdale.—I will only say of the distinguished personage, that Jack of Dover would not pair off with him. This is the true universal science, the oracle of *La Dive Bouteille.*

Mr. Gryll.—It is not exactly Greek music, Mr. Minim, that you are giving us for our Aristophanic choruses.

Mr. Minim.—No, sir; I have endeavoured to give you a good selection, as appropriate as I can make it.

Mr. Pallet.—Neither am I giving you Greek painting for the scenery. I have taken the liberty to introduce perspective.

The Rev. Dr. Opimian.—Very rightly both, for Aristophanes in London.

Mr. Minim.—Besides, sir, we must have such music as your young ladies can sing.

The Rev. Dr. Opimian.—Assuredly; and so far as we have yet heard them rehearse, they sing it delightfully.

After a little more desultory conversation, they adjourned to the drawing-rooms.

[Where Miss Gryll and Miss Niphet sing ballads to their own accompaniment, the second ballad dealing sadly with love and age.]

Miss Ilex.—That is a melancholy song. But of how many first loves is it the true tale? And how many are far less happy?

The Rev. Dr. Opimian.—It is simple and well sung, with a distinctness of articulation not often heard.

Miss Ilex.—That young lady's voice is a perfect contralto. It is singularly beautiful, and I applaud her for keeping within her natural compass, and not destroying her voice by forcing it upwards, as too many do.

The Rev. Dr. Opimian.—Forcing, forcing seems to be the rule of life. A young lady who forces her voice into *altissimo*, and a young gentleman who forces his mind into a receptacle for a chaos of crudities, are pretty much on a par. Both do ill, where, if they were contented with attainments within the limits of natural taste and natural capacity, they might both do well. As to the poor young men, many of them become mere crammed fowls, with the same result as Hermogenes, who, after astonishing the world with his attainments at seventeen, came to a sudden end at the age of twenty-five, and spent the rest of a long life in hopeless imbecility.[1]

Miss Ilex.—The poor young men can scarcely help themselves. They are not held qualified for a profession unless they have overloaded their understanding with things of no use in it; incongruous things too, which could never be combined into the pursuits of natural taste.

The Rev. Dr. Opimian.—Very true. Brindley would not have passed as a canal-maker, nor Edward Williams[2] as a bridge-builder. I saw the other day some examination papers which would have in-

[1] Donaldson's *History of Greek Literature*, vol. iii. p. 156.
[2] The builder of Pont-y-Pryd.

fallibly excluded Marlborough from the army and Nelson from the navy. I doubt if Haydn would have passed as a composer before a committee of lords like one of his pupils, who insisted on demonstrating to him that he was continually sinning against the rules of counterpoint; on which Haydn said to him, "I thought I was to teach you, but it seems you are to teach me, and I do not want a preceptor," and thereon he wished his lordship a good morning. Fancy Watt being asked, how much Joan of Naples got for Avignon, when she sold it to Pope Clement the Sixth, and being held unfit for an engineer because he could not tell.

Miss Ilex.—That is an odd question, doctor. But how much did she get for it?

The Rev. Dr. Opimian.—Nothing. He promised ninety thousand golden florins, but he did not pay one of them: and that, I suppose, is the profound sense of the question. It is true he paid her after a fashion, in his own peculiar coin. He absolved her of the murder of her first husband, and perhaps he thought that was worth the money. But how many of our legislators could answer the question? Is it not strange that candidates for seats in Parliament should not be subjected to competitive examination? Plato and Persius [1] would furnish good hints for it. I should like to see honourable gentlemen having to answer such questions as are deemed necessary tests for government clerks, before they would be held qualified candidates for seats in the legislature. That would be something like a reform in the Parliament. Oh that it were so, and I were the examiner! Ha, ha, ha, what a comedy!

The doctor's hearty laugh was contagious, and Miss Ilex joined in it. Mr. MacBorrowdale came up.

Mr. MacBorrowdale.—You are as merry as if you had discovered the object of Jack of Dover's quest.

The Rev. Dr. Opimian.—Something very like it. We have an honourable gentleman under competitive examination for a degree in legislative wisdom.

Mr. MacBorrowdale.—Truly, that is fooling competition to the top of its bent.

The Rev. Dr. Opimian.—Competitive examination for clerks, and none for legislators, is not this an anomaly? Ask the honourable mem-

[1] PLATO: *Alcibiades*, i.; PERSIUS: *Sat.* iv.

ber for Muckborough on what acquisitions in history and mental and moral philosophy he founds his claim of competence to make laws for the nation? He can only tell you that he has been chosen as the most conspicuous Grub among the Moneygrubs of his borough to be the representative of all that is sordid, selfish, hard-hearted, unintellectual, and antipatriotic, which are the distinguishing qualities of the majority among them. Ask a candidate for a clerkship what are his qualifications? He may answer, "All that are requisite: reading, writing, and arithmetic." "Nonsense," says the questioner. "Do you know the number of miles in direct distance from Timbuctoo to the top of Chimborazo?" "I do not," says the candidate. "Then you will not do for a clerk," says the competitive examiner. Does Moneygrub of Muckborough know? He does not; nor anything else. The clerk may be able to answer some of the questions put to him. Moneygrub could not answer one of them. But he is very fit for a legislator.

Mr. MacBorrowdale.—Eh! but he is subjected to a pretty severe competitive examination of his own, by what they call a constituency, who just put him to the test in the art of conjuring, to see if he can shift money from his own pocket into theirs, without any inconvenient third party being aware of the transfer.

[The house party continues, while the comedy is being rehearsed and the theatre being constructed under the expert supervision of Lord Curryfin.]

A SYMPOSIUM.—TRANSATLANTIC TENDENCIES.— AFTER-DINNER LECTURES.—EDUCATION

SOME guests remained. Some departed and returned. Among these was Mr. MacBorrowdale. One day after dinner, on one of his reappearances, Lord Curryfin said to him:—

"Well, Mr. MacBorrowdale, in your recent observations, have you found anything likely to satisfy Jack of Dover, if he were prosecuting his inquiry among us?"

Mr. MacBorrowdale.—Troth, no, my lord. I think, if he were among us, he would give up the search as hopeless. He found it so in his own day, and he would find it still more so now. Jack was both merry and wise. We have less mirth in practice; and we have more wisdom in pretension, which Jack would not have admitted.

The Rev. Dr. Opimian.—He would have found it like Juvenal's search for patriotic virtue, when Catiline was everywhere, and Brutus and Cato were nowhere.

Lord Curryfin.—Well, among us, if Jack did not find his superior, or even his equal, he would not have been at a loss for company to his mind. There is enough mirth for those who choose to enjoy it, and wisdom too, perhaps as much as he would have cared for. We ought to have more wisdom, as we have clearly more science.

The Rev. Dr. Opimian.—Science is one thing, and wisdom is another. Science is an edged tool, with which men play like children, and cut their own fingers. If you look at the results which science has brought in its train, you will find them to consist almost wholly in elements of mischief. See how much belongs to the word Explosion alone, of which the ancients knew nothing. Explosions of powder-mills and powder-magazines; of coal-gas in mines and in houses; of high-pressure engines in ships and boats and factories. See the complications and refinements of modes of destruction, in revolvers and rifles and shells and rockets and cannon. See collisions and wrecks and every mode of disaster by land and by sea, resulting chiefly from the insanity for speed, in those who for the most part have nothing to do at the end of the race, which they run as if they were so many Mercuries, speeding with messages from Jupiter. Look at our scientific drainage, which turns refuse into poison. Look at the subsoil of London, whenever it is turned up to the air, converted by gas leakage into one mass of pestilent blackness, in which no vegetation can flourish, and above which, with the rapid growth of the ever-growing nuisance, no living thing will breathe with impunity. Look at our scientific machinery, which has destroyed domestic manufacture, which has substituted rottenness for strength in the thing made, and physical degradation in crowded towns for healthy and comfortable country life in the makers. The day would fail, if I should attempt to enumerate the evils which science has inflicted on mankind. I almost think it is the ultimate destiny of science to exterminate the human race.

Lord Curryfin.—You have gone over a wide field, which we might exhaust a good bin of claret in fully discussing. But surely the facility of motion over the face of the earth and sea is both pleasant and profitable. We may now see the world with little expenditure of labour or time.

The Rev. Dr. Opimian.—You may be whisked over it, but you do not see it. You go from one great town to another, where manners and customs are not even now essentially different, and with this facility of intercourse become progressively less and less so. The intermediate country—which you never see, unless there is a show mountain, or waterfall, or ruin, for which there is a station, and to which you go as you would to any other exhibition—the intermediate country contains all that is really worth seeing, to enable you to judge of the various characteristics of men and the diversified objects of nature.

Lord Curryfin.—You can suspend your journey if you please, and see the intermediate country, if you prefer it.

The Rev. Dr. Opimian.—But who does prefer it? You travel round the world by a hand-book, as you do round an exhibition-room by a catalogue.

Mr. MacBorrowdale.—Not to say that in the intermediate country you are punished by bad inns and bad wine; of which I confess myself intolerant. I knew an unfortunate French tourist, who had made the round of Switzerland, and had but one expression for every stage of his journey: *Mauvais auberge!*

Lord Curryfin.—Well, then, what say you to the electric telegraph, by which you converse at the distance of thousands of miles? Even across the Atlantic, as no doubt we shall yet do.

Mr. Gryll.—Some of us have already heard the doctor's opinion on that subject.

The Rev. Dr. Opimian.—I have no wish to expedite communication with the Americans. If we could apply the power of electrical repulsion to preserve us from ever hearing anything more of them, I should think that we had for once derived a benefit from science.

Mr. Gryll.—Your love for the Americans, doctor, seems something like that of Cicero's friend Marius for the Greeks. He would not take the nearest road to his villa, because it was called the Greek Road. Perhaps if your nearest way home were called the American Road, you would make a circuit to avoid it.

The Rev. Dr. Opimian.—I am happy to say I am not put to the test. Magnetism, galvanism, electricity, are "one form of many names." Without magnetism we should never have discovered America; to which we are indebted for nothing but evil; diseases in the worst forms that can afflict humanity, and slavery in the worst form in which slavery can exist. The Old World had the sugar-cane and the cotton-plant, though it did not so misuse them. Then, what good have we got from America? What good of any kind, from the whole continent and its islands, from the Esquimaux to Patagonia?

Mr. Gryll.—Newfoundland salt-fish, doctor.

The Rev. Dr. Opimian.—That is something, but it does not turn the scale.

Mr. Gryll.—If they have given us no good, we have given them none.

The Rev. Dr. Opimian.—We have given them wine and classical literature; but I am afraid Bacchus and Minerva have equally—

Scattered their bounty upon barren ground.

On the other hand, we have given the red men rum, which has been the chief instrument of their perdition. On the whole, our intercourse with America has been little else than an interchange of vices and diseases.

Lord Curryfin.—Do you count it nothing to have substituted civilized for savage men?

The Rev. Dr. Opimian.—Civilized. The word requires definition. But looking into futurity, it seems to me that the ultimate tendency of the change is to substitute the worse for the better race; the Negro for the Red Indian. The Red Indian will not work for a master. No ill-usage will make him. Herein he is the noblest specimen of humanity that ever walked the earth. Therefore, the white man exterminates his race. But the time will come, when by mere force of numbers, the black race will predominate, and exterminate the white. And thus the worse race will be substituted for the better, even as it is in St. Domingo, where the Negro has taken the place of the Caraib. The change is clearly for the worse.

Lord Curryfin.—You imply that in the meantime the white race is better than the red.

The Rev. Dr. Opimian.—I leave that as an open question. But

I hold, as some have done before me, that the human mind degenerates in America, and that the superiority, such as it is, of the white race, is only kept up by intercourse with Europe. Look at the atrocities in their ships. Look at their Congress and their Courts of Justice; debaters in the first; suitors, even advocates, sometimes judges, in the second, settling their arguments with pistol and dagger. Look at their extensions of slavery, and their revivals of the slave-trade, now covertly, soon to be openly. If it were possible that the two worlds could be absolutely dissevered for a century, I think a new Columbus would find nothing in America but savages.

Lord Curryfin.—You look at America, doctor, through your hatred of slavery. You must remember that we introduced it when they were our colonists. It is not so easily got rid of. Its abolition by France exterminated the white race in St. Domingo, as the white race had exterminated the red. Its abolition by England ruined our West Indian Colonies.

The Rev. Dr. Opimian.—Yes, in conjunction with the direct encouragement of foreign slave labour, given by our friends of liberty under the pretext of free trade. It is a mockery to keep up a squadron for suppressing the slave-trade on the one hand, while, on the other hand, we encourage it to an extent that counteracts in a tenfold degree the apparent power of suppression. It is a clear case of false pretension.

Mr. Gryll.—You know, doctor, the Old World had slavery throughout its entire extent; under the Patriarchs, the Greeks, the Romans; everywhere, in short. Cicero thought our island not likely to produce anything worth having, excepting slaves; and of those none skilled, as some slaves were, in letters and music, but all utterly destitute of both. And in the Old World the slaves were of the same race with the masters. The Negroes are an inferior race, not fit, I am afraid, for anything else.

The Rev. Dr. Opimian.—Not fit, perhaps, for anything else belonging to what we call civilized life. Very fit to live on little, and wear nothing, in Africa; where it would have been a blessing to themselves and the rest of the world if they had been left unmolested; if they had had a Friar Bacon to surround their entire continent with a wall of brass.

Mr. Falconer.—I am not sure, doctor, that in many instances, even yet, the white slavery of our factories is not worse than the black slavery of America. We have done much to amend it, and shall do more. Still, much remains to be done.

The Rev. Dr. Opimian.—And will be done, I hope and believe. The Americans do nothing to amend their system. On the contrary, they do all they can to make bad worse. Whatever excuse there may be for maintaining slavery where it exists, there can be none for extending it into new territories; none for reviving the African slave-trade. These are the crying sins of America. Our white slavery, so far as it goes, is so far worse, that it is the degradation of a better race. But if it be not redressed, as I trust it will be, it will work out its own retribution. And so it is of all the oppressions that are done under the sun. Though all men but the red men will work for a master, they will not fight for an oppressor in the day of his need. Thus gigantic empires have crumbled into dust at the first touch of an invader's footstep. For petty, as for great oppressions, there is a day of retribution growing out of themselves. It is often long in coming. *Ut sit magna, tamen certe lenta ira Deorum est.*[1] But it comes.

> Raro antecedentem scelestum
> Deseruit pede Pœna claudo.[2]

Lord Curryfin.—I will not say, doctor, "I've seen, and sure I ought to know." But I have been in America, and I have found there, what many others will testify, a very numerous class of persons, who hold opinions very like your own: persons who altogether keep aloof from public life, because they consider it abandoned to the rabble, but who are as refined, as enlightened, as full of sympathy for all that tends to justice and liberty, as any whom you may most approve amongst ourselves.

The Rev. Dr. Opimian.—Of that I have no doubt. But I look to public acts and public men.

Lord Curryfin.—I should much like to know what Mr. MacBorrowdale thinks of all this.

Mr. MacBorrowdale.—Troth, my lord, I think we have strayed far away from the good company we began with. We have lost sight

---

[1] The anger of the Gods, though great, is slow.
[2] The foot of Punishment, though lame,
O'ertakes at last preceding Wrong.

of Jack of Dover. But the discussion had one bright feature. It did not interfere with, it rather promoted the circulation of the bottle: for every man who spoke pushed it on with as much energy as he spoke with, and those who were silent swallowed the wine and the opinion together, as if they relished them both.

The Rev. Dr. Opimian.—So far, discussion may find favour. In my own experience I have found it very absorbent of claret. But I do not think it otherwise an incongruity after dinner, provided it be carried on, as our disquisitions have always been, with frankness and good humour. Consider how much instruction has been conveyed to us in the form of conversations at banquet, by Plato and Xenophon and Plutarch. I read nothing with more pleasure than their *Symposia:* to say nothing of Athenæus, whose work is one long banquet.

Mr. MacBorrowdale.—Nay, I do not object to conversation on any subject. I object to after-dinner lectures. I have had some unfortunate experiences. I have found what began in conversation end in a lecture. I have, on different occasions, met several men, who were in that respect all alike. Once started they never stopped. The rest of the good company, or rather the rest which without them would have been good company, was no company. No one could get in a word. They went on with one unvarying stream of monotonous desolating sound. This makes me tremble when a discussion begins. I sit in fear of a lecture.

Lord Curryfin.—Well, you and I have lectured, but never after dinner. We do it when we have promised it, and when those who are present expect it. After dinner, I agree with you, it is the most doleful blight that can fall on human enjoyment.

Mr. MacBorrowdale.—I will give you one or two examples of these postprandial inflictions. One was a great Indian reformer. He did not open his mouth till he had had about a bottle and a half of wine. Then he burst on us with a declamation on all that was wrong in India, and its remedy. He began in the Punjaub, travelled to Calcutta, went southward, got into the Temple of Juggernaut, went southward again, and after holding forth for more than an hour, paused for a moment. The man who sate next him attempted to speak: but the orator clapped him on the arm, and said: "Excuse me: now I come to Madras." On which his neighbour jumped up and vanished. Another went on in the same way about currency. His first hour's talking carried him just through the Restriction Act of ninety-seven. As we had then more than half a century before us, I took my departure. But these were two whom topography and chronology would have brought to a close. The bore of all bores was the third. His subject had no beginning, middle, nor end. It was education. Never was such a journey through the desert of mind: the Great Sahara of intellect. The very recollection makes me thirsty.

The Rev. Dr. Opimian.—If all the nonsense which, in the last quarter of a century, has been talked on all other subjects were thrown into one scale, and all that has been talked on the subject of education alone were thrown into the other, I think the latter would preponderate.

Lord Curryfin.—We have had through the whole period some fine specimens of nonsense on other subjects: for instance, with a single exception, political economy.

Mr. MacBorrowdale.—I understand your lordship's politeness as excepting the present company. You need not except me. I am "free to confess," as they say "in another place," that I have talked a great deal of nonsense on that subject myself.

Lord Curryfin.—Then, we have had latterly a mighty mass on the purification of the Thames.

The Rev. Dr. Opimian.—Allowing full weight to the two last-named ingredients, they are not more than a counterpoise to Competitive Examination, which is also a recent exotic belonging to education.

Lord Curryfin.—Patronage, it used to be alleged, considered only the fitness of the place for the man, not the fitness of the man for the place. It was desirable to reverse this.

The Rev. Dr. Opimian.—True: but—

Dum vitant stulti vitium, in contraria currunt.[1]

Questions which can only be answered by the parrotings of a memory, crammed to disease with all sorts of heterogeneous diet, can form no test of genius, taste, judgment, or natural capacity. Competitive Examination takes for its *norma:* "It is better to learn many things ill than one thing well;" or rather: "It is better to learn to

[1] When fools would from one vice take flight,
They rush into its opposite.
HOR. *Sat.* i. 2, 24

gabble about everything than to understand anything." This is not the way to discover the wood of which Mercuries are made. I have been told that this precious scheme has been borrowed from China: a pretty fountain-head for moral and political improvement: and if so, I may say, after Petronius: "This windy and monstrous loquacity has lately found its way to us from Asia, and like a pestilential star has blighted the minds of youth otherwise rising to greatness."

Lord Curryfin.—There is something to be said on behalf of applying the same tests, addressing the same questions, to everybody.

The Rev. Dr. Opimian.—I shall be glad to hear what can be said on that behalf.

Lord Curryfin (after a pause).—"Mass," as the second grave-digger says in *Hamlet,* "I cannot tell."

A chorus of laughter dissolved the sitting.

ALGERNON AND MORGANA.—OPPORTUNITY AND REPENTANCE.—THE FOREST IN WINTER

The winter set in early. December began with intense frost. Mr. Falconer, one afternoon, entering the inner drawing-room, found Miss Gryll alone. She was reading, and on the entrance of her visitor, laid down her book. He hoped he had not interrupted her in an agreeable occupation. "To observe romantic method," we shall give what passed between them with the Christian names of the speakers.

Morgana.—I am only reading what I have often read before, *Orlando Innamorato;* and I was at the moment occupied with a passage about the enchantress from whom my name was borrowed. You are aware that enchantresses are in great favour here.

Algernon.—Circe and Gryllus, and your name, sufficiently show that. And not your name only, but—— I should like to see the passage, and should be still better pleased if you would read it to me.

Morgana.—It is where Orlando, who had left Morgana sleeping by the fountain, returns to seek the enchanted key, by which alone he can liberate his friends.

[She quotes.]

Algernon.—I remember the passage well. The beautiful Fata, dancing and singing by the fountain, presents a delightful picture.

Morgana.—Then, you know, Orlando, who had missed his opportunity of seizing the golden forelock while she was sleeping, pursues her a long while in vain through rocky deserts, *La Penitenza* following him with a scourge. The same idea was afterwards happily worked out by Machiavelli in his *Capitolo dell' Occasione.*

Algernon.—You are fond of Italian literature? You read the language beautifully. I observe you have read from the original poem, and not from Berni's *rifacciamento.* [1]

Morgana.—I prefer the original. It is more simple, and more in earnest. Berni's playfulness is very pleasant, and his exordiums are charming; and in many instances he has improved the poetry. Still, I think he has less than the original of what are to me the great charms of poetry, truth and simplicity. Even the greater antiquity of style has its peculiar appropriateness to the subject. And Bojardo seems to have more faith in his narrative than Berni. I go on with him with ready credulity, where Berni's pleasantry interposes a doubt.

Algernon.—You think that in narratives, however wild and romantic, the poet should write as if he fully believed in the truth of his own story.

Morgana.—I do; and I think so in reference to all narratives, not to poetry only. What a dry skeleton is the history of the early ages of Rome, told by one who believes nothing that the Romans believed. Religion pervades every step of the early Roman history; and in a great degree down at least to the Empire; but, because their religion is not our religion, we pass over the supernatural part of the matter in silence, or advert to it in a spirit of contemptuous incredulity. We do not give it its proper place, nor present it in its proper colours, as a cause in the production of great effects. Therefore, I like to read Livy, and I do not like to read Niebuhr.

Algernon.—May I ask if you read Latin?

Morgana.—I do; sufficiently to derive great pleasure from it. Perhaps, after this confession, you will not wonder that I am a spinster.

Algernon.—So far, that I think it would tend to make you fastidi-

[1 adaptation.]

ous in your choice. Not that you would be less sought by any who
would be worthy of your attention. For I am told you have had many
suitors, and have rejected them all in succession. And have you
not still many, and among them one very devoted lover, who would
bring you title as well as fortune? A very amiable person, too, though
not without a comic side to his character.

Morgana.—I do not well know. He so far differs from all my
preceding suitors that in every one of them I found the presence
of some quality that displeased me, or the absence of some which
would have pleased me: the want, in the one way or the other,
of that entire congeniality in taste and feeling which I think essential to happiness in marriage. He has so strong a desire of pleasing,
and such power of acquisition and assimilation, that I think a
woman truly attached to him might mould him to her mind. Still,
I can scarcely tell why, he does not complete my idealities. They
say, Love is his own avenger; and perhaps I shall be punished by
finding my idealities realized in one who will not care for me.

Algernon.—I take that to be impossible.

Morgana blushed, held down her head, and made no reply. Algernon looked at her with silent admiration. A new light seemed to
break in on him. Though he had had so many opportunities of
forming a judgment on the point, it seemed to strike him for the
first time with irresistible conviction that he had never before heard
such a sweet voice, nor seen such an expressive and intelligent
countenance. And in this way they continued like two figures in a
tableau vivant, till the entrance of other parties broke the spell
which had thus fixed them in their positions.

A few minutes more, and their destinies might have been
irrevocably fixed. But the interruption gave Mr. Falconer the
opportunity of returning again to his Tower, to consider, in the
presence of the seven sisters, whether he should not be in the position of a Roman, who was reduced to the dilemma of migrating
without his household deities, or of suffering his local deities to
migrate without him; and whether he could sit comfortably on
either of the horns of this dilemma. He felt that he could not. On
the other hand, could he bear to see the fascinating Morgana
metamorphosed into Lady Curryfin? The time had been when he
had half wished it, as the means of restoring him to liberty. He

felt now, that when in her society he could not bear the idea; but he still thought that in the midst of his domestic duties he might become reconciled to it.

He did not care for horses, nor keep any for his own use. But as time and weather were not always favourable to walking, he had provided for himself a comfortable travelling-chariot, without a box to intercept the view, in which, with post-horses after the fashion of the olden time, he performed occasional migrations. He found this vehicle of great use in moving to and fro between the Grange and the Tower; for then, with all his philosophy, Impatience was always his companion: Impatience on his way to the Grange, to pass into the full attraction of the powerful spell by which he was drawn like the fated ship to the magnetic rock in the *Arabian Nights*: Impatience on his way to the Tower, to find himself again in the "Regions mild of pure and serene air," in which the seven sisters seemed to dwell, like Milton's ethereal spirits "Before the starry threshold of Jove's court." Here was everything to soothe, nothing to irritate or disturb him: nothing on the spot: but it was with him, as it is with many, perhaps with all: the two great enemies of tranquillity, Hope and Remembrance, would still intrude: not like a bubble and a spectre, as in the beautiful lines of Coleridge: [1] for the remembrance of Morgana was not a spectre, and the hope of her love, which he cherished in spite of himself, was not a bubble: but their forces were not less disturbing, even in the presence of his earliest and most long and deeply cherished associations.

He did not allow his impatience to require that the horses should be put to extraordinary speed. He found something tranquillizing in the movement of a postilion in a smart jacket, vibrating on one horse upwards and downwards, with one invariable regulated motion like the cross-head of a side-lever steam-engine, and holding the whip quietly arched over the neck of the other. The mechanical

[1] Who late and lingering seeks thy shrine,
On him but seldom, Power divine,
Thy spirit rests. Satiety,
And sloth, poor counterfeits of thee,
Mock the tired worldling. Idle Hope,
And dire Remembrance, interlope,
And vex the feverish slumbers of the mind:
The bubble floats before: the spectre stalks behind.
COLERIDGE's *Ode to Tranquillity*.

monotony of the movement seemed less in contrast than in harmony with the profound stillness of the wintry forest: the leafless branches heavy with rime frost and glittering in the sun: the deep repose of nature, broken now and then by the traversing of deer, or the flight of wild birds: highest and loudest among them the long lines of rooks: but for the greater part of the way one long deep silence, undisturbed but by the rolling of the wheels and the iron tinkling of the hoofs on the frozen ground. By degrees he fell into a reverie, and meditated on his last dialogue with Morgana.

"It is a curious coincidence," he thought, "that she should have been dwelling in a passage, in which her namesake enchantress inflicted punishment on Orlando for having lost his opportunity. Did she associate Morgana with herself and Orlando with me? Did she intend a graceful hint to me not to lose my opportunity? I seemed in a fair way to seize the golden forelock, if we had not been interrupted. Do I regret that I did not? That is just what I cannot determine. Yet it would be more fitting, that whatever I may do should be done calmly, deliberately, philosophically, than suddenly, passionately, impulsively. One thing is clear to me. It is now or never: this or none. The world does not contain a second Morgana, at least not of mortal race. Well: the opportunity will return. So far, I am not in the predicament in which we left Orlando. I may yet ward off the scourge of *La Penitenza*."

But his arrival at home, and the sight of the seven sisters, who had all come to the hall-door to greet him, turned his thoughts for awhile into another channel.

He dined at his usual hour, and his two Hebes alternately filled his glass with Madeira. After which the sisters played and sang to him in the drawing-room; and when he had retired to his chamber, had looked on the many portraitures of his Virgin Saint, and had thought by how many charms of life he was surrounded, he composed himself to rest with the reflection: "I am here like Rasselas in the Happy Valley: and I can now fully appreciate the force of that beautiful chapter: *The wants of him who wants nothing*."

[Lord Curryfin skates beautifully with Miss Niphet; while Harry Hedgerow, a worthy young farmer, leads a delegation of six other stout fellows in a mass declaration of love for the seven sisters.]

THE TWO QUADRILLES.—POPE'S OMBRE.—POETICAL TRUTH TO NATURE.—CLEOPATRA

In the meantime Mr. Falconer, after staying somewhat longer than usual at home, had returned to the Grange. He found much the same party as he had left: but he observed, or imagined, that Lord Curryfin was much more than previously in favour with Miss Gryll; that she paid him more marked attention, and watched his conduct to Miss Niphet with something more than curiosity.

Amongst the winter evenings' amusements were two forms of quadrille: the old-fashioned game of cards, and the more recently fashionable dance. On these occasions, it was of course a carpet-dance. Now, dancing had never been in Mr. Falconer's line, and though modern dancing, especially in quadrilles, is little more than walking, still in that "little more" there is ample room for grace and elegance of motion. Herein Lord Curryfin outshone all the other young men in the circle. He endeavoured to be as indiscriminating as possible in inviting partners: but it was plain to curious observation, especially if a spice of jealousy mingled with the curiosity, that his favourite partner was Miss Niphet. When they occasionally danced a polka, the reverend doctor's mythological theory came out in full force. It seemed as if Nature had pre-ordained that they should be inseparable, and the interior conviction of both, that so it ought to be, gave them an accordance of movement that seemed to emanate from the innermost mind. Sometimes, too, they danced the *Minuet de la Cour*. Having once done it, they had been often unanimously requested to repeat it. In this they had no competitors. Miss Gryll confined herself to quadrilles, and Mr. Falconer did not even propose to walk through one with her. When dancing brought into Miss Niphet's cheeks the blush-rose bloom, which had more than once before so charmed Lord Curryfin, it required little penetration to see, through his external decorum, the passionate admiration with which he regarded her. Mr. Falconer remarked it, and, looking round to Miss Gryll, thought he saw the trace of a tear in her eye. It was a questionable glistening: jealousy construed it into a tear. But why should it be there? Was her mind turning to Lord Curryfin? and

the more readily because of a newly perceived obstacle? Had mortified vanity any share in it? No: this was beneath Morgana. Then
why was it there? Was it anything like regret that, in respect of
the young lord, she too had lost her opportunity? Was he himself
blameless in the matter? He had been on the point of declaration,
and she had been apparently on the point of acceptance: and instead of following up his advantage, he had been absent longer than
usual. This was ill; but in the midst of the contending forces which
severally acted on him, how could he make it well? So he sate still,
tormenting himself.

In the meantime, Mr. Gryll had got up at a card-table, in the
outer, which was the smaller drawing-room, a quadrille-party of
his own, consisting of himself, Miss Ilex, the Reverend Dr.
Opimian, and Mr. MacBorrowdale.

Mr. Gryll.—This is the only game of cards that ever pleased
me. Once it was the great evening charm of the whole nation.
Now, when cards are played at all, it has given place to whist,
which, in my younger days, was considered a dry, solemn, studious
game, played in moody silence, only interrupted by an occasional
outbreak of dogmatism and ill-humour. Quadrille is not so absorbing but that we may talk and laugh over it, and yet is quite as
interesting as anything of the kind has need to be.

Miss Ilex.—I delight in quadrille. I am old enough to remember when, in mixed society in the country, it was played every evening by some of the party. But *Chaque age a ses plaisirs, son esprit,
et ses mœurs.* It is one of the evils of growing old that we do not
easily habituate ourselves to changes of custom. The old, who sit
still while the young dance and sing, may be permitted to regret the
once always accessible cards, which, in their own young days, delighted the old of that generation: and not the old only.

The Rev. Dr. Opimian.—There are many causes for the diminished attraction of cards in evening society. Late dinners leave little
evening. The old time for cards was the interval between tea and
supper. Now there is no such interval, except here and there in
out-of-the-way places, where, perhaps, quadrille and supper may
still flourish, as in the days of Queen Anne. Nothing was more
common in country towns and villages, half a century ago, than
parties meeting in succession at each other's houses for tea, sup-

per, and quadrille. How popular this game had been, you may judge from Gay's ballad, which represents all classes as absorbed in quadrille. Then the facility of locomotion dissipates, annihilates neighbourhood. People are not now the fixtures they used to be in their respective localities, finding their amusements within their own limited circle. Half the inhabitants of a country-place are here to-day and gone to-morrow. Even of those who are more what they call settled, the greater portion is less, probably, at home than whisking about the world. Then, again, where cards are played at all, whist is more consentaneous to modern solemnity: there is more wiseacre-ism about it: in the same manner that this other sort of quadrille, in which people walk to and from one another with faces of exemplary gravity, has taken the place of the old-fashioned country-dance. "The merry dance I dearly love" would never suggest the idea of a quadrille, any more than "merry England" would call up any image not drawn from ancient ballads and the old English drama.

Mr. Gryll.—Well, doctor, I intend to have a ball at Christmas, in which all modes of dancing shall have fair play, but country-dances shall have their full share.

The Rev. Dr. Opimian.—I rejoice in the prospect. I shall be glad to see the young dancing as if they were young.

Miss Ilex.—The variety of the game called tredrille—the Ombre of Pope's *Rape of the Lock*—is a pleasant game for three. Pope had many opportunities of seeing it played, yet he has not described it correctly: and I do not know that this has been observed.

The Rev. Dr. Opimian.—Indeed, I never observed it. I shall be glad to know how it is so.

Miss Ilex.—Quadrille is played with forty cards: tredrille usually with thirty: sometimes, as in Pope's Ombre, with twenty-seven. In forty cards, the number of trumps is eleven in the black suits, twelve in the red:[1] in thirty, nine in all suits alike.[2] In twenty-seven, they cannot be more than nine in one suit, and eight in the other three. In Pope's Ombre, spades are trumps, and the number is eleven: the number which they would be if the cards were

---

[1] Nine cards in the black, and ten in the red suits, in addition to the aces of spades and clubs, Spadille and Basto, which are trumps in all suits.

[2] Seven cards in each of the four suits in addition to Spadille and Basto.

forty. If you follow his description carefully, you will find it to be so.

Mr. MacBorrowdale.—Why, then, we can only say, as a great philosopher said on another occasion: The description is sufficient "to impose on the degree of attention with which poetry is read." [1]

Miss Ilex.—It is a pity it should be so. Truth to nature is essential to poetry. Few may perceive an inaccuracy: but to those who do, it causes a great diminution, if not a total destruction, of pleasure in perusal. Shakspeare never makes a flower blossom out of season. Wordsworth, Coleridge, and Southey are true to nature in this and in all other respects: even in their wildest imaginings.

The Rev. Dr. Opimian.—Yet here is a combination by one of our greatest poets, of flowers that never blossom in the same season:—

> Bring the rathe primrose, that forsaken dies,
> The tufted crow-toe and pale jessamine,
> The white pink, and the pansie freakt with jet,
> The glowing violet,
> The musk-rose, and the well-attired woodbine,
> With cowslips wan, that hang the pensive head,
> And every flower that sad embroidery wears:
> Bid amaranthus all his beauty shed,
> And daffadillies fill their cups with tears,
> To deck the laureat hearse where Lycid lies.

And at the same time he plucks the berries of the myrtle and the ivy.

Miss Ilex.—Very beautiful, if not true to English seasons: but Milton might have thought himself justified in making this combination in Arcadia. Generally, he is strictly accurate, to a degree that is in itself a beauty. For instance, in his address to the nightingale:—

> Thee, chauntress, oft the woods among,
> I woo to hear thy even-song,
> And missing thee, I walk unseen,
> On the dry smooth-shaven green.

The song of the nightingale ceases about the time that the grass is mown.

[1] DUGALD STEWART, in the *Philosophy of the Human Mind*, I think; but I quote from memory.

The Rev. Dr. Opimian.—The old Greek poetry is always true to nature, and will bear any degree of critical analysis. I must say I take no pleasure in poetry that will not.

Mr. MacBorrowdale.—No poet is truer to nature than Burns, and no one less so than Moore. His imagery is almost always false. Here is a highly applauded stanza, and very taking at first sight:—

> The night-dew of heaven, though in silence it weeps,
> Shall brighten with verdure the sod where he sleeps;
> And the tear that we shed, though in secret it rolls,
> Shall long keep his memory green in our souls.

But it will not bear analysis. The dew is the cause of the verdure: but the tear is not the cause of the memory: the memory is the cause of the tear.

The Rev. Dr. Opimian.—There are inaccuracies more offensive to me than even false imagery. Here is one, in a song which I have often heard with displeasure. A young man goes up a mountain, and as he goes higher and higher, he repeats *Excelsior:* but *excelsior* is only taller in the comparison of things on a common basis, not higher, as a detached object in the air. Jack's bean-stalk was *excelsior* the higher it grew: but Jack himself was no more *celsus* at the top than he had been at the bottom.

Mr. MacBorrowdale.—I am afraid, doctor, if you look for profound knowledge in popular poetry, you will often be disappointed.

The Rev. Dr. Opimian.—I do not look for profound knowledge. But I do expect that poets should understand what they talk of. Burns was not a scholar, but he was always master of his subject. All the scholarship of the world would not have produced *Tam O'Shanter:* but in the whole of that poem there is not a false image nor a misused word. What do you suppose these lines represent?

> I turning saw, throned on a flowery rise,
> One sitting on a crimson scarf unrolled:
> A queen, with swarthy cheeks and bold black eyes,
> Brow-bound with burning gold.

Mr. MacBorrowdale.—I should take it to be a description of the Queen of Bambo.

The Rev. Dr. Opimian.—Yet thus one of our most popular poets describes Cleopatra: and one of our most popular artists has illustrated the description by a portrait of a hideous grinning Æthiop. Moore led the way to this perversion by demonstrating that the Ægyptian women must have been beautiful, because they were "the countrywomen of Cleopatra." Here we have a sort of counter-demonstration, that Cleopatra must have been a fright because she was the countrywoman of the Ægyptians. But Cleopatra was a Greek, the daughter of Ptolemy Auletes and a lady of Pontus. The Ptolemies were Greeks, and whoever will look at their genealogy, their coins, and their medals, will see how carefully they kept their pure Greek blood uncontaminated by African inter-mixture. Think of this description and this picture applied to one who Dio says—and all antiquity confirms him—was "the most superlatively beautiful of women, splendid to see, and delightful to hear." For she was eminently accomplished: she spoke many languages with grace and facility. Her mind was as wonderful as her personal beauty. There is not a shadow of intellectual expression in that horrible portrait.

The conversation at the quadrille-table was carried on with occasional pauses, and intermingled with the technicalities of the game.

Miss Gryll continued to alternate between joining in the quadrille dances and resuming her seat by the side of the room, where she was the object of great attention from some young gentlemen, who were glad to find her unattended by either Lord Curryfin or Mr. Falconer. Mr. Falconer continued to sit as if he had been fixed to his seat, like Theseus. The more he reflected on his conduct, in disappearing at that critical point of time and staying away so long, the more he felt that he had been guilty of an unjustifiable, and perhaps unpardonable offence. He noticed with extreme dis-composure the swarm of moths, as he called them to himself, who were fluttering in the light of her beauty: he would gladly have put them to flight; and this being out of the question, he would have been contented to take his place among them; but he dared not try the experiment.

Nevertheless, he would have been graciously received. The young lady was not cherishing any feeling of resentment against him. She understood, and made generous allowance for his divided feelings. But his irresolution, if he were left to himself, was likely to be of

long duration: and she meditated within herself the means of forcing
him to a conclusion, one way or the other.

PROGRESS OF SYMPATHY.—LOVE'S INJUNCTIONS.— ORLANDO INNAMORATO

WHILE light, fire, mirth, and music were enlivening the party
within the close-drawn curtains, without were moonless night and
thickly falling snow; and the morning opened on one vast expanse
of white, mantling alike the lawns and the trees, and weighing
down the wide-spreading branches. Lord Curryfin, determined not
to be baulked of his skating, sallied forth immediately after breakfast, collected a body of labourers, and swept clear an ample surface of ice, a path to it from the house, and a promenade on the
bank. Here he and Miss Niphet amused themselves in the afternoon, in company with a small number of the party, and in the
presence of about the usual number of spectators. Mr. Falconer was
there, and contented himself with looking on.

Lord Curryfin proposed a reel, Miss Niphet acquiesced, but it
was long before they found a third. At length one young gentleman, of the plump and rotund order, volunteered to supply the
deficiency, and was soon deposited on the ice, where his partners
in the ice-dance would have tumbled over him if they had not
anticipated the result, and given him a wide berth. One or two
others followed, exhibiting several varieties in the art of falling
ungracefully. At last the lord and the lady skated away on as large
a circuit as the cleared ice permitted, and as they went he said
to her,

"If you were the prize of skating, as Atalanta was of running,
I should have good hope to carry you off against all competitors
but yourself."

She answered, "Do not disturb my thoughts, or I shall slip."

He said no more, but the words left their impression. They gave
him as much encouragement as, under their peculiar circumstances,
he could not dare to wish for, or she could venture to intimate.

Mr. Falconer admired their "poetry of motion" as much as all the others had done. It suggested a remark which he would have liked to address to Miss Gryll, but he looked round for her in vain. He returned to the house in the hope that he might find her alone, and take the opportunity of making his peace.

He found her alone, but it seemed that he had no peace to make. She received him with a smile, and held out her hand to him, which he grasped fervently. He fancied that it trembled, but her features were composed. He then sat down at the table, on which the old edition of Bojardo was lying open as before. He said, "You have not been down to the lake to see that wonderful skating." She answered, "I have seen it every day but this. The snow deters me to-day. But it is wonderful. Grace and skill can scarcely go beyond it."

He wanted to apologize for the mode and duration of his departure and absence, but did not know how to begin. She gave him the occasion. She said, "You have been longer absent than usual —from our rehearsals. But we are all tolerably perfect in our parts. But your absence was remarked—by some of the party. You seemed to be especially missed by Lord Curryfin. He asked the reverend doctor every morning if he thought you would return that day."

Algernon.—And what said the doctor?

Morgana.—He usually said, "I hope so." But one morning he said something more specific.

Algernon.—What was it?

Morgana.—I do not know that I ought to tell you.

Algernon.—Oh, pray do.

Morgana.—He said, "The chances are against it." "What are the odds?" said Lord Curryfin. "Seven to one," said the doctor. "It ought not to be so," said Lord Curryfin, "for here is a whole Greek chorus against seven vestals." The doctor said, "I do not estimate the chances by the mere balance of numbers."

Algernon.—He might have said more as to the balance of numbers.

Morgana.—He might have said more, that the seven outweighed the one.

Algernon.—He could not have said that.

Morgana.—It would be much for the one to say that the balance was even.

Algernon.—But how if the absentee himself had been weighed against another in that one's own balance?

Morgana.—One to one promises at least more even weight.

Algernon.—I would not have it so. Pray, forgive me.

Morgana.—Forgive you? For what?

Algernon.—I wish to say, and I do not well know how, without seeming to assume what I have no right to assume, and then I must have double cause to ask your forgiveness.

Morgana.—Shall I imagine what you wish to say, and say it for you?

Algernon.—You would relieve me infinitely, if you imagine justly.

Morgana.—You may begin by saying with Achilles,

> My mind is troubled, like a fountain stirred;
> And I myself see not the bottom of it.

Algernon.—I think I do see it more clearly.

Morgana.—You may next say, I live an enchanted life. I have been in danger of breaking the spell; it has once more bound me with sevenfold force; I was in danger of yielding to another attraction; I went a step too far in all but declaring it; I do not know how to make a decent retreat.

Algernon.—Oh! no, no; nothing like that.

Morgana.—Then there is a third thing you may say; but before I say that for you, you must promise to make no reply, not even a monosyllable; and not to revert to the subject for four times seven days. You hesitate.

Algernon.—It seems as if my fate were trembling in the balance.

Morgana.—You must give me the promise I have asked for.

Algernon.—I do give it.

Morgana.—Repeat it then, word for word.

Algernon.—To listen to you in silence; not to say a syllable in reply; not to return to the subject for four times seven days.

Morgana.—Then you may say, I have fallen in love; very irrationally—(*he was about to exclaim, but she placed her finger on her lips*)—very irrationally; but I cannot help it. I fear I must yield to my destiny. I will try to free myself from all obstacles; I will, if I can, offer my hand where I have given my heart. And this I will do, if I ever do, at the end of four times seven days: if not then, never.

She placed her finger on her lips again, and immediately left the room, having first pointed to a passage in the open pages of *Orlando Innamorato*. She was gone before he was aware that she was going; but he turned to the book, and read the indicated passage. It was a part of the continuation of Orlando's adventure in the enchanted garden, when himself pursued and scourged by *La Penitenza*, he was pursuing the Fata Morgana over rugged rocks and through briary thickets.

"She must have anticipated my coming," said the young gentleman to himself. "She had opened the book at this passage, and has left it to say to me for her—Choose between love and repentance. Four times seven days! That is to ensure calm for the Christmas holidays. The term will pass over twelfth night. The lovers of old romance were subjected to a probation of seven years:—

"Seven long years I served thee, fair one,
Seven long years my fee was scorn.

"But here, perhaps, the case is reversed. She may have feared a probation of seven years for herself; and not without reason. And what have I to expect if I let the four times seven days pass by? Why, then, I can read in her looks—and they are interpreted in the verses before me—I am assigned to repentance, without the hope of a third opportunity. She is not without a leaning towards Lord Curryfin. She thinks he is passing from her, and on the twenty-ninth day, or perhaps in the meantime, she will try to regain him. Of course she will succeed. What rivalry could stand against her? If her power over him is lessened, it is that she has not chosen to exert it. She has but to will it, and he is again her slave. Twenty-eight days! twenty-eight days of doubt and distraction." And starting up, he walked out into the park, not choosing the swept path, but wading knee-deep in snow where it lay thickest in the glades. He was recalled to himself by sinking up to his shoulders in a hollow. He emerged with some difficulty, and retraced his steps to the house, thinking that, even in the midst of love's most dire perplexities, dry clothes and a good fire are better than a hole in the snow.

[The day of the great performance draws near, while Mr. Falconer remains suspended between present happiness and future bliss; and Harry Hedgerow makes progress.]

ARISTOPHANES IN LONDON

RAIN came, and thaw, followed by drying wind. The roads were in good order for the visitors to the Aristophanic comedy. The fifth day of Christmas was fixed for the performance. The theatre was brilliantly lighted, with spermaceti candles in glass chandeliers for the audience, and argand lamps for the stage. In addition to Mr. Gryll's own houseful of company, the beauty and fashion of the surrounding country, which comprised an extensive circle, adorned the semicircular seats; which, however, were not mere stone-benches, but were backed, armed, and padded into comfortable stalls. Lord Curryfin was in his glory, in the capacity of stage-manager.

The curtain rising, as there was no necessity for its being made to fall, [1] discovered the scene, which was on the London bank of the Thames, on the terrace of a mansion occupied by the Spirit-rapping Society, with an archway in the centre of the building, showing a street in the background. Gryllus was lying asleep. Circe, standing over him, began the dialogue.

CIRCE.

Wake, Gryllus, and arise in human form.

GRYLLUS.

I have slept soundly, and had pleasant dreams.

CIRCE.

I, too, have soundly slept. Divine how long.

[1] The Athenian theatre was open to the sky, and if the curtain had been made to fall it would have been folded up in mid air, destroying the effect of the scene. Being raised from below, it was invisible when not in use.

GRYLLUS.'
Why, judging by the sun, some fourteen hours.

CIRCE.
Three thousand years.

GRYLLUS.
That is a nap indeed.
But this is not your garden, nor your palace.
Where are we now?

CIRCE.
Three thousand years ago,
This land was forest, and a bright pure river
Ran through it to and from the Ocean stream.
Now, through a wilderness of human forms,
And human dwellings, a polluted flood
Rolls up and down, charged with all earthly poisons,
Poisoning the air in turn.

GRYLLUS.
I see vast masses
Of strange unnatural things.

CIRCE.
Houses, and ships,
And boats, and chimneys vomiting black smoke,
Horses, and carriages of every form,
And restless bipeds, rushing here and there
For profit or for pleasure, as they phrase it.

GRYLLUS.
Oh, Jupiter and Bacchus! what a crowd,
Flitting, like shadows without mind or purpose,
Such as Ulysses saw in Erebus.
But wherefore are we here?

CIRCE.
There have arisen
Some mighty masters of the invisible world,
And these have summoned us.

GRYLLUS.
With what design?

CIRCE.
That they themselves must tell. Behold they come,
Carrying a mystic table, around which
They work their magic spells. Stand by, and mark.

Three spirit-rappers appeared, carrying a table, which they placed on one side of the stage:

1. Carefully the table place,
   Let our gifted brother trace
   A ring around the enchanted space.
2. Let him tow'rd the table point,
   With his first fore-finger joint,
   And with mesmerized beginning,
   Set the sentient oak-slab spinning.
3. Now it spins around, around,
   Sending forth a murmuring sound,
   By the initiate understood
   As of spirits in the wood.
ALL. Once more Circe we invoke.

CIRCE.

Here: not bound in ribs of oak,
Nor, from wooden disk revolving,
In strange sounds strange riddles solving,
But in native form appearing,
Plain to sight, as clear to hearing.

THE THREE.

Thee with wonder we behold.
By thy hair of burning gold,
By thy face with radiance bright,
By thine eyes of beaming light,
We confess thee, mighty one,
For the daughter of the Sun.
On thy form we gaze appalled.

CIRCE.

Gryllus, too, your summons called.

THE THREE.

Him of yore thy powerful spell
Doomed in swinish shape to dwell:
Yet such life he reckoned then
Happier than the life of men.
Now, when carefully he ponders
All our scientific wonders,
Steam-driven myriads, all in motion
On the land and on the ocean,
Going, for the sake of going,
Wheresoever waves are flowing,

Wheresoever winds are blowing;
Converse through the sea transmitted,
Swift as ever thought has flitted;
All the glories of our time,
Past the praise of loftiest rhyme;
Will he, seeing these, indeed,
Still retain his ancient creed,
Ranking, in his mental plan,
Life of beast o'er life of man?

CIRCE.
Speak, Gryllus.

GRYLLUS.
It is early yet to judge:
But all the novelties I yet have seen
Seem changes for the worse.

THE THREE.
If we could show him
Our triumphs in succession, one by one,
'Twould surely change his judgment: and herein
How might'st thou aid us, Circe!

CIRCE.
I will do so:
And calling down, like Socrates of yore,
The clouds to aid us, they shall shadow forth,
In bright succession, all that they behold,
From air, on earth and sea. I wave my wand:
And lo! they come, even as they came in Athens,
Shining like virgins of ethereal life.

The Chorus of Clouds descended, and a dazzling array of female beauty was revealed by degrees through folds of misty gauze. They sang their first choral song:

CHORUS OF CLOUDS.[1]

I.

Clouds ever-flowing, conspicuously soaring,
From loud-rolling Ocean, whose stream [2] gave us birth

[1] The first stanza is pretty closely adapted from the strophe of Aristophanes: Ἀέναοι Νεφέλαι. The second is only a distant imitation of the antistrophe: Παρδένοι ὀμβροφόροι.

[2] In Homer, and all the older poets, the ocean is a river surrounding the earth, and the seas are inlets from it.

To heights, whence we look over torrents down-pouring
    To the deep quiet vales of the fruit-giving earth,—
As the broad eye of Æther, unwearied in brightness,
    Dissolves our mist-veil in glittering rays,
Our forms we reveal from its vapoury lightness,
    In semblance immortal, with far-seeing gaze.

II.

Shower-bearing Virgins, we seek not the regions
    Whence Pallas, the Muses, and Bacchus have fled,
But the city, where Commerce embodies her legions,
    And Mammon exalts his omnipotent head.
All joys of thought, feeling, and taste are before us,
    Wherever the beams of his favour are warm:
Though transient full oft as the veil of our chorus,
    Now golden with glory, now passing in storm.

Reformers, scientific, moral, educational, political, passed in succession, each answering a question of Gryllus. Gryllus observed, that so far from everything being better than it had been, it seemed that everything was wrong and wanted mending. The chorus sang its second song.

Seven competitive examiners entered with another table, and sat down on the opposite side of the stage to the spirit-rappers. They brought forward Hermogenes as a crammed fowl to argue with Gryllus. Gryllus had the best of the argument; but the examiners adjudged the victory to Hermogenes. The chorus sang its third song.

Circe, at the request of the spirit-rappers, whose power was limited to the production of sound, called up several visible spirits, all illustrious in their day, but all appearing as in the days of their early youth, "before their renown was around them." They were all subjected to competitive examination, and were severally pronounced disqualified for the pursuit in which they had shone. At last came one whom Circe recommended to the examiners as a particularly promising youth. He was a candidate for military life. Every question relative to his profession he answered to the purpose. To every question not so relevant, he replied that he did not know and did not care. This drew on him a reprimand. He was pronounced disqualified, and ordered to join the rejected, who were ranged in a line along the back of the scene. A touch of Circe's wand changed them into their semblance of maturer years. Among them were Hannibal and Oliver Cromwell; and in the fore-ground was the last candidate, Richard Cœur-de-Lion. Richard flourished his battle-axe over the heads of the examiners, who jumped up in great trepidation, overturned their table, tumbled over one another, and escaped as best they might in haste and terror. The heroes vanished. The chorus sang its fourth song.

CHORUS.

I.

As before the pike will fly
Dace and roach and such small fry;
As the leaf before the gale,
As the chaff beneath the flail;
As before the wolf the flocks,
As before the hounds the fox;
As before the cat the mouse,
As the rat from falling house;
As the fiend before the spell
Of holy water, book, and bell;
As the ghost from dawning day,—
So has fled, in gaunt dismay,
This septemvirate of quacks,
From the shadowy attacks
Of Cœur-de-Lion's battle-axe.

II.

Could he in corporeal might,
Plain to feeling as to sight,
Rise again to solar light,
How his arm would put to flight
All the forms of Stygian night,
That round us rise in grim array,
Darkening the meridian day:
Bigotry, whose chief employ
Is embittering earthly joy;
Chaos, throned in pedant state,
Teaching echo how to prate;
And "Ignorance, with looks profound,"
Not "with eye that loves the ground,"
But stalking wide, with lofty crest,
In science's pretentious vest.

III.

And now, great masters of the realms of shade,
To end the task which called us down from air,

We shall present, in pictured show arrayed,
  Of this your modern world the triumphs rare,
That Gryllus's benighted spirit
May wake to your transcendent merit,
And, with profoundest admiration thrilled,
He may with willing mind assume his place
In your steam-nursed, steam-borne, steam-killed,
And gas-enlightened race.

CIRCE.
Speak, Gryllus, what you see.

GRYLLUS.
                    I see the ocean,
And o'er its face ships passing wide and far;
Some with expanded sails before the breeze,
And some with neither sails nor oars, impelled
By some invisible power against the wind,
Scattering the spray before them. But of many
One is on fire, and one has struck on rocks
And melted in the waves like fallen snow.
Two crash together in the middle sea,
And go to pieces on the instant, leaving
No soul to tell the tale, and one is hurled
In fragments to the sky, strewing the deep
With death and wreck. I had rather live with Circe
Even as I was, than flit about the world
In those enchanted ships, which some Alastor
Must have devised as traps for mortal ruin.

CIRCE.
Look yet again.

GRYLLUS.
            Now the whole scene is changed.
I see long chains of strange machines on wheels,
With one in front of each, puffing white smoke
From a black hollow column. Fast and far
They speed, like yellow leaves before the gale,
When autumn winds are strongest. Through their windows
I judge them thronged with people; but distinctly
Their speed forbids my seeing.

SPIRIT-RAPPER.
                    This is one
Of the great glories of our modern time.
"Men are become as birds," and skim like swallows
The surface of the world.

GRYLLUS.
For what good end?

SPIRIT-RAPPER
The end is in itself—the end of skimming
The surface of the world.

GRYLLUS.
If that be all,
I had rather sit in peace in my old home:
But while I look, two of them meet and clash,
And pile their way with ruin. One is rolled
Down a steep bank; one through a broken bridge
Is dashed into a flood. Dead, dying, wounded,
Are there as in a battle-field. Are these
Your modern triumphs? Jove preserve me from them.

SPIRIT-RAPPER.
These ills are rare. Millions are borne in safety
Where one incurs mischance. Look yet again.

GRYLLUS.
I see a mass of light brighter than that
Which burned in Circe's palace, and beneath it
A motley crew, dancing to joyous music.
But from that light explosion comes, and flame;
And forth the dancers rush in haste and fear
From their wide-blazing hall.

SPIRIT-RAPPER.
Oh, Circe! Circe!
Thou show'st him all the evil of our arts
In more than just proportion to the good.
Good without evil is not given to man.
Jove, from his urns dispensing good and ill,
Gives ill unmixed to some, and good and ill
Mingled to many—good unmixed to none.
Our arts are good. The inevitable ill
That mixes with them, as with all things human,
Is as a drop of water in a goblet
Full of old wine.

GRYLLUS.
More than one drop, I fear,
And those of bitter water.

CIRCE.
There is yet
An ample field of scientific triumph:
What shall we show him next?

SPIRIT-RAPPER.
Pause we awhile.
He is not in the mood to feel conviction
Of our superior greatness. He is all
For rural comfort and domestic ease,
But our impulsive days are all for moving:
Sometimes with some ulterior end, but still
For moving, moving, always. There is nothing
Common between us in our points of judgment.
He takes his stand upon tranquillity,
We ours upon excitement. There we place
The being, end, and aim of mortal life,
The many are with us: some few, perhaps,
With him. We put the question to the vote
By universal suffrage. Aid us, Circe!
On talismanic wings your spells can waft
The question and reply. Are we not wiser,
Happier, and better, than the men of old,
Of Homer's days, of Athens, and of Rome?

VOICES WITHOUT.
Ay. No. Ay, ay. No. Ay, ay, ay, ay, ay,
We are the wisest race the earth has known,
The most advanced in all the arts of life,
In science, and in morals.

SPIRIT-RAPPER.
The ays have it.
What is that wondrous sound, that seems like thunder
Mixed with gigantic laughter?

CIRCE.
It is Jupiter,
Who laughs at your presumption; half in anger,
And half in mockery. Now, my worthy masters,
You must in turn experience in yourselves
The mighty magic thus far tried on others.

The table turned slowly, and by degrees went on spinning with accelerated speed. The legs assumed motion, and it danced off the stage. The arms of the chairs put forth hands, and pinched the spirit-rappers, who sprang up and ran off, pursued by their chairs. This piece of mechanical pantomime was a triumph of Lord Curry-fin's art, and afforded him ample satisfaction for the failure of his resonant vases.

CIRCE.
Now, Gryllus, we may seek our ancient home
In my enchanted isle.

GRYLLUS.
Not yet, not yet.
Good signs are toward of a joyous supper.
Therein the modern world may have its glory,
And I, like an impartial judge, am ready
To do it ample justice. But, perhaps,
As all we hitherto have seen are shadows,
So too may be the supper.

CIRCE.
Fear not, Gryllus.
That you will find a sound reality,
To which the land and air, seas, lakes, and rivers,
Have sent their several tributes. Now, kind friends,
Who with your smiles have graciously rewarded
Our humble, but most earnest aims to please,
And with your presence at our festal board
Will charm the winter midnight, Music gives
The signal: Welcome and old wine await you.

THE CHORUS.
Shadows to-night have offered portraits true
Of many follies which the world enthral.
"Shadows we are, and shadows we pursue:"
But, in the banquet's well-illumined hall,
Realities, delectable to all,
Invite you now our festal joy to share.
Could we our Attic prototype recall,
One compound word should give our bill of fare:
But where our language fails, our hearts true welcome bear.

Miss Gryll was resplendent as Circe; and Miss Niphet, as leader of the chorus, looked like Melpomene herself, slightly unbending her tragic severity into that solemn smile which characterized the chorus of the old comedy. The charm of the first acted irresistibly

on Mr. Falconer. The second would have completed, if anything had
been wanted to complete it, the conquest of Lord Curryfin.

The supper passed off joyously, and it was a late hour of the
morning before the company dispersed.

[Theatrical triumph is succeeded by the triumph of love, and nine
lovely brides are led to the altar by nine worthy grooms; but not
before Mr. Gryll has delivered himself of certain pessimistic
opinions with which this selection closes.]

A TWELFTH-NIGHT BALL.—PANTOPRAGMATIC COOKERY.—MODERN VANDALISM

TWELFTH-NIGHT was the night of the ball. The folding-doors of
the drawing-rooms, which occupied their entire breadth, were thrown
wide open. The larger room was appropriated to grown dancers; the
smaller to children, who came in some force, and were placed within
the magnetic attraction of an enormous twelfth-cake, which stood
in a decorated recess. The carpets had been taken up, and the floors
were painted with forms in chalk by skillful artists, under the
superintendance of Mr. Pallet. The library, separated from all the
apartments by ante-chambers with double doors, was assigned, with
an arrangement of whist-tables, to such of the elder portion of the
party as might prefer that mode of amusement to being mere spectators of the dancing. Mr. Gryll, with Miss Ilex, Mr. MacBorrowdale,
and the Reverend Doctor Opimian, established his own quadrille
party in a corner of the smaller drawing-room, where they could
at once play and talk, and enjoy the enjoyment of the young. Lord
Curryfin was Master of the Ceremonies.

After two or three preliminary dances, to give time for the
arrival of the whole of the company, the twelfth-cake was divided.
The characters were drawn exclusively among the children, and the
little king and queen were duly crowned, placed on a theatrical
throne, and paraded in state round both drawing-rooms, to their own
great delight and that of their little associates. Then the ball was

supposed to commence, and was by general desire opened with a minuet by Miss Niphet and Lord Curryfin. Then came alternations of quadrilles and country dances, interspersed with occasional waltzes and polkas. So the ball went merrily, with, as usual, abundant love-making in mute signs and in *sotto voce* parlance.

Lord Curryfin, having brought his own love-making to a satisfactory close, was in exuberant spirits, sometimes joining in the dance, sometimes—in his official capacity—taking the round of the rooms to see that everything was going on to everybody's satisfaction. He could not fail to observe that his proffered partnership in the dance, though always graciously, was not so ambitiously accepted as before he had disposed of himself for life. A day had sufficed to ask and obtain the consent of Miss Niphet's father, who now sate on the side of the larger drawing-room, looking with pride and delight on his daughter, and with cordial gratification on her choice; and when it was once, as it was at once known, that Miss Niphet was to be Lady Curryfin, his lordship passed into the class of married men, and was no longer the object of that solicitous attention which he had received as an undrawn prize in the lottery of marriage, while it was probable that somebody would have him, and nobody knew who.

The absence of Mr. Falconer was remarked by several young ladies, to whom it appeared that Miss Gryll had lost her two most favoured lovers at once. However, as she had still many others, it was not yet a decided case for sympathy. Of course she had no lack of partners, and whatever might have been her internal anxiety, she was not the least gay among the joyous assembly.

Lord Curryfin, in his circuit of the apartments, paused at the quadrille-table, and said, "You have been absent two or three days, Mr. MacBorrowdale—what news have you brought from London?"

Mr. MacBorrowdale.—Not much, my lord. Tables turn as usual, and the ghost-trade appears to be thriving: for instead of being merely audible, the ghosts are becoming tangible, and shake hands under the tables with living wiseacres, who solemnly attest the fact. Civilized men ill-use their wives; the wives revenge themselves in their own way, and the Divorce Court has business enough on its hands to employ it twenty years at its present rate of progression. Commercial bubbles burst, and high-pressure boilers blow up, and mountebanks of all descriptions flourish on public credulity. Everywhere there are wars and rumours of wars. The Peace Society has wound up its affairs in the Insolvent Court of Prophecy. A great tribulation is coming on the earth, and Apollyon in person is to be perpetual dictator of all the nations. There is, to be sure, one piece of news in your line, but it will be no news to you. There is a meeting of the Pantopragmatic Society, under the presidency of Lord Facing-both-ways, who has opened it with a long speech, philanthropically designed as an elaborate exercise in fallacies, for the benefit of young rhetoricians. The society has divided its work into departments, which are to meddle with everything, from the highest to the lowest—from a voice in legislation to a finger in Jack Horner's pie. I looked for a department of Fish, with your lordship's name at the head of it; but I did not find it. It would be a fine department. It would divide itself naturally into three classes —living fish, fossil fish, and fish in the frying-pan.

Lord Curryfin.—I assure you, Mr. MacBorrowdale, all this seems as ridiculous now to me as it does to you. The third class of fish is all that I shall trouble myself with in future, and that only at the tables of myself and my friends.

Mr. Gryll.—I wonder the Pantopragmatics have not a department of cookery; a female department, to teach young wives how to keep their husbands at home, by giving them as good dinners as they can get abroad, especially at clubs. Those anti-domestic institutions receive their chief encouragement from the total ignorance of cookery on the part of young wives: for in this, as in all other arts of life, it is not sufficient to order what shall be done: it is necessary to know how it ought to be done. This is a matter of more importance to social well-being, than nine-tenths of the subjects the Pantopragmatics meddle with.

The Rev. Dr. Opimian.—And therefore I rejoice that they do not meddle with it. A dinner, prepared from a New Art of Cookery, concocted under their auspices, would be more comical and more uneatable than the Roman dinner in Peregrine Pickle. Let young ladies learn cookery by all means: but let them learn under any other tuition than that of the Pantopragmatic Society.

Mr. Gryll.—As for the tribulation coming on the earth, I am afraid there is some ground to expect it, without looking for its foreshadowing exclusively to the Apocalypse. Niebuhr, who did not draw his opinions from prophecy, rejoiced that his career was coming to a close, for he thought we were on the eve of a darker middle age.

The Rev. Dr. Opimian.—He had not before his eyes the astounding march of intellect, drumming and trumpeting science from city to city. But I am afraid that sort of obstreperous science only gives people the novel "use of their eyes to see the way of blindness."

> Truths which, from action's paths retired,
> My silent search in vain required,

I am not likely to find in the successive gabblings of a dozen lecturers of Babel.

Mr. Gryll.—If you could so find them, they would be of little avail against the new irruption of Goths and Vandals, which must have been in the apprehension of Niebuhr. There are Vandals on northern thrones, anxious for nothing so much as to extinguish truth and liberty wherever they show themselves—Vandals in the bosom of society everywhere even amongst ourselves, in multitudes, with precisely the same aim, only more disguised by knaves, and less understood by dupes.

The Rev. Dr. Opimian.—And, you may add, Vandals dominating over society throughout half America, who deal with free speech and even the suspicion of free thought, just as the Inquisition dealt with them, only substituting Lynch law and the gallows for a different mockery of justice, ending in fire and faggot.

Mr. Gryll.—I confine my view to Europe. I dread northern monarchy, and southern anarchy; and rabble brutality amongst ourselves, smothered and repressed for the present, but always ready to break out into inextinguishable flame, like hidden fire under treacherous ashes.

Mr. MacBorrowdale.—In the meantime, we are all pretty comfortable: and sufficient for the day is the evil thereof; which in our case, so far as I can see, happens to be precisely none.

KEY TO CHARACTERS

The reader is advised to use this Key with many grains of salt, as the identification of real and fictional characters is often most tenuous.

HEADLONG HALL

Escot	Peacock
Foster	Shelley
Gall	Francis Jeffrey
Jenkison	Thomas Jefferson Hogg
MacLaurel	Thomas Campbell
Milestone	Humphrey Repton
Nightshade	Southey
Panscope	Coleridge
Patrick O'Prism	Sir Uvedale Price
Poppyseed, Mrs.	Mrs. Amelia Opie

MELINCOURT

Feathernest	Southey
Forester	Shelley
Fax	Malthus

NIGHTMARE ABBEY

Cypress	Byron
Flosky	Coleridge
Listless	Sir Lamley Skeffington
Marionetta	Harriet Shelley
Scythrop	Shelley
Stella	Mary Shelley
Toobad	J. F. Newton

CROTCHET CASTLE

Eavesdrop . . . . Hazlitt
Mac Quedy . . . . J. R. MacCullough
Philpot . . . . MacGregor Laird
Shantsee . . . . Southey
Skionar . . . . Coleridge
Toogood . . . . Robert Owen
Wontsee . . . . Wordsworth

GRYLL GRANGE

Lord Facing-both-ways . . . . Lord Brougham
Falconer . . . . Shelley